Omra saw himself standing in crystal halls, walking through mirrored caves full of marvels beyond anything he had ever imagined—jewels and fountains, alabaster statues of exotic animals. At an intersection of corridors, he stopped to face a holy light so brilliant he could not bear to gaze upon it. Though he could make out no details, Omra knew that this was the Key to Creation, the blessed talisman waiting to be found since the very beginning of the world. Ondun had sent Urec out to find it.

Omra awoke with a start—and a firm conviction. He knew what he had to do.

Hidden somewhere in the undiscovered vastness of the world was this incredible object. Now that he possessed the Map, he had to send someone to find the Key to Creation. Only then would the conflict end. With such a relic in their possession, the followers of Urec would surely defeat the Aidenists.

Kevin J. Anderson

The MAP of all THINGS

Terra Incognita
Book Two

orbit

www.orbitbooks.net

ORBIT

First published in Great Britain in 2010 by Orbit
This paperback edition published in 2011 by Orbit

Typeset in Baskerville by M Rules
Printed in the UK by CPI Mackays, Chatham ME5 8TD

Orbit
An imprint of
Little, Brown Book Group
100 Victoria Embankment
London EC4Y 0DY

An Hachette UK Company
www.hachette.co.uk

www.orbitbooks.net

her way to the harbor to escape the fire, ASHA (one of Imir's wives) finds the injured Prester Hannes; believing him to be a devout follower of Urec because of his tattered clothes and the Urecari relic he took from the burning church, she decides to bring him along and nurse him back to health. As Korastine and Imir sail away in opposite directions, the holy city of Ishalem burns behind them, and both leaders know the war is just beginning. . . .

The young Tierran sailor CRISTON VORA and his new wife ADREA sail his cargo boat from the coastal fishing village of Windcatch to Calay. Criston dreams of sailing the seas and visiting new lands and, though he hates to leave lovely Adrea behind, joins the crew of the new exploration ship, the *Luminara*; CAPTAIN ANDON SHAY plans to sail to the edge of the world and find the lost land of Terravitae and Holy Joron. Criston sells his boat so Adrea will have money to support herself while he's away; she gives him a lock of her hair, and he promises to write her letters, which he'll throw overboard in bottles. The sympathetic magic binding the hair to Adrea should bring the bottles to her. She says farewell, and the *Luminara* sails off. Only after she goes back to Windcatch to live with her younger brother CIARLO (who has a lame leg) and Criston's old mother does Adrea discover that she's pregnant. . . .

Another group of people, followers of neither Aiden nor Urec, are the Saedrans—scientists, craftsmen, philosophers. They believe their ancestors left Terravitae voluntarily, long after the two brothers sailed, and settled on another continent, from which they established a maritime civilization. But the Saedran continent sank beneath the waves, and the only survivors are the descendants of traders who were away from home at the time of the catastrophe. Saedrans have settled in both Uraba and Tierra but don't espouse either religion.

One young Saedran in Calay, ALDO NA-CURIC, is being trained by the old scholar SEN LEO NA-HADRA to become a chartsman (a navigator much in demand by ship captains). Aldo passes his test, having memorized all of the generations of navigational data as well as volumes of the Tales of the Traveler— journals written by a mysterious wandering stranger, said to be either Aiden or Urec himself. Excited to become a chartsman, Aldo goes to the Calay docks, where he meets the con man YAL DOLICAR, who sells him a fake map of unexplored lands. When Aldo eagerly shows Sen Leo his discovery, the scholar denounces Dolicar's map as a forgery, and then proves it by taking Aldo to a secret chamber beneath the Saedran temple. There, covering the walls and ceiling, is an intricate map of everything the Saedrans have compiled about the world: the Mappa Mundi, or the Map of All Things.

In Olabar, Asha nurses the burned Prester Hannes back to health, praying over him, giving him Urecari sacraments. When he recovers his strength and learns that she has fouled him with the hated rival religion, Hannes becomes enraged, kills her, and escapes into the night. Grief-stricken to learn that his young wife was murdered by the mysterious man she tried to help, Soldan-Shah Imir calls out his guards . . . but Hannes is gone.

Omra is despondent over having lost his own young wife Istar, but his father arranges another wife for him, CLIA-PARIA, the daughter of the Yuarej soldan. Though she is

The Story So Far

According to legend, before ONDUN (the creator of all things) departed from the world, He sent out His sons AIDEN and UREC each in a separate great arkship to explore His entire creation, while His third son, JORON, remained behind in the Eden-like land of Terravitae.

Today, the known world has two continents, Tierra and Uraba, connected by a thin isthmus of land, on which the sacred city of Ishalem was built. The people of Tierra believe themselves to be the descendants of Aiden's crew, while Urabans are convinced that their ancestors originally sailed on Urec's ship. The wreck of an ancient vessel sits on a high hill in Ishalem, and each people insists it belongs to them.

After generations of strife, KING KORASTINE of Tierra and SOLDAN-SHAH IMIR of Uraba agree to sign an Edict that divides the world in half, above and below Ishalem. This will remove all need for conflict, and both leaders look forward to peace at last. Korastine sails from Calay, the capital of Tierra, with his young daughter PRINCESS ANJINE and her childhood friend, MATEO. Soldan-Shah Imir sails from Olabar, Uraba's capital, for the formal signing ceremony.

King Korastine and Soldan-Shah Imir meet at the wreck of the Arkship on the hill above Ishalem, accompanied by

PRESTER-MARSHALL BAINE (representing the Aidenist church) and UR-SIKARA LUKAI (representing the Urecari church). The Edict is signed, peace is declared between the two continents, and the celebrations begin.

Back at the Olabar palace, Imir has left his son and heir, OMRA, in charge. Omra's beloved wife ISTAR is pregnant and will soon bear their first child. The sikaras—priestesses of the church of Urec—bless the unborn baby, and Omra is very happy. His cousin BURILO comes from the distant soldanate of Missinia to deliver the head of a slain bandit leader from the Great Desert; the bandits have been plaguing the soldanate for years, but though their leader is dead, Omra knows the problem isn't solved. Before Soldan-Shah Imir can return from signing the Edict in Ishalem, tragedy strikes: Istar collapses and dies from a difficult miscarriage. Omra is devastated.

In Ishalem, we meet PRESTER HANNES, a fanatical follower of the Aidenist church, who has spent years in disguise among the Urecari. He was given this spying mission by Prester-Marshall Baine to gather information about the rival religion. Hannes hates the followers of Urec with a passion. During the celebrations after the signing ceremony, an accidental fire starts and quickly spreads across the city. Both Tierrans and the Urabans assign blame for the disaster and spend more time fighting each other than trying to extinguish the fire. As flames rage through the main Urecari church, Prester Hannes breaks in to steal a religious relic. In the process, he is caught in the inferno, terribly burned, and barely manages to stagger away, delirious.

Korastine flees the city with Anjine and Mateo, while Soldan-Shah Imir calls for an evacuation of his people. On beautiful and ambitious, he cannot bring himself to love her. Instead, Omra fixes his anger on the Tierrans for burning Ishalem. Many in Uraba feel the same rage and call out for war. Soldan-Shah Imir increases production of metals at the Gremurr mines, a secret facility on a rugged coast that should technically belong to Tierra, but is inaccessible to them due to a mountain range. Because Uraba is poor in metals, the people are forced to mine the ores in enemy territory.

Hoping to rebuild Ishalem, Prester-Marshall Baine and a group of volunteers from Tierra set up camp in the burned ruins and set to work clearing away the rubble. They are beset by an angry Uraban soldan, who feels the Tierrans are further desecrating the holy city. Baine and his followers are murdered horribly, and only one man, an Iborian shipbuilder named KJELNAR, escapes to tell the tale. When King Korastine learns what has happened to the well-meaning Aidenists, he has no choice but to prepare for all-out war. Though his ward Mateo is still young, he sends the young man off to be trained in the Tierran military, while his daughter Anjine will have to study to be a leader, the next queen.

Learning of the ill-advised massacre at Ishalem, Soldan-Shah Imir dispatches a diplomat with an apology and a proposed peace treaty to Korastine, but the diplomat is intercepted by TAVISHEL, destrar of Soeland Reach, who brashly takes his revenge against the Uraban man for the slaying of Prester-Marshall Baine and his followers. The retaliatory murder of the diplomat is an atrocity that further inflames the Urabans.

Ignoring his new wife Cliaparia, Omra leads violent raids along the Tierran coast. In Windcatch, as her pregnancy progresses, Adrea misses Criston, who has sailed far away in the *Luminara*; her brother Ciarlo is training to become the next prester of the village. Everything seems at peace, until Omra and his raiders strike Windcatch, setting fire to the buildings, massacring many of the townspeople, and destroying the small Aidenist kirk. Ciarlo, unable to run with his injured leg, barely escapes and hides. The men are about to kill Adrea, but when Omra sees she is pregnant, he thinks of his own wife Istar who died in childbirth, and he spares her. Omra takes Adrea captive, along with many Tierran children, who are herded aboard the Uraban raiding ships. They sail away, leaving the wounded Windcatch behind. Eventually, they reach Olabar, and Omra tells Adrea that this is her new home.

Meanwhile, voyaging aboard the *Luminara*, Criston sees many new and strange things. Captain Shay takes him under his wing, showing off the journal in which he sketches the sea serpents he has encountered. Criston also becomes close with PRESTER JERARD, a kindly old priest. He writes his letters to Adrea, seals them with a strand of her hair, and throws the bottles overboard. The ship has been gone for months, seeing no sign of Terravitae, when they encounter a terrible storm—along with the most terrifying sea monster of legend, the Leviathan. The Leviathan attacks and destroys the *Luminara*.

Criston and Prester Jerard are the only survivors. For days, they drift on a makeshift raft, fighting off sharks. Then a black-and-gold sea serpent devours the prester, but Criston manages to snag it with an iron hook. The enraged beast races through the water, dragging Criston's hodgepodge raft for many leagues before the rope breaks.

Fortunately, the serpent has towed Criston back into Tierran shipping lanes, and he is rescued. When he finally makes his way home to Windcatch, desperate to see Adrea, he finds the town recovering from the Uraban raid. Ciarlo reveals that Adrea was either kidnapped or killed; she is long gone and there is no chance of getting her back. A broken man, Criston leaves Windcatch, rejects the sea, and goes up into the mountains to live alone.

Four years later, Aldo na-Curic is an experienced Saedran chartsman and has sailed on many Tierran ships. When his captain ventures south of the Edict Line, however, the ship is surrounded by Uraban war vessels. Aldo, with his rare talent as a chartsman, is captured and taken to Olabar, where Soldan-Shah Imir asks a wise Saedran woman, SEN SHERUFA NA-OA, to convince the young man to serve Uraba. But both Aldo and Sherufa owe their loyalty to the Saedran quest to complete the Map of All Things, and she gives him all of her information about Uraban geography, then secretly helps him escape back to Tierra, where he can share his knowledge.

Since recovering from his burns and murdering his benefactor Asha, Prester Hannes has adopted a new mission: stranded in a foreign land, he vows to harm the enemy as much as possible. Moving like a shadow, he burns churches, poisons wells, and wreaks havoc among the followers of Urec. They are spooked and assume that the Tierrans have sent many spies and saboteurs among them.

Over the years, Omra has kidnapped many Tierran children and—under the guidance of a sinister and mysterious masked figure, the Teacher—has brainwashed and transformed them into zealous assassins and saboteurs, called *ra'virs*, which he intends to turn loose on Tierra. Adrea is a household slave at the palace, and all this time she has pretended to be unable to speak. She has given birth to Criston's son, SAAN, whom she is allowed to raise; the boy is now almost four, and is being schooled in Uraban ways and the teachings of Urec. Ur-Sikara Lukai informs her that when the boy turns four, Saan will be taken away from her and sent to a special training camp to become a *ra'vir*. Adrea is panicked, but there is nothing she can do.

She accidentally discovers a plot hatched by Ur-Sikara Lukai and VILLIKI, another wife of Soldan-Shah Imir, to poison Omra, frame Cliaparia, and then set Villiki's good-natured and unambitious son TUKAR (Omra's half-brother) on the throne. Adrea reveals the plot to Omra and, as payment for the information, demands that Saan be kept out of the *ra'vir* camps and raised in the palace instead. Their scheme exposed, Ur-Sikara Lukai is killed, Villiki is stripped of all possessions and cast out, and Tukar (who had no real part in the plot) is exiled to live at the harsh Gremurr mines. Saan is brought back to Adrea, but the old soldan-shah is broken by the revelation of the murderous scheme, and so he retires, handing over the leadership to Omra.

After saving Omra's life, Adrea is taken into the new soldan-shah's household. Despite the obvious jealousy of Cliaparia, Omra asks Adrea to marry him as well, and in return he promises to raise Saan as his own. Seeing this as the only way to ensure a future for her son, she grudgingly accepts. But a Tierran name will not do for the wife of a soldan-shah, and Omra insists that she change her name to Istar.

Meanwhile, Criston Vora lives in isolation in the mountains, going to other villages only when he needs supplies. Once each year he makes the trip to the seashore, where he casts another letter in a bottle into the sea, clinging to hope that someday, somehow, Adrea might receive them. ...

Up in Tierra, Mateo undergoes years of military training, including arctic survival with the destrar of Iboria, BROECK. Broeck takes a liking to Mateo, and when his daughter ILRIDA agrees to be the new bride of lonely King Korastine, Mateo escorts her down to Calay. Anjine is thrilled to see Mateo back in the city (they are very fond of each other but cannot admit their feelings), and Korastine is delighted with his new bride, who is fascinated by legends of Holy Joron in Terravitae. As a special gift for Ilrida, the king constructs an Iborian-style kirk so that she can worship as she did in her own land.

Over the years, Omra becomes very fond of Saan and raises him as a true son, despite the boy's Tierran heritage. Adrea/Istar and Cliaparia develop a rivalry as wives: no matter what she tries, Cliaparia can't make Omra love her, and the soldan-shah's true affection is reserved for Istar. He now has three daughters—ADREALA and ISTALA by Istar and CITHARA by Cliaparia, but the soldan-shah still needs a male heir.

Back in Calay King Korastine and Ilrida are very happy together and produce a son, TOMAS. One day, as she prays in the special Iborian kirk that Korastine built for her, Ilrida scratches herself on a rusty nail. The wound becomes infected, and Ilrida dies of tetanus; Korastine is so paralyzed by grief that Princess Anjine shoulders more and more of the burdens of ruling Tierra. Knowing how much Ilrida revered Holy Joron, Korastine announces a quest in her honor: Tierra will build another great exploration ship that will sail off in search of Terravitae. Anjine thinks this is an expensive fool's quest in a time of war, but Korastine takes her to a high tower and shows her a relic that has been kept secret for generations: Aiden's Compass, a magical object that will reveal the location of the lost homeland. Anjine sees that the plan isn't so foolish after all. . . .

At the southern boundary of Uraba, at the edge of the Great Desert, a strange man staggers in from the dunes, speaking no tongue that anyone can understand. The Saedran woman Sen Sherufa eventually learns his language. His name is ASADDAN and he has crossed the Great Desert; his people, the Nunghals, live on the other side of the expanse of dunes. Asaddan becomes a court sensation and convinces Omra to sponsor an expedition so he can return to his side of the desert, using a balloon-borne sand coracle to ride the winds. Saan, now twelve, accompanies him, along with the retired soldan-shah Imir and a reluctant Sherufa (who would rather stay home and read about adventures). The group crosses the desert and is received among the Nunghals. As guests of KHAN JIKARIS, they travel to a large clan gathering on the coast of the southern ocean, a body of water that Sherufa never even guessed existed. From seafaring Nunghals, she obtains maps and begins to suspect that the southern ocean may in fact connect with the coastline of Uraba, far to the north. Sherufa, Imir, and Saan return home with their exciting news.

Prester Hannes continues his depredations against the

followers of Urec, leaving a path of death and destruction behind him as he makes his way back to Tierra. He reaches the burned ruins of Ishalem, which have remained uninhabited for more than a dozen years, and he weeps to see what has become of the holy city. Before he can leave the ruins, though, Hannes is captured by a Uraban patrol, and he is sent with other prisoners to work in the Gremurr mines. They do not know he is the man who has caused them so much harm; they just need more slaves. Hannes toils for a long time, always looking for a way to escape, and finally slips away from the mines into the supposedly impassible mountains that lead to Tierra. No man has ever survived the trek, but Hannes is not like any other man. Frostbitten, starving, and near death, he stumbles into a high mountain meadow, where he is rescued by the hermit Criston Vora. Criston nurses him back to health, and then helps the prester make his way to Calay.

As the Iborian Kjelnar constructs Korastine's new Arkship, Destrar Broeck goes out into the northern wastelands to track down and kill the fabled ice dragon, whose horn supposedly has magical properties. Broeck returns to Calay with the shimmering horn, which will be mounted on the prow of the Arkship. Both Broeck and Korastine intend to sail on the vessel, and Aldo na-Curic will be the chartsman. Before the new Arkship can depart, though, *ra'virs* strike in the night and burn the ship in the harbor. The Tierran dreams are dashed.

Soldan-Shah Omra decides to recapture the barren city of Ishalem for his people and puts together a major assault. His wife Istar gives him a son at last, whom she names Criston, which only increases the jealousy Cliaparia holds toward her. Omra has recently taken a third wife, NAORI, who is also pregnant. The soldan-shah bids them all farewell, and heads off with his armies to conquer Ishalem. His operation works perfectly. Before the Tierran army can respond effectively, Omra destroys the enemy military out-posts and kills all the Aidenist pilgrims. He claims the ash-strewn ground in the name of Uraba.

Back in Olabar, Cliaparia schemes to oust Istar, but she fails ... which only forces her to try even darker treachery. After Naori gives birth to a baby boy—another heir for the soldan-shah—Cliaparia slips a poisonous sand spider into the crib of Istar's year-old son Criston, and the boy dies. Saan returns from the land of the Nunghals to discover that his mother has been nearly driven mad by the death of the baby, while Cliaparia remains smug. When Istar learns that Cliaparia was the murderer, she does not hesitate. Thinking of nothing but revenge, she goes to the market, where she finds Cliaparia laughing with her ladies-in-waiting. She stabs the hateful woman to death in broad daylight and dumps her body into the harbor, then staggers away in shock, covered in blood. As she wanders through the market stalls, Istar is stunned to discover a merchant selling a letter found sealed in a bottle. One of Criston's letters to her.

Having saved Prester Hannes, Criston at last decides to return to his former life. Over the years living alone in the mountains, he has dabbled with making models of sailing ships, exploring different designs. King Korastine and all of Calay are reeling from the heinous burning of the Arkship, but Criston presents himself to the king with new models and offers his services to create, and captain, a new ship.

On the Map of All Things, each life is a kingdom.
    —Tales of the Traveler

Part I

Six Years After the Burning
of the Arkship

1 *Shipbuilders' Bay, Calay Harbor*

Suspended in a rope cradle abeam of the vessel, a grizzled craftsman used mallet, chisel, and rasp to fashion the ornate lettering. He followed charcoal lines drawn on the sanded surface, coaxing the ship's name from the wood.

Dyscovera. The word embodied everything that the magnificent new ship was meant to be, evoking the hopes pinned on her mission and her captain.

Criston Vora stood on the dock in Shipbuilders' Bay, regarding the whole ship. *His* ship. Soon, she would sail across the unexplored seas to find the lost land of Terravitae. And he would succeed this time.

Using hooks and a block-and-tackle, seasoned workers scurried up the shroud lines, stringing a cat's-cradle of ropes to support the masts and spars. From inside and outside the curved hull, caulkers hammered oakum between boards to prevent saltwater from leaking in; carpenters sanded and planed the golden wood that furnished the cabins, while painters and gilders added finishing touches to the exterior, making every detail as beautiful as possible—for Holy Joron.

Even under the bright sun, the late spring air remained crisp and cool. Work progressed on the three-masted carrack, six years after hateful Urecari saboteurs had burned the new Arkship that King Korastine had commissioned. A few blackened hull timbers could still be seen at the bottom of Shipbuilders' Bay, where the ruined exploration vessel had sunk.

But this new ship proved that hope was not gone, merely delayed. This wasn't the first time Criston Vora had resurrected hope from the ashes . . .

The bare-chested Iborian shipwright, Kjelnar, walked up and down the deck, indifferent to the chill. For a man who had grown up in the cold northern reach, this was a balmy day. Waving to Criston on the dock, he yelled over the bustling noise of construction work. "The fittings are ready, Captain! The ice-dragon horn will have its home on the *Dyscovera*'s prow."

Criston cupped his hands around his mouth and called back, "Let's hope your Iborian legends are as reliable as your craftsmanship. We need all the protection we can get." The horn had originally been meant for Korastine's first Arkship; fortunately, the relic had not been installed when the ship burned in the harbor. Now the horn would be kept under guard inside the main Aidenist kirk, until just before the *Dyscovera* sailed.

Feeling a tug on his sleeve, Criston looked down to see his young companion. "Are we going aboard, sir? I want to see what they've finished in your cabin since yesterday."

Criston gave Javian an indulgent smile, feeling a bond with him. He remembered when he himself was fourteen, excited to sail out on fishing boats with his father. He would stare out to sea, imagining mysterious lands just beyond the horizon. "You'll have more than enough time to memorize every splinter and every knot in every deckboard. I suggest you spend your time on dry land while you can, take advantage of what Calay has to offer."

But Javian could not take his eyes off of the ship. "The sea has more to offer, sir."

The young man had lost his mother in the last major gray fever epidemic that scoured the streets of Calay and had run away from his desperate and abusive father. Javian had told Criston how, since the age of ten, he had haunted the docks and eked out a living by doing odd jobs, begging afternoon scraps from fishmongers' stalls.

The young man was curious, determined, and—most important of all—made himself *useful*. During the *Dyscovera*'s construction, if one of the craftsmen grumbled about an unpleasant task, Javian bounded off to do it without being asked. After observing him, Criston had offered to make Javian his personal cabin boy for the voyage.

So much like me, when I was his age . . .

It had been more than eighteen years since the *Luminara* sailed under Captain Andon Shay with similar dreams and determination. Back then, Criston and his crewmates had gone beyond the boundaries of any known map . . . and he had lost everything. Though he survived the shipwreck, his life was forever changed. After many quiet years as a hermit, Criston had decided to face life again and return to the sea. He'd been back among humanity for six years now, but he never stopped feeling alone. His focus, his obsession, set him apart from others: Criston was sure that the *Luminara* had been close, very close, to her sacred destination. With the *Dyscovera*, he intended to go back and search again.

A hush drifted across the docks like an unexpected breeze. A group of blue-uniformed royal guards escorted an old man in plush maroon robes. King Korastine leaned on a carved walking stick, though he seemed embarrassed to be using it. The king had closely watched the progress of the

Dyscovera, from the laying of the keel to the setting of ribs and the mounting of hull planks. Criston knew how badly Korastine wanted to sail away from Tierra. Years ago, the king had planned to go aboard the new Arkship, along with Destrar Broeck, both of them hoping to find peace from the tragedies in their lives. But that was not meant to be.

At Korastine's side walked a smiling ten-year-old boy, blond-haired and thin-faced. Equally fascinated by the ships in the harbor, Prince Tomas often joined his father in Shipbuilders' Bay. The boy's pale hair and eyes reflected those of his Iborian mother, who had died when he was but four.

The king hobbled after his son, favoring his left knee. In recent years, the gout had become so bad that he could barely walk, though he refused to be carried on a palanquin. "What news today, Captain Vora? Are we on schedule?"

Criston bowed formally. "With Kjelnar as our shipwright, Majesty, of course we're on schedule."

Korastine ran his wistful gaze over the lines of the vessel. With a forced smile, he patted his swollen leg. "Much as I'd like to be part of your crew, Captain, I will stay here and await your reports."

Prince Tomas took a step ahead of his father. "*I* want to go along."

Korastine smiled at him. "I don't doubt that would be more amusing than court functions, but the voyage will be too dangerous. You have to stay here in Tierra, where it's safe."

Criston pulled his jacket tight as a cold breeze wove through the docks. By sailing in early spring, the *Dyscovera* should have months of good weather to take them farther than any man had ever gone. "We depart in three weeks, Sire, when the winds should be most favorable for a long westward voyage."

Korastine caressed his beard. "I have high hopes for you, Captain Vora." He squeezed Tomas's shoulder, resting some of his weight on the boy. "Find Holy Joron. We need his aid in the crusade against the evil followers of Urec."

2 *Ishalem*

The great wall across Ishalem blocked the isthmus from the Aidenist enemy. Behind God's Barricade, the holy city would at last be safe in Urecari hands, and on the other side Tierra would wither and die like a branch broken from a tree.

From the high hill where once had stood the ancient wreck of Urec's Arkship, Soldan-Shah Omra watched his construction workers and Tierran slaves continue their labors. The sweating men used log rollers lubricated with mud to pull blocks into place. In the western harbor, a barge rode low in the water, carrying heavy blocks hewn from cliffside quarries.

In charge of the project, Kel Unwar had nearly completed a towering barrier seven miles long, stone after stone after stone, now that the Uraban army had recaptured the blood- and ash-encrusted land. Though trained to be a military leader, Unwar was more gifted as an engineer and organizer, commanding work teams instead of armies.

When Omra first challenged him to build the wall, Unwar had stared off into the distance, then slowly nodded. "No man has ever attempted such a task, Soldan-Shah. It will be magnificent."

Over the years, the enemy had tried—and repeatedly failed—to breach the defenses, and Omra had no intention of ever allowing the 'Hooks to set foot on this sacred ground again. Wearing clean sashes and carrying bright scimitars, soldiers patrolled the rocky landscape north of the boundary line to watch for Aidenist forays. Warships patrolled the harbor and the coast. As the wall neared completion, the enemy grew increasingly desperate—and the soldan-shah felt increasingly secure.

Soon he would be able to go back home to the capital of Olabar, to his family and the palace. But not yet.

His goal was to restore the true glory of Ishalem. The pilgrim camps and the last ruins of burned homes had been replaced by new dwellings made of white and tan stone. Sturdy Uraban horses dredged the debris-choked canals so that water flowed again; small boats could travel inland from the harbors on both the Oceansea and Middlesea coasts. The air resonated with the noises of construction: the clink of hammers, the creak of ropes and rattle of pulleys, the grunting calls of hardworking men. It was a joyful sound, a satisfying racket.

Perhaps Ondun Himself would notice and decide that the people He had left behind were once again worthy. . . .

Riding up next to Omra, Soldan Vishkar from Outer Wahilir slid down from his dapple-gray stallion and somehow managed to bow at the same time. The stallion's showy tack was made of ornately tooled leather, the bit cheek-pieces stylized with plated golden ferns and deep purple tassels.

"A fine afternoon, Soldan-Shah." Twenty years Omra's senior, the new soldan of Outer Wahilir had a square face and barrel chest. His delicately pointed noise and the quirk of his smile always brought a brief sadness to Omra: the man looked so much like his daughter Istar—Omra's first wife and first true love—who had died in childbirth long ago.

Vishkar extracted a long cylinder from his saddlebag, unrolled the paper, and looked around for a place to display the drawing. Finally, he used his horse's flank as a makeshift table; the stallion grazed on patches of grass, unconcerned. "And the day will be even finer once I show you these plans for my church. My Saedran architect has outdone himself. This building will be far more impressive than Huttan's."

"I knew you were up to the challenge. Let me see your designs, even if they were drawn by a Saedran." Vishkar often tried to coax forth details about his competitor's plans, but Omra would not say. "Wouldn't it be better to have a *follower* of Urec design the *church* of Urec?"

Instead of looking abashed, Vishkar shook his head. "No, Soldan-Shah. It is best to use the most talented architect, regardless of his beliefs. And Sen Bira na-Lanis is the best. I intend to win this contest."

In the city's glory days, two churches had dominated Ishalem—an Aidenist kirk on the western side and the main Urecari church on the eastern side. After the great fire, the soldan-shah commanded that the two churches be rebuilt, but this time *both* would be raised to the glory of Urec, and both would display the unfurling fern symbol. The new Ishalem had no place for the Aidenist fishhook.

The neighboring soldanates of Outer and Inner Wahilir had always been rivals, and Omra had challenged each of the two soldans to rebuild one of the grand churches. Stodgy Huttan had complained, while Vishkar vowed to demonstrate his worthiness for such an important project. As the newly installed soldan, Vishkar felt he had much to prove.

Several years ago, after the former leader of Outer Wahilir and his entire family were poisoned by a heinous Aidenist assassin, Soldan-Shah Omra had caused an uproar among the nobles by installing *Vishkar* in the vacant ruling seat. An unexpected choice, but he was a wealthy and stable Olabar merchant—and, as the father of sweet Istar, he was a man Omra respected. Much to the consternation of old-guard noble families, Vishkar ruled the entire rich soldanate with its major coastal cities, its shipyards, and its trading ports.

While his Inner Wahilir rival Soldan Huttan grumbled about the expense of building a new church, Vishkar enthusiastically set to work. Now, pointing to the parchment spread on the grazing stallion's flank, he indicated the turrets and minarets, the vaulted worship chamber with a spiraling walkway. Numerous windows would admit a flood of light. From the highest balconies, sikara priestesses would shout out the scriptures or burn prayer ribbons in braziers. Although this plan was far more ambitious than anything Soldan Huttan had suggested, Omra allowed no hint of reaction to show.

Suddenly, the stallion's head jerked up, ears pricked, as

a thin man ran up the Pilgrim's Path toward the top of the sentinel hill, as if a host of demons were on his heels. Covered with dust, dirt, and powder, he carried a rolled object in his hand. Guards raced behind him, in shared excitement rather than pursuit. Panting and gasping, the man reached the hilltop, bent over, and coughed, resting his weight on his knees.

Vishkar blinked in surprise. "Sen Bira? I hardly recognized you! Sire, this is my Saedran architect."

Bira shook dust out of his tangled hair and tried in vain to neaten his appearance. He gulped a breath of air. "I . . . I should have taken a horse."

The guards arrived quickly beside the Saedran, embarrassed that he had outrun them. "Soldan-Shah! This man has made a discovery—"

"He was about to explain himself." Omra nodded to the man once more. "Go on—my curiosity is piqued."

With an effort, Sen Bira na-Lanis caught his breath and composed himself. "We have been excavating the ruins of the old Aidenist kirk that burned to the ground in the great fire. Today, we broke through a stone wall deep in the catacomb levels and discovered a vault that has remained untouched for centuries." He raised the cylinder—an ancient letter container made of varnished leather.

Vishkar snatched the leather tube and, without opening it, passed it to Omra. The soldan-shah withdrew a well-preserved sheet of parchment, unrolling it with painstaking care, and saw glorious illuminated text. The chart was of a land he had never seen before: islands and reefs along a strange coastline, floating mountains of ice, along with fanciful illustrations of sea serpents and tentacled things.

The writing was so ornate and archaic that Omra had trouble deciphering the letters.

With surprising reverence, Sen Bira said, "It's the Map, Soldan-Shah—*the original Map*. The information it contains, the wonders . . ." He pointed a dirty finger at the coastline but took care not to touch the parchment. "See here, it says TERRAVITAE."

Omra looked at Vishkar, then back at the Saedran. "*Urec's* original Map? The one given to him by Ondun Himself before the two brothers sailed away? The one Urec used in his search for the Key to Creation?"

Sen Bira nodded. "I believe so, Soldan-Shah. It has been sealed in a catacomb, undisturbed, for an impossible amount of time."

"But Urec supposedly lost his map," Vishkar argued. "We know all the stories. That's why he could never find his way back home."

Sen Bira's eyes traveled over the document. "The legends are so old, who can say what is true and what is not? Tales change over the years."

"The truth doesn't change," Vishkar said.

Omra marveled at the map, breathing quickly as his suspicions grew, his sense of wonder shifting to anger. "If this is indeed Urec's original Map, then why was it hidden beneath an *Aidenist* kirk?"

In the city below, war horns sounded from the wall, a fanfare that made the workers pause in their labors. Omra looked up from the ancient relic in his hands, instantly on edge. Vishkar slid a spyglass out of its loop on his stallion's saddle and extended the embossed brass cylinder to the soldan-shah.

Omra passed the newly discovered Map back to the Saedran. "Take this to my residence for safekeeping, but tell no one until I have had time to contemplate it." Without waiting to hear the architect's answer, he pressed the spyglass to his eye, focused, and saw a scout rider on the other side of God's Barricade, galloping along the rough and overgrown old road that had once carried Aidenist pilgrims to Ishalem. The rider raised a fern banner so that archers from the top of the barricade would not shoot at him.

"It's one of our scouts returning, riding hard." Omra swiftly mounted his horse while the guards and Sen Bira milled around in alarm. With an effort, Vishkar climbed back into his own saddle, and the two men kicked their mounts into a trot, making their way down the steep path, whistling and shouting for others to move out of the way.

They reached the uncompleted gap in the tall stone wall, where more Uraban soldiers converged to meet the scout. "Make way for the soldan-shah!" Vishkar bellowed, and the uniformed men shifted aside.

As he pulled up his horse, the scout was flushed, his eyes shining with excitement. Seeing Omra, he sketched a quick bow from his saddle, but wasted no time on formalities. "It's the Tierran army, Soldan-Shah! Ten thousand strong—cavalry and footsoldiers, the largest force they have ever sent against us."

Omra received the news without surprise. "They must be serious this time. When will they arrive?"

"Within days, Sire. Three at the most." A ripple of excitement spread through the people gathered at the wall.

Omra stroked his dark beard. "Then we will be ready for them."

3 Olabar Palace

In the high tower room, the soldan-shah's First Wife Istar—who had been called Adrea, a lifetime ago—sat with her daughters, ostensibly studying verses in Urec's Log. The blue silk curtains were drawn aside, and hot Olabar sunlight gleamed on the polished marble of the open balcony.

From the milling crowds in the square far below, the penetrating voice of Sikara Fyiri wafted upward. Her words were as sharp as a gull's beak, but even gulls weren't so malicious or persistent. "Did Urec not teach us that a mirage can be as deadly as physical danger? He warned us not to trust in *strangers*." Fyiri grew more strident. "Do not fail to recognize the stranger you have let into your own house and into your bed."

Clearly a reference to the First Wife and her role in the Olabar palace. Istar kept her temper in check, pretending to be aloof. The sikaras were never so bold when Omra was present in the city.

Leaning over the cool stone table, Istar pointed to ornate letters on the page, correcting her youngest daughter's mumbled pronunciation. The three girls—Adreala, Cithara, and Istala—were disturbed from their studies by the sikara outside.

Because he spent so much of his time in Ishalem, Omra designated advisers in his absence to monitor the Uraban treasury, agriculture and trade, military preparations, the navy. As the soldan-shah's First Wife, Istar had spent many years at his side listening to complaints of injustices; now he let her handle many of his day-to-day duties at court. Since she was a mere woman, though—and a foreigner at that— many Uraban nobles, priestesses, and commoners were disturbed to see her influence. They circulated rumors that Istar was an Aidenist witch who had cast an unholy spell on the soldan-shah. Utter nonsense. She was more concerned with her daughters' education.

Twelve-year-old Adreala, the eldest, paced around the tower room, bored with the poetry in Urec's Log; she preferred stories of adventures to lyrical verse. She and her little sister, Istala—two years younger—would soon begin schooling in the main church of Olabar, entering the ranks of acolytes at the same time.

Adreala took after her mother, showing a hint of Tierran skin tone; her hair was a lighter brown than Istala's, her figure more wiry. The girl felt no great desire to become a sikara; she had dreams of doing other things in her life besides studying and preaching.

Istala was the other side of the *cuar* coin: olive-skinned, her hair a true blue-black, her demeanor studious. The ten-year-old loved to listen to the priestesses and their music. She perused Urec's Log on her own, wrote out prayers, and burned the paper strips in hopes that Ondun Himself would see the smoke.

The crowd roared outside, incensed by something Sikara Fyiri had said, and Istar glanced up from the thick tome. The third girl in the room, Cithara, at eleven years old, was harder and more moody than her two half-sisters. She turned away from the open balcony with a sniff. "You should not listen, Mother Istar. Sikara Fyiri spreads poison against you."

Despite the knot in her stomach, Istar did not let herself show any distress in front of the girls. "I am proof against her poison. She can talk all she wants." She took the girl's hand and drew her back to the table and their studies.

Cithara was the daughter of the soldan-shah's late wife Cliaparia, whom Istar had stabbed to death in broad daylight. Covered with blood, staggering through the souks, Istar had been horrified at herself, but she had felt no guilt. Cliaparia had killed her baby son . . . Criston . . . the soldan-shah's heir.

Six years ago, when Omra had rushed back from his conquest of Ishalem, the soldan-shah easily found proof of the other woman's crimes. His rage had been thunderous. He dispatched proclamations to all the soldanates absolving Istar of all blame in the killing. "I would have executed Cliaparia myself. Istar was merely meting out the soldan-shah's justice."

Omra had wanted to exile Cliaparia's little daughter—his own daughter—though the girl was much too young to bear any responsibility. But when Istar had looked at the child, something changed inside her. She had caught a glimpse of her humanity again, much as she had upon finding the long-lost note in a bottle from her beloved Criston Vora. "You cannot punish the girl for the sins of her mother," she had insisted.

The soldan-shah was puzzled, for Istar had more reason than anyone else to hate Cliaparia and her family. But she stood firm, and he relented. Instead of letting the girl be exiled, she raised Cithara as one of her own daughters.

Though Omra still didn't understand her motives, the arrangement had worked well for the past six years. The three girls were inseparable.

Outside in the square, Fyiri continued, "Ondun will keep His back turned from us as long as we remain tainted, as long as there are those among us who hide behind masks and whose thoughts are never truly known."

Another veiled reference to Istar. She found it ironic, actually. Masks? With her golden-brown hair, light skin, and blue eyes, Istar could never pretend to be one of them. She had never wanted to be here in the first place; she was born to be a village wife with a Tierran sailor for a husband. But Omra had taken all that from her more than eighteen years ago. Now this was her only life, and she had made the best of it.

"Don't worry, Mother," Istala said in a quiet voice, speaking for herself and her sisters. "When we all become sikaras, we will never hate you, no matter what they try to teach us."

With beautiful cushions piled about her, Istar sat on the dais in the throne room. Acting in the soldan-shah's stead, she waited to receive Soldan Huttan's emissary from Inner Wahilir.

Beside her, a fluted silver pot filled with hot water, fresh mint leaves, and honey was accompanied by a single eggshell ceramic cup. Istar would not waste social pleasantries on the emissary. She had met Ualfor once during a banquet with Omra, but she doubted he had even noticed her; he was a man who saw only the "important" people in a room.

As Soldan Huttan's mouthpiece, Ualfor was delivering a

proposal to annex certain border lands on the edge of Yuarej soldanate, areas that Huttan claimed were ignored by Yuarej and already settled by the people of Inner Wahilir. Istar would accept the document on the soldan-shah's behalf, but she did not intend to render any decision.

Ualfor sauntered in, head held high, a clean white olba wrapped around his dark hair. He smelled of sandalwood and cloves, the scent preceding him by several steps, but when he saw Istar sitting on the dais, the emissary stopped abruptly. "I have been dispatched by Soldan Huttan to speak with the soldan-shah. I have an important petition, for his eyes alone."

"I am his eyes here today."

The emissary clutched a scroll, his grip so tight that he wrinkled the fabric. "I cannot trust a matter of such import to a . . ."

"To one of his wives?"

"When will the soldan-shah return? Tell me."

Istar was put off by his tone and how he presumed to command her. "I do not set the soldan-shah's schedule, and neither do you. By Omra's command, I sit here in court, to receive—and decide—such matters in his absence. You may deliver your document to me, or you may go home with your task uncompleted. It matters not to me."

The emissary turned to two of his retainers who had entered after him. He struck one on the side of the head, berating the man for making him look like an uninformed fool. Without bidding Istar farewell, Ualfor stalked out of the throne room. She could barely keep herself from chuckling in the face of such childish behavior.

*

That night, alone in her spacious bedchamber, Istar lit five beeswax candles and sat cross-legged on the floor beside a low table of polished mahogany. She contented herself with a solitary game of glass spheres and beads. Hearing a soft voice, she looked up to see doe-eyed Naori, Omra's other wife. "Excuse me, Lady Istar—might I speak with you?"

Istar gestured toward the table. "You're always welcome here, Naori."

In stark contrast to the murderous Cliaparia, Naori was sweet and gracious. From the day the soldan-shah had married the girl, Istar and Naori had gotten along well. Immersed in the Uraban culture, Istar had long ago surrendered preconceptions of monogamy, as the Aidenists preached. She had never wanted to wed Omra in the first place, and in her heart—as well as in the eyes of Ondun—she was still married to Criston Vora. Naori was no threat to her, nor to her children. The younger wife had given the soldan-shah two sons, Omirr and Irec, who would be the heirs of Uraba.

Naori arranged her silk skirts so she could kneel at the low table. Istar rearranged the beads and glass spheres, setting up the game for two players, but the other woman looked deeply troubled. "Ur-Sikara Erima came to me again in the church at sunset services. While I was praying, she whispered dangerous things in my ear."

Istar pushed the game pieces away. "What did she say?"

"She said that"—Naori swallowed hard—"she said that you and Saan are going to kill my two sons, so you can rule Uraba. The ur-sikara mocks me for trusting you." When she shook her head, dark ringlets waved from side to side.

Istar rolled her eyes. "Why would I be so foolish? Even

if I managed to put Saan on the throne, he would never be safe. He'd be assassinated within a month. We both know the Uraban people—not to mention the sikaras—would never tolerate him on the throne." Mere logic would not comfort Naori, though. Istar forced herself to remember Cliaparia's treachery. She reached out to pat the younger woman's hand. "I have felt the pain of losing a child. I would not do that to you *or* my son." She lowered her voice. "Or to our husband. I love Saan. Omra loves him. I want him safe and *alive*."

Istar arranged the pieces once more and pushed the blue spheres closer to Naori, encouraging her to pick them up. The game would distract her from the ur-sikara's poisonous accusations. "We are all part of the same household. I love you, Naori, and I have helped raise your sons. Omirr will make a fine soldan-shah someday." She meant it sincerely. "I want your sons, and mine, to grow up and prosper."

4 Olabar Harbor

Saan's little brother loved the colorful ships in the Olabar harbor, the merchants who hawked exotic items from far-off soldanates, and the fishermen who dumped their catch into marketplace tubs. As seabirds wheeled overhead, he kept a firm grip on the six-year-old's pudgy hand and led him through the bustling crowds. "Let's go sit out at the end of the docks."

Zarif Omirr was a scrappy boy with his playmates in the soldan-shah's palace, but he minded Saan. The boy knew full well that bad behavior would result in a day of lessons in his stuffy rooms rather than exploring the city.

The two walked to the end of the wharf and sat on the weathered planks, letting their feet dangle above the water. The low tide had left seaweed and barnacles exposed on the pilings. The brothers wore plain clothes, since Saan did not want to draw attention to himself or to the young zarif.

Back in the palace, advisers complained that Saan was endangering the soldan-shah's heir every time he took the boy into the city. (Naturally, the complainers weren't worried that *Saan* might encounter an accident, since they had never considered him to be Omra's real son.) For years now, however, Kel Rovic, the captain of the palace guard, had trained Saan in self-defense and a variety of fighting techniques. Saan was handy—maybe even a bit cocky—with both a curved sword and short dagger, and he could protect Omirr as well as any uniformed guard. The zarif also had basic training in simple defensive maneuvers.

While his little brother sucked on a hard lump of datesugar bought from a merchant stall, Saan pointed to the bright green sail of an approaching ship. "That one's a merchant vessel, probably from Kiesh. And that one"—he pointed to a blocky and much dirtier vessel that was tying up at a far pier—"an ore carrier from Gremurr, just sailed across the Middlesea."

"I like the red sails best," Omirr decided.

"Those are from Sioara." Saan himself had traveled west to Sioara and all the way east to Kiesh, and many points in between, but never all the way to Ishalem, where the soldan-shah had been for the past month. Since he had no place in government activities, Saan wanted to be a sea captain. Someday, he was sure his father would grant him any ship he wished, and then he'd sail far from here.

Omirr grew restless as soon as he finished his sugar lump. Saan playfully yanked the boy back to his feet and swung him by his arms. "Enough for today. Come on." The two wound their way back through the crowded souks, heading home to the palace. In midafternoon, the crowded buildings cast lengthening shadows.

Navigating the convoluted alleys was more of a challenge than threading the sand shoals off the coast of northern Abilan, but Saan had grown up here in Olabar. He knew the meandering spice merchants' street, the threadmaker's alley, the streets filled with goldsmiths, jewelers, woodcarvers, and potters. They passed booths with henna painters and tattoo artists, rug weavers, ceramic makers, bone carvers. Winding past the noisome tannery district, the two held sprigs of fresh mint to their noses to mask the smell, and then Saan took the boy on a zigzag course to streets filled with vendors of dates, olives, and palm wine, as well as fishmongers and men with caged pigeons or chickens. It was an endless fascinating parade of sounds, colors, and smells.

The two men thought Saan didn't see them as they darted out from a blind alley that smelled of garbage, but he spotted the figures out of the corner of his eye. The pair tracked them with painfully obvious furtiveness, stopping at occasional intervals, pretending to peruse spices or jars of olives, then moving on, casually closing the gap.

Saan picked up the pace, careful not to let the little zarif notice his concern. With his free hand, he touched the fighting dagger in its sheath at his waist. If these men were cutpurses seeking an easy target, they would be in for a surprise. He kept his attention on them, letting Omirr pull ahead.

Despite his alertness, Saan failed to see that it was a double-ruse, a trap.

While he worried about the men behind them, he didn't notice the other two lurkers in the opposite alley. As he and Omirr passed the opening, the hidden men sprang out, knives already drawn. The first man grabbed the boy's arm, clamped a hand over his mouth, and yanked him away so fiercely that his sleeve ripped. Omirr let out a muffled squawk as the kidnappers retreated deeper into the alley.

The narrow passages between the clay-brick buildings connected with other alleys in a winding labyrinth, and Saan knew the men could easily lose themselves—with the zarif— in moments. He drew his dagger, throwing all caution aside, and bounded into the alley to rescue his half-brother.

Just around a sharp corner, Omirr squirmed, but the first man kept a firm hold on him and a hand over himself; he was the smaller of the two, dressed in a green Khenara vest. His fellow cutthroat was tall, with a brown olba tied around his head and a brown sash at his waist. The taller man turned to face Saan.

Most men in such a situation would exhibit caution, study their opponent, take stock of the situation. Saan, though, wasted no time with threats or testing. Yelling like a wild animal, he charged toward the man with the brown olba and slashed hard. The knife felt fluid in his hand; his arm danced back and forth like an embroiderer's needle.

The brown olba was knocked askew as the tall man pressed hard to defend himself with his own dagger. With his left hand, he drew a second curved blade from his sash, standing between Saan and his companion. Still struggling, Omirr yelped, but could not break the captor's grip.

Steel blades clanked together once, twice. Saan withdrew, jabbed with the point, and slashed with a quick reverse to lay open the tall man's forearm along the inside of his elbow. An alarming fountain of blood sprayed from the open artery, drenching his linen tunic and his brown sash. The man backed away in shock. "He cut my arm!"

The shorter man holding Omirr had no olba, his dark hair loose and sticking out in all directions. "You *let* him cut you, idiot." The scrappy zarif grabbed at the man's Khenara vest, popping off two brass buttons that clinked on the alley floor.

Now the pair of decoy stalkers blocked the mouth of the alley with drawn knives. One of the men was as large as a hill bear. They closed in.

Saan glanced over his shoulder at the two new opponents and made a rude sound. "It takes four of you to best one man and a little boy? You must not have a high opinion of your own fighting skills."

The man with the Khenara vest wrapped his forearm tight around Omirr's throat. "It'll take two of us to dispose of your body, and two to cut up the boy here and leave him to be found. After you vanish, it'll be obvious that you killed your own brother out of jealousy, then fled Olabar."

Laughing, Saan pretended not to be concerned. "And I suppose the sikaras are ready to start those rumors?"

At the mouth of the alley behind him, the bear-sized man let out a low chuckle. "And everybody will believe them!"

His wiry companion jabbed him with an elbow. "Nobody said anything about priestesses."

Nobody had to, Saan thought, *but now I know*. The man with the cut arm continued to wail as if he'd received a mortal wound.

Little Omirr thrashed, barely able to breathe in the chokehold. "Cowards! Let me have a knife and watch how I defend my brother!"

The man in the vest yanked his arm tight against the boy's throat. "I'll give you a knife soon enough."

As the two men closed in from behind, Saan made up his mind in a flash. He had been taught never to hesitate, never to let an opponent guess what he had in mind. He hurled himself at the bear-sized man, the one who seemed the greatest threat. Another fighting lesson: Kel Rovic had taught him to concentrate on the most formidable opponent when he himself was freshest and strongest.

Saan had no qualms about killing anyone who threatened his little brother. Using a single stroke before the big man could realize his suicidal audacity, he stabbed the thug in the gut: no finesse, just pain. While the bearish man doubled over, Saan's second jab struck beneath his left ear, through the neck. It was a mortal wound, though the man would be a long time thrashing and moaning in the dirty alley.

While his wiry companion gaped at his fallen comrade, Saan engaged him fiercely, slicing, parrying. The wiry man's own knife was an awkward storm of clumsy attacks and defenses, but by sheer luck, he cut Saan across the chest, and a long line of blood soaked into his tunic.

Seeing his brother wounded, Omirr spat and struggled;

his captor struck him hard in the face, cuffed him again, and bright blood spurted from the boy's nose. The casual brutality against the zarif enraged Saan further.

He faked a slash at the wiry man's eyes, then used the opening to land a ferocious kick to his opponent's crotch. When he doubled over in pain, Saan stuck his knife in the man's throat, yanked it back out. Then he rounded on the zarif's captor. Omirr's battered face and the blood streaming out of his smashed nose made Saan come forward like an angry bull. "You hurt my little brother."

The man held his knife against the boy's neck. "Stop, or I'll kill him right now!" But the look in Saan's foreign blue eyes made him more frantic. "You hear me? I'll cut him right now if you don't—"

Saan slowed, but did not stop. "Omirr, do you remember what Kel Rovic taught you?"

The zarif had been trained well enough. The boy stomped on the man's instep and used the instant of surprise to slip out of his chokehold. Saan grabbed the boy and pulled him away, then kicked the thug's knee. Hard. The kneecap crunched, and the man collapsed sideways with a sharp grunt. A moment later, Saan had thrust his knife through the kidnapper's heart.

Only the whimpering man in the brown olba remained, shocked at the amount of blood flowing from his wounded arm. Wailing, he scrambled headlong out of the alley, nearly tripping over the dead bodies of his co-conspirators.

The battle had lasted only a few minutes, and people clustered in the merchants' street, a few venturing into the alley to look at the slain men. Such assaults were not uncommon in the dark underbelly of the souks.

Saan grabbed his little brother and hurried him out of the alley, eager to get away before a well-meaning shout identified the sons of the soldan-shah. His chest was bleeding, though the knife wound wasn't deep. Flushed, terrified, and excited, little Omirr cupped a hand to his face to catch the red droplets from his bloody nose. Both of them were covered in blood—most of it from their attackers, three of whom lay dead in the alley behind them. *Three dead. I just killed three men.* There was no time to think about it now.

"I want to go home," Omirr said as his shock began to wear off.

In spite of his own pounding heart, Saan pasted an aloof grin on his face to dispel the zarif's fear. "Ha! Those four weren't much of a threat once you and I stood up to them. I'm proud of you."

Saan moved at the best speed the boy could manage, choosing large open streets, working his way back to the palace. "You were very brave. Maybe Kel Rovic should induct you into the palace guard right away."

"I'm the zarif, not a palace guard!"

"Too bad. A zarif doesn't get much practice with swords, but a palace guard carries one every day."

As soon as Saan glimpsed the graceful arches and spires of the palace, he felt great relief. Handmaidens came to greet them, startled to see the torn clothes, the bloody nose, the cut on Saan's chest. "What have you two gotten into now? You're lucky your mothers don't see you this way."

Saan pretended that nothing serious had happened as he passed Omirr to the alarmed women. "Better clean him up before he goes back to Naori."

The boy was already babbling about killers and knives

and fights, but Saan slipped away before the handmaidens suspected he might be telling the truth. Turning the corner, he put on a burst of speed. He had to report to Kel Rovic, one of the few men in the palace that Saan could really trust.

5 *The Pilgrims' Road, Outskirts of Ishalem*

As the large army of Aiden finally reached Ishalem, the sight of the detestable wall lit a fire in the weary and foot-sore men. Ten thousand strong, their shouts rumbled like thunder across the countryside, slamming into the high stone barrier. These men were ready to tear down the blocks with their bare hands.

This time, Mateo promised himself, the soldan-shah's wall would crumble.

On a sturdy horse next to him in the vanguard of the army, Comdar Delnas—the leader of all Aidenist land and sea forces—shaded his eyes, seemingly weighed down by his chain mail and leather armor. "By this time tomorrow, Ishalem will be ours." Because of the heat, he had loosened his chest plates, but he would have his boys tighten the vul-nerable spots before they engaged the enemy in battle.

Delnas was a man who liked his uniform, and he often discussed military matters with overemphasized gravity. Years ago, he had served as an effective administrator in times of peace and stability, but as a wartime comdar, his vision was too narrow. Many brave field commanders had demonstrated their mettle in real battles, but Delnas was little more than an administrator. This would be his first actual engagement with the enemy.

Back in their war council in Calay Castle, stodgy old Delnas had expressed his reservations about mounting such a massive assault with so many troops; he did not want to leave too much of Tierra defenseless for the sake of a precipitous action. But Mateo had disagreed vehemently. "An action is not precipitous when it's long overdue, sir."

After the Urabans recaptured the site of Ishalem six years earlier, the indignant Tierrans had tried to drive them back out. Eight times in the past several years, Tierra had sent small skirmish parties and warship forays down to Ishalem. In every instance, they had been defeated because King Korastine did not send enough troops to do the job. The operations were too small, too disorganized.

It was time to stop underestimating the enemy.

"We're prepared for it, Comdar." Mateo sat high in his saddle and assessed the immense barricade that spanned the isthmus from shore to shore, and the relatively small gap that remained incomplete. "But it will still be a difficult fight."

Though he rarely commented during war councils anymore, King Korastine had said, "Prester-Marshall Rudio tells us that Ondun is displeased to have half of His children cut off from the holy city."

Barely able to control her temper, Anjine had struck her fist on the council table. "I don't intend to wait for Ondun to knock down the wall with a sweep of His mighty hand. Since we know what God wants, it is a sin for us not to act."

With contingents of the standing army drawn from all

five reaches, and after boisterous rallies in Calay to see them off, the soldiers had crowded aboard nearly a hundred ships and set forth with favorable winds and currents down the coast. Though this would be a ground assault with vast numbers of fighters, transport ships were the only way to move them swiftly, before their supplies ran out. The men disembarked at Tierra's southernmost port and began their five-day-long overland journey, while supply trains hurried to keep up with the masses.

As the Tierran army moved, Mateo rode up and down the ranks, talked with them, kept up their morale by fanning the flames of anger against their mortal enemies. This would be their last chance to strike before the Urecari completed the wall. Each soldier knew how much was at stake: if they did not conquer the holy city this time, they would lose Ishalem forever.

For years after the burning of Ishalem, the charred wasteland had remained a haunted place of ashes and skeletons, a reminder of how the followers of Aiden and Urec had offended Ondun. A well-intentioned Prester-Marshall Baine and his flock had gone there to rebuild, only to be hideously murdered by a vengeful soldan. Then, after more than a decade, Soldan-Shah Omra shocked the Tierrans by swarming in with his armies and claiming the abandoned ruins of Ishalem in the name of Urec.

That was when the Tierrans decided they wanted it back.

In the first year, impetuous Destrar Shenro of Alamont Reach had sent an undisciplined group of ninety riders down to the isthmus to sweep away the invaders. All of those brash and unprepared Alamont horsemen had died. The Aidenist church had declared them martyrs, but that was little consolation. Subsequent forays and retaliatory advances fared no better as Soldan-Shah Omra systematically increased his defenses to make Ishalem impregnable.

This time, though, the Tierran military would strike with sufficient soldiers, weapons, supplies, and resolve. This time, they would throw out the "Curlies"—derogatively named because of the unfurling-fern symbol they all sported. This time, loyal Aidenists would tear down the stone wall and raise high the fishhook symbol.

Mateo rode at the head of nearly five hundred cavalrymen, their group commanders, and the young boys who carried their masters' colorful standards. The warriors wore leather armor and chain mail, some of them with fitted breastplates. Behind the mounted vanguard came an army of Tierra's best footsoldiers— archers, swordsmen, and spearmen—in thick leather armor. Their swords were sharp and ready to be blooded.

"Aiden will watch over us." Delnas's horse shifted restlessly, and the comdar's young redheaded pageboy held the bridle. "When we attack, I will ride at the front—I'm going to personally plant King Korastine's flag high on the hill where Aiden's Arkship once stood."

"Yes, sir. May the Compass guide you."

"The Compass will guide us all."

Shifting into position near his troops from Alamont Reach sat General Vanov. The Alamont commander's face was pale and weathered, his skin peeling from a recent sunburn; he sweated heavily in his armor, but stared ahead with steely eyes. Around the campfires at night, Vanov had made no secret that he wanted revenge for the ninety martyred Alamont riders.

The dust of their passage on the worn Pilgrims' Road rose up in clouds, both disguising and exaggerating the size of their forces. The soldiers banged swords against shields and marched forward. Young boys pounded a drumbeat, keeping spirits high. Even the drummers and standard-bearers carried swords, more eager to fight than the seasoned soldiers.

Delnas looked over at Mateo, cleared his throat—a persistent habit the old man wasn't aware of—and said, "Omra must be pissing on his sandals right now. We'll show him and all of the Curlies whose side God is on." He whistled, then raised his voice. "They can see us now. Let's show them who we are. Standard-bearers!"

Mixed among the cavalrymen and field commanders, young boys lifted colorful flags high, proclaiming loyalty to the various reaches. "I want the soldan-shah to see all the colors arrayed against him, that he might be blinded by the rainbow of God's warriors!" Spontaneously, the soldiers let out a loud cheer, a bellowing challenge that rippled across the land.

Delnas was flanked by a pair of young standard-bearers, a blond one and the redheaded page; one flag represented the church with its golden fishhook, the other was a plain scarlet pennant (which Delnas said symbolized the blood of the faithful). Next to Mateo, a young boy carried a flag of indigo and gray, the colors of Calay and the king, which Anjine had given him. The thought of her solidified his resolve.

Atop the looming wall, Urecari defenders moved about in a flurry of preparation; outside the gap, workers scrambled to dig trenches and set up hazard lines of pointed spears to prevent the horses from charging. Vigilant enemy scouts galloped to and fro in front of the gap, waving bright pennants of their own. Shrill horns sounded, and the soldan-shah's troops moved in a practiced, orderly manner, retreating through a temporary wooden barricade, taking shelter inside the city.

Mateo knew that Soldan-Shah Omra couldn't possibly have sufficient soldiers stationed in Ishalem to stand against so many angry Tierrans.

General Vanov removed a gauntlet to wipe perspiration from his brow, then made a brusque comment to the standard-bearer riding next to him. "Keep the flag up, boy. Let them know we're proud of who we are." Comdar Delnas repeated the order down the line.

The raised flags flapped in the wind. Each commander seemed confident. With a glance at Delnas, Mateo said, "We'll throw them out of Ishalem and send them running all the way to the Great Desert!"

6 *Calay Castle*

At the age of twenty-nine Anjine remained unmarried, much to her father's dismay. She could not allow herself to think of romance or husbands in the midst of this war . . . but the conflict showed no sign of ending.

Though Prince Tomas was bright and healthy, and certainly worthy to be in line for the throne, Anjine was King Korastine's successor. Isolated by her royal position, she had never dallied with the schoolgirl crushes her maidservants enjoyed. The war against Uraba consumed her thoughts and erased such giddy ideas from her mind.

Still, she knew Korastine wanted her not only to be married, but *happy*.

Anjine sat in the war council room, poring over summaries from the five reaches. Each day, she waited for a report from Mateo on the front lines, some news about the success of the march against the Ishalem wall.

Her cat Tycho curled up on her lap, finding a way to melt into the valley of her skirts. As he grew older, the cat spent more and more time with Anjine, following her from room to room. Some days, Tycho seemed a perfect sounding board for her to talk through her ideas, especially when Mateo could not be there.

Mateo Bornan, her friend and childhood companion, had risen through the ranks to serve as special subcomdar in the Tierran military, a new liaison position from Calay to the military units. Other men might outrank Mateo, but Anjine trusted him over anyone else.

Her father entered the room smiling, and she could tell that he wanted to talk of husbands or weddings. "My daughter, in these quiet days while we wait to hear from the army, why don't we take the time to discuss other matters that are relevant to Tierra? There is more to life, and to the crown, than war. Sometimes we forget that."

"I don't forget about it, Father. But we have to choose our priorities."

"Yes, indeed we do." Korastine took his seat and leaned forward on the table of varnished Iborian pine. "I just received a letter packet from Destrar Unsul of Erietta, and I am very pleased by his suggestion." He pushed the papers in front of him. "Unsul is a wise and studious man, not given to displays of temper. By building clever windmills to pump water and irrigate the crops, he's greatly increased his yields of cotton and hemp."

She looked up, absently stroking the cat behind his ears. "Good. We always need rope and fabric for our war effort."

Korastine continued as if he hadn't heard. "Such a dedicated man—Unsul worries more about the welfare of his people than about his own personal wealth, or politics in general. I think he would have been happier as an engineer than a destrar. His wife loved the Eriettan horses and was quite an accomplished rider herself, until she was killed in a fall." A cloud-shadow of sadness crossed Korastine's face. "Unsul loved her very much, and now his eldest son Jenirod is a spectacular showman ... takes more after his mother than his father, but I'm sure he's a good man." He lifted one of the letters; the wax seal was already broken. "It would make me very glad if you took this offer seriously."

"And what offer is that?"

"Jenirod is strong, handsome ... and of marriageable age. He comes highly recommended."

Her expression quickly changed. "We're too busy to plan a wedding right now." Done with the subject, Anjine studied an assessment of the Urecari captives that had been sent to the work camps in Alamont and Corag. It wasn't clear whether their unwilling labor produced enough to justify the food required to keep them alive.

Korastine looked dejectedly at Destrar Unsul's letter, tapping his fingers on the words written there. "Forgive a father for wishing his daughter happiness. Having a husband is more than simple political necessity. Ilrida made my life brighter than it had ever been before."

And you were devastated with grief when she died. Anjine nodded. "I realize that, Father, but please . . . not now."

After losing his dear wife, not through treachery or violence but to a simple infection, Korastine had wanted to sail away in search of Terravitae, in search of peace. But the burning of the new Arkship had dashed those hopes, and since then the king spent evenings alone in his chambers, reading the Tales of the Traveler. His swollen, gouty knee had dashed his hopes of sailing to the ends of the earth, and so he explored the world vicariously through the adventures of the fabled wanderer.

"And Tomas . . ." Korastine sat back, smiling. "What a dear boy. With two such wonderful children, what more could a man want?"

Perhaps because of Ilrida's death, King Korastine was overprotective of the boy, fearing any harm that might come to his only son. Anjine remembered the great panic in the castle only five months ago, when her brother hadn't arrived for his lessons on time. No one could locate Tomas—or Mateo, or Obertas, the marshall of the royal guard who was responsible for the prince's safety. Despite a frantic search throughout the castle, Tomas was nowhere to be found.

Though Anjine had tried to downplay the seriousness, poor Korastine's alarm had increased with every hour. He summoned the entire royal guard and city guard, mounting a full-fledged search of the city. The king had melted into relief and nervous laughter when Mateo and Obertas sauntered back to the castle with the boy between them. Grinning, Tomas held up a string with great pride, showing off the four fish they had caught in the bay.

"Can we eat them for dinner?" Tomas didn't understand

what all the fuss was about. "I want the cook to prepare them. They'll be the most delicious fish we've ever had. We used fishhooks and lumps of cheese, and when the fish bit, it almost pulled my arm out!"

While Obertas had begged forgiveness for the inadvertent panic they had caused, Korastine hugged the boy and wouldn't let go. Anjine looked fondly at her friend Mateo, thinking of their times as "Tycho" and "Tolli" when they too had caused the castle staff much consternation.

Mateo smiled sheepishly at her. "We just took your brother fishing. He'd never caught a fish before."

"Can we go again?" Tomas looked up at the king. "I want to go fishing every day. Mateo said he'd take me!"

Korastine shuddered, apparently unable to find an answer, so Anjine replied for him. "Not just yet, Tomas. Next time, let us know where you're going."

Obertas had squirmed in abject apology, but with twinkling eyes, Mateo had added, "Next time, Anjine, we'll even take you with us."

Mateo didn't often appear so happy, but he always tried to make a good show for her, hoping to lighten her burden. Now Anjine hoped he was safe at the Ishalem wall. Maybe, when the soldan-shah faced the large Tierran army—nearly ten thousand troops, gathered for a single attack—he would simply surrender. . . .

Now Korastine studied the letter from Destrar Unsul again; he was certainly persistent. "You could have the same joy, if you would marry."

With a bustle at the door, Anjine's plump handmaiden Enifir came in bearing a small crock of mulled cider. She was of hardy Iborian stock and enormously pregnant, but her condition did not slow her one bit. "I thought you both might be thirsty." Her voice still carried a nasal accent of the northern dialect.

Enifir was one of five handmaidens who had accompanied young Ilrida on her wedding procession from Iboria Reach. The other women had returned to the cold north after the death of their mistress, but Enifir remained in Calay and married a man named Vorannen, who was now the marshall of the city guard. Waddling up to each of them, she ladled warm cider into their mugs. "Drink up before it grows cold." Enifir watched like a hawk until each took a sip, then left the chamber.

Tycho shifted on Anjine's lap, stretched, then dozed again.

"Tomas is about the same age I was when Mateo and I accompanied you on the last trip to Ishalem, to sign the Edict," she pointed out. "Don't you want him to be able to see the holy city, too? Our army is at the gates of Ishalem, Father. We'll conquer it for him—and for all followers of Aiden. With ten thousand soldiers, how can we fail?"

Korastine sipped his mulled cider, let out a sigh. "Once Ishalem is safely in Aidenist hands again, will you take time to plan a wedding?"

7   Southern Ocean, Position Unknown

The tall masts and weathered deckboards creaked as the Nunghal ship swayed in gentle swells. The gray sailcloth sighed and strained as the easterly breeze pushed them along, forcing the helmsman to shift his tack to keep them angling northward. The waves of the open sea rocked the vessel from side to side, rolled it up and down.

Up and down.

Side to side.

Up and down.

Endlessly.

Amidships, gripping the rail with his powerful hands and bunching his arm muscles, Asaddan struggled not to be sick—again. He longed for solid ground that did not lurch and sway under his boots. In the month since their departure from the clan gathering, he had spent more time retching than sleeping.

With a good-natured chuckle, the wiry shipkhan of the vessel, Ruad, came up behind him; he wore no shirt beneath his sharkskin vest. "Cousin, you'll miss the scenery if you spend all your days heaving. We're in waters no man has ever seen."

"The water looks the same to me." Asaddan whistled his sibilants through the gap of his missing front tooth; he groaned as his stomach lurched again.

"That's the way I feel about your grassy plains." Amused, Ruad spread his arms expansively. "It's not even a rough sea."

"If it was a bad storm, I'd be distracted enough to keep my guts inside me." Asaddan stared at the endless ripples of water, the shattered yellow reflection of the sun. He fought down another wave of nausea.

With uncharacteristic sympathy, Ruad lowered his voice. "It's just teasing, cousin—my little revenge for how your clans pestered me mercilessly for *my* clumsiness in riding horses, herding buffalo, and tracking game." The shipkhan drew a deep breath of the salty air. "Ah, I am glad to be back on deck again, where I belong!"

As punishment for wrecking his ship in a storm, which had cost the lives of most of his crew, Ruad had spent a year exiled from the sea among the nomadic Nunghal-Ari. Now he was a joke among his fellow seafaring Nunghals, but he hoped to regain his clan's respect. "We'll go to those fantastic places on the other side of the Great Desert. *If* the oceans take us there."

"They will . . . but it's the long way around," Asaddan said. "You've looked at the maps. There can be no other answer."

After being lost in the sandy wasteland beyond the Nunghal grazing lands, Asaddan had stumbled upon Uraba, a land no Nunghal had ever seen. He had met the soldan-shah, become a sensation at the Olabar court, and eventually convinced his new friends to lead an expedition across the Great Desert. Since that time, Asaddan had made three additional journeys by sand coracle to visit his friends in Uraba.

After hearing Sen Sherufa's theory that a well-provisioned ship could reach Uraba by way of the southern ocean, Asaddan had proposed a scheme. The captain was still considered a great embarrassment to his clan, but if they could complete such a spectacular journey and discover a new route, Ruad's name would be written in gold leaf in all the Nunghal logbooks.

So at the end of the recent clan gathering, Ruad, Asaddan, and a hardy volunteer crew set forth in search of a new route to Uraba. Unaccustomed to long sailing voyages, Asaddan began puking his guts out within the first day.

He had never felt so pitiful, not even during his crossing of the Great Desert on foot. Determined to pull his weight as a crewman aboard the Nunghal ship, he had intended to scrub decks, haul nets, even scramble up a swaying cable ladder. Surrounded by the dizzying openness of the deep sea, he prayed to his gods that they would soon reach the distant Uraban city of Lahjar.

Now the wrenching knot in his stomach tightened, and he vomited over the rail. He coughed and spat the foul taste out of his mouth. Though Ruad tried to restrain himself, he couldn't help laughing.

As Asaddan watched the greenish-pink stain disperse, he noticed a metallic glimmer beneath the waves, a sheen of silver scales that went on and on, then disappeared again. His queasiness forgotten, he shouted, "Ruad, look there!"

Off to the port side of the ship, a large serpent rose from the sea. Water sheeted from its armored hide, and a beard of long spines and seaweed hung from its jaws and chin. Dark blue scalloped fins undulated along its fluidly bent neck.

Ruad did not look at all afraid. "Ha, there's something to keep you distracted, cousin! Silver and blue—never seen one like that before. Must be these northerly waters."

The creature's hinged jaw dropped open, displaying long teeth that could rip a hole in the hide of the largest whale. The serpent emitted a mournful hoot, then a deeper roar; a plume of silvery steam blasted from its blowhole.

"Will it attack?"

"Depends on its mood." Ruad whistled, and the men on deck rushed to their stations. "Load the port cannons!"

Wiry Nunghals pulled on ropes and opened a pair of

gunports in the hull. Crewmen scrambled down the deck ladders and raced to take up positions behind two bronze cylinders that were loaded with firepowder, tamping material, and projectiles.

Asaddan backed away from the rail, wishing he had a longbow, spear, or harpoon. "Looks like it's going to charge."

"That it does. Light torches and fire those cannons!"

The creature hurled itself forward with a speed that reminded Asaddan of a spotted plains viper slithering off of a hot rock.

The Nunghal crewmen touched their torches to the fuses, and two explosions rocked the ship, sending a shudder like thunder through the decks. One of the heavy balls missed the target, and a splashing plume of water appeared far behind the serpent. The other projectile struck home.

The silvery monster snapped in half like a felled tree, its neck severed just below its bearded jaw. With a series of splattering noises, shredded flesh and scales rained down on the water, some striking close to the ship. The serpent's lifeless head, mouth agape but no longer threatening, floated for a moment then capsized. Slowly, the rest of the silver-scaled creature rose to the surface.

Ruad placed his hands on his narrow hips and studied the chunks of meat floating around the hull. "Leave it for the sharks. I've never been fond of sea-monster meat." Asaddan continued to stare, but the shipkhan clapped him on the back once more. "Shall we keep sailing northward? It can't be far now."

Asaddan realized to his surprise that he no longer felt seasick.

8 At the Edge of the Great Desert, Missinia Soldanate

In five years, the settlement at the edge of Missinia's sandy wasteland had grown from a camp to an actual village. Most of the workers still slept in tents, but a permanent administrative dwelling now housed Soldan Xivir and his son Burilo. Deep wells had been dug to provide water for the crews working on the sand coracles, for the merchants and adventurers who flew them, and for the suppliers who brought Uraban goods to be sold at outrageous prices to Nunghal clans on the other side of the Great Desert.

Imposing taxes and tariffs on any goods carried aboard the sand coracles, Soldan Xivir had transformed a rough camp into a civilized town with necessary services, and the road from Desert Harbor to Arikara was well traveled. He was quite proud of his operation.

Once each year, at the seasonal turning of the prevailing winds, intrepid explorers inflated silken balloon sacks fastened to wicker coracles and flew them across the sea of sand. The previous year, nine such vessels had braved the crossing; this year, twelve had launched.

Even priestesses had made the passage, hoping to spread the word of Urec. The Nunghal nomads had listened politely, but showed no desire to change their own beliefs, much to the sikaras' consternation. The Nunghal khan Jikaris had asked a frustrated priestess to become one of his wives. Pragmatic, she had agreed to be his lover on the condition that he convert to the Urecari faith, but Jikaris responded that while the offer was tempting, he didn't find her quite *that* attractive. He preferred his own rough, open churches and his own version of tales of the sailor Sons of God and unexplored lands.

In the past four years, eight Uraban sand coracles had been lost during the hazardous crossing. In one terrifying incident, the wicker basket of a loaded coracle had caught fire from the brazier that kept the silken balloons inflated. As flames engulfed the basket, some men had thrown themselves overboard to their deaths; others climbed up the ropes, clinging to the balloon sack, where they were roasted alive. The burning sand coracle had crashed onto the dunes like an angry meteor.

However, because of the potential for riches and adventure, many merchants still braved the crossing. Each year, the colorful vessels departed from Desert Harbor like a fleet of sailing ships. Six months later, the winds would reverse and blow the sand coracles home. The camp town swelled again with eager caravan leaders and representatives of merchant families ready to receive the unusual Nunghal merchandise.

Any day now, the first sand coracles were expected to come back.

Since the flatlands offered no high points for lookouts, Soldan Xivir had erected a tall wooden tower at the edge of Desert Harbor. All day long, anxious observers stood on the upper platform, scanning the skies with spyglasses, alert to glimpse the first colorful balloon.

Just after noon, a spotter shouted out, "Two coracles! Red and orange balloons!"

Men rushed out of tents, and three eager caravan leaders scrambled up the wooden steps to crowd the observation platform. Soldan Xivir marched out of his headquarters building and turned to the portmaster. "Go, look in your records to see who owns the red and orange coracles."

The small-statured man did not even need to check. "Why, my Lord, the orange vessel carries the former soldan-shah himself. The red balloon belongs to the Gahari family."

The soldan of Missinia felt a wave of relief to know that Imir—his brother-in-law—would soon be returning. He shaded his eyes, looking up. "Prepare a traditional reception feast, and you'd better make it an extravagant one."

Drifting along with painstaking slowness, the airborne vessels took two more hours to arrive at Desert Harbor. Gentle breezes delivered the orange balloon well in advance of the second coracle. High above, the figures in the wicker basket doused the central brazier and let the silk balloon sack deflate. As the coracle descended, the men threw coils of rope down to ground workers who had pounded stakes into the patchy grass.

When the basket was anchored, former soldan-shah Imir swung himself over the coracle's side and dropped to the ground, where he swayed unsteadily on knees unaccustomed to solid land. "What a pleasure to be back on Uraban soil again!"

Xivir came forward to embrace him, sending up a flurry of brown dust and grit from the other man's dirty traveling clothes. "Welcome home."

"Please tell me you have a bath and food—most importantly a bath."

Burilo came up to shake his uncle's hand. "We have already drawn water from the wells, my Lord. Cauldrons are heating it over a fire." Xivir's son was Omra's age—the two had been boys together—and Burilo had already proven himself to be a good administrator, a wise man, and a fitting soldan-in-training to rule Missinia.

The three men walked toward the bath tent. "Was your journey successful?" Xivir asked.

"Oh, yes." The older man's eyes sparkled. "More than I had hoped, more than you can imagine."

When the second coracle drifted in half an hour later, caravan leaders and representatives of the Gahari merchant family swarmed forward with slate boards to tally the goods. Curious camp workers unloaded the cargo, while traders squabbled over the division of the profits.

Imir had made the desert trek three out of the past five years, and by now he had grown quite fond of the nomadic people; he knew their culture, their customs, and had even learned to speak passable Nunghal (though Khan Jikaris teased him for his silly accent).

Given the freedom to travel, and relieved of political responsibilities, the former soldan-shah felt more content now than when he'd ruled all of Uraba. He did not miss the press of advisers and emissaries with their accompanying rivalries, nor the tragedy of scheming wives and assassination attempts. His only disappointment on these trips was that Sen Sherufa na-Oa did not accompany him. The Saedran scholar would have been a great companion during his explorations—not only because she spoke the native language far better than he, but also because Imir was quite fond of her company. However, while she encouraged him to bring back any information about the unknown southern half of the continent, Sherufa didn't personally enjoy the rigors of traveling.

Nevertheless, Imir clung to hope. . . .

Entering the shade of the bath tent, he gulped down a flask of cool well water, then savored a cup of good Missinian wine. Burilo directed servants to pour buckets of heated water into a wooden tub, while a young woman added aromatic herbs and oils.

With a groan and a sigh, Imir shucked his filthy travel clothes, let them fall to the ground, and nudged them away with his toe. "No need to wash the garments—just burn them." He sank into the steaming tub of water with a contented sigh, closed his eyes, and slid his entire head beneath the surface, scrubbing the dirt from his stubbly gray hair and beard. Traditionally, Imir kept himself clean-shaven when in Uraba, but never bothered once he boarded a sand coracle.

He spluttered to the surface again, shaking his head and spraying water from his lips. Burilo and Soldan Xivir pulled up tripod stools with leather seats and waited to hear more of his travels.

Imir's eyes were hard, and his expression had changed from a smile of delight to a predatory grin. "You'll be happy to know that we spotted two bandit camps as we flew over, and I noted their positions."

Burilo looked eager. "We will raid them and crush them, as we've done before. They've been a thorn in our sides for far too many years. In fact, the bandits harassed Desert Harbor only a week ago, but we drove them off."

Soldan Xivir shifted uncomfortably on his stool. "We interrogated one of the captives. Before he died, he told us the name of their new leader: Norgo. Each time we kill one, another springs up. More severed heads for my growing collection back in Arikara, I suppose." He placed his hands on one knee. "But enough of that. You said that your mission was more successful than you had dreamed. What did you mean by that?"

Imir enjoyed the relaxation of the warm water, though he was anxious to join the first caravan back to Olabar, given his vital news for Omra. He blew air through his lips again. "After years of pleading, I finally convinced Khan Jikaris—well, a great deal of gold convinced him—to give me what I wanted." He smiled enigmatically. "I have the recipe and process for making *firepowder*. Now we can blast the Aidenists from the face of the world!"

9 *The Wall of Ishalem*

From the parapets of God's Barricade, Omra stared at the mob of enemy soldiers on the terminus of the Pilgrims' Road. His scouts had given him several days' warning, but the size and speed of the Tierran advance took him by surprise. His scouts had not exaggerated the strength of the oncoming force; the army of Aiden could well crash through the gap in the wall and overwhelm Ishalem.

Previous Tierran attempts to retake the city had been disorganized groups of undisciplined men whose rowdy anger petered out by the time they reached the imposing wall. Kel Unwar had built a remarkable, invincible defense, and the sight of it alone was sufficient to deter most Tierran raiders.

But this was no unruly raiding party, no group of fool-hardy blusterers with more bravery than brains. Omra muttered, "So, King Korastine has finally found his balls."

"Or Princess Anjine found hers." Kel Unwar chuckled beside him. "Tierran females are more like oxen than women."

Omra shot him a sharp glance. "My First Wife is Tierran." Unwar blanched and fumbled for an apology, but the soldan-shah dismissed the comment. "You will be for-given, Kel—if your wall holds."

"It will hold, Soldan-Shah, though I wish they had waited a few months, until construction was complete. As it is, they will try for the gap, and we have to defend it at all costs. I suggest we send men outside to hold it against the 'Hook advance. We can set up obstacles and lure the enemy into range." He looked up and down the wall where groups of archers took their places, stringing their bows; young helpers ran along the parapets, making sure that the tall narrow baskets beside the bowmen were filled with arrows.

Omra nodded his disapproval, but knew he had to pre-pare for the worst. Ten thousand attackers—swordsmen, archers, horsemen! Even the wall might not be sufficient to hold back such a crush. And if they broke through the gap in the barricade and rushed into the city . . .

He had been prepared for this over the past few days. "Mount cavalry and distribute swords to the crew masters at the construction sites. In fact, arm all the faithful Urecari here in the city. And lock away the Aidenist slaves so they can't possibly attempt treachery in the heat of battle."

Unwar scrambled down the scaffolding and whistled for his subcommanders to give them new orders.

By the rockpiles and construction sites, the Tierran slaves began shouting insults to their captors, but after Unwar ordered five of them killed, the rest fell silent. Guards put them into leg irons and herded them into the middle of the city, to the large pit excavated at the site of the former Aidenist kirk. The big hole in the ground would hold them, for now.

Omra paced the top of the wall, studying the colored flags of his enemy, the gleaming armor and snorting horses. From their positions on the parapets, several eager Uraban archers drew back their longbows and let premature arrows fly, though all of them fell short of the front ranks of the army. Omra shouted, "Cease firing! Hold your arrows!"

Unfortunately, the damage was already done. Those impetuous shots now clearly delineated the range of Uraban weapons, and the Tierran commander halted his horses where they were safe. From there, he could issue orders and prepare for the main charge against the wall.

The great stone barrier extended westward down to the breakwater of the Oceansea and east across the narrow isthmus to the shore of the Middlesea, seven miles away. Though the two ends of the wall had not yet met, leaving a point of vulnerability at Ishalem, the gap would create a bottleneck. Even if the ten thousand enemies breached the defenses, they would be limited in how swiftly they could flood through into Ishalem. During the turmoil, Omra's archers could inflict heavy casualties from atop the wall.

But as he watched the angry Aidenists and heard the defiant clashing of sword hilts against shields, Omra realized that heavy losses would not matter to a sufficiently zealous opponent. These Fishhook followers were fanatics who wanted to destroy the unfurling fern wherever they saw it.

The battle ahead would be a grim one, indeed.

However, now that Urec's sacred Map had been found in the vault beneath the ruined kirk, his faith had been reaffirmed. Once he got back to Olabar, Omra would analyze the Map in detail, but he would keep the discovery secret until he had dealt with these Aidenists.

A hush fell over the men atop the wall, and Omra saw a dark-cloaked figure approaching—a mysterious, ominous silhouette that wore black gloves, black robes, and a featureless silver mask. The Teacher showed no hint of his features or his physique; he was a specter, inspiring fear in those who saw him. But Omra did not fear this man. By training and unleashing *ra'virs* on the Aidenists, the Teacher had singlehandedly caused more damage to Tierran morale than any dozen coastal raids or military skirmishes.

The Teacher's voice came muffled from behind the silver mask as he looked out at the massed army beyond the wall. "I shall be interested to watch this."

Nobody had ever seen the Teacher unmasked. Many claimed he must be horribly disfigured, perhaps suffering from leprosy; then again, those might have been rumors fostered by the Teacher himself. Omra considered it more likely the man merely wanted to keep his identity secret: it added to his mystery, increased fear, kept others off balance.

Omra responded with a grim nod. "It will be a bloody battle, and we will be hard-pressed to defend Ishalem. I know how well those Aidenists can fight."

"You have nothing to fear, Soldan-Shah. Urec will take care of his faithful. Without their leaders, even an army of that size will be impotent. Tell your own swordsmen and riders to be ready to charge out onto the battlefield when the moment is right."

"Charge?" Omra looked back at the enormous Aidenist army. "Why should I order the men to leave the protection of the wall?"

"You want to destroy the Tierrans, don't you?" With a swirl of dark garments and a glint of sunlight on the silver mask, the Teacher stalked off down the wall.

Omra stood impatiently while his servants helped him into battle armor, covered with a clean white tunic embroidered with a Golden Fern. His sword was sharp, his shield freshly painted, his olba wrapped tightly around his head. He mounted his battle-ready mare and rode to his forces crowded at the gap in the wall.

As the afternoon light took on a deeper gold, Uraban soldiers stood hooting and jeering from the safety of God's Barricade, trying to lure the enemy closer. The Tierran front lines pushed forward to stop just short of where prematurely fired arrows prickled the ground. Across the flat expanse, battlefield presters walked the lines of Aidenist soldiers, waving their hands in meaningless blessings.

Omra saw the man in the lead, obviously their comdar, with young standard-bearers on both sides carrying bright flags. The old military leader bellowed something in a

challenging voice, words that the soldan-shah didn't understand. Generals and subcommanders called out to their
cavalry, their footsoldiers. Swords and spears were raised.

Omra called out to his men; Kel Unwar issued orders.
The Uraban warhorses trotted forward, a few hundred of
them to make a stand at the gap in the wall. He glanced up
at the wall behind him, saw the Teacher standing there in
silhouette.

When the Tierran battle horns blew, Omra turned to his
well-trained men and yelled, "Stand fast! Protect the wall at
all costs."

Before the archers could begin their deadly rain of
arrows, from atop the high wall came a strange cry from the
Teacher, an ululating wail that pierced the hot, sluggish air.

As the Aidenist soldiers prepared to charge, the two
young standard-bearers beside their main commander drew
their swords. In unison, they ran the Tierran commander
through, plunging their blades between his chestplate and
back guard. They found his vulnerable spot again and
again, and the leader of the Aidenist army fell dead before
the rest of the soldiers even realized what has happening.

Another general, bearing the standard of Alamont
Reach, thrashed left and right, but his young standard-
bearer thrust a blade under the older man's chin, nearly
decapitating him.

It happened in an instant, throughout the Aidenist ranks.
Responding to the Teacher's eerie call, fighters turned on
their own comrades—young men stabbing their military
leaders, killing the Aidenist soldiers on either side of them
with no regard for their own safety.

Ra'virs! Omra realized that the Teacher had planted

dozens of *ra'virs* among the Tierran troops. Serving as pages, flag-carriers, and aides, these boys had gotten close to their unsuspecting leaders. Within the first critical moments of surprise, more than half of the Aidenist field commanders were slain.

As shock, confusion, and horror stalled the enemy advance, Omra knew he had to press his advantage. The Teacher had been right. With their chain of command in shambles, the unwieldy Aidenist army would not know how to react. Now was the time to press his advantage.

He howled the command to charge, and his armed riders rushed through the gap in the wall and plunged into the sudden turmoil the *ra'virs* had created. He spared only one glance back at the proud figure of the Teacher atop the parapets.

Even before he struck his first enemy, Omra felt a glow of warmth inside. This battle would be a bloodbath.

10 *Windcatch*

Before the departure of the *Dyscovera*, and the very real possibility that he might never return home, Criston felt obligated to visit Windcatch, the village that had once been his home. Adrea's home. A place of love and a place of loss, filled with memories, shadows, and ghosts.

Back in Shipbuilders' Bay, while the new vessel's quartermaster saw to loading the supplies and the sailmaster began hanging the sheets on the yardarms, Criston took passage aboard a small merchant vessel that was heading south to his old hometown. Javian asked to go along, so eager to help that Criston could not deny him. "Let me visit your village, Captain. I want to see where the raiders attacked. I promise I'll be helpful."

Criston hadn't wanted any witnesses to the emotional impact the place might have on him, but he agreed to take the earnest young man. On the short voyage, Javian made a point of assisting the merchant ship's captain, intent on proving how well he would serve as the *Dyscovera*'s cabin boy. He ran errands and worked as hard as any member of the real crew, much to their amusement. Criston never regretted his decision.

Four months ago, the two had sat on the dock in Shipbuilders' Bay, eating apples that Criston had bought from a farmer's cart. The young man matched him bite for bite, imitating his movements. Back then, the *Dyscovera* was only a framework in the construction area, surrounded by piles of fresh Iborian lumber. Shipbuilders pounded the planks to the hull supports. Looking at the great sailing vessel taking shape, Criston had mused, "So, boy, would you like to sail on her when she's finished?"

Javian's entire face had lit up. "Of course, sir!"

"I might be in need of a cabin boy, if you think you can handle the hard work."

"I can handle hard work."

"And follow orders?"

"Anything you ask, sir!"

"I'll hold you to that."

Javian had tried to prove himself every day since. . . .

When the small merchant ship docked in the Windcatch harbor, Criston saw an unfamiliar place filled with strangers. Porters lifted crates and unloaded supplies from the hold. Shopkeepers came forward to study the newly arrived wares; villagers hovered around to receive mail packets from Calay and other coastal towns.

Criston drank in the details that were so common and yet so strange. *Home.* The little seaport town seemed the same ... but different. The dozens of houses and shops burned in the raid had been rebuilt, but the new ones didn't look right. The docks had been greatly expanded, but many slips were empty, with most of the fishing boats out for the day's catch. Drying nets hung on plank racks on the gravelly shore.

Criston smelled only the faintest lingering scent of rot. "Lucky we weren't here a month ago. When the migratory seaweed spoils in the water, the stink is so bad it drives even the fish away." He kept a jovial tone in his voice, but his heart ached with the memory of the many times he, Adrea, and her brother Ciarlo had waded out to harvest the kelp. Now that near-forgotten *normalcy* seemed as imaginary as the tales told by grizzled old seamen in dockside taverns.

Over the years since returning to civilization, Criston had gone back to Windcatch off and on. The first few times, he had kept to himself, expecting someone to spot him on the street and call out his name. But no one did. Soon enough, he realized he needed no disguise. The people here no longer remembered much about him, his old mother, or Adrea. Most Windcatch families had lost much in the raid—nineteen years past now—and many other deaths and tragedies had happened since, through violence or natural causes. Hurricanes, fevers, an accidental fire that had burned an entire section of docks. His town had moved on from its tragedies.

When he looked at the young townspeople, the active fishermen, the boys longing to go out to sea, he realized that many of them had not yet been born at the time of the devastating Urecari raid.

Without a word, he led Javian to the end of one of the old docks, not one of the newly rebuilt structures or the expanded wharves. Criston gestured out to the harbor opening and restless waves far beyond. He kept his voice low, musing to himself, although the young man listened with eager attention.

"I used to stand here and watch my father set off to sea every day in his fishing boat. I'd wave to him until I couldn't see him anymore. My mother would always tell him to be careful, and then she'd pray for Aiden to watch over him. But one day my father didn't come back. His boat sank, lost at sea in a storm—or maybe the Leviathan found him."

He blinked furiously, but his eyes continued to burn. When he was younger, he had so wanted to be like his father. He had even purchased his own sailing boat to follow in Cindon Vora's footsteps, taking cargo back and forth to Calay. But that was before the *Luminara* . . . before everything.

"There were times when I'd sit here, on this dock, under the starlight with Adrea. I'd show her the constellations, and we'd talk about the wide world that neither of us had ever seen. The lands and seas seemed endless but reachable. The world was exciting." He looked down at Javian. "So I understand your longing to sail off on the *Dyscovera*, I really do."

The young man frowned and looked away. "We understand each other in many ways, Captain. But I ran away from home for entirely different reasons."

"Are you going to try to see your father again before we depart?"

"No."

Two bulky Soeland ships, former whalers now converted to patrol vessels, came into the harbor and dropped anchor away from the crowded docks; farther out to sea, Criston could see three sailing ships that were clearly of Uraban design, keeping station with two other Soeland patrol vessels; their colorful silken sails were patched, hulls repaired with fresh wood.

The people in town cheered the arrival of the ships. Stony-faced Destrar Tavishel himself rode in the first boat to shore. "Two more enemy vessels captured for the Tierran navy!" When he stepped onto the rocky beach, the people of Windcatch whistled. "Another Aidenist victory— and another seventy prisoners to be put to work in our camps."

Rowboats shuttled the downcast captives to holding areas; the foreign men were tied together in strings like fish on a line, shuffling along, knowing they had no hope of escape. Destrar Tavishel had become a legend for his skill in intercepting Uraban ships, capturing their crews, and delivering the spoils of war to villages along the coast. Tavishel took little for himself, drawing satisfaction from hurting the followers of Urec, wherever he found them.

Javian looked with wide eyes at the captured ships and the many Uraban slaves, and Criston stared, trying to feel moved by the sense of celebration. "When I left here many years ago, Windcatch was a quiet place."

Inside a new inn, he bought the young man a small cup of local kelpwine and a large one for himself, then they shared a bowl of the traditional stew of dried seaweed and shellfish. Criston recognized no one, including the bartender. It had been so many years since he'd left home, eager to sail off on the *Luminara*. Back then, expecting that nothing would change, he hadn't taken the time or trouble to notice his daily life. Now it was too late.

Stepping out of the inn, he looked toward the hill overlooking the town and the rebuilt Aidenist kirk. Yes, he would find Ciarlo there. "Follow me. There's someone I need to see before we go."

The two trudged up the worn path to the house of worship. A cast-iron fishhook as tall as Javian graced the kirk's entrance. The window shutters were open wide to air out winter's leftover mustiness. In the garden beds out front, rows of seeds had been planted in newly turned soil, and fine green tendrils were already sprouting.

A man in prester robes limped out of the door, paused upon seeing Criston, then gasped. "I hoped you would come for one last visit before you sailed off again."

Criston embraced Adrea's brother, but the sudden lump in his throat made it impossible to speak. Finally, he said, "I went away on the *Luminara* because I wanted to see what was out there, but I didn't realize the price I'd have to pay." He stepped back, just looking at the other man. "This time, I have a different reason."

"You can't fool me, Criston. This time, you think you have nothing to lose." Then he broke into a smile. "Just greet Holy Joron for me when you see him, all right? I'll be waiting right here for Ondun to return."

Remembering his companion, Criston introduced Javian. Ciarlo looked at the fourteen-year-old, adding the years in his mind, surely imagining how old Adrea's child—Criston's true son—would be now, if the raiders hadn't taken her. But both Adrea and the baby had probably died long ago. And Javian was much too young.

Turning to hide the tears in his eyes, Ciarlo effusively invited the two into the kirk. There, a dark-haired young boy nearly bowled them over, his arms wrapped around a half-empty cask of oil. Ciarlo reeled out of the way. "Careful, Davic! Spilled whale oil is not a mess *I* have any intention of cleaning up."

The boy gulped and stuttered; he looked to be about eleven years old. "S-sorry, Prester Ciarlo, but you said that once I finished—" He caught himself, noticing the two strangers beside the prester. "Oh!"

Ciarlo laughed. "This is my enthusiastic helper Davic."

"Pleased to meet you." The boy steadied himself, bobbing his head toward the visitors. "I filled all the kirk's lamps, Prester, and I swept your office, like you asked. Then I stacked the books neatly."

"Good enough. Now, put the oil back in the shed. Take a handful of dried peas and plant them in a row outside, and then you can be done for the day." Ciarlo turned back to Criston, shaking his head indulgently. "You aren't the only one to take on a young lad who needs guidance in his life. This boy came to Windcatch six months ago after his family was killed in a Urecari raid on a nearby village. He had nowhere else to go. I found him here in the kirk, wanting to pray." He tousled Davic's dark hair. "He assists in the dawn services each morning. Maybe one day he'll even want to become the town's prester. I could train him just as Prester Fennan trained me."

Criston's expression hardened at the sharp memory. On the day of the Urecari raid, the town's previous prester had sacrificed his own life to give his lame apprentice time to hide.

Though the two boys were separated by only three years, Javian wanted to be considered an adult, while the other boy was more interested in play time, now that his chores were done. Davic bounded away outside, but Javian stayed with Criston.

For a late midday meal, they broke bread in Ciarlo's small parsonage adjacent to the kirk. Criston and his brother-in-law talked about nothing of consequence, basking in the shared company. Though neither man was old, both had lined and creased faces, aged more by harsh memories than by time itself.

When the low sun spilled a golden path across the sea, Criston excused himself and left the kirk. "There's one more visit I have to make."

The graveyard on the hill outside of town had grown in the intervening years; a new section of eleven graves all dug in a single month when the gray fever swept through Windcatch. Criston went to a particular wooden post with its fishhook symbol, where he studied the weathered name of TELHA VORA, his mother. Another nearby post memorialized his beloved Adrea, though her body had never been found. *Maybe* she was still alive. Criston squeezed his eyes shut. He would never know.

As he sat there, saying goodbye for what might be the last

time, Criston renewed his solemn promise to send Adrea letters. He would keep throwing the bottles into the sea, where he hoped the tides would bring them to their destination . . . wherever that was.

There was too much uncertainty. Whether Adrea was alive or dead, whether he would ever come back to Tierra, whether they would find what they sought. After the sinking of the *Luminara*, when Criston had been lost, he had felt like this. Adrift.

Back then he had taken refuge in his prayers, clinging to a fishline of hope that he would get home to Adrea. This time, though, he had no ties to bring him back to the known world. . . .

He and Javian stayed the night with Ciarlo in the parsonage, then before the morning services they trudged back down to the town so they could take passage on the next cargo boat heading back to Calay. The *Dyscovera* would be waiting for them.

11   *Corag Mountains*

On their third day in the rugged Corag mountains, Prester Hannes and his companion found a place to make camp as night set in. The two men had climbed through an open cirque, over a stony pass, and down into another hanging valley. The patches of snow in the high meadow were still too thick for spring flowers to penetrate.

The place reminded Hannes very much of where he'd nearly frozen to death.

Drifting ice glazed the beautiful turquoise lakes. Late in the afternoon, Raga Var caught two small fish, which would supplement the snow grouse he had shot with his arrows. Food for another night—and the two men would push onward. Hannes believed they were close to their destination; he would know when he saw it.

After the abrupt sunset, the temperature fell like a descending ax blade. With instinct born of long practice, the scruffy scout found a good spot amid the talus boulders. Without speaking to his companion, Raga Var gathered dead leaves, dry moss, and a few twigs to start their fire.

Hannes unslung his pack and extracted a blanket, spreading it out on the hard rock so he could have a warmer place to sit. The prester had little need for conversation, and the scout had even less. Hannes liked it that way.

Soon their meal was roasting over the low flames. The blaze did little to warm them, but Hannes didn't care; he could endure any amount of discomfort. He finally broke the silence. "How much farther do you think we need to go?"

Raga Var shrugged his bony shoulders beneath the patchwork furs. "Never been this far before. Never seen these crags." He withdrew the spitted trout and grouse from the flames, poked the blackened skin with his finger, and decided the meat was done enough to eat.

"Can we find our way through to the Middlesea?"

Another shrug. "If such a way exists."

"It exists." Hannes had crossed over the mountains after his escape from the Gremurr mines, though he'd nearly died from frostbite and exposure. The cold had cost him two fingers and three toes. He retrieved the other roasting fish for himself, though Raga Var had not offered it. The men ate in silence, then divided the snow grouse between them.

Absently, Hannes touched the waxy scars on his cheek from the Ishalem fire. He had survived and spent years afterward in the accursed lands of Uraba. After killing a woman who tainted him with Urecari sacraments, he quietly wrought havoc across the soldanates, before being captured and sent to work in the Gremurr mines. But by the power of Ondun and Aiden, Prester Hannes had escaped through the mountains, wandering lost until at last a quiet hermit named Criston Vora had saved him.

Now, years later, Hannes was determined to rediscover the path he had taken—a route that could lead Tierran crusaders to the Uraban beachhead on the shore of the Middlesea. He had pleaded his case with Prester-Marshall Rudio, who sent him to Corag on his quest. In the cliff city of Stoneholm, Hannes had hired this odd and silent guide who came highly recommended by Destrar Siescu himself.

With the spring thaw and the guidance of Raga Var, Hannes was certain he could find a route for Aidenist armies through the trackless mountains to reach the Middlesea. Such a discovery would change the war forever.

After the small meal, Hannes wrapped himself in his blankets and said his prayers before sleep. Raga Var moved about a while longer, gathering the feathers he had plucked from the snow grouse and keeping them in a pouch; later, he would use the feathers to fletch arrows or insulate his clothes.

Despite the hard rock against which he lay, Hannes slept soundly. A righteous man, untroubled by nightmares, he awoke at sunrise, refreshed. He broke the skin of ice on the pot of drinking water and splashed his face, bracing himself against the frigid slap. Then he drew out a razor-edged dagger and began to shave.

Raga Var watched Hannes with interest. The scrawny scout had a patchy beard that extended from cheekbones to collarbones; his hair was long and matted, his eyebrows thick. "I wouldn't put such a sharp knife so close to my throat. Why do you do that to yourself day after day?"

"For the glory of God."

"How do you know God wants you to scrape your face?"

"Because I have seen paintings of Aiden. He alone among the brothers was clean-shaven."

Raga Var frowned. "But how do you know what he looked like? There was no painter aboard Aiden's ship."

"I do not question my beliefs."

Finished, Hannes wrapped his blanket and his few belongings in his pack, and the two men set off once more. Since they had eaten all the food the previous night, there was no breakfast, but Raga Var foraged along the way, always keeping his bow ready in case he spotted game.

The scout picked his own path and moved at a good pace. He knew portions of the Corag mountains intimately—the passes, valleys, peaks, and glaciers. On this trip, Prester Hannes had pushed him farther than he had ever explored, and Raga Var seemed eager to learn a new landscape.

Throughout the day, the two men walked in companionable silence, climbing over rocks, switchbacking up steep grassy hillsides into the tundra. The rocks, cliffs, and peaks began to look familiar, but Hannes said nothing, not wanting to get either of their hopes up.

When two black crags loomed before them, the prester felt a powerful sense of déjà vu. The men picked their way through a notch between the peaks, and an expansive view opened up before them, another series of valleys—and beyond that, the wide deep blue of a great body of water: the Middlesea.

The scout scratched his bushy beard and stared. "I have led you where you wanted to go, Prester."

Hannes clutched the cold black rockface next to him for balance. "You ... and Aiden." He sent a silent prayer of thanks. "I need to see more."

He didn't rest at the top of the pass but pushed forward with renewed vigor. As they descended the rugged valleys and the Middlesea filled their view, Hannes smelled a stink in the air and recognized a smoky pall rising from the mines and smelters of Gremurr. But he had to be sure.

The two men reached the top of a defile and looked down a canyon carved by rushing seasonal streams. Ahead was the shore, the natural harbor. Shaft openings honeycombed the gray cliffsides, and Hannes could make out the antlike figures of slaves carrying buckets of rock. Out in the water, wide barges rode low, heavily laden with metals and finished weapons.

Filled with hatred, Hannes stared for a long time, then finally nodded at Raga Var. "Now we know the way. I have to return to Calay and make my report to the prester-marshall and the king."

12 *Gremurr Mines*

As administrator of the Gremurr mines, Tukar held a position of some power and importance. Nevertheless, he remained an exile from his home in Olabar. He was comfortable enough, yes, but his situation was not so different from that of the workers and soldiers.

The decree of the former soldan-shah, his own father, was clear. Tukar was lucky he hadn't been executed for his mother's treachery.

So he made the best of his circumstances. Though the mines were above the Edict Line on the Middlesea coast, and therefore technically in Tierran territory, this outpost provided vital metals and weapons for the war effort. Since being sent here, Tukar had tried to make amends, prove his loyalty, and make the mines an example for all of the faithful; he owed it to his brother Omra, the soldan-shah of all Uraba.

He had grown accustomed to his eyes burning from the constant haze of black smoke, which even the Middlesea breezes could not sweep away. He no longer noticed the sulfurous stink from the smelters, the soot from the coke ovens, the rock dust that always made his mouth taste gritty. This was his life now, and Gremurr was his home, the place where he had a family. It wasn't so bad.

Even so, Tukar had not forgotten the fresh smells of the Uraban capital city, the perfumes of the palace, or the fine meals he'd once eaten.

Now, Workmaster Zadar led the weekly inspection tour

of the slaves and facilities. Bald and stocky, his body a solid lump of muscle, Zadar was hard on the laborers, though not unfair. They would never love him, but they respected him. He fed the workers enough to keep them strong, and maintained harsh conditions to keep them cooperative.

For the past month, the workmaster had been particularly proud of their ambitious new rolling mills designed to manufacture heavy iron sheeting to armor Urecari warships. Inside the factory, Tukar heard the clanging of metal and the shouts of men pouring molten iron from a crucible into molds. In adjacent smithies, captives chained to anvils hammered on swords, while others stood inured to the spray of sparks from grinding wheels. In the oppressive heat, soot-covered Aidenist slaves hauled still-warm sheets of iron and stacked them into piles; their bare skin glistened with sweat.

Tukar nodded in satisfaction. "Good work, Zadar. Those plates will make our warships invincible."

The workmaster wiped a bare palm across his forehead. "The iron sheets are here, my Lord, but the war galleys are on the Oceansea, on the other side of the isthmus."

"Caravans can carry them overland from Sioara," Tukar said.

"As easy as that?" Zadar gestured toward the rolling mill. "It takes two men just to lift a single plate. How many sheets do you think a horse can carry, on a cart, over rough roads? And how many plates are needed to cover the entire hull of a single war galley? And how many warships does our navy possess?"

Tukar struggled with the math, feeling deflated. He had been excited to see the added output with the new rolling mills, but he hadn't bothered to consider the difficulties of transporting the armor plates away from Gremurr. "It's like a game of *xaries*. I was seeing only one move ahead, while you looked farther."

Zadar brushed aside the compliment. "And the soldan-shah needs to see many more moves beyond that. I don't envy your brother at all."

Tukar's brow furrowed as he tried to think of a brilliant solution to offer Omra, but Zadar pulled him away from the working area, chuckling. "Come, it's not a problem for you to solve. I merely pointed it out to keep you distracted during today's game."

Tukar brightened. Their daily match of *xaries* was a high-light for him. Over the past decade, he had become an excellent opponent, seeing strategic nuances on the board that his wicked mother had never taught him. But Villiki's goal had always been to demean him, while Workmaster Zadar wanted a challenging opponent.

The two men left the dirty industrial area and followed the gravel path up to Tukar's residence. The hints of com-fort and finery in his home here were nothing like what he had left behind in Olabar. Outdoors in a red-and-green-striped silk pavilion, Tukar's dear wife Shetia had spread out a tray of fruit and skewers of roasted songbirds for them. He smiled adoringly at her.

Shetia was quiet and shy, not unattractive, though she wasn't one of the gorgeous noble daughters he might have married. After so many years, however, Tukar wasn't sure he would have wanted it any other way. His kind, loving Shetia never complained about being sent away to this hot and dirty place. She was the twelfth daughter of a wealthy merchant from Lillotha, and considering her own prospects she had married reasonably well. Tukar treated her with respect, even a touch of love and sweetness. She made him content.

Their nine-year-old son, Ulan, ran toward them from the main residence. He grabbed his father's sleeve. "May I play a game with you today? You said I was good enough to challenge Workmaster Zadar!"

The other man looked at Tukar in surprise, his lips quirking in a curious smile. Tukar said, "Yes, I am teaching the boy *xaries*. He was even good enough to defeat me once."

"Twice," the boy piped up.

Zadar teased, "On the other hand, my Lord, defeating you is no great challenge."

Tukar sent the boy away with a fond pat. "You and I should practice a bit more together, Ulan. Let me enjoy my conversation with Zadar for the afternoon. Go play with your puppy." Dejected for a moment, the boy went back to his mother, and the pair retired into the residence. Soon, however, the sounds of barking and a child's laughter changed the mood.

Tukar knew it was unkind to raise Ulan in a place like this, where there were no other children. So when a recent supply ship arrived, and the captain's dog gave birth to a litter of puppies, Tukar took Ulan to see them. Isolated at the Gremurr mines, the boy had never played with a dog before, but he was instantly smitten. After negotiating with the captain, Tukar presented his son with one of the puppies—a bouncing brown energetic mass of fur.

Tukar recalled how much pleasure his own puppy had given him long ago in the Olabar palace . . . for a few weeks until his mother took it away. Villiki did not want him to waste his time with such things. Later, though, Tukar had tended the hounds once owned by the soldan-shah's wife Asha. He wondered what had happened to them since his exile here. . . .

A breeze rustled the silk fabric of the pavilion. Tukar, sitting across the game board from Zadar, touched the carved jet and jade, planning his opening move. The bald workmaster ate one of the skewered birds, crunching the bones. Tukar moved his first piece, and the workmaster responded quickly. The ebb and flow of the game was automatic to them.

They talked about their work. He countered the workmaster's offense with a move his mother had taught him.

Thinking of Villiki, he shook his head. "I cannot forgive my mother for trying to poison Omra and bringing disgrace to the entire royal family. But I miss my father, and Omra, too." He moved another piece, sipped his warm tea. "Things could have been so different. Now I wonder if I'll ever leave here."

"You could ask the soldan-shah to reconsider your sentence."

Tukar shook his head. "No, I couldn't do that, although one day . . . one day I hope to see the new Ishalem that Omra has built."

13 *Nunghal Ship, Position Unknown*

Under the beating sun, Asaddan sprawled on the hot deck, inhaling and exhaling fiery air, wondering when it would ever end. He stared blearily at the sagging ropes of the ship's rigging, at the limp gray sheets of the sails. The air rippled with heat, as if the sky itself had become a giant magnifying lens.

Even wandering lost in the Great Desert hadn't been quite so hot as this.

Around him, the Nunghal-Su crewmen lay fanning themselves, dumping buckets of seawater onto their parched skin for a few moments of coolness, although the water itself was murky and warm. Each day when the sun was high overhead, Asaddan expected the water around the ship to boil and cook them like clams in a pot.

Most of the men were drearily silent, some moaned, and a few whispered a mixture of prayers and complaints. Asaddan had discussed the predicament with Ruad in private, acknowledging that the entire crew was afraid; it had been much too long since they'd sighted land. No one knew where they were going, and worse, the ship had come to a standstill in the doldrums.

Fights broke out as the men squabbled over small patches of shade on deck. Some miserable sailors sulked in the dark cargo hold below, although the stifling heat down there was even worse than in the open air. Their water barrels were nearly empty, tainted with greenish scum and wriggling insect larvae.

This was not at all the paradise Asaddan had promised them during the clan gathering many weeks ago.

A shadow fell across Asaddan, who opened his eyes to see a concerned Ruad standing before him. When the ship-khan squatted next to him, Asaddan groaned, "Could you stand up again, cousin? Your shadow was blocking the sun. Make yourself useful."

Ruad made a rude response and continued to crouch beside the larger man. "The sailors are complaining. They already accuse me of losing another ship and another crew."

Asaddan shaded his face with his hand. "And what solution do they offer? To turn around? What good would that do? We're not moving anyway." He let out a fatalistic chuckle. It had been a week and a half since they'd seen clouds, two weeks since the last rainfall, five days since the wind had died completely, leaving them stranded on an ocean as smooth as glass. "I doubt we'll ever catch a breeze again." Sweat trickled between his squeezed-shut eyelids and stung. "At least I haven't been seasick for days."

"We Nunghal-Su say that God is holding His breath. But even God has to exhale sometime—and when He does, we'd better be prepared."

With another groan, Asaddan turned his head away. Thick strands of seaweed floated on the lethargic currents around the ship. With boathooks and ropes, the men had hauled up some of the strands, but the brown seaweed was inedible, despite the cook's best efforts. Even the fish they caught in these waters looked monstrous, spiny, misshapen. And they tasted foul.

Asaddan heaved himself into a sitting position. Ruad went to the side of the ship and hauled up one of the dangling wooden buckets. He doused his companion without warning, and Asaddan spluttered and rubbed the matted hair from his eyes. In the oppressive heat, many of the sailors had shaved off their hair and beards to keep themselves cooler, but he refused to do so, as a matter of pride.

His skin cooled for a few moments, but the evaporating water left a sparkle of salt-dust that itched and burned. When he took a deep breath, he imagined a blacksmith filling bellows with hot air. "If we keep sailing northward, we get closer and closer to the sun. Is there a chance we might sail into the flames?"

Ruad showed little reaction. "How would I know? No one has ever sailed this far before. But since we know the Uraban lands are to the north, it can't be all fire."

Asaddan gazed around him, fearing that the sails, the ropes, the wood of the deck itself would combust. All of them could roast, and no one would ever know what happened to them. He said, "It's the price, and the excitement, of exploring the unknown. I have to believe there's a way out of this. Sen Sherufa was a wise woman. I knew her well and trusted her. And Saan . . . ah, that boy was clever!"

"I thought so, too." Ruad squinted in the bright sunlight. "But now I begin to doubt their idea. Maybe we made a mistake by believing them."

Asaddan motioned for the shipkhan to lower his voice. "The crew is thinking that already. They should not hear it from us as well."

Ruad gazed toward the prow, as though he could will the ship forward. "Just how long are we going to wait here?"

"As long as it takes. We don't have much of a choice."

The two men fell silent, keeping their hopes and fears to themselves.

Then, as they stared and waited, a breeze tickled the fabric of the sails. Asaddan raised his nose and sniffed. The crew began to stir, also sensing the movement. The canvas luffed, then sagged again, but after a few tense movements it bulged outward once more. The breeze was tentative, but better than anything they'd felt in a long time.

Gradually, the wind caught the sails and pushed the ship forward.

14 *Saedran District, Olabar*

When Olabar came into view over the low hills, the skyline looked so beautiful that Imir thought the caravan had taken a wrong turn and found the way to mystical Terravitae.

He had been away for half a year, but it seemed like ages. The Nunghals were not a particularly cultured people, and their women were not the most attractive in the world. (Sometimes, in fact, Imir had trouble telling the difference between one of the old wives and one of the shaggy buffaloes from their herds.) He couldn't wait to see his people, his city . . . and Sen Sherufa.

After the four-day trek from Desert Harbor, the officials at the palace would want to receive him with a flurry of celebrations and social gatherings, but the first thing Imir wanted to do was visit Sherufa before he got caught up in all that nonsense. He had his priorities.

At the moment, though, he smelled of horse and dust and sweat, and that wouldn't do for the Saedran woman. He had to make himself presentable first. As the caravan dispersed into the merchants' quarter, Imir slipped off his borrowed mount. He paid a young boy three *cuars* to procure new clothing for him while he went to the crowded public baths. By the time the boy returned, Imir was cleansed, freshly shaved, his cheeks, scalp, and skin oiled with a touch of perfume (but not too much). His new clothes fit him rather well, and he realized that he had become leaner during the months of traveling—leaner and more handsome, he hoped.

Walking through the Saedran District, he passed apothecaries, bookshops, and candle makers, until he arrived at the familiar door of Sherufa's home. Tucked under his arm, he carried packets of documents and annotated sketches from the land of the Nunghals; he knew she would consider them finer gifts than any jewelry he might have brought her.

Answering his knock, she pulled open the door, taken aback at first, then surprised and delighted. "Imir! I must have lost track of the days. Are you early, or late?"

He would have preferred a hug and a kiss, an excited exclamation of how much she'd missed him while he was away . . . but that was not, and had never been, in Sherufa's nature. He kissed her on the cheek, though, and couldn't stop grinning as he entered her dwelling. "I was on the first sand coracle to arrive, and I hurried directly here."

Imir placed his packet of papers on the main table that served as both her desk and dining surface. "For you, my dear, I had Khan Jikaris send out riders in all directions. The men kept notes of the terrain, sketching any particular cartographic points of interest."

When Sherufa spread out the brown-edged sheets and bent over to look at the lines and landscape markings, her shoulder brushed against his. Imir intentionally pressed a bit closer; she was too preoccupied to notice . . . or maybe not.

He continued, "Also, at the clan gathering on the

seacoast, I purchased copies of Nunghal-Su charts so you could compare all the details."

Sherufa slid one map aside, stared at the next, then the next. The notations were in the Nunghal language, crude letters with a variety of spellings. "This is the most complete information on the southern continent that any Uraban eyes have ever seen. Thank you, Imir!"

It had been such a long time since he'd talked with her. "After I looked at these charts and spoke to the mapmakers, many of them talked about your idea that the coastlines connect. If a ship sailed far enough, it would eventually find Lahjar."

"*Might* find Lahjar. And remember, that was Saan's idea as well," Sherufa reminded him.

"Oh, the boy doesn't care about the credit."

"And you think I do? Do I appear to be a vain person?"

He lifted his chin. "You're a person who should be honored, among both your people and mine." Sherufa snorted and gazed back down at the charts, but he could see that her lips quirked in a smile.

"In fact," Imir continued, "when I left the clan gathering, our friend Asaddan had convinced Ruad to attempt the voyage."

"Asaddan always loved to tell stories."

"I don't think it was a story, my dear. If they had the determination, they certainly had the wherewithal. Who knows, someday they may show up on our doorstep."

Sherufa noted a few small inconsistencies among the documents. "I'll read the written descriptions in detail later." She leaned over to kiss him on his newly shaven cheek. "Thank you, Imir. Thank you for thinking of me."

"I always think of you. Whenever I see something you may not know, I collect it and bring it back to you." He spread his hands to indicate the maps, then gathered his courage. "You see, I have given you the entire world. *Now* will you consent to be my wife?"

Sherufa was not surprised by the question, since he had asked her repeatedly before. "The entire world is not yet mapped, Imir. Ask me later, when it is."

15 *Ishalem*

It was a bloody and difficult fight, but once the *ra'vir* assassins struck the Tierran commanders, ripples of shock destroyed the Aidenist formations from within. Omra's cavalry and swordsmen had rushed through the gap in the wall and into the confusion, slashing with their curved scimitars. Thousands strong, disciplined and in well-trained formations, the soldan-shah's army caused disproportionate slaughter on the enemy.

After the Tierran forces retreated in disarray, the Uraban wounded were brought back into the city where their injuries could be tended by healers; the Tierran dead and injured were left where they lay on the bloody battlefield outside the wall. Fading moans continued throughout the night, while great cheers rang in the streets of Ishalem as the followers of Urec celebrated their victory.

The next dawn, Omra stood atop the wall again to stare at the churned battleground. He had not slept, not even cleaned himself. He did not feel his numerous cuts and bruises, did not care about the drying red stains on his skin and clothes; his olba had come unwound and hung in loose scraps down his neck. He would leave the myriad enemy corpses to rot on the blood-soaked Pilgrims' Road. Hungry seabirds had already begun wheeling in from the Oceansea, contemplating their feast.

When the shrouded Teacher joined him, Omra spoke to the blank silver mask. "You have done Uraba a great service. Name your reward."

The Teacher bowed slightly. "The blessings of Urec are my reward. The spilled blood of evil Aidenists is my reward. Their cries of pain and screams of fear throughout the night . . . yes, those are my reward."

"And nothing else?" Omra wasn't surprised. The Teacher had always needed little, asked for little, yet performed a great service.

The stranger's identity was secret even from Omra. Years ago, Kel Unwar had delivered mysterious letters written in a firm, unstylized hand, proposing a new method to infiltrate and destroy the 'Hooks from within. "Soldan-shah, I believe you should read these," he had said. "The letters were brought to me by an unknown man. I don't know why he chose me as his conduit . . . but perhaps you should hear his ideas. This could be our path to victory." Omra—only the zarif at the time—had read the suggestions with interest, then amazement.

With Unwar acting as intermediary, Omra had arranged a meeting in a darkened section of Olabar on a moonless night, and the masked figure told him the story of the *ra'vir* bird, which laid its eggs in another bird's nest, and later the hatchlings would kill their rivals. "We can do that with children, my Lord. Tierran children ... malleable minds that we make our own. We need only the material to work with."

And the Teacher had been absolutely right. The turmoil and fear wrought by the secret infiltrators caused as much damage as an outright military assault.

Now, on the wall in the brightening morning sunlight, the face behind the silver mask remained silent for a long moment. He contemplated the proffered reward, then said, "Yes, Soldan-Shah, there is something I would like. Allow me to create a new, larger training camp for *ra'virs* here, not far from Ishalem."

Omra did not hesitate. "I'll have Kel Unwar divert work teams immediately. I leave for Olabar tomorrow, but you shall have whatever you desire."

"Even before the workers finish the wall?"

"We'll whip the Tierran slaves hard enough to do both jobs."

The Teacher nodded slowly. "That is their purpose in the world."

Reaffirming Kel Unwar as the provisional governor of Ishalem in his absence, Omra took the swiftest dromond across the Middlesea, eager to return to his palace, his wives, and his children. Home.

When he arrived in the capital, priestesses set braziers upon the stone steps of the main church, adding chemical dusts to the coals so that bright smoke rose up with tempting scents and unusual colors. Ur-Sikara Erima herself emerged to deliver the triumphal sermon, expressing great passion as she spoke with the lilting twang of her Lahjar accent. "For truly we are blessed, for Ondun sees our great soldan-shah as another son following in the footsteps of His favorite, Urec."

As he made a slow procession back to the minarets of the palace, Omra let his people applaud him, but when he entered his own chambers, he focused his attention on his family. Sweet Naori came to him first, leading their two young sons, overjoyed to have him home. She embraced him but expressed no interest in the politics or the battle.

Omra called his three daughters—Adreala, Cithara, and Istala—who greeted him formally, though he could see by the sparkle in their eyes how glad they were to have him home and safe. Next, Saan bounded in, his straw-colored hair and blue eyes giving him an entirely non-Uraban appearance. "I never had any doubts you would hold Ishalem, Father. The city belongs to us, not the Aidenists."

Omra swept him into a hug. It always amazed him that Saan was a man now. "You will hear plenty of stories about what happened on the battlefield. The soldiers are already spinning tales up and down the docks, looking for someone to buy them cups of wine."

"I'll buy you a cup of wine, Father, if you tell *me* your stories."

"Later." He took a seat on his cushions, relaxing. "I want to know what's happened here in my absence."

"Not much, certainly nothing so exciting as an invading Aidenist army." But the young man's bright gaze flicked away for a moment. "Well . . . there was one incident, an attack on me and Omirr. Thugs in the souks. But we fended it off. Considering what the men said, I suspect the sikaras put them up to it, though I have no proof."

After Saan described the attackers, the conversation, and the knife fight in the alley, Omra could barely contain his fury. He lurched up from the cushions again. "Someone raised a hand against my son!" He caught himself and added, "*Two* of my sons."

Saan shrugged. "There were only four of them, and Omirr did his share of fighting too. Remember, Father, enemies have tried to kill me many times. I'm ready for them."

Omra paced, clenching his jaw. "At least the Aidenists attack us openly. If this is some sikara plot . . ." He let out a long sigh. "I cannot challenge the church without proof."

"Three of the men are dead, and the one who escaped was never found. If he is involved with the sikaras, I doubt we'll see him again. They've probably sent him away to Kiesh by now . . . or we'll find his body floating in the harbor. Kel Rovic is investigating. Maybe he'll find something."

Troubled, Omra sent him away and called for Istar, the person he most wanted to see. Always attuned to his thoughts, Istar detected his mood as soon as she entered the room. She settled in, crossing her legs on a broad cushion, and reported on her meetings with Finance Minister Samfair, Protocol Minister Faan, and Trade Minister Usthra, all of whom tolerated her well enough. Then, with a tone of amusement, she recounted how the stuffy Inner Wahilir emissary had refused to present her with his document from Soldan Huttan, even though she was Omra's court surrogate while he was in Ishalem.

Saan's news had stripped away his feelings of peace and anticipation, and at this further affront, the soldan-shah felt his face grow hot. Going to his writing desk, he snatched a cut piece of rough paper. "By treating you with disrespect, they insult *me*." His words were hard and sharp, like the jagged edge of a spear head. "That, at least, I can stop—I have the power. I will show them what it means to ignore you."

Istar leaned closer as he wrote furiously. "There's no need to overreact."

"I am reacting *properly*, not excessively." He finished his decree with a flourish, set aside the quill, and sealed the inkpot. "This is my summons, to be delivered to all five soldanates. Each soldan is hereby commanded to send his First Wife here to the Olabar court, where all will see the consequences of insulting me—and you."

Istar was troubled. "What is it you plan to do? I want no blood shed over this, Omra."

He merely dusted the fresh ink with powder, tipped a candle over the document to spill drops of wax, then pressed his signet ring into the hot wax to make his mark. "Do not question me, Istar. This is my command. My people have no choice but to obey."

16 *Calay*

Back from Windcatch, Criston and Javian returned to Shipbuilders' Bay and the *Dyscovera*. Broad-backed men filed aboard carrying crates of cured meats, dried fruit, wrapped biscuits, medical supplies, bottles of wine, kegs of heavily hopped beer, cages of chickens, sacks of grain, and many casks of fresh water.

Kjelnar greeted them from the prow, shirtless as usual. "I was hoping we wouldn't have to sail without you, Captain! We're about ready, Aiden willing."

"Well then, let's see if the ship meets with my approval, Shipwright."

He walked the deck, climbed down a wooden ladder into the cargo hold, checked the bunks and hammocks where the crewmen would sleep stacked together like dried apricots, then inspected the brick oven in the galley. Following with undisguised pride, Kjelnar pointed out all that he'd completed during Criston's brief absence.

As cabin boy, Javian would have his own closet-sized room adjacent to the captain's cabin; it was barely large enough for him to stand up in, with a hard shelf for a bed, and another for his reading and studies. Criston had made it a condition of Javian's service that the boy continue his education in letters and mathematics, as well as the Book of Aiden.

At the navigator's station, alongside a traditional magnetic compass and the Captain's Compass whose needle always pointed to Calay, stood Aiden's Compass. The ancient relic would show them the way to Terravitae. Although its needle remained inert and motionless, as it had for centuries, Criston had faith that once they neared the land of Holy Joron, the sympathetic magic would register again.

Criston extended his hand, taking Kjelnar's grip in his own. "I can't say that I have ever seen a more perfect ship, Shipwright. When I first imagined the designs for sailing vessels and carved my wooden models, even my dreams were not as excellent as the *Dyscovera* actually is."

Javian beamed. "And now the greatest captain and the greatest crew will make this greatest mission a success."

Kjelnar's chest swelled. "If faith could float boats, boy, our ship would fly."

The converted warehouse building at the harbor's edge smelled of sawdust, shellac, paint, and tar. The window shutters were open to fill the interior with sunshine. More than a dozen Saedrans toiled in a flurry of finishing touches on the replica; the team of intense craftsmen, led by the famed model-maker Burian na-Coway, would light lamps and work far into the night in order to complete the project in time.

Four feet long from bowsprit to stern, the *Dyscovera*'s sympathetic counterpart was larger and more precise than any of the ship models that sat on shelves in the naval war room at Calay Castle. Sen Leo na-Hadra, the aged but brilliant Saedran scholar, paced around the detailed construction. Burian kept sheet after sheet of notes, constantly measuring, jotting down numbers, and sending runners back to the actual vessel in Shipbuilders' Bay with measuring strings to verify his notes.

When he saw the captain enter, Sen Leo's eyes burned with a new kind of fire. He snapped at his craftsmen, "Back and forth you go! I want every man here to study the real *Dyscovera* at least once an hour. Any flaw you note must be reproduced here. Every rigging rope, every knot."

The old scholar formally introduced Criston to Sen Aldo na-Curic, who would act as the *Dyscovera*'s navigator, chronicler, and cartographer. Criston shook Aldo's hand. "Are you ready for the voyage, Chartsman? We set sail in less than a week."

The dark-haired Saedran crossed his thin arms.

"Captain, I've been ready all my life. I became a chartsman just before the departure of the *Luminara*, and I was chosen to serve aboard the great Arkship, before she burned. Oh yes, Captain, I am ready."

"Sounds to me like you're bad luck," Javian said with a hint of skepticism. Criston nudged the boy into silence.

With balls of string, like the toy ribbons children used during Landing Day celebrations, two Saedran riggers laid down the ropes and tied the shrouds on the model *Dyscovera*, exactly mimicking the ones on the great vessel.

Strands of sympathetic magic wove through the world and connected all things, because—according to the Book of Aiden—every speck of creation had been touched by the hand of Ondun. Therefore, if a model were built with scraps of wood from the same planks that made up the real vessel, if duplicate rigging ropes were strands from the actual ropes, if the paint and shellac came from the same pots, then the two counterparts were inseparably connected. If anything should happen to the *Dyscovera* herself, this model would reflect it, here inside this building in Calay.

"We will do our part, Captain Vora," said the model-maker, looking up from his notes. "Your job is to sail the ship where it needs to go."

Back home in the Saedran District, Aldo na-Curic joined his family for a boisterous meal and an evening of discussions, games, and fellowship. Aldo's wife, Lanni, one of Sen Leo's daughters, greeted him at the doorway with a quick embrace, then ran back to the kitchen to help his mother prepare the meal. Aldo's little son and daughter—aged three and two, respectively—hurried up to him, clinging to his legs. He threw the girl into the air and swung her around, then repeated the process with the boy.

By the time he returned from the *Dyscovera*'s voyage—*if* he returned—the children would be much older. He hated to miss key years of their childhood, but he would not turn down the chance for this voyage. If Aldo discovered the rest of the world, found Terravitae, and helped the Saedrans in their age-old quest to complete the accurate Mappa Mundi—the Map of All Things—then his son and daughter would forgive him.

Aldo's sister, Ilna, who still had no husband though she was well past the age to marry, called them to the table. Ilna was an attractive young woman, though somewhat flighty, and the na-Curic family had enough funds for a reasonable dowry, but she was extremely picky about her suitors.

Aldo's parents, Biento and Yura, unveiled the baked fish with sprigs of herbs and preserved lemons. Lanni passed around a basket of fresh-baked rolls. Aldo took one for himself and reached for a pot of butter, while the children fought over the jam and honey.

Aldo's father called for them all to stop. "Before we partake, we must express our thanks. Tell us what you're grateful for. Ondun may be far away, but we all know He is listening." In the subsequent pause, Biento scanned their faces, then said, "I am grateful for the opportunity my son has been given. He will be the most famous Saedran chartsman in history."

Aldo blushed. Lanni spoke next. "I am grateful for my husband and everything he has given me, including these wonderful children."

Aldo's younger brother, Wen, who wanted to be a chartsman himself but didn't have the fortitude or patience to memorize vast libraries of data, said he was thankful for his new job as a journeyman clockmaker.

When it was his turn, Aldo felt a lump in his throat. "I am grateful for such a wonderful family, and the happy memories you've given me. I will draw upon you for strength when I am far, far away."

As he looked around at his family, their faces made blurry by his own tears, Aldo realized he would miss them very much.

Biento began to serve the fish.

17 *Calay*

Wounded, weary, and dispirited, Mateo and the first group of surviving cavalrymen rode hard, pushing their horses to exhaustion, well ahead of the marching remnants of the army. Though sick at heart, he had to report to King Korastine . . . and to Anjine.

Despite their utter defeat at Ishalem, the Tierran army had inflicted enough hurt on the enemy, thankfully, that the Urecari forces could not pursue them more than several miles from the wall. With a little more preparation and determination, the soldan-shah could have wiped them out.

It was a devastating blow. More than half of the Aidenist field commanders had been murdered.

Mateo finally reached Calay. The sweat running down his forehead stung his eyes in salty droplets much like tears, much like blood. He had seen so much blood in only a few hours. . . .

After the traitors had struck down their commanders at the wall, the Tierrans had fought bravely, outraged, disbelieving. Those innocent-seeming young boys had trained alongside them as soldiers, carried fishhook battle standards, lived in their camps, laughed with their fellows . . . and then fallen upon their own comrades, stabbing, slashing, murdering battle leaders at the most crucial moment.

At the head of the troops, visible to the front ranks of cavalrymen and footsoldiers, Comdar Delnas had been a key target. He was slaughtered like a pig in the first few seconds, to the utter shock of the advancing Aidenists. The standard-bearers continued to stab Delnas until he was a mangled bloody patchwork that tumbled from his rearing horse.

As the soldiers' charge faltered in confusion, more traitors appeared, seeming to strike everywhere.

Mateo had immediately guessed what was happening. The brainwashed infiltrators had caused harm here and there across Tierra, but incidents had been rare over the past several years. Yet they had quietly infested the ranks of the army. No more than a few dozen of the bloodthirsty traitors had been sprinkled among the forces at Ishalem . . . but they had wormed their way into in the most crucial places, ready to strike.

As subcomdar, Mateo was a target, too.

His own standard-bearer was a giggling brown-haired boy with a freckle-splashed face. When the cheerful boy lunged at him from behind, Mateo had thrown himself to one side on his saddle, so that the sharp blade caromed off his shoulderplate. Without thinking, he struck backward with the sword he'd raised to challenge the advancing Uraban soldiers, running its point through the fanatical *ra'vir*'s chest.

As loud roars of surprise and rage boiled up from the front lines, Mateo yelled a warning into the clamor, but not swiftly enough to save General Vanov of Alamont, whose focus had been straight ahead.

Taking advantage of the confusion, Soldan-Shah Omra's mounted Uraban army surged like a flood through the unfinished gap in the wall, holding scimitars high. Thousands of them.

With no one in clear command of the Aidenist army, Mateo did his best to rally the troops, shouting until he thought his throat would bleed. But in the chaos, one other surviving general—Kurda from Soeland Reach—screamed conflicting orders. In the end, there had been no discipline, and the footsoldiers fought one-on-one for their own survival. When Urecari arrows finally cut down General Kurda, Mateo was the only one left. Watching the tides of battle turn, he had no alternative but to sound the retreat. . . .

After long and miserable days of travel, arriving back in Calay with a group of the first men on the fastest horses, Mateo sent his dispirited fighters to get food and drink; some went straight to their barracks and collapsed in exhaustion.

But Mateo couldn't allow himself that relief. His field bandages were dirty, crusted with blood and dust, and he felt feverish. His cuts had been sewn up by an overworked Saedran surgeon. Once far enough away from the isthmus to feel safe, Mateo had removed his heavy, hot armor, discarding it so he could ride even faster. His bruises and cuts would heal, except for the ache in his heart. Many other faithful Aidenist fighters would not.

He did not waste time changing into a clean uniform or making himself presentable. His tunic was torn, stained with road dust and dried blood—his own, mixed with the blood of his comrades and his enemies. He reported directly to Subcomdar Rief, who had been left in charge when Delnas took the ten-thousand-man army south.

Torin Rief was a younger and, in Mateo's opinion, more competent commander than Delnas had been. Rief bore a long scar on the left side of his face, and two fingers were gone from his right hand, the marks of different battles. After the many years of bloody struggle against Uraba, no one remained unscathed.

Standing erect, muddy boots together, gaze directed at the subcomdar, Mateo gave his report like a true soldier. He wanted nothing more than to forget the battle—the horror of watching his friends slaughtered, the sounds of clashing swords, frenzied horses, and screaming men, the mingled smells of urine, feces, and blood—but he did not have that luxury. Though his heart pounded with the memories, he crushed his rising emotions, kept his voice even, and told Rief what he needed to know. He did not embellish his descriptions, nor did he allow himself to break down, but merely stated what he had witnessed, what he had done, and what he had left behind.

It was bad enough.

The other man was pale as curdled milk by the time the report was finished. Though Mateo's knees were weak and he wished he could let himself collapse into a chair, he remained standing because Torin Rief had not dismissed him. He clung to his duty like a fraying lifeline.

Rief snapped out of his shock and lurched to his feet, knocking the wooden chair backward, and took Mateo's arm, careful to grasp below the bandage. "Come with me to the castle. The king needs to hear this directly from you."

An hour later, when Royal Guard-Marshall Obertas ushered the two into the war room, they interrupted a meeting between Anjine, King Korastine, Sen Leo na-Hadra, and Destrar Shenro; documents and charts were spread on the long pine table, and the four abruptly stopped their discussion.

After all the bloodshed and turmoil, what Mateo most dreaded seeing was the look in Anjine's eyes when he confessed his failure. He had let her down. He had promised her Ishalem. Instead, he had lost thousands of Tierran soldiers.

Anjine rose to her feet, taking in Mateo's bedraggled appearance and his wounds. She stopped herself from running to him only with visible effort. Mateo looked away in shame. She shouldn't be concerned just for him; it was her duty to worry what had happened to the whole army, to Comdar Delnas, to all the others slain. He now realized that he should have taken the time to hide the extent of his injuries, to gloss over the damage *he* had suffered so that she could concentrate on the real tragedy.

Subcomdar Rief bowed quickly and wasted no time. "Majesty, our army has been defeated at Ishalem."

Anjine stared at Mateo, her eyes fixed on him to make sure he was all right, but he addressed Korastine and once again told his awful tale. When he was finished, Destrar Shenro hung his head. "I had hoped General Vanov would avenge my brave horsemen slaughtered by the Curlies. Now we have even greater reason for hating them."

Anjine snapped, "We've had enough reasons to hate them for a long time, and now we've lost many of our leaders, including Comdar Delnas himself."

Mateo said, "Many troop commanders, cavalrymen, infantry soldiers are dead. My best estimate"—he paused because the number made him reel—"is that we lost three to four thousand of the ten thousand fighters who marched down to the Ishalem wall." He could hardly look at her through his crushing guilt. "I fear now that we may never recapture the holy city."

He remembered the shine in Anjine's eyes not so long ago when she called for the offensive against the Ishalem wall. None of them had imagined a circumstance in which he would return in such utter defeat.

Cool and professional, Rief attended to important business. "Majesty, the rest of our soldiers are making their way back to Calay, some on ships, others on the road. Over the next week, they'll straggle into the city, exhausted and hungry. Many of them must be sorely injured. We should get help to them with all possible haste. I ask permission to dispatch wagons of supplies and field doctors."

King Korastine clawed fingers through his gray-streaked brown hair and hung his head. "Yes, yes. Do so immediately."

Mateo could not remain silent. He spoke without using

the proper titles, but no one noticed. "I failed you, Anjine. You placed your faith in me and the other commanders. They've died for it." He swallowed. "I have no choice but to offer my resignation."

Anjine pushed aside Destrar Shenro's records and placed her fists upon the table. Sparks seemed to fly from her gaze. "Stop being ridiculous, Mateo. Those damnable *ra'virs* caused our defeat. It took only a few of them to kill key military commanders at our army's most vulnerable moment. It took only a few of them to burn our new Arkship right here in Calay harbor." She looked around the room, demanding answers. "How do they continue to infiltrate our towns, our army? How do they know so much about us that they can live among us undetected?"

"We've captured several over the years, but they reveal nothing, Princess," Torin Rief said.

"But are they not all young men? Orphans?" Shenro said. "That gives us a clue."

Mateo shook his head. "We need soldiers, especially now! Should we turn away all young men from military service because some of them might be *ra'virs*? Even in this recent debacle, there were no more than a few dozen traitors among ten thousand."

"Only a few, yes, but look how much harm they caused," Sen Leo pointed out.

Mateo could see that Anjine was outraged at how they had hurt her people, but even more upset at the danger they had posed to *him*. "I hate them—*hate them* more than I can express! How many more lurk among us, unsuspected? They have infested our armies like spreading weeds, and we must root them out. We have no greater priority than to identify and be rid of them." She pointed directly at Mateo; everyone there knew she spoke for the king. "That is your new mission. Find a way to identify these monsters hidden in our midst—whatever it takes."

18 *Calay*

Destrar Broeck had made many trips down from the cold north, but each time he returned to Calay he felt a pang of sadness for his lost daughter. He still remembered bringing Ilrida here to marry King Korastine, never guessing that something as simple as an accidental scratch could end years of happiness.

As their ship pulled into the harbor, he watched the wonder on the face of his nephew Iaros. The eager young man had never before left Iboria Reach, but if he was going to be the new destrar, he would have to understand more of the world. "Can we go to the castle straightaway, Uncle? I want to meet and serve the king."

Broeck wondered if he had looked like such a bumpkin his first time in Calay, but that was long ago and under a different king. "Don't be impatient, lad. Korastine will see us in his own time." He pointed a stern finger, knowing the admonishment would not sink in. "Do not forget that you make a better impression the more you *listen* and the less you say."

"I won't say anything unless it's important. I won't ask questions. I won't speak up. I'll just be quiet and learn what I can. I've been practicing."

"I hadn't noticed."

Iaros was a full-grown man, well-muscled, almost as handsome as he *thought* he was, but his innocence gave him a childlike air. After the ship tied up to the dock and the two men disembarked, Iaros licked his palms and smoothed back his thick reddish hair. Then, with great care and concentration, he used his fingertips to straighten the mustache that spread like a rooster feather across his upper lip and down his cheeks.

Not long before, Iaros had sported a full flaming-red beard, which he had constantly washed, combed, and trimmed, preening in front of anything that reflected his face. Tired of such displays of vanity, Broeck had commanded his nephew to shave his chin. Though horrified, the young man could hardly disobey his destrar, so he had followed the instructions precisely: he shaved his *chin*, but left the huge mustache in place.

The ridiculous style made him look like one of the walruses from the high ice banks of the north, but Iaros was convinced that it appeared dashing—so convinced, in fact, that he persuaded his swordsmen to shave themselves in a similar fashion, so that now mustache-sans-beard was quite popular in Iboria Reach. Broeck didn't think he'd ever get used to the look.

Leaving the docks, the two men made their way on foot across the bridges to the Royal District, trudging up cobblestoned streets. His nephew would rather have brought a large retinue of warriors, but Broeck had countermanded that suggestion. "We're *Iborians*, lad—not some effete lordlings from Erietta or Alamont! What do you need bodyguards for? If you can't defend yourself against a few pestering street merchants, maybe I should pick a different successor."

"No need, Uncle. We will make a grand impression all by ourselves." Iaros puffed out his chest, placed his hand on the hilt of his sword, and strode alongside the destrar, determined to look fearsome.

On their way to the castle, though, they sensed the somber mood of the city, heard gossip about the recent defeat at Ishalem, and saw ragtag groups of returning soldiers, many of whom wore red-stained bandages. Growling and angry, Broeck demanded explanations from people on the street. Appalled by what he learned, he clenched and unclenched his fists, picturing Urecari throats. He picked up the pace, storming toward the castle. "With me, Iaros—the king needs us!"

Inside the castle, the two visitors found King Korastine spending the afternoon in a small sunlit office. He sat at a writing table where he had spread out reports from his financial minister, studying the costs of the war and the expenses of running the country, but he didn't seem to be paying much attention.

When they entered the warm room, Broeck was startled to see his old friend's worn appearance. Though he and the king were approximately the same age, Korastine now carried a mantle of *oldness* around him, a weight of years and pain. The king simply looked used up, like a boiled soupbone that had been too long in the pot.

But the smile of relief that crossed his face was real. "Broeck, my friend!" The king struggled to his feet with a wince, placing a hand against his swollen left knee.

Broeck caught him in a bear hug, supporting him, then

eased the man back down to his chair. "Sire, allow me to introduce my nephew Iaros, who will be our next destrar—if he learns enough about the job. He is the best of the choices I have. With a bit more training and another survival trek up in the north, I suppose he'll be an adequate leader."

Iaros stumbled to make a formal bow; he flushed so red that his cheeks almost matched his mustache. The king looked the lad up and down, assessing him. He gave the requisite compliments, commenting on Iaros's striking mustache, which gratified the young man immensely. "These days we have nothing but troubles, young man. I trust you have a strong spine and a solid constitution? You'll need it."

Iaros nodded vigorously but said nothing, squirming as he forced himself to remain silent, as his uncle had advised. Broeck leaned closer to him. "It is all right for you to answer when the king actually speaks to you, lad."

"Yes, Majesty!"

Before they could begin their casual discussion, Anjine burst into the room leading a gaunt, knife-eyed man who looked like a thundercloud in human form. He wore a clean and well-maintained prester's tunic as well as a stylized fish-hook pendant at his throat. Waxy burn scars covered one cheek and both his hands.

Paying no attention to Broeck or Iaros, even as the destrar's nephew struggled to make a formal bow to the princess, Anjine blurted, "Father, Prester Hannes has important news. He's just returned from the mountains of Corag, where he discovered something that will change the war."

Korastine glanced down at the financial papers before

him, as though to avoid whatever message the prester had. "Very well, tell me."

Hannes explained that he had discovered the long-rumored pass through the rugged crags and down to the Middlesea. "The Urecari have a large base there, on our shores. They have built extensive mines above the Edict Line, worked by hundreds of Aidenist slaves. For years, they have excavated *our* iron and copper, manufacturing swords and armor for their armies. The weapons that recently killed our soldiers at Ishalem came from there." He nodded grimly, taking a deep breath to compose himself, but his voice dripped with hatred. "I know. I was held prisoner there for a long time before I escaped."

Anjine looked at her father, and her voice was full of urgency. "We cannot allow the enemy to keep this foothold—especially after what just happened at Ishalem. We must take back those mines! We *must* hurt them as much as they hurt us."

At her urging, Hannes produced a packet of papers bound in a waterproof oilskin. "I kept careful notes, and the Corag scout will lead others to mark out a better-defined path." He added a note of caution. "It is a route, but by no means a road. It would be impossible for a large military force to cross that land. Horses, carts, and supply wagons could not survive the rigors."

Standing there in the room with the princess, Broeck smiled as an idea formed in his mind. "Sire, what if we use beasts that are accustomed to the snow and the cold? If the people of Corag can mark out a clear path, Iboria Reach can provide an army that will strike terror into the hearts of the Urecari."

*

That night, Korastine was pleased to invite his old friend to dinner in his private chambers. The fire in the hearth was roaring and hot, and the king sat in his padded chair with a poultice of herbs wrapped around his knee. On a serving-board sat a platter of roasted pheasant for the two men to split, apples baked with whole cloves (smuggled from below the Edict Line), and pumpkin pastries fresh from the castle's kitchens.

Now, with a flurry of loud voices, Broeck entered the king's chambers with Kjelnar in tow. The destrar had turned his eager young nephew loose on the city to sample the taverns, restaurants, and anything else he might find amusing. Iaros was only too happy to comply.

Now he placed a hand against the shipwright's back, nudging him forward. "Forgive me, Majesty. As the *Dyscovera* makes its last preparations to sail, Captain Vora requests the use of the map on the sea-turtle shell. He needs it for his voyage."

The Iborian shipwright glanced away self-consciously. "I apologize, Sire. I didn't mean to intrude upon your evening with my destrar."

Korastine waved away Kjelnar's embarrassment. "Nonsense, Shipwright. Anything to help guarantee the success of the voyage. The Saedrans have already studied and copied the drawing, but Captain Vora should have the original."

From his chair, the king looked at the faded leathery shell on which some unknown lost sailor had etched a crude map of unknown continents and mysterious shores. Years ago, Sen Leo had brought the amazing object to the king while he mourned for Ilrida, and that discovery had shone a ray of hope upon his despair. Now his face wore a pensive expression. "Take it. I hope the map helps guide the *Dyscovera*."

As Kjelnar lifted the object carefully from the stand, Broeck said, "Once you've found Terravitae, the king and I will follow on the second voyage."

Korastine's lips curved in a wistful smile. "You know that's not likely to happen."

"Ha! It wasn't likely anyone would find a map etched on a sea-turtle shell in the first place. And it wasn't likely that Captain Vora would survive a Leviathan attack and come back to lead a new expedition. We don't base our lives on what is *likely*, Sire, but on what we are determined to do." Inhaling the delicious aromas of the dinner laid out before them, Broeck turned to Kjelnar, spoke with comradely gruffness. "What are you waiting for? You have what you wanted, now leave the king and me in peace."

After the shipwright hurried off with the shell, Broeck closed the wooden door, then dropped heavily into a large chair at the king's side. He tore off a drumstick from the well-cooked pheasant and snatched up one of the spiced apples, placed both on a pewter plate, and handed it to Korastine. "Let no one say that I hesitate to serve my king."

Korastine groaned at the joke. Broeck served himself, anxious to talk about his unusual plans for moving an army through the Corag mountains, but the king raised a hand. "Let us just be friends tonight, Broeck. I spend too many days with nothing but business. Grant me a few hours without that."

The two men ate a relaxed meal, talking of old times. After they finished their dinner, Enifir brought Prince Tomas to the king's chamber. Broeck lurched out of the chair at the sight of his grandson. "Tomas! Look how big you are." He snatched the boy up and held him above the floor. "You might grow tall enough to be considered an Iborian after all!"

The ten-year-old struggled playfully to get down. "Will you take me out in the snow? We can hunt another ice dragon."

"Oh, I'd rather leave them alone, so the ice dragons can continue to protect all of Tierra." He set the boy down and held him at arm's length. "Here, I've brought you a gift." From his belt, Broeck removed a fine steel dagger with an ornately carved hilt. "This is a knife for a man, for a fighter, and for a prince. The handle is made from mammoth ivory." He extended it to the wide-eyed boy. "It's your own knife, an Iborian knife. Carry it proudly." He lowered his voice teasingly. "The mammoths and ice bears will be afraid of you now."

After Enifir took the boy away to put him to bed, the two old men sat together in each other's quiet company before the fire. Great love showed in Korastine's eyes. "Thank you for that, Broeck. Tomas will treasure the knife." He cleared his throat, trying to find his voice again. "Now let us talk about great days, when our future was bright and when Ondun smiled on us."

Broeck bowed his head. "Whatever my king commands."

19   *Middlesea Coast, Outside of Olabar*

Back from the Nunghal lands, Imir announced that he had something to show Soldan-Shah Omra—an intriguing "special demonstration." His skin still looked pale from recently shaving his hair and beard. "My travels aren't just for my amusement and enrichment, you know. I never stopped thinking about how to strengthen Uraba."

Together, they rode away from Olabar accompanied by a retinue of guards and advisers. "But the Tierrans also strengthen themselves. We fight them, they fight us," Omra said. "We need to do more than just be strong, Father—we need a way to win."

"Then I may have your solution. Just you wait." Imir grinned and kicked his horse to a faster pace. "Have I told you stories about my father and his attempted raid on Tierra by riding overland north of the isthmus?"

"Many times," Omra said, but it didn't stop Imir from continuing.

"Your grandfather Shieltar took a hundred horsemen into the hills, convinced he could find a way around the old Pilgrims' Road and strike deep into Aidenist lands before anyone knew they were coming. But the hills were rugged, the weather terrible, and as they pressed northward from Ishalem, the terrain forced them west, back toward the coast. Shieltar encountered a small cluster of homes—not even big enough to call a village, I suppose—and they set fire to a few buildings.

"But the Tierran farmers came out and defended themselves. One of them shot an arrow into Shieltar's breast . . . a lucky shot, no doubt. Not a fatal wound, but a debilitating one, and your grandfather was forced to call a retreat. His riders withdrew, avoiding pursuit . . . but got lost in the foothills. By the time they found their way back to Sioara, the soldan-shah's wound was infected and festering. A sikara healer cauterized it and saved his life, but it pained him until the end of his days."

"Yes, I remember him complaining and telling the story when I was just a boy," Omra said. "He never stopped blaming the Aidenists."

Once he got started, Imir loved to tell his stories. "And then there was your great-grandfather, Soldan-Shah Untra, who fought an amazing naval battle against Tierran warships off the coast of Khenara."

Before his father could go into detail, Omra broke in. "And before that, Oenar had *his* clashes . . . and each one was in response to something the Tierrans did to us. This conflict with the Aidenists is a constant spiral, eagreing out of control. But my war is different from those previous generations'. This isn't just a few skirmishes. This could be the end of all things. Unless we change it."

"Oh, we will." Imir grinned. "I needed to take you far away so no one else sees this. I expect it to be rather spectacular."

They rode for an hour along the coast, finally approaching a small camp in dunes that were covered with salt grass and low succulents. A handful of industrious men stacked a large pile of wooden barrels out in an open area. Omra couldn't tell what they were doing.

A mousy Saedran man fussed over the barrels, rapping them with his knuckles, leaned close to sniff the contents. When they arrived at the camp, the Saedran man approached them, bowed to the soldan-shah, then looked at Imir with palpable awe. His voice cracked and stuttered as he spoke. "My Lord, my *Lords!*" His hair stuck out in brown patches around his ears. "The demonstration is ready! We have never tried an experiment so large—I hope we do not crack the world itself."

Omra raised his eyebrows in surprise, and Imir laughed again. "We'd better sit far away. Omra, this man is an apothecary, Killin na-Fas. This recipe he's brewed—according to my instructions—will change the face of the world."

"Or crack it in half," Killin repeated soberly.

Brushing the apothecary's concerns aside, Imir pointed to a high dune in the distance. "We can observe from there." The group of advisers followed them as they rode off to the rise of sand.

Below, Killin na-Fas checked the piles of barrels one more time, then laid out a long cord that extended well away from the kegs. The nervous Saedran shooed the other workers away, and they all ran to dunes on the outskirts.

Omra shaded his eyes, trying to see. "What is he doing?"

"Hush. Just watch!" Their horses nuzzled the succulent weeds but did not find them appetizing.

With a flint and steel, Sen Killin struck a spark on the long rope. As soon as a tiny curl of smoke rose from the fuse, he ran for his life, sandaled feet kicking up clouds of dust and sand.

Omra chuckled at the comical sight, but the Saedran apothecary looked genuinely frightened. The soldan-shah leaned over the pommel of his saddle, watching as the smoke crawled along the cord toward the piled barrels.

Imir leaned close, spoke in a conspiratorial voice. "I've already told you about Nunghal firepowder. Remember how they use it to make brilliant fireballs in the sky for their own enjoyment?"

"You haven't stopped talking about it for five years."

"Well, Khan Jikaris finally gave me the recipe." Imir

hunkered deep into the saddle, heels down, grabbing pommel, mane, and reins. "Watch what it can do."

The smoking line reached the barrels. The explosion was like all the thunderclaps of a thousand, thousand storms. Fire blasted in every direction, heaving a pillar of smoke and displaced sand into the air, higher than the towers of the Olabar palace.

The group of horses shied, reared, and screamed, their eyes rolling in fear. Omra, sitting too high out of the saddle, was nearly thrown and barely managed to keep hold of the reins. Next to him, having been prepared for the explosion, his father was laughing like a delighted child.

The workers nearest the detonation fled as far and as fast as they could, shielding their heads. After he had wrestled his horse back under control, Omra stared in awe as black smoke rolled toward them like a sandstorm. Seconds later, they were pelted by an unexpected rain of dust, clods of dirt, and splinters of barrels. When the smoke and dust began to clear, he nudged his skittish mount into a gallop to see the aftermath.

On the edge of the blast area, Killin na-Fas stood dumbly with eyes wide, his face coated with dirt and sand, hair sticking out in all directions like a dandelion puff. At the soldan-shah's approach, Killin tried to smear his hair down, which only made it worse. "My Lord, were you impressed?"

"Extremely so."

Where the kegs had been piled, a wide crater yawned in the sand, a giant scar gouged into the world. Omra stared into the deep hole, where water began to seep into the bottom, leaking from the nearby Middlesea.

Imir laughed uproariously as he rode up behind his son. "It was magnificent!" He clapped his hands. "Imagine the Aidenist army facing that, eh! They'll be so terrified they'll drop their fishhooks where they stand."

Omra remained fascinated as the water continued to fill the bottom of the crater. In the back of his mind he mused about something else. "Work crews would have taken days to make such an excavation ... yet this was blasted in an instant." He gave the former soldan-shah an enthusiastic smile as plans began to form in his mind. "Your firepowder may have other uses as well, Father."

20 *Calay*

Since it was nearly time to leave, Criston sought out Prester Hannes, whom he had rescued and befriended in a high mountain meadow so many years ago. Fully aware of the tribulations the prester had endured, and how his faith remained a bright candle throughout the most furious storms of suffering, Criston knew the measure of the man. He did not doubt Hannes's strength.

The *Dyscovera* needed a man like him.

In Calay's main kirk, as the soldiers continued to come home from the Ishalem battlefield, Prester-Marshall Rudio had changed the usual droning tone of his sermons, replacing it with real anger. A fire of indignation had been lit under the old church leader as he now realized—as did all Aidenists—that the enemy would continue to hold and desecrate the holy city.

Trying to rally the faithful, the prester-marshall assigned groups of young presters to pray in shifts around the clock, constantly begging Ondun to help the faithful against the heretics that had infested Ishalem. They beseeched God to swoop down with His holy sword and exterminate all the followers of Urec.

But Criston had other business at the kirk.

The presters and scholars were surprised when he asked to see Hannes, but they invited him through the echoing stone halls to the seminary quarters. "He has few visitors, sir," said the skinny young man who escorted him. "In fact, he has few friends even among the presters."

Criston gave a sharp answer. "Hannes has endured more tribulations than you can imagine. Do not judge him so harshly."

The young man looked abashed. "I am sorry, sir. I will ponder that during this evening's devotions."

When the door opened, Criston saw that his friend's cell was small, dim, and austere—perfectly suited to a solitary man's tastes. By the glow of a stubby candle, the prester hunched over two large books, the Book of Aiden and a weathered copy of Urec's Log, in which he furiously wrote comments and refutations. In recent years, Hannes had become an expert in the opposing faith, using his knowledge to point out the rival book's numerous flaws and contradictions.

When Hannes glanced up with a scowl at the interruption, Criston instantly remembered how close the man had come to death before being coaxed back from the brink. Though the prester remained gaunt and haunted-looking, the hollows were not so dark around his eyes, and his flesh had filled out, but his tense posture still showed a ready combativeness to defend his beliefs.

Hannes's expression changed to one of surprised recognition. "It's . . . you!" He stood, showing a genuine smile. "I haven't seen you in years."

Smiling warmly, Criston stepped into the cell. "We've both changed a lot since those hard days."

"These are still hard days." Hannes closed the book, as Criston caught a glimpse of the extensive scribblings in the margins. "Have you heard? I just found a way through the Corag mountains. I went back, retraced my steps, and came back with my faith stronger than ever."

Criston could never forget finding the man, dressed in tatters, frostbitten and starving, in one of the high mountain meadows. Criston had nursed him back to health, heard his tale, and delivered him safely to civilization again.

Floating in the wreckage of the *Luminara*, Criston had endured an ordeal as horrific as this man's. Lost far out at sea, he had never truly believed he would be rescued, and yet Prester Jerard had helped him cling to hope. Few others could understand adversity, and salvation, the way he and Hannes could. They shared a bond.

"That's why I came. You survived where anyone else would have died. You achieved the impossible."

Exactly what the *Dyscovera* hoped to do.

Hannes showed no pride. "I had to. Aiden kept me alive for a purpose."

"That's why I need you. I don't doubt that you stayed alive for a reason—and now that reason is clear to me."

Now the prester was interested. "Ondun speaks to you as well?"

"Doesn't He speak to everyone, in His own way?" Criston sat down on a wooden stool, the only piece of furniture besides the narrow sleeping pallet. "When I heard that you had just returned to Calay, I knew it was a sign from Ondun. The *Dyscovera* will sail shortly, and we need you."

Hannes seemed distracted. "The new ship? Yes ... I heard about that." It was obvious the prester had been paying little attention to the outside world.

"I am her captain. And I require someone familiar with the Book of Aiden. Someone I know ... someone whose faith I need not question."

Hannes was astonished. The last they'd seen of each other, Criston had lived alone, tending sheep in the isolated mountains. "You're the captain of the *Dyscovera*? But you were just a ... hermit. A shepherd."

"I'm a different man now. I've emerged from the darkness, and the king has given me the mission of finding Holy Joron. I want you to join my crew. Sail with me to the edge of the world."

Hannes scarcely knew what to say. "But the Gremurr mines, the path through Corag. Nothing can stop the armies of Aiden now."

"You have already shown them the way. But if we rediscover Terravitae, if we stand before Holy Joron—isn't that a greater victory against the enemy? Ask yourself, which is the better use of your abilities?"

Hannes's eyes shone with a different light now. "Yes, if Joron still has the powers that Ondun gave him, and if we tell him all the atrocities committed by the Urecari, he will surely rise up and ally himself with us!"

The stubby candle flickered from a stray breeze that crept through a loose casing in the window. "Yes, I will go with you to Terravitae. I'll be your crew's spiritual guide, and I will be Aiden's emissary to Joron. After all the tribulations in my life, I've earned it."

21 *Bora's Bastion, Alamont Reach*

The slave camp covered—and ruined—acres of fertile river flatlands that would have been better used for growing crops, Shenro thought. Inside the fences lived more than two thousand followers of Urec who had been seized in raids of their coastal towns or captured along with their ships at sea. Within the sturdy fences, the provisions were meager, the tent shelters squalid, people crowded in conditions that the Alamont destrar would not have inflicted on cattle.

On the other hand, cattle had a definite value.

And after what he had just learned of their race's treachery at the Ishalem wall, turning what should have been a glorious reconquest of the holy city into a humiliating rout, Shenro was not of a mind to show sympathy to these pathetic Curlies.

Now that winter was over, the prisoners required little in the way of shelter; besides, Urecari didn't deserve comforts. After all, up and down the Tierran coast, countless murdered Aidenist villagers were not "comfortable" in their cold graves. None of those recently betrayed soldiers at Ishalem were "comfortable."

No, he would not show any sympathy. There must be some way to make them pay, to balance the accounting sheets, for what the Urecari had done.

With a pinched look on his face, Shenro rode the fence-line with his guard patrol. Because he sat on such a fine horse, every camp prisoner could tell that he was an important man. Some even recognized him as the destrar, the man who controlled their destinies.

Shenro rode a gradual circuit of the perimeter so that he could see their haunted expressions. The sharp smoke from small campfires could not mask the odor of all those close-packed human bodies. His men provided the captives with shovels to dig their own latrines; the shovels were inventoried and collected nightly, so the prisoners could not dig their way out and escape. No follower of Urec could be trusted.

Every day, carts brought barrels of river water for the camp's cooking, bathing, and drinking needs, but that was all Shenro provided. If the captives wanted food, they had to work. He would not whip them into toiling in the wheat fields or marshy rice paddies. The Book of Aiden denounced slavery, and therefore the prisoners' work had to be voluntary.

But if they didn't work, they didn't eat.

Another "volunteer" crew filed through the gates, escorted out to the crops under the watchful eyes of a dozen archers. Outside the main entrance, Shenro had erected a newly commissioned bronze statue of a brave horseman, symbolizing the ninety vengeful riders who had raced from Bora's Bastion to Ishalem to overthrow the Urecari invaders . . . only to be slain by the enemy. The people of

Alamont were proud of those fallen warriors, and the statue was a reminder of why the prisoners had to be held inside the fences, why these Urabans had to atone for the crimes of their people.

The foreign prisoners, though, looked on the statue with an entirely different emotion, hating what it symbolized. The work crew shuffled past, few of them even glancing at the sculpture. This group would spread buckets of human and animal manure onto the croplands; other teams would pull up spiny thistles with their bare hands. Once they put in a day of work, the captives received a meal of watery porridge and perhaps some leftover catfish from the river markets. Shenro found it a gratifying irony to see these enemies of Aiden planting and harvesting crops to feed the army that would defeat them.

A handful of Urecari fanatics steadfastly refused to accept the work option. Although occasionally workers smuggled food to them, most of the fanatics remained defiant to the last and refused to eat. With no qualms, Shenro let them die.

After three cases of cholera had appeared in the past month, Shenro grudgingly set up sick tents and encouraged better hygiene in the camp. As Urabans, they were naturally infested with vermin. He and his men rode along with a sharp eye on the crowds, alert for any signs of fever or malady. While their health mattered little to him personally, a plague in the camp might spread to Bora's Bastion and his own people.

From behind the fence, a woman stared at him, her shadowed eyes ablaze with hatred. Shenro did not flinch, but rather met her stare. It was easy to maintain his resolve by remembering that nearly four thousand good soldiers had recently fallen at the Ishalem wall because of Urecari treachery. The enemy played by such inhuman rules, they couldn't possibly be considered human.

Destrar Shenro had developed his own plan to make the Curlies pay for what they had done. He hated to waste resources, but some things were required by a higher morality. . . .

Satisfied with what he had seen, the destrar rode back to his tall main house, which overlooked the boat and barge traffic on the river. He called for Captain Jillac, the manager of the prison camp. The two often met to discuss the prisoners and the daily tasks required of them to earn their food. Today, however, Shenro had something else in mind.

Jillac arrived, his garments moist with sweat from his day at work, but Shenro didn't mind. The destrar poured them each a glass of good Alamont wine. "How many prisoners currently reside in our camp, Captain?"

Jillac didn't pause to consider. "Two thousand three hundred and sixteen, although we may have lost a few more since this morning, when we hauled out five bodies."

"What did they die of? Cholera again?"

"Starvation, I think. Or just plain stubbornness. I don't worry too much about a dead follower of Urec."

Shenro pressed his lips together, deep in thought. The galling defeat at Ishalem—the haunted look on Subcomdar Mateo Bornan's face—convinced him what had to be done. "I have long been a student of military history, Captain, but I've never heard of atrocities that match what the Curlies have inflicted on us in this war."

Jillac nodded. "You'll get no argument from me, my Lord."

"All those prisoners—we've fed them, given them a new home, even offered to instruct them in the light of Aidenism. We could have executed them outright instead of taking them under our wing."

"They are primarily civilians, sir, not enemy soldiers."

Shenro set down his goblet with a hard click. "Any person who wears the unfurling fern is an enemy soldier in his heart, even if he carries no weapon."

"I wasn't making excuses for them, Destrar."

"Unfortunately, we need those workers, and Destrar Siescu in Corag will be assigning others to hard labor. I can't waste them all, but an accounting still needs to be made." Shenro leaned back in his chair. "Distribute numbered discs to each person inside the fences. Every camp guest from captured soldiers and old men to women and children—all two thousand three hundred and sixteen of them."

Jillac began scribbling on a small slate board he kept with him, frowning as he worked out the details in his mind.

"Let me know when it's finished, and then I would like to address the prisoners. Please see that we have a Urecari translator available."

"Yes, Destrar." Jillac departed, and Shenro remained wrapped up in his hard decision while he finished his wine.

As the sun set behind rolling hills, Shenro stood atop a wooden platform that had been built outside the camp's front gate. The blaze of color in the sky gave a rich, fiery glow to the new bronze statue of the martyred horseman.

From twenty feet above the ground, Shenro could see the squalid tents and cookfires inside the camp fence. Beside him, a wide-bellied cauldron held chits marked with numbers identical to the ones distributed among the prisoners.

He addressed the captives from his perch. "Four hundred of you will be chosen for a special duty." Beside him on the platform stood a Uraban merchant, a simpering and cooperative man who hoped to improve his status in the camp. The translator repeated the words in Uraban gibberish.

A separate fenced area like a large corral had been set aside adjacent to the main camp. There were no facilities, since the holding area was only temporary. That day, bearlike Sazar had unloaded three large riverboats, which remained tied up to the docks at Bora's Bastion. Seeing the empty riverboats, the prisoners muttered amongst themselves, convinced that the four hundred chosen would be taken elsewhere. Shenro thought it best to keep them guessing.

As he called out numbers one at a time, those selected came forward, some of them trading numbered discs because families wanted to stay together. Some insisted on staying in the Alamont camp, while others begged to be allowed to go. Amongst two thousand people, it was hard to find a particular number when someone refused to come forward; out of impatience, Shenro soon had the men grab any person at random.

It was full dark by the time the separate stockade was crowded with the chosen ones. Captain Jillac lit torches around the camp. As the captives grew restless, the buzzing of their jabber increased. They were hungry, impatient, fearful.

At last, the selection was done. Four hundred people out of 2,316. The Book of Aiden called for a payment of debts, especially blood debts, but Shenro could not justify one for one. Four thousand loyal Aidenist soldiers had died at Ishalem. One Uraban captive would have to atone for ten Tierran warriors. He did not see these captives as innocents—even the women and children.

He raised his voice to a shout. "Four thousand good soldiers recently died at Ishalem because of Urecari deceit. They sacrificed their lives trying to regain the holy city in the name of Ondun." The destrar spoke with such fervor that the stumbling translator had difficulty keeping up.

As the Uraban merchant repeated the announcement, the selected captives in the corral began to guess what Shenro meant to do, and the uproar grew louder. Mothers grasped their children. Inside the fences, the Urecari prisoners began hurling their numbered discs, which pattered around the wooden platform.

Shenro did not flinch as he finished his well-considered speech. "For Ondun's sake, we must balance the scales. There can no longer be such an unjust deficit of lives."

Four hundred . . . it was not such a large number. One for ten. And it was just.

Captain Jillac's fifty archers, each with a full quiver of arrows, surrounded the separate corral. "Draw your bows!"

The merchant translator on the platform quailed and begged Shenro not to do this, but the destrar cuffed him on the side of the head, then pushed him off the platform. The man tumbled twenty feet to the hard-packed ground, and Shenro heard a snap of bone as the merchant's ankle broke.

The man began wailing in pain, no longer concerned about those trapped in the corral.

The selected ones tore at the fence, trying to rush forward.

Shenro issued the command himself. "Loose your arrows!"

With a singing hum from above, the strings twanged and a merciless rain of arrows lanced into the pen. A second volley came close after the first, and then a third, showering down on the four hundred prisoners. The unfortunate captives dropped like scythed stalks of wheat. Some men or women attempted to shield their children and died, their backs prickling with the deadly quills. More arrows came, more bodies fell. Men, women, children—they were all the same. Numbers.

Inside the larger camp, the remaining Urecari howled in outrage, but Shenro's soldiers used cudgels to beat back the mob. There would be plenty of them left to send to Destrar Siescu in Corag; he would get his road through the mountains.

The blood looked black in the orange torchlight. "Archers, continue until every one of these prisoners has fallen. Four hundred—that is the price Ondun demands."

After it was done, he sent footsoldiers in among the fallen with daggers to dispatch any who still lived. Many Alamont soldiers looked queasy about what they were asked to do, but Shenro felt no sympathy for them; as members of the Tierran army, they would need to become hardened to the horrors of a battlefield.

The merchant translator was still squirming on the ground with his broken ankle; Captain Jillac thrust a sword through his chest to silence him.

On his high platform, Shenro felt detached and distant. His skin prickled with the powerful realization of what he had done, but he could feel nothing inside. Though he no longer had a translator, he spoke again. "That is the blood you owe for Ishalem. That is the price you must pay for your crimes against Tierra and your sins against God."

Shenro climbed down from the speaking platform and walked back to his main house that overlooked the river, his gaze fixed forward. He did not doubt that he would have to balance the scales again.

22 *Calay, Military District*

After picking over a roast mutton dinner inside Calay's military headquarters, Mateo continued the discussion with Guard-Marshalls Obertas and Vorannen. They all had the same orders from Anjine, and they would talk long into the night, until they found a way to expose the infiltrators.

Mateo laid out the problem. "Any of our soldiers might be a *ra'vir*, especially the young trainees. If we don't root them out, they could betray us at any time. They know our ways. They hide among us. They are indistinguishable from any true Tierran. Where do they come from? How do we identify them?" He looked at the other two men. "The task seems impossible."

Vorannen shifted in his chair. "As a first step, we should make note of every single Tierran soldier returning from the Ishalem battle. Take their names and keep them in barracks separate from the other soldiers."

Obertas looked offended. "Those fighters risked their lives for Tierra! They almost died at Ishalem. It's preposterous to suspect them."

Vorannen shook his head. "I don't. Any real traitors would have turned on us in the fight when they had the chance. All the *ra'virs* were killed on the battlefield. Therefore, anyone returning from the battle is almost certainly *not* a *ra'vir*. We begin with them, a pool of fighters we know to be true."

Obertas picked a particularly stringy piece of meat from his teeth and flicked it to the side of his plate. "We'll have to interrogate everyone else, make them swear on the Book of Aiden."

Mateo set aside his plate, no longer hungry. "And what would stop them from lying? They are already pretending to be something they are not."

"Well . . . we could insist that parents accompany their sons to the recruitment stations, prove that they aren't infiltrators from Uraba," Vorannen suggested.

Obertas disagreed. "Many of our recruits are young men who have run away from home to join the army. Just because they cannot show us their parents doesn't mean they are traitors."

Vorannen's shoulders slumped. "And we can't condemn all orphans. Thanks to the raiders, we have plenty of children without fathers or mothers—and they have more reason to fight the Curlies than most do."

"And yet some of them are *ra'virs*—a dozen of whom just caused the greatest defeat the Aidenist army has ever experienced." Mateo's brow furrowed as he puzzled through the possibilities. "Poor kidnapped Tierran children who've been manipulated and confused by Urecari captors. After all these years, and so many of them, how is it possible that not one of the *ra'virs* has seen through the lies and come back to Aidenism? Do they not remember their old lives?"

"The Teacher must have a deathly hold on them," Vorannen said. "You saw how the few survivors reacted during interrogation."

Obertas lowered his voice, leaned closer to Mateo. "What would your father have done in such a situation?"

"I don't know, Obertas. He never faced anything like this."

Marshall Obertas now performed the same job that Ereo Bornan had held for many years, charged with the protection of King Korastine. Mateo's father had been killed in the line of duty, and Korastine had raised Mateo in the castle alongside Anjine, almost as a surrogate son.

Since he'd taken Ereo's old job three years ago, Obertas occasionally joined Mateo for meals, wanting to hear stories of his predecessor. "I wear the same uniform as your father," he had said. "It would be honorable to carry on that grand tradition."

So Mateo had told him all the stories he remembered, though he had only vague recollections because he'd been so young when the former guard captain died. Not content with sketchy details, Marshall Obertas had delved into the castle archives and brought dusty tomes to Mateo, so the two of them could spend days poring over records. Like miners searching for gems, they dug out entries and reports that Ereo had written himself, as well as other references to what the brave captain had done (when he was too embarrassed to write them objectively). Together, Mateo and Obertas had gotten to know Ereo Bornan much better.

But those old stories did not help them now.

The royal guard-marshall rested his elbows on the plank table as he shifted the discussion. "Suspicions are causing as much damage as the *ra'virs* themselves. I've seen great unrest in the royal guard barracks. Fights have broken out, two knifings."

Vorannen picked up a hard roll. "My city guard says the same thing. Neighbors are reporting neighbors. They dislike anyone with strange speech or different ways. One wood-carver with a Soeland accent was turned in because someone thought he 'sounded Urecari.'"

Mateo wrestled with frustration. "Our society is tearing itself apart. The damned Curlies don't even need to have spies among us anymore—we're doing it to ourselves." He had to find a solution, for Anjine, for Tierra.

"And yet there *are* spies," Vorannen growled.

One of the blue-uniformed city guardsmen burst through the door to the military headquarters building. "Sirs, there's been another attack at the shipyards!"

Their long-cold meal forgotten, the three men grabbed cloaks and hurried from the building into the chill spring night. Shouting city guards ran through the street, carrying torches or lanterns and heading toward the docks south of the castle.

Mateo felt a leaden weight in his stomach. The Arkship had burned just prior to its departure, and now the new *Dyscovera* was almost ready to sail. He had ordered extra guards posted and kept the docks brightly lit throughout the night, but what if he had underestimated the *ra'virs*? He increased his pace, breathing cold air into his lungs until his throat burned.

To his great relief, though, he saw that the glorious three-masted carrack remained tied up in her slip, and extra guards stood on the gangplank, swords drawn and ready for battle.

The commotion, however, came from the other side of the narrow bay. Crews scurried around two smaller merchant ships, shouting for buckets, pumps, and carpenters; men scrambled down ladders into the holds. The ships were foundering, tilted at odd angles, riding low in the water.

After crossing the bridge to reach the crippled ships, Vorannen demanded a report from a guard. "*Ra'virs* again, sirs. Empty merchant ships aren't as closely guarded, I suppose, so the little cockroaches went into the water, swam below the waterline, and used augers to drill holes in the hulls. The holds are already flooded and the ships are sinking—can't patch them in time. A damned mess!"

Mateo turned his back on the wallowing merchant ships and pointed to the large exploration vessel. "Double the guards over at the *Dyscovera*! Inspect and inventory all supplies already loaded aboard to be sure no one has poisoned the rations or turned snakes loose belowdeck."

He felt anger pounding within him and knew he had to speak with Anjine—and King Korastine—as soon as possible. "We have to launch the ship without further delay. The only way to protect *Dyscovera* from another *ra'vir* attack is to get her safely out at sea."

23 *Olabar*

More than a week after his return to Olabar, the soldan-shah went without fanfare to the main church, ostensibly to pay his respects to the ur-sikara, but he had another motive. "I would like to see the Amulet of Urec. I wish to study it for myself."

Erima looked alarmed and confused. "That is highly irregular, Soldan-Shah. The Amulet is a sacred object."

"Yes, and it belonged to my ancestor, Urec. I am your soldan-shah. You would deny me this?" He had heard Istar complain that the sikaras denigrated her whenever he was not in Olabar, and he knew Saan's suspicions that the priestesses had been behind the recent attack in the souks. He didn't trust them.

Still, the dark-skinned woman balked. "I must consult with . . . with other priestesses."

Baffled by her attitude, Omra kept his voice steady. "You are the ur-sikara. You make the final decisions."

Without waiting for her to respond, he simply walked into the large sanctuary, prepared to summon his guards if necessary, but he hoped Erima wouldn't force him to do that.

He stood alone at the altar, perusing the gold medallion that had been passed down from generation to generation, protected in the church. This object was a direct link with Urec and his crew.

During his father's reign, Ur-Sikara Lukai had delivered

the talisman to the prime Urecari church in Ishalem, where it had nearly been destroyed in the great fire, but an unknown pilgrim had rescued it. The amulet's edges and markings had been softened and blurred by exposure to the intense heat, but he could still read the symbols and recognize the marks.

The same ones as on the Map that Sen Bira na-Lanis had found beneath the ruined Aidenist kirk.

It was all Omra needed to see, but he remained there for several more moments, staring and pondering before he finally went back to the palace. He had no doubts that the Map was real.

That night, unable to sleep though he was home at last, Omra lit a brass oil lamp and closed the door to his private office. By the flickering warm light, he withdrew the beautiful Map. The Saedran architect had translated all the descriptions and labels, writing them on a separate parchment. The archaic and nearly incomprehensible text gave Ondun's blessings and directions to his "sailor son."

According to the original legend, Ondun had given His son Aiden a compass that would always point the way back to Terravitae, but He had given Urec a detailed chart to guide his voyage. This chart revealed undiscovered lands, hidden coasts, far-flung islands—and clues about the Key to Creation, a miraculous object that Ondun had hidden in the world when He created it, a special prize for the most worthy of men, a talisman of great power. In their teachings, the sikaras were vague about what, exactly, the Key to Creation was; different sects and experts disagreed on their interpretations of Urec's Log.

Long ago, the Map had been lost. The official church story was that it had been swept away in a storm at sea. According to some apocrypha, however, an Aidenist spy had destroyed it to prevent Urec from completing his quest, thereby cutting him off from Terravitae—and the Key to Creation—for all time. Conversely, the corrupted Aidenist version of the story said that Urec was so arrogant, wanting no direction from his father, that he had discarded the Map.

Given that the Map had been found in an Aidenist kirk, Omra didn't know which story to believe.

Though this treasure was of immeasurable value, Omra was convinced he had made the correct decision to keep it secret. No doubt Ur-Sikara Erima would demand that the Map be given to the church, and Omra had no intention of doing so. He had too many questions of his own.

Fully awake while the palace slept, he stared down at the lines, imagining those mythical shores, the cliffs and reefs, the whirlpools and strong tides. The currents could have taken Urec to so many different places on his voyage across the unexplored world, but he had landed *here*, and he and his wives, along with the crew and their descendants, had become the Uraban people.

Omra touched his fingertips to the ancient ink and sensed a leftover aura of power. Those words could well have been written by the hand of Ondun Himself. He continued to stare by the flickering lamplight until his eyes burned and he could no longer remain awake. Unsettled, he went back to his bed, where the night breezes sighed against the silken hangings. In the hour before dawn, he finally drifted into a restless slumber, in which he had a vivid dream. . . .

Omra saw himself standing in crystal halls, walking through mirrored caves full of marvels beyond anything he had ever imagined—jewels and fountains, alabaster statues of exotic animals. At an intersection of corridors, he stopped to face a holy light so brilliant he could not bear to gaze upon it. Though he could make out no details, Omra knew that this was the Key to Creation, the blessed talisman waiting to be found since the very beginning of the world. Ondun had sent Urec out to find it.

Omra awoke with a start—and a firm conviction. He knew what he had to do.

Hidden somewhere in the undiscovered vastness of the world was this incredible object. Now that he possessed the Map, he had to send someone to find the Key to Creation. Only then would the conflict end. With such a relic in their possession, the followers of Urec would surely defeat the Aidenists.

24 *Calay*

Ever since Destrar Broeck had slain the ice dragon and delivered its horn to Calay, the pearlescent relic had rested in a felt-lined cradle inside Calay's largest kirk. According to scripture, the spell Aiden had placed upon the dragon Raathgir was a powerful bane against sea serpents. Broeck had obtained the horn as a talisman to be mounted on the prow of the new Arkship, but *ra'vir* saboteurs had burned the vessel before the horn could be installed. Now Raathgir's horn would join the *Dyscovera* on her voyage of exploration.

On the last day, old Prester-Marshall Rudio led the crowded service to bless the ice-dragon relic. As late-morning sunlight streamed through the kirk's colored glass windows, the old man stood behind the altar, intoning a long prayer, then he raised his scratchy voice. "Because all magic draws its power from Ondun, we will keep part of the horn here in the holy church, while the other half sails with our greatest ship, the *Dyscovera*."

He lifted the horn, to reveal that it had been sawed neatly in two along its axis; half of it remained in its cradle. The audience muttered, surprised. From the front bench, next to Broeck, Anjine, and a fidgeting Tomas, Korastine nodded.

"Though separated, all things remain one," Rudio intoned from the Book of Aiden.

Sen Leo had approached him with the idea weeks ago, reminding him of how sympathetic magic worked; the king had been skeptical at first, but the arguments were convincing. The two pieces would draw strength from each other, joined with the threads of magic. The Saedran sympathetic model of the *Dyscovera* in the guarded warehouse would also receive a long sliver of the horn, mounted on its prow.

Once the prester-marshall completed his invocation, King Korastine struggled to his feet, helped by Destrar Broeck's hand on his elbow. The two men stood together to receive the half of Raathgir's horn Rudio handed them, and they raised the pearlescent object before the transfixed worshipers.

"Though separated, all things remain one," Korastine repeated, and this time the audience cheered.

Aware of the schedule they had to keep in order to meet the following day's departure, Broeck handed the relic to Kjelnar as soon as the service was over. The big shipwright, looking very uncomfortable in formal clothes for the kirk, bowed vigorously to the king, the destrar, and the prester-marshall, before he rushed down to Ship-builders' Bay to install the finishing touches on the *Dyscovera*.

On the last day before the launch of the *Dyscovera*, Aldo na-Curic spent every possible moment with his family. He doted over his two children, listened to his younger brother Wen mooning about how he wanted to be a sailor too. His mind rattled with numerous details, and he compiled lists of things to add to his pack, items to leave behind, people he wanted to see, farewells he needed to say.

In his studio, his father worked on a painting that showed Aiden at the prow of his Arkship, casting away the sea serpent Raathgir. To the group of sailors depicted there, Biento added a brave crewman whose features looked exactly like his son's.

When a knock came at the door, Sen Leo na-Hadra greeted him with a large wire cage full of restless pigeons. "Sen Leo! Come in—I had hoped to see you before the ship sailed."

Lanni ran to hug her father, and Aldo's mother came forward, perplexed by the caged birds. "Are those for us, Sen Leo? Even with Aldo gone, I don't think we'll be reduced to eating pigeons!"

The scholar made a tsking sound. "If you eat *these* pigeons, the elders will be quite upset. We developed them as an experiment." He tapped the cage, making the crowded birds flutter again. "*Rea* pigeons are a breed whose eggs commonly have a double yolk. These birds are all twins—one here in this cage for Aldo to take aboard the *Dyscovera*, its counterpart back in a coop on the roof of the Saedran temple."

Aldo understood. "Sympathetic magic!"

"I'll show you how to tie a message to their legs. When you release a bird, it *should* find its way home to its counterpart. The theory is sound, but in practice ..."

The children ran around pestering their grandfather before Wen shooed them all away, herding them into their own room. Aldo's mother whispered something to his sister, who marched off into the kitchen. "You will stay for dinner, of course, Sen Leo."

Bending slowly, as if his joints ached, the scholar sat down at the table beside the birdcages. "Of course. We will have much to talk about."

Late at night, after the children were put to bed, each with a loving kiss on the forehead, Aldo sat up talking with his parents and Lanni, and spending a few private moments with his old mentor.

Sen Leo sighed, turning away to hide his reddened eyes. "Aldo, I taught you to be a chartsman. You know of the Mappa Mundi. Every place you explore, every new coastline and island you chart, will bring us closer to finishing our great task."

Aldo nodded, trying to be serious, but his excitement got the best of him. "And when we have completed the Map of All Things, Ondun will return."

Sen Leo cocked his eyebrows, nodded pensively. "It may

just be a legend, it may be the literal truth, or some combination of both, garbled and distorted by time. And you know the story of our origin, the lost people, the sunken continent. As you sail into the unknown, keep your eyes open for where our race once lived before it sank beneath the waves. Who knows, you just may find it, eh?"

"I've already prepared myself by studying all variations of the legend recounted in the Tales of the Traveler."

Sen Leo made a chiding sound. "Now, now, you know that many Tales of the Traveler are not entirely believable. Learn whatever you can. Find the truth."

Aldo promised him. "That is what the voyage is all about, sir."

While most of the ship's crew enjoyed one last night on land, Criston remained in his cabin aboard the *Dyscovera*. On the dock itself and in boats anchored nearby, a barricade of nervous city guards protected the vessel from harm, after the recent sabotage. But Criston did not mind being alone on the ship.

Anxious to set sail, young Javian had wanted to stay with him, but Criston insisted that the boy go into Calay. "Eat whatever treats you enjoy best, walk past the old homes and shops, smell flowers and trees—and *remember them*. Those memories are the most important things you can pack with you. At times, they may be all you have."

Though he appreciated the young man's dedication, Criston wanted solitude to consider the imminent departure, the dangers, the hope and responsibility. This voyage would be much different from the previous one. . . .

Long ago, before sailing on the *Luminara*, Criston had

made love to Adrea for the last time aboard his own small boat. Years had only added a warm glow to the memory of that final moment together, when they had believed in the future, trusting their decision as husband and wife, both ready to wait as long as it might take. God had smiled on them all. Neither Criston nor Adrea had imagined the span of years that would separate them, the gulf of time and tragedy.

On that last night, they had held each other belowdecks in their small cabin aboard the *Cindon*, the boat he had named after his father who had been lost at sea. That night each moment with Adrea had been fresh, and even after nearly two decades of longing, those memories remained vivid in his mind. Now in his darkened captain's cabin on the *Dyscovera*, he was alone but not lonely, because Adrea was there with him in spirit.

Logically, he knew that his wife must be long dead at the hands of the Urecari monsters. The raiders had destroyed everything they touched. And yet his heart clung to hope, and he still wrote her letters, sealed them in bottles, set them adrift. . . .

Restless, he walked the quiet deck and stopped next to the three compasses. The ancient relic of Aiden's Compass was polished and lovingly restored. With his fingernail, he tapped the crystal, but the needle did not move, even though it had been set back into place and carefully balanced. The compass had either forgotten its way, or Terravitae was simply too distant, the magical bonds too thin and frayed.

May the Compass guide you. Aidenists used that blessing to focus their very lives. In the morning, when they sailed out of Calay harbor, the Compass, and Criston's own skills as captain, would guide them across the unexplored seas.

It was late by the time Sen Leo left the na-Curic household. The Calay streets were quiet, and the air smelled of a cool harbor mist; the lamps on street corners and lintels were haloed in the fog. Inside the temple, he opened the hidden door behind the complex mosaic and descended the stone staircase. Down below, he could hear the muttered voices of learned men engaged in a heated discussion. The Saedran elders were waiting for him in the secret underground chamber.

Dozens of candles illuminated the intricate painted cartography that covered large portions of the chamber's smooth walls; constellations spanned the vaulted ceiling. *The whole known world.* Though the sum total of Saedran geographical knowledge covered these walls, significant areas remained blank. And time was running out, if the cryptic prophecies and old writings could be believed.

Six revered scholars sat at the table with their parchment notes, their inkpots, and their perennially furrowed brows. The drawings traced from the sea-turtle shell lay in front of them, along with a few questionable outlines, additional scratched landmasses that had become visible on the shell after the Saedrans gently applied chemical powders to enhance contrast.

"Sen Aldo na-Curic has all the information and assistance we can give him," Sen Leo announced. "He will send his reports via the bonded pigeons, and each letter will tell us more about unknown geography."

Portly Sen Belos scowled. "A chartsman should not

write down his observations, but keep them solely in his memory. What if someone else should intercept these notes?"

"And what if the ship sinks before Sen Aldo returns? What if we lose everything he has seen up to that point, as we did with the *Luminara*?" Sen Furic interrupted.

Sen Cherr always had a sleepy-sounding voice, but it carried great power. "I consider it an acceptable risk, Belos. Aldo will, of course, write his letters in our coded language. It is imperative that we complete the Map of All Things."

Sen Leo pointed to the Mappa Mundi on the wall. "And don't forget, we are speaking of Aldo na-Curic. Thanks to his connections with Sen Sherufa na-Oa in Olabar, he delivered detailed descriptions of all five soldanates of Uraba, and brought us the southern coastline beyond the land of the Nunghals. Because of Aldo, in one generation, Saedran knowledge of the world has unfolded dramatically. I would not dismiss his likelihood of success." He looked around at the other elders. "We must complete the Mappa Mundi as soon as possible. You all know the reasons why."

Cryptic lines from the Tales of the Traveler, the Book of Aiden, Urec's Log, and Saedran scriptures yielded a convergence of prophecies that suggested the arrival of humanity's final days ... that Ondun had given them only so much time to explore and unveil His entire creation. If they did not complete the Mappa Mundi soon, the world itself might be torn asunder.

"All Saedrans have the same goal, Sen Leo," said Belos, trying to be conciliatory. "If the pieces can be brought together, our information will be complete."

Sen Leo closed his eyes, but the image of the Map

remained before his imagination. "Then we will be able to save the world."

25   *Olabar Harbor*

Saan enjoyed any excuse to walk with his father, particularly along the harbor with all the lovely sailing ships, barges, and supply galleys. Soldan-Shah Omra knew the young man's interest.

For the past year now, Saan had made a habit of chatting with merchants and sea captains when they came to port; he bought pennants and seals from various Uraban cities he hoped to see someday with his own eyes. He had already been struck with the yearning to travel to distant lands. It was in his blood.

When he was only twelve years old, Saan had crossed the Great Desert with his grandfather and Sen Sherufa; he had seen the Nunghal steppes and the Southern Sea. Once back home, he had traveled as far as Sioara, but he had never visited Ishalem or the rugged western shoreline of the Oceansea. Someday, though . . .

The two men strolled along the sloping cobblestoned street toward the wooden piers that extended like fingers into the water. People whispered as they walked by; some bowed or stepped back, recognizing the soldan-shah. Kel Rovic and his closely following guards could be summoned on a second's notice, should assassins try anything foolish, but for now, Saan was alone with his father.

Having noted the ships coming into port and the larger

vessels at anchor in the deeper harbor, he turned to see a preoccupied look on the soldan-shah's face. At the moment, Omra was noticing none of the things that fascinated Saan. "Are you worried about matters of state, Father?"

His train of thought broken, the older man turned to him, his dark beard framing a smile. "A soldan-shah always worries, Saan. Consider yourself fortunate that such a fate isn't on the game board for you."

"I don't envy the zarif. Omirr will have to bear that responsibility when he gets older, but I've never wanted to rule Uraba." The very idea seemed impossible and foreign to him.

"That is exactly why you're so important to me." His father reached out and surprised him with a warm hug. "When I spend time with you, I can be just a man with his son . . . and friend. A soldan-shah has too few friends. With you, I have someone who just listens and speaks with honesty, not an agenda."

Saan felt his cheeks flush. "I try, Father."

They paused at a wooden table where a blind man had set up piles of colorful seashells, including large milk pearls harvested by the famous reef divers of Lahjar. Omra studied one of the pearls on display, then looked at Saan again. "I'll be very sorry to see you leave Olabar," he said. "It's going to be a long trip."

Saan felt a sudden fear that he had done something wrong, that he would be exiled too, like Omra's brother Tukar. "What?"

The soldan-shah wore both a sad and slightly mischievous expression as he continued walking down to the ships tied up to the Olabar docks. "For some time, I've been concerned about all these threats on your life. Too many people have too many reasons to want you dead—some to hurt me, some because they hate you or your mother, and some despise what you both represent to the church. They say you still secretly worship the Fishhook."

"I am as devout a follower of Urec as anyone in Uraba!"

"I believe you, but the priestesses would still prefer to get rid of you. We both know the threat they pose."

With a hearty laugh, Saan dismissed the idea. "I've been in danger ever since I was a little boy. Remember when I outfoxed the mercenaries, *and* I found the Golden Fern? That means I have a great destiny. I won't be killed on some street corner. I can take care of myself. Kel Rovic says I'm one of the best fighters he's ever trained."

"And Rovic does not give unwarranted compliments." Omra faced Saan. Two burly fishermen staggered by, hauling a crate of feebly twitching silver sardines. "But no matter how skilled you are with a blade, someone could slip poison into your food or drink, or they could set a sand spider in your bed, as they did to your baby brother."

Omra walked on in troubled silence for a few moments, then continued. "Worse, your very presence may endanger my other sons—my true heirs. You saved little Omirr from the assassins, but if it hadn't been for the threat they see in *you*, the zarif might never have been in danger at all."

Saan knew his father was right. "The last thing I want is for harm to come to Omirr." The words caught in his throat, but he forced them out. "So . . . you are sending me away? You'll exile me to where I don't pose any further threat?"

The soldan-shah chuckled gently. "Exile? Oh no, my son. Not like that! I need you to find something for me."

When Omra stopped at one of the outer piers, Saan noticed a large, new two-masted ship tied to the docks. Her great silken sails hung loose, both squares and lateens, dancing gently in the harbor breeze, a large Eye of Urec on the mainsail. Saan was intrigued by the ship's lines, her size and sturdy curves. Though not a large ship, she was fast and strong. Her draught was shallow enough to nimbly approach rocky shores, but her hull was thick and her masts set sturdily enough to weather difficult crossings.

"She's a beauty. From Kiesh?"

"Yes, newly commissioned. She is the *Al-Orizin*." He glanced over to watch Saan's expression. "And she is yours."

It felt as if the boards of the dock had dropped out from beneath him. His own ship? "Mine? But I'm too young to be a captain."

"You'll have experienced sailors with you. Come aboard and have a look around."

Taking him by the arm, the soldan-shah led him up the gangplank. The deckboards were newly scrubbed, the voluminous cargo holds fresh and aired out, all hatches open to the breezes. The *Al-Orizin* was virtually empty, with only a handful of men on deck, concentrating overmuch on their work. Saan guessed that his father must have arranged for this visit ahead of time.

Saan still couldn't believe what he was seeing, but he did not want to argue. He pictured himself standing at the bow, issuing orders, turning to face the endless horizon, exploring the world. *Captain Saan* . . . "But where would I go?"

Omra led him aft to the captain's cabin in the stern. The small shelves were empty, the tabletop clean, the bunk neatly made. Removing a leather cylinder that he kept tucked in his sapphire-blue sash, the soldan-shah unrolled the ancient Map of Urec on the small charting table. His hands trembled with true reverence. "This was found in Ishalem. It is genuine—Urec's Map." To Saan's astonishment, he explained how the Saedran architect had uncovered the relic deep in the ruins, and how he had kept the news secret, for the time being.

He pointed to the Map. "I want you to make a voyage that could save Uraba ... and one that will be the stuff of legends for many generations."

Saan grinned. "I like the sound of that."

"Take the *Al-Orizin* and sail east, follow the Middlesea, go beyond Kiesh—farther than anyone has ever gone. There, you will find Terravitae ... and the Key to Creation."

"The Key to Creation? But no one knows what that is."

"Urec was searching for it, on orders from Ondun. If you can find the Key for Uraba, how can we fail to achieve victory against our Aidenist enemies?"

Saan tore his gaze away from the ancient chart and saw a shine of moisture in his father's eyes. "You'll be undertaking the most important quest since Urec sailed at the beginning of time. Whom else would I choose for this?"

26 *Calay Harbor*

With all sails set to catch the dawn breeze and the ties loosed from dockside stanchions, the *Dyscovera* pulled away from the wharf. The crew, including Captain Vora, the chartsman Aldo, and the cabin boy Javian, waved furiously. Burly Kjelnar, now designated as first mate, stood at the prow like a figurehead behind the ice-dragon horn, exuding pride in his ship, his masterpiece, as they sailed toward the two lighthouses at the harbor's mouth. From the stern, Prester Hannes watched the cheering crowds, his face chiseled from stone, as if his own prayers propelled the ship along, rather than the winds and the outgoing tide.

Five of Destrar Tavishel's sturdy Soeland warships escorted the three-masted carrack to the open Oceansea. The Soeland vessels were refitted whaling ships that now patrolled the seas, attacking any Urecari ship they encountered, seizing prisoners and booty. The bearded destrar, whose determination seemed to match Hannes's own, would guide the *Dyscovera* beyond the Soeland islands to the edge of known waters.

As fanfares played and people whistled and cheered, an oddly silent King Korastine watched the glorious vessel depart. Without him. Even the king of Tierra could not have all that he wanted. He had known it would be impossible to join the crew, but he still dreamed of the historic voyage. Now he sat on a padded chair with a blanket wrapped around his left leg. It ached so, and this morning he had been unable to bend his knee at all.

Standing beside his father, cheeks flushed pink by excitement as well as the morning's chill, Prince Tomas waved and shouted, trying to make the crew notice him.

Anjine looked regal, her honey-blonde hair caught by stray breezes. "It's a great relief to see the ship safely launched, Father." She looked down at him, her expression serious. "If we had protected the Arkship more carefully six years ago, you would have made it to Terravitae."

"And I would have been back by now." Korastine gave his daughter a wistful smile. "If I decided to come back at all. Maybe I would have remained with Holy Joron for the rest of my days." His voice trailed off. Tears misted his eyes as the departing ship passed the two tall lighthouses on the headlands.

"Will they find Terravitae?" Tomas asked.

"For all our sakes, they will have to try." There was no other option than to *try*; he had learned that much. He had tried to establish a peace with the Urecari. He had tried to rule Tierra wisely through the hardest times and the greatest tragedies. He had tried to find happiness in marriage.

And we must never stop trying.

Destrar Broeck wore an ermine-lined cape for the occasion. "There she goes! How I wish we could have joined them." He squeezed Korastine's bony shoulder. "But adventures are for younger men."

"We were young enough once, Broeck, but we missed our opportunity. Don't begrudge them their chance." His heart ached. "I wanted to do this for Ilrida. I wanted to see Joron, face him ..." His voice cracked. "I wanted to ask him why Ondun allowed so much sadness into the world."

"Ondun also created love."

"Yes, and that's what makes the sadness even more painful."

Anjine frowned at them both. "You two talk like a pair of old women. See what you *have*, not what you've lost."

Korastine patted his daughter's hand. "Of course, my

dear. I know full well I would just have been another anchor aboard the *Dyscovera*."

Tomas shaded his eyes, continuing to watch the disappearing ship. "Will I be old enough to go on the second voyage to Terravitae? After they return?"

"I guarantee it, Tomas." Korastine stared after the *Dyscovera*, his eyes sparkling. "Someday, we will all see Terravitae."

The next morning, the servant Enifir carried a tray containing a traditional breakfast of fresh-baked scones, potted berries, and two boiled eggs to the king's chamber. At first, Korastine had argued that he was not an invalid and did not need to eat his meals in his bed, but soon it became obvious that he took so long to dress himself and make his way down to the banquet hall that Enifir no longer asked permission. She simply came to the king's quarters with his food, and he grudgingly accepted it.

Enifir granted him an extra hour to sleep, for he had seemed especially weary the previous evening, after seeing off the *Dyscovera*. When she knocked and received no response, she couldn't believe he was still dozing. She worked the latch and opened the door, deciding to wake him.

King Korastine lay in his bed, his leg stretched out, arms atop the down comforter. The candle at his bedside had burned out in the middle of the night, and a large leatherbound volume of the Tales of the Traveler lay beside him, its well-thumbed pages open to the story of Terravitae. His eyes were closed, his expression peaceful. His fingers rested lightly on a picture of bearded Joron surrounded by imaginary animals.

Enifir knew immediately that he was dead.

King Korastine had held on just long enough to see the *Dyscovera* sail, before he had made his own journey beyond the horizon, following a different course.

With warm tears heavy in her eyes, Enifir stood for several minutes, gulping long breaths, placing her hands across her rounded belly. She spoke a quick prayer, then hurried out, running through the castle halls to find Anjine.

Part II

Part II

27 *Sioara, Inner Wahilir*

After Soldan Huttan read the curt letter, he retreated to his quarters for the evening and sent the servants away so he could let his rage show freely. He paced the chamber, fuming as he considered the summons from Soldan-Shah Omra.

He was commanded to send his First Wife, Kuari—and good riddance to the shrew, too, though he still hated to be required do it. Soldan-Shah Omra was making a lot of demands, and the soldanate of Inner Wahilir seemed to be bearing the brunt of the costs and obligations.

Huttan undressed himself for the evening with abrupt, distracted gestures, threw his fine new clothes in a pile on the floor, then donned a comfortable silken robe with the most beautiful embroidery. The garment had been given to him by Yuarej merchants, wise men who could see the shifting tides of power. They recognized changes that might be coming to the neighboring soldanate.

Impatient, Huttan shouted for his servants, and an old woman scuttled in, pretending to be meek, though he knew she despised him. She collected the discarded clothes, as she did every night, and retreated from his chambers.

Crowds would be waiting outside the front door of Huttan's villa, hoping to receive his soiled clothes. Since he was the soldan, he had made up his mind never to wear the same garment twice, and so as a generous gesture his representatives offered the discarded clothes to beggars at the gate, who were honored to wear garments that had touched his skin. It gave him great pleasure to know that the citizens of Sioara, even the beggars, were the best dressed in all Uraba.

His First Wife Kuari appeared at the door without being sent for. It was not her night, and Huttan had five other wives, all more attractive than this sturdy and sharp-tongued woman—a marriage that had given him political benefits and his first two sons, but not a great deal of affection. She walked boldly past the guards, though they'd been told not to let anyone disturb him; alas, the guards were more afraid of Kuari than of him.

"Why are you here?"

"I'm here because you need me to be here. I want to be sure you don't make another mistake."

"I am the soldan. I don't make mistakes."

"Call them what you will." She took a seat on the piled cushions without asking permission. "Your emissary Ualfor has always been a man with a narrow mind and a loud voice. He has insulted the soldan-shah's First Wife, and that insult has come back to bite you."

A pot of fresh tea sat on his writing table. Huttan looked meaningfully at it, waiting for his wife to pour him a cup. She didn't.

He irritably glanced at the rough paper and the soldan-shah's broken wax seal. "It appears the viper will bite you instead. *You* are the one I must send to Olabar. You will have to face the soldan-shah's wrath."

Kuari did not seem concerned. "It may go better for Inner Wahilir if you make a point of reprimanding Ualfor. Send an apology to Lady Istar and be as abject as you possibly can."

"I'm a soldan, born of nobility. All of Inner Wahilir is mine. I don't apologize."

Kuari shrugged. "The fact remains that your emissary speaks in your name, and he offended the soldan-shah's First Wife. Therefore, *you* have offended the soldan-shah's wife."

Huttan paced the room again. "Who cares about wives? We are speaking of serious things."

"Don't let your pride bring you down—like a water ox sitting on your head."

Her disrespect startled him, as it usually did. He often threatened to send her into exile, to break the bonds of their marriage, even to have her meet with some accident, but she called his bluff every time. Kuari had been trained among the sikaras, taught their wiles as well as their religion, but she had left the church to marry him, by her father's command. Now he wished she had stayed among the scheming priestesses.

He tapped a ringed finger on the paper. His fingers were plump, and the gold bit into his flesh; he hadn't been able to remove the ring in some years. "The crucial thing is that the soldan-shah never received my request to annex parts of Yuarej. Now, what am I to do about the border settlements? And the money I need to build the ostentatious church that Omra has demanded in Ishalem? It'll bankrupt me. Maybe I should speak to the soldan-shah myself, seek some kind of relief or concessions."

"Read the words in the summons, husband. He specifically requires *my* presence. If you go instead, you'll only offend him further."

Huttan grumbled. Kuari's network of spies was widespread and damnably accurate. Even though she knew the pressures a soldan had to face, she showed him no sympathy. Instead, his wife pestered him like a crow, always pointing out his failings or taking an opposite point of view. One day she would push him too far, and he would have one of his guards strangle her in her sleep. Maybe he would even do it himself. One day . . .

If he was lucky, Soldan-Shah Omra would take care of the matter for him.

He slumped wearily on his cushions, but not too close to Kuari. Again he looked meaningfully at the pot of unpoured tea, and again she ignored him. "I miss my cousin Attar. Now *he* was a worthy rival."

"You hated Attar. You cursed his name for years and reviled him. Don't expect me to believe you've changed your mind just because he was poisoned."

"At least Attar was of noble blood," Huttan spat. "This new Vishkar—a *merchant*! A useful enough man, someone with wealth and influence, but not with the stuff to be soldan of Outer Wahilir. That upstart soils the office."

However, Vishkar had so much support from Olabar that Huttan didn't dare move against him. Instead, he had turned his sights on the much weaker soldanate of Yuarej. Over the past two years, he had sent his people up to the border hills to build settlements in the wilderness territory, establishing a foothold over the line. Huttan had ignored the complaints of Soldan Andouk. The Yuarej soldan was a broken man, without ambitions—his own people did not respect him. Huttan wasn't worried about any threat from Andouk, but he needed the soldan-shah's seal of approval to complete his plans . . .

Kuari got to the heart of the matter. "Wouldn't it be

embarrassing if Vishkar builds a far more glorious church than *you* do? How goes the project, by the way?" Her words twisted like knives.

"That is why I need the money from Yuarej!" He held his temper with difficulty, as though he were speaking to a stupid child. "I need to collect more taxes and tariffs—and I need to annex those lands. Ualfor was supposed to deliver my request!"

"The soldan-shah did not deny your request, my dear husband. He merely ignored you."

Impatient, Huttan poured his own cup of tea and glared at Kuari while drinking it. He rudely wiped his mouth on his sleeve. "Since your spies have told you the content of the soldan-shah's message, what are you waiting for? Pack your things, gather your entourage, and depart for Olabar." He fluttered his ringed fingers at her, to make her go away. Then he mumbled the traditional Urecari blessing. "Follow the Map."

"It is the middle of the night, my dear husband. I'll leave Sioara in due course."

"The soldan-shah commands, and you must go with all due haste. Take your chattering servants and head for Olabar. I expect you to be far, far away from me by the first light of dawn."

28 *Calay, Military District*

When the skinny young woman came nosing around the barracks, asking where she might find Mateo Bornan, her arrival caused a stir in the Military District. She couldn't have been more than fifteen or sixteen years old. Her skin was much too pale and covered with a coppery splatter of freckles; her hair was red and wild, as lustrous as a frayed old paintbrush. She was not attractive by any stretch, nor would she be—definitely not the sort of young woman the subcomdar was often seen with.

"Let me see Mateo Bornan." She actually stamped her foot on the ground when the soldiers regarded her with amusement. "In private. I need to talk with him."

Mateo had just arrived back from upriver, where he had escorted a group of fresh Uraban captives to the Alamont prisoner camps. Returning to Calay, though, he had heard the news of the king's death. Mateo's next sad duty would be attending Korastine's funeral.

When informed of the redheaded girl's presence outside the barracks, he said, "Send her away. We have too much else to do. The king is dead." With a quick salute, the young guard left to give the girl a gruff dismissal.

As couriers spread the news around the five reaches, destrars would rush to Calay so they could attend the old king's final ceremony and be present for Anjine's formal coronation (although she had been the de facto ruler of Tierra for several years now). Mateo longed to go to Anjine—as a friend. She had always been able to talk with him about her greatest concerns, her inner doubts, her dreams. They were childhood friends, bound by years of memories and shared experiences. But this was a time of vulnerability for her. Perhaps he shouldn't allow himself to get closer. She would be the queen now, and he was just a soldier. . . .

When they were children, politics hadn't mattered

much—though Anjine's mother had never been keen on the close friendship between the princess and a lowborn boy taken into the castle. She had tried to separate the pair, and they had rebelled, finding surreptitious ways to run off, creating imaginary identities for themselves and having their own adventures out in the city. Later, as Anjine assumed the formal mantle of princess and he became a career soldier rising through the ranks, Mateo had needed to distance himself from her. Social expectations came into play.

Once Anjine was queen, *his* queen, the gulf between them would be even vaster. She couldn't just cry on Mateo's shoulder; the loss of her father wasn't just a skinned knee. She was *Queen Anjine*. The words formed a lump in Mateo's throat as he thought them.

If nothing else, he would be first to bend his knee and swear loyalty to her, offering his heart and life alike, for her . . . and for Tierra.

King Korastine had been a patient and loving mentor to him, practically a father. The king's wisdom, benevolence, understanding, and generosity had also made him a great ruler in times of prosperity, keeping his people on an even keel. But he was not molded from the right stuff to face a never-ending war. The violence, repeated tragedies, and simmering hatred had ruined him. Now perhaps Korastine would find peace; he certainly deserved it. But that only meant more heartache and backbreaking responsibility for poor Anjine.

He would help her however he could. He could not let her be ruined too.

The young guard returned once more, flustered. "I'm sorry, sir, but the girl won't leave. She even gave one of the troops a black eye when he tried to move her against her will. She calls you a fool if you won't listen to her."

Despite his sad thoughts, an intrigued smile quirked Mateo's lips. "She gave one of *my* soldiers a black eye?"

"Yes, sir. Shall we lock her in the stockade?"

"Do you think you can?" Mateo gave a small chuckle. "Better send that soldier back to training if he can be bested by a girl! How old did you say she was?"

"Looks to be fifteen or so." The rest of the sentence was weighted with unspoken meaning: *Much too young for you.* And certainly too old for her to claim to be his daughter.

"All right, she's sparked my interest. Let's see why she feels the need to cause so much fuss."

The girl came in looking indignant. Her clothes were rags, and her face needed a good scrubbing; she seemed to be a stranger to regular meals. As Mateo inspected her, she flashed a hot glance at the soldier who had escorted her in. "I said I needed to speak to the subcomdar *alone*."

The soldier gave Mateo an uncertain look. "Will you be all right, sir?"

"I'll try not to let her give *me* a black eye." Doubtful, the soldier left and closed the door behind him. Sitting back at his desk, Mateo regarded the redheaded teenager with some amusement. "What's your name, girl? We haven't been introduced."

"Tira."

"And your last name?"

Her bony shoulders bobbed once. "Don't have one." In response to his skeptical frown, she let out an impatient sigh. "You'll understand soon. I don't have a family that I remember. That was all pounded out of me. They try to make you forget, especially fond memories. They scour everything away, everything but the mission."

Mateo perked up. "What mission?"

Tira squared her shoulders and met Mateo's gaze straight on with her greenish brown eyes. "I'm a *ra'vir*."

The information took him completely by surprise. Mateo stared, ready to call for the soldier again, but the girl interjected, "A former one. Captured eight years ago from my home, brought down the coast of Uraba with many other children, marched overland, and trained for years."

Behind the desk, Mateo's hand strayed toward the dagger at his belt. He could call for guards at a moment's notice, but he let Tira continue to talk. "Explain yourself. How do I know you're not a *ra'vir* anymore."

"Urecari raiders captured a lot of us. Our training was ruthless, rigorous, relentless. Most children don't survive long—not the right material or not susceptible to the Teacher's manipulations. Some of the failures are sent to the soldanates as slaves. The rest are killed for their failings. The ones who complete *ra'vir* training are the best of the best, hardened warriors in the cause of Urec. They want to destroy anyone who worships the Fishhook. I was one of them."

Mateo remained silent, waiting.

"After three years, the Teacher sent me back to Tierra. Alone—most *ra'virs* are. Don't know where any of the others might be. We were encouraged to scatter. The Teacher ordered us to inflict damage and keep you in terror." She lowered her chin, swallowed hard. "I heard what happened at the Ishalem wall."

The reminder made Mateo's anger flare. "And you

expect me to believe you?" With the king's death still raw in his mind, he thought of how *ra'virs* had burned the Arkship in Calay harbor, destroying Korastine's dreams of sailing to Terravitae.

The redheaded girl shrugged again, made no apology. "Never found the right time or place to strike . . . but I did find friends. Aidenist friends, kindhearted Tierrans, good people, devout and sympathetic folks who helped me without knowing a thing about me. Even though I thought it was burned out of me, and the Teacher taught me to hate Aidenists, I started to remember my family. My real family. The raiders that captured me murdered my parents first. I remembered that I loved them, how kind they were. I remembered being a Tierran . . . but I can't forget that I'm a *ra'vir*. So I hid. I worked. I stayed alive. But I did nothing else."

Mateo leaned forward. "Why did you come to me? And why now?"

Her milky skin flushed a bright red. "On the streets, I recognized a young man. I'm sure he was from my childhood village—probably escaped the raid somehow." Tira sniffed. "He was living the life I could have had." She shook her head. "When I heard about those Tierran soldiers killed at the Ishalem wall, I should have felt glad, but I didn't. It felt wrong."

Fascinated, Mateo realized that he could neither turn away this potential boon, nor entirely trust her. At least not yet. "You say you can't identify any other *ra'virs*? So how can you help me?" The few captive *ra'virs* he'd interrogated had been no help at all.

"We don't have a secret sign or code, but I have suspicions

about a few people." She gave him a winsome smile. "And I know a way you can root them out."

29 *Lillotha, Yuarej*

"It appears that I am to lose everything, my love," Soldan Andouk said to his first and only wife. A courier riding an exhausted horse to the capital of Yuarej soldanate had delivered the soldan-shah's summons. "Honestly, I didn't expect Omra to take so long to act against us. It's been years since Cliaparia's ... crimes."

He had been about to say Cliaparia's *death*, but that wasn't the part the soldan-shah would react to. He had unequivocally forgiven Istar for murdering Andouk's dear but treacherous daughter. Cliaparia had deserved to be killed.

Sharique tucked her feet beneath her as she curled up beside him on the bedcushions. She stroked his hair, kept her voice gentle. "Have faith, husband. Perhaps Omra has something else in mind. His letter makes no mention of revenge for what our daughter did."

Soldan Andouk was a thin, rabbitlike man, who had good reason to be nervous. He shook his head, unconvinced. His eyes were weary, his shoulders bowed by the invisible weight on them. "I suppose I should give thanks for these last six years, though I have not enjoyed them. The soldan-shah could have sent his men here to execute us at any time. How can a man forgive the murder of his firstborn son?"

"This is a summons for *all* First Wives," Sharique pointed out. "It is not targeted at you, or me. I think someone else must have offended him."

Leaning back in their bed, Andouk let out a long sigh. Torches burned in their holders outside the stone archway. The faint buzz of insect song in the forested hills, normally a peaceful sound, now grated on his nerves.

Years earlier, he and Sharique had reached the pinnacle of happiness when their lovely but far too ambitious daughter was chosen as a new wife for Zarif Omra. Andouk had thought the fortunes of Yuarej were improving, a new sun rising upon the small and peaceful soldanate. But he'd been oblivious to schemes Cliaparia worked to gain power in the Olabar palace. Even as a girl, she had been power-hungry. He had been blind to his daughter's flaws.

And someone had to pay for it.

Devastated to learn of Cliaparia's murder, Andouk had at first cried out for revenge, but he quickly learned the truth of the matter. After that, Andouk was a broken and shamed man, living in fear that armed soldiers would arrive one day to seize him and his wife.

Now this unexpected and ominous summons . . .

Sharique read the document herself, again and again. She was an educated woman, though she remained silent at court, advising her husband only in his private chambers. The two kept to themselves, tending the business of the soldanate. Far from relishing his position as soldan, however, Andouk longed for the peaceful, unremarkable life of a normal man. Taxes on the silk trade, which supplied so much fabric to the war effort, allowed them a comfortable existence.

As a consequence of his quiet lack of ambition, wealthy merchants grew wealthier; Andouk had no doubt that they were cheating him of taxes, altering numbers in their ledger books. They had made him irrelevant, a figurehead. And he didn't have the power, influence, or stamina to call them to account. So long as the Uraban army and navy received its required goods, the soldan-shah did not interfere with the running of any individual soldanate.

Year after year, Soldan Andouk brushed aside the small slights. Not wanting to spark a confrontation or draw attention to himself, he remained in mental retreat from what his daughter had done. But, like slivers being whittled away from a piece of wood, each affront he ignored exposed more egregious behavior. By establishing settlements on the northern border of Yuarej, however, his rival Soldan Huttan was practically declaring war. Andouk had sent repeated complaints to Olabar, to no effect.

And now Omra had commanded that all soldans send their First Wives to the palace. As hostages? As sacrifices?

The sikaras and nobles had long pressured Andouk to take additional wives who would give him sons and heirs. But Sharique was his only wife, because he wanted no one else. She satisfied his needs. After Cliaparia's treachery, Andouk wasn't sure he *wanted* other children. . . . He did enjoy his visits with his granddaughter Cithara, but since the girl was raised by Istar, Andouk was sure he had lost her, too.

He looked over at his beloved. "What am I to do?" Perhaps he should just abdicate, move into a home in a small village somewhere, run a mulberry grove for the silkworms.

Sharique lifted her chin and looked as brave as Andouk wished he could feel. "You are going to send me to Olabar, and I will stand proudly before the soldan-shah, for I am the wife of the Yuarej soldan." She kissed him. "Don't worry, husband. You are a good man, and I believe the soldan-shah is too. Urec will watch over us all."

30 *Olabar Palace*

The new clothes had cost him a fortune, not to mention the requisite jeweled rings, the tourmaline clasp for his cloak, and the strand of milk pearls that hung from his neck like a badge of office. In Tierra, only women wore pearls, but Urabans considered them a sign of importance and wealth for men as well. His dark hair was cut in the latest fashion, and his brown eyes and tan skin allowed him to pass as either Tierran or Uraban, which had served him well.

Every detail was part of Yal Dolicar's disguise.

For days, he had liberally spent money around Olabar in order to build up his mystique. Dolicar had to ensure that his fame preceded him when he appeared before the soldan-shah. Over the years he had developed many innovative ways to part people from their riches, but this was his most ambitious scheme yet.

He had to deliver every part of his story with the weight of absolute veracity. Soldan-Shah Omra was not a man who would be easily duped.

Dolicar had handed his petition to the court chamberlain, along with a hefty bribe, explaining that he had an

item of tremendous historical interest (and value) that the
soldan-shah simply must see.

It was midmorning by the time the crier summoned him
into the audience chamber. Yal Dolicar gathered his robes,
manufactured a demeanor of both supreme importance
and humility, and walked into the immaculately appointed
room. Advisers and ministers stood around the perimeter,
regarding him incuriously; he was the ninth supplicant so
far this morning.

Omra sat on a dais from which he dispensed orders and
justice. On his left sat his First Wife Istar, the unmistakably
Tierran woman who caused so much consternation among
the sikaras, and on his right sat a handsome young man
with blond hair and blue eyes, also obviously Tierran. His
adopted son Saan. Yes, Dolicar had done his research.

Sinking to his knees on the floor of polished driftwood
tiles, he spread his arms forward in full obeisance. "My
Lord Soldan-Shah, I have brought you an artifact of great
magnificence."

"So my chamberlain says." Omra leaned forward on the
dais as Dolicar extracted a long leather case dyed blood-red
and carved with intricate designs. Dolicar had spent as
much to create the extravagant container as on the supposed relic inside, but the investment would pay off. He
untied a string, removed the cap, and pulled out a weath-
ered-looking parchment with ragged edges. Part of the
paper was stained, and the bottom left corner had been
burned off. It appeared to be very old, very ornate, and very
important.

Still on his knees, Dolicar unrolled the parchment on the
polished wood. The map showed strange islands and open

seas, embellished with waves and fanciful creatures, tentacled monsters and fanged serpents. The labels were written in archaic and indecipherable script. (Yal Dolicar had no idea what the words were supposed to say, since he had just made them up.)

"My Lord, this was found in a hidden cave in the cliffs above Lahjar." His breathy voice dripped with awe. "The original Map of Urec—lost so many centuries ago! As soon as I discovered the relic, I rushed here to deliver it to you alone. I suffered great tribulations crossing Uraba, and arrived here all but penniless . . . save for this great treasure of history, and of our faith."

At Omra's gesture, Kel Rovic took the map from Dolicar's hand and carried it to the dais. As the soldan-shah stared at the parchment, his expression darkened, which Dolicar found extremely odd. "And you found this map yourself? In a cave you say?"

"Yes, in the ruins of an ancient city. Some of the structures had been looted by bandits, but this was untouched. It is a true relic."

"Someone with great talent created it." Omra looked up. "Most unfortunate that it is a forgery."

Gasps rang around the court, and Dolicar goggled. "Soldan-Shah, certainly you—"

"*Certainly* I know that this is a fake and that you are trying to cheat me." He summoned Kel Rovic. "He is to be executed."

As guards came forward to seize him, Dolicar sprang to his feet. "My Lord, why do you say such things? This map is no forgery!" The guard captain slid his curved scimitar half out of its sheath, and Dolicar squawked, "If there has been a falsification, then I swear I've been cheated as well.

When I bought the map from a merchant in Lahjar, he assured me that—"

Omra's expression remained cold. "Bought it? You told me you found it yourself."

"I did—I mean, the men took me to the place where it was found. I had every reason to believe it was real. Look at the drawings, the letters. You must admit there's a chance—"

"There is no chance, none at all. This map is a forgery." The soldan-shah sat back, revealing his own secret. "I already have the real Map."

Dolicar knew he was doomed.

As an enthusiastic Imir marched her to the throne room, Sen Sherufa bustled alongside, curious. He had practically dragged her from her home that morning, insisting that Omra wanted to see her. "He has an incredible announcement to make. I want you to hear it."

Other supplicants were waiting for their names to be called, but Imir whisked her past them without a second glance. As he pushed his way into the presence of the soldan-shah, tugging on her arm, she dug in her heels on the slippery floor. "We should wait, Imir. It isn't our turn."

"I was the soldan-shah, my dear. I never learned how to wait."

The throne room was in the midst of a commotion, the guards struggling with a man who wailed and thrashed, pleading for his life. Sherufa was astonished to recognize him, though his clothing was different and years had passed. The prisoner spotted her too and cried out, pointing wildly. "That woman—the Saedran woman! She can vouch for me! Sen Sherufa na-Oa knows that I am true to my word."

Irritated, Omra snapped to Kel Rovic, "Cut out the man's tongue if he will not be quiet."

The prisoner clamped his mouth shut, but continued to point urgently toward Sherufa.

Imir, scandalized at the man's audacity, put a protective arm around Sherufa, but she stood straight and said calmly, "Yes, Soldan-Shah—long ago, I asked this man to deliver a message to a . . . far-off friend." She didn't want to reveal that she had paid him to deliver secrets to her fellow chartsman, Aldo na-Curic, *in Calay.*

"And I did exactly as I was told! I went straight to the Saedran District. The house belonged to a man named Biento na-Curic, and he was the most famed painter in all of—"

Sherufa cut him off in alarm. "I have already said I know who you are. But I know nothing about the trouble you've caused now."

"There, that settles it." Though puzzled by her behavior, Imir pushed her toward Omra on his dais, wrapped up in his own excitement. "Tell Sen Sherufa your announcement, my son."

From the right of the dais, Saan smiled at Sherufa; he too seemed ready to burst with news he was anxious to share. She, Saan, and Imir had formed a strong friendship during their arduous journey over the Great Desert and through the lands of the Nunghals.

Omra raised his voice so his words would carry throughout the room. "We were getting to that, Father. I was about to explain myself to this man." He scowled at Dolicar, who swallowed hard. "Your map is a forgery because *I* have Urec's original Map. It was discovered in a vault beneath the

Aidenist kirk in Ishalem." He clapped his hands, and within moments the actual relic was brought into the throne room, and Omra revealed it at last for the amazed spectators.

"This map—the *true* Map—shows the way to Terravitae, as well as the location of the fabled Key to Creation, which even Urec could not find. I have chosen my son Saan to undertake a new expedition." He reached over to place his hand on the young man's shoulder. "If he can find the Key, then we will become invincible in our struggle against the Aidenists."

Now the muttering became excited, intrigued. Imir blurted out to Sherufa as he squeezed her in a hug. "And you, my dear, will go with them as their chartsman and see mysterious lands with your own eyes! The greatest voyage in the history of Uraba. You'll thank me for years to come."

Sherufa was astonished that the idea would enter his mind, and the thought of such a long and dangerous expedition made her heart quail. "No . . . no, I am not the best choice. There are better, younger, and more eager Saedrans. I've already seen my share of the world."

Imir clucked at her. "Oh come now, my dear. You always encourage me to take notes about new and uncharted places. I know your fascination. This is your chance to expand the boundaries of the known world. What more could any Saedran desire?"

Sherufa couldn't think of a reply. How could he be so oblivious to her desire to stay at home, to read only the adventures that *others* had undertaken? Or maybe he was wily after all. Could this be a ploy to get her to marry him so that she could stay home?

But Imir dispelled that idea as he continued, bubbling

with excitement. "How I wish I could go with you, my dear. The adventures we'd have! But alas, I have other obligations." He grinned wolfishly. "Soldan Xivir and I are going to hunt down the desert bandits once and for all."

From where the guards held him, Yal Dolicar shouted, "I'll go! Take me with you on the voyage! I have seen much of the world, both Uraba and Tierra! No one is as well versed in foreign lands. I journeyed to every reach in Tierra before the war began and to all the soldanates in Uraba. I have knowledge and experience that would be crucial to the success of such a long and dangerous voyage."

Sherufa decided to speak on his behalf, although reluctantly. "I have reason to believe this man is indeed well traveled as he claims." Dolicar would not have known the name of Aldo's father unless he had actually traveled from Olabar to Calay.

Though Soldan-Shah Omra frowned at the charlatan's continued protests, Saan apparently saw something worthwhile in his earnest charisma. "There's truly no telling how he got that map, Father. What if he was tricked himself? He wouldn't be the first person to buy a false chart from an unscrupulous merchant."

Omra remained skeptical, but Saan continued. "You yourself said that I will need an experienced crew aboard the *Al-Orizin*. Sen Sherufa and I can't do it ourselves! The voyage will be long and difficult, with no guarantee of a safe return. And if it is this man's fate to die, should he not die out there instead of here at court?"

Yal Dolicar fell to his knees once more. "Such wisdom in a young man! I will be a fine sailor—I have much experience aboard ships."

Omra was displeased but resigned. "I could never deny anything you request, Saan. This is your decision, and you will have to live with it. The captain of a ship must abide by his choices." The soldan-shah tapped his fingers together in contemplation. "Still, this man tried to cheat me, and he must face some punishment. I will not have you talk me out of that." He dismissively gave the order to Kel Rovic, "Cut off one of his hands. That'll be enough to remind him never to handle stolen goods again."

Dolicar wailed, trying to escape, but the guards held him firmly. "No, not my hand, not my right hand! No!"

As he was dragged away, Sen Sherufa stood numb next to a grinning Imir. "I appreciate the gesture, Imir—I truly do—but I'd rather stay home and study maps. And if you aren't going along on the voyage to watch over me . . ."

He leaned closer, whispering in her ear. "Ah, you'll miss me, I know. Never fear, I will be thinking about you as well. And when you come back home, my dear, you'll have many new stories to tell me."

Omra spoke to everyone in the throne room. "Send the announcement across all of Uraba. The *Al-Orizin* will set sail as soon as Saan gathers the rest of his crew."

31 *Nunghal Ship*

When the Nunghal lookout sighted land, he shouted until he was hoarse. From the starboard rail, Asaddan saw nothing more than a smudge of gray uncertainty on the horizon, another mirage or perhaps a line of storm clouds.

Though the bulky vessel had been moving along at a good clip for days now, their supplies were low, water barrels nearly empty, and tempers short. The seafaring Nunghal-Su were accustomed to long voyages, but only in familiar waters. It had been more than a month since the last known landmark.

Ruad took his place next to Asaddan at the prow, crossing his arms over his sharkskin vest. "Well, we have made it here, friend . . . wherever *here* might be. This land is not on any of our charts."

Asaddan still couldn't make out a coastline, but the lookout's enthusiasm and certainty could not be denied. "We can hunt fresh food on land. My stomach longs for the taste of meat again, and I am sick of eating fish. No wonder your clan members are always thin and sallow-looking."

The shipkhan let out a rude snort. "At least fish don't stink the way your buffalo herds do."

"That is open to debate."

After turning the rudder and setting the accordioned sail to make the best possible speed, the Nunghal crew guided the ship toward the mysterious shore. The details of cliffs and coves soon became more apparent, and barely submerged reefs made a milky froth of the water.

Ruad held a spyglass to his eye, examining the coastline. "I see a settlement, maybe even a large city." He passed the spyglass to Asaddan, who spotted an unlit lighthouse on a spire of rock, as well as whitewashed wooden buoys floating near underwater hazards. He also made out pale buildings crowded close to each other, like stone tents at the largest clan gathering.

As the gray-sailed ship picked its way through the reefs

toward the strange city and its harbor, they encountered seven feluccas, shallow-draught boats with a single mast and large sail that extended so far out to the side that the vessel looked sure to overbalance and capsize. Brown-skinned men aboard the anchored feluccas wore only loincloths as they dove over the sides, swimming deep. When they broke the surface, sputtering water and flinging dark hair from their eyes, they reminded Asaddan of otters at play as they waved a friendly greeting at the Nunghal ship.

"Better anchor here before those reefs rip our hull open," Ruad said. "We'll take the ship's boat to meet with the divers and find out where we are. Asaddan, you'll translate, since you are the only one aboard who speaks the language."

"If they are indeed Urabans," Asaddan said.

Concealing swords by the gunwales, he joined the ship-khan and four burly sailors as they rowed over to where the divers trod water alongside their feluccas. Asaddan cupped his hands around his mouth and shouted, "Hello! Do you understand me? Do you speak Uraban?" Remembering the traditional blessing, he added, "Do you follow the Map?"

One of the divers shouted back, "Yes, we follow the Map." The accent was so strong that Asaddan had difficulty comprehending it. "Welcome, strangers!"

One man dove deep and remained submerged for so long that Asaddan feared he would drown. Then, with a surprising splash, he popped up right next to the ship's boat, smiling as he lifted a handheld net to spill rough oysters into their boat. "A gift for you, strangers." He barely sounded out of breath at all. "I'd wager at least two of these hold milk pearls."

Ruad nudged Asaddan. "What is he saying?"

"He says these oysters have pearls in them."

"Now that's a fine start, but find out where we are. Ask them the name of this place."

Asaddan said, "What is the name of this city? We have had a long voyage. Can you tell us where we are?"

The man found this outrageously funny. "How can you make a journey and not know where you are or where you should be?"

Asaddan sniffed. "Not all journeys have an obvious destination. We are where we are, and we will be wherever we go."

"Then you've arrived." The diver laughed. "Welcome to Lahjar."

32 *Calay*

Returning from the somber at-sea funeral for King Korastine, Anjine stood beside her brother at the stern of the escort ship. Black smoke from the pyre vessel rose high into the cloudless sky as it continued to burn, drifting far away.

"If he's with my mother now, do you think he's happy?" Tomas asked, sniffling. "I'm not happy that he's gone." Though he struggled to fulfill his role as the prince of Tierra, he looked incredibly young.

Anjine wondered if her little brother remembered Ilrida's funeral, a similar pyre barge set adrift out on the Oceansea. "Death is not a happy thing, but it happens, even though we almost never expect it." She forced a wan smile. "At least our father lived long enough to see the launch of the *Dyscovera*."

Tomas brightened, making a visible effort. "If the ship reaches Terravitae, do you think Captain Vora will find Father there waiting?"

Though Anjine didn't believe it, she wouldn't dash her brother's hope. "There's no telling what the *Dyscovera* might find, or what miracles Holy Joron could perform."

Up at the bow, in his finest military uniform, Mateo stood proudly with the heads of the city guard and the royal guard, along with a solemn contingent of soldiers, all of whom had come to see the dead king on his final voyage. Mateo's hair blew in the salty breeze, and his face was pale.

He had loved King Korastine greatly, and Anjine knew that to a certain degree, Mateo felt the loss as keenly as she did. He was like a brother to her, a son to Korastine, but he was also well trained as a soldier, and he performed his duty to perfection now. Anjine looked longingly at her friend, standing so far away, but since the loss of the king he had increased his distance from her, treating her more formally. Perhaps that was for the best. She had to turn her attention to the kingdom's other leaders and advisers.

All of the destrars attended the funeral aboard the escort vessel: Broeck from Iboria, Tavishel from Soeland, Shenro from Alamont, Siescu from Corag, and Unsul from Erietta; even Sazar, the leader of the rivermen—who considered himself a destrar, in duties if not in title—had come. Now that she considered Unsul more closely, she saw that the destrar was indeed the man her father had described— quiet and intelligent, with weak eyesight and a gracious personality. No wonder Korastine had suggested the man's son as a worthy marriage prospect.

Of all the destrars, Broeck was as close to a friend as Anjine had. Tomas's grandfather said to her, "You are queen now, Anjine. While we're here in Calay, you should call a council of the destrars to discuss the matters that lie before us. Siescu and I must finalize our plans for crossing the mountains to invade the Gremurr mines, and we may need laborers from the Alamont labor camps to build the road."

Anjine's voice was hard. "The destrars will cooperate. Not a one of them has any love for the Urecari."

"Yes, my Queen." Broeck nodded his shaggy head and stepped back respectfully to give her and the boy a moment of privacy.

My Queen. The words suddenly struck Anjine, and she had to grip the rail and close her eyes to stop herself from sobbing out loud. Responsibility and *fear* welled up inside her. *Queen.*

For the past several years, she had served as Tierra's ruler in many capacities, writing proclamations that her father then signed. Throughout her life, Korastine had taught her how to wear the crown, but now that he was gone, she felt the gulf of knowledge she did not possess. It had never been so apparent to her before, and there were so many questions she'd never thought to ask.

As the deck swayed in a gentle swell, she reached out, wrapped her arm around Tomas, and squeezed him tightly. Her brother trembled, grappling with his emotions; he tried to be brave, tried not to show his grief—but failed.

The ship passed the comforting guardians of the two

lighthouses at the harbor mouth, and Anjine looked back out to sea. Most of the smoke had been borne away on the winds, as the blazing pyre ship dropped below the horizon.

Anjine thought of the nights she had left her father alone to read his books, to dream of what lay out there unexplored. Korastine must have been so lonely. How she wished that she'd spent more time with him talking about important things—political decisions, family connections, trade and taxes ... even unimportant conversations about the weather, or which flowers to plant in the castle courtyard. Everything, anything.

Had her father lived another thirty years, she would still be wishing for more time with him. There would always be things they should have said to each other. But Anjine was queen now. She had to be strong.

Turning away, she walked to the prow to stand silently next to Mateo during the ship's entry into the harbor. He stayed close, saying nothing, but they shared a deep and silent grief. They didn't need to speak the words aloud. If so many others hadn't been there watching, she would have clasped Mateo's hand, just for the closeness. Instead, the two remained formal, a guard and a princess. No, a queen.

She looked toward Calay, her city, her kingdom. King Korastine's spirit may have found his way to Terravitae, but she still had a land to rule.

The city of Calay observed a period of mourning for seven days after the funeral, but Anjine could not allow herself such a personal luxury. Broeck had made a good suggestion, and she used the opportunity to call all five destrars for an important strategy meeting inside the castle.

Prester-Marshall Rudio joined them at the long pine table, along with newly promoted Comdar Rief and the subcomdars of the army and navy, as well as Sen Leo na-Hadra. Mateo, though, had departed immediately after the funeral, riding out to the military camps.

After the prester-marshall delivered his invocation for the meeting, Anjine spread out the mountain maps of Corag Reach, which showed the potential route down to the Middlesea shores. Though little had actually changed in the way she conducted a meeting, Anjine felt strange, too aware that this was her first session as the queen of Tierra, instead of just a surrogate for her father. It made a difference that her father was not at her side. Anjine would have to fill the void with her own advisers; she would have to make her own decisions.

She did not try to color her words or soften the pain of their recent setbacks. "We failed to capture Ishalem. That loss wounded us deeply, and we must learn from it. Our first and highest priority is to seize the Gremurr mines from the Urecari. The enemy believes the Corag mountains to be impassable. They aren't aware that we know the mines exist, even though they are in our territory."

These men had all heard Broeck's plan to cross the mountains and attack Gremurr from the rear. His nephew Iaros sat beside him, his large mustache bristling. The young man held his silence with difficulty; he fidgeted, eyes bright, as he listened.

Pale and gaunt Destrar Siescu of Corag pounded a fist on the table. His translucent skin showed the faint purplish lines of blood vessels. "The mines must be *ours*."

Destrar Shenro seemed particularly incensed. "And think

of all those poor Aidenist slaves they keep in pens, like animals."

The Corag destrar looked at the drawings of his mountains, nodding and mumbling to himself. Though it was a warm spring day, Siescu wrapped himself in furs, even inside the castle chamber. "My scout confirms the route, and I dispatched him with some of our mining engineers to assess the challenge. Given sufficient workers and equipment, we could hack out a path to get our army through the tightest places."

"It will need to be a wide road for the beasts," Broeck said.

"We will make it as wide as need be, but we'll require more slaves." Siescu looked around meaningfully.

"I will contribute as many as you like," Destrar Shenro said. "I recently lost four hundred of them, but I still have far more Curlies than I need."

Contemplative, Destrar Unsul said, "It's not simply a question of *having* the slaves, but of feeding, clothing, and guarding them. We're sure to lose some during the labor in the mountains. We will need replacements."

Destrar Tavishel stroked his square-cut beard; perspiration glistened from his shaved head. Unlike the Corag destrar, the leader of the windy island reach seemed overheated in the chamber. "My ships will increase their raids and bring as many captives as you need. If we venture far enough south, the followers of Urec are there for the taking."

At the head of the table, Anjine remained stern and strong. "When we strike Gremurr, the Urecari cannot know we are coming. Our greatest challenge is a practical one—

how to get a large army, with all of our weapons, mounts, and armor, over the mountain passes and carry out a massive attack, while maintaining complete secrecy?"

"Raga Var will lead you," Siescu promised with a predatory smile.

"We can do it," said Shenro, "provided we find a way to flush out the infiltrators in our military."

Anjine answered with a smile that showed confidence, but no warmth. "We have a way," she said, thinking of Mateo's plan. "We will find them and purge them from our army."

33   *Military Camp, Alamont Reach*

As night settled over the training camp near Bora's Bastion, comforting fires burned brightly; off-duty soldier-recruits sat around the blazes, telling stories of their home reaches. Mess tents served generous portions of porridge, bread, and cheese—the bounty of Alamont. The first-year recruits were exhausted from vigorous practice sessions, while the more hardened ones enjoyed the quiet time with their comrades. In recent months, however, the campfire groups had grown smaller, the cliques tighter, as suspicions spread like rot through their ranks.

Mateo felt the dark mood, like jagged cracks in a pane of windowglass. An army whose soldiers mistrusted their comrades was already defeated. . . .

After the former *ra'vir* Tira had explained the suffering the Teacher inflicted on captive Tierran children—

pummeling them, torturing them, and forging the ones he didn't murder into fanatical tools of assassination and sabotage—Mateo had a much better idea what drove those traitors. He even felt a hint of sympathy for them. It wasn't their fault that the evil Curlies had turned them all into venomous snakes that slithered back into the Aidenist fold.

But he also recalled what they had done to the Tierran military commanders at the Ishalem wall, how they had burned the Arkship, how they fostered a general fog of anger and suspicion among the entire Tierran populace— and his sympathy faded. They had to be found and stopped.

During the past few weeks, he had kept the *ra'vir* girl's revelation secret from all but Anjine and a select few of his commanders, letting everyone else imagine his romantic or paternal connections to her. Only his most trusted men were aware of the scheme the girl had suggested. He was confident. He knew there were more *ra'virs* in his army. Having confessed and helped Mateo, Tira felt frightened for her life.

Inside his command tent now, he sat in a canvas chair behind the field table. Whale-oil lamps shed a glow as bright and welcoming as any fire; having grown up in Calay, Mateo didn't mind the fishy smell the oil exuded. Placing his elbows on the hard planks of the table, he regarded the young recruit who sat across from him. Mateo kept a firm sense of authority about him, and the trainee viewed him with respect.

This young man, Rickar Fenn, came from one of the smaller islands in Soeland Reach. Having heard gruff Destrar Tavishel's accounts of battles at sea, Fenn was anxious to fight the Curlies. At the end of his training, he hoped to be assigned to one of the Soeland patrol ships; in the meantime, though, the young man had to learn how to fight alongside the rest of the Tierran army, wherever the battles might take him.

When Mateo called him into the command tent, Rickar Fenn was nervous, but he relaxed as their conversation continued. The young man finished the proffered cup of wine. "I swear to help you root out the evil followers of Urec, sir, wherever they may be."

"That's what I am personally asking every soldier." Mateo took the smallest sip from his own goblet; he had already spoken to eleven young men so far, and he had many more meetings scheduled before he could retire for the night. He couldn't drink too much. "I'm glad we've had this chance to get to know each other. Dismissed. Now, would you please send in . . ." He paused to look down at his list of names. "Dawson Orin, from Erietta."

"Yes, sir." The trainee hopped to his feet and pushed the tent flap aside. On his way out, Fenn walked with a jaunty stride; if nothing else, the recruit's enthusiasm would boost morale in the training camp.

Mateo set the bottle of wine on the side of the table, turned the label out of view, and set an empty goblet next to it. Within moments, the next young man poked his head inside. He had shaggy brown hair and a thin face. "Excuse me, Subcomdar? Dawson Orin, reporting as you requested."

"Come in. I'm trying to meet as many of my troops here in Alamont as I possibly can. We'll all depend upon each other in days to come."

Self-consciously, Dawson ran his fingers through his hair and brushed the front of his uniform tunic. He took the indicated seat across from the field table as Mateo studied his ledger book. "So, you come from Erietta Reach, near Peliton?"

"Nearer the coast than the river, sir. There aren't many towns worth the name, so I had to put something on my recruitment papers. I was eager to join the army, of course."

"Of course. Would you care for a glass of wine? I want this to be an informal conversation."

The young man's eyes lit up and he nodded, amazed by his good fortune. "Yes, sir, I'd like that very much."

Mateo handed him the empty goblet. "This is your second year in the army, is it not? Or your third?"

"Second, sir. I was first assigned to Corag Reach, and then Alamont. Next year, I'll be home in Erietta."

Before pouring, Mateo casually turned the wine bottle so Dawson could see the label. He topped off his own glass, inspected the bottle, and smiled. "This wine was confiscated from a Uraban ship in our waters. Tavishel took the whole crew prisoner, appropriated their cargo. It's what the Curly merchants deserve, if they try to trade above the Edict Line." Mateo shook his head. "I just opened the bottle this evening. The wine is quite good, though I have no idea where it's from."

He extended the bottle to pour for Dawson, but the young man's eyes were fixed on the incomprehensible Uraban lettering. He raised his hand abruptly. "On second thought, sir, maybe I shouldn't. I'm exhausted after a long day of training."

"Come now, how often do you get a chance to talk with your commander like this, and enjoy the spoils of Uraba?" Mateo poured wine into the goblet. "Drink up."

In numerous camps across Tierra, his loyal field commanders were doing the same thing, meeting with their troops, having similar conversations.

The young man stared. "I'm afraid I can't, sir, I . . . I've decided not to have any drink until I've completed my prayer cycle for the holidays."

"Only a moment ago, you were glad to share a cup with me."

"My apologies, sir. I-I appreciate your generosity."

"Of course you do." Mateo whistled sharply, and the quietly waiting soldiers—all survivors of the Ishalem battle—burst in through the back flap in the tent. "Arrest him. He has already condemned himself in my eyes."

Dawson sprang to his feet. "I don't understand!" He thrashed his arms as the soldiers grabbed him. "What is this, sir? I'm a loyal recruit, I—"

"No one else here can understand Uraban scribblings, but you recognized that this mark here"—Mateo tapped his fingertip against the brown glass—"denotes 'slow poison.'"

Out of the twelve recruits Mateo had interviewed so far, only Dawson Orin had reacted to the writing on the bottle, believing the confiscated wine to be deadly. Yes, Tira had been right. . . .

As the guards pulled the young man toward the tent's rear flap, so that other camp members could not see him, Dawson spat a stream of incomprehensible words, Uraban curses, which were cut off as soon as the men wrestled a gag into his mouth.

"We've caught a spy." Mateo sighed, but he did not feel triumphant. "And now, alas, our army is also decreased by one."

34 *Olabar Harbor*

Word of the *Al-Orizin*'s quest spread across the five soldanates. Would-be crewmen, curiosity seekers, and fortune hunters streamed to the capital city and volunteered their services. Taking his captain's duties seriously, Saan insisted on vetting all the candidates himself.

So far, though, he'd found only a few men that he considered acceptable.

After interviewing dozens of sailors, he could easily spot the dreamers, those wide-eyed men more enamored with the *idea* of such a voyage than with the reality (and with little, if any, experience). He knew full well that such volunteers would sail away with great enthusiasm and sparkling eyes, blowing kisses to their loved ones, eager for a great adventure . . . but after a few days of hard work and bad weather, they would be worthless. "Ballast with mouths to feed," Saan called them.

On a dangerous voyage like this, some captains would accept any crewmen, even prisoners. While Yal Dolicar was technically a prisoner, Saan felt he had a spark of persistence, determination, and perhaps creativity that most other men lacked.

So he kept looking, but he wasn't desperate yet. The *Al-Orizin* wasn't ready to sail, and he had found twelve men already. He needed a crew of forty-five, but could make do with forty, if he had to. Saan had decided he'd rather have fewer good men than a full complement of mediocre ones.

They would depend on one another for their lives, so he refused to relax his standards.

His mother had told him, "A wise man does not trust his weight to a rope that is already frayed." When he asked if that was a quote from Urec's Log, she had looked away, mumbling that it was just an old saying. Saan supposed that the line came from the Book of Aiden, but he didn't press his mother. Istar— *Adrea*—had been raised on the deceptions of Aidenist presters and still hadn't forgotten all of their teachings.

He set up a recruitment pavilion out on the sunny docks, surrounded by the bustle of ships and cargo haulers, the creak of oars and rigging, the chatter of sailors and merchants. Hour after hour, men came in full of bluster and departed looking dejected.

A large shadow appeared on the flapping silk walls as a burly man stepped through the pavilion entrance. "You are Captain Saan? My name is Grigovar, and I deserve to be part of your crew." His voice had the rich musical accent of far-off lands.

"I'll be the one to decide that." Saan sized up the man, liked what he saw. Grigovar had dark skin and thick black hair, enormous muscles, and a leather vest that seemed too small for his broad chest. A round gold earring dangled from one ear.

The man crossed his arms. "It's your choice, sir, but if you turn down my service, then you aren't a wise enough captain to be in charge of this voyage."

Saan wasn't sure whether to laugh or be offended. "Well, I am looking for confident sailors, but I need more than brave talk. I need experience, strength, and common sense."

Grigovar flexed his muscles. "Do I look like a poet?"

"I don't need a poet. What is your accent? Is that Lahjar I hear?"

"I am one of the famed reef divers." He slapped his chest. "My lungs can hold a breath for six minutes. By diving deeper than my fellows, I made myself wealthy from the bushels of milk pearls I harvested off the coast of Lahjar."

Though he was already more impressed by this man than by any candidate so far that morning, Saan pretended to be dubious. "If you possess such riches, why would you want to sign aboard the *Al-Orizin*?"

"I want to see the world."

"Why?"

The reef diver scratched his thick hair. "You've heard the saying, 'From Lahjar to Kiesh'? From one side of the world to the other. I started at Lahjar. I had already made up my mind to see all the soldanates, to make my way to Kiesh at the far end of Abilan, but then I learned of your voyage. Now, I enjoy your city of Olabar. Your women are beautiful and, better still, they find *me* exotic and attractive. But I've had enough women and enough wealth. It's time for something more. The *Al-Orizin* can take me to Kiesh ... and beyond."

"Why not settle down, take a wife, have children?"

Grigovar rocked back on his heels. "I'd rather have good drink and listen to an amusing joke."

"You'll not be drunk aboard my ship."

"I drink. I'm not a drunk. Diving deep for pearls puts enough pressure on my skull. No need to add a hangover on top of it."

Saan stood up from behind his small table. "One more question—did you bring along any companions from Lahjar? I could use more crewmen like you."

"One of me is worth ten of your other crewmen," Grigovar said.

"Then welcome aboard."

It took the better part of a week, but Saan did gather forty-two crewmen—enough for him to announce that he was ready to sail. Then he received an unexpected and unwelcome visitor.

In a swirl of red robes, Sikara Fyiri appeared at the boarding ramp with her dark cinnamon-brown hair blowing loose in the breeze. Standing atop a crate as he supervised the loading of supplies, Saan looked at the haughty woman and greeted her with exaggerated cheer. "Good morning, Sikara! Have you come to bless the *Al-Orizin* before our departure?"

Fyiri regarded him coldly. "I have come to join your crew. The ur-sikara chose me to serve on your voyage."

"Really?" It took all of his effort to mask his automatic scowl. "I don't recall asking for a sikara aboard." Though he considered himself a devout believer in Urec's Log, Saan had nothing but disdain for the women who had so often targeted him and his mother with their scorn.

"And we did not ask your opinion. This is a voyage to seek the Key to Creation, perhaps even to find the original home of holy Urec. You must allow a high-ranking priestess aboard. The church's mandate is clear."

Saan considered challenging her, or asking the soldan-shah to intervene, but that might cause more problems than it solved. Once the *Al-Orizin* sailed, Fyiri would be greatly outnumbered and her influence would be marginal. "If you come along, don't expect any special treatment."

"I expect what is my due—a private cabin and the respect of your men."

Saan mentally rearranged sleeping quarters. Briefly, he considered having Fyiri share a cabin with Sen Sherufa, but dismissed the idea. He was too fond of Sen Sherufa to do that to her. The two women would be as compatible as oil and vinegar—with Fyiri definitely more vinegar. "I can find you a room, but you'll have to earn the respect of my men for yourself."

As the remaining crates of supplies came aboard, Kel Rovic and two guards led a prisoner to the docks. Though Yal Dolicar's legs were in chains, he walked with as much of a jaunty step as he could manage. The stump of his right arm was bound up in white gauze, ending abruptly where his hand had been.

Rovic warned, "Keep him locked in the brig until you're well out of the harbor, Captain." Saan found it amusing to hear his old friend refer to him as "Captain."

"I won't give you any trouble," Dolicar said. "Trust me. Truly, Captain, I am grateful for this exciting opportunity."

Saan showed the prisoner aboard. "You're in good spirits, considering your circumstances."

"I try to make the best of a situation. Could have been much worse." Dolicar held up the stump of his right arm. "Your minister of punishment was adept at his work, his blade was sharp, and your Olabar physicians know how to tend an amputation." Standing there in his chains and tattered clothes, with his wrapped wrist, the charlatan actually smiled. "I would have preferred not to lose my hand, but I'm lucky to be alive. I owe my life to you, Captain."

He frowned at the stump, where blood seeped through the bandages. "Losing my hand limits my ability to be a good sailor and fighter, but all is not lost. I sent word out—your guards were very accommodating." He nodded at Kel Rovic. "I commissioned an assortment of tools. I'll have a hook like many sailors wear, and a carved wooden hand for situations that require a bit more decorum, and even an attachment with a built-in dagger, in case you need me to fight."

Saan was impressed at how thoroughly the man had thought his situation through. "I appreciate your good humor. You will have to practice doing things with your left hand now." He motioned for Rovic to take the prisoner belowdecks, where he would be held until after they sailed away.

Before he ducked into the hatch, Dolicar called in a conspiratorial whisper, "It's not so bad." He raised his stump. "After all, I was never right-handed."

35 *The* Dyscovera

One uncharted sea looked much like another, but Criston knew that at any time the curve of the horizon could reveal mysterious shorelines, rugged continents, exotic islands—or the edge of the world itself. So far, though, he saw only water stretching out in all directions . . . day after day after day.

After leaving the escort of Soeland ships, the graceful

carrack continued westward, chasing the sunset into waters that no living man had ever seen. As captain, he had chosen a different course from the wide-ranging path the *Luminara* had sailed on her disastrous voyage.

Each morning at dawn, Prester Hannes summoned every member of the crew to listen to his sermons. He was grim and fiery, quite unlike the soft-spoken and avuncular Prester Jerard from the *Luminara*. But Hannes had been shaped by the painful experiences he'd endured, and Criston felt close to the man, understood him. He himself was very different from the optimistic young sailor who had climbed aboard the *Luminara* nearly two decades ago. . . .

Hannes shouted into the clear, moist air and inflamed the sailors, but out on the open sea, the men had no place to vent their anger. Rather, the prester had to content himself with focusing their energy and determination on finding Terravitae and forming an alliance with Holy Joron to crush the enemy. Prester Hannes continued to remind the crew how much was at stake on this mission. "Though we sail far beyond the eyes of mortal men, do not assume we are safe. Always remain alert for Urecari treachery."

Impressionable Javian was alarmed to hear such talk, but Criston let the prester spew all the invective he liked. He could never forgive or forget what the Urecari raiders had done to Windcatch, his old mother, or his beloved wife Adrea and their unborn child. . . .

While the *Dyscovera* sailed smoothly along under high white clouds, Criston sat at the table in his cabin and marked the ship's charts. After a brisk knock, Javian pushed open the door, his face flushed with worry. "Sir, there's trouble brewing!"

Only a few steps behind the cabin boy came big Kjelnar, clearly angry. "It's a decision for you to make, Captain. It shouldn't have been a problem at all, if you ask me. One of the crewmen, sir—a man named Mior. The men don't like him. They're suspicious."

Criston frowned irritably. "A crewman isn't required to be liked, just to do his work. Haven't these others ever sailed before?"

Kjelnar kept his voice low. "Even so, Captain, there could be something to their suspicions. Mior is quiet, keeps to himself, has secretive habits."

He followed the two out onto the deck, where he saw his sailors milling about uneasily. In the hot afternoon sun, the other crewmen had stripped to the waist as they worked on deck, but the one named Mior remained fully clothed in shirt, pants, and headband. He must have been abominably hot in such garments.

"He never shows his skin, and that's passing strange, especially in this weather," Kjelnar grumbled. "Some of the crew think he has scars from the lash on his back, and he's ashamed of them."

"Or that he has fern tattoos, showing his allegiance to Urec," Javian interjected.

Criston rested his fists on his hips as he observed. "Has he actually done anything wrong?"

"He completes his tasks like any other sailor, better than some. He causes no trouble, but still . . ." Kjelnar rubbed his face. "Nagging questions make the men uneasy, and uneasy men are more difficult to control."

Growing angry, Criston walked with a determined gait across the deck. "Then we'll put an end to this now, for good." Some of the sailors turned away, cowed, while others raised their voices in a cacophony of indignant shouts.

Mior stood apart, glowering at them, his back to three large barrels.

Criston regarded the thin young man, who seemed only a year or so older than Javian. "I will have no secrets among my crew. We'll face unknown perils together. We must trust one another."

But Mior stood rigid, shaking his head. "No, Captain. A person has a right to privacy, even on a crew. Why should these men care how I dress?"

"You're right, they shouldn't care." Criston swept a stern gaze across the men, showing his own disapproval before he turned back to Mior. "But they do. And once the question has been raised, it can't be taken back. Considering what the *ra'virs* have done over the years, the crew has good reason to be suspicious. It's a small thing, and you are *all* ridiculous to argue about it." Criston raised his voice sharply, looking at them again, then back at Mior. "Including you. Will you take off your shirt?"

"No, Captain. Please don't make me."

"It's the fastest way to put an end to this distrust." Impatient, Criston gestured to two of the men. "Off with the shirt. We'll all see if he's hiding scars or fern tattoos— and then everyone can get back to work!"

Mior struggled even after the captain's command, and the open defiance concerned Criston even more. But when the cloth ripped and the fabric fell away from the white unblemished skin, they saw no lash scars, no tattoos . . . only a pair of small, rounded breasts.

36 *The* Al-Orizin

The soldan-shah decreed a day of rejoicing and prayer for the *Al-Orizin* before their departure. Plumes of colored smoke wafted from every Urecari church as sikaras burned prayer strips begging Ondun to keep His watchful eye on the ship; some even remembered to include Captain Saan in their words.

Under bright sunshine on the day of sailing, Saan stood at the prow wearing a golden fern pendant that little Omirr had given him; his sisters had made a hand-painted silk Eye of Urec pennant, which now flew from the top of the main-mast. The crew gathered on the deck waving at the audience, blowing kisses. Sikara Fyiri stood at the ship's stern resplendent in scarlet robes, as if demanding to be the center of attention, but the other sailors crowded in with their exuberance, particularly the muscular reef diver Grigovar.

The shackled but grinning prisoner Yal Dolicar was released from the hold below, and a blacksmith came aboard. With a loud clang, he struck the bolt from the shackles and freed the man, then carried the chains back off the *Al-Orizin*. Dolicar rubbed his sore ankles with his one hand, then straightened and waved as vigorously as any other crewman, holding up his beautifully carved wooden hand.

Old Imir strode up the boarding ramp, walked straight to brown-robed Sen Sherufa, and swept her into his arms for a wet, enthusiastic kiss. The crowds whistled and cheered. Saan couldn't tell if the Saedran woman was startled more by Imir's unexpected act or by the catcalls that erupted from the hundreds of observers. Sherufa blushed furiously but didn't pull away too quickly. Imir laughed as she extricated herself and still managed to pat her rear before he bounded back to the docks.

Soldan-Shah Omra stood on the dock with his two wives, three daughters, and two young sons. Saan waved to his mother with such confidence that some of the worry actually faded from Istar's expression. He had already said goodbye to his family, taking special care to speak earnestly with Omirr. "You are the zarif, brother. Help our father take care of Uraba until I come back."

Raising his hands, Omra shouted above the crowd noise, "Urec will guide you! Let his eye on your sail see only untroubled waters and brisk winds to carry you to your destination. Follow the Map and find what all men are meant to find. Find the Key to Creation!"

When Omra finished his speech, two sailors withdrew the boarding ramp, and dockworkers loosed the ropes. Saan and his crew threw long rolls of ribbon toward the crowd, keeping hold of one end as the ship drifted away from the main dock. The colored streamers shot out like the tails of falling stars, and the gathered people ran forward to catch them. They held the ribbons that grew tighter and tighter as the *Al-Orizin* moved off, until finally the ribbons snapped. One young man held on even when his ribbon didn't break, and he was pulled off the dock into the water, to uproarious laughter.

As the ship began to sail away, Saan stared at the broken

fabric strands, then looked up and waved farewell to his family again.

The crowds diminished on the docks as the *Al-Orizin* headed out into the deep Middlesea, her colorful sails dwindling in the distance. And Istar was left behind again. She remained on the lonely dock long after most people had dispersed, keeping her three daughters close. None of the girls spoke now, having yelled themselves hoarse as the ship launched.

Istar felt herself crumbling inside, shaking. She had prepared for this, but she had not expected how the emotions would overwhelm her. She had thought those feelings long buried, but she had been fooling herself. They were not forgotten.

First Criston . . . and now Saan.

For the past five years, she had carefully kept her secret from the soldan-shah, an old waterstained letter written in the familiar hand of her first love, her *true* husband in the eyes of Ondun and Aiden. Though she had long ago surrendered to affection and appreciation for Omra, she had always reserved a special part of her heart and her dreams for Criston. That letter had saved her in more ways than one; she read and cherished it whenever she needed to. Even when Omra was away, Istar was never truly alone.

On that last day in Calay, when Criston and his fellow crewmen had waved from the decks of the *Luminara*, she had given him a lock of her hair . . . golden strands that symbolized the bonds of sympathetic magic, and of their love. He had vowed to write her letters and seal them in bottles along with strands of hair so that they would be drawn back to her. And he had done exactly as he promised.

But she had been taken from him, thrown unwillingly into a different life, a life that she had *accepted*. But Istar—*Adrea*—had never forgotten.

Each time she studied the already memorized words Criston had written aboard the *Luminara*, so long ago, she felt as if she were cheating on Omra. But Criston didn't know where she was—or whether she was even alive—just as she had no idea if he had been lost at sea like his father . . . or if he had found someone else to love.

Now Istar barely recognized her own life. Once she had made her desperate bargain and married Omra to protect her young son, the soldan-shah had treated Saan as his own and accepted Istar as a true First Wife. But she had never forgotten about her fishing village of Windcatch . . . or that horrific day when Omra and his Urecari raiders had ended her world. The letter anchored her to those other days. . . .

Once, she had carelessly left the door to her palace chambers unattended, considering herself alone as she pored over the letter. Cithara had come in to ask her to play a game with the girls. Istar had tried to hide the brittle, waterstained pages, but not before the quiet girl had seen the Aidenist writing. Cithara had stared, wide-eyed, her expression full of questions. When Istar was clumsy in making excuses, Cithara had merely said, "Don't worry, Mother Istar, I didn't see anything."

Since that bloody day in the souks down by the docks, Istar had made it known to all Saedran merchants and arriving traders that she was interested in seeing any letters found in bottles. Twice, men had brought her possibilities, but they were obvious forgeries and certainly not written by Criston. She had no further word from him.

After long consideration, she had shown the letter to Saan and again told him the full story of her past life. Having been raised in the Olabar palace and taught only the religion of Urec, her son had difficulty understanding her wistful memories of Tierra. He knew the facts, realized that his mother had been taken against her will, but saw only that her life had been much improved from what it would have been as a poor fisherman's wife. Omra was a good husband and a good father, and she could not argue with that.

Now that the *Al-Orizin* had sailed away, however, she regretted not telling Saan more about what his real father had done, how their son was unwittingly following in Criston's wake. How similar they were! Young Saan was so brave, happy, incredibly handsome and strong, chasing after a true dream in his heart. Just as Criston had.

She understood perfectly well the political reasons why Omra had sent the young man away; not only did it make pragmatic sense, it was something that needed to be done . . . and something Saan *longed* to do.

But as she stood on the dock and looked toward the horizon, no longer able to see the ship, Istar couldn't help thinking about the day that her brave young Criston Vora had sailed away in the *Luminara*, leaving her behind.

37 *The* Dyscovera

Once exposed, the young sailor Mior thrashed like a hellcat, grabbing the remnants of her torn shirt and trying to cover herself. Javian gaped, as if he'd never seen naked breasts before. The other crewmen recoiled, taken aback by this surprise that did not match any of their dark suspicions.

Prester Hannes's eyes flashed, and he opened his mouth to spout a condemnation that could not be taken back, but Criston cut him off with a loud warning. "*I* am captain of this ship, Prester!" He swept his gaze across the crew. "Any man here—no matter what his station—who presumes to command this ship in my stead will find himself cast overboard!"

The prester tensed, fighting back the anger flaring in his eyes, then relaxed his stance. He deferred to Criston with a visible effort. "As you say, Captain Vora."

"How did a woman get aboard our ship?" Kjelnar demanded, as if this were his failing as first mate.

"The same way the rest of you did." Mior glared, staring down the crew, her body coiled and ready to fight. "By signing up for the voyage and doing my work."

But Criston was not through with his scolding. "You deceived your captain and your crew, young woman."

She remained unapologetic. "Only by hiding my gender, not my abilities. If I had signed the roster as a woman, you never would have allowed me as part of your crew."

"Of course not." Kjelnar barked a laugh.

"And why not?" Mior rounded on him, her whole body shaking with anger. "Can only young men dream of going off to sea?" She swung like a skilled duelist squarely upon her next opponent, Prester Hannes. "Aiden brought plenty of women aboard his great Arkship at the beginning of history."

The prester's expression remained stony. "As passengers, not as crew."

"Does the Book of Aiden say that? I can read—the scriptures are not specific. During Aiden's long voyage, do you believe the women aboard never lifted a hand to help? Never aided the sailors?"

Kjelnar scratched his full beard, still angry but uneasy. "In Iboria, women help herd the mammoths. Some of them even fell trees and work the logs as they float down to Calay."

Javian spoke up. "She's right, Captain. We would never have let her join the crew if she told us up front."

"And good thing, too," one of the sailors grumbled.

Mior sniffed. "I knew I could do the work, but you would not have given me the chance. So I had to pretend to be what you expected. Have you found fault with my work in any way?"

Prester Hannes seemed torn. "There is some merit to your claim. I too had to hide my identity when I lived among the Urecari, Captain. My deception was for the greater good and the glory of Ondun. But what is your true purpose here, young woman? Urec also brought women aboard." His countenance darkened, and he turned back to the captain. "This girl has already deceived us once. How can we know where her heart truly lies? If she tricked her way aboard because she wanted to see the world, then her deception was for her own wants and needs—not for the glory of Ondun."

With a soft expression, Criston regarded Hannes. "Truth be told, those are exactly the reasons I signed aboard the *Luminara* when I was but a young man. There's no fault in that. In light of this revelation, I rather doubt she's a Urecari spy. What is your real name, girl? Come now, I'll have the truth."

"It's Mia." She stared down the angry, uncertain sailors and Prester Hannes in turn, then back at Criston. "I did what I had to, Captain."

He pondered in silence for a moment. "We can argue all day, but there is a practical matter to consider. We've gone too far to turn back, and we are not close to any shore whatsoever. What are we to do with her?"

"We can always throw her overboard," said a sailor named Enoch Dey.

"It is an option to consider," Hannes pointed out. "She may bring ruin upon this expedition."

Mia glared at them. "Throw me over the side and leave me? Like the crew did to Sapier? Remember your own tales, Prester! Ondun watched over Sapier, and he caught a sea serpent with his fishhook. Sapier made it home safely, but the men who wronged him faced severe punishments."

"It's not so easy to catch a sea serpent with a fishhook." Criston laughed in spite of himself. Every crewmember knew how he had survived after the sinking of the *Luminara*.

Javian seemed upset and confused. "We should give her a chance, Captain. If she turns out to be a *ra'vir*, we can still put her ashore the first time we make landfall."

Hannes remained uneasy. "I need to ponder this and study my Book."

"Prester, you may be the spiritual leader of the men, but *I* make all final decisions in regards to the crew of this vessel." He couldn't simply kill Mia, nor could he let her be a festering wound among his crew. "I see no reason why a young woman cannot haul ropes, set sail, scrub decks, and pump out the bilge like the rest of you. *Princess Anjine* does a good enough job ruling Tierra along with King

Korastine—would any of you dare speak out against the princess?"

The men shook their heads with great vigor. Criston strode back to his cabin. "It's settled, then. Now get back to work. We've got a whole world to explore."

38 *Calay*

In private, Queen Anjine pondered how to be the best leader possible. Tierra demanded it, her father's memory demanded it, and she demanded it of herself. She would make the challenging and painful decisions that Korastine had often avoided. He had been a kind man, a ruler bred for times of peace. Anjine had not thought of him as weak, merely compassionate. But these difficult times had little place for compassion.

Anjine spent her days in a small writing room that had been one of her father's favorite places in which to mull over decisions, read decrees, and meet with representatives. Tycho, a fixture in the castle for many years, loved to find a patch of sun here and sprawl out while she did her work. She would often read documents aloud to him, practicing the language of her written responses, talking through her own thoughts and pretending that the cat listened or cared.

Despite her natural reluctance to accept the change, castle carpenters had furnished Anjine's rooms as the primary royal bedchambers. She had refused to move into the suite her father had occupied, first with her mother, then with his beloved Ilrida, and finally alone.

The work of the kingdom, however, demanded that she spend many hours attending to business, and she settled into the well-lit withdrawing room Korastine had used as his office. Piles of documents and unsigned replies still haunted his desk. Unfinished business. Toward the end, just before the sailing of the *Dyscovera*, Korastine had ignored all but the most urgent matters ... and his definition of "urgent" had grown more and more restrictive over the years.

Anjine lifted each paper and scanned the writings, reading aloud to Tycho. "Acting as destrar of the river clans, Sazar has asked for a relaxation of his heavy obligations in carrying war supplies from the outer reaches." She gave a quick snort, looking down at the cat. "What do you think? He claims that his riverboats no longer have any room for commercial goods, and so the clans can't make a living. At the same time, Comdar Rief requests *more* riverboats to deliver food and raw materials that the army vitally needs. One way or another, someone is going to be unhappy."

Tycho stretched, closed his eyes, and rolled onto his back.

Anjine knew the needs of her army and would not reduce the flow of vital materiel despite the river clans' complaints. However, in a gesture that would mean a great deal to Sazar, while costing Tierra nothing, Anjine wrote a proclamation that officially acknowledged the big man's title as destrar.

"We'll grant him rank and standing, as well as jurisdiction over the flowing rivers and all of his boats. Any boaters not part of the river clan will have a right of free passage, so other Tierrans won't notice a difference in their daily lives. But Sazar will certainly appreciate being acknowledged, and the responsibility implicit in his new title should outweigh any reluctance to keep shipping military supplies." She petted Tycho, then wrote and signed the brief document, pleased with the solution.

In another missive, Destrar Shenro suggested that since a large share of Alamont's cropland was devoted to growing food for the army, and since his prisoner-of-war camps provided all the labor for such efforts, his taxes be adjusted accordingly. "Quite reasonable," Anjine said. "He makes a good case."

The cat signified his agreement by yawning.

Mateo sent her a note from a distant military camp, describing his successful testing of young soldiers to root out *ra'virs*. Though his tone was formal and businesslike, she read the letter with avid interest, smiling at subtle hints she found between the lines.

Because Mateo had given her the little kitten years ago, she read the letter to Tycho. "'It's getting more and more difficult to keep this task secret, Majesty. In all the camps, we have caught fourteen of the traitors so far. The method developed by our new ally has been quite successful, but she has been so long away from the other *ra'virs* that she is not familiar with their current numbers or training techniques.

"'*Ra'virs* generally operate independently, each one brainwashed and sent to Tierra with the intent of causing harm to all followers of Aiden. But most of the hidden traitors must have realized what we are doing, and thus are not so easily fooled. We may have to devise another way.

"'I wish I could be there to report in person. When you and I pretended to be Tycho and Tolli, we took those identities as a game—but this is no game. I've questioned the young *ra'virs*, using all the interrogation skills I know—

including some that I am ashamed of—but the captives reveal little. They have a consistent dread of someone they call "the Teacher," whom they obviously fear more than any torture. I just don't understand them. Living in Tierra again, how can they not see the goodness of our ways? Why don't we have more turncoat allies, like Tira? And how do we find them? I do not doubt that you and I could figure it out together, Tolli, if I were there.'"

She read the letter twice more to herself, smiling as she thought of Mateo writing it. Even though his news gave little reason for hope or optimism, she knew she could count on him. If only she had more subjects like Mateo ... if only she could spend more time with him.

But that was not in her role as queen.

As she settled into her work, Anjine became engrossed in the papers until finally, like tripping over a rut on a path, she found a set of documents that her father had compiled: a list of potential husband candidates for her.

She stared at them, stung. Korastine had so desperately wanted her to marry, to have a happy family, to bear heirs. Anjine had always thought there would be plenty of time. Though she was older than a typical unwed woman, she had never felt the urgent pull of the matter. And now her father was gone.

She did not daydream about finding a dashing and handsome young husband, as her handmaidens did. She had always seen herself as a future leader, not a giggly romantic, but she had watched Enifir fall in love with Guard-Marshall Vorannen. Soon, the handmaiden would have her baby, and all the other women would coo and praise the infant, just for being an infant.

And Korastine had certainly adored Ilrida. Because Ilrida had given him so much happiness in the years they were together, Anjine could see the power and joy of a genuine love. But she hadn't allowed herself to believe that it could happen to her. Queens were obligated to marry and have heirs, but she did not expect more than that.

Even Mateo had often had trysts over the years, a succession of girlfriends, none of them serious. Oddly, Anjine had felt a pang of jealousy each time she heard of a new woman who had caught Mateo's eye (though he rarely spoke of them to her, apparently embarrassed to mention it). The jealousy was surprising and inappropriate, and it made her wonder whether she could experience the same sort of romance as any other person. . . .

Anjine stared at the papers for a long time, feeling like a helpless child. She wanted her father there so she could ask him more about these men he offered as suitable husbands. What were they like? Which was most compatible with her own personality? Now she'd have to make the decision herself.

With a sigh she looked at the names and notes written in Korastine's familiar spidery hand. Having studied the merits of the candidates, playing upon his friendship and compatibility with the Eriettan destrar, the king had made his recommendation. He very much wanted Anjine to marry Jenirod.

She wished she hadn't been so resistant to marriage while her father was still alive. Regardless of the glow Ilrida had shone on Korastine's life for the few years they'd had together, such things were hardly important, especially now. In choosing a husband, she would use only dynastic and political merits as selection criteria.

She would not second-guess her father's wishes. If he had studied the options and chosen Jenirod, then she would accept that. Perhaps she and Jenirod would truly fall in love, as her father and Ilrida had. Perhaps not. It made no difference to her. Anjine's greatest regret was that she hadn't agreed years ago, because that would have made Korastine so happy.

Determined now, Anjine took out a blank sheet of paper, opened the inkpot, and mixed a small amount of ink. She sharpened the tip of the pen and began to write a letter to the Erietta destrar, announcing that she wished to accept his eldest son as her future husband.

"Assuming this is acceptable to you," she wrote, "my party will come in three weeks' time, so that Jenirod and I can formally meet." She paused, pondering what to write next. "I do this to strengthen Tierra. If you and your son are amenable, I suggest that the wedding take place within the year. In these troubling times, we should not delay."

She signed with finality, before she could lose her nerve. After applying her seal, she rolled the document, tied it with ribbon, and called for a fast courier to take it to Destrar Unsul. If Mateo were here, she would have had him deliver the letter, since she knew she could count on him, although she might have felt an odd reluctance to tell him what she had decided. A husband . . .

Rushing in response to her summons, the guard looked concerned. "Dire news, Majesty?"

"Not at all. Good news, very good news." She forced a smile. "And please send Tomas to me. I have a special job for him."

When she told her brother that she had decided to

marry, he beamed. He'd studied Tierran history and loved to hear legends of brave rulers. She felt a pang when he said, "It's been a long time since we've had a king *and* a queen."

"I never thought of it that way, Tomas."

"We have to tell everybody in Tierra!" The boy found the black-and-white cat sprawled on a window-bench and sat down to pet him; Tycho endured the attentions as his due.

Anjine sat beside her brother in the window-bench, and they stroked the cat in mutual silence for a few minutes. "You can help me spread the word. You're old enough now. It's time that you take on more of your duties as prince."

The ten-year-old's eyes shone. "Father always said I would grow into a fine prince. What should I do?"

"Be my very own emissary. Take the royal cog and sail up and down the coast, stop at villages, and make the announcement. Guard-Marshall Obertas will go along as your personal guard."

Tomas threw his arms around his sister's neck. She hugged him tightly. "I know it's not as good as joining the crew of the *Dyscovera*, but I need your help, and I can't think of anyone better to send."

39 Calay

Returning from his tour of the military camps, Mateo spent days at the army administration offices, assisting Comdar Rief in assuring that the men had adequate food, uniforms, boots, armor, and weapons. After the Ishalem disaster, the Tierran military had to be rebuilt, both in strength and in morale. Though he had recently eliminated many hidden *ra'virs* among the troops, he knew they had not found them all.

Down in the Metalworkers' District, small forges and smithies clustered near where the riverboats unloaded raw metal from the mines in Corag Reach. In a city the size of Calay, blacksmiths had plenty of work shoeing horses, repairing farm equipment, fashioning cookware. However, for a generation now, the smithies had devoted most of their output to the manufacture of swords, knives, shields, and armor.

Mateo went regularly to the largest such operation, which filled an entire neighborhood. Ammur Sonnen had produced more finished blades than any other smith in Calay, and he oversaw dozens of apprentices and journey-men, but the heart of the operation was his clever daughter Vicka, who had as keen an eye for business as her father had for steel.

As Tierra's wartime demand increased, Vicka had encouraged her father to take on more workers, rather than attempt to fill all orders by himself. This expansion had increased their productivity and profit enough that Ammur bought out one of the neighboring blacksmith shops and its accompanying forge, then others in turn. Now the Sonnens owned a veritable empire of swordmaking establishments, though Ammur never spent a day away from his anvil and bellows. Vicka was the one who had seen how they could increase their output by combining forces with the smaller operations.

Mateo had watched the young woman for a long time. Even when her face was smudged with grime and smoke, or shone from sweat in the heat of the forge, she was beautiful (though he had a hard time imagining Vicka in a gown and jewels instead of work clothes). She had dozens of workers wrapped around her finger, including her father.

This bright morning, Mateo walked past the ornate wrought-iron gate and heard the clanging of hammers on anvils, the hissing of hot iron quenched in barrels of scummy water, the huff of pumping bellows, and the good-natured banter among apprentices and journeymen. He stopped to look at a crate of newly fashioned swords, each one polished and oiled, its edges ground to a bright silver line. One young apprentice, intent on his sharpening wheel, seemed hypnotized by the shower of orange-yellow sparks.

Mateo could hear Vicka's rich voice chiding a group of journeymen who crowded around a paper proclamation that a royal errand-boy had just nailed up on the public street post. "Come on, boys, you can cry in your soup tonight! The queen would never have chosen any of you, so it's no loss. Make her one hundred fine swords for a wedding present."

Mateo came closer to see what Vicka was talking about, and she noticed him. "Come to look over our shoulders again, Subcomdar? You visit me so often, you must like my company."

"I do like your company, but don't let it go to your head. My attentions are strictly business-related."

"Of course they are." Vicka flashed him a smile. "What kind of business, though? That, I'm still trying to figure out."

The journeymen stepped aside so Mateo could read the proclamation. He scanned the words and realized he had actually stopped breathing. "Queen Anjine is getting married? Who is—" He leaned closer. "Jenirod?"

Vicka shrugged. "I hope she's at least seen his portrait. The queen deserves a handsome husband. She's pretty enough herself."

Stunned, Mateo read the proclamation again, but the words did not change. He hadn't managed to meet with Anjine since returning from his tour of the military camps. Though the queen had many political advisers, Mateo had always considered himself one of her closest personal friends—*just friends*, he reminded himself. Still, he had thought she would tell him something this important.

Over the years, as a dashing and respected soldier, Mateo had dallied with many girlfriends, but had never had anyone special. With all his travels from reach to reach, as well as his sailing patrols, he had not been able to settle down and have a family. With a bittersweet smile he remembered his first love from his training days in Soeland. *Uishel.* The name still evoked music within him, still made his heart ache. It had been a ridiculous boyhood crush. When Uishel had found another young soldier, the depth of his heartache could only be measured in relation to his youth, naiveté, and inexperience in love. Anjine had been so understanding then, such a good friend, writing him letters, holding his hand across the distance.

Obviously, though, she had made up her mind without him. As a loyal servant to the crown, he would support Anjine and give her, as well as her husband-to-be, his best wishes and his loyalty. She was like a dear sister to him, and that was the closest—the only—possible connection. He had always known that. "Jenirod is a very lucky young man, that's all I can say."

When Vicka stood close to him, she smelled of smoke and leather, polishing oils, and simple soap, rather than perfumes. "Considering the war, and all the destrars who complain about their taxes, I wouldn't imagine that being queen is all honey and cake. It's hard enough to keep *this* lot in line, and they only have one job to do." She nudged the journeymen to get back to work, then took Mateo by the arm and walked with him into the clamor of the active smithy. "From the look on your face, you must have wanted to be king yourself."

The comment surprised him. "I have no desire to become king, and that's Aiden's truth."

"Oh, not for the title, nor the power," Vicka teased. "I think you've taken a shine to Queen Anjine."

"Absolutely not!" Mateo retorted so vehemently that it convinced neither of them. But he looked at Vicka in a different light. Putting pieces together in his mind, he thought of the banter he enjoyed with her, realized how often he came to see her when he could easily have delegated the job to someone else. "What time do you take your evening meal? And would you like some company?"

"Why Mateo Bornan, have you finally taken it into your head to court me? There must be romance in the air."

He blushed furiously and gave an unconvincing shrug. "A man has to eat. Is it any surprise that I find your company more pleasant than a mess hall full of soldier-recruits?"

"My, aren't you full of compliments!"

Her father strode over, wearing only old breeches and a

scarred leather apron that hung below his knees. Ammur had heavy black brows, a thick dark mustache, and a shaved head (since sparks had caught his hair on fire too many times). "Thirty more swords today, Subcomdar! Even better than yesterday."

"And I bet you'll do better tomorrow. I've never met a man who worked as hard as you, Ammur."

Vicka smiled. "Subcomdar Bornan is joining us for dinner, Father. We'll eat with everyone else at the big tables, but he does want to sit next to me."

The blacksmith saw nothing unusual about the request. "Good enough. I'll tell the cook—we can squeeze in one more."

Having a meal with Vicka surrounded by a dozen or more boisterous and grimy apprentices or journeymen wasn't exactly what he had in mind, but it would do.

"Do we have business to discuss, Mateo?" Her voice had a charming lilt, like a tiny fishhook catching him, pulling him along.

"Maybe . . . or maybe just conversation."

Two days later, Queen Anjine's betrothal procession met at the eastern end of Calay, where the wide river opened into the bay. She and her party boarded a ribbon-bedecked boat that would take her upstream to Peliton, the capital of Erietta Reach. Royal couriers arrived well ahead of time, and Destrar Unsul had already sent back an exuberant acceptance of her proposal.

Mateo joined the crowds seeing her off, but he did not try to catch her eye. If he had gone to the castle, Anjine would have insisted he join her group—as part of the formal military escort. But since learning of her betrothal, he'd felt an odd reluctance to see her. Given his duties as subcomdar, he was very busy, but he promised himself to give her his best wishes once her party returned.

He hoped that Anjine found Jenirod to be a worthy husband, someone who would help lead Tierra. When he'd been stationed in Erietta, Mateo had been in a large camp of soldiers; he'd seen the destrar's son a few times, but only from a distance. The young man had always been running his horses, or hunting, or racing, while Destrar Unsul was out building his windmills and designing irrigation trenches, leaving the training of soldiers to his professional military men.

As the colorful boat began to move upstream, rivermen used thick poles to push the craft along. Mateo waved like everyone else, silently wished Anjine well ... and still pretended that the news didn't bother him.

40 *Olabar Palace*

By Soldan-Shah Omra's command, the First Wives of all five soldans arrived in Olabar, one by one. Some brought showy retinues of assistants, handmaidens, hairdressers, and clothiers; by contrast, Sharique from Yuarej soldanate came alone, meek and deferential. Aini, the squarish and brusque wife of Soldan Xivir from Missinia, wore ill-fitting riding clothes and had brought only a small satchel of necessary items on the caravan north; Soldan Vishkar sent his wife Hakri, mother of the original Istar; sharp-tongued Kuari came from Inner Wahilir, relieved to be away from Soldan Huttan; Tesha, the young wife of the Abilan soldan, had never been outside of Kiesh and now looked frightened by the size of Olabar.

Kel Rovic met each woman and took her to separate quarters, keeping them isolated; guards stood at the doorways, blocking them from palace activities. A few of the First Wives were sensible enough to be nervous, fearing Omra's temper; others remained oblivious to their peril.

On the night before he intended to meet with the five women, Omra dined with both Istar and Naori. The fact that his two wives got along so well amazed the former soldan-shah, since Imir's various wives had caused him nothing but heartache or confusion. But sweet Naori was warmhearted and utterly unambitious, and Istar found no reason to dislike the mother of the soldan-shah's two heirs.

The two women sat opposite Omra, daintily eating with their fingers. Istar remained on edge, worried about what he intended to do to the First Wives. "Our daughter Istala has expressed her desire for a pilgrimage to Fashia's Fountain. If I and the other girls accompany her, we will be gone for per-haps two weeks. That might be a good time for cooling off—"

Omra's mood grew edgier. "You and our daughters will go to Fashia's Fountain, but we will decide this matter first. Although an insult to you is enough to provoke my wrath, the emissary's behavior points out a fundamental flaw in the way our government functions. In times of peace, lax rules were not a fatal weakness, but now I will not tolerate it. All five soldans must hear me, loud and clear, and their First Wives provide the best way for me to send the message."

Naori nibbled on a piece of golden-brown bread. "Why

not just have Istar help me raise your two sons, my Lord? They'd benefit from two mothers, and it would keep her away from those who resent her presence in court. Wouldn't that ease tensions?"

Omra smiled at the young woman's earnestness. "Sweet Naori, if only everyone were as kind as you! Of course my sons would benefit from Istar's experience and attention, but that is not the point. *I* am the point. And I have made my decision. Those I choose to trust are not dictated by mere soldans or their emissaries."

"Or the sikaras," Istar muttered.

Omra raised a scolding finger. "One problem at a time. Tomorrow morning, I meet with the First Wives and the current emissaries of the five soldanates. Naori, remain with the children, but I want Istar at my side, so that all can hear my pronouncement."

The five anxious women were escorted into Omra's audience chamber precisely at sunrise, as the soldan-shah had ordered. Though they arrived on time, looking to each other and to the flustered official emissaries for answers, they saw only an empty room.

An hour later, Omra and his First Wife arrived casually, making no apologies to those who had been made to stand for the entire time. As he and Istar took their places on the cushion-strewn dais, a servant entered with a tray of steaming coffee. Istar poured a cup for Omra, then one for herself. She sat beside him and waited. They both drank.

Omra scanned the audience, and the five women regarded him, some confused, some frightened, others merely curious. He noted that those who looked the most nervous were the ones who had done nothing to offend him at all. Kuari, the wife of Soldan Huttan, was well aware of what her husband had done, yet she seemed resigned to whatever fate awaited her.

Crowding the large room stood attendants, handmaidens, and functionaries, as well as Omra's own representatives and ministers, all of whom waited to see what he would do. The five primary emissaries—including the oblivious Ualfor from Inner Missinia—wore their finest garments, looking official and important.

Omra enjoyed his small cup of coffee, directing his cold hard gaze at each First Wife in turn. They remained quiet and tense, afraid to speak until he had stated his purpose. Next to him, Istar looked particularly pale.

Finally, Omra set his empty cup aside and rose to his feet. He stretched out his hand to raise Istar up beside him. Her face was drawn, and she squeezed his hand, imparting a silent message, begging him to show restraint and mercy. Omra remained stony and intimidating. When he spoke, his words were quiet, and all the more powerful because his tone contained no threat whatsoever. "Why do you not bow before your soldan-shah?"

Like marionettes with their strings severed, the five women fell to their knees on the floor, along with everyone else in the chamber.

While they prostrated themselves on the driftwood tiles, he said, "I rule all five soldanates of Uraba. I am a direct descendant of Urec himself. And this is my First Wife, Istar." He raised her hand. "I chose her to be my wife, and when I am not in the palace, she speaks in my stead. She is my eyes, my ears, and my voice in Olabar, and I expect my people—my soldans and their representatives—to treat her with the deference they would show me."

Now his voice became the snap of a whip. "But this has not happened!"

The entire audience remained kneeling, heads bowed. At last, he saw that every one of them understood just how serious he was. "I will not tolerate it. Every single ambassador and every emissary currently assigned by the five soldans is hereby relieved of duty. Their work is unsatisfactory to me. I will appoint new ambassadors to speak in their stead."

Gasps rippled through those present, though they remained bowed and fearful. The First Wives glanced sidelong at one another, afraid to look up. The dismissed emissaries stared, speechless.

"As of today—Sharique of Yuarej, Kuari of Inner Wahilir, Hakri of Outer Wahilir, Tesha of Abilan, and Aini of Missinia— I appoint *you* five to be my new representatives. You, the First Wives of my soldans, will carry messages to and from your husbands. The other emissaries are no longer required."

Istar smiled with relief. Sharique squatted back on her heels, her smile bright with gratitude. Kuari wore a satisfied grin, her eyes gleaming as though she already imagined how her husband would react to this new turn of events. The other three women jerked up in shocked disbelief.

"You will all sign oaths of loyalty that bind you and your husbands to me. The five soldans must understand that *your* lives are forfeit, should you ever offend me in the way the previous ambassadors did. I will require formal acknowledgment and an oath from each of them in return."

The women, unable to believe what they had heard, whispered to each other. The original emissaries did not look pleased.

Istar stood like a confident queen at his side. "The soldan-shah is exceedingly wise. I find these new emissaries to be most acceptable, my husband. I trust that they will not let politics interfere with their common sense."

Omra said, "You may all rise." The five women sprang to their feet, and the stunned audience also rose, not sure what to say to one another. The soldan-shah was certain that his message had gotten across.

Istar gave him a grateful smile. "That was a solution even Urec would have been proud of."

"The unruly soldans have been sufficiently chastised. Now you may make arrangements to take our daughters to Fashia's Fountain, and I can return to Ishalem, where I have important work to do. I am taking a shipment of Nunghal firepowder there to begin a very large new project."

Istar looked concerned, then forced herself to ask, "You will use the explosive against the Aidenists if they attack the wall again?"

"If necessary . . . but I have another purpose in mind."

41 *Kiesh, Abilan*

After six days of calm sailing, the *Al-Orizin* reached Kiesh, the easternmost Uraban outpost on the Middlesea. In the uncharted waters beyond, sand shoals, treacherous currents, and unpredictable storms discouraged all ships.

"This would be the end of most voyages," Saan said to Sen Sherufa as the sailors threw down hawsers and Kiesh workers tied them up to the docks. "But we're just beginning. From here on out, we follow in the wake of Urec."

Eager to visit the taverns and inns, not knowing when their next landfall might be, the crew rushed down the ramp. Grigovar paused, delaying the men behind him as he savored the moment. "I've made it, Captain—*from Lahjar to Kiesh.*"

Sikara Fyiri imperiously pushed her way around the reef diver. "Move aside. I have messages to deliver from Ur-Sikara Erima." The isolated church in Kiesh would host a lengthy service, and the priestess wanted Saan to attend, but he made excuses, much to Fyiri's consternation. She promised to pray for him nevertheless.

Saan turned to the Saedran woman standing beside him. Sherufa had been drinking in the details of Kiesh, but he noted her uneasy demeanor. "You still look unhappy about our voyage."

"Not because I don't want it to be done." She gave him a rueful smile. "I'll go to the Saedran District and ask my colleagues. Maybe I'll find a chartsman who knows about the waters to the east. Any information will be helpful."

While dockworkers reprovisioned the ship, adding fresh food and water, Saan joined the local soldan, Huref, for the midday meal, and as they shared hot sweet tea, the soldan spoke dire warnings. "Your ship will be grounded east of here on sand shoals if you aren't careful. Farther north, the storm patterns are the worst in all the Middlesea. Many ships have tried to fight their way past, but none has ever returned." Huref shook his head.

Saan, though, did not change his mood. "Then we'll be the first. After all, we have Urec's Map."

After the ship sailed from Kiesh into a deceptively bright sunrise, Fyiri called Saan to her quarters. In the first week she had already made the cabin into her own nest by tacking silken hangings on the walls and ceiling to make it look like a tent rather than a wooden-walled room. Symbolic ferns stood on stands.

As if he were a mere acolyte she had summoned, Fyiri said, "Now that we are on our way, let me show you how we can stay in contact with Olabar, wherever we go." She placed a leather-bound book on her small writing desk, a volume that looked both new and ragged at the same time. She opened the cover to reveal that each page had been torn in half, but only the top half was bound into the book. The rest was gone.

"Through sympathetic magic, this book is linked to an identical one in the main church in Olabar. Each copy is bound with leather from the same calfskin. Every piece of paper was split in half—one bound into this volume, the other half into its counterpart. The journals are perfectly bonded."

She pointed to a line of text on the first page, then another line below it in a distinctly different handwriting style. "On these pages, I will write reports of our voyage, and my words will appear on the journal within the Olabar church, where they can be read by Ur-Sikara Erima. When she writes on the pages of *her* journal, her words will instantly appear here.

"And she *will* share all of our messages with the soldan-shah?" Saan said pointedly. "Does my father know about this?"

"The sikaras will, of course, pass along all relevant news."

"I wish you had thought to inform me of this earlier. I would like to write messages myself, to have direct contact with the soldan-shah."

She shut the book with finality. "This is a very delicate matter of sympathetic magic, Captain. Only a highly attuned sikara, or someone adept in tugging the threads that bind all things, can write such messages." She pulled the leather-bound book toward her. "You may rely on me."

He didn't believe her for a moment.

42 *The* Dyscovera

Though Aldo stared through the crystalline cover of Aiden's Compass, the hovering golden needle did not twitch. Javian stood next to him, his face flushed. "I saw it move, I swear!"

The cabin boy had run up and down the deck, shouting. Both Captain Vora and Kjelnar hurried over to the station that held the three compasses, but neither man spotted anything.

"I did see it move!"

"I don't doubt you, Javian." Captain Vora's smile was confident, but the boy didn't seem reassured.

As soon as he heard the young man's excited call, Aldo

felt sure they had come close enough to Terravitae for the sympathetic magic to take hold. "Depending on the winds and the currents, and the orientation of our ship, it's possible we picked up a flicker of connection."

Captain Vora saw the sailors eagerly awaiting news. "Back to your duties! We haven't found Holy Joron yet."

Returning to his private cabin, Aldo set out papers and charts, leaving the door open to the daylight and fresh breeze. Before sailing from Calay, the captain had given him all available navigation records, but the *Dyscovera* had sailed far beyond the usefulness of those charts. Propped in front of him was the crudely sketched map on the old sea-turtle shell. Though mysterious and amazing, Aldo could not guess how accurate the scratched map drawing might be. Nevertheless, it provided clues to an undiscovered part of the world.

Captain Vora entered the chartsman's cabin carrying a battered and waterstained old volume. Aldo knew what it was. "Come to add to your sea-monster book?"

"I still think of it as Captain Shay's book." He opened to a blank page. "This morning one of the men sighted a sea serpent of unusual size off the starboard bow. I wanted to make an annotation."

The *Luminara*'s captain had recorded detailed observations of the creatures he encountered on his voyages. It had been Captain Shay's intention to publish a practical guide to sea serpents, but he'd never gotten the chance.

The captain flipped the pages, revealing detailed sketches made by the old captain and newer ones done in his own hand. "This volume reminds me how much there is still to discover out in the world. It reminds me of my friends and fellow crewmen—all destroyed by the Leviathan." Across two adjoining sheets, he had drawn a terrifying picture of the monster, based on his own experience. He stared at it now, transfixed, lost in his own memories.

He looked up, met Aldo's gaze. "This is a long voyage, and though we've had smooth sailing so far, we will encounter perils sooner or later. Aboard the *Luminara*, we lost our Saedran chartsman and all the knowledge he had. A wave swept him overboard, and we never saw him again." Captain Vora leaned closer. "I know chartsmen don't draw maps or write down observations, but I have good reasons, and you'll need to accept that. If we should lose you, I must have the means to bring my crew back to Tierra. The Captain's Compass may not be enough."

Aldo was torn between his responsibilities to his captain and to the Saedran elders, who insisted that he keep all geographical knowledge inside his head and never commit it to paper. However, Aldo could not deny the need for a written document. "I understand, Captain."

He bent over the naval charts and began making diligent notations; as soon as the *Dyscovera* returned to Calay, he would have to destroy the records, or Sen Leo would be very disappointed in him. Aldo realized how much he missed the old scholar ... which led to a pang of homesickness for Lanni and their two children, as well as his parents. He had been voyaging for thirty days now. Thirty days ... "Captain, perhaps I should write a summary of our voyage and dispatch one of our *rea* pigeons? It's been a month."

"Send your note, Chartsman. Even though we've made no great discoveries, we did promise to stay in close contact."

*

The cage containing the ten bonded pigeons sat surrounded by sturdy supply crates and dirt-filled pots where the cook grew herbs and vegetables. Inside the wire coop, the pigeons contentedly pecked at the squirming weevils that sailors picked out of their biscuits and fed to the birds.

Mia, who preferred to work alone away from the scorn of the other sailors, nonetheless enjoyed the company of Aldo and Javian. "Time to feed them, Chartsman?" She was barely sixteen, but spunky enough to hold her own against the grumbling sailors. Since it was a solitary job, Mia liked tending the pigeons. As the lone Saedran on a ship full of Aidenists, Aldo also understood how it felt to be different.

"I'm going to set one free, send a message home. You can help me attach the note." He grabbed the closest pigeon and held the wings close to the soft feathery body while Mia tied the small scroll to its leg. She secured it with a second string.

He set the bird free, casting it into the air. The pigeon spread its wings and flew off into the open sky.

Mia said, "Sooner or later, we'll have something exciting to tell."

They still had nine more chances to send messages back home.

43 *Peliton, Erietta Reach*

After three days' travel upriver, Anjine's riverboat docked at Peliton, the capital of Erietta Reach. As the queen and her royal party prepared to disembark, Destrar Unsul walked down the wooden wharf to greet her, accompanied by his three younger sons, the eldest of whom was only eight years old. "Peliton is honored to have you here, my Queen. These are my boys—Gart, Renny, and Pol."

When Unsul nudged each son forward, the three young men bowed so deeply and stiffly that Anjine imagined their tutors must have made them practice again and again. She received them graciously. "And where is Jenirod?" Unsul's eldest son had been an adult when their mother was killed in a fall from a horse; these young boys had been raised by their father with more emphasis on studies than on horse shows.

"Majesty, he was so excited about the betrothal that he prepared a triumphal horse cavalcade in your honor. Tomorrow is Landing Day, and Peliton is ready to celebrate with our annual market fair, but Jenirod insists on marking both the holiday and your visit with a show that minstrels will sing about for generations. He has been riding and training since we received your offer of marriage." Unsul seemed to be asking her indulgence. "This means a great deal to him. You'll certainly see his enthusiasm, if nothing else."

"I am pleased to hear it, though I would rather have met him first." She had seen horse shows before, had watched cavalry soldiers put their mounts through complex regimented maneuvers. Though impressive, the demonstrations usually went on far too long for her tastes.

The destrar gave a tolerant smile. "When Jenirod gets an idea stuck in his head, it's difficult to make him slow down. I'm sure he'll be disappointed you couldn't have seen all the classes, since the beginning."

"I'm sorry too," Anjine said, not meaning it for a moment. "But plenty of hours remain."

Destrar Unsul led the queen's party into Peliton. The shops and homes were festooned with garlands and ribbons to symbolize the ropes with which Aiden had first tied his Arkship to the shore of this new land. Children ran through the streets, flailing their strings; several draped colorful yarn across lintels as a prank.

In trampled fields outside the city, fences enclosed a wide racetrack and performance arena. Open wooden seats were crowded with spectators, none of whom seemed to mind the dust-choked air, the baking sun, or the sharp smell of horses and manure. The people cheered and clapped as a heavy-boned warhorse cleared a final combination of difficult jumps as part of a course.

When Unsul led the queen and her party to seats shaded by a colorful awning, Anjine sat primly. Several horses thundered past on the track behind the pavilion, their riders waving streamers and whooping. The destrar raised both hands to signal a crier standing on a high observation platform. Taking his cue, a thin and small man with a huge voice shouted, "Erietta Reach is pleased to welcome Queen Anjine, who has come to observe our cavalcade and meet her betrothed—*Jenirod*!" The people in the stands cheered and whistled.

Launching through the arena in-gate, a man charged forth on a powerful bay mount and galloped in a wide circle to the accolades of the audience. The lines of Jenirod's mount clearly showed her distinctive Uraban bloodlines. Uraban horses, refined in physical build, were much swifter and more maneuverable in battle than the heavier Tierran animals. Over the course of the war, the Aidenist army had made a priority of capturing enemy horses—war mares in particular—to integrate into ambitious Eriettan breeding programs.

As to his own breeding, Jenirod was broad-shouldered and muscular, and his grin was an integral part of his square jaw. He raised one gloved hand, which acted like a lodestone to draw further cheers. Basking in the attention, he rode up to the stands where many women called his name. He swooped his hat into an overextended bow, then trotted proudly toward the destrar's pavilion, halting his spirited horse with a flourish.

The turnout of both horse and rider was painfully resplendent. Jenirod wore a broadcloth burgundy tunic sporting silver buttons that held a white plastron in place. A strip of embroidery ran down the outside leg of his black breeches, and his black boots gleamed from extra polish, despite the dust of the track. His gloves and hat were of the same fine leather, and a saucy feather stuck out of the brim. Scarlet and gold ribbons had been woven across the horse's browband and noseband. The thick mane was in an intricate continental braid, and a second braid finished its tail.

"I am pleased to meet my bride-to-be," Jenirod called, a little too loudly.

"Thank you for holding the show in my honor," Anjine said.

Taking that as permission to continue the performance, Jenirod wheeled his horse about with flair and cantered away. The show went on.

*

Anjine had attended many tedious court meetings and waited through high-holiday Aidenist services in the main kirk. She knew how to sit still and endure, even when she was bored; she had developed silent games to amuse herself, and now she pondered decisions of trade and taxes that would affect all five reaches. The interminable horse show lasted hours; even Destrar Unsul seemed to be daydreaming.

When the conclusion came at last, Anjine leaned close to him. "Excuse me, Destrar, but my party and I are weary from the long river voyage. Would it be possible to see our quarters in the city and rest a bit before tonight's banquet?"

"But, my Queen, the banquet is here." Unsul gestured to a large area of tents under which long tables had been erected. Busy servants were setting out trenchers and preparing food.

Jenirod rode up again to the pavilion. Covered with dust and dirt, he dismounted, handing the reins to a page. He waved toward the stands, invoking another round of cheers, then strode to Anjine and his father. "I trust you were impressed, Queen Anjine!" He extended his hand in a manly gesture to clasp hers. He smelled strongly of horse, sweat, and leather oil.

"You didn't need to make such an effort on my behalf." She didn't know what else to add. "I assume you'd like to clean up, so we can sit together at the banquet?"

"I'll just wipe off the worst of it. My father can show you to the banquet tent. I'll be along in a few minutes." He strolled away, followed by the page and his horse.

*

At the banquet table, a fine roast of beef was served, large hunks carved off and presented alongside cheese and fresh bread. Jenirod served himself, then handed a full plate to Anjine. "There's a nice rare piece. Eriettan beef is the best in all of Tierra." He joked with the others at the table and often yelled back and forth with friends.

Destrar Unsul sat on the other end of the table with his three younger sons, as if he felt the need to isolate them from their older brother. Anjine picked up more subtle details now, reading shades of meaning in their family inter-actions. She could only imagine what Unsul's wife must have been like—vivacious, athletic, thrilled to perform—and Jenirod had followed her example much more than his father's. Unsul seemed intent on raising his three younger boys more in his own mold.

During the banquet, when Jenirod spoke to Anjine, he didn't really *converse* with her, nor did he show any real intent to get to know her. He talked about the tack on his horses, breeding stock in the stables, a hunting trip he'd taken. He told an embarrassing story about one of his fellow riders who had fallen headfirst into a mud puddle, and she laughed politely, though she had little interest. Jenirod was the center of attention, at least in his own mind. Anjine had seen other young women practically swooning over him, but though he smiled and flirted, she wondered if Jenirod ever actually talked *with* the well-dressed ladies, rather than *to* them. Maybe he didn't consider it necessary.

The thought only hammered home how much she appreciated Mateo. With a pang, she wished her friend had come along on this procession. Right now, during this ban-quet, he would have been a savior.

"I hope you enjoyed the day, my Queen. Once we're married, we'll have many such pageants. Think of what we can do for our wedding celebration!" Jenirod hit his fist on the table with a loud bang that rattled silverware, goblets, and plates. He glanced over at Unsul with a poorly disguised expression of scorn. "Erietta is known for its fine horsemanship—not windmills and irrigation ditches."

"But I haven't shown her my windmills yet," Unsul said. "A good queen understands the need for increased agricultural production in order to feed the land and the army."

"The army needs cavalry soldiers even more than it needs pretty flowers." Jenirod laughed at his own cleverness. He reached over to squeeze Anjine's shoulder, and she gritted her teeth, suddenly wondering if her father had ever *met* Jenirod. She began to fear that she had made a mistake.

But the queen of Tierra had to abide by her decisions. Anjine considered that she might need to break and train Jenirod, the same way he trained a wild and unruly horse. She didn't look forward to the prospect.

Jenirod kept talking, without regard to whether he had her attention. "Erietta's cavalry continues to train. Our soldiers will form the backbone of the Tierran army, so we can make overland assaults. We've relied too much on the navy, and the Curlies turn all their defenses toward the sea. I think Subcomdar Hist should run the army with as much strength as Ardan runs the navy. In fact, I have many ideas in the matter." Jenirod leaned closer to her. "When I am king, things will change. The war will finally—"

Anjine cut him off with words sharper than the carving knife used on the roast. "You misunderstand, Jenirod. I haven't asked you to be *king*. You will be the consort of the *queen*. Nothing more."

Jenirod's mouth snapped shut, and the conversations around them died quickly. Destrar Unsul put a palm to his face in shame. Jenirod paused for a long moment, befuddled, then laughed, as if Anjine had told a joke.

But she kept staring at him, and he realized that *everyone* was looking at him with decidedly icy expressions.

Anjine continued, "I shall have to assign protocol ministers to spend time with you, Jenirod. You have much to learn before our wedding in Calay."

44 Calay

The population of Calay prepared for Landing Day for weeks: decorating buildings, cleaning the streets, whitewashing homes, and stringing celebratory ribbons and banners from slanted eaves. The main kirk held services three times daily, rather than just the traditional sunrise ceremony.

On the piers, children dangled hooks and strings into the water to catch a special fish for the holiday feast (though most of the fish in the harbor tasted like mud). Vendors sold pastries and tarts. Farmers wheeled in carts of barrels filled with sour pickles, a traditional Landing Day treat. Well-to-do families kept model Arkships inside their homes, which the mothers brought out from storage crates and dusted off, filling the small cargo holds with candy.

On street corners, young presters told the already familiar legend of Aiden's voyage from Terravitae, the perils he had endured and the exotic places he'd seen before his ship landed on the isthmus. Farther south in Uraba, the people claimed that *Urec* had landed there; they celebrated a different Landing Day, but all Tierrans knew the truth.

Mateo walked through town with Vicka Sonnen, staying close to her as they perused merchant stalls filled with interesting items, including old pilgrims' badges from days when the faithful could travel to Ishalem and back.

Vicka liked to poke through the jewelry, appreciating the fine metalwork. "It takes nimble fingers to make a thing like this." She picked up an ornate fishhook pendant made of polished Corag silver. He was eager to buy it for her, but she merely laughed and set the pendant back on its display, to the disappointment of the merchant. "I was just looking. I don't think I'd have the patience to make something so intricate and delicate."

"You've shown me enough patience of late. So much business at your father's forge ..." Mateo had been going to the Sonnen smithy on various pretexts at least four times a week. More often than not, he coincidentally arrived at the time of the evening meal, which he then ate with Vicka.

She cocked her eyebrows. "Was it truly business, or just an excuse to see me?"

"Anything to make the Tierran army as strong and prepared as it can be."

"Such attention to detail. At least you gave me the opportunity to fix your armor. Its condition was shameful." She made a tsking noise. "If you'd been killed by a Urecari sword thrust, I'd have been embarrassed."

"I appreciate your concern for my well-being," Mateo said with a rueful smile.

"I was thinking more of my reputation than your well-being."

He laughed. "In that case, I'll make an effort to stay alive—if only to protect your reputation."

They strolled past scribes who offered to take down letters or write Landing Day wishes in fine calligraphy. Mateo bought a pickle on a stick, which he and Vicka shared, passing it back and forth, taking nibbles. The astringent tang made his mouth pucker.

Since he took such frequent meals at the Sonnen smithy, obviously focusing his attention on Vicka, the young apprentices and journeymen knew full well what was going on. Ammur, though, didn't notice anything amiss; in fact, he spent most meals droning on about how many swords he planned to make, which types or lengths of blade he would choose. Recently during meals, Vicka had chosen to sit with Mateo inside the smithy building so they could have some privacy. When she gave her father the poor excuse that Mateo was "distracting the other workers," Ammur actually believed her.

In fact, Mateo realized with a start, he'd been spending so much pleasant time with Vicka that he hadn't worried about Anjine and her betrothal since she'd departed for Peliton.

A crowd gathered around a juggler who tossed colored glass bottles in loops, making a humorous show of stumbling and nearly dropping the delicate objects on the cobblestones, but catching each one just in time and balancing it on his knuckles or elbows before finally popping it into the air again. Vicka's laugh was a deep-throated sound of delight.

Mateo regaled her with stories about sailing aboard the patrol ship *Raven*. When he described his clashes with Urecari raiders up and down the coast, he didn't boast about the number of enemy fighters he'd killed; he stated it as a fact, which impressed Vicka more than any braggadocio would have.

They paused to hear a young, straw-haired prester whose voice squeaked a little as he told his story. "And after Aiden had exiled Raathgir up to the icy wastes of Iboria, the Arkship sailed on and on. His wife and crew began to wonder if Ondun had made other lands besides Terravitae, or if they would voyage forever, finding no landfall at all. Rain gave them water to drink, and they continued to have plentiful harvests of fish from the waters, but there came a time when not a single fish appeared in the nets. The waters were barren. Aiden feared that they had sailed beyond where Ondun had created fish." The young prester leaned forward. His listeners, mostly young boys, crowded closer in rapt attention. "But that wasn't the reason at all."

"It was the Leviathan, Prester Dilora!" one child whispered.

"Yes, the Leviathan had scared away all the fish—and now the monster was coming for Aiden's Arkship. The most terrible beast in the sea, so awful that after Ondun fashioned it, He realized that He didn't dare create a mate for it, or their offspring would devour the world!

"The Leviathan rose to the surface in a storm. The huge beast had long tentacles, a single blazing eye, and a giant maw filled with sharp teeth. It wanted to eat the Arkship and swallow Aiden whole." Prester Dilora extended a finger. "And do you know how he saved himself?"

The children were hushed, in thrilled awe of the story. Vicka was smiling.

"Why, Aiden leaned right over the bow to stare into the Leviathan's eye! 'Leave us, for I am the son of Ondun. What has been created can always be *un*-created!' he said. Hearing the truth and the power in Aiden's voice, the monster was even more afraid of him than the other way around. The Leviathan sank beneath the waves and did not bother the Arkship again."

The young prester challenged his titillated listeners. "Would you have been so brave? Would your faith have been strong enough?"

One of the boys blushed as he admitted, "I would've been scared." His companions teased him.

Vicka elbowed Mateo in the ribs as they strolled away. "I'll bet you would have been brave enough."

More children ran down the streets, flailing lengths of yarn as they tried to rope each other. Laughing, they tossed their yarn over Vicka and Mateo and ran off, leaving them caught. Mateo took one of the blue strands and threw it in a loop around Vicka's waist. "There, now I've got you ensnared."

She stepped in closer. "You've been trying to snare me for some time."

For a moment, he thought guiltily of Anjine, knew that even now she was in Erietta discussing her wedding plans with Jenirod. But he pushed the vision of her face aside and gazed at the beautiful woman directly before him. "And have I been successful?"

She shrugged and teased him more gently. "Time will tell."

"I'm a soldier, and an impatient man. I'd like to know now." He drew her closer, tugging the string more tightly, and looked into her eyes. He blurted the words before the thought had even crystallized in his mind. He had certainly not intended to ask, but at the moment, with her next to him, the question seemed the most natural thing in the world.

The words startled her enough that it took her a long moment to compose a response that was not at all as flippant as she apparently intended it. "I expected a man like you to be able to think of a more impassioned proposal, but if that's the best you can do ... I suppose it's the thought that counts."

Mateo flushed. "I'll try to think of something better, and I'll ask you again at a more appropriate time."

But she wouldn't let go. "No need for that. The answer would still be the same. Yes, of course I'll marry you."

She put her arms around his neck and kissed him.

45 *Ishalem*

Each time he returned to Ishalem, Soldan-Shah Omra felt a sense of triumph to know that the great city was firmly under Urecari control. The new buildings, the repaved streets, the faithful pilgrims gave him a sense of satisfaction unlike any other. When he looked out over the city from the hill, where Urec's gigantic Arkship had rested for so many centuries, the concerns of the five soldanates seemed unimportant.

Omra admired the enormous foundations and rising frameworks of the two new Urecari churches, one on each side of the city. Quarries delivered shipments of stone blocks to each worksite, and scaffolding laced the walls as they grew higher. Soldan Huttan urged the crews to build his eastern church with greater speed, while Soldan Vishkar and his Saedran architect appeared to be falling behind because they devoted more time to study and planning. Nevertheless, both landmark churches were rising high, the work of generations being completed in a handful of years.

As Omra turned in a slow circle to behold all of the works in Ishalem, Kel Unwar gave his report. "Those projects continue at such a rushed pace, my Lord, that we often run short of supplies. We've used so much stone over the past five years that two of our quarries have petered out, which means that shipments must travel a greater distance. The shortages are causing some dissent. Each building site is like a hungry nestling with its beak wide open, demanding more and more."

Omra nodded. "I will send my new emissaries to command their soldanates to supply more raw materials with all due speed. Their husbands will listen—it is their duty to Urec." He stroked his dark beard. "And of course, any wealth or materials seized from trespassing Tierran ships shall be added to our own resources. The interlopers can consider it a tax."

"At least God's Barricade is complete, Soldan-Shah. The 'Hooks are forever denied access to Ishalem." After the recent Aidenist charge against the wall, Unwar had pushed the work teams to exhaustion, causing the deaths of many enemy slaves.

"I know of no other man who could have managed such an impossible project, found all the necessary stone, built ramps and scaffolding as far as the eye could see, arranged the cranes and pulleys, guided the work crews and slaves. God's Barricade is a legacy that will preserve your name in history, Kel Unwar."

The man turned away. "I don't do it for history or personal glory, my Lord, but to hold off the heretics. All of my passion has been devoted to completing this project. I don't know what I'll do with myself now that it's finished."

Omra crossed his arms over his chest. "What if I were to propose an even more ambitious scheme?"

Unwar didn't flinch. "It would challenge me, my Lord."

"Good." Omra gazed as far as he could see, mentally measuring the width of the isthmus. "You've already built a wall. Now I need you to dig a canal." Though they were alone atop the Arkship hill, Omra lowered his voice, sharing a secret. "Only seven miles of dry land separate the Middlesea and the Oceansea. I propose that we excavate a path straight across the isthmus."

Kel Unwar's eyes widened in disbelief. "Sunder the two continents?"

Excitement had been building in Omra ever since he had conceived the idea. "It is time-consuming and impractical for caravans to cross the isthmus with loads of material. The Gremurr mines produce heavy shipments of armor for our war galleys, but it must be hauled by slow, overloaded wagons from one shore to the other. If we build a waterway connecting both great seas, however, our ships will be able to travel from Kiesh all the way to Lahjar."

Unwar took several deep breaths. "But ... it is seven miles of solid land, Soldan-Shah! The hills, the rock—it would take centuries, and thousands of slave teams to dig such a trench."

"We have something better than slaves, and faster." Omra stared toward the blue-gray haze of the Middlesea off to the east. "Nunghal firepowder can remove as much dirt in a single blast as large work crews excavate in days. The hardest bedrock will crumble under the explosion."

Unwar reconsidered. "That changes a great deal. And where am I to get hold of this miraculous substance?"

"I brought a shipload of firepowder with me, and we can manufacture much, much more."

Kel Unwar shook his head as he realized the true ramifications. "I have always assumed that the world is the way it is because Ondun created it so. He connected the continents of Tierra and Uraba by an umbilicus of land."

"Now we must sever that umbilicus—and leave Tierra stillborn." Omra's eyes gleamed above his confident smile.

"I shall begin surveys immediately, Soldan-Shah, to determine the most efficient path to be excavated, utilizing lakes and existing canals. I accept your challenge."

"Then we had best begin manufacturing more firepowder—a great deal more." Omra clapped the man on the back. "I am glad Urec gave me men such as you."

A sudden flare on the western coast caught his eye, flames rising from what had once been Aiden's Lighthouse. Omra pointed. "A signal fire. Are we under attack?"

Unwar shaded his eyes. "It's not a call to arms. Someone has spotted a ship, but ... it doesn't seem to be a Tierran war vessel."

"It must be one of our own ships, then, from Khenara or Tenér."

But the kel shook his head. "We have a different-colored signal for that. This is ... I don't know what it is. A strange ship."

Omra and Unwar touched spurs to their horses and rode down the steep Pilgrim's Path, working their way toward the sentinel lighthouse on the Aidenist side of Ishalem. There they could see a bulky ship with accordioned gray sails gliding majestically into the harbor.

"She does not display the Eye of Urec, and she's definitely not Tierran."

Many strange-looking men crowded the vessel's deck, waving as they came in sight of shore. Omra sensed something unusual about the people aboard, noting their thick, dark hair and squarish bodies.

The newcomers threw out lines for curious Uraban workers to tie to pilings. One of the men aboard pushed his way to the plank ramp as soon as it was angled down to the pier. His grin showed a gap in his front teeth. "Soldan-Shah Omra, you came to greet us in person. What an honor!"

Omra recognized the Nunghal visitor who had survived a trek across the Great Desert. "Asaddan! I didn't expect you here—and on a sailing ship, yet!"

The big man stepped proudly onto dry land. "There are many ways around the world—and we've just discovered a new one."

46 *Fashia's Fountain*

With both Omra and Saan gone, Istar took her three daughters on their pilgrimage to Fashia's Fountain. The city of Olabar was stable, the five soldanates cowed by the soldan-shah's stern warning and his dismissal of the previous emissaries. Old Imir had already departed for the edge of the Great Desert, where he planned to hunt bandits with Soldan Xivir.

Istar looked forward to a quiet and meaningful trip with the girls. With an unobtrusive escort provided by Kel Rovic, they followed the best roads and carried plentiful supplies across Uraba to the Oceansea shore.

She was surprised, however, by the wave of emotions the trek awakened in her. Scars had covered her deep-seated pain, and she had tried to forget, tried to move on, first for the sake of her son . . . and then for other reasons. Just as watching Saan's departure on the ship had dredged up long-buried sorrows and memories, she once again found herself reliving terrors from her past life.

As they crossed the caravan road from Inner Wahilir to Outer Wahilir, how could she forget her similar journey a lifetime ago, as part of a group of Tierran prisoners dragged across unfamiliar Uraba? Still stunned after witnessing the murder of friends and family in Windcatch, the Aidenist prisoners had been forced to plod along for days, driven like livestock. She had been Adrea Vora then, pregnant with the son of her beloved Criston. To the rest of Tierra, the woman named Adrea had died on that journey.

Istar was another person entirely, with another life, and a wall around her heart that could not completely block out her regrets. The love letter in a bottle from Criston that she kept hidden in her chambers served as a private shrine to that past life and love. She hoped and prayed that Criston remained safe, although she had accepted that she could never return to him.

Her daughters knew nothing of her painful past, though. They were excited to visit a fabled shrine, and she had to play the good wife and mother. . . .

Catching a small pilgrims' ship from Khenara, she and eleven other devotees dropped anchor off the coast and took a rowboat to the mouth of a rugged gorge nestled in the coastal cliffs where they were let off at a small, rickety dock.

High up in the narrow canyon, nestled amongst arid hills, a silvery spring bubbled from a crack in the rocks, pouring out in a thin waterfall to form a mirrorlike hanging lake. Pilgrims came to purify themselves in the frigid waters, and priestesses blessed them.

According to legend, Urec had anchored his Arkship here on the way to Ishalem. His crew, hungry and thirsty, desperately needed supplies of fresh water. Urec's childless wife Fashia led a group of sailors up into the narrow defile in search of water, but when they reached the end of the gorge, they stared in dismay, for the stone wall was bone dry. However, when Fashia called out to Ondun and struck the rock with the flat of her hand, water burst forth. Generations later, a group of devout sikaras built a shrine there and established a holy place, attended by a hundred priestesses.

Now, during the long uphill hike to the hanging lake, the group of pilgrims spread out, some rushing ahead, while others lagged far behind. Istar and the girls toiled up the hillside path together, one footstep after another. The way was steep and difficult, but none of them complained.

Though she was the most studious of the three girls, Istala needed no encouragement to keep going. When they paused for a brief rest, she pointed out, "A pilgrimage is supposed to be difficult. That's why you earn your reward when you reach the end."

By contrast, the destination held no special anticipation for Adreala, who was more excited by the rugged scenery, so unlike the lands around Olabar. Gracious and obedient, Cithara was just pleased to have been included in the expedition.

Istar and her daughters felt great satisfaction as they climbed over the last headwall to see the beautiful lake, the feathery waterfall, and lush greenery all around. The first few pilgrims ahead of them had informed the white-robed sikaras that Omra's First Wife and three daughters were coming up the path.

The priestesses raised their hands in blessing and welcomed them with pitchers of water taken fresh from the spring. Having been raised as an Aidenist, Istar didn't entirely believe the legend of the shrine; nevertheless, she was glad for the refreshing draught. The three girls drank deeply.

Her youngest daughter looked all about her, awestruck. "I so wanted to see this place. I can't believe I'm here."

Istala went to the lake's edge and dipped her fingers into the cold water. "Thank you, Mother." The sincere gratitude on the ten-year-old's face made every trudging mile and every uncomfortable day worthwhile.

The fountain priestesses lived in small rock dwellings that ringed the clear lake. They had laid out a path of interlocking white stones, tracing an unfurling spiral on the ground, at the center of which stood a brazier with smoldering coals. Farther from the sacred fountain and pool, pilgrims' quarters and changing rooms crowded together.

"You may cleanse yourself in the waters," said the lead priestess, a thin old woman named Luaren. "I believe Soldan Vishkar will join you."

Istar was surprised. "Vishkar is here?" He was the father of the original Istar, Omra's first wife, for whom he still felt a deep love, long after her death . . . so much so that he had asked her, Adrea, to take the same name.

"The soldan arrived three days ago, tired and troubled, overwhelmed by responsibilities. Now he has a new sense of clarity." Luaren smiled. "That is what Fashia's Fountain does."

"I hope it does the same for me." Istar led the girls to the stone-walled structures, where white linen gowns awaited them. Few children made the arduous pilgrimage, and though her daughters searched for the smallest robes, the garments hung overlarge like tents on their shoulders.

Together, they walked barefoot out to the deep pool, where several pilgrims sat in the frigid water, their white robes soaked. Hot and tired, Adreala plunged in with enough of a splash that other visitors frowned at her rambunctiousness. With breathless anticipation, her sister Istala slid into the pool, dunked her head, and came up with water streaming down her hair; she gasped from the cold. Cithara held Istar's hand as they eased themselves into the lake.

Istar recognized Soldan Vishkar, who sat submerged up to his shoulders near the stream from the fountain itself. She hesitated as she considered the uneasy link between the two of them. *She* had been Omra's Istar for fourteen years, but this man could not help but be reminded of his daughter.

Vishkar saw her and moved closer, while she let the three girls amuse themselves in the water. "Lady Istar, I don't believe we have formally met." He seemed a good-natured man, but his eyes held a shadow of pain. "I understand that you've brought great happiness to the soldan-shah. Omra must trust you, if he allows you to manage the court for him while he is at Ishalem."

Though at a loss, she realized the most important thing Vishkar needed to hear. "I have done my best as First Wife, but I can never take the place of your daughter in his heart. Omra still talks about her often. He loved her greatly."

"We all did." Vishkar turned away, but not before she saw the tears welling up in his eyes.

Though the events were unrelated, the tragic death of the first Istar had come close upon the burning of Ishalem. Such shocks had wrought a fundamental change in Omra's personality, hardening him, sharpening his reactions. Those tragedies had made him into a much less tolerant man than Soldan-Shah Imir ever was. She contemplated sadly that if the first Istar had not died when she did—for reasons that had nothing to do with Aidenists—the war might not have continued with such viciousness. Maybe Omra wouldn't have inflicted senseless pain upon Tierra by raiding coastal villages . . . taking prisoners. Her own life might have been entirely different.

Vishkar sat in the water and stared at the mossy cliffs nearby. "Lady Istar, I have learned one thing in my years as a successful merchant, as a grieving father, and as a soldan. The days flow forward, not backward. We cannot live our lives in yesterdays. We must live in today." He turned to smile at her. "And I am happy the soldan-shah found you."

Omra had often spoken of how much he appreciated this man. "He's glad to have found you as well," Istar said. "After Soldan Attar was poisoned, all of his other candidates were entangled in politics and schemes. You are a man he knows he can trust."

Vishkar looked at his pruning fingertips. "Considering the responsibilities weighing on my shoulders, I'm not convinced that he did me a favor. The other soldans dislike me and see me as a power-hungry upstart, even though I never asked for the position. In order to become soldan, I was forced to surrender my business to my brother and nephews."

"You would rather have stayed in Olabar? As a merchant?"

"Yes, I would. That new church is sure to bankrupt me! But I am a loyal Uraban, and I do as my soldan-shah asks. I'm happy enough. I am content. My sons are helping to manage our new estates in Outer Wahilir. My remaining daughters have gotten married—and now I hear that Hakri has just been appointed my own emissary to the palace!"

Istar nodded. "Yes, the paths of our lives take us to some very strange places."

Later, after they had emerged from the small lake, young Istala asked the priestesses so many questions that the old head sikara finally took the girl under her wing and showed her around the site.

At the meager evening meal, at which pilgrims gathered for quiet conversation or silent meditation, Istala sat between her mother and Sikara Luaren. Summoning her courage, the girl broached a subject with her mother. "When I finish my training in the church, I'd like to be assigned here. Luaren says I can be one of the hundred priestesses." She worked very hard to control the pleading tone in her voice. "Do you think that would be all right?"

The old sikara was full of pride and gratitude. "We would be glad to have the soldan-shah's daughter join us, my Lady. You can see that it is truly her heart's desire."

Istar nodded slowly. "We will have to ask her father, but I don't believe he'll be averse to the idea." She hugged her youngest daughter. "Someday, this will be your home."

47 *Windcatch*

In the parsonage beside the Windcatch kirk, Ciarlo awoke and sat up in bed with the dream still resounding in his thoughts. Adrea's face had been so vivid, her need calling out to him. Why did the dreams keep haunting his sleep? The rest of Windcatch had moved on, with new lives, new homes, new families in the two decades since the raid.

Ever since Criston Vora had come to say farewell to him, Ciarlo had felt unsettled but determined. Each year, Criston still sent Adrea a letter in a bottle, showing the ache of his love for her. Now Criston had sailed off again, chasing the unknown, in search of *something*.

Just after his brother-in-law's unexpected farewell visit to Windcatch, Prester Ciarlo began to experience compelling nightmares, flashbacks to that awful time when Urecari raiders had swept into the village. The memories refused to let go.

He had never seen Adrea again, and her body had never been found. Even if the raiders had taken her alive, Ciarlo very much doubted she had survived. A pregnant woman would have been too much of a burden for those evil men.

But the recurring nightmares demanded that he reconsider. Why did he keep dreaming about her? A conviction grew within him, and when at last he understood the reason, it left him breathless.

Adrea might still be alive in some distant, foreign land. *Someone* had to go after her. His heart pounded as he realized what he must do.

Swinging himself out of bed with a well-practiced move, he rubbed his thigh, stretched ... winced. It was a reflex from the pain he had felt all of his adult life. The poorly mended bone had never lost its deep-seated ache, but he couldn't be bothered by that now. Ciarlo hobbled across the wooden floor, reaching the door just as Davic came up the path with his breakfast basket—a warm roll fresh from the village bakery, two boiled eggs, and an apple.

The boy saw him moving stiffly, shook his head in disappointment. "I prayed again last night, Prester Ciarlo. I asked Aiden to bless you and take away your pain. But he doesn't seem to listen."

"Aiden always listens, young man, but he makes his own decisions. He has given me blessings in many other ways—including your companionship." Ciarlo swept the boy into a hug and stepped back. Aiden had been speaking to him through dreams for some time now, sending him mystic messages.

Though Adrea might be across the world, she was *still alive*. Despite the pain in his leg and the potential length and dangers of the arduous journey, he had to go find her himself.

As Ciarlo shared breakfast with Davic, the boy talked about the exciting news of Prince Tomas's impending visit. A mail ship had just brought the announcement of Queen Anjine's betrothal, along with the schedule of the prince's procession, which would stop at the major towns on the west coast of Tierra—including Windcatch.

Ciarlo tried to get the boy to focus on his studies from the night before, the passages he had read in the Book of Aiden. For months now, he had taught Davic how to read scripture, just as Prester Fennan had once taught him. Since the parsonage was so small, Davic preferred to sleep inside the kirk itself, sprawled on one of the wooden benches. Ciarlo gave the poor boy privacy, knowing that he must suffer from nightmares of his own, powerful recollections of the Urecari attack that had killed his family and sent him wandering up the coast as an orphan.

When Davic finished reading aloud the story of Aiden and the Island of the Sirens, he wore a troubled expression, as if a thought had just occurred to him. "Prester, if no one ever told the followers of Urec these true stories, how are they supposed to know?"

"That is a sad thing, Davic. But with the war, it's even more difficult for ships to take missionaries to Uraba ..." Ciarlo's voice trailed off as the last gear in the clockwork of his thoughts fell into place. Missionaries ...

Yes, when he left Windcatch to find Adrea, he would take the word of Aiden with him and make his way overland to Uraba. He would spread the truth to any Urabans he encountered so that they could have a chance for salvation as well. If the quest became too difficult, Aiden would assist him.

As the boy continued jabbering about the impending arrival of Prince Tomas, Ciarlo could not concentrate on lessons or princes or betrothals. He had to think about his own journey. Now that he had made up his mind, he was eager to go. Adrea had waited and suffered so many years already. Had she given up hope? Ciarlo couldn't delay any longer.

He startled the boy. "Davic, I'll be departing from the village as soon as possible. You'll have to take care of the kirk while I'm gone."

"Where are you going? What do you intend to do?" Davic was both alarmed and confused. "And what will become of me?"

"The villagers will take care of you." Ciarlo went to his small office and pulled out a clean sheet of paper, mixed his ink, sharpened his pen. Everything moved with swift inevitability now. "This is a letter to Prester-Marshall Rudio, requesting that a new prester be sent here to captain the Windcatch flock. In the meantime, take care of the gardens, open the kirk for services. The people know how to pray by themselves." He drew a deep breath, feeling giddy. "Can I count on you, Davic? Can I trust you to do what's right?"

Though the boy was uneasy, he gave a vigorous nod. Ciarlo folded the paper and sealed it with wax. "Make certain this is sent aboard the next ship bound for Calay. It's a very important letter."

"But, Prester Ciarlo, you won't be here when Prince Tomas arrives. Don't you want to stay for that?"

"I can't wait for several weeks. My sister is in the hands of the Urecari. You'll have to greet Prince Tomas without me."

"How long will you be gone?"

"Until I find what I seek." Ciarlo tousled the boy's shaggy hair. "You are much too young to be the next prester, but I've asked my replacement to continue your instruction. You are a good, devout boy, Davic. I know I can count on you."

Still limping, but no longer noticing it, Ciarlo returned to the parsonage. With great care, he set out his clothes, supplies, and a small stash of money, then prepared to depart for the strange and distant continent of Uraba.

48 *The* Dyscovera

Surveying the dark night sky above the unexplored ocean, Prester Hannes saw God's handiwork in the stars. Aldo na-Curic might be able to navigate by the positions of those bright lights, but the Saedran chartsman did not recognize the majestic purpose there. Ondun had placed the stars into constellations, forming patterns that only He could fully comprehend.

Hannes didn't know the secret message there, but he could still view it with awe. He was a devout and holy man, but not so arrogant as to expect divine instruction whenever he asked for it. Nevertheless, he knew the Book of Aiden, and he knew the correct and moral path.

It was his greatest joy—his *duty*—to see to it that others heard and followed that path as well. He led Javian out onto the deck, alone in the peaceful, open night. The young man, nearly fifteen years old, served Captain Vora well, and the boy occasionally listened to the prester's dawn sermons, but not with sufficient resolve or fervor. Hannes hoped to change that.

"I want to show you the constellations, tell you the story that Ondun Himself painted in the stars. Do you see that pattern there, the Anchor?" He pointed, tracing a majestic arc overhead.

Javian briefly gazed upward. "Every sailor knows the Anchor. The three stars in the crossbar point from north to south."

Hannes frowned. "That may be true, but the reason the pattern is *there* is to remind us of the story of how a great whale once grasped the anchor of Aiden's ship like a gigantic fishhook and dragged the holy vessel far off course. At the time, Aiden thought they were being attacked, but in truth the whale guided the Arkship safely around an area of treacherous reefs."

Javian shrugged. "I've heard that story since I was a boy."

"Hearing a story and *knowing* it are two different things."

Hannes reached into the pocket of his dark robe and withdrew a leather thong from which a symbolic copper fishhook dangled. "I want you to have this." Though Javian showed no particular enthusiasm for the blessing, the prester slipped the thong over the young man's head. "This is to remind you of how Aiden's voyage and landing created our civilization in Tierra, and how his grandson Sapier formed the bedrock of the religion that is the Truth for all men."

Dubiously, Javian touched the symbol at his neck. "I've been to the kirk, and I've listened to your sermons. What more do you want from me?"

Hannes smiled at the young man in the starlight. "I just want you to think about it. Captain Vora insists that you continue your studies—is that not true?" Javian gave a wary nod, as if afraid of being caught in a verbal trap. "Then should you not include the study of Aiden? The captain is a devout man—I know this, because Ondun appointed him to save me in the mountains during my own tribulations."

Most of the crew was asleep at this late hour, except for the skeleton watch, though Hannes had seen neither of the two men on patrol. Dim lantern light burned from the captain's cabin, and low laughter came from belowdecks where a few crewmen played games.

Pointing to another constellation, Hannes walked with Javian toward the stern, near the wire coop that held the Saedran's *rea* pigeons. In the stillness, they heard some faint sounds—a thud on the deckboards, the scuffle of feet, a whispered voice hissing a warning . . . then more sounds of struggle.

Hannes strode boldly toward the noise, and Javian

sprang ahead. In the dim shadows near the pigeon coop, they saw two figures on the deck: a large man and a smaller, slender form that thrashed and kicked.

"You, man, what are you doing there?" Hannes shouted.

Startled, the larger sailor bolted upright and whirled with a glare. Hannes recognized the burly man as Enoch Dey, a rough crewman who never failed to attend the sunrise services, always nodding and growling when Hannes described Urecari crimes. Next came a low groan, followed by a muffled burst of incomprehensible words.

"It's Mia!" Javian cried.

Hannes spotted the girl on the deck, a rag stuffed into her mouth. Her wide eyes glinted in the starlight as she thrashed to free herself. A dark splotch of blood stood out on her forehead from where she had been struck. Then Hannes realized that the girl sailor's trousers were missing; at the apex of the struggling girl's bare legs, he saw a thatch of dark hair. Enoch's trousers were pooled about his ankles. When he turned toward the interruption, his erection protruded like an embarrassingly small yardarm.

With a yelp, Javian launched himself at the big sailor. "Stop!"

When Hannes realized what was happening here, rage erupted within him like a blast from an active volcano. He shouted in the stentorious voice with which he harangued crowds in the kirk, "Captain Vora! Sailors—to arms! We have caught a vile criminal!"

The boy leaped on Enoch's back, riding him like an Eriettan bull. The big sailor thrashed and knocked Javian to the deck, but the trousers around the man's ankles tripped him up. He fell backward.

In no time, Mia had managed to get to her feet, grab her own trousers, and yank them on. When she saw the large crewman fall on his back, she took a light step toward him, drew her foot back and kicked him hard in the crotch, putting everything she had behind it—physical, mental, and emotional. Enoch let out an alarming high-pitched shriek.

As the *Dyscovera*'s crew raced up from the hatches below, Captain Vora threw open his cabin door and strode out, holding a lantern. "What's going on out here?"

Hannes stabbed an accusatory finger at Enoch Dey, who lay curled on the deck, half-naked. "This man is a rapist, Captain! We barely caught him in time to save the girl's virtue. There is no question as to his guilt. He has broken the laws of God."

Collecting her dignity, Mia finished pulling her clothing back into place and spat the rag from her mouth. "Thank you, Prester. Thank you both." Her voice was husky. She wiped at the blood on her forehead with her gag, before tossing it dismissively over Enoch's genitals.

Javian went to her. "Are you all right?"

"Better than he's going to be." She glared at her attacker.

Hannes felt disgust and loathing as he noticed that Enoch Dey also wore a fishhook pendant, much like the one he'd just presented to Javian. The prester reached down, grasped the thong, and yanked it away. "This no longer belongs to you. I can only hope Aiden forgives me for offering it to such an unworthy follower."

The next day at noon, Hannes was still in the captain's cabin, with the door tightly closed and the windows shuttered. They attempted to keep their voices low, sure that the curious sailors would try to eavesdrop. This grim matter concerned them all.

Since being revealed as a female, Mia had stopped sleeping belowdecks with the rest of the crew; instead, she spent nights wrapped in a blanket on the open deck near the pigeon cage. Enoch Dey and the other man assigned to the night watch, Silam Henner, had planned to knock Mia senseless while she slept, then gag her and rape her, each in turn while the other man patrolled the deck. Both Enoch and Silam were now in irons down in one of the brig cells.

"They didn't think their plan through very well." Criston shook his heavy head. "How could they believe they wouldn't get caught? Did they honestly think Mia would be too intimidated to report them?"

"Stupidity is no excuse for criminal behavior, Captain. The law is clear. Aboard ship or on land, rape is a capital crime. Aiden brought his wife and many other women as passengers aboard his Arkship. They had to be protected, just as we must now protect that girl."

"I thought you didn't even like her, Hannes."

"I was offended by her deception, but the law does not apply only to those whom I like. Ondun placed us here to improve the world. Crimes like this only delay His return."

Criston remained pensive. "Given what happened last night, I see why she felt the need to hide who she was. Just as you did when you lived among the Urecari."

Hannes still did not like the comparison. "I was doing Ondun's work."

"And how do you know Mia isn't?"

"Because she isn't."

Criston frowned. "You sound very certain, my friend."

"I have never had a problem with certainty." He sniffed. "That isn't the issue before us. Those two men are guilty. You must punish them—severely."

Criston stroked his fingers through his beard, the decision whirling in his mind. "Captain Shay never faced a problem like this."

"Your Captain Shay had no women aboard his ship." Hannes clenched his hand into a fist and rested it on the tabletop. "I am your spiritual adviser, Captain. I believe wholeheartedly in the love of Aiden, but I also believe in the inflexibility of his law. Our civilization hinges on it. Your role as captain aboard this ship hinges on it. We cannot tolerate rapists, thieves, arsonists, or murderers, else the ship of our society will crash upon the rocks and sink with all hands lost." Hannes leaned closer, dark eyes blazing now. "You must act decisively *now*, if you wish to put an end to this problem."

"This is a long voyage," Criston said, his voice raspy. "I expected to lose crewmen through storms or hazards at sea, but not because of this."

"And yet they are lost to you. You must do what is necessary, for all our sakes." Hannes sat back, utterly calm. "If it helps, do not think of them as crewmen. After what they did, they are merely garbage in the eyes of Ondun."

49 *Calay*

Although the criers in Calay described the queen's meeting with her fiancé Jenirod as a spectacular event, with a marvelous horse show and feast, Mateo immediately sensed that he was not hearing the whole story. Anjine had cut her trip to Erietta short, and her attendants made excuses. Mateo was concerned for her.

When she summoned him for a private meeting in the castle, ostensibly to discuss military matters, he was very eager to see her. With a formal bow, Mateo presented himself at the door to the queen's private sunlit office. Anjine rose quickly to her feet, and her face lit up. "It's so good to see you! I wish you had come along with me to Erietta."

Most people wouldn't have noticed it, but he heard the tinge of sadness in her voice. "I didn't think you'd want me there, or I would have volunteered."

"Of course I wanted you, Mateo!" She suddenly looked like a shy little girl. "Or can I still call you Tycho?"

He reacted with a comical wince. "We're well beyond childhood nicknames, Anjine. I can't very well call you *Queen Tolli*, now can I? What would the other nobles think? From now on, Tycho is just the cat I gave you."

The feline Tycho sprawled atop documents on the table, centered in a skewed rectangle of sunlight that poured in through the window. The cat was oblivious to politics or conversation, though he did expect to be petted.

"So . . . you met Jenirod? The betrothal ceremony went well?" Mateo forced a light tone into his voice, though he wasn't sure he wanted to hear the answer. "Do you approve of him as your future husband?"

"My father made his choice quite clear. As I said, I wish you'd been there." Anjine brushed the matter aside, clearly not wanting to talk about it, and Mateo could not ask why. Her demeanor changed, and she got down to business. "Now then, I read your report on rooting out the *ra'virs* among our soldiers. Excellent work. Bring me up to date."

Mateo took a seat, pulling together his formal manner as a military officer instead of a friend. "With Tira's help, we discovered and arrested six more *ra'virs*, but I believe word has spread about the ruse. They may suspect that some former *ra'vir* is helping us. Now it's even more difficult to find them."

Anjine paced the room, edgy and angry. "Damn them all! They are vipers in our beds. No, they're worse—who can hate a snake? It is what it is. But I *hate* these Urecari, Mateo. I *hate* everything they stand for. I wish Ondun would just strike them all dead with a bolt of lightning." She slumped into a chair and put her head in her hands, obviously disturbed by more than she was saying.

He wanted to put his arms around her to comfort her, but knew that would not be appropriate. She managed to mount an unconvincing smile on her face. "Enough of that. It's been such a long time since I've seen you, Mateo. Cheer me up—you've always known how to do that. Tell me good news. Surely something exciting has happened in your life while I've been gone?"

Mateo wondered if she had already heard his news. He felt a sudden twinge of guilt, but he wanted to be the one to tell her. "Did ... uh, you ever meet Vicka Sonnen, the daughter of Ammur Sonnen?"

"The blacksmith?"

"Yes. I've come to know Vicka rather well. She's intelligent, beautiful—" He began to blush, and Anjine laughed.

"Why, you're sweet on her!"

"I ... asked her to marry me, and she accepted."

Anjine's grin froze suddenly, and her surprised silence lasted a second longer than it should have. "Why, Mateo, congratulations! I'm so happy for you." She hurried to give him a chaste, sisterly embrace that he found very awkward. "You must bring her to the castle. We'll have a banquet so I can get to know her better." Anjine became a flurry of motion. "This isn't something we can take lightly. I insist that you be married in the main kirk. Prester-Marshall Rudio himself will officiate."

Mateo was deeply embarrassed. "That's too much, Anjine . . . my Queen. Just a simple ceremony is—"

She cut him off. "Simple is not good enough for my friend Mateo. This wedding is what I can give you, and I insist."

Mateo felt a pang as he watched her working particularly hard to make him happy, because it was all too clear that *she* was not happy.

The royal cog prepared to sail with an enthusiastic Prince Tomas. For days now, the boy had done nothing but talk about his goodwill voyage. Regardless of what had happened in Erietta, the queen insisted on going forward with her plans for marriage, and Tomas would appear at all the seaside villages.

Banners flew from the ship, showing off the colors of all five reaches; a larger flag displayed the Aidenist fishhook. Already on deck, Obertas and his ten royal guardsmen wore their best uniforms and brightest polished armor. The guard-marshall's hair was pulled back in a tight ponytail, slicked with pomade, and tied with a thin green ribbon.

Mateo, whom Anjine had selected as her formal escort for the event, now walked stiffly with her and the prince down the dock, up the boarding plank, and onto the deck of the royal cog. Tomas's blond hair caught the wind. Despite the early summer warmth, he wore a heavy red velvet cape lined with spotted Iborian ermine, a gift from Destrar Broeck.

Once they stood on the deck together, Anjine faced the gathered crowd and held her young brother by the shoulders. Standing at attention beside her, Mateo recalled how the two of them had sailed with King Korastine down to Ishalem for the signing of the Edict, when they were just a bit older than Tomas. His throat went dry as he thought of how many tragedies had flowed from that well-meaning visit. . . .

Anjine, for the moment, seemed unhaunted by memories. She smiled down at her little brother, spoke gently to him. "You represent Tierra on this voyage, Tomas. On my behalf, spread our goodwill from village to village. Let the people know that their queen remembers them."

Tomas did a masterful job of controlling his excitement over the pending voyage. He nodded with comical solemnity. "I won't forget. I'm the prince. I'll make all of Tierra proud of me."

"All of Tierra already is proud of you—and so am I."

After presenting his guards, Obertas removed his hat and bowed to the queen. "He shall be safe with us, Majesty. I'll coach him on his speeches during the voyage south. Tomas is a fine prince."

Before they could walk down the ramp, Mateo asked her quietly, "Would you like me to go along as well, Anjine? To help protect him? In times like these, one can't be too cautious."

Tears sparkled in her eyes. "No, Mateo. It would shame Marshall Obertas if he thought I was belittling his abilities." She took her friend's arm in his capacity as her formal escort, and they left the ship with heads held high. The crowds cheered, and Mateo wondered why Jenirod himself hadn't come to Calay for the celebration.

Turning to watch as the cog's square sails were set and the ropes thrown off, Anjine added, "Besides, you can't always think of your duties, Mateo." She forced a smile. "You have your own wedding preparations to attend to."

After Prince Tomas had sailed away, Guard-Marshall Vorannen called upon Mateo with grim news. "I think she was a friend of yours, Subcomdar. We left her where she was, just in case ..." He shrugged. "Well, I don't know why."

Mateo felt ice in his stomach. "Who are you talking about?" Several possibilities came to mind, the first and most urgent of which was Vicka Sonnen.

"The redheaded one, the skinny girl who always came to pester you in the barracks."

At first Mateo couldn't move, and then he was away from his desk and moving with a brisk stride. "Show me. What happened?"

Down in the smelly, green water of the Butchers' District, the gangly body floated up against one of the sluice docks where the slaughter yards dumped offal. Workers came to the harbor to empty their waste every evening, so Tira could not have been in the water longer than overnight, but the fish had already begun nibbling on her pale skin. Her mouth was open, as were her sightless eyes. Her red hair was matted with algae. Her throat had been slit in a grotesque grin, side to side.

As Mateo stared, Vorannen said, "Is there someone we should inform, sir? We don't know where she lives, or who her family is."

"She had no family. No last name."

"But how did you know her, sir?"

"She ... helped the Tierran army."

Vorannen accepted this with a nod. "It was likely a cut-purse ... she wandered into the wrong place at the wrong time."

Mateo shook his head. "No, this was no robbery, but I doubt we'll find who killed her." He looked away from Tira's sad corpse. "Take the body and have her cleaned up. I want a nice funeral service with a prester. She should be buried in an Aidenist graveyard with a fine fishhook to mark her place. I'll pay for it all." He looked down again and closed his eyes. "She's earned it."

50 *Iboria*

Up in the frozen steppes, Destrar Broeck and his nephew spent each night alone and cold in camp after camp. This was not one of the survival quests Broeck enjoyed so much; this was for the defense of Tierra.

In the early summer most of the snow and ice had melted, leaving marshes and standing pools that became breeding grounds for mosquitoes and biting black flies. The two men wore thick furs and covered their exposed skin with a soapy salve that discouraged the insects from biting, though not from flying maddeningly around their faces.

On their sixth day of wandering the open landscape, following beaten trails and prominent spoor, the two finally came upon the mammoth herders they'd been seeking. Iaros spotted the shaggy beasts while he and Broeck were trudging up to their ankles through the cold muddy waters of an extensive bog. "I knew Iboria was big, but I didn't know it'd be so hard to find these creatures. Look at how big they are!"

"Don't celebrate yet. We'll need at least a dozen herds like this."

Iborian nomads used the entire landscape as their domain, wandering the steppes in clan units, hunting woolly deer, harvesting lichens and shelf mushrooms, herding mammoths across the open grasslands. Broeck and his nephew stopped to survey the distant herd; he counted seventeen beasts grazing on shoots in the marsh. A black curl of smoke marked the herders' camp.

With evident excitement, Iaros led the way, sloshing heedlessly along, intent on reaching the camp of clustered hide tents. Broeck picked his path with greater care, not surprised when his nephew slipped through a matted covering of grasses and plunged up to his waist into peaty muck. Iaros laughed at his own misfortune and clambered out, wiping the mud off of his breeches. He kicked his leg to shake his hide boots, but water continued to slosh inside them.

"We'll be at the camp soon enough," Broeck said. "You can warm yourself by a fire then."

The mammoth herders spotted the visitors when they were still a half-mile away. The vegetation was sparse, and the voracious beasts had already cleared much of the underbrush. In the camp, a group of women sat together next to piles of rushes they had harvested, peeling cattails and adding them to a stewpot, while others wove the dried leaves into mats.

The men were out keeping watch over the beasts, though if any steppe predators attacked, the mammoths could protect themselves far better than their herders could. Some of the beasts were tame enough that the Iborian boys could ride them; several mammoths stood munching on willow shoots, untroubled as herders used combs as big as rakes to brush the rust-colored woolly hair, collecting the strands for their own uses.

These clans generally followed the movements of the herd, instead of actually training or directing them, but Broeck intended to change that.

He and Iaros raised their hands in greeting. The herders were not suspicious people as a rule; out on the steppes, they had plenty of room and few rivalries, and they were far from the nightmares of war. Visitors were unusual enough that the herders left the grazing mammoths and came in to join their families.

Broeck slapped his fur vest. "I am your destrar, and this is Iaros, my nephew." The herders greeted them in return, showing no awe or deference. Tierran politics had little to do with the life of the nomads. "We have come to purchase your mammoths."

"How many?" asked the gruff clan leader, not surprised.

"All of them—and any more you can find."

"If you buy all of our mammoths, then what will my clan do?"

"You'll wander the steppes and find another herd," Broeck said simply.

The man pursed his lips. The destrar reached into his pack, removed a leather pouch swollen with gold coins. "Queen Anjine has given me full access to the royal treasury in Tierra. With this, you can go to Calavik and buy a year's worth of food and supplies for every member of your clan. That should give you plenty of time to gather and adopt a new herd."

The chieftain regarded the gold, adding sums in his mind. The money itself didn't impress him, for the nomads had few possessions and little need for commerce, but he did understand how gold could make their lives easier.

"It is a challenge to find unclaimed mammoths these days." He leaned back on his woven grass mat, smoking a rolled cylinder of leaves. "Then again, our lives have been quiet lately."

While the destrar negotiated with the clan leader, the women prepared a feast of stringy meat from a grandfather mammoth that had been culled and butchered. Old men squatted around smoky peat fires, using tools made of durable Corag metal to etch and carve bits of mammoth ivory.

Iaros played with the children and told loud jokes with some of the men. The mammoth herders had five girls of marriageable age, all of whom giggled and flirted with him, impressed by his long walrus mustache. Iaros would normally have preened, but now he turned away, blushing. He didn't know what to do with the attentions of the young women. At first he seemed flattered, but as the girls pressed closer, stroking his bare arms and his fine (but mud-spattered) fur vest, he seemed to panic. One of the stocky girls nuzzled him, poking him with a finger like a cook testing meat to see if it was done. "Stay here. I'll take you as my husband."

A second girl crossed her arms over her breasts in indignation. "Oh, but he's mine. I saw him first."

The first young woman didn't seem bothered. "We can share. It gets lonely enough out here, and there are too many cold nights."

Iaros swallowed hard, and his voice cracked. "But I am the next destrar of Iboria!"

"I'm sure you can make babies like anyone else."

"I . . . I'll have to consult with my uncle." They laughed as he fled back to Broeck, trying to strut like a proud man but almost running in his haste. He brushed down his bristling mustache and attempted to regain his dignity, but the flush had reddened his entire head.

Broeck had seen his nephew fell large trees, hunt narwhals, and stalk the white bears, but his shy reaction around these girls was unexpected. Iaros had seemed a vain and self-confident man, but now he was tongue-tied. Broeck lowered his voice. "You do know you're going to have to get married and have children someday?"

Iaros remained embarrassed. "Let me face only one fear at a time."

The clan leader finished counting the gold and stored it securely. Each season, herders brought domesticated mammoths into Calay, where the beasts were put to work hauling logs or pulling blocks of stone. Even so, the clan leader seemed surprised. "You ask for so many mammoths, Destrar. We have never heard of such a need. Is there a great construction project in Calavik?"

"These beasts won't be hauling logs or dragging sledges." Broeck's eyes took on a far-off gleam as he imagined the reaction of an enemy that had never laid eyes upon such creatures. "No, these mammoths will be outfitted for war."

51 *Stoneholm, Corag Reach*

Deep in the mountain fastness, Destrar Siescu walked alone, carrying a lantern. The glow stretched ahead into the dark tunnels and threw long shadows behind him. Year after year, Corag miners delved deeper into the living rock, tunneling into the heart of the mountain itself, searching for new veins, gems, or subterranean mysteries.

Siescu's skilled miners claimed they could smell a vein of metal ore and follow its winding path through solid stone. Every Corag destrar had encouraged them to excavate more and more extensively until the mountain range was as riddled as wormwood. Siescu, though, had his own goal in directing the miners to dig deeper shafts.

Holding the lantern before him, he wound his way endlessly downward. Even wearing leather gloves and wrapped in thick furs, he still felt cold. Always. For some unknown reason, Ondun had given his body a smaller, weaker internal spark than other men possessed. His pale skin reddened easily if he spent too much time under the sun; he kept himself covered, even indoors.

Beyond the pool of lantern light, the darkness was intense and impenetrable, but he didn't mind . . . so long as it was warm. The tunnels were like a womb. Reaching a low point in the shaft, Siescu removed his left glove and reached out to touch the rock with his bare skin, pressing his palm hard against the rough surface.

He thought he felt a warmth there, a residual heat. Somewhere far below, beneath strata of rock, lay the Fires of Creation. Once his tunnels reached them, Siescu would move his main throne room to the heart of the world, where he could finally be warm. He stood for a long time at the tunnel's end, trying to sense the elusive fires through the palm of his hand. His workers would just have to dig deeper and deeper.

Siescu did not know how long he had been away from the main city above, but he saw torchlight, heard footsteps, and turned to see two of his councilors, hurrying to find him. "Destrar! Raga Var has returned with the report you requested." Both men looked uneasy. Siescu was not surprised, since most men disliked the unruly scout. For his own part, Raga Var was just as uncomfortable among people inside the stone walls of the mountain city.

Reluctantly, Siescu drew his hand away from the warm rock and tugged his glove back on. With a sigh, he followed the two councilors.

Inside his meeting chamber, a pile of dry logs formed a roaring blaze in the man-sized fireplace. The heat felt like a glow of sunshine on his body, and Siescu opened his fur wrap to let the warmth play across his skin.

The scrawny scout was already seated at a dark wooden table with a platter of food before him. He chewed enthusiastically on the leg bone of a roast mountain goat. Though Raga Var had stripped off all of his clothing save for a loincloth, he still sweated in the firelight. His body was all wiry muscle and sinew, and ribs showed at his sides, but he didn't look unhealthy. The shaggy hair and long beard were tangled, like the wool on a mountain sheep. Siescu's barbers had once offered to shear him, but Raga Var vigorously declined.

Seeing the destrar enter, the scout straightened his bony shoulders. "Didn't think you'd get here before I finished my meal." He licked his fingers and wiped the back of a hand across his forehead. "Why do you keep it so hot all the time?"

"I keep it comfortable." Siescu took a seat next to him. Dirty, handmade patchwork clothes lay in a pile beside the table; Raga Var must have shucked them off in layers as he waited near the fire. "After spending so much time frozen out in the mountains, I doubt you know what warmth feels like."

"I know what it feels like now—and I could do with less of it." He went back to eating while Siescu watched him, smiling indulgently.

The destrar had always liked this man who paid no attention to courts, rivalries, or formalities. Raga Var was an aimless scamp, thrown out of his village because the other families considered him untamable. Siescu had suggested that the near-feral man take up a career of wandering the unexplored mountains, living off the land, and reporting back to the destrar whenever he found something interesting.

Self-sufficient out in the wild, Raga Var didn't need money, but a profession gave him something to do. Whenever he came to Stoneholm, the scout was in awe of the huge caverns and titanic stone-walled chambers, though he didn't like to be inside for very long.

Finished with his meal, Raga Var lounged back and gave his report. "I've sneaked over to the Gremurr mines four times now. I found two distinct routes an army could use to cross the mountains. Each has its own advantages, but I know which route I'd recommend."

"Then I'll accept your recommendation."

The scout shrugged as though he'd expected nothing less. "It'll take a lot of work. You have strong crews?"

"We have plenty of Urecari prisoners to assign to the labor. Destrar Shenro is sending workers up from his Alamont camps. We'll clear the route before the snow starts to fall again."

Raga Var picked something out of his teeth. "I can't draw you a detailed map, you know—I'm not a Saedran. I'll have to lead the way myself."

"I *want* you to lead us. We'll mark the route, then slave teams with pickaxes and shovels will clear the way. Destrar Broeck is due to bring his mammoths in a few months. The road must be ready by then."

Raga Var's bony shoulders bounced up and down in another shrug, as if he didn't care. "So long as I don't have to do the work, I can show you the way."

"I'll organize the teams and equipment we need. Can you come back in a week and take us up there?" He didn't expect Raga Var to stay in Stoneholm for the intervening days.

"I'll be here when you need me."

The scout pushed aside his finished meal, wiped his mouth and beard with his hands, and gathered his discarded clothes in an armful. "I've got to be going, so I can find a place to make camp before nightfall."

Siescu didn't bother to suggest that quarters could be found for him inside the mountain city. He bade the scout goodbye, then summoned his chief metalworkers. From now on, his smiths would have to forgo work on decorative jewelry items and concentrate on making armor ... enormous armor.

52 *The Great Desert*

Once Imir had retired as the soldan-shah, the soft life in the Olabar palace no longer appealed to him. The desert called to him now: the sands, the heat, the bright yellow sun, and winds so dry they made his skin crackle. He liked being in the settlement at the edge of the dunes, sleeping in a fabric-walled shelter not far from the sand coracles that had recently returned from the Nunghal lands.

Today, though, the balloon-borne ships would not embark on a trade voyage. Instead, they were going to war.

For most of his rule, the despicable bandits had plagued the soldanate of Missinia, and now Imir would finally hunt down and eradicate the vermin, once and for all. He drew a deep, hot breath and grinned with anticipation.

A squad of mounted soldiers had ridden down from the

Missinian capital of Arikara on sturdy desert horses, ready for the follow-up assault across the barren dunes. Two of the sand coracles had been repaired, their wicker baskets reinforced with thin sheets of metal to protect against any high-flying arrows.

Imir dressed himself in a buffalo leather jerkin and went out to stand beside Soldan Xivir, who stared upward with a hard expression. Fires inflated the silken balloon sacks, and the coracles strained against the thick ropes and wooden stakes that held them to the ground.

Xivir sat astride a restless black horse. He wore loose, pale desert garb and a dusty white olba wrapped about his head, with the end of the cloth trailing as a scarf he could tuck around his mouth and nose. He didn't look at all like his sister, whom Imir had taken as his First Wife long ago. The only good thing he could say about Lithio was that she had given him Omra as a son . . . and that was a good thing indeed.

"Today will be a good day," Xivir said.

"Not for the bandits." Anxious to get aboard, the former soldan-shah swung himself into the basket of the coracle that he would be guiding. Three Missinian archers were already there.

With great care, two nervous camp workers lifted aboard a basket of hollowed-out gourds, each one filled with explosive firepowder. "Please keep these far from the burning coals in the brazier, my Lord."

Imir chuckled. "I'm the one who showed you the precautions."

In the saddle, Soldan Xivir wrapped the reins around his hand. "My horsemen are mounted and ready. Scouts have marked the direction of tracks where the desert bandits have made raiding forays."

"Burilo and I will find them from the air and direct you. I intend to start dropping our firepowder bombs as soon as we see the camp, but your men on the ground can mop up any stragglers."

"So long as we get Norgo himself, I'll be satisfied." Xivir's black horse stamped restlessly. The rest of the desert cavalry squad had mounted up, ready to race off into the wasteland after the bandits.

"Hah, you think too small! We will eliminate them all. I'm tired of waiting for the sand dervishes to get them." Inside the basket, Imir called over to Omra's cousin, who had climbed into the second coracle. "Ho, Burilo!"

The other man called back to Xivir, "We'll save some for you, Father! The men need to keep in practice, after all. Let's be off while the morning breezes are still strong." Burilo signaled for the ground crews to loose the tether ropes.

The two coracles sprang into the air, climbing higher and catching the invisible currents. When Burilo's coracle drifted off to the east, he and Imir used polished metal mirrors to signal each other with a code they had developed for the purpose. On the ground, Soldan Xivir and his horsemen followed along the untracked sand dunes, keeping the bright coracles in sight.

After three hours of slow travel above the hypnotic sandy landscape, a glint from the scout mirror in Burilo's coracle attracted Imir's attention. "They've found something." He turned to one of the archers. "Drop down to find a westerly air current—we have to get ourselves over

there." As the archer covered the heat from the central brazier, Imir felt as anxious as a child, leaning over the edge of
the basket to scan the ground. "Look there, trampled paths.
We're close."

Both balloons approached the bandit encampment. In a
sandy depression lined with protruding rocks, he spotted a
cluster of tents, tethered horses, and a small water seep surrounded by hardy vegetation. It was a pathetic place. Imir
had hoped for a more worthy target, a sturdy fortress rather
than this squalid collection of tents and dung-burning
campfires. Regardless, Norgo and his bandits were vermin
and they would die as such.

The men below had seen the balloons high in the sky.
Defiant, they gathered their weapons, shook their spears
with impotent threats, and shot arrows as high as they
could, though the arrows fell well short. Only one of the
shafts struck with a weak—sounding thump on the bottom
of Imir's basket.

"Archers, indulge yourselves." With a gleam in his eye,
the former soldan-shah watched the Missinian fighters
shoot back, raining death upon the scurrying men below.
Some of the panicked raiders threw themselves onto their
horses and fled out into the sands, scattering like beetles
from beneath an overturned rock.

"Time for something more impressive." Imir grabbed
one of the powder-filled gourds, twisted the thin cloth fuse,
and touched it to the coals of the brazier. He tossed the
smoking bomb over the side of the basket and watched it
tumble through the air. Two of the bandits looked up to see
what it might be.

The gourd exploded only a few feet from the ground,

spreading fire, smoke, and shrapnel in a bright burst that bowled the men over. From the second coracle, Burilo's soldiers also began throwing explosives. Thunderous eruptions blasted craters in the ground, destroyed the encampment, and split the rock spring, spilling water out into the churned sand.

The bandits' horses screamed and plunged at their tether lines; some broke away and galloped pell-mell into the dunes. Terrified men provided good target practice for the archers; soon, many bandits sprawled facedown.

In hindsight, Imir realized he should have restrained himself so that Soldan Xivir could retrieve the stolen property, but he was so infuriated by these parasites that he did not try to check his anger. He used every one of his explosive gourds and wished he had more, though there was nothing left to wreck. What had been a camp now looked like the cratered face of the moon. Bodies lay strewn about, and only a few of the bandits had escaped. His grin was so broad that it made his face ache. "This was most enjoyable."

As smoke continued to curl into the sky and shouts faded into dying moans, Soldan Xivir and his horsemen finally reached the site of the carnage, but saw little left for them to do.

When the bodies were counted, there was no way to identify which one might be the infamous and violent leader, but Imir didn't care. They would launch the coracles again until they had hunted down all the illicit camps, and they would obliterate each one just as they had the first. Within a week, there would be no more desert bandits left in Uraba.

53 *Ishalem*

The explosion rolled out, and Kel Unwar watched from a safe distance as dust and shattered rock showered down. Clods of dirt pattered on the wooden slats of the covered supply shed in which Unwar stood. While his men flinched and covered their ears, Unwar merely watched. He smiled. "Soldan-Shah Omra is right. The firepowder changes everything."

Shipments of raw chemicals arrived daily, mined and harvested from deposits scattered around Uraba. Since the firepowder was so volatile, the Saedran chemist Killin na-Fas manufactured great quantities right at the canal worksite, rather than transporting the dangerous mixed components.

When the brisk breezes cleared the smoke and dust, Unwar emerged from the shelter to survey the new wound in the isthmus. This was the sixth such crater excavated so far. Spaced close to one other, the pits formed a dotted line that marked the future path of the huge watercourse. The deep incision would cut off the continent of Tierra like a gangrenous leg.

Perhaps the whole landmass would sink. He hoped so. How he hated the Aidenists ...

Unwar chased the work supervisors out of the slatted shelter. "Tell your men to take their shovels and clear the debris. Have the prisoners set up the next stack of fire-powder barrels." So far only one of the volatile kegs had exploded unintentionally. The unstable firepowder mix had killed three workers, but they were only Aidenists, and far enough away from the larger explosive stockpile to avert a complete disaster.

When the work leaders did not move fast enough for him, Unwar's temper exploded like firepowder. "Move, all of you—or you'll be in chains alongside the Tierrans! I can always use the extra labor." The men scurried off, knowing that Unwar did not issue false threats.

He sat down in the shade of the supply shed, unrolling the terrain map of the isthmus. He calmed himself by studying the hills and trees, the gullies, the network of already dug canals that he intended to stitch together for this new waterway, as well as a swamp that could be flooded and a small lake deep enough to allow ship traffic. And several miles of new digging and blasting. Several segments of the excavation were happening at the same time.

Staring at the plans made his temper fade away. The project engrossed Unwar, challenged his abilities even more than the immense wall had. Concentrating on orderly plans had always helped him to control his emotions. In equations and blueprints he saw precision, clear answers, and a direct refutation of the barbaric hatred and violence of the Aidenists.

Wiping dust from a wooden writing surface, he used his protractor, straight edge, and abacus to map out blasting zones, add notations for work crews, and organize the excavation schedule for the next weeks. He calculated the amount of firepowder he would need and wrote urgent requisitions for the chemical ingredients that were still lacking. Sen Killin had sent orders many days earlier, but the Saedran chemist was ignored; Unwar, however, would make sure that *his* demands were met immediately, or the soldan-shah would hear about it.

In the middle of the isthmus, stony areas would require more blasting, while nearer the Middlesea coast the loose sand necessitated bricks or some kind of support to prevent the walls from washing away once the water began to flow. The completed canal would allow direct trade from the Middlesea to the western coastal cities of Khenara, Tenér, and Ouroussa, but Unwar's task was not to fill the pockets of merchants.

For him, the canal's greatest purpose was to allow the passage of an invincible war fleet. Displaying the Eye of Urec on their sails, the armored vessels would glide smoothly through and miraculously appear in the Ocean-sea, astonishing the unprepared Aidenists. The new warships could set fire to the entire coastline of Tierra and blockade Calay itself. He would hang Queen Anjine and the Aidenist prester-marshall on one of their own fishhooks. The thought pleased him greatly, but even that would not make up for what the 'Hooks had done to his sister.

Setting aside his plans and tools, Kel Unwar walked out into the bright sun. Seeing him, the work captains scurried about, yelling at the slave workers, but their progress still was not swift enough to satisfy him.

Astride fine Abilan horses, Soldan-Shah Omra led Asaddan and Shipkhan Ruad as they trotted along the enormous ditch Kel Unwar had dug. Below them, at the bottom of the trench, sweating slaves—some of them skeletal and ready to collapse— continued to dig, widening the channel. Only an hour before, an explosion had blasted another great crater.

"We never thought to use our firepowder like this, Soldan-Shah," Asaddan said, whistling through his teeth. "Nunghal cannons are powerful enough to fend off sea serpents, but your ambitions belong on an entirely different level."

Ruad made a comment in the Nunghal language, and Omra waited for the translation. "The shipkhan says that you should see all of his clan's sailing vessels. The Nunghal-Su have nearly a hundred vessels like the one we brought here. He calls it a city on the waves." Asaddan lowered his voice, even though his companion couldn't understand him. "My cousin Ruad thinks a bit too much of his clan, but he's not exaggerating. He is already anxious to sail back home with his triumphant news."

"Why so soon? You only just arrived."

"*I'm* glad to be on solid ground again, where the only rocking motion comes from the horse or woman I'm riding. But Ruad wants the satisfaction of returning to his own clans with a tale that will earn his reputation back."

Omra understood. "Who can blame him? He has done a singular thing." The Nunghal shipkhan regarded them curiously, scowling when Asaddan did not immediately translate, but his companion ignored him. The soldan-shah continued, "Make sure he understands the significance of this, Asaddan. Once this canal is finished, your Nunghal ships can sail from the southern ocean to Lahjar, up the Uraban coast, and then into the Middlesea all the way to Olabar."

"Oh, Ruad understands, Soldan-Shah." When Ruad complained about not understanding the conversation, Asaddan shushed him. "He is about to become the richest shipkhan of the Nunghal-Su. We will come back, without doubt and as soon as possible. Now that we've discovered the sailing route, we'd better take advantage of it. We intend to arrive home in time for the next clan gathering. You'll give us a cargo of valuable, exotic items to entice them?"

"You shall have the best Uraban goods." Wheels turned in the soldan-shah's mind as the three horses ambled along the side of the trench. He glanced up at the deceptively sunny sky. "And if a hundred Nunghal-Su clan vessels were to join with the Uraban navy . . . I would pay a handsome reward for their support. Will you convince him to join us?"

Ruad's interruption was sharp and impatient, demanding to know what the two men were talking about. When Asaddan quickly summarized their conversation, the shipkhan pursed his lips. Omra fidgeted as the two foreigners talked, and finally Asaddan said, "Ruad believes his fellow shipkhans could be convinced to join in a battle or two. It's an exercise they don't often have when sailing the southern ocean."

Omra felt a weight lift from his shoulders as if new possibilities were the wings of birds.

54 *The Al-Orizin*

With Kiesh far behind them, the ship followed the sandy and uninviting coastline into silty waters. Standing on deck, always studying, Sen Sherufa watched the sea change from blue to green to murky brown. The knot in her stomach had not loosened in days as she watched the distant shoreline, knowing that each hour took her farther from her comfortable home.

But there was also excitement, and curiosity finally caught up with the Saedran woman.

Imir had given this voyage to her, thinking it a special favor. At first, she'd chalked it up as another reason not to accept his repeated marriage proposals, since he obviously knew so little about her. But then Sherufa began to wonder if he was genuinely doing this for her, to force her out of her shell, to push her out of her quiet, sheltered life . . . regardless of how much she *liked* her quiet life.

Sen Sherufa wished Imir had come along with them. She missed his laugh, his company, his interest in everything she had to say, his fascination with all the stories that she had to tell. He did make her feel safe, even when they were in far-off lands, crossing an unexplored landscape. If only he were here . . .

She would have to do her best alone on the *Al-Orizin*. No, not alone, she realized; Saan was also an excellent traveling companion.

In her own mind, she enlarged upon the Mappa Mundi. With Saan's permission, she had pored over the antique Map of Urec. Though it was an excellent chart, Sherufa could do nothing with it until she matched the landforms with her own knowledge. So much of the world remained a mystery. . . .

Sikara Fyiri came out on deck, as she often did, to assess the men as though they were cattle. She had already taken several of the sailors as lovers, most frequently Grigovar, although the reef diver considered it *his* conquest rather than Fyiri's. Most priestesses took their first lovers when they were in early training, and Fyiri had already heaped scorn on Sen Sherufa for remaining a virgin so late in life. "It's an insult to the way Ondun created us."

Sherufa had always been more interested in her books than in men. She had responded quickly and coolly, "Why do you complain, Sikara? My choice leaves you free to service every man aboard this ship without competition. You can have them all."

The comment had not endeared her to the priestess, but she knew Imir would have loved it.

When the sun reached its zenith, Sherufa used her Saedran instruments to measure its position, carefully noting the time of the zenith. She added the detail to all of the other numbers in her head and frowned.

Each night she also studied the moon's path across the star patterns. Throughout the voyage, she had been comparing her mental charts and star positions with the carefully tracked sun's path. Today's measurement gave her the vital last piece she needed to evaluate a suspicion that had been building in her mind. Adding the data to the tomes of astronomical records she had memorized, Sen Sherufa realized that the paths of the sun and moon were intersecting, coming together above the *Al-Orizin*'s course as the ship headed northeast into the expanse of the Middlesea.

Sherufa had heard of this phenomenon in the ancient writings, but no one in living memory had ever witnessed it. Lunar eclipses were common, when the full moon became dark and coppery, engulfed by an encroaching shadow. But this . . . this would happen in the daytime. In four days.

She looked up at a scattering of clouds that covered the sky, then set down her instruments. Noticing something in her expression, Saan asked what was bothering her and listened carefully as she explained her prediction. "You mean the sun will disappear in the sky?"

"All my measurements point to it, Captain. It's a natural phenomenon, but the crew is bound to be terrified, so we had better warn them."

Fyiri pushed her way into their conversation. "An eclipse? Saedran nonsense."

Saan scowled at her. "Sen Sherufa has a great deal of knowledge. I wouldn't call her ideas 'nonsense.'"

Sherufa demurred. "No need to argue. We'll see in four days if I'm right."

That evening, after the men sat down to eat their rations, Saan addressed them with Sherufa at his side. "Our chartsman believes we may encounter an eclipse in a few days. The sun will be dark for a time."

"There's nothing to fear," she assured them. "It is just an astronomical event, like a comet or a shooting star."

"But comets and shooting stars are evil omens," Grigovar said, mainly for the chuckles he elicited.

Fyiri stood at her cabin door, holding her copy of Urec's Log. "Ever since the chartsman made her ridiculous suggestion, I have studied the scripture for any entries that could relate to our situation. There is no basis whatsoever for such an eclipse. Do not listen to the Saedran—she does not share our faith."

Sherufa, very much annoyed, did not back down. "This is not a matter of faith or scriptures. If you don't trust me to know the stars and our ship's position, then you should pick another chartsman."

*

Three days later, the *Al-Orizin* sailed on under a bright sun—a sun that grew dimmer throughout the morning. The men began to whisper and point, squinting against the glare. "It is like a Leviathan in the sky, devouring the sun." Grigovar was no longer joking.

"It is nothing of the sort," Sherufa snapped. "It's the moon passing before the sun, just as if you put your big bulky body in front of mine, you'd block the light."

Saan watched in awe as the sun dwindled in the sky. "This is truly a wonder, Sherufa—provided it goes away as quickly as you say."

"I promise it will."

Fyiri had shut herself into her cabin, but as more and more of the sun disappeared into shadow, the sailors pounded on her door, beseeching her to call upon Ondun for help. Sen Sherufa took no joy in being proved right.

Everyone aboard the *Al-Orizin* fell silent as the eclipse became total, leaving only an eerie pearlescent halo around what appeared to be an impenetrable hole where the sun had been. Grigovar actually held his breath.

Then a flare of dazzling light flashed from the opposite side of the moving shadow. The moon continued on its path, and the sun's light returned with full glory. The men cheered, some collapsing in relief. Saan hugged Sen Sherufa.

At last, Fyiri emerged from her cabin and proclaimed, "Take heed and be thankful. I have prayed to Ondun and Urec, and they have restored the sun to us. We will be safe now."

Though Sherufa grimaced, she kept her comments to herself. Fyiri flashed the Saedran a nasty smile and retreated into her cabin.

55 *The* Dyscovera

At sunset Criston called all hands to the *Dyscovera*'s deck. To him, the necessity of taking this action meant that he had failed as a captain.

On the orders of First Mate Kjelnar, the cowed prisoners were brought up from the brig. When Enoch Dey and Silam Henner saw Mia standing next to Javian, they glared at her, as if their current situation were her fault alone. She glared right back, saying nothing. The wound on her forehead had scabbed over, but a darkening bruise spread around the skin.

A hush fell when Criston spoke; he didn't need to raise his voice. "You two men know what you did. Mia told us of your crime. Prester Hannes and my own cabin boy witnessed it."

"But I did nothing, Captain!" Silam moaned. "I was on watch!"

"Shut up!" Enoch growled. "The whore has told them lies."

The other men began to shout, but Mia's mocking voice pierced the babble. "You tried to rape me—and that makes me a whore?"

"Quiet, all of you! Enough." Criston's heart ached, and a slow drumbeat pounded in his ears. "Silam Henner, because of your part in this plan to harm a shipmate, you shall be bound to the mast and suffer twenty lashes, administered by First Mate Kjelnar."

There was a soft indrawn gasp amongst the other crewmen; they knew that the skin on the man's back would be cut to ribbons before the first mate was through with the whip. Enoch Dey relaxed somewhat, however, as if suddenly taking hope. But that was short-lived.

"Your crime was far greater, Mr. Dey. Because you have broken Aiden's law, you will be cast out. Your place aboard this ship is forfeit." He felt sick as he said it. "You will be thrown over the side. Let the ocean currents take you where they may."

The man's jaw dropped. "No, Captain! I beg your forgiveness."

"There can be no forgiveness for you." Prester Hannes's instant venomous pronouncement shocked even Criston.

Enoch pleaded. "But she's a woman aboard our ship! What does she expect? By your own orders, Captain, we stripped her shirt, bared her breasts! We've been gone from land for months. How can any man—"

"You are not animals!" Hannes roared, stalking forward. "The Book of Aiden says, 'He who harms any helpless woman or child shall be considered to have committed such crime tenfold.'" Enoch quailed, more terrified of the prester's wrath than of the captain's.

"I am the captain, and I have made my judgment." It felt as if someone else were speaking the words. Criston jerked his hand toward the railing. "Enoch Dey, you will be cast overboard into the deep. Sentence to be carried out immediately." The pronouncement came much more easily than he had expected, and he realized that he could do it again if he must.

The nervous sailors grumbled. Enoch struggled, his knees wobbly as he was dragged toward the back of the ship. "Mercy, Captain! Mercy, please!"

At the stern, the condemned man reached out beseechingly and grasped for the large fishhook pendant at Hannes's neck. "Give me Aiden's blessing, Prester! Grant me forgiveness!" The sailor's hands trembled so much that the barbed point of the hook cut into them.

Hannes pried the man's bleeding fingers away. "Forgiveness is not for me to dispense. You must ask Aiden yourself. You'll see him soon enough."

Noting that many of the crewmen looked sidelong at Mia, blaming her, Criston snapped, "This woman is part of my crew, as you all are. A crime against her is a crime against all of you."

"But we still don't know who she is! What if she's a *ra'vir*?" Enoch wailed. Kjelnar punched the man into silence.

"At least we know she is not a rapist," Prester Hannes said.

Criston added, "I grant you this one mercy—it is your choice. Will you take a stone?"

Enoch's face turned gray; sweat streamed down his forehead. He waited a long moment before he nodded. "Yes, Captain, I'll take a stone."

Javian solemnly lifted one of the spare weight blocks that attached to the depth-sounding ropes. After being thrown overboard, a man could drift for days in the watery emptiness, fighting the waves, starvation, dehydration, sharks, sea serpents. It would be a long, slow death . . . unless he chose to hold on to a weight, which would drag him down until he drowned. It would be swift, and far kinder than dying in pieces.

Javian extended the flat round stone. The condemned sailor stared as if he couldn't remember what it was for, then reached out to take it.

"May the Compass guide you," Criston said.

Enoch stared over the railing, as the deepening dusk seeped out of the sky, giving way to night. He waited for so long that the hushed crewmen began to mutter. Kjelnar stepped forward, squaring his chest, ready to throw the man overboard if he wouldn't go willingly.

With a last defiant glare toward Mia, Enoch Dey stepped onto the rail, clutched the stone tightly to his chest, and jumped off. He landed with a splash. Watching with all the other crew, Criston saw him disappear at once, descending into the depths, dragged down by the stone he held.

"May the Compass guide us all," Criston said again.

Silam Henner fell to the deck, sobbing.

Criston had hoped to feel the heaviness lifted from him now that the decision was made and carried out, but he felt no pleasure, no satisfaction. Javian and Mia stood together, surrounded by a protective silence. The young woman did not appear vindicated or pleased. Hannes held his fishhook pendant and meticulously wiped off the specks of blood from the cast-out man's fingers.

With another splash, far behind the ship, Enoch burst to the surface once more, gulping great breaths of air, gasping as he flailed his hands. "Help! Come back! Save me, please!"

"I should have known he wouldn't have the courage," Mia said.

The other men began to mutter uneasily.

"Save me!" Enoch's voice degenerated into wordless shrieks.

Each cry from the condemned man thrust like a blade into Criston's gut. They could easily drop anchor and send out the ship's boat. After this ordeal, the man would cause no further trouble.

Prester Hannes, perhaps sensing his doubts, said in a low voice, "If you lose your resolve now, Captain, what lesson do you teach the rest of the faithful? For the sake of your ship and for our mission, you cannot be lenient."

Criston looked at him. "You can say that? Enoch was one of the most devout followers of your dawn services."

Hannes shrugged. "By breaking Aiden's law, he proved that he was not a true follower."

The wails were growing fainter now. "Save me . . ."

The *Dyscovera* sailed on into the deepening night, and Criston walked heavily toward the three compasses mounted next to the captain's wheel, trying to shut out all of his unsettled thoughts.

Before long, the sigh of waves and rustle of sailcloth enveloped and smothered the ever-diminishing pleas for help.

56 *Windcatch*

On the morning Prester Ciarlo left Windcatch to find his long-lost sister, young Davic watched him turn his back on the kirk and bid farewell to the villagers. Though they understood the prester's calling, the people were sad to see him go on such a dangerous errand.

Ciarlo had tears in his eyes as he hugged the boy he had taken under his wing. "I'll miss you, Davic."

"And I will miss you." He pressed his face against the prester's shoulder. "How can I thank you? You taught me about Aiden."

Ciarlo smoothed the boy's hair. "Yes, and if I can do the same for the Urabans, there will be peace in the world, and even Ondun will be happy. You'll be safe here. Give my blessing to Prince Tomas when he arrives in a few weeks."

"I will. I promise." Davic had no intention of staying that long.

After the prester departed, Davic remained at the kirk for the rest of that day, doing his familiar chores. A lonely old woman invited him to live with her, but he shook his head. Fishermen brought food. A baker gave him several loaves of bread, two of which weren't even stale. "You sure you'll be all right, young man?"

"Aiden will watch over me."

The baker wiped a smear of flour from his cheek. "I understand, but you can always come to me, or anyone else in town, if you want companionship."

Davic waited until nightfall, counting down the hours, and finally as darkness set in he made his own preparations. He gathered the preserved food in the parsonage, stuffing it into a satchel; he took all the coins from the collection box.

He still had Ciarlo's letter to Prester-Marshall Rudio,

requesting that a replacement prester be sent to Windcatch. After making sure that no one was watching, Davic stood before the kirk and in a burst of anger tore the paper into many small pieces, scattering the scraps into the cold night winds.

Moving methodically now, he carried the heavy Book of Aiden that had sat on its pedestal for years, the volume that Ciarlo himself had saved from Urecari raiders during their sacking of the town. Davic threw it on the dirt in front of the kirk, then went back inside to retrieve all the other holy texts. He had been taught everything he needed to know, long before arriving at Windcatch.

Carrying a candle from inside the kirk, he knelt before the pile of books and set fire to the volumes, fanning the blaze until the paper was consumed in cheery flames. He watched the words disappear into ash and was not sorry to see it.

He would have liked to set fire to the kirk and burn the structure to the ground, leaving only smoke and a pile of ashes, but such a blaze would have attracted too much attention from the village, and people would have rushed up to extinguish the flames, to "help" him. Davic did not want anyone to notice ... not yet. This small blaze was sufficient to destroy the heretical books.

He intended to be far away from Windcatch by daybreak. The nosy Aidenists would come to look for him before long, but he doubted they'd search too hard even after they discovered what he had done. Nevertheless, he would use all of his skills to hide his trail.

He regretted not having taken the opportunity to stab Ciarlo in his bed; he'd had plenty of chances. He hoped the

Teacher wouldn't be too disappointed in him. The news he had to deliver was vital to the Urabans.

Taking his pack, supplies, and stolen money, Davic headed south into the night, picking his way by moonlight toward Ishalem.

Part III

Part III

57 *Peliton, Erietta Reach*

After the queen and her party departed early from Erietta, Jenirod listened to the muttering amongst the staff and functionaries in his father's offices. At first, he assumed some government matter must have called Anjine back to Calay, but slowly it dawned on him that the all-important betrothal meeting must not have gone as well as he'd imagined. Puzzled, he relived that first day over and over again, but he couldn't quite put his finger on what he'd done wrong.

The horse cavalcade had been one of the finest in Erietta's history, his own performance impeccable. He knew he cut a handsome figure on his horse. All his life, women had swooned whenever he showed off; they would blush and giggle, making him feel giddy. Not so with Queen Anjine. He had never met a woman who made him feel so insignificant.

From his first glimpse of Anjine in the stands, he realized that she was a beautiful woman with a fine figure, smooth skin, lovely hair; she would certainly bear many strong children. He supposed she must be intelligent too, not to mention wealthy and powerful—more than acceptable as a bride. He had certainly been satisfied.

But he must have done something wrong. Jenirod grappled with the inexplicable idea that the queen apparently found *him* deficient in some way. Ever since she and her retinue had left Peliton, Destrar Unsul had moped about, avoiding him. It was such a fantastic turnabout to think that the bookish destrar might be disappointed in *him*. Jenirod knew he had to get to the bottom of this. Though he had never particularly understood his father's odd interests, he wished the man would just *explain* to him what had gone wrong.

Unsul met him out in the stables, an obvious, weary weight on his face and shoulders. "You should be at your instruction. The court tutors say you've left classes. Now, of all times, why can't you pay attention to what is important?"

Each day since Anjine's departure, Jenirod had been forced to endure hours of instruction from the cultural ministers she had left behind. He grudgingly studied courtly manners, learned how to hold delicate eating implements, memorized insipid phrases that supposedly demonstrated good breeding.

Unsul shook his head. For several years now, the man had withdrawn from his eldest son, concentrating instead on the younger three. "Your behavior was rude and embarrassing. The queen left those teachers here for you so you can learn to be a better husband."

"A better husband?" Jenirod laughed. "Queen Anjine is not a wilting flower. Why should she care about such nonsense?" He couldn't imagine his own mother paying any heed to that when she chose a husband. Jenirod missed her very much; his mother had been the right kind of woman, a spectacular rider, someone who knew how to put on a show to please the people.

Jenirod saddled up a spirited young stallion that needed the extra energy run out of him. "I'm tired of that. I need to go for a ride."

Unsul said, "No one questions your horsemanship. You

need to improve your statesmanship. Understand your place, learn the politics, grasp the subtleties you will need at court in Calay."

This wasn't at all what Jenirod wanted to hear. "With manners and dances and pretty phrases? Shall I write her poetry? Love letters scented with lavender? I can't accept that Anjine would want to turn a man like me into a . . . a gelding! There must be some other way to win her over."

Jenirod swung into the saddle and went tearing off down the dirt roads and up into the hills, leaving his father standing at the stable door. At the top of a grassy hill, he pulled the horse to a halt and looked at the windmills that pumped water during the dry season. When he settled in Calay, it was going to be difficult for him to ride off his own energy, and unless the queen warmed up to him, he certainly wouldn't be riding off that energy in the bedchamber.

He dismounted near some bushes so he could take a piss, still pondering his situation. When he finished, he went back and scratched the horse's head, looking into the animal's large brown eyes. "What could she possibly want from me, eh, boy?"

Queen Anjine was a tough woman who had endured hardships and made difficult decisions. She had sent armies into war and recently lost many thousands of fighters in the disaster at Ishalem. But *she* had proven her mettle. Maybe she would let Jenirod lead a new offensive, so he could do it right.

No matter what his father said, he knew he was worth a lot more to her, and to Tierra, with his own skills. He had been born to lead, and people respected his presence, his panache.

A brisk wind rustled the drying grasses and shrub leaves. The horse snorted, jerking his head around, ears swiveling for danger. The answer suddenly occurred to Jenirod: yes, Queen Anjine was a woman of substance, of action. She was not the sort who would swoon at a fine uniform or a complicated trick in a horse cavalcade. Of course not! Queen Anjine needed real, concrete reasons to accept him.

In Calay, she was surrounded by hundreds of show-offs and flowery talkers, and in her eyes, Jenirod was probably just another such buffoon, a man who could fire arrows accurately at a gallop and vault on and off a horse's bare back without so much as a stumble. But such a man added nothing to the worth or defense of Tierra. Anjine would want more from her husband.

Jenirod needed to do something profound to change her impression, to make the queen appreciate his strength and bravery, his manliness, his military prowess. She must want him to make his mark and demonstrate how valuable he would be against the evil Urecari.

Why hadn't she just said so outright? Women often had trouble communicating what they really wanted.

He mounted again and let the stallion have his head, running freely back toward Peliton and the stables.

Brusquely informing his father that he was leaving, Jenirod gave no explanation other than, "You and Queen Anjine will both be proud of me when I return triumphant." Her etiquette teachers would just have to find something else to do in the meantime, or go back to Calay.

Jenirod packed up his gear and rode off downriver. It was a two-day trip to the coastal town where Destrar

Tavishel and his Soeland patrol ships regularly stopped to resupply. Jenirod passed herds of grazing cattle, spent his nights in small villages where he told stories to the ranchers. Their daughters flirted with him and he smiled at them, but because he was betrothed, he remained faithful to Anjine, no doubt disappointing all the young women.

At the seaside village, Jenirod boarded his horse at a livery, paying a stable boy to care for the animal while he was gone. He asked around until he learned that Destrar Tavishel's ships were due to return in four days' time.

When the sails were sighted, the town's bells rang and the shopkeepers prepared their wares. The Soeland destrar had a standing order, so that the necessary supplies were packed and piled at the docks, ready to be loaded as soon as his ships docked. While he was on patrol, Tavishel was not a man who liked to be delayed.

Jenirod greeted the gruff captain as he strode ashore, introducing himself as the future husband of Queen Anjine. Tavishel was a stern-looking man with a square-cut gray beard, shaved head, and leathery skin from time spent in the harsh winds of the open sea. He looked Jenirod up and down. "You rode a long way to greet me."

"Not to greet you—I want to join you. I'd like to propose a mission in the name of the queen."

"A mission?" Tavishel crossed his arms over a muscular chest, his skeptical gaze sizing up the younger man.

Jenirod drew a deep breath, sure he would not be found lacking by the Soelander. "You sail your patrol ships in a great circle from Calay up to Erietta, west to Soeland, and back south below the Edict Line. Let me suggest something more than a patrol. Before I marry the queen, I want to demonstrate my prowess to her—to give her a victory against the Curlies as my wedding present."

Now Tavishel was interested. "Oh? Such a victory could be a wedding gift from Soeland Reach as well. What did you have in mind?"

"It's got to be meaningful and spectacular, a raid that destroys something of great importance to the Urecari, so they feel the hurt as much as they've hurt us."

Tavishel nodded with a sly smile. "I know just the place. I've been eyeing it for a long time. I merely needed an excuse."

"I hope I've given you one. I'd like to be off as soon as possible—time moves swiftly past us."

The Soeland destrar stroked his beard, already formulating the plan. "After we reprovision, we can set off with tomorrow's tide."

58   *Gremurr Mines*

When he left Ishalem, Omra was so pleased with the progress of the canal and the potential alliance with the Nunghals that he ordered the captain to sail to the Gremurr mines. The soldan-shah had complete faith in what he was doing, and it was foolish to wait to construct his armored war fleet. He wanted to be ready with his ships as soon as Kel Unwar completed the excavation.

He also wanted to visit his half-brother. Omra had not seen Tukar in the fourteen years since his exile. He hated the political reasons that had forced him to remain estranged from his poor brother, but treacherous Villiki was long gone. *Omra* was the soldan-shah, and he could make his own decisions. Tukar should have been pardoned years ago.

During the voyage, Omra opened several record scrolls and studied the columns of numbers, assessing just how many tons of iron and steel the mines had produced under Tukar's management. This one operation was responsible for more vital metals than all five soldanates combined—and right under the noses of the Tierrans.

It was ironic that when Ondun created the world, He had placed so many valuable metals on Tierran lands, while leaving Uraba nearly barren—no doubt to challenge the resourceful and intelligent descendants of Urec's crew. Though Tukar had gone to the rugged northern coast in disgrace, Omra was certainly satisfied with the work his brother had done in the intervening years. Now he had to find some way to show his appreciation.

The thought of his estranged brother made Omra ponder how Aiden and Urec must have felt about each other, separated for so long on their voyages. Over the many centuries, their followers had experienced a great schism, but how did the brothers *themselves* actually regard each other? And what about Joron, the brother who had remained behind in Terravitae?

It was time for Tukar to come home.

Soon the Middlesea coast came into view, hazed with smoke and the sharp brimstone smell of refineries. When the soldan-shah's dromond arrived at the docks, flying the unfurling-fern banner, the Gremurr workers and guard staff were astonished. Soldan-Shah Omra had never set foot here before—had never, in fact, touched Tierran soil at all.

Tukar and his bald workmaster raced down to the docks, trying to adjust their already clean clothes on their way to greet the important visitors. Workmaster Zadar fitted a formal sash across his chest, looking worried. Tukar, however, wore a wild grin as he trotted along the dock.

Omra disembarked to stand before his brother and found himself at a loss for words. Tukar looked much older, his features roughened by the hard years here, but Omra could still remember him as a boy. As Tukar opened and closed his mouth like a fish trying to sing, Omra embraced him. "Brother, it has been too many years!"

Zadar looked relieved that the soldan-shah had not come to express his displeasure. The mine guards and Uraban soldiers stood in awkward ranks, clearly unaccustomed to military drills. Only a skeleton crew of armed guards remained with the slave workers, who had paused in their labors to stare at the spectacle, until cracking whips forced them back to their tasks.

Tukar blurted, "I haven't seen you since . . . I wanted to apologize for what my mother did. I had nothing to do with it."

"I know that. Even without the letters you wrote to me, I know that." Villiki had always schemed for her son's benefit, willing to kill Omra so that Tukar could advance. But her plot had failed. "She can no longer harm us. It is time for me to meet your wife and son."

In Tukar's private residence, Shetia worked with their only household servant, an old man named Firun, striving to prepare the best meal with the supplies she had on hand. She managed a worthy fish dinner made with a few local spices and berries picked from bushes in the canyons; old Firun served the meal with as much formality as he could muster.

Rummaging through his possessions, Tukar found an old sealed bottle of brandy, which he presented with great ceremony. "It's the best I have, Omra. I'll share it with you."

The soldan-shah smiled and relaxed on the cushions. "If we like it, I'll send you a case on the next ship from Olabar."

Tukar flushed with embarrassment. "I didn't mean to beg. I have everything I need—"

Omra waved aside his brother's concerns. "It will be my pleasure."

After Shetia's merchant father had paid a significant fee so that she could marry Tukar, Omra had never taken the time to meet her. As he got to know the woman, he found her pleasant and certainly devoted to his brother. Their son Ulan, his nephew, was both energetic and shy, and he seemed awestruck once he realized who the visitor was. The boy made a point of showing the soldan-shah his puppy, and Omra laughed as the dog licked his face. Shetia took her son and the puppy away so the two men could talk.

As they relaxed together, Tukar peppered his brother with bashful questions about things he remembered from Olabar—the tangerine trees in the palace garden, the silk merchants who brought colorful cloth from Yuarej, the old man who made the best grilled lamb down in the marketplace. Omra could hear the wistfulness in his brother's voice.

Firun shuffled in bearing a serviceable but plain silver

pot of steeping tea. Shetia poured the tea while Omra described his remarkable project to dig a canal across the isthmus. Tukar was astounded. "Cutting the two continents apart? It cannot be done!"

"Kel Unwar believes he can succeed, and I've seen the excavation so far. You haven't witnessed the explosive power of Nunghal firepowder." He paused as another thought occurred to him, and he made a mental note to ship some of the explosives here, where they could also prove useful in blasting rock for the mines. The workmaster would have to show the mine prisoners how to mix the chemicals here.

Tukar bit his lip, deep in thought. "If such a canal could be dug, if ships could sail directly from the Middlesea to the Oceansea, then all of the armor plates we produce could be delivered directly and immediately." His face lit up and he stared at Omra.

The soldan-shah said, "*That* is why I came to Gremurr, brother—to give your workmaster a new mission. We can armor Uraban warships right here, at the mines, and then sail them directly through the canal to the Oceansea. When we return to Olabar, I will send several large ships up here, so their hulls can be plated with Gremurr iron."

"We have one large vessel in the docks right now," Tukar pointed out. "We could start with that one!"

Omra had seen the sturdy vessel when his dromond pulled up to the docks. The cargo ship could just as well be used for carrying soldiers and weapons. "Agreed. That will be my first great armored warship to sail through our completed canal at Ishalem."

"But what if Kel Unwar doesn't complete his task? All of that metal will have been wasted."

"He will not fail. Judging by his progress already, he will be done before the year is out. When your ship is fully armored and done, Zadar can rechristen her the *Golden Fern* and send her to Olabar."

"The *Golden Fern*, that is a good name." Tukar bobbed his head, but he looked a little hurt. "Zadar is a fine supervisor, but . . . do you not trust me with this job?"

Omra finished his tea and sat back, content, utterly unable to hide his growing grin. "Certainly, brother. But you won't be here. You're coming back with me to Olabar. It is time you took your place in the palace again."

The expression of joy on Tukar's face nearly overwhelmed him. He opened and closed his mouth several times. "I never thought . . . I had stopped dreaming of it. My wife and son deserve to be there. They have been so patient with me."

Omra felt a sweet warmth fill his chest. "I think we should open that brandy and celebrate."

But Tukar paused and sat back down. He swallowed hard, nodded slowly to himself, and came to what must have been a very difficult decision. "Not yet, Omra. Yes, I long to go back to Olabar. I will be very happy there . . . but my first duty is to Uraba. These mines are my responsibility, and you have just brought us a tremendous new task. I will go home across the Middlesea, and bring my family with me—but only after I see the armored war fleet to its completion."

"That is not necessary. I will make certain all the arrangements are made."

Tukar shook his head. "I insist. It is one final way for me to show my loyalty. Those ironclad vessels will destroy the

Aidenists. Then Shetia and Ulan, and everyone else in Uraba, can have peace at last."

Omra saw that his brother would not budge. "I admire your dedication. All right, see this mission to its end, and then come back to the palace. We will have fine quarters waiting for you there."

"I won't let you down, brother." Tukar snapped his fingers to call his servant back. "Meanwhile, we can open the brandy."

59 Olabar Palace

Istar and her daughters returned home from Fashia's Fountain to find a rather officious announcement from the church that Adreala, Cithara, and Istala were to be accepted into the ranks of acolytes as soon as possible. The proclamation was signed by Ur-Sikara Erima herself. It made Istar's heart sink, but she had been expecting it.

The three girls gathered around their mother to read the notice with varying degrees of enthusiasm. Though their ages ranged from ten to twelve, the ur-sikara had decided that all of the soldan-shah's daughters would enter the church at the same time.

Istala, the youngest, glowed. All the way back to Olabar, she had chattered about her dreams of joining the white-robed priestesses at the shrine; she couldn't wait to finish her acolyte training. Sikara Luaren had given her a thin bracelet to wear, an item donated by one of the pilgrims, and the girl treasured it.

Since she was the proper age to become an acolyte, Cithara had been prepared to begin her studies. "I'll miss you, Mother Istar, but I am also glad that I will stay with my sisters. Together, we won't be so lonely in such a strange place."

Adreala, on the other hand, was not at all excited. Though she had been scheduled to enter the church the previous year, she had made excuses, dragged her feet, and cajoled her mother into delaying her entry. "There is so much else I want to do."

Istar sympathized. "We can't always go where we choose to go. Sometimes we're just flotsam drifting in a storm." Her own existence certainly hadn't followed the course she had plotted—a different life, in a different place, with a different husband—but she had tried to be happy here.

Since Omra was still away, Istar invited the former soldan-shah to a special benediction banquet for the three girls. Imir had just returned from a gloriously successful expedition to root out desert bandits in Missinia, and he was delighted to join them. He arrived with his head and cheeks freshly shaven, his garments laundered, but not in the traditional cut and style of Uraban royalty. Instead, he had donned an ornate furry jerkin made from buffalo suede, embroidered with gold threads; it was sleeveless, to show off the muscles of his bare arms (though not to good effect). The jerkin barely tied across his belly.

He hugged Istar before turning to gaze upon his three granddaughters. "Please stop growing, girls—you make me feel old! I can't possibly be the grandfather of such fine and mature young women."

Cithara thanked him, Istala blushed, while Adreala wrinkled her nose at the rough jerkin. "That's the skin of some animal, and it stinks."

"It was a gift from Khan Jikaris. Next time I return from the Nunghals, I'll bring a bit of preserved buffalo meat. That's all the Nunghals eat. You've never tasted anything like it."

"I thought you complained about having to eat buffalo all the time," Istar said.

"It's just a matter of degree. I enjoy the meat, but it gets a bit tiresome for every single meal."

For years now, Istar had enjoyed a comfortable relationship with the soldan-shah's father. Not only had she been Omra's wife for a very long time; before that, as a household slave, she had exposed the murderous plot of Villiki and Ur-Sikara Lukai. Yes, Imir liked her well enough.

Over the course of the meal, Imir talked about how he intended to go back to the Great Desert as soon as Omra came back to the palace so that he could be ready for the next season's departure of sand coracles to the Nunghal lands.

Adreala perked up. "You're leaving so soon?"

He waved a hand. "The winds wait for no one! I want to oversee the construction of new coracles so I can bring more cargo back—maybe even Khan Jikaris. He keeps saying he'd like to visit Uraba, but he isn't anxious to leave his tents or his wives."

Adreala turned to her mother with respectful excitement. "I'd like to go with my grandfather and see those far-off lands. Besides, I can visit Grandmother Lithio in Arikara!" She looked pleadingly at Imir, who had flinched at the mere mention of his long-estranged First Wife. "Won't you take me with you?"

Imir didn't know how to respond. "This isn't a court game, young lady. There are hardships—"

"Now, you know that's just an excuse to avoid training with the sikaras." Istar pushed aside her small plate, which now held only olive pits and a dot of honey next to the bones of a small roasted bird. "All three of my daughters have been accepted into the church as acolytes. I doubt Omra would let her go."

"Can't we make an exception?" Adreala dug in as stubbornly as she dared. "I'd rather go traveling with my grandfather."

Her youngest sister sounded surprised. "But you made excuses last year, Adreala. The sikaras will grow angry if you keep avoiding them."

Old Imir waved dismissively, now that he'd had a chance to think. "Oh, sikaras find reasons to grow angry with every tide." He looked at Istar, serious now. "Does she want to go? Truly *want* to go?"

"Yes!" Adreala's voice was practically a shout.

Imir leaned across the table. "How old are you now, girl? Twelve? Saan was that age when he accompanied me on our first trip across the Great Desert." He sat up straight, coming to his own conclusions. "It would do the girl good, Istar. I can't imagine you want *all* of your daughters to be sikaras?"

Istar definitely did not, but she couldn't say so aloud. Yet Imir himself seemed to be offering an alternative. She looked at Adreala seriously. "The journey will be hard and dangerous."

Imir brushed crumbs from his buffalo suede vest. "Oh, it's safe enough now. We've made the crossing five times, and the sand coracles are much improved. And I saw to it that the desert bandits were eradicated. What's the harm in letting her go?"

"Please, Mother!"

When Istar saw the hopeful excitement on her daughter's face, it reminded her of Saan's sheer joy when he had sailed off in the *Al-Orizin*. "The soldan-shah will have to decide, but I'll put in a good word for you. Not every woman is made for the church, no matter what the sikaras say."

Returning from the Gremurr mines, Omra felt pleased and satisfied, both because of the Ishalem canal and also for finally granting Tukar forgiveness. He knew old Imir would be overjoyed to hear that his exiled son would be coming home as soon as the new fleet was armored.

Even though many ministers needed to see him after his long time away, Omra set aside all matters of state. This was his family time. He played games with Omirr; he bounced little Irec on his lap. Naori brought him tea and just sat at his side, happy to have him home. Istar welcomed him with a warm hug, and the two younger daughters bubbled over with excitement about being allowed to enter the church as sikara acolytes together.

But Adreala clearly had something on her mind. With perfect manners, she asked to see her father alone to make a request, and he indulged her. Omra took a seat on the cushions beside his oldest daughter. "Now, what's on your mind?"

He didn't even take a breath before she spilled out her request to go on a long journey with her grandfather, rattling off arguments and justifications with such enthusiasm and confusing energy that Omra had to laugh and sit back. "So you'd rather cross the Great Desert than be taught by the priestesses?"

Adreala raised her chin in a regal expression. "Wouldn't you?"

He laughed at that. "You may be right." She looked so mature and beautiful, sure of herself ... much like her mother.

"And you let *Saan* go when he was my age. Grandfather Imir says he'll take care of me. He'll protect me—or I can protect him, if he needs it. After I've seen part of the world and had some adventures, *then* I'll go to any schooling you require of me. Please, Father?"

Omra kissed the top of her head. "My dear daughter, I am the soldan-shah. I am not required to give the priestesses everything." He sat up more formally now. "And your grandfather has promised to watch over you?"

"He has."

"Very well, then. I can tell from your persuasive speech that you have already developed valuable skills in diplomatic negotiation. Therefore, I as your soldan-shah command that you continue your education in matters of state. As I have appointed the First Wives as my emissaries to the five soldanates, you will be my special emissary to the Nunghals—apprenticed to your grandfather, of course. Travel with him and see the world."

Adreala leaped off the cushions and threw her arms around her father's neck, kissing him with childish enthusiasm. "Thank you, thank you!"

Omra reveled in the pure affection for a few more moments, then shooed her away. "Now I need to have a few words with your grandfather."

He joined the former soldan-shah outside in the courtyard as the moon rose. The evening air was cool and still. By lantern light, they sat under the night-blooming lilies and set out a game board with pieces of gold, jasper, and jade. They played a game of *xaries* while they talked, but Omra could barely concentrate on his moves. "I have just seen Tukar, Father. It has been a long time since his exile."

Imir moved a piece on the *xaries* board, leaving himself open for an attack by Omra's sea serpent. "Poor Tukar . . . not cut out for leadership at all."

"He's an honorable man, Father. I offered him forgiveness, asked him to come home to Olabar—but he wants to stay at the mines until he finishes the task I gave him. He's very dedicated."

A tear appeared in the corner of the older man's eye. "I know Tukar wanted nothing to do with his mother's schemes. But tragedies have little bearing on what is *right*. Ondun has His reasons, and we don't all have a map to follow in order to understand them."

"But some injustices can be rectified." Omra paused for a long moment. "I told him he can come home."

The old man looked up from the game, startled, and tears began flowing down his cheeks.

60 *Main Urecari Church, Olabar*

While Adreala made preparations to depart with her grandfather, her younger sisters said their farewells and approached the looming church as new acolytes. Istala and Cithara went by themselves, as was tradition, leaving all past connections behind.

The girls presented themselves as meek supplicants at a tall wooden door designed to intimidate and dwarf all who entered. Looking at the imposing barrier, Istala quoted from Urec's Log: "All are insignificant before the glory of Ondun."

When the doors opened, the two passed through into echoing halls where the priestesses welcomed them, blessed them, and asked the girls to scribe their names onto a ribbon of clean white silk, which they tossed onto a smoldering brazier. As the smoke curled up, one old sikara said, "Now your names and lives are sealed in service to Urec and his church."

Despite the girls' breeding, the priestesses gave them no special consideration. The church was their only family now, but Istala and Cithara understood politics well enough to know that they would rise quickly in the hierarchy. This was the surest way for a woman to gain power, prestige, and importance in Uraba.

For the first three days, the girls were assigned traditional duties as newcomers: emptying chamber pots, scrubbing dishes, working in the laundry. They bedded down on pallets in a communal sleeping chamber. Cithara realized that such humble activities were designed to teach acolytes obedience, and she performed them dutifully.

On the fourth day, the two girls were ushered to an office deep inside the church. In the windowless room, Ur-Sikara Erima sat at a desk lit with scented candles. The church leader was tall and gaunt, with prominent cheekbones and dark woolly hair cropped short except for two long locks that dangled at each side, weighted with red beads. Large gold rings hung from her ears, contrasting with skin the color of mahogany, and her brown eyes had a glazed and distant appearance. She spoke in a tumble of words, as if she had memorized what she was supposed to say. "I welcome my two newest acolytes into the joy of service to Urec and his teachings."

Istala bowed with great reverence. "Ur-Sikara, I have dreamed of becoming an acolyte in your church."

Erima paused for a long moment, as if drifting. "Not *my* church, child. Urec's church." Cithara noted that the ur-sikara seemed drugged, her words faint and slurred. "You are both important to us, as well. You must learn the secret ways of the priestesses. We will be watching you."

Distracted, the ur-sikara picked up a lutelike musical instrument with three strings and a long curled neck. She plucked the strings, creating a wailing atonal sound that pleased her, though Cithara found it jarring. Erima had apparently forgotten the girls were still there, and two red-robed women hurried in to usher the girls away. They were sent back to their studies and given documents to copy and memorize.

The next week, Istala and Cithara were assigned to different groups to learn, to sing, and to study. While saddened that they couldn't continue together, the girls did as they were told.

For several days, Cithara was tested alone. Priestesses questioned her about her life in the Olabar palace, her relationship with Mother Istar and her two half-sisters. She was asked to describe how the soldan-shah regarded her, what she remembered about her true mother, Cliaparia.

In a calm voice, she answered every query as fully as she could, but as one sikara after another continued to press for details, the girl began to wonder why the church had such a specific interest in her former family life. Cithara didn't believe that every acolyte was the subject of such scrutiny.

Finally, the girl's patience reached its limit. Her repeated answer became, "I simply wish to become a sikara." But the priestesses did not find her responses acceptable.

On the fifteenth day, her questioners led her through the winding stone halls, and she recognized the way into the ur-sikara's main chamber. Again, Erima sat at her table looking sleepy and distant. When the church leader did not deign to notice her, Cithara asked boldly, "Why am I being asked so many questions?"

Erima's gaze swiveled toward her with apparent effort. "You have a special role in the church."

"What special role?"

She merely repeated, "A special role in the church."

Cithara decided she would get no further answers from this woman. In earlier years, when addressing huge crowds, the ur-sikara had been an intimidating woman with a strong personality. Now Erima seemed like a shell, a rudderless ship.

Abruptly, an older priestess appeared at the doorway and took Cithara's arm in a firm grip. "Come with me, girl. It is time for you to begin a more important phase of your instruction."

Wanting answers, the girl turned her back on the ur-sikara and followed. "Why am I being treated differently from the other acolytes?"

"You have other obligations. Now be silent."

Without further conversation, the woman led her to a door that opened to a steep stairwell where torches lined the walls. They descended more and more stairs until they were surely belowground, and for the first time Cithara began to grasp the scope of the church's catacombs.

At last they arrived at another candlelit chamber, where

plush tapestries covered the walls to disguise the fact that this isolated cell was far from the open air and sunlight. Decorative stands displayed polished fern fossils.

A woman waited for her, older than Erima and with a greater presence. Her hard eyes held an inner fire. Cithara instantly guessed that *this* woman was the real power in the Urecari church.

"I've heard great things about you, child. We believe you have the power to save Uraba from certain doom."

It took Cithara a moment to recognize the face from a painting she had seen in a section of the Olabar palace. "I know you. Everyone believes you are dead." It was not a question, and there was no fear. "You are Villiki."

This woman, the wife of Soldan-Shah Imir, had been banished long ago, turned out into the streets, and was presumed to have perished.

"Exiled. Not dead." Villiki smiled, pleased to be remembered. "You may recognize my appearance, child, and you may know my name, but do not presume that you know *me*. That will happen in time, as I devote extra care to your training. You, Cithara, have a very special destiny."

61   *The* Dyscovera

"Monster! Monster off the port bow!"

High in the lookout nest, Javian yelled with such alarm that Criston bolted out of his cabin. The *Dyscovera* crew scrambled to their stations or crowded the port rails, shading their eyes to see.

Far off in the distance, a knot of dark clouds hovered in an angry localized weather pattern that moved like a shadow, a sudden squall that could easily bear down on an unsuspecting ship. Criston surprised the men with his odd request. "Pull up the fish nets! Pull them up, *now*!"

Running faster than the others, Mia was the first to turn the crank at the ship's stern, and a couple of other men joined her to haul up the nets that trolled in the *Dyscovera*'s wake. Instead of the usual day's catch of flopping fish, the nets came up empty except for a few strands of seaweed.

Criston paled, knowing what that meant. "It's the Leviathan." He began to breathe faster with excitement, and he scrambled up the rope ladder to join Javian in the lookout nest. The boy pointed. "It's huge, Captain. And horrible. I've never seen such a thing."

Criston extended his brass spyglass and placed the lens to his eye, scanning the knotted storm. In the murky grayness of choppy water, he spotted the enormous creature that had given him so many nightmares over the years.

"You've never seen such a thing because there is only one." *Leviathan.* The terrifying lord of the seas.

The monster's blunt, mountainous head rose out of the water, glaring at the world with its single milky eye. Its maw opened so wide it looked like a cave filled with mammoth tusks. Masses of serpent-headed tentacles thrashed about as the creature moved along.

On the deck below, Kjelnar glared at the distant storms. "This ship can withstand any sea-monster attack, Captain."

Criston was not convinced. The horrific beast continued to swim away, accompanied by storms that manifested from its own anger and loneliness. But the Leviathan was *not* coming to attack them. Miles ahead, off the port bow, the monster dove to prowl the depths, moving toward the horizon. It had not seen the *Dyscovera*.

Javian laughed with giddy relief. "We're safe!"

"Not safe." Criston handed the spyglass to the young man, who took a last look. "No sailor will ever be safe so long as that thing remains in the oceans of the world."

Before dawn the next day, when the cook lit the breakfast fires in the galley, Criston knocked on the prester's cabin. "You have your anchor to carry, Hannes, your own tragedies in life. That monster is mine. Would you preach the story today? The crewmen cannot be allowed to forget what we face out here."

In the lantern light, Hannes's burn scars were quite visible. "Each man has his own Leviathan to face, Captain. Yours happens to be the real one. I will remind the men of the evil that still lurks out in this world."

When dawn broke on calm seas, the crew gathered to hear Prester Hannes. Criston stood close to Javian, who squirmed with the thrill of fear. Hannes had so much angry passion within him that he painted a story of terror and fury as he spoke, fascinating his listeners.

"The Leviathan is a creature of destruction, a manifestation of all the evil that Ondun was unable to eradicate from mankind. *We* can defeat the Leviathan and all it stands for by keeping our true faith. The enemies of Aiden are monsters as terrible as that one, but we can overcome." He paused for effect. "Our captain has already encountered the Leviathan—and lived."

As Criston listened, one hard and stubborn part of him

wanted to face that beast again, to throw a sharp-ended harpoon into the center of that hateful eye, as Captain Shay had tried to do. The Leviathan had destroyed his life, killed his friends and crewmates. Though he had survived the wreck of the *Luminara*, the monster had ultimately taken away what should have been his perfect and happy life with Adrea.

But for the monster's senseless attack on the ship, Criston would have returned home to fight the Urecari raiders. He would have defended Adrea and their unborn baby, or he would have died at their sides. Either way, it would have been better. Now he was left without them. It was too late.

But he could look forward to another encounter with the Leviathan, a chance to repay the pain that the creature so richly deserved. . . .

Hannes raised his voice. "If we must face the Leviathan, the spirit of Aiden will help our fight." He grasped his pendant, squeezed it in his fist. "The most terrible creature of the seas can be killed by something as small as a fishhook!"

The *Dyscovera*'s crewmen cheered, bolstering their confidence. The prester wrapped the men in his spell, inspiring passion and dedication. But Criston knew that no one could match *his* passion to kill the Leviathan.

62 *The* Al-Orizin

In the weeks after the eclipse, Saan steered a course northeast across the Middlesea, far beyond the sand shoals outside of Kiesh. Despite studying the Map of Urec, he could not determine where they were, or how they might find the Key to Creation. He expected to encounter the northern shore many leagues east of Gremurr, but the body of water grew wider and wider, with no end in sight. The *Al-Orizin* sailed on.

Saan was sure they would encounter foreign lands and strange peoples, not unlike the Nunghals on the far side of the Great Desert. Sooner or later, the ship must find another coastline ... unless they had exceeded the reach of Ondun's creation, and nothing but water filled the rest of the world. That was an intimidating thought.

Ahead, foamy water churned around a line of reefs out in the middle of the empty sea. Cautious lookouts leaned over the sides of the ship, watching for underwater hazards that might tear open the ship's hull.

Grigovar strode up to the young captain, tossing his black hair. "Captain, those reefs are sure to offer a feast of mussels, oysters, and urchins. If you're as sick of eating fish as I am, let me dive down to see what I can find."

Sen Sherufa shrugged. "It is our task to explore. Who knows ... maybe Grigovar will find an undersea kingdom?" She said nothing more about the legendary Saedran origins or their sunken continent.

Sikara Fyiri announced herself in typical fashion, with a sweeping proclamation. "There are no undersea kingdoms." Stepping close, she stroked Grigovar's broad shoulders, though the reef diver was much more interested in peering into the clear water than in her romantic attentions.

Ultimately, Saan knew his crew needed something to distract them from their endless voyaging. "Drop anchor here. I admit I'm tired of salted meat and boiled fish. Grigovar, take one of the ship's boats so we don't endanger our hull around those reefs."

The reef diver stripped off his shirt and secured a dagger to his waist for prying shellfish loose. After two crewmen had lowered the boat into the water, Grigovar rowed over to where foamy water marked the reefs. He tied a small mesh bag to his waist-wrap, then slipped over the side of the boat, stroking down deep. When minute after minute ticked by and he still did not reappear, the men began to mutter. "Something's eaten him, I think."

"No man can hold his air that long."

"No *normal* man. You've heard him sing as he pulls on the ropes—Grigovar's got lungs as big as his ego."

With a welcome splash, the diver surfaced again, holding aloft a bulging mesh bag. "Oysters! Dozens of them!" He emptied the sack into the boat, heaved several deep breaths, then dove again. He rose three more times, emptying his haul each time. "A feast for us all!"

Grigovar crawled back into the boat and rowed farther toward the reef's edge. "A better bed!" he yelled, then dove again.

The man in the lookout nest began to shout. "Sea serpent!"

Excited, the crew rushed to the starboard side of the *Al-Orizin*, and Saan spotted the sinuous line of a scaly creature gliding along. It reminded Saan of a deadly snake knifing through the grasses of a salt marsh. Its neck rose up, displaying coppery spots on pale blue scales. Its snub head was nearly as large as the ship's boat.

"Bring pots and pans!" Saan shouted. "Make a lot of noise— we might drive it away."

Some men rushed to the galley, while others grabbed anything that could be used as a weapon. Yal Dolicar mounted the fighting dagger onto his wrist stump, though such a blade would do little against a sea serpent. Sikara Fyiri stood her ground, as if she could drive the creature away by sheer force of will. The spotted serpent continued to glide through the water, making no threatening moves . . . yet.

Unaware of the commotion, Grigovar burst to the surface and threw another sack full of oysters into the boat. He yelled, "We'll have fine eating tonight, Captain!"

Drawn to the noise, the serpent streaked toward the reef diver like a thrown spear.

"Watch out!" Saan shouted. The crew ran around the deck with their pots and pans, setting up a tremendous racket, but to no avail. The serpent's attention was fixed on its prey.

The racket did get Grigovar's attention. He saw the monster bearing down on him, its fanged mouth gaping open. Flailing in the water, he brandished his long dagger, but the serpent was not impressed with the threat. He tried to duck behind the small boat, but the serpent struck down and grabbed him out of the water, raised him into the air like a pelican with a fish, and swallowed him whole. Closing its jaws, the monster dove back under the water.

The men aboard the *Al-Orizin* howled curses. Tears streamed down Sen Sherufa's face, and Fyiri looked sickened. "Weapons, everyone! Set the sails!" Saan couldn't believe what he'd just seen, couldn't believe Grigovar was gone. After swallowing its meal, the serpent moved fluidly through the water. Even with favorable winds and masterful piloting, they could never catch the beast. But Saan knew he had to do something.

The lookout kept a sharp watch as the *Al-Orizin* started to move. Saan stood at the bow for a tense ten minutes, burning with disappointment and guilt. Their easy voyage had lulled him into forgetting how many dangers lay out in the unexplored waters. Grigovar had been lost for no good reason. Oysters? The idea nauseated him as they sailed away in hopeless pursuit.

From above, the lookout shouted, "Captain, I see the serpent, two points to starboard! It's . . . just lying there on the surface."

"Maybe it sleeps after a meal," Dolicar mused. "Like a jungle python."

Saan bristled. "Then we'll make it sleep permanently. Everyone, ready weapons. As soon as we're within range, kill it!"

As the *Al-Orizin* approached, however, Saan realized that something was amiss. The spotted serpent drifted like a dead fish carcass. It hung suspended, its head underwater, its blowhole venting no gases.

The men held their harpoons, and archers nocked metal-tipped arrows to their bows. Everyone expected the serpent to rise up and attack, but the water was stained red by clouds of scarlet blood dissipating around its neck. As it drifted, the spotted monster began to roll over, and Saan could see a long gash down its throat—surely a mortal wound.

With a sudden splash, a man surfaced in the water nearby. Grigovar wheezed, covered with gore and slime. Saan stared, speechless, and the crew set up a loud cheer. Looking stunned, the weary reef diver raised a hand. "As soon as you're done staring, could somebody throw down a rope?"

When they hauled Grigovar aboard, the sailors were astonished to find him uninjured, though shaken. "I got stuck in the serpent's throat." He made a jabbing motion with his blade. "I slid over its meaty tongue and down into the gullet, but I sliced my way out and made a new exit for myself. A shortcut, you might say, though it took a long time to saw a hole through those tough scales." Grigovar laughed aloud.

Two crewmen hauled up a bucket of water and dumped it over the man's head to wash off the slime.

"But we saw the dead serpent when we sailed over here," Saan said. "Where were you?"

Grigovar stroked his dagger's hilt with pride. "After cutting myself free, I dropped my knife in the commotion. I couldn't leave such a lucky blade behind. I had to dive five times before I finally found it. The water's deeper here."

Yal Dolicar sat on a barrel, shaking his head in astonishment. "Though I saw the events myself, even *I* wouldn't be brazen enough to tell such an outrageous story!"

Saan gave orders to head back to the reefs so they could retrieve the ship's boat. "And the oysters," Grigovar insisted. "I worked too hard to get them."

63 *Reefspur*

The royal cog sailed south from Calay, pausing at each main village. The captain was in no hurry, and Prince Tomas enjoyed the slow progress, spreading the joyous news about his sister's betrothal to Jenirod.

Day after day, the ten-year-old stood on deck, drinking in the scenery of cliffs and inlets, forested hills, and thundering waterfalls that plunged into the sea. Over the past two weeks, he had seen many villages, but each one remained distinct in his memory. It was about time he experienced more of the world. Guard-Marshall Obertas was also a stern taskmaster, insisting that Tomas continue his studies inside his cabin, learning his letters, his numbers, and his history. As a prince, not just a boy, Tomas had a duty to make himself as knowledgeable as possible about all aspects of Tierra.

Outside the coral breakwaters of Reefspur, a local pilot rode out to meet the cog, guiding the captain safely into the sheltered harbor. Tomas stood amidships, watching and waving.

"Time to change into your formal clothing, my Prince." Obertas had already donned his royal guard uniform again and slicked back his hair into a ponytail under a dark felt hat. "Make yourself presentable."

In his cabin Tomas rummaged in a cedarwood trunk to find one of the clean (but uncomfortable) formal outfits, as well as the heavy cape lined with Iborian ermine. During days at sea, Tomas wore casual garments, just like the other sailors, but as soon as they approached the docks, the Reefspur villagers would come out to see him. It was his job as prince to cut a fine figure, which they would remember for a long time.

Tomas was eager to meet the villagers, but even more eager to sleep on a solid bed in one of their inns. He'd never been able to get much rest in his narrow shipboard bunk, nor in the swaying hammocks the sailors used. Despite his excitement for the voyage, the boy had been queasy for the first several days, until Guard-Marshall Obertas gave him a bitter-tasting root to chew, and that had quelled his sea-sickness.

Obertas was as much a teacher as a personal guard. When they approached each landfall, he made a point of instructing Tomas about the town, its environs, and its history. He listened closely, aware that a prince should know all about Tierra. When the royal cog entered the harbor, Tomas asked, "Wasn't Reefspur the site of a great battle a few years ago?"

"Yes, my Prince. Our ships defeated and burned a pair of Urecari war galleys. It was a great victory for Aiden, one of many."

Again and again, Tomas heard accounts of how enemy raiders struck coastal settlements, but each time the resilient Tierran people had recovered. Blessed by Aiden, they clung to the Fishhook for strength and defied the enemy by rebuilding. Even so, the tales of devastation left Tomas shaken and angry. He fingered the ivory hilt of the dagger his grandfather Broeck had given him. "Why do they hate us so, Obertas? Why would people do such things?"

Obertas merely gave a somber nod. "Because they are Urecari animals."

In their own boats, the people of Reefspur rowed out to welcome the royal cog as the ship entered the sheltered harbor. Everyone had been prepared for the prince's impending arrival, and he had another ten days of the procession before the ship reached the southernmost town in Tierra, after which the captain would change course and take them home.

Now, with the spotted Iborian cape over his shoulders, Prince Tomas crossed the wide plank onto the Reefspur docks, head held high. He raised his hands to greet all of the villagers who had come to see him. Obertas hovered close, tall and implacable, though silent. Aboard ship, the guardsman engaged in frequent casual conversation with Tomas, but in public Obertas held himself distant.

The small village was thriving. Most of the homes looked new and sturdily built, with a coat of fresh whitewash in preparation for his arrival. Chunks of coral adorned the walls and gardens, as well as dried starfish and polished shells from the reefs. The Reefspur people wore simple clothing, though their coral necklaces would have been the envy of the wealthiest women in Calay.

The town leader approached, clasping his hands. "May the Compass guide you, Prince Tomas! As you can see, Reefspur recovered from the enemy attacks some years ago, and our village is now stronger than ever. Thanks to the Tierran navy, we feel protected and safe."

"And because of Aiden's protection, too," Tomas said.

When the townspeople talked casually with him, he found the lack of formality refreshing. The prester came forward and invoked a quick blessing. In the village square, the people had set out long trestle tables, and pots of boiling salted water hung on sturdy tripods over cookfires. The fishermen had brought in a catch of sardine-like fish, which they dumped into the cauldrons. Using wire baskets, sweating men and women scooped out the cooked fish and drained the briny morsels onto platters, one of which they presented to Tomas. Boiled onions and carrots simmered in other pots.

After watching the boisterous town mayor take the first few bites, Tomas picked up the silvery fish and devoured them whole, bones, heads, and all. At the table close to his side, Obertas ate two whole plates of fish; he had eaten enough camp food and military rations that he would not let a good meal go to waste.

When the conversation died down, the mayor called on Tomas to give his speech. The prince stood, wearing a proud grin. "Most of you already know—my sister is going to be married to Jenirod, the son of Erietta's destrar." The people cheered and whistled, though it was old news by now.

He felt very much an adult as he continued his well-rehearsed words. "Queen Anjine wishes she could visit you herself, but she sent me in her place. I am so happy to meet you all, and to see your fine villages." Though he was stuffed and already a little sleepy, Tomas knew he'd be expected to spend the afternoon touring the town and greeting villagers, shopkeepers, bakers, and fishermen. He said, "May the Compass guide us all."

Their response was resounding: "May the Compass guide us all."

64 *Fashia's Fountain*

Three sturdy Soeland patrol ships anchored just off the rocky Uraban coastline, far below the Edict Line. The look-outs remained on high alert to make sure no Urecari vessels saw them. Up against the cliffs, a small pier and marker obelisks indicated a stony path that wound into the narrow gorge. Destrar Tavishel was sure that this was the right place.

Flushed with excitement, Jenirod watched the determined Soelanders take up their weapons and prepare to go ashore. "Are you sure we need all these men, Destrar? Fashia's Fountain isn't a military outpost, just one of their unholy shrines."

Tavishel gave him a cool look. "Do you fault my thoroughness?"

Jenirod shook his head. "No, we both have too much riding on this operation. Let us do it in the name of Queen Anjine."

The Soeland destrar barked gruff orders, but the men already knew what they were doing. Creaking ropes lowered the small boats over the side, and the men rowed to the lonely pier, disembarked, then sent the boats back for additional shore parties. Jenirod sat aboard the second boat, anxious to fight. Tavishel arrived with the very last group. The Soelanders, though eager, were professional warriors.

Years ago, after the heinous slaughter of Prester-Marshall Baine's pilgrims at Ishalem, Tavishel's ships had intercepted a Uraban diplomat en route to Calay. After killing the man and his crew, Tavishel had desecrated the proposed peace treaty and sent the corpse-filled ship into the Tenér docks. The Soeland destrar was not a braggart, but it had been too long since he'd done something significant.

Now Jenirod was only too glad to help him—and earn the respect and adoration of his bride-to-be. He grinned to think of how impressed the queen would be. Previously,

Jenirod had fought in mock battles and tournaments, but he suspected this experience would feel different from a colorful equestrian cavalcade. He was anxious to see the color of Urecari blood; he had heard so many stories that questioned whether they were even human . . .

As the last boat tied up to the dock, Tavishel stepped off. He was a humorless man, but they had a grim task ahead, and it was good for grim men to do it. The bearded destrar strode to Jenirod. "Are you ready?"

Jenirod's eyes gleamed over his enthusiastic smile. "I've been waiting for this all my life."

Unimpressed, Tavishel trudged up the steep path, holding his sword in a firm grip. The hardy Soelanders followed at a swift pace, and Jenirod found it difficult to keep up; he was a horseman, not a footsoldier. His own sword was heavy, but it would feel lighter once coated with Urecari blood.

During the mile-long climb into the gorge, the Soelanders spread out and paced themselves to save strength for the real attack. Along the way, they came upon two women who were astonished to see an armed Aidenist party heading toward the shrine. Tavishel did not bother to speak to them, since nobody understood the gibberish of Urecari language anyway. The pilgrims were too shocked even to raise an alarm before the first soldiers ran them through and pushed the bodies down the slope.

Jenirod stared, but the Soelanders pressed on with great vigor, now that first blood had been spilled. He furrowed his brow as he kept up with Tavishel. "Those were unarmed women. That wasn't sporting."

Tavishel turned toward him in angry amazement. "This

isn't sport—this is retribution in the name of Aiden! If you have no stomach for it, go back to the dock and wait while we strike. There'll be plenty more women killed before the day is out."

Jenirod wavered, realizing that he had not thought through everything they would be doing. He had imagined great battlefield glories, a victory over the heinous enemy, not just a slaughter of helpless pilgrims and priestesses. And yet they were the enemy.

Jenirod squared his shoulders and pushed ahead. When the path leveled off near the hanging lake and its waterfall, the men raced forward, raising their swords and howling bloodcurdling cries. Fourteen pilgrims were at the sacred lake, eight in the water and the other six on the shore. More than twenty white-robed priestesses hurried out in sheer astonishment as the attack party burst upon them. The Urabans screamed and raised their hands, some pleading, some hurling curses. In the end, the result was the same.

Though he couldn't understand anything the people were saying, Jenirod was sure they invoked the protection of Urec, expecting lightning bolts to come down from the sky and incinerate the invaders. Apparently, Urec was not listening to the priestesses today.

Tavishel's fighters sloshed into the pool, wading up to their waists and swinging swords. The pilgrims tried to swim out of reach, but the lake was small and they were hindered by their sodden white robes. With grim ruthlessness, Destrar Tavishel sprinted along the rocky shore to catch two pilgrims seeking shelter behind the downpour of the falls. The spray ran red for a few moments before the blood was rinsed away.

His killing spirits high, Jenirod cut down a slow old woman— no doubt an evil priestess—then rushed onward in search of other victims. They were easy to find, since the people cowered and screamed. Momentum swept him along now, the adrenaline, the red haze that made him focus in the same way he concentrated on winning during a great tournament. He didn't view them as victims, or even humans. They were Urecari. They were the *enemy*. And he discovered that Urecari blood was red after all.

The slaughter lasted less than an hour. Tavishel and the Soelanders, streaked with blood and gore, surveyed the butchered bodies. One of their men strode to the lake's edge and urinated into the sacred water with exaggerated formality; the other men laughed, and many followed suit.

As one of the men bent to sew up a wound on Tavishel's arm, the destrar smiled with satisfaction. "Search every-where. I doubt you'll find any more Curlies left alive, but there might be treasure. Take all of their gold or artifacts."

"This is a shrine." One of the Soelanders sounded super-stitious. "Everything will be marked with the sign of the Fern."

Tavishel's voice was heavy with scorn. "Does it look like Urec is protecting his people? We'll melt it down. Gold is gold."

The men smashed open the doors of the priestesses' dwellings and gathered a pile of jewels, gold icons, and *cuar* coins, donations to the shrine. Finding stockpiles of food and sacramental wine, the men had a satisfying feast, throwing bones and refuse into the lake. They set fire to anything com-bustible, then headed down the trail to the ships before the sun began to set, each man carrying a portion of the spoils.

Tavishel's smile was genuine now. "Is this what you expected, Jenirod? Are you pleased with the outcome?"

"I accomplished exactly what I set out to." Jenirod admired a ring he'd collected to prove his devotion to Anjine. This truly was a gift fit for a queen, a victory that would rock the Urecari to the core, and *he* had suggested it. If Anjine did not respect him after this, then there was just no pleasing the woman.

65 *Ishalem*

Every *ra'vir* learned how to blend in with the people he loathed most; the Teacher made certain of that. The kidnapped Tierran boys and girls who survived the training might look innocuous, but they were tough, tempered into hard steel.

During his escape from Windcatch, picking his way along the rugged unpopulated shores and highlands, Davic survived on grasses, a few berries, tiny fish he caught in tide pools, and a bird he snared. When there was no food, he did not eat; he made his way ever southward.

Finally, the determined boy reached the towering wall that cut across the isthmus from Oceansea to Middlesea, blocking any Aidenist incursion. God's Barricade. All alone, he gazed at the piled stones in awe. During his secret life with Prester Ciarlo, Davic had heard rumors of the great wall Soldan-Shah Omra was building. And though he had glanced at maps and knew the width of the isthmus, he had never imagined that the project could be so titanic. He tried to comprehend the amount of labor and raw materials that had gone into constructing this line of stone. Surely Ondun Himself would notice it.

Near regularly spaced guard towers, he saw Uraban soldiers in clean uniforms, colorful sashes, and olbas wrapped around their heads. Fern banners rose from the crenellations, rippling in the breeze. Davic smiled, feeling great relief. At last, he had returned to a place where he could feel at home.

He was just a boy and looked completely harmless. Men pointed at him; archers unslung their bows. The guards on patrol probably considered him a foolhardy Tierran pilgrim who had come to see the holy city, and he feared they would use him for target practice before he had a chance to report. Davic was willing to die in the service of Urec, but he refused to let himself be killed before he could deliver his news. He yelled out in clear Uraban, "I follow the Map!"

In the trampled dirt outside the wall, he took a stick and quickly sketched a crude spiral—the sign of the unfurling fern—on the ground where, not long ago, Aidenist invaders had been killed by other brave *ra'virs* like himself. He stepped back and held out his hands to show that he carried no weapon.

A guard shouted out in Uraban, "Who are you? Why are you here?"

Davic spread his arms, blinking in the bright sunlight, dazzled by the glory of Ishalem. "I have come from Tierra with news. Send for the Teacher—then you will know who I am."

Invoking the name of the Teacher struck fear into the guards, and some of the men disappeared from the wall.

Before long, the nearest wooden gate clanked and shuddered as the huge crossbolt was pulled aside. With a groan, the door opened, and two guards hurried out to grab Davic by the arms. He did not struggle or argue with them and let the men hustle him through the gate, which closed behind him with finality.

Suspicious that the boy's arrival might be a trick, the lookouts continued to scan the landscape beyond the wall. But Davic was alone. "I have important news for Soldan-Shah Omra."

"The soldan-shah has returned to the Olabar palace," said the lead guard.

"Then take me to the provisional governor. This news cannot wait. In the name of Urec, we must act quickly, or we won't be able to act at all."

Kel Unwar rushed to the main governmental tower, still clad in dirty work clothes from the canal excavations. When Davic was brought before him, the kel shot an angry glare at the guards. "A boy? You made me cease work on the soldan-shah's canal because you found a *boy*?"

"Not a boy, Kel Unwar. A *ra'vir*."

Davic straightened. "I am a student of the Teacher. I've been pretending to be an orphan in the 'Hook village known as Windcatch. I lived among them, but never lost my hold on the true faith. And now I bring urgent news. That is why I made the long journey."

Unwar's brow furrowed, and he could barely force his words through his deepened scowl. "I've heard enough bad tidings recently."

"No, I bring opportunity." Davic could not hide his satisfied grin. "Tomas, the young prince of Tierra, is making a celebratory procession down the coastline to announce Queen Anjine's impending marriage. I know when he is due to arrive at various villages and towns. I saw the schedule." Davic narrowed his gaze. "I know how you can intercept him."

Unwar's angry expression became one of calculation. His nod was slow and thoughtful as the variables coalesced in his mind. "Maybe it's time we took action of our own."

66   *The* Dyscovera

Under a sparkling veil of stars, the *Dyscovera* sailed on. Javian shared the midnight watch with Mia. They no longer had any worries about a rapist being abroad during the night hours; the two of them looked for outside threats.

Since revealing her identity, Mia had endured many surly comments from other sailors, but Javian accepted her, seeing the young woman as another outsider, someone who might share a common bond with him. She was a quiet person and rarely initiated conversation, but when they were all alone on the sleeping ship, with crewmen snoring belowdecks or out in the open, Javian and Mia fell into a tentative, comfortable companionship.

She stared up into the darkness where a shimmering blue-green aurora flickered and crackled across the sky. Javian had never seen such a thing before. "Maybe it's dust blowing free from the stars. What do you think it is?"

She shrugged. "Just another of Ondun's wonders. I don't have to understand it to admire it."

Mia rested her elbows on the ship's rail, listening to the whisper of waves, the creaking of the lines, the rustle of sail-cloth like a mother spreading a blanket for her children. While Javian considered her answer, two streaks of light shot across the sky, like fingernail scratches making sparks on the night.

"What if it *is* dust leaking through?" Mia looked over at him. "What if the heavens themselves are crumbling? I've heard Prester Hannes say that these are dangerous times, maybe the End Times. Do you believe that, Javian?"

"It doesn't matter if I believe it. We are all in Ondun's hands, and He will sort the evil from the righteous. Nothing we do can make a difference."

"I don't believe that. If we find Holy Joron, that would change everything."

In an awkward moment of silence, Javian asked the question that Mia had known he would raise sooner or later. Though at times he seemed naïve and starry-eyed, he had his own scars, like hers. "So what did you leave behind in Calay? Why did you really want to disguise yourself and be a sailor?"

"Can't I have dreams like anyone else?"

"Nobody's dreams are the same. Nobody's reasons are the same. I just wanted to know yours." She turned away to stare at the dark waters, but Javian didn't back down. "I don't think you're here to visit exotic lands. I think you wanted to get away from Calay. I can see it in your eyes—you're hiding something."

"How would you know?"

He shrugged. "Some people can tell."

She glared at him, expecting Javian to keep pestering her,

but he held his silence, waiting her out. Finally, she said in a quiet voice, "I came because I had no good choices, and this was the best of the bad ones." Her words were nearly drowned out by the wash of waves against the *Dyscovera*'s hull.

"My father was a woodcutter, but he injured himself, lost his hand and lamed his leg. He couldn't work anymore, so he brought me and my little brother to Calay, hoping to find someone to take mercy on us. But our situation just got worse. Even as a beggar, he could barely get enough coins to keep us from starving.

"My brother was too young, but I tried to find work to help us. I tried my hand at being a seamstress, but I had no skill. I volunteered to empty offal buckets in the Butchers' District, but they laughed at me and said a girl couldn't do that work. They said they had Urecari slaves to do the worst jobs and they'd rather see *them* covered with blood, guts, and slime." She gazed out at the horizon with an angry, troubled stare. "Oh, they had plenty of *other* ideas for me. My father told me it was perfectly acceptable for me to be a whore, if that was the only way to keep my family fed."

Javian stared at her, amazed. "There had to be some way to earn money. I ran around doing little jobs, and I always managed to find something. That's how I survived after I ran away from home." He seemed to be accusing her for not having tried hard enough.

She whipped around on him with fury. "You're a boy. You don't know me, you can't know my situation."

He held up his hands, backing away in surrender. "Sorry!"

"But I refused to become a whore, and my father beat

me. I refused again, and when he tried to strike me, I hit him back. I ran away." Her voice hitched. "That's why I decided to dress as a young man and come aboard the ship. This was my only chance. It's no surprise that a *boy* wants to be a sailor, and I didn't want to risk being turned down for a stupid reason." She looked at him with clear eyes and a defiant smile. "I'm glad I don't have to hide anymore."

The cabin boy was surprised by this. "But I see how badly they treat you. They taunt you mercilessly."

Mia chuckled harshly. "I don't care. At least I can be myself."

The door to the captain's cabin opened, shedding a sudden pool of lamplight on the dark deck. Criston Vora emerged, not seeing them standing together in the shadows. The captain walked to the opposite rail, carrying a bottle in his hand. A wine bottle? Javian wondered. Perhaps the captain drank from the ship's stores in order to ease his troubled dreams.

But no. Captain Vora held the bottle with a kind of reverence. He pressed the cork in tighter, then threw the bottle as far as he could out into the water. It tumbled and splashed into the unknown sea.

Javian knew exactly what he was doing.

Mia startled him. "Captain, are you all right?"

Captain Vora turned to see them in the gloom. "I was just . . . adding a letter to the others I've sent. It's an old habit of mine." He rested his elbows on the rail. "Long ago I lost my wife. While I was on the *Luminara*, I promised Adrea I'd write letters and put them in bottles, hoping that the currents would bring them to her."

From his pocket, he withdrew a soft calfskin pouch,

which held a very small clump of golden hairs; Javian saw that only a few strands remained. "She gave me this lock of hair before we set sail from Calay. I place a strand with each letter, hoping that the sympathetic magic will bind them. So far, though, I've no reason to believe she's received any of them ... if she's even alive." He shrugged and looked away. "It's quite likely Adrea's already dead. When the Urecari raiders came to my village, they killed so many." He seemed embarrassed to admit such a sentimental thing. "Nobody knows for sure. I do it now because of my promise, not out of any actual hope, but I am still devoted to Adrea. I know it's silly to believe."

Javian lashed out with a fervent retort. "Don't talk like that, Captain! No truly held belief is silly. Ondun knows your heart. Don't ever doubt what you believe."

When Criston looked at him, tears added starlight to his eyes. He swept his arm around Javian's shoulders, hugging him. "Thank you for that, boy."

Together, the three of them looked over the side of the *Dyscovera*. Under the pale eerie glow of the aurora, they watched the sealed bottle drift away.

67 *Calay, Saedran District*

Suspicious guards stood posted outside the shuttered warehouse near the Calay docks, ready to stop any saboteur from causing mischief. Secure inside, the large sympathetic replica of the *Dyscovera* was the most faithful representation of any vessel that Burian na-Coway had ever built. The

Saedran model-makers had done their absolute best, and Sen Leo had approved every step. It was perfect.

Belatedly, however, the old scholar realized that such absolute accuracy posed its own danger. Such a strong connection between the two ships—original and model—might create a significant vulnerability for the real *Dyscovera*.

After years of studying sympathetic magic, Sen Leo believed that the greater the size and complexity of a twinned object, the stronger the link through the fabric of the universe. Burian na-Coway's craftsmen had made this model very large, seven feet long from bow to stern, for the best possible accuracy. With its clear sympathetic connection, they could monitor the condition of the real vessel.

Last night, though, Sen Leo had awakened abruptly with the shocked realization of what should have been obvious: the bonds of sympathetic magic traveled *both* directions. If the horrid *ra'virs* were to break into the warehouse and destroy the ship model—especially such a large model— might that not damage the actual *Dyscovera*?

At sunrise, he rushed to the castle, demanding to see the queen. Although she had not yet emerged from her bedchambers, the scholar's obvious urgency alarmed the castle guards, who went directly to the royal chambers. Anjine was awake and alert when she entered the main hall, pulling a robe around her shoulders. Sen Leo waited there, fidgeting. "There is an unexpected danger, my Queen. We need to protect the *Dyscovera* model with all the resources we have."

After he explained his concern, she dispatched Marshall Vorannen with a troop of his trusted city guards down to the warehouse. "If you can figure this out, Sen Leo, then Urecari spies may come to the same conclusion. No one is ever to be left alone with the ship model. Station three guards there at all times."

Fortunately, no *ra'virs* had manifested themselves. Yet.

Following Vorannen and his flushed men down to the warehouse, Sen Leo looked at the intact construction, relieved. Each morning, as was his habit, he made a slow circuit of the model, studying it for any signs of damage to the hull, a crack in her mast, a tatter in her sails. It was the only way he could infer the disposition of the *Dyscovera*. So far, the exploration ship seemed unharmed. They had been gone for more than five weeks.

The scholar scratched his chin, but made only a non-committal sound to the model-maker who hovered next to him. He complimented the guards for keeping the model safe, told the Saedrans to continue their watch, then returned home to his wife, bleary-eyed and tired. He bought a loaf of bread and two smoked sausages from a vendor on his way.

After the two shared a pleasant lunch next to the open window in their kitchen, Sen Leo climbed the wooden ladder to the roof, where he kept the special *rea* pigeons. Well-fed and healthy, the birds rustled and cooed, spreading their wings in restless exercise. Sen Leo had built them a spacious cage, much larger than the one Aldo had aboard the *Dyscovera*. He poured kernels of grain into the feed dish, and the birds stirred again, but not because of the feed.

The scholar looked into the sky and was surprised to see another pigeon winging in. The weary bird swooped low, flapping its wings to alight on the plank roof of the coop. Another *rea* pigeon, identical to the ones inside!

With a gasp, Sen Leo spotted a tightly rolled ribbon of

paper tied to its leg. Though he had been expecting this for some time, the old scholar was shocked now that it had actually happened. The connection between the birds had worked. He grasped the pigeon's wings, holding it gently. The bird was trembling and exhausted; its flight must have been long.

He imitated its cooing noise. "Hush, you made it, my friend. You're here, safe and sound." He stroked the bird, calming it, then with unusually nimble fingers he untied the strings and removed the paper note. He placed the tired pigeon in the coop with the others, where it could eat and drink after its long voyage. The pigeon quickly found its twinned counterpart, and the two seemed inseparable.

Only after he had seen to the courier bird did Sen Leo turn his attention to the strip of paper. Holding it carefully, he made his way down the ladder to the bright main room, where his wife was still cleaning up from their lunch.

"Aldo sent a message!" He unrolled the paper, holding it flat on the table so he could read the tightly written letters in the Saedran coded language. Squinting, he scanned the description of the *Dyscovera*'s voyage so far, thrilled to hear the report.

As he read in fascinated silence, his wife pestered him with questions about Aldo, and he answered her curtly, still absorbing the message himself. When he was done, Sen Leo had three things to do: First, he would go to the Mappa Mundi in the main Saedran temple and mark the coordinates, an entire swath of Aldo's discovery to incorporate into the Saedran chart of the world. Then he would go to the na-Curic household and show the note to Aldo's family. Finally, he would go to the castle and present the news to Queen Anjine.

68 *Off the Coast of Tierra*

After nearly three weeks of visiting every coastal village worth the name, Tomas felt he had seen and met half the population of Tierra: presters, mayors, fishermen, shop-keepers, craftsmen, farmers. It gave him a sense of how the land and people fit together under the sign of the Fish-hook.

Even so, he was glad when the royal cog reached the southern end of the processional route, then headed out to sea and to catch the northerly current that would carry them back home to Calay. Finished with the formalities, Guard-Marshall Obertas untied his hair and packed away his dress uniform, which would not be needed again until they pulled into the home harbor.

Tomas stood next to the royal guardsman on the open deck to catch the fresh breezes. The past few weeks had changed the young prince. How much older he felt! He had carried the queen's news, broken bread with the people of Tierra, met with to the village leaders. A real prince ... and also a real sailor. He knew King Korastine would have been proud of him.

Obertas relaxed next to him on the deck, listening to the wind stretching the sails, the hiss of spray dancing from the bow and across the hull. "It was a worthy mission, my Prince. And it was accomplished well."

"What's next after we get home? Do you think Anjine will send me inland by riverboat to Erietta, Alamont, and

Corag? Or off to the Soeland islands? I want to see all the reaches."

"I thought you were anxious to sleep in your own bed again."

Tomas considered this. "I suppose I'd like to settle down at home for a while—but not too long."

From atop the mainmast, the lookout shouted, "Sails ho! Two points to port."

Tomas and Obertas shaded their eyes and tried to spot the ships farther out to sea. Since the royal cog had encountered plenty of merchant and fishing vessels, the crew reacted with little excitement until the lookout cried out again, his voice cracking. "*Colored* sails! I see the Eye of Urec!"

Obertas let out a shrill whistle. "To arms, everyone!!"

"But we're far north of the Edict Line," Tomas protested. "They shouldn't be here."

"Five Uraban ships," the lookout confirmed. "And they've spotted us. They're coming around to bear."

Obertas ran to the cog's captain. "The prince's safety is our greatest concern. Run before the wind! We'll fight only if we have to."

The captain had a pale, queasy expression. "We can try to run, sir, but those ships are lighter, faster, and more agile than we are—and they're war galleys, crewed by oarsmen to add speed. They can turn quickly and go whichever direction they want without being at the mercy of the winds."

Obertas told his fellow guards, "Don your armor and get ready for the fight of your lives." With the painted Eyes blazing on their sails, the enemy warships closed in.

*

After the *ra'vir* boy had provided vital information about the prince's procession, Kel Unwar took no chances. He had been charged with the defense of Ishalem, both as provisional governor and as chief engineer of the wall and the canal. He knew his priorities. In less than a day, he selected five of the best and fastest warships anchored in the Ishalem harbor, picked seasoned crews, and set off after his prey. He vowed that the Tierran prince would not slip through his fingers.

According to Davic, Prince Tomas sailed with only a small contingent of guards, foolishly believing himself safe in Tierran waters. Unwar, though, did not believe in safety. Confidence was an illusion; protective measures and pre-conceptions were irrelevant against a powerful enemy. He knew what he wanted to accomplish, in Urec's name, and he wasn't afraid to take risks.

His five war galleys struck out to sea from Ishalem, riding the swift northerly current up into Tierran waters. Unwar had to intercept the royal cog when it was most vulnerable. Heading back to Calay after a successful voyage, the crew and the escort guard would be complacent, weary, thinking only of getting home.

As soon as they sighted the cog, Unwar had his captain signal the other four vessels in the attack group, pulling them closer, running up the sails and telling the oarsmen to prepare for careful maneuvering in a close fight. Under a sunny sky in calm waters, they could never take the cog unawares: this would be an outright race, and a fight.

Unwar peered through the spyglass as the distance narrowed. Noting the flurry of the Aidenist crew, the extra sails being raised, he laughed. "Ah, they've seen us—but too late. It's only a matter of time."

The Urecari fighters sharpened their scimitars on whet-stones and donned bright clothes; every man wore an emerald sash of Yuarej silk. As the ships closed, Unwar reminded his crew, "Prince Tomas must be taken alive at all costs, and preferably unharmed. Other than that . . . do what is necessary. Any prisoners we take will be set to work digging my canal. Kill them if you must, but I'd rather have them laboring for the glory of Urec than simply feeding the fishes." Using coded signal flags, he dispatched a similar message to the nearby ships.

Unwar watched as the war galleys surrounded the other ship. The royal cog was a large, older vessel, heavy and spacious, while the five sleek Uraban ships sliced the waves like predator fish. Kel Unwar had his men take to their benches and use the oars to add speed for the final charge. At the prow of each war galley, a sharpened beak of cast iron gleamed in the sun. With Unwar's ship in the lead, the others flanked the cog, turning to block its passage.

Drumbeats pounded and the oarsmen pulled hard. Unwar's galley rammed the side of the Tierran cog, and the iron beak battered through the hull. As soon as the ships clashed, the Urabans threw boarding hooks and leaped across the gap.

On deck, the small group of Tierran guards stood to meet them, swords raised and ready to put up a valiant defense. Unwar took up his own scimitar and, adding his yell to those of his men, boarded the cog, looking for Prince Tomas.

Watching the enemy ships close in, Tomas's growing terror made him sick. With a grim face, Obertas gave the prince reassurances, but they were not believable. Finally, he admitted, "I won't lie to you, my Prince. This will be a hard fight."

Knowing that battle was imminent, Obertas coached his men and rallied all of the crew. They were outnumbered at least three to one. The man in the lookout nest kept scanning the waters, hoping to spot a Tierran patrol ship. Had they been closer to shore, they could have signaled one of the lighthouses, but out here they were all alone.

As soon as boarding hooks grappled the ships together, the Tierran men shouted out to reinforce their confidence.

"Stand firm, shoulder to shoulder, swords raised!" Obertas yelled.

Tomas drew the dagger his grandfather had given him. His palm was sweaty on the hilt of mammoth ivory. "I can fight, too."

Obertas looked at him with admiration and regret. "No, my Prince. We have sworn to give our lives for your protection. You must let us defend you."

The Urecari came now, howling, blades flashing, but the royal guardsmen did not flinch, did not break ranks. The anxious Tierran sailors were the first to meet the impact, swinging boathooks, jabbing with harpoons and spears, attacking with makeshift clubs. More than a dozen enemy raiders fell to the deck, bleeding, but the cog's crewmen suffered even greater losses.

The attackers who survived the first clash pushed toward the group of royal guards at the stern. More Urecari men boarded, and more.

A second war galley crashed into the cog's bow with a sickening crunch, and the other three enemy ships closed in for the kill. Within moments, Tomas could see they would be overwhelmed.

Though flushed, Obertas wore an implacable expression, knowing exactly what he had to do. As his guards struck the first raiders who came at them, he pushed Tomas roughly into his cabin. "Barricade yourself inside. Block the door and don't come out!"

Tomas still held his dagger. "I can help defend myself. If we've lost anyway, let my blade—"

"Don't argue with me. You are the prince, and you must be protected at all costs. *Go!* Block the door *now*."

After Tomas backed into the small cabin, Obertas said, "We'll guard this door with our lives, but if the enemy should manage to get past me, I promise to hurt them enough that you can take care of the rest of them with your dagger, all right?"

"Yes, Guard-Marshall, thank you. May ... may the Compass guide you." Tomas slammed the door and threw the crossbar. He then moved his chair, his cedarwood trunk, everything he could against the door. It formed a meager barricade at best.

From the other side of the door, he heard the battle cries, the bone-rattling sound of steel against steel, wet chopping sounds and groans of pain that seemed to go on endlessly. Uraban voices dominated the babble more and more with every moment. He heard Obertas snapping orders, rallying his men ... then Tomas didn't hear the man's voice anymore.

The sounds of battle fell into a lull, but Tomas knew it wasn't over.

Heavy fists pounded on the cabin door, creaking the boards, pushing against the crossbar. Shoulders slammed against the barrier, and the wood splintered. With a startling thunk, the blade of a battle ax smashed through the door. With repeated chopping, the weapon broke a hole through the planks. Heavy hands tore apart the splintered wood and reached inside to grab the crossbar.

Tomas darted forward with his dagger, slashing at the hands, making them retreat with unintelligible curses. But it was only a brief delay. More men smashed the door open at last. Tomas backed into a defensible corner as Obertas had taught him, brandishing his bloody dagger before him.

Now the enemy faced him. Outside, he could see bodies strewn on the deck: familiar men who had traveled with him on the procession. Even Guard-Marshall Obertas lay among the corpses. All had died to defend him, refusing to be captured.

The lead Urecari man grinned at the boy, seeing no threat from the prince's ivory-handled dagger. Tomas slashed and danced forward, intending to sell his life dearly. "You won't take me alive!"

The Urecari man merely struck his arm a stinging blow with the flat of his scimitar. The boy's hand went numb, his fingers useless, and the dagger flew aside. Tomas was not a warrior, just a young boy. A prince.

Laughing, the Urecari swarmed forward to grab him.

69 *Ishalem,* Ra'vir *Compound*

Though he was only eleven years old, Davic had already achieved great things in his life. After living with Prester

Ciarlo for months, pretending to be a faithful Aidenist (and loathing every minute of it), he now recognized how clever the Teacher's training had made him. He had never lost sight of the truth. Now, thanks to the boy's information, Kel Unwar was off to capture Prince Tomas—what a devastating blow to the enemy that would be! And *Davic* had made it possible. A true blessing from Urec!

Before setting off in his warships to go after the prince, Unwar had sent Davic to the large new *ra'vir* camp established just south of Ishalem. Accustomed to taking care of himself, the boy needed no escort. He eagerly looked forward to announcing his triumph to the Teacher himself.

When he approached the outskirts of the mock Aidenist town, two horsemen on patrol challenged him. They wore yellow sashes across their chests and bright yellow olbas. Davic held up a sealed letter of verification from the provisional governor. "I am a *ra'vir* returned from my mission. I need to see the Teacher."

The guards inspected Unwar's letter, conversed with each other, then handed back the document. "Congratulations. The soldan-shah will be proud of what you've done. We will take you to the Teacher now."

"I'll go there myself, without an escort." The boy gave them a disarming, waifish grin (something the Teacher had taught him), and it worked as well on these Urecari men as it had on the fools in Windcatch. "Let this be a surprise."

He bounded into the faux Aidenist town, saw the boys and girls like himself, unremarkable street scamps, all supposedly orphans—and they *were* in fact orphans, because they'd been rescued from 'Hook parents who would have raised them to be damned. Davic knew none of the other children, because all of the *ra'virs* in his training group were already assigned to various Tierran villages, some even to Calay.

Most of the children stolen from Tierran villages did not survive *ra'vir* indoctrination. Any boys or girls who clung to their false beliefs, or who wailed in despair at having lost their former lives, or who refused to accept the Truth of Urec—those were killed, often as practice victims for the other children. *Ra'virs* learned early on never to consider unbelievers as God's children. Only the best candidates— the smartest, the purest—survived their instruction. Oh, some tried to trick the Teacher, secretly keeping their Aidenist beliefs, but the ominous silver-masked figure always found them out.

During his years of indoctrination, Davic had suffered beatings and bruisings, even broken bones, but he had recovered, and the ordeals strengthened him. He had deserved those punishments because he had made mistakes. His errors were not intentional or deceitful, but mistakes were nevertheless a blot in the eyes of Ondun, and the boy had learned never to make them again.

Given his success, Davic was sure the Teacher would dispatch him to Tierra on another assignment, though he longed to stay here in Uraba with people he understood. He wanted to worship freely, wear an unfurling-fern pendant for all to see. He didn't want to have to pretend, but he was a master at it. Ondun would reward him, either in this life or the next.

As he made his way to the Teacher's permanent headquarters tent, he realized for the first time that he *looked forward* to seeing the fearsome figure. Approaching the tent,

Davic straightened his clothing, smoothed his hair, adjusted the concealed knife that the Teacher himself had given him on his graduation. *A ra'vir must be ready to fight for his faith at any time.*

Preoccupied with his triumphant news and anxious to deliver his surprise, Davic parted the tent flap and bounded inside. "Teacher, I have returned!" He did not try to suppress the excited grin on his face.

The Teacher spun quickly with an indrawn gasp and bark of anger. Davic saw the silver mask lying facedown on a small table, the black cowl slipped down to the shoulders.

Davic stared, paralyzed with shock, then slapped his hands over his eyes—but too late. He recoiled, trying to drive away what he'd just seen. "I'm sorry! I did not mean to look!"

The Teacher snatched up the silver mask, pressed it back into place, adjusted the robes and cowl once more. "You should not have come here."

Davic kept his eyes averted, his face flushed with shame. "I merely wanted to report to you. Kel Unwar sent me here." A deep-seated fear bubbled like lava in his stomach: for *this* error, he knew he would suffer far more than a thrashing. "I didn't mean to ... I will never reveal what I have seen!"

"*That* much is certain." Tugging the gloves back on, the Teacher grabbed a long knife from the table and brandished it. "As a *ra'vir*, you know it is vital that secrets be kept."

"I will keep the secret, Teacher—as I have kept all the others. I swear it on the Golden Fern!"

But the dark form was already moving with deadly swiftness. The long knife sang in a swift arc.

Davic's reflexes kicked in. He had spent years undergoing the Teacher's own training, and he knew how to defend himself. Instinctively, the boy whipped out his own blade and met the Teacher's, edge to edge. They danced, parried. Davic could not read the Teacher's face behind the silver mask, but he *knew* a cauldron of anger must be simmering there.

He had done a terrible thing. He had seen what he should not have seen. He had committed a terrible mistake, and he deserved to be punished. But the Teacher had also trained him to protect himself. Davic ducked and spun nimbly, remembering his incessant training, avoiding the other blade again and again.

The Teacher jabbed, slashed, breathing heavily behind the silver mask. The boy whisked his knife back and forth, keeping his opponent at bay, but afraid to do any real harm. "I'm sorry, Teacher! I am sorry!"

The Teacher's blade came dangerously close to sticking him, but the boy squirmed, ducked backward, then slithered close to the cumbersome dark garments that hindered the Teacher's full range of motion. He spotted an opening and could have slashed his opponent's forearm through the dark sleeve, but instead he retreated to the tent flap, still holding up his blade. "Teacher, believe me! I meant no harm. I came only to deliver vital information—I was excited. I did not mean to intrude."

Still keeping the dagger raised, the Teacher paused. "What information?"

Anxious to be pardoned, the *ra'vir* boy told his tale in a rush of words. The Teacher listened and nodded. "I am proud of your accomplishments, Davic, and I will speak to

Kel Unwar about them myself. Prince Tomas will be a fine prize—if your information is accurate."

"You'll know the truth of that soon enough. And I . . . I will tell no one what I have seen."

"Swear it!" The voice sounded sharper than the honed dagger blade.

"I swear! In the names of Urec and Ondun!"

The Teacher raised the dagger in a silent salute. "Very well, I believe you. You have done a great service for Uraba. I have tested your determination, your faith—and you proved yourself worthy." Placing the dagger back on the table, the Teacher took a seat, turning the implacable blank mask toward him. "Now go blend in with the *ra'vir* recruits. There is a bunk for you in the third barracks. Rest and recover. Soon, I will find a new mission for you."

Joyful and relieved, Davic bounded out of the Teacher's tent and went to join his fellow *ra'virs*.

That night in the barracks, gliding through the shadows, the Teacher moved along the line of beds, inspecting the faces of the Tierran children. So innocent looking, yet so deadly. Because the young ones worked so hard on their training and believed in their mission, the *ra'vir* trainees slept well.

Content to be back in Urecari lands, Davic sprawled on his pallet, face turned up, mouth slightly open; periodically, he let out a faint snore. Looming over the narrow bed, the Teacher regarded him for a long moment, then extended a gloved hand to pour a small pile of white powder onto the open palm. Moving with utter silence, the Teacher lifted the silver mask, held the powder close to Davic's face, and blew sharply. The powder clouded around the sleeping boy's head. Automatically, Davic inhaled, snorted, and began to cough.

The Teacher straightened once more and replaced the mask as the boy's gasps and struggles awakened other *ra'vir* children, who were startled to see the dark figure in their barracks. Davic jerked and convulsed. After several long choking gasps, his eyes bulged, and he stared up at the featureless silver mask. He clawed at his eyes, his throat … unable to believe what was happening—and then slumped back. His last breath came out in a long, wet rattle. Davic twitched a few more times before he lay still.

All the other children had awakened and now stared in awe and fear. Masked in shadows, the Teacher did not speak until Davic had fallen silent in death. "His faith was insufficient."

The dark figure turned and stalked out of the barracks, leaving the dead boy in his bunk, and the *ra'vir* children stared after the receding form.

70 *Calay, Main Aidenist Kirk*

The preparations for Mateo's wedding day were more complex and grandiose than the plans for a large battle. Once Queen Anjine assigned her protocol ministers to the job, Mateo found the decisions taken entirely out of his hands. Vicka Sonnen didn't know what had happened either; she'd been surprised when he asked her to marry him in the first place, but she never imagined the uncontrolled hurricane that the wedding ceremony would become.

"It does us no good to fight against the queen's commands," he told her, good-humored and resigned. He found it odd that Anjine talked very little about her own wedding; she seemed more interested in his.

Vicka's father was delighted, though a bit confused, when she told him about the impending nuptials. For months, he had remained oblivious to the attraction between the two, never imagining Mateo's true reasons for his frequent visits. Ammur Sonnen was a man who took things at face value. Now the blacksmith didn't understand the need for such complex wedding preparations, or for the tailors who continually drew him away from his forge so he could be measured for garments that befitted the father of the bride. Ammur was so distressed that his output of swords and armor decreased noticeably.

Prester-Marshall Rudio consulted with Mateo and Vicka in his high-ceilinged offices inside the main kirk. In his service to the queen, Mateo had already met the old religious leader several times, but Vicka was so in awe of Rudio that she could barely stammer a few words in the man's presence. Mateo teased her as they walked out of the kirk offices. "I've never seen you speechless in front of someone."

She just looked at him with her large brown eyes. "Pinch me, so that I can be sure this is all real."

"There'll be time enough to pinch you later. For the time being, we have to maintain a certain sense of propriety."

When the day finally came for the service, Mateo looked dashing in his military dress uniform, complete with his high rank insignia as well as marks from the Tierran navy. He and Vicka had rehearsed the ceremony with other presters, who guided them through the motions, preparing them for what Prester-Marshall Rudio would do. Mateo felt like a game piece being moved around a game board, but when he looked at Vicka and saw how happy she was, he had no regrets at all.

Now in the giant, crowded kirk, he walked forward, accompanied by Marshall Vorannen of the city guard, who stood up for him. As the successor to Mateo's father in the royal guard, Obertas would have been a more appropriate choice to stand beside the groom, but Prince Tomas and the royal cog had not yet returned from their procession along the coast.

With appropriate fanfare, Mateo stood at the center of attention near the great altar, where the shining half-horn of the ice dragon rested in its cradle. Among the audience in the kirk, he recognized the grinning faces of friends and comrades, ship captains, army commanders. He felt swept away by the day.

Before the ceremony started, Queen Anjine entered with her retinue of handmaidens and retainers. She was dressed in her finest gown, her golden-brown hair piled up beneath a jeweled tiara. Anjine wore an expression of complete joy. Just looking at her gave Mateo a pang; he had never realized how stunning she was. She smiled at him with more friendship than formality as she took her seat in the reserved front row on his side of the kirk.

However, from the moment Vicka glided forward in a shower of white lace, with tiny white flowers adorning her hair, Mateo could see her and only her. Wearing a gold necklace and earrings that sparkled with jewels, she walked with one hand on her father's muscular arm, the other carrying a glad spray of sweet-smelling blossoms.

Before he realized it, she was next to him, her gaze riveted to his. She whispered, "I didn't know you could be so dashing. Are you sure you're the man I agreed to marry?"

"Are you sure you're the woman I proposed to? You're so beautiful, you take my breath away!" They seemed tied together, like a ship bound to a dock. The two faced each other in front of the altar, and the prester-marshall pointedly cleared his throat to see if they were done chatting. Vicka blushed.

The audience fell silent as the old man read a long passage from the Book of Aiden. Other town presters had better speaking voices, but Rudio was the head of the Aidenist church. Mateo stole a nervous glance backward at Anjine, feeling strangely embarrassed. He wondered how he was going to feel several months hence, when it was his turn to sit dutifully in the kirk while Anjine took wedding vows with Jenirod.

Then he returned his attention to Vicka, scolding himself. He loved Vicka; he loved everything about her. She was beautiful, smart, independent, not at all shy, and ready to be his equal. She was almost everything he wanted ... and she could do nothing to alleviate her lone failing, that she was *not* Anjine.

Prester-Marshall Rudio prayed, blessed the couple, then began a long, rambling sermon that drew parallels between the tale of Sapier and the fishhook, and how love could bind hearts together.

As the church leader continued to talk, a man entered the back of the kirk, dressed in a courier's uniform. Keeping to the side of the main chamber, he did his best to be unobtrusive, darting to the front benches, where he knelt next to the queen. Despite his attempts to be quiet, all eyes turned to the man. Rudio droned on without interruption. When the courier whispered to Anjine, her face darkened. She rose, as did her retinue, quietly filing to the side and exiting with as little fuss as possible.

On the dais next to Mateo, Marshall Vorannen tensed, obviously wanting to hear the news, but Prester-Marshall Rudio didn't seem to notice. Vicka squeezed Mateo's hand tightly, and his heart sank as he saw Anjine go. Rudio caught their attention again and handed each a large symbolic fishhook, plated with gold, four inches long. "With these, you join yourselves together."

Vicka and Mateo linked the hooks and pulled them tight. The action forced them to face each other once more, and when he saw his bride again, his concerns faded away. *His wife.* Then the word was given, and he found himself leaning forward to kiss her. Ignoring all politics and other concerns, Mateo simply let himself be swept along with the celebrations.

71   *Calay Castle*

Anjine reached the castle angry, offended, and in no mood for courtesy. A messenger from Uraba would have made her wary under any circumstances, but because his demand to see her had interrupted such a special occasion, she had half a mind to let the man cool off for a few days in a squalid cell.

She hated leaving Mateo's wedding ceremony. Being

there for him as a friend meant so much to her. But she was also the queen of Tierra. No one understood that better than Mateo.

Nevertheless, this had better be important.

The Uraban messenger claimed that his news had something to do with Tomas. Fortunately, a patrol captain out in the coastal waters, recognizing the importance of this man's message, had called Tierran warships to surround the strange vessel and escort it directly to Calay harbor. Anjine knew full well that if it had been Destrar Tavishel who intercepted the foreign ship, he would have sent the courier to a prisoner camp without bothering to interrogate him.

Anjine needed to hear what he had to say.

Flushed and annoyed, she took no time to compose herself; rather, she strode in front of her guards and retainers through the castle's grand foyer and directly into the throne room like an unexpected windstorm blowing in from the sea.

Her abrupt arrival startled the Uraban emissary, who turned. He did not seem to know whether to bow or abase himself. The foreigner wore baggy silken clothes of blue and brown, slightly faded; his odd-looking olba had been rewrapped tightly around his dark hair.

In short, he was not at all what Anjine expected—no haughty or supercilious man wearing the jewels and ornamental trappings of his office. Rather, he looked like a poor merchant or fisherman, completely unaccustomed to dealing with political leaders. He was nervous, and his dusky skin had a gray cast. His lips opened and closed like the mouth of a gigged fish, but no sound came out.

Anjine spoke curtly as she walked forward to take her

place on the throne. "For years, the only communication we've received from your countrymen has been in the form of swords and schemes. Who are you? What is it you need to say to me, and how does it concern my brother?"

The man bowed, struggling to gather his wits. "My name is Khalig, and I have come directly from Ishalem. I am a sailor, a merchant." He tugged at his Uraban tunic, which seemed clean enough, though not an expensive cut.

"And you are the best envoy Soldan-Shah Omra could send? What is it? Speak up, man!"

"I ... I come here on behalf of Kel Unwar, who is the provisional governor of Ishalem in the soldan-shah's absence. I apologize that I am not a person of greater importance. I was chosen because I had the first available ship. I merely bring a message concerning Prince Tomas." Again, he kept his eyes averted.

A lump of terror formed in Anjine's chest, but she refused to show any weakness, especially in front of this man. "What about my brother?"

Khalig could sense that his life hung in the balance. "Kel Unwar instructed me to inform you that the royal cog was captured on the open sea. In retribution for atrocities committed by Aidenists, Prince Tomas of Tierra is being held prisoner in the governor's residence in Ishalem, and the surviving members of his crew have been sent to Urecari work camps."

Khalig continued to speak, even though an instant uproar drowned out his words. Anjine's eyes crackled as she rose from the throne. She was now a thunderstorm in feminine form. "How dare you accuse *Tierrans* of atrocities, after what the Urecari have done to us, year after year! How dare you take hostages! How dare you lay a hand on my brother!"

"I am just a messenger, Majesty. I-I was not present."

All she could think of was how excited Tomas had been to embark on the voyage down the coast. Marshall Obertas had gone along to protect the boy, and she knew the royal guard would never have surrendered. "How do we know this isn't another instance of Urecari trickery? What proof do you offer?"

Khalig fumbled with a leather pouch tied to his belt, and the guards in the throne hall stiffened as he withdrew a dagger with an ornately carved handle of mammoth ivory. Tomas's dagger. Anjine's heart fell as she recognized it immediately. She did not need to see it more closely. The guards came forward now, hands on their own blades.

Khalig finally lost his resolve and collapsed to his elbows and knees, abasing himself. "It is but the message I was commanded to bring, Queen Anjine. Prince Tomas lives and is unharmed, but by the Eye of Urec, I had no prior knowledge of what Kel Unwar did. Please do not kill me!"

Anjine felt coldness seep through her veins now. "Your life is not forfeit, Khalig—not yet. Tierra is a *civilized* land, and that is not how we do things here. We are not monsters."

Khalig looked up, his face a tangled mixture of disbelief and indignant anger. "You say that after what Tierrans have done to our innocent people?" He rose to his knees in defiance, ready for a noble execution.

Anjine ground her teeth. First and foremost, she had to get her brother back unharmed, whatever the cost. "And what ransom does your governor demand?"

"He . . . he did not say, Queen Anjine. He merely told me to inform you. I-I am certain other messages will be forthcoming."

Anjine felt fury roiling up within her and feared it would outstrip her reason. If she faced this worthless man a moment longer, she might be provoked to actions she would later regret. That might even be part of the Urecari plan . . .

She spoke in a very low voice, heavy with threat. "You will take a message to Kel Unwar, or the soldan-shah, or whoever holds our prince: We demand to know what ransom he asks. Guards, please escort Khalig immediately back to his ship. No one is to harm him, but I want him gone with the outgoing tide."

The men shoved and hauled the Uraban roughly from the throne room.

Anjine returned to her seat and sat back, lacing her fingers together. *This is not the way we do things in Tierra.* She wondered if the very nature of the war had changed.

72 Ishalem, Governor's Residence

Inside the high sandstone tower, a ring of narrow windows let in strips of sunlight that traveled around the round room every hour of the day like the hands on a Saedran clock.

Tomas pressed his face against an open window. He'd always wanted to visit Ishalem, but not like this. He had seen paintings of the city's glory before the terrible fire destroyed everything. Ishalem was sacred to both faiths, but

now the followers of Urec had taken over the entire site—
built a wall to block out Aiden's faithful, filled the Aidenist
district with foreign-looking buildings.

Outside the tower, a rumbling boom heralded an explosion near the canal construction site. Looking out one of the
window slits, Tomas saw a plume of smoke and dust rising
into the air. He had heard repeated explosions since his
capture.

The boy had been left alone for eight days now. Everyone here spoke only Uraban, and he could not understand
them. When he made hand gestures and used expressions
to communicate with the guards, he was sure they knew
what he meant, but the men refused to respond.

Each day he received plain food—bread, rice, fish—and
water to drink, probably the same rations given to the labor
crews at the numerous construction sites around Ishalem.
From the high tower, Tomas could see the work on two
giant churches being erected on the sites of the original
Aidenist kirk and Urecari church.

With a rattle of keys and the creak of hinges, the wooden
door to his tower room opened. Tomas marshaled his anger
to glare at the man who had led the raid and captured the
royal cog. *Kel Unwar.* Remembering that he was the prince
of Tierra, the only son of King Korastine, Tomas drew a
deep breath and said, "I don't recognize your authority.
You're just an acting governor of a city. I wish to speak to
Soldan-Shah Omra."

The kel replied in heavily accented Tierran, "Not his
decision. I lead Ishalem. *I* captured you. Soldan-shah does
not know."

Tomas's nostrils flared as he demanded, "Where are the

other members of my crew? Did you murder them?" He still felt sick at having seen the bodies of Obertas and so many brave Aidenist sailors on the deck.

Kel Unwar spoke Tierran surprisingly well, despite his accent. "They are slaves for Uraba. They work. They build."

Tomas reddened. The very idea made him angry. "They are prisoners of war! You have no right to treat them so."

Unwar merely gave him a sour look. "You have slave camps too. Uraban prisoners."

Tomas bristled. "We didn't start this war. It's only right that Urecari prisoners work to make up for the damage they have done."

The man gave the prince a withering, hate-filled glare. "I do not argue with a child. You are only a pawn. I send a message to your queen—but she does not know how much I hate Aidenists."

"You have no reason to hate Aidenists. We are good people."

His words ignited a genuine fury in the man's dark eyes. "All Aidenists lie. But since you are a child, I will teach you about 'good people' who follow Aiden." Unwar stalked farther into the room, looming over Tomas.

"My home city is Ouroussa, a shipbuilding port. I was happy there when I was young . . . before I knew Aidenists. My sister, Alisi, was a kind, cheerful girl, twelve years old, almost a woman. She was beautiful. Boys paid attention to her. Merchants and noble families considered her a good marriage prospect. She had a bright future. This was before the war, before Ishalem burned.

"One night Alisi went to the docks to find a merchant

ship from Yuarej. Our mother gave her money to buy a bolt of scarlet cloth. But a Tierran ship was in port, and Aidenists stole Alisi. She fought, but they took her on their ship.

"I followed my sister to make sure she bought the right cloth, and I saw the men take her. They laughed when I tried to save her. They threw me back to the docks and sailed away." Unwar's hands clenched and unclenched. He looked at Tomas as if he resembled one of the men who had kidnapped his sister.

"I called for help, but no one believed me until too late." He shook his head. "My parents were not powerful, not wealthy. We demanded action, but City Leader Fillok would not risk insult to Tierran merchants for only one girl." He drew a deep breath and straightened.

Tomas was incensed. "Aidenists would never do something like that!"

"And yet they did." Kel Unwar scowled at the prince, his body trembling with barely contained violence.

The boy remained silent, sensing that the slightest provocation would unleash Unwar's misplaced vengeance. The provisional governor backed toward the door, visibly struggling to calm himself. He paused at the threshold. "And that is why I hate your people."

73 Olabar, Main Urecari Church

As the swollen orange sun set to the west of the capital city, Istar accompanied Kuari, the newly designated emissary from Inner Wahilir, to the main church of Urec. The First Wife of Soldan Huttan was a pragmatic woman, and Istar enjoyed her company.

The two high-ranking women attended sunset services accompanied by guards and attendants. Despite their status, though, they moved through the crowds like any other suppliants, inching their way around the processional spiral, pressed close to everyone else.

Traditionally, the soldan-shah's retinue had a special right-of-way and separate passages and balconies inside the church, but Ur-Sikara Erima had recently decreed that Ondun considered all of His people equal, that no one should receive special privileges. Such a pronouncement was enforced only when Istar attended services, however.

She refused to take offense at the obvious insult. She might wear gowns and jewels, but she had been born in a small fishing village in Tierra. She never forgot where she came from. She thought wistfully about walking up the dirt path to the small kirk on the hill above Windcatch, listening to Prester Fennan read from the Book of Aiden. Being snubbed by these officious priestesses in the huge church of Urec meant little to her.

Entering the main worship chamber, Kuari walked beside her, shoulders back, chin held high. She wore a gown of maroon silk and a gold chain belt around her waist. "Never before have I had to wait with the crowds. It seems you have few friends in the church, my Lady."

Istar was surprised by her own sharp retort. "The sikaras consider themselves more important than they really are. Much of their arrogant attitude is to keep the people from looking at them too closely."

Kuari responded with a scandalized chuckle. "You are very perceptive, my Lady! I was trained among the sikaras for years before I realized *that*."

"I've had to be perceptive, in order to survive all these years among enemies."

Though she had been in Uraba for two decades and did what was expected of her, Istar had never wholeheartedly embraced the rival faith. She had seen enough zealous violence to taint her view of the followers of Urec.

True to his word, Soldan-Shah Omra had genuinely cared for Saan, kept him safe, given him a good life . . . but Omra also condoned and committed atrocities that she found unforgivable. Nevertheless, she could not deny her appreciation, her respect, even her affection for him. Her heart was like a boat in heavy seas, rocking back and forth, always in danger of being capsized. Was there such a thing as a beloved enemy?

This was her life now.

She glanced around the chamber, hoping for a glimpse of her two acolyte daughters, but apparently Istala and Cithara did not participate in the major services. Or perhaps, knowing that Istar herself would be attending the ceremony, the stern sikaras had kept the girls away out of petty spite. . . .

When the two women completed their spiral journey, they moved to a front row, from which they would be able to hear the ur-sikara speak. Before the service started, Istar leaned over and whispered to Kuari, "So you were raised as a sikara, but you became a soldan's wife?"

The other woman was not terribly interested in the ceremony. "I can't say which was the greater ordeal, or the most eye-opening experience." She smiled. "I do know, however, that anyone who truly follows the path of goodness described in Urec's Log is at a distinct disadvantage among the priestesses."

"How did you discover that?"

"Early in my training, I saw two of my friends, the most devout acolytes in our entire group, ignored in favor of far more ambitious young women. When I saw what was happening, it was like a bright lamp being lit in a dark room. That was the beginning of understanding for me." Kuari raised her eyebrows. "Once I grasped the politics, I realized I could have made quite a career in the church for myself— if I played that game."

"But you didn't."

Kuari shrugged. "I found it tedious. After I finished my training, I was a good marriage prospect. My father was a wealthy merchant, and he arranged for me to marry a soldan." She smiled. "But that hasn't been so glorious either."

"Maybe you've found your true calling as emissary to the Olabar court," Istar said. "You're certainly preferable to Ambassador Ualfor."

Kuari made a moue of displeasure. "You place me on a high pedestal indeed!"

Istar wanted to laugh but stopped herself. Still, Kuari's words worried her. Just what were her daughters learning behind these impenetrable stone walls? Maybe it was a good thing that Adreala had not entered the church after all.

Walking with a slow, ponderous tread, Ur-Sikara Erima emerged from the gilded doors behind the altar. The woman from Lahjar appeared to have been carved from dark wood. She stood, haughty, imposing, shielded from all distractions, the center of the universe—and the attendants in the church treated her as such.

Erima carried a heavy, ornate amulet cast from gold. It had age-softened edges, details blurred from exposure to tremendous heat in the burning of the main church in Ishalem so many years before. The ur-sikara lifted the Amulet of Urec, kissed its back, and placed the sacred relic on the altar behind her.

When Erima finished a brief homily, she lifted a large tome and set it upon the podium from which she preached. Istar's attention centered on the book, knowing what it was. *This* was why she endured the demeaning behavior of the sikaras.

"We have received another message written by Sikara Fyiri aboard the *Al-Orizin*. Hear now what she tells us." Erima opened the book, flipped past several of the torn pages, then read aloud, "As Urec watches over us, we have had continued smooth sailing. Each sunset, I lead the crew in prayers and I keep them on the proper path. We voyage for the glory of Ondun. We shall find the Key to Creation. I have faith in the crew. Pray with me."

Fyiri's log entry described weather patterns and strange fish, even a glimpse of sea serpents far away, but the distant sikara's message was bland and said little. Although Istar hung on every word, she felt empty and disappointed when the ur-sikara finished reading. "She does not mention my son," she muttered, "not once."

Kuari touched her arm. "And that surprises you? It is very intentional. Fyiri would only mention Saan by name if she had worked some victory or found some complaint. Take heart that she has found no way to use him."

Istar considered this. As the rest of the congregation began a shared prayer of benediction, she smiled as she mouthed the words, content with the subtle inference that Saan was all right.

74 *The Great Desert*

Traveling with a large caravan, Adreala enjoyed the rolling countryside of the Missinia soldanate while her grandfather regaled the merchants with stories of his journeys. Adreala had heard the tales before, but she listened anyway with a new perspective. She was on an adventure herself now. Whenever she got hot, dusty, or uncomfortable, she reminded herself that her sisters were spending their days in the church studying Urec's Log. Compared to that, even the biting flies were tolerable.

They arrived at Desert Harbor near sunset. Imir pointed out a cluster of sturdy canvas tents, a few pavilions of colorful silk, and three permanent structures made of wood and stone. He explained to Adreala that the population of the camp town had swelled in preparation for the next departure of sand coracles as soon as the winds turned.

"Each year this place grows busier and busier." Imir nodded with satisfaction. "I see we have fifteen coracles ready to go— five brand new, and ten repaired and refurbished."

The soldan's son Burilo, who administered the camp

town, emerged from the main building and regarded Adreala in surprise. He had tried to grow a full beard, but it remained patchy, though well combed. "So, this gangly girl is my cousin? Ah, I remember Omra was scrawny when he was your age, too."

Adreala returned his teasing. "Would you rather I was a fat horse-maiden? Then I'd never fit in a saddle, and I intend to travel far and wide."

Soldan Xivir came strutting up, guiding Imir and Adreala to the main administrative house. "I promise you a fine meal and a comfortable bed—enjoy it. Aboard a sand coracle, you'll barely have room to stand, much less sleep."

Throughout dinner, Imir continued to tell stories about his adventures among the Nunghals, bragging that he was the first true Uraban ever to gaze upon the southern ocean. But Adreala had heard a different version of the events from Saan. "I thought my brother and Sen Sherufa were the first to see the ocean. Didn't you come up afterward, Grandfather?"

Imir flushed. "A matter of semantics, my dear girl. Sherufa is a Saedran, and Saan—much as I love the boy— has a Tierran mother. And so, by default, I am the first true *Uraban* to have laid eyes upon the new sea." Adreala rolled her eyes at the frivolous distinction.

Later, her grandfather tucked her in as if she were a little girl, but Adreala didn't mind. She found the attentions comforting. Though tired, she slept restlessly, excited about the impending dangerous voyage across the Great Desert. Despite all his exuberance for the upcoming trip, Imir slept deeply and Adreala could hear him snoring in the next room.

Just before dawn, she crawled out of bed and pulled on her traveling clothes. She stood outside in the dry coolness, watching the first faint light of dawn seep into the eastern sky. Lamps burned in a few of the pavilions, in the windows of the main offices, and the cookhouse. A handful of early risers worked among the coracle baskets, which had been packed with cargo and supplies the previous evening. Two groggy merchants went in search of cookfires where they could find a cup of tea to accompany their morning meal.

As daylight brightened and people began to stir, Adreala watched the glow of a burnished gold sunrise spill across the dunes. She saw movement. Silhouetted figures rose like ants from behind the sandy slopes. Men on horses. First a dozen, then twenty, then more, in a long line. At least a hundred riders gathered there at the desert's edge, looking toward the camp city.

At first she thought they must be riders that Burilo had sent out to patrol the wasteland, but something seemed ominous about this group. Finally a merchant pointed them out to one of the local workers, and the man yowled an alarm. "Urec protect us—bandits! *Bandits!* We're under attack!"

The alarm acted as a signal to the strange riders. Adreala heard their leader whistle, and with a loud rumble the line of bandits rode down into the camp. The girl added her own screams of warning as the people in Desert Harbor scrambled about in panic. Guards, merchants, and harbor workers burst out of their pavilions and tents, grabbing weapons.

The bandits charged into the camp, slashing with swords, shooting arrows, creating total chaos. They kicked at campfires, hacked down tents, killed anyone in their way. Behind the first group of raiders came a second line of fifty men, carrying torches. Whooping, laughing, and goading each other, the bandits threw the burning torches onto the pavilions, igniting the cloth. With shouted curses, men scrambled to and fro, trying to save what they could.

Adreala saw that the raiders' target was the cluster of fifteen sand coracles that were packed and ready for departure. Striking down any man who stood in their way, the horsemen tossed fiery brands into the wicker baskets. The silk balloon sacks caught fire, and the flames grew larger and hungrier.

Adreala looked desperately for somewhere to hide in the turmoil. Burilo, Soldan Xivir, and her grandfather burst out of the main building and tried to rally the guards. Waving to get their attention, Adreala heard a galloping horse close by and turned to see a hideous rider bearing down on her. He had black paint on his face and clumps of red dye in his matted hair. His sword was raised, his eyes wide and gleeful, but when he saw her, he thrust the scimitar back in his sash and swooped an arm down to grab her.

Adreala crouched, ready to fight, although she had no weapon. She tried to jump out of the way, but the bandit second-guessed her. As his horse thundered past, he grabbed her roughly by the waist and threw her like a rolled rug onto the saddle in front of him. She struggled, but he grabbed her hair and yanked her head back so fiercely that the pain sent a thunderclap through her skull. She tried to claw him, but his grip was like iron. The horse kept running.

Attackers poured through the camp in an unstoppable wave. Another bandit rode up alongside, regarding her with scorn. "She's a child, Norgo—why waste time on her? Slit her throat and save the weight for supplies we can steal."

The painted bandit growled, "Think about it—why would a *girl* be here? Must be someone important."

"You have sand in your brain. Do what you will. I'm grabbing more wineskins." The other bandit peeled off. Many of their comrades continued to wreak destruction. When Desert Harbor was in flames and bodies lay strewn on the ground, they all wheeled around and raced back into the open dunes, their horses laden with wine, food, and stolen goods.

Behind them, all fifteen sand coracles were engulfed in fire and smoke.

75 *Southern Ocean*

Though Asaddan still suffered from bouts of seasickness, the return voyage was far less harrowing than their uncertain outbound trip. This time, they knew the voyage was *possible*. At Ishalem, Soldan-Shah Omra had filled their cargo hold with exotic goods to awe and tempt the other Nunghal-Su. Considering the gold, jewels, and silk fabrics stowed belowdecks, Asaddan concluded that the results were worth a few weeks of discomfort and nausea. Every man aboard was going to be rich upon returning to the Nunghal clans.

Triumphant, Shipkhan Ruad was an entirely different person from the man who had been disgraced by the wreck of his ship. Now his crew treated him as a hero, forgetting his mistakes. Ruad loved to stand at the bow of the ship, looking at the curling waves and daydreaming.

Asaddan stood beside his Nunghal cousin. "Aren't you glad you listened to my advice and dared to take this voyage? You'll be celebrated among the clans—you know that, don't you?"

"That was my plan, friend. There's gold and jewels in our treasure chests, but I'll take my treasure in respect and prestige among the Nunghal-Su."

"Oh, does that mean you grant me your share of the profits?"

Ruad laughed. "I wouldn't go *that* far!"

They voyaged south for weeks and rounded the coast, heading east until they entered familiar waters. After dispersing from a clan gathering, Nunghal-Su ships wandered the waters in a loose confederation, living off of the sea.

Ruad's ship finally encountered a group of fourteen vessels from allied families. The shipkhan sent up signal flags to request a meeting of clan elders. Some of the other shipkhans were gruff or skeptical, making snide comments. "So, Ruad, lost any ships lately?"

But Ruad paraded across the deck of his own ship, wearing colorful clothing given to him by the soldan-shah. "I lost nothing and gained much. My ship voyaged far past any explored coastline, headed north, and discovered a route to the land of Uraba."

One of the captains scoffed. "Did you find sea witches and mermaids as well?"

"I was too busy filling my cargo hold with riches. Would you like to see?" Planting his hands on his hips, Ruad commanded his sailors to carry a sample of the chests over to the other ship to show the bounty Omra had given him. "Uraba is a wealthy land, and the people are eager to trade with us. I can lead you there, if you're interested in being rich."

The proof of Ruad's claims immediately changed the attitude of the clan elders. He continued to tempt them with the promise of riches. "We braved the unknown and marked our charts. Soldan-Shah Omra and the Urabans are our friends and allies—not to mention rich trading partners. Once we reprovision, I intend to go back there. We invite you to accompany us—if you have the balls for it. I promised the soldan-shah we'd bring more Nunghals next time, but if the dangers worry you too much . . ."

"The Urabans are in the middle of a war and need fighters," Asaddan interjected. "The soldan-shah promises to pay well for any man who is not afraid of an adventure."

"This will require a council meeting." One of the stern older shipkhans shook his head. "That isn't where we had planned to sail."

Ruad rolled his eyes with a confident, lighthearted disrespect he would never have dared show the elders before. "And where did you plan to sail? Nowhere! I know what courses you set. Your families move across the waters like aimless buffalo move across the plains. Why not choose a destination with a purpose?"

Next to Ruad, Asaddan gave a nonchalant shrug. "Of course, if *you're* not interested, we'll find other Nunghal-Su ships whose shipkhans are fond enough of profits."

Ruad directed his sailors to pack up the samples of treasure, then he and Asaddan headed back to their own ship. When they were out of earshot, the shipkhan whispered enthusiastically to his friend, "They will join us—I saw it in their eyes!"

"Why stop there? There must be other groups out in the waters. Let's assemble the largest flotilla possible."

"By our course, I can make sure we encounter more clan groupings before we head for Lahjar again. By the time we leave, even those who don't decide to go with us will have heard of my travels. The story will spread, and the rumors will grow. The great Shipkhan Ruad—*that's* what I want."

Asaddan chuckled. "In that case, cousin, I shall help spread the rumors myself."

76 *The* Dyscovera

Rising up from the waves, the black-and-gold serpent blasted spray from its blowhole. Its jagged fins sawed like notched sword blades through the water as it warily circled the *Dyscovera*. The creature looked exactly like the one that had attacked Criston in the wreckage of the *Luminara*, devoured poor Prester Jerard, and dragged the rickety raft for leagues across the uncharted sea.

He raced across the deck, yelling, "Damn you and your kind!" He kept a white-knuckled grip on his dagger, ready to stab the monster if it should snatch him from the deck. "Grab your bows and harpoons! When it gets closer, aim for the soft flesh inside its maw!"

"I don't want to *see* the inside of its mouth," Kjelnar growled as he knocked off the lock to the weapons storage chest.

Sailors scrambled to grab bows and arrows as the first mate handed them around. Without any sort of military precision, the men strung the bows, nocked arrows, and let fly even as the sea serpent threw out another challenge. The shafts bounced off the ebony scales, provoking the creature to rush closer in a froth of splashing foam.

At a run, Prester Hannes bolted past Criston to the bow, his countenance ablaze with fervent purpose. The wind flapped his clothes, and he clenched his fishhook pendant. "By the power of Aiden, I command thee *begone*!" From memory, he shouted out verses from the Book of Aiden that included stern invocations against evil.

The creature lurched toward the *Dyscovera* like a serpentine spear. Seeing the telltale lash of its head, Criston yelled, "Brace yourselves! It'll charge." The archers loosed another volley; this time one of the shafts struck inside the monster's mouth, which only enraged it further.

But as it drew close, the sea serpent thrashed and hesitated, raising its long and supple body high out of the water. It stopped its charge, as if it had run up against an unseen barrier.

Kjelnar pointed wildly toward the *Dyscovera*'s bow. "The horn! Look at Raathgir's horn!" The milky, knurled shaft shone with a cold blue luminescence.

The monster thrashed from side to side, intimidated. It was close enough that Criston could see runnels of water pouring from its black-and-gold scales, but it could not cause any damage. The beast opened its mouth, as if its jaw had come unhinged. Its forked tongue flailed back and forth like a whip, but it refused to come closer to the glowing horn.

Etched with verses from the Book of Aiden, the relic was

connected through sympathetic magic to its counterpart on the altar in the main kirk in Calay. Until now, Criston had not entirely believed Iborian tales of the ice dragon's magic, but the power came from somewhere—protecting the ship from the sea serpent.

Criston stood at the side of the ship, staring it down, looking right into the slit of its reptilian eye. He had seen an eye like that, much too close, just before a similar beast had killed kindly old Prester Jerard. Criston did not waver now.

The monster strained against the invisible barrier, but could not attack as the *Dyscovera* sailed on. Defeated, the thwarted serpent snorted an indignant burst from its blowhole and dropped its head into the water again, cutting a path in the opposite direction as it sank slowly.

Laughing, the Iborian shipwright hammered his chest with one fist. "Raathgir has protected us!"

Prester Hannes looked patiently at the first mate and gave a slow shake of his head. "It wasn't your superstition about the horn but my prayers that drove the monster away."

Criston intervened before the two could argue. "We are protected by the grace of Ondun, whatever form it may take. What matters is that the *Dyscovera* is safe, and we can continue our voyage."

77 *The* Al-Orizin

All across the uncharted Middlesea, Saan saw nothing but water, endless water . . . until a trio of golden sea serpents approached. The lookout bellowed an alarm, and crewmen raced to the bow, taking up spears.

Grigovar held a harpoon in each hand. "You will find me a difficult mouthful to swallow! Ask your brother, who lies dead back in the reefs." But the monsters did not react as he brandished the weapons.

Yal Dolicar tugged at leather laces to secure the knife-blade prosthetic to his stump. "If one of those things tries to swallow me, I'll cut my way out, just like Grigovar did."

Saan stared at the three serpents. "Hold a moment, you two. Let's not provoke them just yet."

The three creatures were gorgeous, their wet scales reflecting the yellow sunlight. Curious, they circled the strange vessel, blasting vapors from their blowholes, then dropped beneath the waves and swam away.

Relieved, Saan turned to Sen Sherufa. "That's enough excitement for one day."

"Another story to tell Imir, when we get back home."

Fyiri emerged from her cabin, holding a large golden fern in one hand. Saan wondered if she intended to take credit for driving away the monsters, but she had lost her moment. Instead, the sikara took a stance of authority and caught the attention of all the men. "Not all sea serpents are dangerous, but they have a cursed origin. Such monsters are the offspring of Bouras—the gigantic serpent that girdles the world, an enormous beast that no man's imagination can fully encompass. The Father Serpent is the personification of evil that thrives in our world."

She glared at the crew, as if blaming each one of them. "Long before He departed from our world, Ondun attempted to stop Bouras and his deceit. He commanded the Father Serpent to bite his own tail, so that he could no longer speak lies. He must remain trapped like that until he is freed. After countless centuries, Bouras has grown so large that he encircles the entire world."

Fyiri gestured across the open water, to where the three golden creatures had disappeared. "If you fear *those* serpents, remember that they are just the tiniest offspring, the infant children of Bouras. Pray that our voyage does not take us across the great monster's path."

When the crew muttered with fear and anxiety, Saan was annoyed with Fyiri for preying upon their superstitions. He laughed, showing just what he thought of such nonsense. "Well, then we'll keep a sharp watch!" He sent a second man up the mainmast to the lookout nest. "If the Father Serpent girdles the entire world, then he had better get out of our way. No monster is going to stop this voyage."

The sleek ship sailed on into uncharted waters, under blue skies and with no threat of sea serpents. For all the excitement and fear of sailing into the unknown, Saan lounged on the deck, waiting for something to happen. They had traveled countless leagues, but he didn't feel any closer to finding the Key to Creation. Even Sen Sherufa remained unable to interpret the Map.

Yal Dolicar often wore a frilly white shirt despite the heat of the sun, while most of the *Al-Orizin*'s crew stripped down to keep cool. Dolicar had affixed the carved wooden hand to his wrist, and now rubbed it self-consciously. "I listened to Sikara Fyiri give her report from the Olabar church last night." The priestess often read pleasant but meaningless words that appeared on the pages of the sympathetic journal. The mere fact that she remained in communication with Uraba reassured the men. "She makes it sound as if there is no news and no conflict back in Olabar. Everything seems to be right with the world. Suspiciously so, don't you think?"

"What do you mean?"

With a shrug, Dolicar hunkered down alongside his captain. "Sir, do you actually *know* what the sikaras have written, back and forth? Have you looked at the sympathetic journal yourself to see what the words really say?"

Saan frowned. "That's Fyiri's business. Same as my captain's log is *my* business."

Dolicar chuckled. "Don't kid yourself, Captain. You should be more suspicious."

Saan tapped his fingertips together as he considered. Fyiri did have sole control over the sympathetic journal, and she could be writing anything, spreading false rumors to the ur-sikara. She could also be distorting, or completely falsifying, the reports that supposedly appeared in the volume. Saan sat up straighter as the wheels began to turn in his mind. "Thank you for your concern, Dolicar. I'll take it under advisement and make a decision."

Unwilling to remain in her quarters all day, a restless Sikara Fyiri walked the deck, visited the cargo hold and the crew bunks. She spent time in the galley criticizing the cook, though he pretended to be deaf to her complaints.

When she was gone, Saan boldly walked to the door, worked the small latch, and entered the priestess's private room. Fyiri had left small candles burning in covered lamps—a fire hazard aboard a sailing ship, but the stern sikara believed that she operated outside of rules. It would be good to remind her of her place.

Saan found the sympathetic journal and opened it, flipping the sheets of paper that were torn in half. He scanned the letters written on each page—lines in Fyiri's strong and determined script, and other words written in a more formal hand.

He saw immediately that Fyiri was indeed withholding information, just as Yal Dolicar had suspected. She had not recounted any of this news to the *Al-Orizin*'s crew. He read entries describing Soldan-Shah Omra's ambitious scheme to dig a great canal across the isthmus, news that Saan's half-sister Adreala had gone south with her grandfather to visit the Nunghals, and that his other two sisters were now acolytes in the church.

When he read that Cithara was being groomed for a "special mission," the wording raised Saan's suspicions, and he studied more closely, flipping through the later entries as Fyiri's mysterious correspondent grew more careless with her reports. When he finally read the writer's name, the word struck like an icicle in Saan's spine. *Villiki!* Villiki was still alive!

The woman had gone into hiding and somehow worked her way into the main church; now she was using the sympathetic journal to communicate with the sikara aboard the *Al-Orizin*.

Fyiri had kept all this from him.

The cabin door opened, and he heard the woman laughing seductively; Fyiri held Grigovar by the arm, leading him into her cabin with obvious intent.

Saan closed the journal with a loud thump. When the

sikara saw him lounging at her writing desk, her face blazed with fury. "What are you doing in my quarters?"

Saan kept his demeanor cocky and confident. "Your quarters, perhaps, but *my* ship. I can do as I wish." He held up the journal.

Fyiri lunged wildly for it. "How dare you!"

He rose to his feet, all nonchalance gone. "You have withheld information from your captain. You exchange private messages with a woman who attempted to poison the soldan-shah. It seems the church of Urec now gives this traitor secret sanctuary." He tucked the book close under his arm. "Obviously you cannot be trusted."

Fyiri clutched Grigovar's arm and snapped at him. "Well, what are you going to do about this? Aren't you going to defend me? Look what he's doing!"

Grigovar burst out laughing. "What am *I* going to do? Why, I'm going to follow the captain's orders! You think you control me just because I sleep with you?" He guffawed at the thought. "You have a very high opinion of yourself, Priestess. If a woman's bed turns cold to me, my hand is warm enough. You place too great a value on your skills as a lover."

Fyiri was dumbstruck, and Saan couldn't help grinning. "I am confiscating this journal, Sikara. Obviously it is too powerful and too tempting for you."

"But only I can use it! You will never be able to send messages back." She gave a haughty sniff.

"If our messages go into the hands of Villiki, the messages are of no use to me. There is nothing I wish that woman to know. Besides, Sen Sherufa is perfectly capable of transmitting any words that I deem necessary."

"Sen Sherufa! A Saedran woman?"

"Yes. And I trust her far more than I trust you."

78 *Olabar Palace*

Soldan-Shah Omra remained in the palace for only a few days before departing for Inner Wahilir and then continuing to Yuarej to discuss the border dispute with Soldans Huttan and Andouk. As he prepared to leave again, Omra grumbled to Istar, "Maybe I should just let their First Wives resolve the issue between them."

"Women solve problems differently than men do," she said.

"Sometimes that is a good thing," he said. "Sometimes it isn't."

"I could talk to Kuari and Sharique, let them prove themselves as your emissaries." Since being placed in their new positions, the five First Wives had begun to take great interest in matters of politics.

"Let me try it my way first." And then he was gone with the morning tide, sailing westward along the coast, leaving her to manage the affairs of Uraba. No one questioned Istar now when she received visitors and discussed matters of state with various ministers of trade, finance, and culture. The First Wives came and went, bearing messages from the soldans, accompanied by Olabar guards.

Omra had been gone for two days when a stunned and frightened-looking traveler stumbled into the Olabar court, exhausted from his long journey. The man, a gaunt pilgrim, looked as though he hadn't eaten in some time. With a sickened expression, Kel Rovic hurried him forward. "My Lady, listen to what this man has seen."

The anxious traveler supported himself on Rovic's arm. Though befuddled to see her instead of the soldan-shah on the dais, he fell to his knees. "Fashia's Fountain has been desecrated! Aidenists, my Lady—they attacked, slew all of the priestesses. The temple is burned, the fountain and pool fouled."

Istar sat bolt upright, her fingers clutching the fabric cushions so tightly that her knuckles turned white. Hot blood pounded in her ears. "How do you know this?"

The man hung his head, shuddering. "I went on pilgrimage there to cleanse myself of my sins. The boat dropped me off with three fellow pilgrims. There were no other boats, and we saw no one else on the trail or at the landing. We thought it odd, because the shrine is usually crowded this time of year. When we hiked up the path, the stench ... the bodies were bloated, pieces floating in the pool. ... It must have been days since the attack."

The traveler continued, glassy-eyed with shock. "The birds had already found the bodies. No one was alive. No one. And the fountain itself, the smell!" He began to sob. "I knew I had to come to Olabar straightaway. I used all my money—joined a caravan, bought a horse, paid passage on three different ships. I traveled for more than a week, but I could not get here any faster."

Istar struggled to find her voice. She had seen that beautiful place less than a month before. "How do you know Aidenists were responsible?" She had to control herself, to keep from screaming. Of course, there could be no other answer.

"This was on the altar at the fountain." The man reached into his clothing, withdrew a silver fishhook pendant, and tossed it to the floor ahead of him. "They left it, like a taunt."

Istar sat rigid with horror and outrage as she struggled to control her inner turmoil. She did not want to taint her memory of the lovely shrine, the peaceful, devoted pilgrims, the shared experience with her daughters. And poor, determined Istala had thrown herself into her church studies so she could become one of the special priestesses chosen to serve at Fashia's Fountain. She might have been among those slaughtered. . . .

Istar closed her eyes against the thought and found herself breathing heavily, her heart pounding. The loud conversation in the throne room receded to a droning buzz in her ears. She felt a surge of fury toward the violent barbarians who had caused so much harm, who had violated such a sacred site, the damned Aidenists who had slaughtered those innocent—

She trembled uncontrollably as she realized what she was thinking, torn between her identities as Istar and Adrea. Long ago it had been the other way, with hateful Urecari raiders killing all the people in Windcatch, burning the small kirk on the hill. She had lost so much . . . her life, her whole future.

But she had also gained this, and her lovely daughters. And Omra, a man who also loved her. How could an *Aidenist* do such an awful thing? She felt as if her heart might rip itself in half.

Istala could have been murdered there!

Tears blurred her vision, but she dashed them away, rose

to her feet. "Kel Rovic, see that this man is fed, given fresh clothing, and comfortable chambers. I will send riders out to find the soldan-shah and bring him back to Olabar with all due speed. He needs to deal with this himself."

Istar paid no mind to the hubbub around her as she retreated to her private chambers, where she refused all visitors. Anxious to reassure herself, to find some kind of stability, she went to the special aromatic chest that held her private things and, after rummaging among her keepsakes, withdrew the battered and waterstained old letter, crumbling pages that had withstood long months or years in a bottle that drifted across the sea.

Although she had read the words so many times that they were burned into her memory, she loved the act of touching the long-faded ink and the words that her husband had written to her. It helped her heart slow its furious beating, but also left an empty longing that could never be filled. Tucked into the handwritten pages was a single strand of hair, brittle and pale—*her* hair—from a lock she had given Criston when he sailed on the *Luminara* twenty years earlier.

Now life was more confusing than ever, with so many echoes of violence. If Criston could be here with her now ... or if only Omra hadn't gone away. And those thoughts only increased her confusion.

The next morning, she awoke from a sleep that had soaked her pillows with tears. Thinking of her daughters, especially Istala, she dressed and made her way to the main Urecari church, followed by four palace guards. Though Omra, Saan, Imir, and Adreala were gone, she felt an urgent need to be with her family. But Istala and Cithara were still close by, and she had not seen them since they became acolytes. Oh, the sikaras sent sketchy reports of the girls' progress, but Istar longed to look deep into their eyes so she could know their hearts.

The news about Fashia's Fountain had already spread throughout the city. Groups of angry citizens demanded retribution in squares and from balconies. The sikaras chanting in the streets of Olabar, not content merely to burn prayer strips in braziers, built large bonfires, into which hundreds of people tossed handwritten messages. These fires roared in every public square, surrounded by infuriated followers of Urec. The messages on the prayer strips beseeched Ondun to come forth and wipe out all Tierrans.

Hearing this, Istar knew that many Urabans were thinking of her as well, blaming her. When angry men and women saw her in the streets, they saw a hated *Tierran*. But she walked along with determination, ignoring the cold glances, as she always did. Could they not see that she was hurting just as much as they were?

At the formal entrance to the main church, a mid-ranked priestess greeted Istar with cool civility and poorly hidden scorn, which was not surprising after the many critical sermons the sikaras had given about her. Istar had no patience for that nonsense. "I will see my daughters," she commanded with a voice surprisingly steady and even. She didn't care whether or not the priestesses liked her. She was still a mother and the soldan-shah's First Wife.

The woman at the doorway frowned at her. "Your daughters are acolytes now. They belong to Urec."

"Then Urec can let me borrow them for a few moments. Summon Cithara and Istala."

The priestess continued to scowl. The guards in Istar's entourage shifted uncomfortably; they too had heard the ur-sikara's spiteful sermons, and while they knew that Istar had Omra's blessing and protection, they did not want to openly challenge the church.

A second sikara who outranked the first came to the doorway. "Cithara is unavailable, fasting and in private contemplation. She cannot be disturbed. I can, however, bring Istala to you. But it must be a brief visit, for she has prayers and scribing duties of her own."

"I would not wish to hinder her progress in the service of Urec. I just need to speak with her."

"Wait here." The two priestesses closed the door in her face, making Istar and the guards stand outside for long minutes until they returned leading the girl between them. Young Istala brightened when she saw her mother, bowed formally, then accepted a quick, strong embrace.

"I'm so glad to see you. After what happened at Fashia's Fountain, I just wanted to reassure myself that you were safe."

The girl barely held her composure. "It was horrible news, and I can't stop thinking about poor Luaren, but I *am* going to be a sikara, Mother. The Fountain will be restored, and I *will* go there."

One of the priestesses stood frowning at the church doorway. "There is nothing to fear. She will have Urec's protection."

Istar pointed out, "The slaughtered sikaras also had his protection."

Nevertheless, having seen and touched her daughter, she felt calm again. Cithara would also be safe within the walls of the church. And Adreala was with her grandfather, who would never let anything happen to her. She tried to convince herself that they would all be safe, happy, and contented.

But she did not succeed.

79   *Olabar, Main Urecari Church*

Despite her secret influence within the church, Villiki felt imprisoned, and while her hatred gave her focus, it did not grant her freedom. Many years had passed since she had been stripped, exiled, disgraced—but the people of Olabar had not forgotten her. Certainly not Omra. Certainly not Kel Rovic or the palace guards. Certainly not the Tierran slave woman who now called herself the soldan-shah's First Wife.

Villiki had not forgotten either.

Oh, she had comforts in her lavish quarters deep underground. She had exotic food and fine Abilan wines, treasures, clothes, comforts. But she was neither happy nor free.

By the light of several large bright candles scented with cardamom oil, Villiki sat at her desk and opened the twinned counterpart of the ship's journal aboard the *Al-Orizin*. She perused the earlier entries Sikara Fyiri had written in her cabin far away on the other side of the world. Why had she stopped? Something must have happened.

A priestess guard rapped at Villiki's door, disturbing her. "Your forgiveness, my Lady. Ur-Sikara Erima has come to speak with you. She begs your indulgence."

With an annoyed sigh, Villiki closed the journal and concealed it. The ur-sikara was wrapped firmly around her finger, but the woman asked far too many questions, required too much assistance. Villiki longed for the days when her predecessor Ur-Sikara Lukai—a strong, like-minded woman—had served the church. Erima was . . . far less than that.

The tall, dark-skinned woman entered the underground chamber and stood before Villiki's desk with a deferential bow, but her dark eyes sparkled with a sheen of anxiety. "I came because I was anxious to see you, my Lady, and to serve the church."

Of course you did. Villiki began to calculate just how many innat seeds it would take to keep Erima complacent.

When this woman from distant Lahjar had been chosen to take the place of Ur-Sikara Lukai, Erima had been viewed as an acceptable compromise among the factions within the church. Every priestess formed alliances and rivalries, but because she came from so far away, Erima was seen as separate from the core of church politics, far from squabbling partisan sikaras. Though considered a safe choice, the Lahjar candidate was a lukewarm alternative and spoke with a thick accent. People considered Erima unambitious, a bumpkin from a far-off and uncivilized land.

By rights, Villiki should have been ur-sikara herself, but that would never be possible. She had been forced to cement her influence in some other way.

As Erima waited, tense, a few droplets of sweat appeared on her brow. "I am ready to deliver the sermon you wish, as soon as it is written. Shall I summon the faithful so that they may anticipate a major address at this evening's sunset services?"

Villiki pretended not to know what the other woman really wanted. Just to emphasize Erima's subservience, she shuffled some papers on her desktop, moved items around to no real purpose, while the ur-sikara waited. Finally, with a sigh, Villiki reached into a drawer and removed a pouch made of soft calfskin. Slowly and tantalizingly, she undid the tie and spread open the pouch, drifting her fingers through the tiny dark seeds inside. With her fingertips, she pulled out a few and dropped them into the palm of her other hand. "I suppose a few more innat seeds will help you to concentrate so you can give a more passionate address."

"Yes, my Lady." Erima's gaze was fixed on the seeds. "Most assuredly so!" She was too anxious; perhaps Villiki had accomplished her goal too well.

"But if you consume too much, you might not be focused enough." Villiki reconsidered, then dropped two of the seeds back in the bag, to Erima's profound disappointment.

Before Villiki had first secretly offered them, Erima had never experienced the rush that innat seeds released in the body. Villiki had cautiously consumed only one or two, to demonstrate their safety, and the new ur-sikara had liked them … far too much. Villiki was magnanimous, giving Erima frequent doses of the seeds, so that the other woman was now thoroughly addicted. Villiki paid substantial bribes to the guards and priestesses to ensure that Erima did not find an alternate supply of the drug. She had to come here to beg, in order to satisfy her longing. That was the way it should be.

"I want you to appreciate what you have, Ur-Sikara. I want you to revel in the sunshine, enjoy your freedom to walk in Olabar." She tied the pouch again, put it away. "Every time you do so, think of me here, unable to see the light of day." On some nights, when it became unbearable, Villiki dressed like an old poor priestess and slipped out to walk the streets of Olabar. She kept her disguise close, but rarely risked using it.

Erima continued to stare at the seeds in her hand. "Someday I will secure a pardon for you, my Lady. Soldan-Shah Omra cannot rule forever."

"And I won't live forever, either!" Villiki tapped several sheets of paper on which she had written another invective-laden speech. "Here is what I want you to tell the people. You may have these few seeds now, and once I hear your degree of passion in delivering the sermon, I will calculate your reward."

Erima backed away. "Thank you, my Lady. It shall be done exactly as you say."

After the ur-sikara departed, the inner-circle priestess guards ushered in the young girl. Cithara was quiet and shy, with beautiful features that would someday blossom into a seductive loveliness just like her mother's. However, with Villiki's careful instruction, Cithara would not make the poor decisions, and would not be left defenseless, as Cliaparia had been. Only a weak and unskilled woman could have allowed her husband's love to fade, especially when competing against a worthless Tierran slave like Istar.

The girl bowed. "I am here for my lessons again, Lady Villiki."

"I'm pleased with the progress you are making, child.

Have you read the passages in Urec's Log that I pointed out to you?"

"Yes, I studied them carefully. The words of Urec cannot be questioned."

Villiki folded her hands before her on the desk. "Yes, and I am the one to interpret them for you." Cithara always seemed so attentive, so interested.

Each afternoon, Villiki spent hours grooming the girl, turning Cliaparia's daughter into a special weapon, an operative who could live right under the soldan-shah's nose. She had already told the girl what sort of woman Istar truly was. Even though the former slave had adopted Cithara and pretended to love her as much as she loved her own two daughters, she was still a *Tierran* woman, an Aidenist. And Aidenists always lied.

"This story will be painful for you, child, but you must hear the truth. Urec's Log tells us that we mustn't be afraid of the truth."

Cithara sat cross-legged on a rug on the hard stone floor and listened attentively.

"You know that *Istar* murdered your mother while your father was away conquering Ishalem for the glory of Ondun. *Istar* followed your mother to the docks and stabbed her once, twice, three times." Each time she said the woman's name, she added a heavy emphasis. "Poor Cliaparia could do nothing to defend herself. *Istar* pushed her dying body against the nets and fishhooks, then dumped her into the water, like nothing more than a bucket of fish guts."

Cithara sat stony-faced, troubled by the story. Villiki leaned farther over the desk. "And that isn't her only crime, you know. When she was just a slave girl, she lied and conspired against me and Ur-Sikara Lukai. She arranged for Lukai's poisoning, and she worked a spell on the former soldan-shah so that he banished me.

"You and I have reason to hate Istar more than anyone else, my dear child. She was just a slave, and an Aidenist at that . . . and now she fancies herself the soldan-shah's First Wife. But you can help me change all that. You can save us all."

Cithara nodded, listening with rapt attention.

80   *The Great Desert*

With Desert Harbor in disarray and the sand coracles nothing more than smoldering shells, Imir tried to restore some kind of order. Workers shoveled sand onto the fires, but the silk balloons had been consumed, the reinforced wicker baskets charred, all the trade goods destroyed. Surviving merchants fell to their knees, clutching their heads and wailing.

Two dozen guards, traders, and camp workers were dead and many more injured. The bodies of several hideously ugly bandits, their faces disfigured by ornamental scars and tattoos, were piled off to one side like garbage. Furious, Soldan Xivir muttered, "Apparently, we have more bandits to kill!" He ordered the bandit corpses propped up on crossbars so that desert vultures could come in and feed.

Burilo was not convinced. "I doubt that will be a deterrent, Father. We've wiped out their leaders and their camps many times, yet they come back to prey upon us. The bandits won't fear a handful of rotting corpses."

Xivir's face contorted with disgust. "No ... but *I* will appreciate it."

Imir stalked among the permanent structures and tents, calling out for Adreala. He had seen her when the raid first began and hoped that she had found someplace to hide. With a sinking dread, he prodded all the mutilated bodies lined up on the ground. He bellowed her name, but she did not answer, and a thorough search by all the guards revealed no sign of her.

Finally, one of the traders called him over. The smaller man sat hunched and sweating, while the camp surgeon used a needle and tough silk thread to sew up a bleeding gash on his shoulder. The trader winced, but the surgeon paid no attention, sticking the needle in and tugging on the thread. "My Lord, I saw—I saw the girl! After one of the bandits wounded me, I fell and tried to scramble out of the way. I remember seeing a rider snatch up your granddaughter and throw her across his horse. He was the ugly one with red dye in his hair and black paint on his face."

Xivir's face flushed with fury. "That was Norgo himself."

"Why would the bandits take her? She's just a girl!" Imir looked around, demanding explanations from all those listening, but he didn't have to press for an answer. He could make his own guesses. "Xivir, mount up everyone who can ride. We are going in pursuit of the bandits *now*."

Burilo turned an awkward look at the wreckage of the camp and the number of wounded, but he did not argue.

He ran to fetch horses, while Soldan Xivir looked at his notched scimitar and cast it aside. "Bring me a new sword and one for the soldan-shah—and make sure they're sharp! All capable men, arm yourselves. We will ride these bandits into the sand and bury them!"

The knot in Imir's stomach pulled even tighter. He didn't let his despair show, but he knew very well that if they did not rescue Adreala within the first day or so, there might not be anything left to save.

By midmorning, the winds had picked up, stirring the loose sand and dust. The riders raced out of Desert Harbor before breezes erased the trail.

The bandits rode through the heat of the day and into the deepening dusk. Adreala never ceased struggling, never stopped trying to escape, although if she did manage to roll off the bandit leader's horse, she would surely die out here in the middle of the empty dunes. She didn't care.

Norgo had lashed her hands together in front of her; her wrists were raw and bleeding because she kept trying to break the bonds. Six times, she managed to get an elbow or foot into position where she could deliver a sharp blow to Norgo. Each time, in response, he slapped the side of her head.

Still, Adreala did not give up. Finally in disgust, Norgo struck her again, much harder. "You refuse to learn, girl!"

She wrenched herself around and spat at him, but the saliva flew past his face. "You are not my teacher."

Norgo looked at where she'd spat. "Not good to waste water out here." Then he laughed, slapped her again with a hint of playfulness, and rode on.

Though the bandits had spread out, they knew their common destination. After dark, the riders converged on a seemingly unremarkable hollow in the dunes. There was no spring here, no rocks, just sand.

Norgo dumped Adreala off the horse and she fell unceremoniously into the dust. It knocked the wind out of her, but she refused to cry out. She pulled her knees up to her chest and sat in a defensive posture, wary, watching.

The bandits camped under the light of the moon; they built no fire. After the horses were hobbled, Norgo squatted down and spoke with his men. Though they had lost some of their comrades at Desert Harbor, the bandits were satisfied they had inflicted much more pain and damage on the enemy.

The men ate stringy dried meat from their saddlebags, sipped from a waterskin they passed around, offering nothing to Adreala. Finally, Norgo approached her holding the waterskin. "Now, who are you, girl? You must be somebody important. Why were you at that camp?"

She refused to answer.

He jiggled the waterskin, tempting her. "Tell me your name, and I will give you a drink of water."

Adreala's throat was parched, her stomach rumbled, but she worked hard not to show her desperation. "My name is worth more than a sip of water."

He sloshed the water enticingly. "The value of a sip of water increases out here in the desert. Before long, you may think the price is not so high."

"Before long, I'll be rescued—and you will be dead in the sand with vultures pecking out your eyes!"

Norgo sat back and laughed. The other bandits guffawed

as well. "Then we'd better make use of you in the meantime. But what can you do for us? You're unskilled, scrawny . . . probably lazy, too."

"That's why I told you to leave her behind, Norgo," one of the men said. "Better off carrying another waterskin."

"You'll never know what I'm worth," Adreala said. "I'm not staying with you."

"You don't have much choice, brat." Norgo grinned. "I think you'll learn to like it out here in the desert. Ah, the freedom! We go where we want, take what we want. All this land is ours!"

"It's only sand." Adreala remained defiant, but her voice cracked because she was so thirsty. "You broke the commandments of Urec's Log. You have slain other Urecari. You stole from Ondun Himself by stealing the blessings He bestowed upon the people in Desert Harbor."

At this, Norgo and the others laughed louder. The black paint on the leader's face was beginning to peel and streak from his sweat. "My gods are the winds and the sand, girl— not some old ship's captain. I believe in what I can see and do."

Adreala was shocked. Though she felt no great calling to become a sikara, as her little sister did, she had never heard such outright blasphemy. Even the Aidenists believed in God. "You will die for what you have spoken and done."

Norgo gave her a dismissive gesture, then drank greedily from the waterskin in front of her, before sealing it and tossing it back to his comrades. "My people were here, eking out an existence in the Great Desert, long before any ancient ships came. We have nothing to do with your Urec or Ondun. To us, they don't exist."

Norgo's statement astonished her. She expected Ondun Himself to rise up from the sands to swallow these bandits because of the hateful words they spoke. She sat back against the dune and waited for divine intervention.

A capricious night breeze blew grains of stinging sand into her face, but she had expected much more of a response. Adreala was disappointed.

81 *Gremurr Mines*

On the ship's hull, the overlapping new armor plates looked like the polished scales of a sea serpent. Tukar had to shade his eyes from the reflected sunlight. "Workmaster Zadar, you have done a fine job, and Soldan-Shah Omra will be proud as well. The *Golden Fern* is going to be the most powerful warship in the Uraban navy."

The burly workmaster was not accustomed to excessive compliments. He had pressed the Aidenist slaves hard, but after so many years he was good at controlling them. "I simply did as the job required." However, Zadar could not hide the fact that he too was pleased. His new smelters and rollers had produced iron sheets that made the ship virtually indestructible. Her hull could not be smashed by reef or ramming vessel.

Feeling a sting of tears in his eyes, Tukar drew a deep breath, coughed, and turned away to cover his emotion. Yes, now he deserved his brother's forgiveness. All past crimes, suspicions, and questions would be washed away when the *Golden Fern* arrived in Olabar harbor. "The wind must have caught the fumes from the smelters." He wiped his eyes. He and his family would be going home as soon as the other ships were finished.

At first, when the Aidenist slaves learned that their work was to armor a Middlesea vessel, they laughed, knowing there was no passage to the Oceansea. The battleship would be a magnificent juggernaut, but it seemed ludicrous for Tukar and his men to waste so much metal and effort on a ship trapped on the wrong side of the isthmus.

But when new Tierran captives from Ishalem spread the news about Kel Unwar's great canal, the rest of the slaves understood what their enemies intended. The Aidenist workers resisted, and a few even tried to sabotage the rolling mills. Though it was not Zadar's policy to waste manpower, the point needed to be made, and he executed the three ringleaders and increased guards in the factories. Soon enough, the work routine returned to normal.

Omra had dispatched seven more ships to Gremurr, which were now tied up to special docks. As soon as the *Golden Fern* was finished, Tukar would begin work armoring the other vessels. And after that, he, Shetia, and Ulan would sleep in the palace, eat fine foods, visit the markets and the souks. He could raise his boy with all the advantages he deserved, and Ulan could have as many puppies as he wanted.

Tukar walked the deck of the *Golden Fern*, pretending to inspect the joints and bolts. He rapped the iron cladding with his knuckles and listened to the pleasant ringing sound. Much heavier than before, the vessel rode low in the water, but she had been designed for hauling metals and ores.

When he pronounced the vessel fit for launch, Tukar

summoned the mine workers to celebrate its completion. The slaves dutifully complied, but their cheers were not as enthusiastic as Tukar would have liked. How these Aidenist captives must hate what they had been forced to do! At least the Urecari guards applauded sincerely.

Tukar brought his wife and son to the docks so they could watch the final touches to the first ironclad ship. Shetia and Ulan stared with wide eyes as the crews used ropes and pulleys to align a jagged attachment of cast iron, like a saw blade, along the prow.

"It looks like the teeth in a sea monster's jaw," Ulan cried. "That ship will cut through an Aidenist vessel like a gutting knife cuts a fish!"

"That's the reason for the design, son." Tukar regarded the other seven vessels ready to receive similar plating. "Before long, the soldan-shah will have a fleet of invincible ships."

"Does that mean the Aidenists will all die soon?" Unlike Tukar, the boy did not long to go to Olabar; Ulan had never known any life other than here at Gremurr.

"I don't like all this talk about death and killing." Tukar's wife tugged the boy's arm. "However, if these ships end the war sooner, I'll be happy enough to go home to Olabar."

When the sails were hoisted, the Eye of Urec stared out from blood-red silk. The crew stood at the rails and waved as they departed for the capital city, where the *Golden Fern* would inspire all Urabans. As soon as the Ishalem canal was completed, this vessel would lead the Uraban fleet on a decisive strike.

Tukar touched his wife's shoulder. "Once the other ships are completed, we can sail away from Gremurr, and we'll let

Zadar have this place. He can rule here as long as he likes, even in peacetime. Uraba will always need the metals from these mines."

The bald workmaster chuckled. "Why would I want to leave my home? I'd rather smell the forge than perfumes and incense."

82 *Iboria*

Plodding along on the fourth day of the overland march, Destrar Broeck surveyed the vast unbroken steppes that were still dotted with patches of snow even in high summer. Even after many days of travel, they could barely see the gray outline of mountains on the horizon. His boots were sodden and his feet were cold as he splashed through muck and bogs, but the large force of soldiers and shaggy beasts still had a long way to go.

"I didn't realize that mammoths had such an ... odor about them," said Iaros, wrinkling his nose above his drooping mustache. Around them, the restless herd thundered along toward the foothills. "I've never seen so many mammoths together in one place."

Broeck drew a deep breath, not minding the musky smell of the beasts. "Never in history has there been such a herd. No, not a herd—an *army*."

In searching the steppes, he and his nephew had succeeded beyond their wildest expectations. More than a hundred of the enormous creatures lumbered along, churning the ground, stripping the landscape of anything edible.

A few nomadic herders had come on the trek to tend the beasts, but most of the work was done by Tierran soldier-trainees who had been assigned to Iboria Reach. This long march was not part of their traditional training, but Broeck's task was to prepare young soldier-recruits for war in whatever form it might take.

The mammoths moved at an unhurried pace, pausing to munch tall grasses or drink from scummy ponds. Some beasts slurped the thick green algae as if it were a delicacy. A dozen of the bull mammoths were already partially domesticated, and Broeck set the herders and his young soldiers to work taming the rest. Like any army, brute strength was not enough; they would need discipline to crush the enemy.

Trotting along beside the mammoths, four young soldiers grabbed the russet-colored hair and hauled themselves up onto the beasts' backs, encouraged by the nomadic herders. Two of the big creatures shied at the disturbance, shuffling from side to side, but the soldiers held on, whistling and yelling to each other. Some mammoths didn't mind being ridden and kept walking amiably at a steady mile-eating pace. Even so, Broeck had no idea how well the beasts would tolerate the heavy armor that Destrar Siescu was even now fashioning. . . .

Up ahead, the lead cow mammoth lifted her large head and unleashed an earsplitting bellow, which was echoed by two more mammoths, then all of them. Their trumpeting thunder rolled across the steppes.

Iaros trudged along on the ground, working to keep up with his uncle and the mammoths. It was midafternoon, but the temperature had already begun to drop. He wiped sweat from his brow. "We've made such good progress in the past few days, maybe we should stop early tonight, Uncle. All of us could use a rest, even the mammoths."

"Look around you, Iaros. With a herd this large, how much food do they leave behind? They're stripping the ground bare as they move along. If we stop for too long, the beasts will get hungry and restless. Do *you* want to try and control a restless herd?"

Iaros looked at the trampled ground, the stubble and gnawed roots that remained after the herd had passed. He swallowed. "Yes, we'd better keep moving."

Broeck pointed toward the distant mountains. "We have many leagues to go before we stop for the day. Many leagues." He knew that once they reached the mountains, the temperatures would get colder, and there would be less food for them to eat.

By the time they reached the Gremurr mines, the hundred mammoths would be hungry and ornery—and very dangerous.

83 *Corag Mountains*

Bundled in furs and thick gloves, Destrar Siescu sat in the base camp near where the slave crews had been laboring for months to carve a route through the rugged crags. Raga Var had found the easiest path in the cold mountains, marking a way for the Tierran army to cross snow-patched bowls and high hanging valleys. But along the tight passes and sheer cliffs, a road needed to be chiseled out—a path wide enough to accommodate the enormous beasts that were on their way from Iboria.

By now, swarms of Urecari prisoners from the Alamont and Corag internment camps had cleared a large portion of the path. Sullen teams of slaves wielded heavy hammers, shovels, and pickaxes to widen the rock ledges. Twenty laborers had died already from exhaustion, mishaps, or rockslides, but Siescu could always replenish his work crews.

A large fire blazed in front of the destrar's tent, and he hunched close for warmth. Scavenging wood was not easy above treeline, but Siescu's men regularly delivered cartloads of split logs from the forests below. Thus the new road had already proved its worth.

A scrawny man trotted up to him wearing a large grin and patched furs; a long bow hung across his shoulders. His hair was a matted mess, and his beard stuck out in all directions. He tossed a fat marmot on the ground near the campfire. "Here, Destrar. We'll skin it and roast it for dinner."

"Thank you. I'll have my chef prepare a succulent feast." Siescu had always found marmot meat to be greasy and gamey, but it was better than the lizards and lichens the scout had brought the day before. Raga Var was like a pet cat who brought offerings to please his master, and the destrar found the dedication both amusing and endearing. Siescu did not discourage him; the scout seemed to thrive on demonstrating his skills to all the people of Corag, though he still preferred to be alone in the wilderness.

With a longing thought of the warm, heated chambers of Stoneholm, the destrar waited for his daily report. "So how close are we to completion? Now that we've spent weeks chopping our way through this damned pass, don't tell me you've discovered an easy route."

Raga Var glanced up at the pale gash that the workers had hacked through the mountainside. "That *is* the easy way, Destrar. Within a few days, we'll reach smooth traveling again. After that, only one more major section of rough rock to clear and we'll be on the doorstep of the Gremurr mines." He hunkered down near the fire, extending his hands to warm them, though he had never been troubled by the cold before.

"Destrar Broeck should arrive with his mammoths and soldiers soon. If I can carve a road through a mountain range, he can lead a few shaggy beasts on a country walk." He sat closer to Raga Var, not bothered by the man's thick bodily smell. The two had an odd but solid friendship. "We have to be finished before the snows of autumn make the mountains impassable, and before someone from the Urecari mines discovers what we're doing. Is there any way we can speed up the work crews?"

Raga Var was eager to be moving again. "Let's go look." His grin showed bad teeth. He added with uncharacteristic humor, "Maybe you can give the slaves a pep talk, Destrar."

Siescu responded with a rude snort.

Leaving the camp, the two men headed up into the jumbled talus where workers toiled on the trail. The bright crystalline clink of hammers, pick blades, and wedges rang out in a discordant melody. The destrar's guards growled at the slaves to work harder and faster, but to little effect. A rush and rumble of rocks slid down a cliffside as haulers dumped pallets of debris. The vanguard of the roadbuilding crew pressed ahead to move some of the rubble;

individual men scrambled out on the rocks, scouting the way.

As Siescu studied the workers strung out along the cliffside, he mused about how—after their conquest of the Gremurr mines—he could use this road for regular caravan travel from the Middlesea back up into Corag. If the illicit Urecari mines were as productive as Prester Hannes claimed, then this new trade route would be a boon for all of Tierra.

The guards whistled an alarm, pointing far ahead and brandishing swords. One of the Urecari slave laborers had been sent forward along a treacherous section of cliff to mark the path, and now he bolted. Far from the main mass of slaves, the prisoner scrambled over the rocks, leaving his companions behind.

Siescu shaded his eyes. "Where does he think he's going?"

"Home. We're close to the last pass."

Concern made the destrar's face flush. "If he gets to the Gremurr mines, he'll sound the alarm, ruin our element of surprise, and give the Curlies time to build defenses."

Raga Var secured his bow on his shoulder. "Don't worry. He won't make it." Without another word, the scout sprinted off, dropping away from the main path where the soldiers were scrambling after the escaped prisoner. He bounded like a mountain goat from one boulder to another, slipping expertly down a steep rockface until he reached another ledge, then trotted along the unstable talus as if it were a wide country lane. He climbed hand over hand up a rock chute. Large stones bounced and tumbled behind him, but he kept moving, unconcerned.

Without a backward glance, the fleeing slave slipped and stumbled, but miraculously avoided any serious injury. He slid down a grade, no longer paying attention to the marked route. Terror and desperation added speed to his flight, but Raga Var closed the gap with an easy loping pace.

Watching from a distance, Siescu already knew the outcome of the chase. The scout had the situation well in hand.

Raga Var stopped at the edge of a boulder field and unslung his bow. He nocked an arrow and, in a movement so fluid that he didn't even seem to aim, let the arrow fly.

The shaft caught the slave in the back of the thigh. He grabbed his leg with a yelp, reeled, and fell onto a boulder that shifted beneath him. He tumbled off the edge of the cliff, crying out as he fell, until he struck the rocks below.

During the spectacle, the remaining Urecari workers had halted their labors. Though they made no sound, they must have been silently cheering the man, praying for his escape. Now they stared in horror.

One of the guards came up to Siescu, face flushed, eyes deeply troubled. "We should have watched the workers more closely, Destrar. Shall I shackle the rest of them? We dare not risk another escape."

"Chains will only hinder their progress, and we have a schedule to keep." Siescu shivered, but not in disgust at what he had just seen. He longed to be back in warm Stoneholm. "They've just seen what will happen if they try to run. Raga Var is our best deterrent."

The scout came bounding back, grinning with pride. Siescu congratulated him. "I knew I could count on you. May I offer you a reward for such fine service?"

Raga Var simply shrugged. "When have I worked for rewards or pay? If there's ever anything I need, I'll ask."

"And you shall have it. For now, though, it's best if you make yourself visible to the other slaves. Let them know you're watching, and that they can't get away."

"I will, Destrar. Enjoy your marmot dinner." Without waiting for further gratitude, Raga Var moved off, climbing up into the mountains. He never liked to be in the camp with too many people, preferring instead to huddle alone next to a boulder at his own meager fire.

After shouts and threats from the guards, the slave crews went back to work. Siescu was glad to know the scrawny scout was out there.

84 *Ishalem*

No one dared to challenge the Teacher on the streets of Ishalem. The dark figure glided past sweating work crews at the canal construction site, around the towering Urecari churches under construction, and arrived at the residence and headquarters of the provisional governor.

"I am here for Kel Unwar." The uneasy guards parted to allow entry, and the Teacher brushed past them.

When the visitor appeared at his private chambers, Unwar looked up from the scrolls, construction diagrams, and abacus on his desk and responded with a warm smile. "Close the door. We can speak in private here." After he pulled thick curtains to cover the windows, Unwar sat back down. "Relax and be comfortable."

The Teacher reached up and gratefully removed the smooth silver mask. Unwar heaved a long sigh. "It's good to see you without your trappings, sister."

The Teacher pulled back the hood and shook out her raggedly cropped dark hair. She rubbed her face. "That mask is who I am, and the mystique is my persona."

"You're beautiful, Alisi. You shouldn't have to hide."

"I'll stop hiding when all Aidenists are dead, for what they did to me."

Unwar poured his sister a goblet of golden wine. "We all hate them. I know what happened to you."

"You might know the words, but you don't *know* the depth of the wounds. No one can." Alisi pulled off her gloves and sat back. She took a grateful sip of wine, then ate some bread and grapes from a platter, but her deep scowl did not fade. "You have heard what those monsters did at Fashia's Fountain? The desecration? The slaughter? Typical of them."

"Yes, we received reports a few days ago. I sent a group of volunteers by fast ship to help the sikaras cleanse the site." His voice could not convey the revulsion and disbelief he had felt upon learning the news.

"It will never be cleansed ... nor will I. That's why we must inflict all the harm we can upon them, in the name of Urec." The dead spot inside her felt cold and leaden. Alisi could no longer recall how it felt to be a happy girl, a carefree daughter, a dedicated sister. It was like looking at the ashes of a long-dead fire and trying to find warmth and light. It had been there once, but not anymore.

Her heart and soul had been extinguished that night the crude Tierran sailors stole her from the Ouroussa docks. When she had tried to scream, they gagged her; when she struggled, they tied her legs and hands and carried her like a burlap sack of grain up the gangplank to their ship. The captain had laughed. When the ship had cast off and drifted out into the Ouroussa harbor, Alisi was sure she had heard her brother calling for her ... but no rescue ever came, and they sailed far out of sight of the Uraban coast.

The Tierran sailors had locked her in a small lightless cabin for days, starving her, until her spirit was broken. The Aidenist captain was a man named Quanas, his ship called the *Sacred Scroll*. He had kept her as his special pet, refusing to let the lusty crewmen do more than grope and leer at her. She had been so innocent then, a virgin, with very little knowledge about what was supposed to happen between a man and a woman. The stories she had heard about love-making made it sound like a joyful thing, but what Captain Quanas did to her was not joyful at all.

For the first month, he beat and raped her. Alisi fought back, but her struggles only made the treatment worse. After two months, the captain grew bored enough with her that he occasionally sent her to his officers or crewmen as a special treat.

All along, Quanas taught her his language and his religion in an attempt to "save" her. He forced her to rise every dawn and stand before their short-statured and broken-toothed prester, who preached from the Book of Aiden. They made her wear a fishhook pendant, though she had been taught the symbol would burn her skin if she touched it.

When Alisi could speak Tierran well enough, Quanas taught her to read Aidenist scripture. If she refused a lesson, he beat her, once even hard enough that he broke ribs. If she made mistakes, he would beat her again. Eventually, she had learned.

The captain corrected Alisi's pronunciation and grammar, he forced her to eliminate any trace of an accent, intolerant of the slightest errors. She didn't understand why, since he never let her off the ship, never showed her to outsiders. He locked her in the cabin whenever the ship came to port.

He told her to be grateful for what he was doing. "I am saving your soul. I am giving you knowledge and blessings—the knowledge and blessings that Aiden conferred on all of his people. Appreciate the fact that I am treating you as a potential human being, rather than a Urecari animal."

And then he had raped her again.

When she inevitably got pregnant, the captain regarded her with disgust for months, until she came to term. She gave birth with very little help, but the baby was stillborn. Captain Quanas threw it over the side of the ship.

Held prisoner for more than two years, Alisi learned a great deal. She studied the captain as he forced her to repeat his lessons. She never tried to escape while they were in port, never caused trouble; the captain even believed she had converted to their offensive fishhook religion. As time passed, Quanas and his crew grew lazy, careless.

One night, when the *Sacred Scroll* sailed along the Tierran coast just after a successful trip into port, Alisi saw her opportunity. She broke a glass bottle and slit the captain's throat as he slept. Because she was allowed to wander the ship whenever they weren't in port, the night watchman didn't even acknowledge her as she walked out on the deck. She killed him too, this time with the captain's knife. During that quiet night, Alisi slew the five men who had treated her worst, including the prester. Then, before she could be caught, she dropped over the side into deep, dark water and swam to the coastline, where she saw tiny lights in the distance.

She washed up on shore the next morning and was found by a beachcomber collecting mussels. The old woman clucked over her condition, helped her to her feet, and placed an arm around her shoulder so the two could make their way to a nearby village. Since Alisi spoke perfect Tierran, the people there accepted her, and no one ever suspected that she was truly Uraban.

She lived among them for some time, considered an orphan with a terrible past—abused by the Urecari, they assumed. Alisi continued to watch and learn. Finally, when she had absorbed everything she could from that place, she stole food and money and made her way back down to Uraba. . . .

Now, many years later, Alisi possessed a great deal of knowledge about life among the Tierrans. She spoke their language, knew their religion, their customs. She knew how to *be* one of them. And she could teach others.

She loathed the Aidenists. They had killed all of her feelings inside, except for the hatred that blossomed daily with renewed strength. They had stolen her childhood, and now she took joy in stealing their children.

Returning in secret, in shame, she had lived with her brother, explaining her plan for revenge, and Unwar had presented the ideas to Omra without revealing Alisi's identity. As the Teacher, Alisi used her knowledge to create *ra'virs*, and she had even taught her brother to speak their language. For years, with her silver mask and black robes, she had wielded fear over others, casting herself as an enigma. She indoctrinated the captive Tierran children, taught them, tested them, shaped and tempered them, and selected only the most fanatical candidates. No one suspected who she truly was, and that was how it must be.

She finally spoke again. "I came here, Unwar, because you have to make your decision about Prince Tomas before the soldan-shah learns what you have done. Once Omra knows, the choice will be out of your hands." Alisi took up her mask and placed it back over her face. Her voice was muffled once more, a stranger's. "I would like to see the boy. Show me this Aidenist prince."

Unwar led her up the winding steps to the tower cell, where the boy shot to his feet, looking at them with fearful hope. His angry defiance was clearly feigned. Alisi could see how terrified he was.

Staring at him through the burnished hemisphere that covered her face, the Teacher didn't speak. She knew the effect her eerie silence had on people, and she waited for the uneasiness to make him crack.

Tomas cried out, "What do you want? How long are you going to hold me here? When will my sister send her answer?"

The two chuckled as Tomas's questions increased in desperation, and finally the boy broke down and began to sob.

Alisi turned her mask toward Unwar. "Pathetic. Worthless. I wouldn't even try to train him as a *ra'vir.*"

Her brother closed the cell door and bolted it as they walked back down the stone-walled corridor. "*You* know what must be done," she said. "The boy is here. He should be made to pay for what the Aidenists did at Fashia's Fountain."

"That child had nothing to do with the desecration."

Alisi shrugged. "Nevertheless, it provides all the justification we need. How can Omra disagree? It's best if you don't give him the chance to make the wrong decision." When her brother still looked uneasy, she snapped, "Have you already forgotten all those sikaras slain in cold blood?"

Unwar's expression darkened. "I won't forget that. I can never forget."

"And will you forget the atrocities that the Aidenists inflicted on *me*?"

Unwar turned white. "Never!"

The Teacher glided off down the corridor. "Then you know what Urec's justice demands. Why wait for the soldan-shah?"

85 *The Great Desert*

The expanse of dunes was an open ocean, marred by few landmarks. As Imir's pursuit party rode on and on for days, rationing food and water, the former soldan-shah wondered how the bandits could have disappeared. Where could they possibly hide out here? He assumed they must have split up into smaller groups, but he doggedly pressed on, following the main concentration of hoofprints.

The shifting winds stirred up small dust devils that blurred the traces of Norgo's passage. The desert men had gotten too great a head start, but Imir did not give up.

Stinging grains of sand caught in his teeth, scoured his cheeks, made his eyes burn. When he stared toward the horizon, a golden glare reflected off the undulating dunes, but he saw no sign of hope.

The horses were all weary. Even the hardy desert breed could not go on indefinitely; by necessity, their water rations had been cut as well.

Riding alongside him, Soldan Xivir remained grim and quiet. Several times he had started to speak, but stopped himself. Imir knew what the man intended to say, but he didn't want to think about it, didn't want to give up. At last, Xivir pointed out, "Even if we turn around now, we will be sore pressed to make it back to Desert Harbor. Our supplies and water are almost gone. Our horses will die. We will die."

Imir looked at his brother-in-law, narrowing dust-reddened eyes. "Once we find the bandit camp and rescue Adreala, we will take our supplies back along with *their* supplies. We'll have all we need." It was their only hope.

Xivir fell silent, and they rode on into the dusk as the dunes grew higher, like shifting mountain ranges. Unstable surfaces yanked at the horses' hooves. Imir didn't want to stop and camp for the night, but the men were exhausted. One of the horses had already died, leaving its rider stranded so that he had to share another mount. Very soon, Imir knew, they would all begin to drop.

He hardened his heart and made a difficult decision. They would ride all night and continue to search, but once the sun rose he would have no choice but to turn around and hope that most of them survived the return journey.

Even though Adreala was still out there.

At midnight, under sharp starlight that silvered the dunes, they topped a rise and saw, unbelievably, an orange glow in the distance. Imir pulled his horse to a halt and stared. "By the Eye of Urec, we've found them!"

Soldan Xivir was nearly asleep in his saddle, but he perked up at the sight. "They're still a long way off, but if we get there before sunrise, we'll surprise them in the darkness." He looked at Imir, and a decision flashed between them. They knew what a gamble this was—a gamble they had to take, and *win*.

The former soldan-shah spoke. "All right, men. Drink the last of your water, give your horses as much as you can. We need our strength right now, and the bandits will give us all we need for the trip back home." Imir could only pray that the bandits were not as short of supplies as their hunters.

Feeling stronger from the water and food, as well as from the surge of hope, they picked up their pace and closed the distance. Norgo and his bandits had grown careless. After so many days, they must have convinced themselves that their pursuers had given up—and most men would have given up.

But Adreala was Imir's granddaughter. He had promised to keep her safe.

The campfire was small, just a few embers of dried horse dung, but in the utter emptiness it burned as bright as the blazing eye of a demon. Not far from the camp, the pursuers pulled their horses to a halt and whispered together. Imir let Soldan Xivir command his men. They would spread out, encircle, then converge upon the camp, striking simultaneously from several directions.

"Our most important goal is to save the girl," Imir said. "Kill every one of the bandits if you can, but if there is any choice as to what you must do, *Adreala* is your priority. She is the daughter of your soldan-shah."

The men muttered their agreement and drew curved swords, ready to charge. Imir raised his own blade in front of him. With his heart pounding and blood boiling, he was ready.

They approached quietly. The riders prepared to move in from several directions as soon as they heard the bandits' animals snorting and shifting. One of the groggy rogues rose to see what was troubling their mounts. Before the man could sound an alarm, Imir yelled, "Adreala! We're coming!"

Taking advantage of their surprise, the Missinian horsemen pounded forward to the tiny camp. As he rode into the hollow in the dunes, Imir saw a few rocks and a small seep of water that reflected the weak flames. Black soot marks of old campfires suggested that the bandits used this oasis often, though the spring wasn't enough to support more than a few scrawny weeds and a bit of algae.

The astonished bandits leaped up from the sands, grabbing for their weapons. Imir enjoyed the ironic turnabout. Now *they* were the bold raiders sweeping down on unsuspecting sleepers in a desert encampment. The pursuers closed in, swords flashing, and struck down several of the bandits within the first few seconds. One of Soldan Xivir's men had the presence of mind to yank loose the picket line that tied the bandits' horses and began leading them off so the desert men would have no easy means of escape.

With a burst of joy, Imir spotted his granddaughter lying against a soft dune face, propped up, bound but not gagged. The girl looked gaunt, frightened, and exhausted—but alive and uninjured. She struggled against her bonds and shouted with savage glee, "I told you they would come!"

The bandits tried to rally, and Imir identified ugly Norgo by the remnants of paint on his face. When he saw the former soldan-shah coming, the rogue leader flashed a crooked grin, then scrambled up the soft side of the dunes behind him. He fled into the night, leaving his men to fight for themselves.

Though Imir wanted to skewer the bandit leader on the tip of his scimitar, his priority was to free his granddaughter. Slipping off his horse, Imir raced to the girl. "Are you all right? Did he hurt you?"

Adreala had already managed to loosen her bonds, slickening them with the blood that oozed from scrapes on her wrists. "He tried to, Grandfather—but I gave him a few bruises and a cracked rib."

"Thank Ondun!" Imir finished cutting her ropes and lifted her to her feet.

Adreala swayed, her legs weak from excitement and privation, but her gaze seemed to burn. Her eyes suddenly widened. "Look out!"

A bandit lunged toward him, brandishing a dagger; Imir knocked the girl out of the way and struck with his scimitar. Before he knew what he was doing, Imir severed the man's hand at the wrist. The bandit continued to thrust his bleeding stump forward, then saw that he had lost not only his dagger, but his hand. Shrieking, he collapsed, and Imir neatly dealt him a finishing blow.

Adreala struggled back to her feet. "Norgo's getting away!"

Convinced that his granddaughter was safe, Imir peeled the dagger from the limp fingers of the bandit's severed hand on the ground. He handed her the weapon. "Take this, use it if you have to. Stay with the soldan's men—I'm going after Norgo."

Imir slogged up to the dune top at the edge of the bowl. When he finally crested the rise, he saw the man's dark shape several ridges away, racing across the peaks and slipping down into the valleys between dunes. Norgo was nimble, able to dance across the shifting sand before ascending another line in a sidelong, zigzag motion.

Panting hard, Imir ran after him, but his throat and lungs were burning. Still weak from reduced rations and lack of water, he tumbled down a dune face and saw the bandit leader's footprints leading off into the emptiness. His heart sank with the realization that he would not be able to capture the man. He cursed himself for not having taken his horse, but he wasn't thinking clearly.

Still, he nodded to himself with bittersweet satisfaction. Without a horse or rations, the bandit leader would not last long. He could never survive out here.

Far behind, Imir could still hear the remnants of fighting, and with a heavy heart, he decided to go back to Adreala. That was most important to him.

By the time he made his way to the pitiful oasis, the bandits had been slain, their horses captured by Xivir's men. The exhausted Missinian soldiers were sharing out the food supplies they had seized. Some filled waterskins from the seeping spring, nudging aside the horses that were trying to drink.

Soldan Xivir looked at the dead bodies sprawled on the sand. Every one of the bandits was dead, either killed in battle or executed afterward. With a pragmatic shrug, he said, "We didn't have the wherewithal to take prisoners back to Desert Harbor."

Imir wasn't concerned. "Why waste time? I would have ordered their execution anyway." He regarded the small spring, the old campfires. "Before we go, I want this water blocked, the seep plugged up and buried so that bandits can no longer take advantage of it." Imir looked over his shoulder and comforted himself with the fact that Norgo would perish from hunger and thirst, a long and lingering death out there in the sands.

As he fled into the vast wasteland, abandoning his camp and his men, the bandit leader laughed. The arrogant Missinians had surprised him, and his comrades had fought well, though not well enough.

Norgo had seen the old man chasing him, but no civilized man would ever catch him out here. Those soft people didn't know anything about surviving in the wasteland, about the resources there, or the dangers, the mysteries, the stories. He knew he could always gather another group of like-minded men. The desert belonged to him.

The night was silent, all sounds drowned out by the emptiness as Norgo kept running. Far away, he could still discern the secret spring where he and his men had camped, but he could no longer hear the cries of pain, the clash of swords. By now, all of his comrades would be dead or captured. He no longer concerned himself with them.

Ahead, Norgo heard whispers, even laughter. Voices . . .

female voices! He had never heard such a thing before, especially not out here. He wondered if it could be another camp, an oasis. He grinned. They would give him food and water. That was all he needed.

The laughter sounded like music, the voices like song, and a chill ran down his back. Maybe the women had husbands, warriors he could recruit. Or maybe they had no husbands at all and he would have them all to himself. Norgo wasn't sure which he would prefer.

He kept plodding. Each footstep seemed to take longer, and the sand sucked him down, but he pushed forward, attracted by the thought of soft company. He didn't recognize the language, but the voices were seductive. He had to get to the dune crest so he could see.

The wind picked up, and small dust devils skirled across the dune face. Finally, he climbed to the top of the rise from which he could stare down into the dell ... but he saw no camp, no women, no sign of habitation.

The night had fallen silent again, and he turned in a slow circle. From this high ground he should have been able to see anything. There were no fires, no structures, no people. "Hello!"

The tinkling laughter began again, carried on the wind. He looked behind him, saw nothing. Another dust devil whipped through the valley below and vanished, losing its energy. Confused, even a little angry, Norgo turned once more, still seeking the source of the sounds.

The voices seemed to be coming from the sand itself.

The dunes stirred beneath his feet, crumbling, and he began to slip down the slope. Around him, the eerie female voices grew louder, the music more intense, giving him new reassurance. He heard so much loneliness behind the sounds that his heart lifted. They were so happy to see him!

Through a dust-fog in his brain, he vaguely remembered frightening tales that superstitious men told each other on desert nights when the storms whipped up. Sand dervishes, spirits that haunted the dunes ... forlorn demons seeking company for all eternity, lovers that would never let go.

He had always laughed at those tales.

A desiccated hand reached up from the soft sand and clutched his ankle. Norgo ripped it away and looked down, startled to see other figures stirring, vaguely human shapes rising from beneath the dunes. The winds picked up and swirled around him now. As the voices grew louder, their songs reached a higher note, a hypnotic spell, and his fear was smothered, leaving only a fuzzy wonder and desire in his mind.

Norgo no longer saw the blackened, leathery skin or the mummified remains—he heard only love. As the whirlwind encircled him, it felt like soft fingertips caressing his face, his hands. He barely even felt his flesh being scoured away.

Ethereal bodies climbed out of the dunes, angelic spirits clothed in diaphanous veils ... skeins of dust. The hands embraced him, the winds tightened.

Giddy, Norgo opened his arms and invited them. He could not refuse the call when they promised to love him forever. When he tried to express his own love, though, he coughed and choked—his mouth filled with dust. When he inhaled he drew in no air, only sand.

He felt a glimmer of fear, but the music and voices soothed him again. Norgo was beyond struggling when the dervishes sucked him down into the sands.

86 *The Border of Uraba*

After Prester Ciarlo had walked for days across untracked lands, he did not let the old pain in his leg slow his pace or diminish his determination. The pain merely reminded him that he was alive, and Ondun wanted everyone to experience both the good and bad things in this life. With prayers and resolve, Ciarlo kept going. In His mercy, Ondun could always take away the pain.

Ciarlo carried his abridged Book of Aiden, but he had already memorized all the inspirational parables he needed. He wanted to share the wonders of his beliefs with the people of Uraba—those who, in their innocence, had not yet heard the truth.

Leaving the Pilgrims' Road and crossing grassy hills to the east, he stayed with Tierran farmers or shepherds he encountered. As he traveled down the narrowing isthmus, the small cottages became harder to find. Living so close to the Uraban border, those who did offer hospitality were increasingly suspicious, but when they saw Ciarlo's fishhook pendant, they welcomed him and asked for his blessing. Later, he set off once more, limping toward Ishalem and beyond.

As soon as he saw the holy city shining under the sun like the contents of an open treasure chest, Ciarlo approached with more caution. He traveled only at night now, working his way through the hills, as he came toward the towering wall that extended to the edge of the land. The barrier was tall enough and the water deep enough to block any large army, but a lone man could find his way around it.

After midnight, when the moon had set, Ciarlo walked down to the white sand beach, secured his shoes and belongings in an oilskin pack, and waded out into the warm Middlesea. He had never touched the legendary waters before, but now he could think only of bypassing what the Urecari had named "God's Barricade," as if Ondun would ever approve of separating faithful Aidenists from the holy city.

Ciarlo swam out into the deeper waters, beyond the stone wall. Having grown up in Windcatch, he was a strong swimmer. Though his leg hindered him on land, he could make good progress in the sea. Through the hours of darkness, he drifted and swam with the currents, gliding past the city and the boats docked there. His calling pulled him onward, to the heart of Uraba.

As a lone prester preaching the word of Aiden, Ciarlo decided that Ishalem itself would be too dangerous; instead, he would begin his work in outlying villages, talk to small groups, plant seeds so that the common folk would know Aiden and better understand the tribulations that Sapier had endured before founding the church.

For two more days he traveled along beaches and paths until his supplies ran out. His faith had sustained him thus far, but he would need food. Ciarlo's greatest barrier would be language. Having studied the most ancient scriptures of the Book of Aiden, he knew the old forms of the language, from which much of the foreign tongue was derived. Over the years, he'd taught himself a few important Uraban words and phrases, but he would have to become much more fluent in order to inspire these people.

He met a small family camped next to a beached fishing boat. Though they couldn't understand much of what Ciarlo said, they offered him some fresh fish, which he ate thankfully. After he was done, he showed them his fishhook and tried to communicate his important message. The family suddenly turned cold and scowled at him, and after the father made threatening gestures, Ciarlo got up and limped away.

The next morning, he reached a coastal village composed of drab huts and a small church built out of twisted chunks of driftwood. Most of the people were at work, but a few toiled near their homes. Ciarlo grasped his pendant, held his book in the crook of his right arm, and walked boldly among the curious villagers. He spoke with great sincerity, using his few Uraban words and expanding on them, telling familiar stories from the Book of Aiden. The Urabans quickly grasped who he was and what he was saying. When their mood turned dark and they shouted at him, he responded with a peaceful smile.

A plump, square-faced sikara emerged from the driftwood church and regarded him. Upon seeing their priestess, the townspeople grew more vociferous, throwing things at Ciarlo to drive him out of town, and he had no choice but to limp slowly toward the hills, discouraged.

Long after he left the outskirts of the village, in the middle of the afternoon, he spotted a figure riding up behind him on a small pony. He heard the plodding hoofbeats and stopped, knowing that he couldn't outrun mounted pursuit. But the pony was just a working beast, not a warhorse, and the rider appeared to be a woman. He soon recognized the sikara from the village he had just left, and he supposed she had rallied the people against him, to beat or perhaps murder him. Remembering what had happened to Prester-Marshall Baine and the martyrs in the ruins of Ishalem, Ciarlo feared they might string him up on a fishhook and leave him to die in the sun.

But the sikara's expression was kindly. When she drew up next to him, Ciarlo saw wonder and concern on her face. She shook her head. "Apologies. Bad welcome from people." Her Tierran was as rudimentary as his Uraban.

Ciarlo held up the Book of Aiden. "I came to preach, to tell your villagers about Aiden." After several attempts, he and the sikara understood each other well enough.

She shook her head. "Do not want this." She extended her hand to touch his pendant, hesitating briefly, as though afraid it might burn her. She pushed the Book back against his chest, firmly shaking her head. "Go home. No fishhook here." She untied a sack from her pony's saddle and offered it to him. It contained dried fish, dried fruits, and a small wineskin. "You brave. But be careful."

"Why are you doing this? Everyone else afraid, angry." He was frustrated that they could not communicate more freely.

The priestess turned her pony back toward the village. "Don't hate you," she said, then gave him a very warm smile. "All are children of Ondun."

87 *Calay Castle*

When the unlikely Urecari courier sailed back to Calay with his answer from Ishalem, Guard-Marshall Vorannen intercepted him at the docks, surrounded him with city guardsmen, and then marched Khalig directly to the castle.

For two weeks, Anjine had lived in anger and anxiety while awaiting word from Tomas's abductors. She could not sleep, imagining her brother being held prisoner in some awful dungeon. No one in Tierra would have inflicted such treatment on a noble Uraban captive, but she expected no less from those animals. In a way, she was glad that her father had not lived to see such a disheartening moment.

When a nervous Khalig was presented to her, Anjine sat on the throne and glared down at the haggard Uraban man. His clothes were dirty, and he looked terrified; he clenched a leather satchel in his left hand. His skin had a grayish cast; she could smell his sweat from where she sat.

As the man came forward on shaking knees, she was ready to respond to any demand. Preparing herself for an outrageous ransom payment, she had already met with her treasurers; she had also asked Comdar Rief to develop a military plan should it become necessary to send troops to rescue her brother.

She raised her voice. "Speak your message! What word do you bring from Ishalem? I demand to know the ransom for my brother." Anjine had resigned herself to pay whatever was necessary to bring Tomas back safely.

She watched the man's Adam's apple bob up and down. He visibly steeled himself, then swirled his faded brown cape to one side. "I have been commanded to deliver a second message from Kel Unwar, provisional governor of Ishalem."

Annoyed that Soldan-Shah Omra himself could not be bothered with such an important matter, Anjine gestured irritably for him to go on. "I want my brother back. What is Kel Unwar's response?"

Trembling, Khalig closed his eyes and uttered words mechanically. He had memorized a speech, word for word. "He says . . . he says, that this is just the smallest retaliation for the monstrous acts Aidenists have perpetrated on Fashia's Fountain and the innocent sikaras there."

"Fashia's Fountain? I've never heard of it. Explain what you're talking about. What were Unwar's words, exactly?"

"He says . . . 'While we negotiate these complex matters, we are sending back part of Prince Tomas as a good-faith gesture.'"

With a drunken slowness and wooden fingers, Khalig opened the satchel at his side and tipped it to spill out a rounded, discolored object the size of a large melon. An abominable stench filled the air. Bloody clumps of blond hair. Open eyes stared at Anjine.

Someone screamed. The guards rushed forward. A man vomited at the side of the chamber.

Anjine felt all life flood out of her, like blood from a severed artery. She couldn't blink, couldn't tear her eyes away from the ghastly object.

Khalig threw himself to the floor, weeping for mercy, and the guards dragged him away. Marshall Vorannen tore off his own cape and threw it over Tomas's face, but the appalling image would be forever burned into Anjine's mind and heart. At the rear of the throne room, Enifir began wailing.

Anjine could not feel her own heartbeat. She seemed to have stopped breathing. Her warm blood had turned to icy meltwater in her veins. She was unable to cope, unable to accept what she knew and saw. She couldn't process the truth . . . but she had to be the queen. The queen!

Tomas . . .

Even though the guard-marshall's cloak left only a shapeless lump on the floor, she still saw her brother's face. Shouts of anger filled the throne room along with cries of grief and shock, but Queen Anjine could hear none of it. She could not react.

As if she were no more than a wooden marionette, she raised herself to her feet, refusing to let the horror and grief show. Without a word, she walked out of the throne room, returned to her private quarters, and locked the door behind her.

It seemed that only an instant had passed before she heard a loud pounding, a man's shouted voice. "It's Mateo—let me in!" How could he have heard so quickly? "Anjine, open up!" She sat on her bed, staring at her hands as though she'd never seen them before. "Tolli, it's me! Please open up!"

She moved like a wraith, but it seemed to take her forever to reach the door; she had no energy, no knowledge of what she was doing. When she lifted the crossbar, the door burst inward and Mateo pushed his way into the room. He flung the door shut once more, stood before her.

His reddened eyes bore witness to tears already shed. "Oh Tolli, I'm so sorry, so sorry . . ." For a long moment she didn't understand what he meant. "I should have gone with . . . I could have guarded him! I needed to—"

"No!" She trembled, wrestling with the idea, forcing the words out in a hoarse whisper. "Then I would have lost both of you."

Mateo threw his arms around her, drawing her close. He kissed her hair. She saw the image of Tomas's face again, the horrible trophy the Urecari courier had brought.

... part of Prince Tomas as a good-faith gesture ...

Sobs flowed out of her like a sudden squall, a hurricane powerful enough to wreck ships, but nothing could sink the juggernaut of her despair and regret. Mateo held her tight, muffling the long, guttural sounds that seared like branding irons into his shoulder. He kissed the top of her head again.

She choked out the words when she could breathe. "Tomas was a candle of innocence." Mateo stood there, an unbreakable sea wall, steadying her, letting her cry. "Damn, damn, *damn* them all!" She pounded her fists against him. Her legs collapsed, but he held her upright.

He began trying to comfort her, making soothing sounds, guiding her back to reality. "Oh, Tolli, this world has become a terrible place for us." He couldn't think of his duties, nor of Vicka, nor the *ra'vir* threat, nor the wall of Ishalem. He thought only of Anjine. He held her for what must have been hours.

Finally, when she finished unleashing her sorrow, Anjine drew a deep breath and straightened, completely drained.

And now it was Mateo's turn to grieve, for Anjine had become like a statue in his arms. She pulled away from him gently, composing herself. She dashed away the remaining tears and walked over to her basin. She heaved another shuddering breath, poured water, and pressed a cold towel to her eyes and face.

Anjine looked at him from across an impassable distance, her expression cold, her face blotchy and red. She looked like a stranger—and perhaps she was, fundamentally and forever changed. Mateo stared at her with his dark expression, but she let no warmth into her own gaze. "I'm finished, Mateo. Don't ever speak of my moment of vulnerability. I can't afford to show weakness. The Urecari must never know how deeply they have hurt me."

Mateo opened his mouth, thought better of it, and came forward to place his hands on her shoulders for one moment longer, before the woman he had known slipped away forever. "You're human, Anjine. That doesn't mean you're weak."

"I can't afford to be human when we face enemies who are such monsters. I have to be *queen*, and that is all I can be."

Mateo nodded. "I will keep any and every secret you ask of me, my Queen . . . Tolli."

"Never call me that again. Tolli died today, along with Tomas." She stepped away and sat at her bureau, where she arranged her toiletries in a mindless distraction of her hands. She needed something, even something trivial, to keep her hands busy.

"I am the queen. I wear the crown. I surrendered the soft part of me when I became the ruler of Tierra in the midst of this terrible war. Now leave me." She swallowed hard. "I need time to think of an appropriate response."

Part IV

88 *Olabar Harbor*

Shortly after his son's seventh birthday reception, the soldan-shah took Omirr on a walk to the docks, just the two of them. Lookouts in the watchtowers had already sighted the approaching sail from Gremurr, discerning through their spyglasses that this was a different sort of ship. Omra couldn't wait to see what Tukar had accomplished.

The zarif was bouncy and full of energy, pulling on his father's hand to make him hurry. "Saan always used to take me down to see the ships. When will Saan be back?"

"It depends on how big the world is and how soon he finds the Key to Creation."

"I hope it's soon. I want him to be here."

"I miss him too." Sometimes when Omra realized how much he loved Istar and how he had tried to do right by her son, he also remembered that bloody day in the village of Windcatch. If she hadn't been pregnant—like his original wife Istar—Omra never would have spared her life, never would have felt a moment of mercy or pity for a mere Tierran woman. That split-second decision had changed his entire life and led to his happiness. But had she ever truly forgiven him? And did she truly love him? He knew there were holes from her first life that he could never entirely fill.

Istar seemed content as First Wife, though it had taken her a long time—years—before any sort of warmth melted the ice of her resentment, and even longer still before she actually began to show feelings for him. By now, Istar had accepted her new situation. Twenty years in Uraba! While Saan was the son of her long-lost Tierran husband, she also loved her two daughters by Omra, and she even showed genuine compassion for Cithara—a fact that still astonished him. Perhaps it was something one learned from the Book of Aiden? Omra couldn't recall any *sikara* ever preaching such acceptance or unconditional forgiveness.

And though she did not speak of it, the soldan-shah knew Istar had never forgotten about her first love. . . .

That noon, there had been a special feast for the boy in the palace courtyard. Naori was aglow with excitement for her son, holding Irec against her hip. All the handmaidens circled around, celebrating Zarif Omirr's special day, and Istar had helped with the celebration. Afterward, during their walk down to the harbor, the boy preened beside his father as if he were also a man of some importance. Omra found it particularly charming.

They reached the harbor and watched the ironclad vessel sailing toward the dock, where spectators waved and cheered. Seeing the majestic warship, the soldan-shah envisioned a whole fleet of such armored ships sailing through the isthmus canal. The *Golden Fern*. What a perfect name.

Omra squeezed the boy's shoulder. "Look, my son. This is your birthday present from all of Uraba."

The boy looked at his father in awe. "That's my ship?"

"Not yours alone. But I want you to be the first to board it with me."

Curious fishermen and dockworkers crowded close to see the unusual vessel. As soon as the boarding plank was laid, the soldan-shah and Omirr walked up to greet the captain, who seemed embarrassed by all the attention. "Soldan-Shah, my Lord, you honor us."

"And you honor all of Uraba by bringing this magnificent ship. How did she sail?"

"Beautifully. She is like an indestructible creature of the sea. I would pit the *Golden Fern* against the Leviathan."

"I'd rather you pit her against our true enemies. How goes the armoring on the other ships for our new fleet?"

"Work has begun on all seven. Your brother Tukar and Workmaster Zadar have dedicated crews of slave laborers to this project. You won't be disappointed, Soldan-Shah."

The *Golden Fern*'s deck, masts, and rigging revealed her origins as a Middlesea cargo ship. Eventually, Uraban shipwrights would have to design new vessels capable of sailing comfortably on both bodies of water, with a hull configuration built to withstand the weight of the armor plates.

Delighted to be aboard the ship, the boy ran up and down the deck, greeting the sailors, all of whom indulged him. "Saan should have taken this ship to go exploring! That way he could fend off storms and sea monsters. I wish I could have gone with him."

It always warmed Omra's heart to remember how well Saan and the zarif got along, like true brothers. Yes, that was how brothers should act toward each other. The same thought gave him a pang about how faithful Tukar had been for all these years at the mines. He couldn't wait until his brother returned from his exile. It made no sense any longer.

As soon as the other seven armored ships were dispatched from the Gremurr mines, Omra would bring Tukar back himself, if his brother did not return immediately. It was something he should have done years ago. . . .

Leaving the *Golden Fern*, Omra headed back toward the palace with the young zarif at his side, moving through the marketplace as guards cleared the way. With a clatter of hooves, a courier on horseback rounded a corner and tore down the narrow street to intercept them. "Soldan-Shah, I bear a message from Ishalem!" He held a rolled document in his clenched hand.

Omra was immediately on his guard. Though Kel Unwar often dispatched reports on the progress of the canal excavation, none were so urgent that a courier had to rush through the streets to find him. Perhaps the Aidenists had attacked the wall again, or maybe they'd committed another atrocity like the one at Fashia's Fountain.

He snatched the paper from the man before the horse had come to a halt. When he broke the seal and unrolled the document, the news within drove a blunt dagger into his chest.

Unwar's dispatch proudly described how—on his own initiative—he had intercepted the Tierran royal cog, killed or captured all the crew members, and taken the young prince prisoner. The final sentence seemed to blaze off the parchment: "In retaliation for the recent atrocities at Fashia's Fountain, we have executed the boy and sent his head back to Queen Anjine, so that she may know the cost of her terrible actions."

His fingers went numb, and the dispatch fell to the street.

Omirr bent down and grabbed the paper. "You dropped this."

The soldan-shah merely walked along without seeing or hearing, staring ahead as a whirlwind rushed through his mind. This was too much like what had happened after ambitious and foolhardy Soldan Attar had massacred the prester-marshall and his builders in Ishalem.

Frustrated by the lack of attention, the zarif tugged at his father's arm. Omirr looked so innocent, so bright-eyed. Looking down at his beloved son, Omra tried to imagine the pain Kel Unwar had just inflicted upon Queen Anjine.

No matter what the Book of Aiden taught about forgiveness, he knew what Anjine would think. And the Tierrans would never, *never* forgive such an act.

He had to sail for Ishalem immediately.

89 *Calay*

If he ever managed to get back to Calay, Jenirod was certain he'd be welcomed as a hero after the destruction of the Urecari shrine, but Destrar Tavishel seemed to be in no hurry whatsoever to go home.

The successful raid on Fashia's Fountain had shown the Curlies just how strong were Aiden's faithful. By now, word must have spread across Uraba. The followers of Urec would tremble when they learned how utterly their beliefs had been crushed. That would show them!

Leaving the desecrated shrine, the Soelanders had sailed their ships far from the rugged coastline, dropped anchor, and feasted (and prayed, of course). The next day had dawned bright with clear skies and a warm sun—a sign that Ondun approved of what they had done. Jenirod couldn't wait to tell Anjine.

But he was the only landsman aboard the Soeland ships, and Destrar Tavishel wasn't finished yet. The coppery smell of shed blood and the musical sound of Urecari screams had infected all of the sailors. Instead of setting course back to Calay harbor, they wanted to hunt again.

So for weeks, while Jenirod stewed with impatience, they patrolled the open waters for any colorful sail that dared to glare at them with the Eye of Urec. In all that time, they encountered only two far-ranging fishing boats, which they boarded and seized. After capturing and shackling the crews, they'd sailed the foreign boats north to the nearest Tierran port and traded them for supplies so they could go out and prowl the waters again.

Jenirod grew increasingly anxious to get back to Anjine with his news, but each time he expressed his eagerness, the surly Soeland destrar merely frowned at him. "You are welcome to disembark at any village and make your own way to Calay." Though Jenirod was tempted to purchase a horse and ride it to the capital, who would notice a lone man riding into town on a dusty road? No, he longed to appear in the harbor with appropriate glory, standing at the bow of a proud ship and dressed in Eriettan finery. Oh, people would talk about that! So he had no choice but to wait for the ships to sail back to Calay.

By the time they sailed into the harbor at last, Tavishel

had actually warmed to Jenirod, considering him a comrade. "If you ever get tired of horse dung and stables, young man, you have a place in my crew."

Even though Jenirod took the invitation as a compliment, he said, "It's not what I was born to. I long to smell the dry Eriettan grasses in the heat of the day, to feel a good stallion beneath me running unhindered across the landscape. Would *you* surrender your ships and spend your days riding on the plains and in the hills?"

Tavishel scratched his beard. "Now why would I want to do that, when I have this?"

"Now you understand. Likewise, I wouldn't give up my home or heritage." In his cabin, Jenirod trimmed his hair while looking into a small mirror, then changed into his best clothes and most colorful cape. He bounded onto the dock as soon as the Soelanders had tied up.

After weeks of anticipating this moment, he had built up a clear and glorious vision of what should happen. Taking ideas from the Eriettan horse cavalcades and Landing Day festivals, he pictured people lining the streets, waving ribbons, cheering, throwing flowers at his feet. He grinned to imagine all the young ladies who would blow him kisses, and all the young men who would be jealous of the attention. But no matter how much the women flirted with him or called his name, he would walk straight to the castle where Queen Anjine would be waiting for him, a smile on her face like a precious gem, her arms open wide to greet her husband-to-be.

As he made his way to the Royal District, though, no one paid him any particular notice. The city seemed quiet, even subdued. The merchants didn't yell as loudly when hawking their wares; many vendors' stalls were closed or abandoned. Jenirod noticed banners and black ribbon buntings, signs of mourning, and wondered idly who'd died—probably a high-ranking prester or some such. He was in no mood for gloomy news right now, however; his report to Anjine would likely be all the more welcome for bringing cheer to the royal court.

He announced himself to the guard at the castle's entry-way. "I am the queen's betrothed. I apologize for my unexpected arrival, but I would like to speak with Anjine." He used her familiar name quite intentionally.

Jenirod expected a smiling welcome, but the guard was somber and formal. "I will send word to the queen, but she hasn't held court in days, and receives few visitors."

Jenirod chuckled. "She'll receive me."

"Perhaps . . ."

The guard guided him down the corridors, and Jenirod noticed small bouquets of flowers on the window seats, sprays of white baby's breath that traditionally indicated a birth in the castle. "Someone has had a baby?"

The guard seemed distracted. "Oh, yes, the queen's handmaiden and Guard-Marshall Vorannen. Their first child was just born."

"Then I must issue my congratulations!"

Jenirod swept his cape behind him and strutted into the throne room, eager to see Anjine again. Obviously, his behavior during the horse cavalcade and the banquet had not impressed her, but now the queen could not help but recognize his maturity and bravery. The victory at Fashia's Fountain must be proclaimed in all the history books.

He walked forward, head held high—and ground to a

halt, as he actually looked at Queen Anjine. She sat motionless on her throne, her skin as pale as limestone. She wore a simple black gown with no jewelry.

Well, she obviously needed cheering up! Jenirod swept a graceful bow and straightened. "My Queen, my dear Anjine, I bring news of a great victory for the glory of Ondun and Aiden." He lowered his voice, pretending to be bashful. "Though in truth I did it for you."

When Anjine showed no interest, he explained in great detail—with only slight embellishments—how he had convinced Destrar Tavishel to take him on an exciting raid and how they had struck the sacred Urecari shrine. At the end of his story, he produced an ornate jeweled ring he had taken from the spoils and gave it to her to mark his achievement. Smiling, he took a step back, straightened his shoulders, and waited for her praise.

Anjine was even whiter now. With fury. "The Uraban courier spoke of war atrocities. Fashia's Fountain. He talked about the massacre at their shrine, said that was the reason they exacted their revenge on Tomas—*because of what we did to them*. I didn't know what the man was talking about. Now I do."

She raised herself to her feet like a demon about to attack. Jenirod was startled, upset, even frightened. He didn't understand. This wasn't at all the reception he had expected. Anjine was on the verge of hysteria, and he wished he could find some way to make her calm down.

Her blood seemed to be boiling beneath her skin. "Because of your foolhardy, unsanctioned actions, my brother is dead. They cut off his head and delivered it here!"

Jenirod could not believe his ears. The prince dead? That couldn't be right. "What?" A deepening dread began to replace the feeling of affront.

"Because of *you*." The words caught in her throat, and she could no longer speak. She stared at the floor near Jenirod's feet, as if she saw a stain there.

He opened his mouth to tell her she was wrong, that she needed to understand the good news he had brought her, but the ring flew past his head, bounced on the floor and skidded across the chamber. Riffling through the papers on a small document table beside the throne, she yanked out a parchment that had been signed and sealed with both her stamp and that of Destrar Unsul of Erietta.

"I asked for our betrothal agreement to be brought to me. But now—" She glared at Jenirod with such an icy fury that he had to look away. She held the document in front of his face, then tore it in half and continued to shred it into small pieces, flinging the tatters all around her throne.

"You have broken any reason I had to trust you. You acted without permission, against my wishes. You have destroyed me as surely as I have destroyed this." She cast the last pieces to the floor. "Leave me, *now*, before I order your execution."

Jenirod wanted to go to her, to try to soothe her and tell her that she was overreacting, but she yelled for the guards. "Get him out of here! Remove him! Send him home!"

The befuddled man was escorted briskly out of the castle.

*

When Jenirod was gone, Anjine sank back into her throne, feeling the hard wood against her back, listening to her heart pound. Bitter and deadly, she sat staring for long moments. The handful of remaining courtiers looked nervous, horrified by what they had heard. Jenirod's triumphant confession had reawakened all her revulsion and sorrow from recent days.

Anjine finally spoke aloud, issuing orders to no one in particular. She didn't need to. As queen, she had no doubt she would be obeyed.

"Find one thousand Urecari. Gather them from the camps. Capture more if you must. *One thousand*. Then I will deal with them."

90 *Soeland Patrol Ship*

After delivering the impatient Eriettan lordling to Calay, Tavishel was more anxious than ever to prowl the seas for Urecari criminals. As destrar of the isolated island reach, he'd never been fond of big cities. Tavishel craved neither power nor its trappings, and he had already lost everything he'd truly cared about after the gray fever took away his family.

Now he satisfied himself with inflicting pain upon the enemies of Aiden—and the world was full of them. Tavishel had only to sail the open seas until he found a Uraban vessel. He needed someone to blame for the ache inside him, whether or not there was any real connection.

Some of his crew wanted to set course northwest for the

Soeland islands, but Tavishel's own reach did little to call him anymore. Drawing a breath of the fine salty breeze, he said, "Two more weeks, lads, then I'll take you home to your wives and families. Just bear with me a little longer. We have Aiden's work to do."

The ships caught the strong southerly current that took them back toward the Edict Line. The hiss and whisper of waves split along the bow and rushed past the sides of the ship. The destrar studied his charts, taking position measurements so he could see when they crossed the invisible boundary. Though King Korastine and Soldan-Shah Imir had sealed the agreement long ago by applying their own blood to the wood of the ancient Arkship, Tavishel did not feel bound by those terms, because the Urecari had broken them so many times.

Over the next week, hunting in enemy territory, Tavishel and his crew seized three more Urecari boats. The prisoners were kept in chains belowdecks, fed fish offal, and given tepid water to drink. The Urabans grimaced in disgust at the fare, but they slurped it down when they grew hungry enough. It was a waste just to kill all of the enemy captives; better to send them to the work camps in Alamont or Corag, where they could make amends.

Tavishel returned to the Tierran coast with his captured fishing boats and miserable prisoners. At the harbor town of Windcatch, they herded the weakened captives to handlers who would escort them inland to the nearest camp. He exchanged the foreign vessels for all the supplies he needed. Though the harbormaster kept an account for him, the Soeland destrar knew that no good Aidenist would ever turn down reasonable requests for supplies or materials. If he and his crew had kept the booty for themselves, they would have been wealthy men, but Soelanders did not do this work to acquire fine objects or gold; their treasure consisted of performing good deeds in the name of Aiden.

While docked in Windcatch, he gave his crew a day of shore leave and rest, but Tavishel had no taste for the local kelp liquor and no curiosity for news or gossip. With the afternoon to himself, he wandered into the hills and found the village cemetery.

Tavishel stood among the markers, looking at the wooden posts carved with names and symbolic fishhooks. All these people ... and so many slain by vile criminals who followed Urec's Log. The destrar understood Windcatch's pain and loss all too well. Surveying this hillside with all its grave markers, he was reminded of a stony windswept cemetery in his own home of Farport on the main island of Soeland Reach.

Because the scattered shores of Soeland were bleak, and the weather cold and difficult, Tavishel's brand of Aidenism was darker than the more forgiving beliefs preached by soft presters in wealthy towns. He himself was a religious man and had taught himself to read the entire Book of Aiden.

His beard, once dark and magnificent, was now the gray of woodsmoke. Tavishel used a wide, very sharp gutting knife to shave his scalp, so that no one knew his hair had begun to thin. He remembered that he hadn't wanted to look old for his wife, but she hadn't minded either way. He should have paid more attention to her ...

In times past, he had spent much of the year captaining

a whaling ship. Each season, he said goodbye to his wife and children and returned months later with a hold full of oil and preserved whale meat. One year, though, not long after the burning of Ishalem, Tavishel came home from his voyage to find his wife and children all dead from an epidemic of gray fever. The sickness had killed a quarter of the villagers on the main island, and the fires from burning fever-houses had stained the sky. Farport itself looked like a ghost town.

Tavishel had arrived four weeks too late to say farewell. His entire family had perished. He hadn't seen them die, hadn't been able to read aloud from the Book of Aiden as their bound and weighted bodies were given back to the sea with the outgoing tide.

Stone cairns outside of Farport commemorated those who had died—their own cemetery, just like this one in Windcatch. The gray fever was an impersonal thing, sweeping in and killing good and bad alike, Aidenist or Urecari, wherever it touched. That hadn't seemed fair to him. Tavishel needed someone to blame, so now he took out his anger by hunting down the followers of Urec, making them pay because they *must* have invoked the wrath of Ondun.

For so many years, Tavishel's ships had chased, caught, and killed whales; now he hunted Urecari vessels. Blood still flowed, but there was a difference: the whales had done nothing to deserve their deaths, but all Urecari most certainly had.

Seeing the sun near the horizon, Tavishel walked away from the cemetery. Since he was the Soeland destrar, he had dutifully taken another wife back in Farport, but had sired no further children. That part of his life was over.

He felt very little love inside himself, not for his second wife, not for the Soeland people he ruled, not for anyone. But with the continuing war and his mission to protect Tierra, Destrar Tavishel did feel a kind of peace, because he knew he was doing the right thing. He vowed to continue his work. He wanted to sail again, soon.

91 *Alamont Prison Camp*

Mateo obeyed the queen's command, no matter how uneasy her instructions made him. He understood her heart, and he couldn't fault the logic of what she was doing. Even so, it was a terrible thing.

Mateo had dispatched word throughout the Tierran military camps: every captive *ra'vir* being held for interrogation was to be summarily executed. And good riddance. He didn't know if any of them had been involved in poor Tira's murder, but it didn't matter. They were all guilty, and should all die. The oldest one identified was fifteen.

And those didn't even count toward the queen's thousand.

Every time he thought of poor Tomas, Mateo had to close his eyes and draw deep breaths.

When he took river passage to Alamont Reach and handed Destrar Shenro the royal decree, the other man studied it, frowning. "That's a great many slaves, Subcomdar, and I've already sent hundreds up to Corag to work on the mountain road. What am I going to use to tend our fields?"

Mateo spoke more sharply than he intended, but he could not keep the anger back. "Considering what happened to Prince Tomas, would you tell the queen you'd rather keep a few extra farm laborers?"

Shenro courteously handed the order back. "You're right, of course. In fact, I'm glad to get rid of some useless mouths to feed." He averted his gaze. "I don't envy you your task, Subcomdar. It is a difficult thing."

As a young recruit, Mateo had listened to the Alamont destrar teach Tierra's military history, but none of the historic struggles and civil wars could compare to the crusades between the Aidenists and Urecari. Mateo showed no hesitation. "I am proud to do whatever my queen commands. Destrar Sazar is sending riverboats to load the captives. They should arrive this afternoon. We'll take the river route as far south as we can, then do a forced march down the Pilgrims' Road."

Later that day, the fence gates were thrown open, and riders herded the prisoners out of the camp, while men with slate tablets kept a careful tally of them. Driven toward the docks, the Urecari grew increasingly angry and apprehensive.

Shenro watched them with a cold smile. "They think I intend to have my archers shoot them—again."

Mateo was impatient with him. "Have your bowmen stand back. No need to panic them."

The destrar reluctantly complied, but the captives did not calm down. Mateo watched them file aboard the wide riverboats. The man with the slateboard muttered to himself, making one mark after another. "You'll need more than a thousand, Subcomdar. Some are sure to die along the way, unless you intend to pamper them."

Mateo realized the truth of this. It would be a hard trek, and food supplies would need to be reserved for the Tierran soldiers. He looked at individual forlorn Urecari faces, but all compassion faded when he again thought of Tomas. "No, exactly a thousand. Anjine never said they had to be alive when they reach their destination."

The man with the slateboard shrugged and continued to mark the numbers. A few foolish captives tried to break away and run, but Alamont guards rode them down, beat them severely with whips, and forced them back into line. Right now, every person counted. Subcomdar Hist was already setting up a large temporary holding camp not far from the Ishalem wall. That was as far as they needed to go.

Aboard the first riverboat, Mateo shook the beefy hand of Destrar Sazar, whose beard was an impressive black spray that covered half his barrel chest. The few times Mateo had met the river destrar, Sazar had been full of loud laughter and out-of-tune singing. He had a battered old violin that he scratched more than played. Now, though, Sazar looked offended by the dragging Urecari footsteps as prisoners shuffled across the boarding ramp and onto the decks of his beloved barges. The gruff, hearty man seemed to have lost his sense of humor.

"My father taught me how to captain this boat, and *his* father plied the currents before him, and so on for generations. We have proud traditions of hauling cargo, but these days I've got far too much human cargo. I don't like trading in goods that weep and wail and beg for mercy."

"It's the queen's orders."

The man continued to stare at the slaves being pushed aboard. "My people of the River Reach are as loyal as any other Tierrans. I'll take these captives without complaint. I'm just telling you, I draw no satisfaction from it."

At the holding camp on barren ground not far from Ishalem, groans of misery rose into the air like odors from a cesspit. On the first night there, Mateo summoned his administrators into a command tent that was pitched as far upwind as possible.

Subcomdar Hist gave his report, though Mateo was supposedly his equal in rank. "We have achieved our goal." The numbers didn't exactly match up, but no more than fifty Urabans had died on the journey to the camp, and their bodies had been carried along on separate carts and wagons, then piled outside the fences.

The camp administrators looked grimly at each other, not wanting to be the first to express their concerns. Finally, a man from Bora's Bastion said, "Subcomdar, they are starving, sick, and restless. We don't have supplies to feed so many. Do we expect the food to arrive soon? The prisoners grow worse every day."

"They are Urecari murderers," groused one of the other men. "Let them starve and rot, for all I care."

"We won't let them starve," Mateo said. "And we won't need supplies." He looked down at Queen Anjine's harsh decree once more. She had set down the words in her own hand. Mateo had studied it over and over again, but the document did not change. He drew a deep breath. "We will carry out our orders without further delay."

92 *The* Al-Orizin

Drenched and shivering in the pouring rain, Saan held on to the mainmast. For two days now, the storm had increased in strength, battering the *Al-Orizin*, hurling them farther into unknown waters.

While Sikara Fyiri had locked herself inside her cabin to pray for safe passage, his crew had to work together on deck even in the worst wind and driving rain. Saan had chosen the men well. Though frightened, several sharp-eyed volunteers climbed the mast and lashed themselves into the lookout nest. They could see little through the clouds, spray, and rain, leaving the ship completely helpless should they encounter submerged rocks or the unknown shore of a rugged continent. But Saan trusted in the vastness of the sea.

"Urec went through worse than this on his voyage!" he bellowed over the howling wind, then he laughed at the storm.

Finally, when the weather abated and the skies cleared, Saan stood on the slick deck watching the sun rise through the clouds. Sikara Fyiri emerged from her cabin wearing a bright red robe. "My prayers were answered. Urec has guided us to safety."

Saan rolled his eyes. Daily, in the privacy of his cabin, he read the sympathetic journal as the sly Villiki wrote more and more urgent comments to Fyiri, asking for a response, never suspecting that *he* might be reading them. He maintained his silence, not wanting to tip his hand.

From the lookout, Grigovar called out, "Land ho! Island ahead, just off the starboard bow!"

Amazed crewmen rushed to the side in such a crowd that Saan thought the ship might capsize. Overhead, he noticed two gulls wheeling in the air, the first birds they'd seen in a long time. Prominent in the now calm water was a rugged but verdant island covered with jungles. He didn't understand how this speck of solid ground could be out here in the middle of the open sea. Just as the question formed in his mind, Grigovar shouted again, this time in alarm: "Reefs! Reefs, Captain!"

Ahead, the water had a foamy look, indicating treacherous lines of rock just beneath the surface, jagged edges that could chew the *Al-Orizin*'s hull like hungry mouths.

"Drop anchor!" Saan shouted immediately.

Yal Dolicar ran to the capstan and knocked out the block, letting the anchor drop. The chain rattled through its channel and struck bottom in only a few seconds. Saan's heart skipped a beat at this proof of how shallow the water must be.

The lush island seemed to call to him, offering much-needed fresh food—fruit, game, water. He didn't want to risk sailing closer, though; they would take longboats to shore.

"That could be Terravitae itself!" Yal Dolicar said. "I shall change into my best clothing. I want to look nice for Holy Joron."

Sizing up the small island, Sen Sherufa said, "I expected Terravitae to be bigger."

"I will accompany the first party." Sikara Fyiri's sentence was not a request, invited no argument.

Saan chose Grigovar and Yal Dolicar to accompany him, as well as another pair of crewmen and the insistent sikara; Sen Sherufa remained behind, for now. With the men at the oars, the longboat plied its way through the reefs, and as they glided closer to the island, Saan saw what appeared to be branches sticking up out of the water. Looking more closely, he was astonished to discern the upthrust masts of sunken vessels that had wrecked upon the rocks. He counted at least five ships.

"We were lucky indeed, Captain." Yal Dolicar leaned over the side to peer into the deceptively clear water. "If the storm had blown for another hour, we would have been shipwrecked as well."

"You see, Ondun is watching over us," Fyiri said. "As I requested."

Dolicar spotted a wisp of smoke and the faint flames of a fire—a bonfire on the shore. "It's a signal, look!"

Grigovar pulled on the oars, not even out of breath. "If any of those ships wrecked recently, there might be survivors on the island, Captain."

When the longboat approached the shore, Saan bounded over the side and waded up to the sandy beach, where two figures waited for them, waving with joy. They were not haggard shipwrecked crewmen, however, but a pair of women: an old crone with wrinkled skin and clumpy gray hair, and a willowy young lady with a lovely face and innocent eyes. The girl's long, pale hair had a greenish-blue sheen and was plaited with strands of seaweed.

The old woman spoke perfect Uraban, though with an archaic accent and syntax. "Such a ship we have not seen in many a year. You are most welcome here, most welcome.

My name is Iyomelka, and this is Ystya. Forgive my daughter's awkwardness. She has no experience with the company of others."

The young girl looked like a startled doe, but Saan came forward with a reassuring smile and a gallant bow. He experienced a surprising, almost magnetic attraction for the girl. "And I am quite inexperienced with such beauty. I am Captain Saan of the *Al-Orizin*. These are my crewmen: Grigovar, Yal Dolicar—"

The priestess pushed her way forward. "I am Sikara Fyiri."

Leaving the beached longboat, Iyomelka led them up the shore, through a line of palm trees, and into a beautiful glade where stood a house made of piled stones, driftwood, and dried palm fronds. Though ancient and withered, with a bent back, the crone appeared strong and spry.

Yal Dolicar looked around, curious, but saw no one else. "Are you two all alone? How did you ladies get here? And how long ago?"

Ystya opened her mouth to answer, but the old woman cut her off. "That time is long past, and we have lost track of the days. Many a ship is blown off course and smashed on the reefs, but only we survive here."

"It's a miracle we weren't wrecked ourselves," Saan said.

"Yes, truly a miracle," Iyomelka said.

"We're searching for the land of Terravitae," he continued. "We have voyaged across the world to find it. Do you have any charts—any knowledge that might help us find the land of Joron?"

The crone seemed both startled and amused. "The shores of Terravitae are far from here, and we cannot help you find them. Alas, we have no maps, nor do we have any use for them. We came here to escape such things."

"And yet they found us, Mother," Ystya said.

Sikara Fyiri interrupted, pressing her own priorities. "Do you know Urec? Have you read his log?"

Iyomelka offered a mysterious smile. "Oh, yes, we knew Urec very well."

Wandering around the fringe of the clearing near the hut, Dolicar yelped with excitement and ran back to join the others, interrupting them. "Captain, look at this! Whether or not they can give us maps, this island is more than worth our while. I've never seen the like!"

Outside the glade stood a gleaming mound of treasure: piles of gold coins, carved goblets, jewel-encrusted plates, strands of pearls, rings. Astounded and laughing, Dolicar used his good hand to poke through the breathtaking objects.

Iyomelka explained in an aloof voice, "This island is like a lodestone. Currents, winds, and storms draw ships toward it, and their cargo washes up on our shores."

Dolicar laughed. "I think I like this place."

Ystya spoke in her shy, ethereal voice. "It's all pretty, but not very useful."

Intent on his mission, Saan said, "I'd trade all this wealth for a good set of charts to show where we are and where we need to go."

Iyomelka gave a curt reply. "The treasure isn't yours to trade."

"We did not come seeking treasure," Fyiri interjected. "We are in search of knowledge. We wish to find the Key to Creation and the land of Terravitae."

"The Key to Creation?" Ystya asked, looking at her mother.

Saan was embarrassed to admit that he didn't exactly know what it was he sought. He flashed a smile at the beautiful young woman. "In a larger sense, we were given a quest to explore the world. If we can find the Key to Creation, we hope it will prove useful in helping us defeat the followers of Aiden."

"But Aiden and Urec were brothers," Ystya said. "And Joron."

"We follow the teachings of Urec," Fyiri said. "Not the corruptions of Aiden."

Saan couldn't tell whether Iyomelka was amused or annoyed by the priestess. She said, "It appears that a great deal has changed in the outside world."

With a spring in her step, Ystya led them away from the treasure pile and back to the hut. "We will share a fresh meal with you, if you like." She seemed giddy from the company.

Hanging back, Dolicar whispered quickly to Saan, "Captain, as overjoyed as I am to see that treasure, something is not right here. *I* know when a person isn't telling the truth. I would not advise trusting that old woman."

"That's one of the reasons I brought you along." But Saan chuckled as they approached the small stone house, from which the two women carried fresh fruit they had gathered from the trees. "However, many people have told me I shouldn't trust *you* either, Yal Dolicar—and that girl is a lot more attractive than you are."

Dolicar snorted. "You'll get no argument from me on that point."

93 *Olabar*

With all the sand coracles destroyed, the annual merchants' voyage to the Nunghals was canceled. Imir was glad simply to have Adreala back safe, though the girl remained disappointed. "When will I see the Nunghals?"

"You wanted to come on an adventure, girl, and I gave you an adventure. Granted, it wasn't what you expected, but haven't you had enough excitement? An adventure is *supposed* to be unexpected." As they headed back to Olabar, he realized that he himself would be glad to be back at the palace.

Upon entering the capital city months earlier than expected, the former soldan-shah paid a few *cuars* to boys who ran through the streets to announce his return. Soldan-Shah Omra had recently left for Ishalem to deal with yet another emergency, and once again Imir did not regret for a moment that he had retired. He was happy to present Adreala to her mother, safe and sound. Even so, he had plenty of explaining to do.

Istar came to greet them in the main reception hall, accompanied by a breathless Naori with her two little boys in tow. Despite the obvious relief on Istar's face, she propped her hands on her hips and gave Imir a stern but silent reprimand. "I thought you would be on the other side of the Great Desert by now! What happened?"

Before Imir could soften the explanation, Adreala piped up, sounding as enthusiastic as Saan once had. "Bandits raided Desert Harbor, Mother! They burned the camp and the coracles. They dragged me off into the desert, but my grandfather saved me. Look, I have a bandit's knife." She held it out, beaming.

With a disingenuous smile, Imir resigned himself to her mother's hard, questioning gaze. He shrugged ruefully. "We'll have time for the full tale later. For now, take heart from the fact that Adreala experienced a fine adventure! The most important part is that she has returned to Olabar safely."

Istar folded the girl in her arms, but Adreala soon pulled away and took up a firm bargaining stance. "I need to go again next year, Mother. I didn't get to make the full trip to the land of the Nunghals. My father appointed me an emissary in training."

Not wanting to think of how Omra would react to the news of his daughter's ordeal, Imir changed the subject. "Has there been any word from Saan and the *Al-Orizin* ... and, uh, Sen Sherufa?"

Istar averted her face, but not before he saw her troubled frown. "The sikaras receive occasional messages through a sympathetic journal, but Sikara Fyiri says very little in her reports. The ship is safe and continuing the voyage, but I know none of the details."

"Priestesses don't usually offer details," Imir groused.

Once back in his private quarters, he changed into clean, comfortable clothes; because of his travels, Imir no longer had the patience for royal finery or gaudy trappings.

Wanting fresh air, he stepped out onto a high balcony and looked out upon beautiful Olabar. His peace was disturbed by the roar and murmur of a crowd. Down below,

Ur-Sikara Erima was giving a sermon, and the words wafted up to the high balcony. Imir rarely listened to sermons, having no interest in the droning petulance and superiority. He'd been married to Villiki, a former sikara herself, and knew all too well the poisonous internal politics of the church.

The dark-skinned woman continued her speech, and it took him a moment to realize that she was not inflaming the people against Aidenists; rather, Erima was disappointed in *Urabans*, saying that they were cursed because of the "foreign temptress and stranger to the Truth who exerts too great a hold on the palace." How ridiculous!

He remembered hearing Istar complain, but the former soldan-shah was shocked to hear such an obvious challenge to Omra's First Wife. He doubted the priestesses spoke out so sharply when the soldan-shah was in the palace, but the ur-sikara was apparently emboldened by his absence.

Imir listened for a few more minutes, deeply disturbed. Istar/Adrea may have been an Aidenist captive taken in a raid long ago, but such things were in the past, and as First Wife she had certainly proved her worth. She had given the soldan-shah two fine daughters—not to mention the baby son murdered by Cliaparia, who was a follower of *Urec*. Treacherous Villiki was also a follower of Urec. Thus, the ur-sikara could not say that foreigners were the root of all evil. Imir doubted Erima understood the irony.

The more he thought about it, though, the more troubled he became. This was not right at all, and something needed to be done. The priestesses needed to be reprimanded. As soon as Omra returned from his latest emergency, Imir would insist that his son seriously look into the problem. The church had definitely gone too far.

94 *Olabar, Main Urecari Church*

Cithara's special training was complete.

As Villiki sat in her office deep within the main church, she noted the difference in the girl's dark eyes, the shine of determination that had not been there a month earlier. The child's features reflected her mother's beauty, but that was not sufficient. *Cliaparia*, despite her striking beauty, had been unable to hold on to Omra's heart. Some people said that Istar had worked an evil Aidenist love spell on the soldan-shah, but Villiki didn't believe such nonsense.

Cithara would be better than her mother was, thanks to Villiki's careful teaching and coaching. Best of all, Istar would suspect nothing.

The girl stood before Villiki, attentive and pliable, yet supported by a steely inner strength. The older woman folded her fingers together. "It's time for you to return to the palace for a visit, child. Your mother Istar misses you very much."

Cithara's voice was cold. "She is not my mother."

It had been a test, of course. Villiki smiled. "Do not forget that. She will lie to you and try to trick you, just as she has done to your father."

"I understand what to watch out for, my Lady. You warned me of Istar's tricks."

Villiki felt warm satisfaction in her heart. This girl was

perfect. "Traditionally, acolytes are allowed to visit their parents before they embark on the next stage of their training. Istar expects this and looks forward to seeing you. Now will be the perfect time, since Soldan-Shah Omra is in Ishalem."

The girl lowered her head in perfect submission. "Will my sister Istala accompany me home to the palace?"

"No, it isn't yet her time. You will go alone."

Cithara paused for a moment. "I hear that Adreala has returned from the Great Desert. Will I see her?"

Villiki began to grow impatient. "Adreala is irrelevant. *You* are the special one, Cithara." She unwrapped a bundle on her desk. The blade of the small dagger shone silver in the light of the oil lamp; the edge had been ground so fine that it trembled with sharpness. "This dagger was a gift to the church. I give it to you now to aid you in your holy work. You *know* that Istar murdered your mother. You *know* how Istar hunted her down in the souks and stabbed her before dozens of witnesses, yet never paid for her crimes."

Cithara flushed. "You told me the story many times, Lady Villiki."

"Istar is a blight upon the Urecari faith! She has brought much pain and trouble to our land ..." She caught her breath and calmed herself. "This is what you must use, child. Slip into your false mother's chamber when she least expects it. Stab her, as she stabbed your own dear mother. It is the only way to make Urec pleased with us again."

Without further encouragement, Cithara accepted the special dagger, looked at it with detached curiosity, then rewrapped it in the blue cloth. "I look forward to my return to the palace, Lady Villiki." She bowed and left the chamber.

After Cithara left, the older woman sat back in her chair, content. She still had a large sack of innat seeds reserved for Ur-Sikara Erima. She considered consuming a few herself, to foster this inner glow, but decided against it. Revenge would create a much stronger euphoria.

Two days later, after being welcomed back to the palace with great warmth, Cithara moved through the darkened corridors toward her adoptive mother's private quarters. The moon was full, shining silver through the arches and windows, but few lamps or candles were lit at this late hour. Cithara's shadow was long, and her footsteps entirely silent.

Her mother Istar had been full of questions about the girl's religious instruction, about how the priestesses were treating her, and about Istala. All smiles, Naori had come to greet her as well, asking many questions of her own, but Cithara had always been a quiet girl. Fortunately, exuberant Adreala wanted to talk and talk about her experiences with the desert bandits, and Cithara was able to avoid answering.

Walking in the shadows, the girl encountered Kel Rovic as he patrolled the corridors. The guard captain, though always alert for treachery or secret invaders, simply smiled at the girl. "Restless night, Cithara?"

"In the church, we learn to do without a lot of sleep, and I know that my mother Istar is often awake at this hour."

Rovic shook his head. "I saw her lamps extinguished two hours ago."

"I'd like to see for myself. If she's asleep, I'll be careful not to wake her." Rovic bade her goodnight and left her as he continued his patrol.

Istar's doors were neither barred nor guarded, and Cithara was able to slip quietly inside. She had been here so many times that she could have worked her way to the bed-chamber with her eyes closed. The balcony curtains were open, stirring in the faint breeze like gauzy specters.

Istar lay peacefully on her bed, alone because Omra was gone. Her head was propped on a silken pillow, her golden-brown hair spread out and mussed by sleep. Cithara approached without a sound and drew Villiki's silver knife from where she had hidden it in her garments. She stood over Istar, the hilt of the blade cold in her hand.

Istar stirred, muttered in her sleep, and let out a long, soft sigh . . . a contented sigh. Cithara realized she was about to change everything, perhaps in all of Uraba.

"Mother Istar, please wake up."

The woman's eyes flew open, reacting as she spotted the dagger. "Cithara?" Her blue eyes focused on the blade.

"There is something you need to know." The girl extended the dagger with a gentle motion, turning the hilt to hand it to Istar. "The sikaras are plotting against you, and they tried to train me to murder you in your sleep. They want you dead." She paused. "They are controlled by Villiki."

Istar bolted upright in bed. "*Villiki?*" She took the blade from the girl's trembling hands. "How can that be? She was banished, turned out—"

"She is in the church, Mother Istar. The priestesses are shielding her. She controls the ur-sikara. Villiki says terrible things about you." Cithara started to cry softly. "I pretended to be convinced, but I did not believe what she said."

Istar felt a great wash of love for the girl, and knew also that this was a crucial turning point. She faced Cithara calmly. "Some of her claims may be true. I have never denied that I killed your mother. You know what she did to my baby."

"I know. The events may be true, but you have always been my true mother."

Without any hesitation, Istar pulled the girl close into a tender, sincere embrace, kissed her dark hair, then drew a deep breath to slow her pounding heart. She pulled on a robe and shouted for Kel Rovic. With a great clamor, guards bounded into the First Wife's chambers, scimitars drawn, expecting assassins, but they saw only Istar and Cithara.

With exaggerated care, Istar began lighting lamps around the chamber. "Call your men, Kel Rovic, and summon the former soldan-shah. We have important work to do this night."

95 *Ishalem Wall*

His face ashen and his thoughts heavy, Mateo led a grim convoy under the hot noonday sun. In the distance, out at sea, thickening clouds hinted at a storm to come—a large one—but the darkness hanging over the travelers was more oppressive than any storm.

Weeds had overgrown the rugged Pilgrims' Road because so few traveled it any longer; ruts and rocks made the cart wheels thump and wobble as they groaned forward under their heavy loads. The horses were restless from the cloying stink.

At least they were away from the sounds of the hungry, desperate, and terrified Urecari captives.

The accompanying soldiers shambled along in a self-protective daze that numbed them to their own memories. There were no words here. To a man, they were appalled by their own actions, and the necessity that had driven them. Only another hour before they delivered their gift to the soldan-shah.

Mateo felt queasy, suffocated by his own responsibility in this. Though the worst was over, he doubted he would ever again sleep without nightmares . . . if he slept at all.

By the queen's command . . .

In desperation, he tried to think of sweet Vicka. She would be back in Calay at her father's smithy, scolding and supervising their numerous young apprentices. She would have dinner with her father, without Mateo, but he knew she would think of him. Vicka would be managing the constant production of weapons and armor. When she stood beside the flying sparks of the grindstone, did the thought cross her mind what those fine Sonnen blades would be used for . . . sharpened to a well-honed edge that could chop through the neck of any Uraban prisoner who had the misfortune to be captured at the wrong time?

He forcibly drove Vicka's face from his memory, because he did not want to associate thoughts of her with *this*. He moved forward in solemn silence.

Destrar Shenro had ridden down from Alamont to join this mission, to honor the martyred Alamont horsemen who had bravely—foolishly—died in an ill-conceived attempt to recapture the holy city. But his drawn face showed clear regret. He already bore guilt for executing hundreds of work-camp prisoners in retaliation for the betrayal at the Ishalem wall.

And then there was poor Tomas.

And now these Uraban victims.

Would the cycle never end? The momentum of hatred swept them along like the foamy waters of an uncontrolled flood. This war had changed both Tierran and Uraban, followers of Aiden and followers of Urec alike. It left scars so thick and ugly that not even victory could make them fade. . . .

With hopeless dread, Mateo knew that today's actions would not stop further vengeful bloodshed. But there was nothing he could do about it, nothing he could change . . . perhaps nothing he even *wanted* to change . . .

Before setting out·from Calay Castle, he had met with Queen Anjine and begged her to reconsider. "I understand your sorrow and your hatred . . . but if you do this, you step over a precipice. You can never take it back."

He expected her anger to flash, but her eyes remained oddly dull. "Take it back? Can they take back what they did to Tomas? They murdered him in cold blood, took that poor sweet boy and chopped off his head. A thousand Urecari are not enough to pay back that pain, but I will be merciful."

He had raised his eyes with a glimmer of hope. "Mercy?"

"Yes . . . I will stop at one thousand. That is all the mercy I'm prepared to show them." Anjine had looked up at him, her expression softening to reveal a hint of the woman he had once known so well. "My decision is made. I *need* you. Mateo. I need you to do this for me."

He had bowed, partly to hide his face. "I have always sworn my heart and my life to you . . . my Queen."

He had tried not to see the faces as he carried out his orders: men begging, women wailing, children crying, all pleading in a language he didn't understand. He had tried to see Tomas instead of these victims, to remember why he was doing this.

As commander, he was not required to bloody his own sword. He could have ordered his soldiers to do all of the killing. But that would not have kept his hands clean. He was a part of this. Mateo had killed thirty-seven captives himself, with strong, clean strokes of his own sharpened sword . . . the one that Vicka had given him. With each death, he hoped it would make up for Tomas, but it didn't.

And it didn't.

Nor did the next . . .

Ahead now, they could see the towering stone wall that barred faithful Aidenists from Ishalem. God's Barricade, the Urecari mockingly called it. Within clear sight of the imposing barrier, Mateo called a halt to the procession.

A commotion occurred atop the wall as soldiers took up bows and waited to see if this was some sort of enemy attack. Next to Mateo, Shenro covered his nose. "Let's be done with this, Subcomdar, and get far from here."

"Not yet. Give them time to call the city governor or the soldan-shah, if he's there."

When all the carts were pulled forward into a line, Mateo gestured to the soldiers. "Abandon the wagons and cut the horses free. We'll have to ride swiftly, once the Curlies see the harvest we brought them."

"There he is!" Destrar Shenro pointed out a man wearing pale robes, with a clean white olba wrapped around his head and a glint of gold at his neck. Clearly, a person of some importance.

Mateo nodded grimly. "Good enough. *Now.*"

The men strained as they rocked the wagons and overturned them to spill their contents on the ground. Cartload after cartload of severed Uraban heads rolled like lumpy, rotten gourds into the dirt outside the Ishalem wall. Men, women, children.

One thousand of them.

Even at that, Anjine did not consider it sufficient payment for what these monsters had done to the prince.

Mateo wheeled his horse and whistled to his men, as howls of outrage erupted behind them from the Ishalem wall. Soon the gates would open and war chargers burst forth. Mateo did not have the army to fight them. They rode away at a gallop along the old Pilgrims' Road, to where ships awaited them at the temporary prisoner camp, miles north.

In front of them, at the now abandoned camp, towering clouds of black smoke already rose into the air, marking the huge pyres that burned the headless bodies. Mateo hoped the Tierran ships were ready to depart as soon as they arrived at the anchorage. He wanted to go home, to Calay, to Vicka, and to the queen.

But he would never leave these memories behind.

96 *Calay Castle*

Buried in grief, anger, and regret, Anjine stopped noticing the sun in the sky, the changing weather, or the dark clouds of a large storm approaching from the Oceansea. By now, she was sure the horrific deed must be done—she could count on Mateo. She couldn't change her mind, couldn't call him back . . . didn't want to.

He had tried to talk her out of it—begged her, in fact, to reconsider—but she had refused. It might not have been the right decision, but it was the only decision she would consider.

Anjine had not held court for nearly two weeks, preferring to remain in her private chambers. She didn't want to face any unwanted but well-meaning visitors. She could not bear their sympathy or grief, their growls of outrage, or their vows of vengeance upon the enemy. She was the queen. She wore the crown. She had made her decision.

Anjine climbed the dusty stone stairs to the tower room where King Korastine had kept Aiden's Compass for so many years. Without the Compass, the room was just a dusty chamber with narrow windows that overlooked the harbor. Her cat followed her, wanting attention but also showing her a kind of love that none of her other subjects did. It was what she needed. She scratched Tycho's ears absently, and he lifted his head to accept the affection.

In the upper room, she stood at the segmented panes of

glass, surprised by a sky knotted with black clouds. Safe and sheltered in the castle, Anjine had been unaware of the worsening weather. But she saw that down at the bustling harbor, ships were already lashed tightly to the docks, their sails tied up securely. As she noted the activity, she wondered how long the storm had been brewing.

Sen Leo na-Hadra knew exactly where to find her.

The Saedran scholar had been a close friend to her father and tried to continue in that role with the queen. Anjine appreciated the old man's advice, though she had not been in the mood for company, conversation, or counsel since the Uraban emissary had delivered his answer onto the floor of the throne room.

She hadn't been in the mood for much of anything at all.

Sen Leo cleared his throat at the doorway to the tower room. "Majesty, I must speak with you. I sympathize with your grief and anger, just as I shared Korastine's pain after the death of Ilrida. I understand how difficult this is, but the people have not seen you for days. As queen, you don't have the luxury of uninterrupted grief, as a normal person does. As your heart goes, so goes the entire kingdom—and Tierra cannot afford empty despair. Not now."

Anjine's eyes were burning and puffy, yet she couldn't remember the last time she had actually cried. No matter which direction she looked, she was confronted by memories of Tomas. How she wished Mateo could be here with her. But she had sent him away. . . .

Her expression hardened. "So you think I ask my subjects to indulge me too much?"

Sen Leo scratched his gray beard. "no, my Queen, but I

do think you need to open your eyes and heed what is occurring around you. I care about you. You have lost your father to illness, your brother to unspeakable crime, but you still have your people. They need you to be strong, to care for them, to be a true leader. Tierra is beset by threats other than the Urecari."

She stiffened coldly at that. "What threats?"

"Majesty! Have you not looked outside? The hurricane has been approaching for days. Ships raced in from the Oceansea seeking the protection of Calay harbor. Fishermen report horrific winds and waves far out at sea, worse than anything they've seen in generations. And the storm is coming here. My Queen, Calay has to prepare, or we'll all be washed away. You must call out the city guard, issue instructions, have your city hunker down, so that it can survive the whirlwind that is to come."

Tycho strolled up to the Saedran scholar, but the old man gracefully dodged him. Anjine picked up the cat, held him close, and he melted into her arms, where he belonged. "If Ondun is lashing out at us with a storm, how can I stand against His will?"

"Ondun would be happy for us to prepare and take care of ourselves. Here is what Guard-Marshall Vorannen can order." The scholar ticked off items on his fingers. "First, we should reinforce the dockside buildings and warehouses, batten everything down, shutter the windows. All the ships in port must prepare for the gale. Vorannen should send the entire city guard out to assist the people. And you must give them strength and encouragement, too. Dark days are ahead of us."

His words were just noises, and she could not grasp the

relevance. "Dark days are already here." Keeping her back to him, Anjine stared out at the dark clouds, trying to imagine the howling gales and turbulent waters that were churning the depths of the Oceansea. "The storm only mirrors what I feel in my heart. Maybe I even summoned it myself."

"I don't believe that, my Queen—and neither do you. The people grieve with you for the loss of Prince Tomas, but please don't let them lose everything else. Summon the resources of the city!"

She thought of sailing away herself, as her father had always longed to do, aboard a large, beautiful vessel that simply charted a course to the edge of the world—perhaps going beyond the boundaries of all maps and looking for Terravitae ... as the *Dyscovera* had done. Thinking of the ship, she felt a new fear. "How far might this storm reach? What about Captain Vora and the *Dyscovera*?"

Sen Leo gave her a reassuring nod. "For now the ship is safe. I checked the model in its warehouse building, and there's not a splinter or thread out of place. After months of sailing, the *Dyscovera* should be far beyond the reach of this storm. But we do need to protect the model from any damage the storm could cause. I added reinforcements to the walls, doors, and shutters, and the building is as strong as we can make it."

"Then how far will this storm reach?"

"All of our signs and weather instruments show it could be the worst storm in generations. It will affect the entire Tierran coastline."

A chill ran down Anjine's back as she pictured Mateo having to struggle through the gale to come home to her.

But he wouldn't let a mere storm stop him ... even after what she had asked him to do.

Shifting Tycho in her arms, she turned to the Saedran scholar. "Very well, Sen Leo. Your wisdom is clear, as always. Call Marshall Vorannen and tell him, on my authority, to dispatch all of the city guard to assist in making necessary preparations. And before the worst weather hits I will walk through the city and address the people, encourage them, strengthen their resolve. It's time they see they have a queen again."

97 *The* Dyscovera

Javian called down from the lookout nest, "Captain Vora, there's something ahead!"

After long weeks with no land in sight, and not even an encounter with sea serpents to interrupt the monotony, the crew scurried across the deck, shading their eyes to peer off into the waters. Criston shouted up, "What is it—a reef? An island?"

Javian paused a long time, staring through the spyglass. "No, sir—it looks like ... towers! Buildings under the water!"

Kjelnar brayed with laughter. "Towers? The boy's gone sunblind."

Criston placed his own battered spyglass to his eye, swung the lens across the water ahead, and frowned. Near the horizon, he did see pointed objects protruding from the waves ... artificial structures. Rooftops? Pinnacles? He suspected it was just a cluster of weirdly shaped coral or pointed rocks, but he couldn't be sure. "Kjelnar, set our course three points to port. We came out here to see what there is to see."

Prester Hannes joined them. "Perhaps this is a signpost that Aiden left to guide us to Terravitae. If that tower is the Lighthouse at the End of the World, then our quest may be at an end."

The Saedran chartsman joined him, his face filled with curiosity. "Isn't that just a legend?"

"Many things sound like legends to unbelievers," Hannes said with a sour expression.

"I'm not an unbeliever," Aldo said in a mild tone. "I just don't believe what you believe." He had always enjoyed sparring with Sen Leo na-Hadra, but Prester Hannes seemed to find it more annoying than intellectually stimulating.

Aldo ignored the prester's pinched expression and continued to stare toward the distant structures. Since sailing beyond the reach of his known charts, he'd had little to do. Each day Aldo took measurements of the sun's zenith and marked the stars at night, but the constellations had long since shifted out of their familiar patterns. After such a long voyage, he had little to show for their explorations other than a map of empty waters.

Appearing suddenly alongside the ship, lissome gray forms rose in graceful arcs, then dove again. Mia called from the starboard rail, "Look at the dolphins. Dozens of them!"

As the *Dyscovera* turned toward the sunken towers, the dolphins followed them all the way like a formal escort, bounding through the waters and then streaking ahead. The sailors cheered them, laughing. They all felt excited, optimistic. Seamen had long considered dolphins to be good luck.

Even with fractured sunlight reflecting from the waves, Criston could discern structures under the water—geometrical shapes in the crystalline depths, large buildings many fathoms down. A ... sunken city. The pointed structures protruding from the surface became the tops of ornate spires that reached out of the water, the tallest of which appeared to be the peak of a great palace.

Kjelnar climbed to the prow, leaning out over the ice-dragon horn to peer downward. "Careful there! Edge a bit starboard—I'll not have my *Dyscovera* wrecked because one of you sailed her into the top of a building!"

The dolphins encircled the *Dyscovera* with chattering laughter. Shimmering forms streaked through the water around the buildings, darting to and fro ... but they did not look like fish. Mia called out, "Captain, do you see it?"

"I'm not sure what I'm seeing."

After swimming around the ship one more time, still frolicking, the dolphins dove beneath the waves, where the depths distorted their forms. A few moments later, figures splashed to the surface, astounding the crew. *Human figures.* Young men and women, barely clothed, dove and splashed and peered up at the large sailing ship.

Reeling back from the sight, Prester Hannes made a warding sign and grasped his fishhook pendant. "If they are demons of the deep, we must fight them. The Book of Aiden warns us about deceivers."

Kjelnar paced up and down the deck, alert and suspicious. "I've heard stories of merfolk, Captain. They tempt ships onto the rocks, get them lost in storms."

But Criston heard no threat in the voices as they laughed and called out in an eerie, musical language. "Don't forget why we came, Hannes, and what we are charged to do. These are all children of Ondun. Aren't you curious to learn what they know of Aiden's original voyage?"

The prester frowned at the captain in surprise. "We already know everything we need to know. Aiden left it for us." His brow furrowed as he studied the swimming people. "I cannot tell if they are ignorant savages who need saving, or if they are already damned—like the Urecari."

Criston was not concerned. "We'll be cautious, but I won't pass up a chance like this. Maybe these people can tell us the way to Terravitae." He raised his voice. "Drop sails! And keep a sharp eye out."

The sunken city was all around and below them now. The buildings were made of ancient stone marked with unusual glyphs and designs, ornamented with scrollwork. Everything seemed perfectly intact, as if someone took care of it.

Scrutinizing the marks on the towers, Aldo na-Curic straightened in shock. "Captain, I—I recognize that writing! The letters are archaic, but there's no doubt ..." He blinked. "They're *Saedran*, sir! This city, those buildings—they're of Saedran origin!"

Below, the swimmers continued to laugh and wave and chatter amongst themselves. Aldo shook his head in wonder. "I have heard the stories all my life, but I thought they were just fanciful tales. Now it's true—it's true! This city—everything that lies beneath us—is the original Saedran continent that sank beneath the waves ages ago."

98 *Iyomelka's Island*

After so long at sea, the *Al-Orizin* sailors were excited to set foot on dry land again, and the two longboats made several trips, delivering parties for shore leave. The old crone and her willowy daughter welcomed the visitors, offering a bounty of fresh fruits and fish, but the men had had enough of fish. Laughing, they ventured into the forests and soon returned with a wild boar, which they roasted over coals in a pit.

Iyomelka happily tore into the meat with her crooked teeth. "What a feast! Ystya and I are unable to hunt such large game."

Saan took every opportunity to flirt with beautiful Ystya, whose shy innocence fascinated him in a way that typical Uraban girls did not. Her features were neither Uraban nor Tierran, but he was attracted by more than her exotic beauty. Growing up in the soldan-shah's palace, Saan himself had always felt like an outsider because of his blond hair and blue eyes. He knew what it was like to be different, to be considered strange among other people. This young woman, with her ivory locks plaited with green strands, combined the wide-eyed charm of a newborn fawn with the majesty of a princess.

He relaxed next to the young woman as they ate their roast boar. "If you like this meat, just wait until we take you and your mother back to Olabar. You'll have all the delicious feasts civilization can provide. Our master chefs make honeyed lamb skewers, roast game hens stuffed with preserved lemons, and pastries you can't even imagine."

Grigovar let out a sound that was halfway between a groan and a sigh. "Stop, Captain! We still have a long voyage ahead of us—and only ship's rations."

Saan moved closer to Ystya. "But I'm just getting started. There's a whole world to describe to this girl." Entirely unaccustomed to so much attention, the young woman listened with fascination to Saan's stories.

"Careful, Captain," Yal Dolicar said around a mouthful of savory roast boar. "With all the treasure on this island, they could *buy* the Olabar palace directly from your father. When we take them from this island, we'll have to make room in our cargo hold for all the gold and jewels. These two will be fabulously wealthy from the moment they set foot on Uraban soil."

Iyomelka turned with narrowed eyes toward Saan. "Do not believe us ungrateful, Captain, but Ystya and I have no wish to be rescued. As remarkable as your coming may be, this island is our home."

Saan used as much charm as he knew, grasping Ystya's slender hand. "It is a crime to keep such a lovely young woman away from the rest of the world. She needs to be with people her own age. She needs to have a life of her own. We can show her the world. You would not keep your own daughter from that?"

The old woman said, "Ystya is unlike other young women. You misunderstand, Captain. I brought her to this island for a reason."

Dolicar nearly choked. "You *want* to be stranded?"

"Why do you assume that we are stranded?"

"We thought you were shipwrecked," Grigovar said.

"Oh, those other ships crashed on the reefs much later," Ystya said gently. "My mother came here quite intentionally. And my father joined us later."

Sen Sherufa frowned in puzzlement. She had been listening and observing, but holding her silence. "Some of those wrecks are centuries old. Exactly how long have you been here?"

Iyomelka avoided the question. "When time matters not, one stops marking it."

Sikara Fyiri's question was much more of a challenge. "Have you been able to study Urec's Log? Do you follow his teachings?"

The old crone laughed derisively, tossing aside a bone. "His teachings? We came here long before Urec and Aiden sailed on their little boats."

Yal Dolicar nearly choked on his food. Even he wouldn't have made such an outrageous claim. "I find that hard to believe."

Iyomelka stroked her daughter's long silken hair, adjusting the seaweed plaits. "Whatever you believe, another person will believe something else. My husband and I left the rest of the world and came here . . . where we meant to raise our only daughter. You will see that this island is endowed with an aura of power."

Fyiri rose to her feet, her demeanor confrontational. "If you know Urec and Aiden, do you know Ondun, then?"

Iyomelka made a dismissive gesture. "My husband's name was Ondun—but that was long ago."

Grigovar laughed aloud. "Now *that* is quite a tale!"

Iyomelka's expression darkened. "Guests should not speak ill of their hosts."

"And you should not speak sacrilege against Ondun and Urec," Fyiri snapped.

Saan cut her off before the discussion could escalate. "We meant no offense, Iyomelka, but you must admit that your claim is difficult to believe. You've been on this island longer than all of recorded history?"

"Longer than *your* recorded history." The withered crone did look as if she could be thousands of years old.

Young Ystya said in a mild tone, "Just because something is difficult to believe does not make it untrue. I have been here as long as I can remember. Who is to say how long that has been?"

Iyomelka regarded all of them as though they were mere children and she a teacher who had almost given up on them. "The wellspring of this island's power originated from my husband. His whole body was infused with it, and he could create things, change things. I had powers, too, but he was by far the stronger." She gazed wistfully up at the sky. "After many millennia, even the greatest love fades, and here all alone on this island, he and I eventually grew tired of each other. But now I miss him very much."

"What happened to him, then?" Saan asked. Fyiri looked greatly offended, not wanting to hear the answer at all because it contradicted her core faith.

The old woman levered herself to her feet, leaving the rest of the boar carcass over the still-warm coals. "Follow me to our spring at the heart of the island. Then you will know why I am so old, and why . . . much has changed over the centuries."

Iyomelka moved through the jungle at a surprisingly rapid clip, following a well-worn path flanked by crowded weeds. Saan walked at the head of the group, curious to see what the old woman had to show them, and Ystya stayed close to him.

Iyomelka continued to talk, over her shoulder, as she brushed leaves and vibrant flowers aside. "The soul of this island is contained in a spring of pure water that bubbles up from great depths. For most of our lives, after Ondun came here to join us, my husband, my daughter, and I took our water from this source, and it kept us young and powerful and content."

As the path wound uphill through thick underbrush, it gave way to pale limestone outcroppings. Iyomelka took them to the top of a rise, the crest of which had been cleared of vegetation, where lovingly placed white rocks encircled a hole seven feet wide.

When Saan peered over the edge, he saw that the hole vanished into darkness, like an empty well. The old woman stood at his side, regarding the dry shaft. "This spring was once a silvery fountain, a bubbling source of life—and death. My husband fell into the spring and sank to the bottom. He drowned, and his body still lies there, far below." She didn't seem much bothered by the fact. "However, the magic in his body infused the water, so when Ystya and I partook from the well and bathed in it, the water revitalized us, nourished us, restored our youth."

Iyomelka knelt at the edge. "But you can see something has changed. The water level in the spring dropped, and we can no longer purify ourselves. That is the only reason I have begun to grow old. Ystya remained a mere child for countless centuries, an innocent young girl, such a joy . . . and now, as you can see, she's matured."

Saan looked admiringly at the young woman. "Yes, I can see that very well."

Dolicar grinned. "Well, the passage of many years does tend to make one grow old."

"The passage of years had no effect on me, until the water was gone," Iyomelka retorted.

Sen Sherufa made no comment, taking in the information; Fyiri, though, did not hide her scorn. "Foolish superstition. That is not the way the blessings of Ondun are given to humans."

"And who said we were human, Priestess? Ystya and I weren't created in the same way as the rest of you."

The haughty sikara was not at all intimidated. "Perhaps the spring dried up because of your false beliefs—as a retaliation from the true creator. A curse."

The crone lowered her gaze. "Perhaps there was a cause. Perhaps there was a retaliation. I do not know why the magic faded, why it forsook us. But see what has become of me." Iyomelka indicated her wrinkled, spotted hands, her large-knuckled fingers, then turned her imploring gaze to Saan. "That is why I cannot leave this island, Captain Saan, because the last remnants of power here are the only things that keep me as strong as I am."

Yal Dolicar dropped a pebble down the well, listening as it plunked into water far below. The splash was quite clear, amplified by the narrow stone walls. "Ah, there *is* still a spring down below. Maybe we can lower a bucket?"

"It would not be enough," Iyomelka said. "The water level continues to drop."

As the others crowded around the well, Dolicar whispered to Saan, "Captain, we might have an opportunity here. The old woman is convinced, yes, but . . . just because the spring is drying up doesn't mean there's a curse, or any kind of magical explanation. We could rig a rope and have someone climb down to investigate. There might be a blockage we could fix." He shrugged. "If it's a fountain of youth, shouldn't we try it for ourselves? I'd give it a go."

Saan called out to the old woman, but directed his smile toward Ystya. "Iyomelka, I have a proposal for you. If my men and I discover a way to make the water flow again, would you be grateful for that?" He glanced at Dolicar, knowing full well what the other man would do. "Would you offer us some kind of reward?"

The crone's expression was of hope laced with caution. "Captain, if you can fix the spring for us, I will let you take any treasure on this entire island."

"Any treasure?"

Grigovar and Yal Dolicar gasped and clapped. "Now that's a worthy incentive!"

"Any treasure," the old woman said, "so long as you and your ship are on your way afterward. This place is not for you."

99 *Uraba*

Making his way across the strange continent, Prester Ciarlo learned not to count on the kindness of strangers. Often he felt hurt and disappointed by the treatment he received from the followers of Urec, but he did not let his determination dwindle. "Struggle creates strength," said the Book of Aiden. More often than not, he bedded down alone in the forest by a small campfire.

His leg ached after wandering for so many leagues over hills and through unexplored forests, but the pain was nothing compared to the good work of spreading the word of Aiden . . . if he could ever get these poor people to listen to him. If he converted only one soul in Uraba, the reward would be great enough.

And he still hoped he could learn some small hint about Adrea, but the Windcatch raid had occurred twenty years ago, and it didn't seem possible that any slave could remain alive after so long. Even so, he had the afterimage from a dream; Aiden had given him a message. Hope grew inside him like an oak sapling, and he would water and nourish it with his faith, just as he would continue to believe that Aiden wanted him to spread the Word.

Ciarlo received a cool welcome in the port city of Sioara. The villagers regarded him with blank stares or angry scowls.By his appearance, strong accent, and fishhook pendant, all could see that he came from Tierra, and therefore they didn't trust him. It baffled him that others did not delight in the tales of Aiden's voyage or the tribulations of Sapier, but he didn't let himself be discouraged.

Ciarlo wandered across the landscape, wherever his feet took him. He had no map and no particular destination, though the closer he came to Olabar, the better his chances of learning something about Adrea's fate. He assumed that Aiden would give him an invisible compass and guide him where he was destined to go.

After gathering nuts and one soft brown apple that had fallen to the ground, he found a good place to camp. As the darkness deepened in the hesitant hush of the forest, he sat by himself to enjoy his scraps of food and study pages in the abridged Book of Aiden.

The stranger came out of the trees so silently that he startled Ciarlo when he stepped into the circle of firelight. He was an old man with a pleasant face, white hair, and a long beard. Though his clothes had been patched many times, the garments looked well-worn and comfortable, not tattered. He grasped a walking stick in his right hand, and he raised his left hand, palm open, in a gesture of peace.

Ciarlo returned the smile. "In the name of Ondun, you are welcome at my fire." His grasp of the foreign language had grown significantly. Uraban and Tierran were not, in fact, so different; both were based on the same ancient root tongue, which he had learned from Prester Fennan long ago.

"And in the name of Ondun I accept your hospitality." The old man had a strangely accented voice that sounded neither Uraban or Tierran.

"Are you a hunter or a beggar?" Ciarlo inquired.

"Just a traveler who seeks to see the world. And you?"

"I could say the same, I suppose." Ciarlo's fishhook pendant hung at his throat, and the Book of Aiden sat open beside him in the firelight, so he saw no reason to avoid the subject. "I've come to spread the word of Aiden. These people know only of Urec."

The old man slowly took a seat on the opposite side of the fire. "It is not good to know only one brother or the other. Are you learning about Urec, as well, in your time here in Uraba?"

The question surprised Ciarlo. "I do not mean to convert to the Urecari religion, if that is your question."

"That was not my suggestion at all. Simply a reminder that Aiden and Urec were brothers, along with Joron. They had much in common and many adventures together before they set sail from Terravitae to explore the world."

Ciarlo glanced at the gnawed shreds of the apple core. "I'm afraid I don't have any food to offer you. I am limited by what I can easily find and catch." He rubbed his palm against his thigh. "My leg pains me. It is an old injury. The bone broke when I was just a boy."

The stranger undid a fuzzy bag of sewn rabbit skins at his side "You have already built the fire. Since I share your warmth, you may share some of my food." He withdrew strips of dried meat, a handful of morel mushrooms, and three small plums. "The world was created in such a way as to provide what a person needs, if he knows how and where to look."

Ciarlo accepted the offer. He received so much scorn that at times he lost hope for these people ... but then he encountered someone like the benevolent sikara from the seaside village, or this old traveler. He knew that there *was* good in these people, despite their false beliefs.

Ciarlo looked down at his open book. "I have only read about Aiden's voyage. I know what happened on the Arkship and how he came to Tierra to settle there. I confess I've heard very few legends about the two brothers in Terravitae."

"Three brothers. You must not forget Joron," the old

man chided. "There are stories, and some are fanciful, I agree. My particular favorite is a tale of when Aiden, Urec, and Joron were young, and the three boys embarked on an adventure to explore Terravitae."

"A childhood story of the three brothers?" Ciarlo had never heard such a thing.

"Yes, the brothers went off alone, assuming the land was safe, because their father Ondun had created everything. Why would He create something dangerous? The boys followed a river inland. They plucked ripe fruit from the trees whenever they were hungry, or fish leapt out of streams and flopped on the banks so they could be roasted over a campfire. Aiden, Urec, and Joron finally reached a great smoking mountain where the rocks were hard and sharp. Cracks leaked lava like the fiery blood of the world.

"Wise and cautious Joron warned them to be careful, but Aiden and Urec raced each other to the top of the mountain so they could look down into the crater. There from the bubbling lava, a fiery orange worm rose up to hiss at them, spewing sulfurous smoke from its nostrils. Suddenly, Aiden and Urec were afraid and realized that perhaps they had gone where Ondun had not meant for them to go after all. Joron had been right to warn them.

"The worm emerged from the lava crack and slithered after them. The boys stumbled over sharp black rocks on their way down the mountainside. Seeing their danger, brave Joron called out to their father for help, and before the glowing worm could strike the boys, Ondun Himself arrived. Moving swiftly and with terrible power, He shielded Aiden and Urec. Putting them behind Him, He sent the fiery worm back into the lava pit.

"'You should not have come here,' Ondun said to the boys. 'Yes, I created the world, but I was not finished with this part yet.'

"Aiden, Urec, and Joron said that they were sorry, that they only wanted to see their father's creation. So Ondun bade them to watch His labors as He remained at the volcano for a day, a night, and a day, pushing the rocks and cracked earth together, sealing the wound, and covering the flaming blood of the world. The fiery worm was never seen again.

"Ondun planted trees in the volcanic soil, and very soon there was not even a scar to show where the volcano had been. 'You will explore the world someday,' Ondun said to the boys, 'but not today.'"

Ciarlo listened to the story with delight. "I had not heard that before."

"There are so many stories." The old man ate one of the plums, and comically puckered his face at the sourness. "You must have some tales of your own. Tell me."

Ciarlo blushed. "I know what is written in the Book of Aiden."

"Not those stories. *Your* story."

Ciarlo was reticent as he began to explain how Windcatch had nearly been destroyed in the Urecari raid, how Adrea had been taken, and how he had become the town's prester. The stranger listened and encouraged him until Ciarlo felt the tale drawn out of him, blossoming from his memories and his imagination.

It was late when he was through. Ciarlo felt drained, his throat dry and raspy. The old man stretched out on the other side of the fire. "We both deserve a good rest now.

Thank you for sharing your tale with me, and for the company."

Realizing just how sleepy he was, Ciarlo lay down on the soft dry leaves. With a safe, contented feeling, he began dreaming almost immediately. . . .

In the morning when he awoke, the fire was cold gray ash. He stretched on the hard ground, rubbed the scratchiness from his eyes, and saw that his visitor had gone, leaving only a mark on the matted leaves where he had slept. Ciarlo sighed with disappointment. He had liked the old man and hoped that they might travel awhile together.

Still fuzzy with sleep, Ciarlo saw that his guest had left a leather-bound book next to his pack. Curious, he reached down to pick it up, wondering if it might be some religious text, but when he opened the cover, he saw it was merely a journal, tales the old man had written about his own adventures.

They seemed to span years—*centuries*.

He felt a chill. Handwritten lines filled page after page, and Ciarlo read the adventures and ruminations with growing amazement. Everyone knew stories of strange hermits, old men who traveled the wilderness and appeared at unexpected times.

This book was a new volume of the Tales of the Traveler.

Ciarlo was so astonished he wasn't sure what to believe. He had never asked the stranger's name, and the old man had revealed little about himself or his identity. Ciarlo's unexpected visitor might have been the ancient Traveler himself—Aiden (or Urec, as the Urabans believed) wandering the world. Ciarlo looked around for some sign of the man, wondering where he had gone. But the forest was quiet and empty.

He brushed crumpled leaves and a few strands of dry grass from his pants, got to his feet—and froze in unraveling astonishment. He bent down, then straightened. He touched his leg, just now realizing what was missing.

The intense aching pain deep in his bone had vanished. *Gone*, for the first time in as many years as he could remember. It was a miracle. He held the journal of the Traveler's tales reverently against his chest. *Another* miracle.

He walked around the camp, stepped up on a log then down again, bent over, stretched. The pain had been with him for so long he'd stopped noticing it, but now he wanted to dance, to run.

A modest man, Ciarlo couldn't accept that he deserved such a blessing. Nevertheless, the change in him provided all the determination he needed to push forward into Uraba, to keep spreading the word, to keep searching for Adrea— all the way to Olabar, if necessary.

100 *Olabar*

Roused by hushed but urgent alarms, Imir hurried to the First Wife's quarters, still groggy with sleep. At first, he blurrily wondered if desert bandits had attacked the Olabar palace. "What is it? Why all the fuss?" Many people stirred in the corridors. Something bad must have happened. "Where is the emergency?"

Meeting him near Omra's quarters, Kel Rovic wore a

grim expression. "I will allow Lady Istar to explain, my Lord—this is serious news indeed."

The former soldan-shah had hoped to have no more nights like this, after retiring as the leader of Uraba. He remembered his own father's weary face, when Shieltar had gratefully surrendered the ring of leadership to Imir, so many years ago. "A soldan-shah's life is never his own, my son. The land and the people are yours now ... and all that comes with them." Old Shieltar had not lived to enjoy his later years, though; the old arrow wound still pained him, and he had died in his sleep six months later. ...

With no other choice, Imir easily slipped back into the role as he accompanied Kel Rovic into Istar's quarters. With a glance he saw the girls Cithara and Adreala sitting together, frightened. Naori came running in with her two young sons in tow, her eyes wide; young Irec began to cry, and Naori tried to shush him.

Istar soothed Omra's other wife, "It's all right now, Naori. We're safe."

Imir barged in. "Safe from *what*?" He didn't like not knowing what had happened.

Raising her head, as if it took great effort, Istar met his gaze squarely. "Cithara was sent here to assassinate me. We must act quickly, while the sikaras still think they might have succeeded. This is all Villiki's scheme."

"The sikaras? *Villiki*?" As Imir stared in disbelief, Cliaparia's daughter came up to him, knelt in respect, and held out a sharp silver dagger.

"With this knife, I was commanded to kill Mother Istar."

The former soldan-shah turned his glare toward Kel

Rovic and took half a step backward from the point of the dagger. "Then why does the girl still have the blade?"

Istar held up her hand. "Because I gave it back to her. I trust her. She is, and always has been, a true daughter to me."

Shaking his head, Imir slumped onto the pile of cushions on the floor. "By the Eye of Urec, please tell me what is going on ... although I'm already sure I won't like it. Somebody start from the beginning."

As Cithara recounted her tale, he listened with growing anger. His face burned, and his hands clenched into hard fists when he learned that Villiki was not only alive after all, but still active in the church, and still very much attempting to destroy her rivals. "I knew I should have executed her when her crimes were revealed, but I couldn't do it. She was my wife, the mother of Tukar—and he too paid the price." He curled his hands together, as if wrapping them around her neck. "It was a mistake to show mercy to her."

"Her heart is poison, but it is she who made the mistake," Istar said. "When you banished her, Villiki *could* have made a new life for herself, *could* have found a place in the world, *could* have found contentment. Instead, she chose to do this, and the church of Urec supports and shelters her. According to Cithara, the priestesses are actively aware of her schemes—even the ur-sikara herself."

"The rot goes deep, but I'm not surprised." Imir heaved a sigh. "There was a reason why I turned the ring over to Omra. I am disgusted with such politics. Right now, Adreala and I should be feasting with the Nunghals."

Istar's voice was steady. "You may have retired, Imir, but

you will always be a soldan-shah. You can't hide from Uraba."

Adreala spoke up. "What about Istala? She's still an acolyte. What if they hold her hostage? We need to get my sister out of the church."

Imir looked fondly at the girl. Adreala had matured greatly during her brief time away from the palace. "I already rescued one granddaughter from desert bandits. Now we must save another from a treacherous snake that lives right here in Olabar. And there is no time to lose."

Kel Rovic had listened to the entire discussion. "We must be swift as well as cautious. I will prepare my men for immediate action."

When Imir drew himself up, he felt like the soldan-shah once more. "There is no time to summon Omra from Ishalem—we need to do something tonight. Villiki expects an assassination. She ordered Cithara to make her move quickly, and she will have her spies everywhere."

"If she's hiding in the main church, how do we find her?" Istar said. "The sikaras will protect her." From her expression, she looked perfectly willing to tear down the doors and walls of the great stone building to get inside.

"I command loyalties that you do not, Lady Istar. Leave it to me." He'd had his own issues with the priestesses during his rule, and Villiki—his Second Wife—had been a former sikara. He knew their tricks and their schemes. Fortunately, since he was no longer soldan-shah, Imir did not have to pander to them; he could take immediate action and not worry about the consequences. And it was about time.

He raised his voice. "We will go immediately, with as

many men as we can muster. The sikaras may think themselves safe inside their church, but no church will protect a woman who sends a child to do her killing! Long ago she tried to assassinate Omra, and now his First Wife. Kel Rovic, tonight we march on the main church, rescue Istala, and arrest Villiki."

A hundred armed soldiers spilled out of the Olabar palace and into the shadowy streets, their booted feet ringing on the paving stones. Behind darkened windows, lamps and candles began to shine like glowing eyes as the commotion awoke sleeping citizens. The men pressed forward in hushed ranks faster than rumors could spread.

Imir and Kel Rovic took the lead, with Lady Istar and her daughters close behind. Adreala's face wore a fierce look, and she kept her own dagger at her side. She had insisted on going along. "I fought desert bandits, Mother— I can hold off a few priestesses. We've got to get Istala away from them."

Once they got inside the towering stone edifice, they would rely on Cithara to take them directly to Villiki's lair deep within the labyrinth of the main church. The former soldan-shah did not intend to tolerate any delays. He had made the mistake of compassion once, and he didn't intend to let his venomous former wife slip away again.

Having set her scheme in motion, the vile woman would be expecting to hear that Lady Istar had been murdered, or that Cithara had been caught and possibly killed in the attempt. Knowing Villiki's arrogance, Imir was sure she could never imagine that her plot would fail entirely and that soldiers were already on the way to seize her.

Imir and Istar were not trying to exact revenge against all the priestesses of Urec, only against Villiki and those who had tried to destroy Omra and his family. Regardless, whatever happened this night, the former soldan-shah realized it was likely to crack the Urecari church open to its spoiled core . . . and few people would thank them for it.

But so it must be.

The palace troops marched to the giant church with its numerous spires and looming thick doors. Orange braziers shone from many arched windows, and silhouetted figures looked down at the armed men who crowded the streets. As whispered word spread through the church, windows and doors were hastily shut.

Coming to a halt, the soldiers stared at the great building with religious awe. When three tall sikaras appeared on the balconies above, wearing their red robes, some of the men uttered quick prayers, begging Urec for forgiveness.

At this hesitation, Imir spoke harshly to the men. "Do you think *Urec* asked for this? Do you think his word tells us to train children to kill their own mothers?" Pushing forward, he led the first ranks of guards up to the tall wooden main doors.

Kel Rovic hammered with the rounded hilt of his scimitar. "Open up! Open these doors in the name of the soldan-shah!"

Close behind, Lady Istar whispered, "They'll think you're bringing news that I was murdered in my sleep. That's what they expect."

"They will learn the truth soon enough."

Rovic hammered on the door once more, and it finally

opened a crack to reveal an elderly sikara. "This is a holy place. You may not enter!" She glanced at the soldiers and the former soldan-shah, but when she noticed Istar, she recoiled visibly.

Imir pressed his advantage, pushing against the door, though the old priestess pushed back. "Open up, woman!"

"You have no authority here!"

"I have all the authority I need. We know the church is harboring the traitor Villiki, who has been banished from the land. We've come to take her into custody." Then he added in a deeper warning growl, "Any sikara who appears to be in league with Villiki will be stripped of her rank and publicly scourged. For starters."

Kel Rovic and several soldiers added their weight. Unable to stand against the pressure, the old woman stumbled back, and the church doors crashed inward. Armed soldiers flooded inside, searching for Villiki.

101 *Olabar, Main Urecari Church*

A breathless acolyte interrupted Villiki in her underground rooms. She had waited all night for the delicious news, not even attempting to sleep. At any moment, her pet Cithara was due to strike.

As soon as she saw the distraught face of the acolyte in the bobbing lamplight, however, Villiki knew that something had gone wrong. "Soldiers broke into the church, my Lady! They are desecrating the halls—searching for *you*! They know!"

Villiki quickly pulled on a robe. "Istar has to be dead, but how could they know about me?" They must have tortured poor Cithara, forced her to reveal Villiki's involvement. Her mind was already spinning, making emergency plans. She still had time. "Stall them. They can't possibly find me down here."

The acolyte vigorously shook her head. "They will find you, my Lady—Cithara is leading them here!"

Villiki froze, her hand on the sash of her robe. "Are they forcing her?"

"No, her mother is with them. The girl *cooperates*."

"Her mother is *dead*, you fool!"

The acolyte fell back, groveling. "I mean the Lady Istar—and the former soldan-shah Imir is here as well. They are coming for you!"

Villiki could not get past the first revelation. *Istar was still alive!* Now a real rage flashed through her mind as she grabbed a few belongings and shoved them into a bag. "They have all been corrupted by that Tierran witch!"

The acolyte's eyes were as wide as saucers. "Only Urec can protect us now."

Villiki rounded on her. "Urec commands us to protect ourselves!" She rummaged through her baskets, pulled out the drab clothing that she wore as a disguise whenever she ventured out on her nighttime prowls. She knew the catacombs and the chambers throughout the vast church, and now she had to slip away quickly. Her old husband Imir would never allow her to live this time.

Before she fled, however, there was one last task to perform. Villiki grabbed the sack of innat seeds that she kept securely locked away. One more diversion ... "Come, we

must go to the ur-sikara, *now*, so that I can give her instructions before these soldiers try to arrest her."

The acolyte rushed along, her bare feet whispering
across the cold stone tiles. Villiki followed her with great
determination, pulling on the drab robes.

In her central suite, Ur-Sikara Erima was dressing herself in formal church garments, as though preparing for a
ceremonial reception. She draped a heavy fern amulet
around her neck. She seemed in a daze, terrified and unable
to move faster. Her face lit up when Villiki arrived. "There
are soldiers in the church, my Lady. Tell me what I should
do."

"They are coming for me, and you must stop them. This
is *your* church, Erima. You are the ur-sikara. Urec has presented *you* with this trial. The responsibility is *yours*, all blame
falls on *your* shoulders."

The other woman was staggered by the weight of this.
"But you must give me your counsel. You are the one
who—"

"You are the ur-sikara! No one commands you." Villiki
couldn't believe that she still had to coach this woman. "I've
assisted you and the church as much as I can, but now I fear
for my life. The former soldan-shah wants to execute me,
and now *you* have to stop him. You must command him to
leave."

Erima wobbled, clearly afraid.

Villiki advanced on her. "No one but *you*. I need to go
now, but this is my gift to you." She extended the sack of
innat seeds, jiggled it, and Erima snatched it from her.
"These are the last I have. These are the very, very last innat
seeds you will ever find. There are no more. After these,

they are gone forever. You have served Urec well, and this is your reward."

"The last . . . gone forever." The ur-sikara's dark brown eyes widened in a desperately hungry look. She yanked open the sack and stared at the precious seeds.

Given Erima's lack of restraint, Villiki knew what she was likely to do, and didn't care. In fact, she encouraged it, for it would throw the whole church into even more of an uproar. "Ration them carefully. You will never have any more, ever again. Take only what you need for strength."

"Never any more." Erima seemed not to notice when Villiki spun and hurried out of the suite.

Shouting voices rang up and down the stone corridors of the vast church. Few men were ever allowed into the main sanctuaries, only occasional male lovers brought in under blindfolds to service the priestesses. The soldiers should have been hopelessly lost in the maze, but the traitorous Cithara could—and apparently would—lead them directly to her underground rooms.

Villiki didn't have time to go into the central chapel to break open the collection boxes and steal *cuars*, but she had her own stash of money, jewels, and secreted artifacts. She had a secondary plan, a desperate gamble she had never wanted to consider, but now that the soldan-shah's guards were rushing through the church, she had very few options left.

Down stone steps and twisting halls, she made her way through the shadows, ducking along corridors that had no torches or candles, until she reached a locked beggar's door that had not been opened to the public in decades. Villiki unsealed the door, slipped out, and closed it behind her to find herself in a dim alley that smelled of garbage and excrement and rustled with rats. In the streets nearby, she could hear awakened townspeople wondering about the hubbub.

Villiki hurried toward a main street, and once she passed out of sight of the church, she slowed her pace to that of a limping beggar. After being exiled from the palace years ago, she had spent a long time eking out a living, stealing, keeping to the shadows. Now she fit uncomfortably in her rags, and she knew how to hide. She made her way toward the harbor

With the church in the distance behind her, Villiki reached the docks, where she found a dirty barge tied up to the moorings, due to sail the next morning. It was an ore-carrying barge, and she knew it could only be destined for the Gremurr mines, where her son lived.

She would go there—and Tukar would have to take her in.

With Imir close behind him, Kel Rovic ordered his men to break through the crude barricade that blocked the ur-sikara's main suite. The other priestesses had already been driven into their chambers and left to curse ineffectually at the men, but their shrill complaints fell on deaf ears. Cithara had already led them to Villiki's spider hole, and even the most uneasy soldiers saw proof that the sikaras themselves had harbored the banished woman. Their guilt was obvious.

Lady Istar shouted, "Search the acolytes' chambers and find my daughter. I want Istala brought before me now, and *safe!*"

Given the commotion, Imir was not surprised that Villiki had managed to escape. She was a slippery one, willing to sacrifice any person to the hunters following her, just to keep herself safe. The vile woman had used Cithara, his granddaughter, as a tool ... just as she had tried to use Cliaparia years ago as a scapegoat in her plan to poison Omra.

Now she had used Ur-Sikara Erima, too.

The ur-sikara had to be aware of what occurred within her church. She must have known and approved of the plot to hide Villiki. Such things could not possibly be kept from the leader of the church. Erima needed to be held accountable, just as Ur-Sikara Lukai had been, years ago.

Inside the church leader's suite, though, they found the statuesque woman dressed in formal clothes, looking pristine and beautiful, sitting at her main desk. A sheen of perspiration coated her skin. She was barely breathing.

Rovic strode forward, his scimitar drawn. "Ur-Sikara Erima, you are to be taken into custody for crimes against the soldan-shah."

But the dark-skinned woman simply sat in a stupor, staring. A slow rattle came from her throat, and she slumped onto the desk. In front of her, an empty pouch and a few dark seeds lay on her writing surface. Kel Rovic picked one up and sniffed it, wrinkling his nose in disgust.

Cithara came in to stand next to Adreala and Istar. "The ur-sikara likes to consume innat seeds. Villiki provides them to her."

"She has consumed a huge amount." Rovic held up the empty sack and looked down at the heavily perspiring woman. "Too many."

Imir shook Erima by the shoulders, but she was unresponsive.

"She ate them all," Lady Istar said quietly. "Rather than face you, she killed herself."

Cithara looked deeply saddened. "The ur-sikara was a great woman, but I think Villiki broke her."

"Villiki *poisoned* her," Imir corrected in a black and impotent fury. He turned on Kel Rovic, his voice deadly. "Everywhere. Search *everywhere*. Tear the church down to stones if you must. Find Villiki."

Ur-Sikara Erima died of her overdose within the hour, without ever speaking another word. She lay dead in her suite by the time Kel Rovic and his soldiers delivered young Istala to her relieved mother.

The soldiers ransacked the church, searched every chamber and corridor, overturned every bed, opened every cupboard and closet. They uncovered many things that the priestesses would have preferred to remain hidden—but they did not find Villiki. The woman had vanished.

102   *Corag Foothills*

With the vivid memory of dead Urecari eyes haunting his thoughts, Mateo left the military ship when it docked in Windcatch harbor. A terrible storm was bearing down on them from the northwest, and the Oceansea had become an angry mass of whitecaps and churning gray water. The captains didn't want to sail farther north into the black clouds and blowing wind; all ships were rapidly grounded or tied up to moorings, hoping to ride out the weather.

While the soldiers and crew took refuge in Windcatch until they could sail north, Mateo left. He did not want to go back to Calay yet. He could not bear to look into Anjine's face after doing as she asked.

After receiving a formal report, he made up his mind to join Destrar Broeck's ambitious operation that used mammoths from Iboria for an invasion over the Corag mountains. Though Mateo felt sickened and soiled from slaughtering the Urecari prisoners, his hatred toward the enemy had not altered. He wanted a *real* fight; he wanted to face the Curlies in battle at a real military outpost, not kill helpless civilians. Then he could go home to his wife, and to his queen.

Under a sky that spat raindrops from the storm he intended to outrun, Mateo used the Tierran army's letter of credit to purchase a farmer's horse and some supplies. He rode away from Windcatch and up into the hills toward Corag, hoping to meet up with Broeck and his mammoth army before they swept down and captured the Gremurr mines. The Iborian destrar in command of the operation would not turn down another seasoned fighter, especially not Mateo.

After two days of riding inland, he sat in a makeshift camp in the rain, taking shelter under a tree, and tried to nudge more life out of a smoky fire of damp wood. He saw another rider coming—a big-shouldered man hunched over a black horse, leading four pack horses behind him. He rode directly toward Mateo's campfire and called out as he approached, "Are you Subcomdar Bornan? The people of Windcatch told me I'd find you along this road."

"It's not much of a road." Mateo stood, brushed damp leaves from his trousers. His horse snorted a welcome to the arriving mounts. The rain began to pick up. "Yes, that's me. There's enough shelter under here, but I won't promise it's dry."

The newcomer's horses were fine Eriettan war chargers, thick-boned and draft-bred, yet light enough that they could be easily maneuvered in battle. The rider dismounted and meticulously hobbled all the mounts beneath the shelter of some adjacent trees. Stooping over as he ran against the downpour, he came to the campfire, removed his leather hat, and shook the water droplets away.

Mateo recognized Jenirod, the son of the Eriettan destrar—the man Anjine had chosen to marry. "I know you," he said simply.

Jenirod hunkered down and held his hands over the fire. "And I know you. There are enough stories about both of us, we should have met before now." The destrar's son hung his head and looked grief-stricken. "Because you were such a dear childhood companion to Anjine, I'd hoped we might become friends, but none of that matters anymore. I doubt I'll ever see the queen again."

This was news to Mateo. "But you are betrothed."

"She tore up the document and threw the scraps in my face. Now she hates me. She thinks that my actions caused the retaliation— the *murder* of her brother. And she's probably right." He looked up with large, heavy eyes. He shook his head, his jaw trembling. Mateo thought the man might burst into tears. "I acted with brawn and bravery, but I didn't think. I didn't know that the Urecari would take their revenge on poor Tomas!"

Mateo's voice was quiet, but heavy with threat. "You'd better explain yourself."

Jenirod took food out of his sodden pack, chewed on strips of tough beef jerky. Barely able to force his words out, he explained what he and Destrar Tavishel had done, hoping to achieve a triumph they could show off to Queen Anjine. "I was so pleased when I told her of our victory at Fashia's Fountain. I thought I was doing a good thing by eradicating a nest of heretics. But after what they did to poor Tomas, I see that the Urecari aren't just enemies— they are truly evil! I don't understand why Ondun doesn't just wipe that blight from His creation." Mateo didn't know how to respond. Jenirod sat in silence; his eyes were red-rimmed. "I wanted to impress Anjine with my bravery. I wanted her to think I'd be a good husband."

"If you are a good man, Anjine would have recognized it. You should have trusted her. The queen is wise and good—" Mateo cut himself off as longing swelled within his chest. Here was Jenirod, who—for a while at least—had been given something Mateo had always wanted, but could never have: Anjine had accepted the big oaf to be her husband. Jenirod had thrown away all the blessings a man could ever want. Mateo would never get that chance, so how could he not resent the Eriettan man for being chosen in the first place and for hurting Anjine, not to mention causing the death of poor Tomas?

"I heard about all those Urecari prisoners. It must have been horrible for you," Jenirod said, then his face paled.

"Me, I can't stop thinking of the priestesses at Fashia's Fountain, how they looked when Tavishel and his men—all of us—fell upon them with our swords. We hacked those poor misguided pilgrims to pieces."

Mateo poked at the smoky fire with a green stick, looking away from Jenirod. A weight of guilt descended upon him too, and he made himself remember his own beautiful Vicka, who awaited him back in Calay. Vicka still ran the blacksmith shop with her father. She kept herself busy, but Mateo knew she worried about him when he went off to war.

In Windcatch, he had given a letter for her to the captain of the next ship bound for Calay, but with the strengthening hurricane, no vessels would be sailing for some time. He should have taken his horse and headed home on the overland route. Instead he had ridden into Corag.

"Why did you come *here*?" he asked Jenirod.

The other man shrugged woefully. He raised his head again. "Now I want to join the fight, I want to follow Broeck and his army over the mountain pass. That's why I brought all these horses, to join the charge. It's all I have left to offer, to pay for my mistakes. I thought maybe you and I could ride together."

Looking through the rain, Mateo saw the strong horses and knew they could be useful to the Tierran military force heading down to the Gremurr mines. "Have they been trained for battle?"

Jenirod's chest swelled with pride. "These are Eriettan horses, the champions of five different cavalcades."

Mateo looked at his companion and came to a difficult

conclusion. The rain had begun to peter out, but the air remained cold and damp. A breeze rustled the trees, catching misty cloud remnants and blowing them away.

"I'm happy to have your company, Jenirod. Let's hope that we each find what we seek."

103 *Calay Castle*

The windows and doors of Calay Castle were shuttered and barred as the hurricane bombarded the city. The hard rain hissed and pattered, and the impatient wind struggled against the barriers. Servants moved through the castle with their voices hushed, browbeaten by the intimidating storm.

Walking like a specter through the dim halls, Anjine stopped at the threshold of her father's cold, dusty royal chamber and stared at the large bed, the empty fireplace, the burned-out candles beside the chair where Korastine had read his books, the shelves where he had displayed his keepsakes.

The hollowness of loss drove her away. She couldn't even bear to set foot inside the room.

The long war, tragedies, and harsh decisions had debilitated Korastine, so that in his last years he could only dream of searching for sunny lands beyond the horizon. He had left the kingdom in her care—but had Anjine taken care of Tierra? Had she honored the responsibility of the crown?

A thousand heads . . . a thousand innocents . . . a revenge that could never bring back her little brother. And yet she had done it without allowing herself any regrets, any second thoughts.

Her cat found and followed her, seeking attention, but she didn't pick him up as she wandered instead to Tomas's room. Tycho rubbed against the edge of the open door to her brother's quarters. When Anjine hesitated there, the cat strolled in, curious to explore a familiar room that had been closed off. Tycho walked a circuitous route around the prince's keepsakes, furniture, clothes chest, wardrobe cabinet. The cat's confident strut thawed Anjine's joints and she followed him inside.

"He's not here anymore, Tycho," she said aloud. The sound of her voice startled her. The winds outside pushed against the shuttered window, muffled by the thick walls into a weary sigh. *"He's gone."*

The words were so simple, but as vast as all of the unexplored seas.

Anjine knelt on the rug that covered the stone floor and gathered the cat up, pulling his warm body against hers. Tycho melted into her arms. He began to purr, a homey calming sound.

Memories streamed through her mind. Days ago, Mateo and the soldiers would have dumped a thousand Urecari heads at the Ishalem wall. Even when she pictured the look of shock and horror that must have showed on the soldan-shah's face, Anjine did not find it satisfying.

She closed her eyes and whispered, "What have I done, Tycho? I can't take any of it back."

She had hoped to feel more, a sense of closure, of justice ... but every one of those slain prisoners was also someone's child. Uraban women would feel the same loss, their little sons or brothers killed as unintentional game pieces in this terrible war. She had wanted them to feel her pain. She had needed to inflict the same hurt upon them, to make them understand the depth of the wound she had suffered.

But Anjine doubted the revenge would stop there. What would Omra do once he learned of the slaughter? What revenge would *he* take? What if the Urecari killed *ten* thousand Tierrans in an escalating retaliation? What if her own need to inflict pain ended up sparking even more bloodshed from the soulless enemy? How would she comfort the grieving families after the next wave of Uraban butchery?

As queen, Anjine was supposed to protect her people . . . but had she actually made them safer?

Tycho wanted to get down, and she let him onto the floor, where he took an interest in a set of carved wooden figures that had been stored on a bottom shelf with other old toys. She recognized the wooden ships, sea serpents, horses, carts—the paint was chipped and faded now, but she remembered when the colors were bright . . . when Tomas played with them as a little boy.

Sniffing and bumping his head against a sea-serpent figure, Tycho knocked the pieces down with a clatter that startled him.

Anjine's throat clenched with the raw pain of unvoiced sobs. She could not express the whirlwind of contradictory thoughts and yearnings inside of her. She could not break down the thick, protective wall she had built around her heart and mind. . . .

Some hours later, Enifir found her there on the floor just

staring at the wooden figures. Speaking with stern compassion, the handmaiden led her away from the small room filled with shadows and ghosts.

To drive away the persistent gloom, servants had built roaring fires in all the main rooms. In her damp withdrawing room, with a beeswax candle burning beside her and the cat curled on her lap, Queen Anjine listlessly studied documents, but she had been shuffling through the papers for more than hour, unable to focus on the words.

Enifir sat with the queen, cradling her newborn baby and letting the little girl suckle at her breast. "If there's anything you need, my Queen, I will bring it to you."

Anjine pretended to be engrossed in the document. "No thank you. I am fine."

Enifir kept talking, as if she assumed the queen needed to hear more human voices. "I'm worried about my Vorannen. He's out in the streets, keeping watch over the city, but no man should be out in that storm. The sound of that wind and rain makes me want to hold somebody."

"Vorannen needs to be here with you—is there any way to call him back?"

"No, Majesty. He knows his duty, as do all the city guard." Finished nursing, the handmaiden walked around the room with the baby on her shoulder. She paused in front of the queen, who looked up at the baby. Enifir's expression softened. "Would you like to hold her, Majesty?"

Hesitantly, Anjine took the infant wrapped in blankets and gazed down at the small face. She reflected on how tragic life was, how clearly she remembered holding her baby brother, how much joy Tomas had brought to

Korastine and Ilrida. Yet even with so much sadness, so many times when hope and perseverance were knocked to the ground, fresh hope returned and life went on.

Fleeing her own thoughts and afraid she would break down and cry, she handed the little girl back to Enifir. Tycho adjusted his position, making a warm nest in Anjine's skirts, and she petted his head. He didn't like the storm either.

Sen Leo entered the sitting room, looking worried, as he always did. Anjine finally gave up on the document and set it aside. "Shouldn't you be in the Saedran District with your family, Sen Leo?"

He made a grimace of impatient frustration. "I've been here for two days, my Queen. I don't dare leave the castle now, but ... yes, I am concerned for my wife." He slumped in one of the hard chairs. "She's never been a fool, though I doubt she'd say the same thing about me. She knows how to take care of the house and herself. I just wish I could be with her." He paused, then shook his head. "Be thankful, Majesty, that the headlands shelter the harbor from the worst of it. The Oceansea must be a great cauldron, boiling and churning, stirring things up from the depths."

"This is how Ondun washes the stains from the world," Anjine said quietly.

"Is that a quote from the Book of Aiden? Prester-Marshall Rudio said the same thing to me an hour ago."

Anjine was surprised. "He is here too?"

"He came to perform services when the storm began, and he remained in the castle rather than returning to the kirk. I don't think he wanted to get wet."

As though responding to his name, the old prester-marshall appeared at the workroom door. When a particularly loud gust rattled the shutters, Rudio winced, ready to duck should the stone walls blow in. Embarrassed, he tried to disguise his reaction as a bow of respect. "My Queen, on such a long stormy day, I came to see if you would like me to pray with you?" He glanced at the Saedran scholar, a bit intimidated. "And of course Sen Leo na-Hadra is welcome, if he would join us."

"Thank you for the offer, Prester-Marshall, but I prefer to pray by myself." Sen Leo smiled over at Anjine. "While we've been cooped up inside the castle, Rudio and I have had many interesting and insightful discussions. It reminded me of my times with Prester-Marshall Baine."

The prester-marshall's expression soured. "Sen Leo is a wise Saedran, but no matter how many times I show him Aiden's words as proof, he still clings to his own beliefs."

The old scholar responded with a humble shrug. "I was about to give a similar assessment of you, Prester-Marshall."

Acutely aware of the hollowness inside her, Anjine was in no mood for banter. "To answer your question, I have already done plenty of praying, but no matter how benevolent Aiden is, he won't find a way to place my brother's head back on his shoulders, or to gather all the innocent blood our enemies have spilled." Anjine extricated Tycho from her lap and set him on the stone hearth near the fire. She walked over to the shuttered window, feeling drafts whistle through the cracks. The wind reminded her of a cold, moaning whisper of grief. "We are beyond prayer. Now we must do our worshiping with a sharpened sword."

104 *Iyomelka's Island*

Considering the possibility that the sacred wellspring might be repaired, Iyomelka was anxious to provide any assistance. Even though the magic-infused water had not started flowing yet, the crone already looked healthier, charged with excitement. Grigovar was ready to row back to the *Al-Orizin* so they could gather the equipment needed to fix the well.

Saan grinned teasingly at Ystya as they returned to the longboats on the beach. "If we fix your spring, I hope the water doesn't turn you back into a child."

The young woman looked at Saan with wonder in her eyes. "Do you think that could happen?" Ystya was so strange and exotic, so beautiful ... so different from the women in Olabar who flirted with him only because their fathers wanted closer connections with the soldan-shah. Saan laughed, but he didn't know the answer to her question.

On impulse, he gave the old woman his most pleasant smile. "Lady Iyomelka, your daughter might like to see my ship. We have many Uraban objects that would seem strange and wonderful to her. Would you let her join me, while I gather a few items for exploring the well?"

Ystya brightened. She could see the beautiful *Al-Orizin* anchored out at the edge of the reefs. "Oh, please, Mother—let me see it."

Iyomelka turned stony. "No. My daughter must remain here, under my care."

Saan was more hurt than indignant. "We'll be gone no more than a few hours. Do you think I would harm the girl in some way?"

Ystya clung to the older woman's arm. "Oh please, Mother! I'll never have a chance like this again! I've seen the sunken ships out by the reefs, but never a vessel when it was intact." She blinked her large eyes. "They'll sail away soon enough . . . and I'll always wonder."

Grigovar was impatient to go. "Well, make up your minds, one way or the other. If we don't get the equipment soon, there won't be enough daylight to try to fix the fountain."

The crone's resolve wavered. "Very well. But return her to me safely—and swiftly." She touched her daughter's slender arm, lowered her voice. "Do not be tempted by the strangeness of it, Ystya. You will gaze upon many objects from the outside world that you have never needed."

Saan helped situate the young woman in the front of the longboat, then he and Grigovar pushed it off the beach into the water. Ystya held on to the gunwales as the boat rocked. When the big reef diver climbed aboard, he set the oars into the locks and began to row. One of the green seaweed plaits in Ystya's ivory-colored hair came unraveled and blew away, and she laughed.

Saan touched her hand. "Look behind you. Look at your home."

Ystya turned to see the receding shore and caught her breath. "I can see the whole island from here!"

"That spot of land is the edge of your world, all you've ever known." Then Saan directed her gaze out toward the *Al-Orizin* and the great ocean beyond. "But the real edge of the world is far, far from here. That's where my crew and I are going—to find Terravitae and the Key to Creation."

"You must have seen many wonderful things."

"Not enough of them, not yet. We still have a long voyage ahead of us." As if sharing a secret, Saan described Olabar and the palace in the brightest possible terms. He told her the story of finding the real Golden Fern in the forest when he was just a boy; he described crossing the Great Desert in a sand coracle, and how he had lived among the Nunghals as they herded buffalo across the plains. He talked about the seafaring Nunghal-Su, whose families lived aboard hundreds of ships that crossed the Southern Sea. With each description, Ystya grew more amazed, and Saan didn't even have to exaggerate.

When the longboat pulled up alongside the *Al-Orizin* and crewmen tossed down the rope ladder, Ystya touched the hull. "This was built by your people?"

"Yes. There are many such vessels in Olabar harbor."

Once on deck, Ystya looked around, touching everything as if to convince herself it was real. While Grigovar and other crewmen busily loaded ropes, tools, and enclosed lanterns aboard the longboat for work on the dry well, the young woman asked the names of the simplest objects. Even ropes, sailcloth, stanchions, hatches, and winches were exotic to her.

In his cabin, Saan unrolled the colorful ancient Map of Urec, and her eyes widened with unabashed amazement. "Ondun gave this Map to Urec?" Her slender finger traced the outlines of Terravitae, the mysterious continent, the archaic words that she seemed able to read perfectly well. "Did it lead you here to our island?"

"The winds and storms had more to do with that. Even Sen Sherufa hasn't been able to use the Map as a navigational tool—yet. But we hope it'll lead us to the Key to Creation."

"But you don't know what that is?"

"I'll know when I find it." Saan never doubted his resolve or his abilities. "Urec was searching for the Key, and we will carry on his mission."

He reverently rolled the Map, sealed it away, and led her out to the deck again. Saan felt such an odd connection to this young woman. "There's so much I wish I could show you. It's a shame to hide you away on that island."

"I *want* you to show me. I want to see." Ystya shook her head, turning away from the view of the island. "That place is like a prison. I've memorized each rock, each tree—but it's like knowing one grain of sand, while ignoring the rest of the beach. I want to know the rest of the world."

Saan heard the longing in her voice. "Then come with us."

"My mother would never allow it!"

"Then we'll just have to figure out a way." She did not seem convinced by his reassuring smile, but he knew that Yal Dolicar could probably come up with a dozen suggestions, right off the top of his head. Saan was sure he could think of something himself.

He took her to the captain's wheel. "On this one voyage, I've seen that Ondun's creation is vaster than I imagined." He leaned very close to her and whispered, "And maybe all the things I've experienced are still just a grain of sand. Think of how much more might await us."

105 *The* Dyscovera

From the deck high above the crystal waters, Criston Vora watched the sleek people frolic around the sunken city as if humanity had been shaped for the oceans instead of land. Their skin, while pale, had an iridescent sheen like an abalone shell; it caught the light before the young men and women dove underwater again and swam deep. A few minutes later, a new group of dolphins appeared beside the boat, chattering and splashing, but Criston saw no sign of the mer-people anymore. He couldn't believe they had changed their forms so swiftly, but his sense of wonder made all things seem possible.

The discovery of this undersea city pointed out to Criston how many mysteries and wonders remained in the sprawling seas. The rush of exhilaration reminded him of the fresh thrill of discovery he had sought for most of his life. That was why he had gone to sea in the first place.

Another group of the water people had gathered only a few feet above the wavetops on the balcony of the highest spire. A regal-looking man emerged to stand in the bright sunshine. He was bare-chested, with broad shoulders and a pale, thick beard tinged with a watermark of green. Criston realized that, from the undersea perspective, this pinnacle was immensely tall, a fitting place from which an important man could survey his domain.

The bearded man shouted across the water, and while

Criston could not distinguish the words, the meaning was clear. "We'll take a boat. Prester Hannes, I want you with me. These people may know of Aiden or Holy Joron. Sen Aldo, if they don't speak Tierran, perhaps you can understand them."

The prester gave a skeptical and uneasy frown. "The chartsman seems to think they are of Saedran descent."

"We all came from Terravitae, in the beginning," Criston said.

"We have a common origin," Aldo said, his eyes shining. "Many common things. And if they are descendants of the first Saedrans. . . ."

"Can I go, Captain?" Javian piped up, seeming as full of wonder as Criston himself felt. "I can row as well as any other sailor."

"Then come along." Criston was already moving toward the ship's boat. "Kjelnar, you have command of the *Dyscovera*. Let's see what these people know of Terravitae."

"May the Compass guide us," Hannes said, keeping his voice low.

Sleek young swimmers gathered around the small boat as it was lowered. They laughed and splashed, watching the clumsy men make their way into the rocking craft. Watching the watery people swim closer, Aldo settled onto the wooden seat. He could not deny that he detected a hint of Saedran characteristics in their features—the set of the brow, the curve of the jaw.

Javian grasped the oars and began to row, but before he could go far, the mer-people gathered around, gripped the sides of the boat, and propelled them with strong kicks of their legs. Laughing, the cabin boy lifted the oars out of the water and held them up. Aldo held on for the ride as four dolphins splashed along beside them. Once they delivered the representatives from the *Dyscovera*, the escort swimmers and dolphins darted away.

The regal, bearded man rose from his ornate chair on the open balcony just above the ocean surface. He spoke in a deep rumbling voice that seemed designed for underwater communication, though with a heavy accent and an ancient and formalized manner. "I am called by the name of Sonhir, and I rule these children of the sea. My people. Hail and welcome to you strangers from a far-off land, in the name of Ondun, creator of us all."

"The accent is definitely Saedran," Aldo whispered.

"I can understand him—mostly," Criston said, also lowering his voice. "Reminds me of the language in old books."

Prester Hannes pulled out his fishhook pendant, laid it prominently over the fabric of his shirt, and opened the Book of Aiden in his lap. A cloud of skepticism crossed his face as he raised his voice, speaking before anyone else. "Anyone can speak the name of Ondun, but not everyone *believes*."

"You are free to believe as you choose," Sonhir retorted. "As we do."

Aldo spoke quickly before Hannes could take over the conversation. "Greetings, King Sonhir. Allow me to present Criston Vora, captain of the exploration ship *Dyscovera*. We sailed from far-off Tierra in search of new lands and new people."

"I am greatly impressed with your ship," the mer-king said. "A tremendous effort to do a simple thing."

"Our quest is not simple, sir," Criston said. "It is perhaps the greatest effort mankind has ever mounted."

King Sonhir seemed amused.

The prester lifted his fishhook pendant. "We come on behalf of Aiden and Sapier. If you do not know the Word and the Truth, we will enlighten you."

Sonhir's gaze barely skated over Captain Vora's and he pretended not to understand Prester Hannes; he seemed most interested in Aldo. "I sense in you a kindred spirit, young man. What brings you here with these people?"

Aldo wished Sen Leo could have been here, both to see this and to advise him. "I am Sen Aldo na-Curic, the Saedran chartsman of our voyage."

"A Saedran!" The figures swimming in the water nearby chattered with great excitement. "The Lost Saedrans have come home!"

"Our son has returned to us."

"One of them, at least." Sonhir raised both hands and stepped to the edge of the balcony, looking down at the drifting rowboat. "We welcome you back among us, Sen Aldo na-Curic. Our orphaned siblings have wandered from the sea far too long."

Despite his skepticism, Aldo had no choice but to accept that parts of the fantastical Saedran origin tale were true— the sunken continent, the survivors adapted to a life in the sea. "We tell tales of your people, but the details may have been lost over the course of time." In a steady voice, Aldo recounted the legend as he knew it, while the young swimmers around the boat chuckled.

The mer-king gave him an indulgent smile. "In the telling, your story is so garbled! You make it sound as if what happened to us was a tragedy. Have you forgotten that we Saedrans discovered a way to transform ourselves—to live in the sea as well as on land? What does it matter if our cities are built in the dry air or submerged beneath the surface?"

Aldo had a hard time grasping the idea. "You can transform yourselves?"

"So you can breathe underwater?" Criston asked.

"Is it not more miraculous to breathe invisible air? Water at least can be seen and felt." Sonhir laughed again, returning his attention to Aldo to the clear exclusion of the others. "Alas, your legend also lacks a key fact—that we Saedrans *sank our land intentionally.*"

Prester Hannes frowned, not sure he had heard the answer correctly. Taken aback, Aldo asked, "You caused the island to drop beneath the waves *on purpose.* But why?"

"Why?" From the balcony, Sonhir extended his arms. "Look at you, little helpless creatures aboard a floating boat. We are unhindered by such restrictions. We have all the seas as our domain. The entire ocean floor is Saedran land. What more could we want?"

Dolphins splashed next to the rowboat, making Hannes glower as he wiped spray from his face. The dolphins dove again and human-looking swimmers took their places seconds later.

Sonhir's voice grew more sonorous. "Our people have returned to the cradle that Ondun made for us, while the rest of you are exiled on land. But we rejoice that you have come. We welcome back our lost children."

Prester Hannes could no longer restrain his angry words. "We are not your lost children." He held up his copy of the Book of Aiden. "Ondun first created the lowly creatures of the seas before He made mankind. By returning to the sea, you and your people have not advanced—you have *regressed*! You Saedrans have become lowly creatures once more."

A dark expression crossed Sonhir's face, but Captain Vora interceded. "Prester, please do not challenge these people. We're trying to learn from them and have them help us. Let the chartsman talk to them."

"But if they are damned, Captain, we risk—"

The captain lowered his voice, "I have already risked plenty for the voyage of the *Dyscovera*, and these Saedrans will never lead us to Terravitae if you offend them."

Sonhir crossed his arms over his bare chest. "We would prefer to converse with Sen Aldo na-Curic. Dispatch him to us alone, and we will have much to discuss."

The captain turned to Aldo, anxious to cool the situation. "Chartsman, I delegate you to be our representative. You are the best person for the job. For now, it's time we rowed back to our ship."

Sonhir was easily mollified; he didn't seem interested in the other men from the ship anyway. "Return to us on the morrow."

As Javian took up the oars once more, Prester Hannes chewed on his very beliefs, barely containing his resentment. Criston cast a stern gaze toward the prester. "Patience, my friend. If we find Holy Joron, even you will be satisfied."

106 *Farport, Soeland Reach*

The worst of the hurricane struck the Tierran coast from Erietta southward, barely grazing the islands of Soeland Reach. And Soelanders did not let such weather deter them from their activities.

When he finally learned what the abhorrent Curlies had done to Prince Tomas, Destrar Tavishel swiftly set course for home. His mood was black with the need for vengeance. Though the news inflamed his rage, Tavishel did not shout in anger or smash things. Instead, he locked himself inside his cabin, where he could think. And they tried to place the blame on *his* actions? Those animals would have found another reason to cut off the boy's head even if he and Jenirod hadn't struck the heathen fountain.

The queen's retaliation of dumping a thousand Urecari heads was a good start, but not enough. He had ideas of his own. By the time his patrol ships anchored at Farport, he already had rough drawings completed. He was not an engineer like Destrar Unsul of Erietta, but the concept was plain. He would find someone to build it.

Once in port, Tavishel halted all unnecessary work, and his carpenters spent weeks building mangonels—compact but powerful catapults—from any suitable wood, cutting down the island's remaining tall trees or commandeering fresh Iborian wood from the lumberyards. Nothing had a higher priority.

While the storm churned the Oceansea and then petered

out as it moved inland, Soeland work crews anchored the broad-based mangonels to the decks of the patrol ships. Tavishel had seen what such devices could do against solid barriers, and he saw no reason why the small catapults could not be used from his sturdy ships, provided his men reinforced the top decks and anchored them securely enough. The Soeland carpenters added so many thick support beams underneath the main deck that the crewmen had trouble moving about below.

During the refit project, Tavishel barely spoke to his second wife, who was a stranger to him anyway. He slept only a few hours each night, eager to sail for the isthmus as soon as the modifications were completed. His anger was not a capricious thing that faded easily. Even so, he did not want to delay.

From his stone house overlooking the rugged port, Tavishel listened to the sounds of hammers, saws, and winches. Since he never took his meals in the dim, echoey dining room, Tavishel's wife brought him a tureen of chowder in his study. Though they spoke little to each other under any circumstances, she joined him for the meal. He dutifully complimented his wife's cooking, but she seemed like a faint shadow to him. His original wife and children still felt more real. . . .

Burnet, his master carpenter, summoned him down to the docks. "The first mangonel has been completed and installed, Destrar, and is ready to be tested. I've anchored and reinforced the throwing arm and base, but no one quite knows what will happen until we use it."

"We shall see for ourselves. I'll gather a skeleton crew, and we can head out to deep water for a test."

His men loaded the decks with hundreds of small whale-oil casks, which could be set aflame then hurled from a catapult basket to smash into enemy fortifications. The whaling season had just ended, and their oil stockpiles were at their peak; this year, Soeland Reach would not be selling all of the harvest to Calay and other Tierran ports.

When the catapult ship sailed out of Farport, the water was choppy, the breeze scouring and cold. Goosebumps prickled the destrar's shaved scalp, more from anticipation than chill.

Groaning and laughing with the strain, the bearded Soelanders cranked their winches, tightened ropes against the pulleys, and drew down the catapult's throwing arm. The metal wheel clanked, one tooth at a time, until the bent and resilient wood quivered with pent-up energy. A redheaded sailor hefted a small keg of whale oil, set it into the catapult's basket, and used his flint and steel to strike a spark on a wadded rag thrust through the bung hole. As soon as the rag smoldered, the redheaded sailor scrambled backward.

Tavishel did not wait. "Launch, before the whale oil explodes."

The master carpenter released the throwing arm, and the mangonel swung upward with a great groan and crack. The keg of whale oil sailed through the air, reached the top of its arc, and tumbled toward the water. It caught fire midway down, and when the flaming keg struck the water, it shattered, spilling ignited oil across the waves.

"Imagine if that were to fall onto Urecari rooftops," Tavishel growled to Burnet. They could anchor off the coast of Ishalem, out of arrow range, and bombard it for days, if necessary.

His crews had much to learn about this method of warfare, but those skills would come with practice. Once all ten ship's catapults were installed, Tavishel would float empty barrels out on the waters and have his crews practice hitting their targets. While sailing the refitted ships down to Ishalem, he would drill his crews repeatedly. Fortunately, the flaming oil made absolute accuracy unnecessary. He simply needed to hurl the barrels into the city. Anywhere.

The master carpenter knelt on the deckboards, where the body of the catapult had been anchored, and ran his callused fingers along a fresh crack in the wood. "We're not ready yet, Destrar. Even with the additional crossbeams, the force of the release is going to cause damage. We can use each catapult four, maybe five times before we destroy the deck."

Tavishel frowned. "That won't be enough. What is the solution?"

"Iron crossbars, I believe. Thick plates to distribute the stress to the ship's ribs and deckboards. I'll make it work, Destrar."

He squared his shoulders in resignation. "Well even if you cannot . . . four or five shots of flaming barrels, coming from ten ships, would spread enough whale oil and fire to bring Ishalem down again." Tavishel showed his teeth as he actually smiled. "I want to sail soon. Can your work be done in a week?"

Burnet remained silent as he did mental calculations. "I'd need extra men."

"You will have every person on the Soeland islands, if you need them."

"Then I'll be done within a week."

Tavishel had seen the site of the holy city when it was merely a barren, burned wasteland—a terrible place, bleak and hopeless. But a blackened scar was preferable to having it possessed by Urecari heretics. "If we soak the earth with enough blood, even Ishalem will become a fertile place again."

107 *Ishalem*

From atop God's Barricade, Soldan-Shah Omra stared at all the dead faces dumped like overripe melons at a rubbish heap—the harvest of Kel Unwar's foolish action.

After Unwar's rash decisions to kidnap and kill the hostage prince, Omra could only guess the terrible consequences his people would have to face. Considering what was done to Tomas, he had expected a ruthless response, but Queen Anjine's sheer venom stunned him nonetheless. Omra had arrived back in Ishalem in time to watch Tierran soldiers deliver cartloads of severed heads. One thousand innocents!

Now the kel stood beside him, blind to how he himself had been a catalyst for this tragedy. "Even after the appalling massacre at Fashia's Fountain, I did not imagine the Aidenists could possess such untapped depths of cruelty." Unwar's voice was raspy, his throat apparently still sore from the shouting and weeping he had done upon hearing the news. "Look what they have done!"

Omra's fury flowed through him like molten metal from

the smelters of the Gremurr mines. He wanted to grab the man by the neck and hurl him off the top of the wall for his ill-considered action—he had provoked this! But Omra needed the man, and he couldn't even publicly reprimand him: Aidenist barbarities had nearly driven the Urabans mad with the need for retaliation, and killing the young prince now seemed insufficient by far.

The brewing unrest in Ishalem was like a firepowder bomb, primed to explode. Unable to restrain themselves, slave masters had executed dozens of Tierran captives before Omra sent guards into the work camps with a written command to spare the prisoners—not out of mercy, but because the laborers were needed to excavate the great canal. Instead, the guards and supervisors settled for whipping the slaves bloody and driving them to the point of collapse.

He and Unwar were alone on the top of the wall, looking down at the mound of heads. Crows and gulls had settled in for the feast, and by now most of the eye sockets were empty, the flesh rotting in the hot summer sun. "You know what instigated this, Unwar. I am not pleased that you acted without my guidance. You have guaranteed many more years of war."

The provisional governor was not apologetic. "Fashia's Fountain was the spark that caused this, Soldan-Shah. Not I."

Omra scowled. "And the Aidenists would cite something else before that, and before that, and before that. No one remembers the first spark anymore." His shoulders slumped.

"Rest assured that we were not to blame, Soldan-Shah.

I will send soldiers to gather up the heads. We'll build a memorial pyre—"

"No, leave them there. This wall is God's Barricade, but the Aidenists have given us a second barrier. Let it be a wall of skulls. If ever they approach Ishalem again, these bleached bones will remind them of what they have done."

When fishing boats raced into the western harbor to announce the approach of many fearsome vessels, Omra raised the alarm. The Tierran navy had come to capture Ishalem. Gongs were struck, bells rung. The Aidenist prisoners were locked away in their pens once more, while Kel Unwar rallied his soldiers. Faithful Urecari streamed over to the Oceansea docks and launched any vessel that could sail, to protect their holy city.

Omra took his place at the bow of a war galley and the crew pulled at the long oars and rowed out of the harbor. As the jagged bow sliced through the water, he called to his men, "We will turn the harbor red with Aidenist blood!"

The men cheered, the drums pounded, and the ships moved forward to meet the oncoming fleet.

With surprise, Omra realized that the strange vessels were sailing up from the *south*, by way of Lahjar and Ouroussa. He saw dozens of sails, perhaps as many as a hundred ships. He used a spyglass to study the rigging, the shape of the hulls, the accordioned gray sails, then grasped the war galley's rail to steady himself in surprise and relief. A hundred well-armed ships, a formidable force. "It's the Nunghals—Asaddan and Ruad have returned!"

*

Foreign vessels filled the Ishalem harbor and anchored out in the deeper water. Cheering Urabans welcomed their guests and built fires in braziers at the sites of the churches under construction, adding powders to color the smoke.

Omra opened the storehouses, having workers haul out barrels of honey and casks of wine. Bakeries worked around the clock. Cows, sheep, and pigs were butchered and roasted. After long months at sea, the Nunghals fell to the strange repast with great gusto.

"What did I tell you?" Asaddan shouted above the clamor of the gathered Nunghals in the huge banquet hall. "Was I exaggerating?" Even though he had constantly told stories about the wonders of Uraba, the Nunghals were awestruck by the unusual sights in Ishalem.

During the voyage from the southern sea, Asaddan had flitted from one ship to another, like a popular man at a clan dance. No longer suffering from seasickness, he taught the shipkhans and crew a few words of the Uraban language, while also proclaiming the (exaggerated) exploits of Ruad. The once-disgraced shipkhan was clad in fine garments now, a hero among his people, and the soldan-shah gave him and Asaddan seats at the head of the main table.

"It was a close thing, Soldan-Shah." Asaddan gnawed on a rib bone, peeling off a few scraps of meat. Though he'd consumed a great deal of red wine, his goblet kept being refilled. "These other men were skeptical, remembering how poor Ruad had crashed his ship long ago." He reached over to wrap his arm around his friend's shoulders, giving him a vigorous hug, even though Ruad understood little of what he'd said. "Now all that is forgiven and forgotten."

Omra picked at his food, thinking of the tragedies that had occurred since Asaddan's last visit here. "You could not have come at a better time."

The next morning, he led a representative group of Nunghal shipkhans out to view the canal across the isthmus. With Asaddan translating, Omra said, "Someday soon, my fleet of ironclad warships will sail from the Middlesea out into the ocean. And with your hundred vessels added to our own navy, we will at last overrun Calay harbor and squash the blight of Aidenism."

Next, he took them to God's Barricade. The towering seven-mile-long wall astonished them; neither the nomadic clans nor the seafaring families had ever built anything so massive or enduring. From the wall, Omra told them the horrific story and showed them the decaying heads of innocent Urecari prisoners strewn on the ground. "What more do you need to know about how evil the Tierrans are?"

The Nunghal captains muttered to each other, and Asaddan spoke for them all. "Urabans are our friends and our new trading partners. Of course we will help you against your enemies."

108 *Iyomelka's Island*

When the longboat came back ashore, Iyomelka was waiting on the beach, weak with relief to see her daughter safely returned. "There was no need to worry," Saan insisted, careful to keep the annoyance out of his tone. "No follower of Urec would ever overpower a girl and take her against her wishes. It goes against our teachings."

As he spoke, though, Saan wondered what his mother would have said about that, considering that *she* had been taken against her will from a Tierran village. Istar had told him her story, and Soldan-Shah Omra had never denied the facts. Saan didn't quite understand what had really taken place, so many years ago.

Ystya, however, had made it clear to him in quiet words that leaving the island would not be entirely against her wishes . . .

With Grigovar carrying the heavy tools and equipment they needed for exploring the dried-up well shaft, Saan took a few items and headed back up the hill to the failed spring. On the way, Ystya couldn't help describing to her mother all the wondrous things she had seen.

Her mother, though, had eyes only for the ropes, pulleys, pry bars, and tools they carried. "We will have time enough to talk about it later, daughter, after these men have sailed far away. For now, I am eager to see if Captain Saan can fix our spring." She looked hungrily into the open mouth of the well. "Then everything will be right with the world again."

Saan cautioned, "Remember, we made no promises, Lady Iyomelka. We said only that there *might* be a way to make the water flow again. Yal Dolicar has ideas, but if the cause is truly a curse—"

Dolicar hurried up, soothing the old woman. "But your offer of treasure gives us all the incentive we require. If there's a way to do it, we will succeed. We're ingenious and resourceful, you'll see."

"I think Saan can do it," Ystya said without a shred of doubt in her voice.

Grigovar dumped the equipment and began setting up the ropes and pulleys, while an anxious Iyomelka followed his every move.

While they were gone, Dolicar had paced around the circle of stones and studied the dark shaft, igniting bits of tinder and dropping them down into it, to see if he could make out any details. Now he took Saan aside for a quiet consultation. "From what I can determine, Captain, there is an obstruction blocking the flow from an underground aquifer. I wouldn't stake my other hand on it, but I suspect that a rockfall diverted the water to another outlet, perhaps an undersea cave. Since water flows along the easiest path, all we have to do is make it *easier* for the water to bubble up here. Nothing magical about it, but we can certainly impress the old woman."

Saan dropped his coil of rope onto the ground. "You sound like an expert. Are you just talking again, or do you genuinely have knowledge about wells and irrigation?"

The other man glanced away abashedly. "I am embarrassed to admit that I was once arrested in Abilan—falsely accused, I swear!—but the magistrate would not hear my defense. I was sentenced to a year of digging irrigation trenches. I had to climb down wells to clear dried or clogged shafts. But it was the will of Ondun, and I'm pleased that my unfortunate experience has given me an opportunity to help these dear ladies."

"*And* gain treasure for yourself."

Dolicar gave a charming shrug. "That, too. As I said, the will of Ondun."

Grigovar tied off one of the ropes on a sturdy palm tree. "Enough talking over there. Best way is to go down and see for ourselves."

Yal Dolicar held up his hook with an exaggerated expression of disappointment. "Unfortunately, due to yet another unpleasant circumstance, it's not possible for me to climb down a rope. You'll have to do it for me."

Grigovar fastened the other end of the rope around his waist. "I'll climb down. No need for you to come along, Captain."

"Perhaps not, but I will." Saan wanted Iyomelka to see his earnestness. "Wish us luck."

"May Ondun's blessings be upon you." The old woman's voice carried an unexpected and inexplicable undertone of sarcasm.

Shrugging, Saan secured himself with another rope while his men lit three enclosed lanterns, attached them to lengths of twine, and carefully dropped them into the shaft's dark depths, shining the way. The big reef diver lowered himself over the edge and soon disappeared into the darkness.

With a quick wink at Ystya, Saan stripped off his shirt and dropped after him, resting his weight on rough rock outcroppings. Holding on to the rope, he glanced up to see faces crowding the pool of sky above. Accustomed to climbing the masts and rigging of the *Al-Orizin*, both men descended without difficulty.

The well was deeper than Saan had expected, and it remained bone dry. Though he was dubious that the waters had magical powers to restore youth, he couldn't deny the excitement and hope on Iyomelka's face. *She* certainly believed. More importantly, his men had seen the treasure, and Saan already knew what reward he wanted.

At last, he and Grigovar reached the seeming bottom in mud and moisture, but the well wasn't dry. The shaft curved horizontally in an abrupt gooseneck, at the bottom of which they found a pool that seemed to extend much deeper, a channel that curved out of sight. While Grigovar untied the lanterns dangling from the twine and set them all around for light, Saan inspected the pool, frowning. "I don't see how we can pump this water all the way to the top of the well shaft."

"Maybe something is blocking it below. I'll dive down to see." Grigovar began heaving great lungfuls of air, preparing himself. He flashed an encouraging grin at Saan and pointed into the curved shaft. "It'll be just like sliding down the throat of a sea serpent." Without another word, he dove in so smoothly that he barely made a ripple.

Long minutes later, when the reef diver returned, he tossed his shaggy wet hair out of his dark eyes. "Follow me, Captain—I want you to see this for yourself. It's only four body-lengths down."

Saan filled his lungs, then followed the reef diver into the pool's depths. As he immersed himself, he sensed no magical energy tingling on his skin—just water. But Iyomelka certainly expected the spring to have amazing properties.

They swam deeper, and in the fading glow from the lanterns above he saw Grigovar pointing. Yes, tumbling rocks had blocked the narrow mouth at a bend in the shaft, sealing off all but a trickle of water. Without too much trouble, they could move some of the stones and clear the obstruction so water could flow again.

Grigovar touched Saan's shoulder and pointed to the ceiling of the underwater chamber they had entered. Saan was so startled by what he saw that the air nearly exploded from his lungs.

The pale body of an old man floated there, caught in a pocket at the chamber's ceiling. But the flesh had not swollen or decayed. Rather, the man seemed perfectly preserved, like a wax figure. If Iyomelka's story was true, this had to be her husband.

Saan's lungs ached and burned, and he stroked quickly back to the surface of the pool. He gasped much harder for breath than Grigovar, who rose beside him. The two stared at each other, and the reef diver had a tinge of awe in his voice. "Have we just laid eyes upon Ondun?"

"Well, His body would be free of corruption and suffused with magic. That could be what seeped into the spring water, gave it the potency Iyomelka says." Saan intended to scoff, but he did feel a strange awe. This island held far too many mysteries—the old woman and her daughter, and those shipwrecks around the reefs. "Ondun supposedly left the world to create other places. What if He simply left Terravitae and came here to this island with His wife? What if He had a daughter here and then drowned in the spring? That would explain why Ondun never returned to the world."

Grigovar climbed out of the pool, getting back to business. "I'll leave that for the sikaras to decide. *Our* job is to clear that blockage and get the spring flowing. If we use pry bars and work together, we can shift those stones."

Saan tied stone weights around his waist so he sank faster to the obstruction of rocks, which gave him an extra minute or so to work underwater. Grigovar's lung capacity was nearly three times his, and the reef diver kept laboring by himself even when Saan had to swim back to catch his breath. Together, they pushed on pry bars, moved boulders, and worried away the smaller stones, loosening the rubble, bit by bit. The obstruction began to crumble, and they felt a strong, cold current flowing through the cracks.

On their fifth descent, Saan and Grigovar pushed aside a key boulder, and the force of the surge knocked away the rest of the blockage. Around them, the water plunged into darkness as the rising pool flooded the upper chamber and extinguished the lanterns.

Releasing the weights around his waist, Saan flailed, trying to reach the surface. Rushing water swept him upward like a geyser. He needed to breathe but could not open his mouth. Frothing water swirled all around him. He tried to swim toward the bright sunlight above. He bounced against the side of the shaft, struggled out to the churning center.

He felt a hand against his, a cold arm—and saw the preserved body of Ondun tumbling alongside him, propelled toward the surface like a projectile. All of the air burst out of Saan's lungs.

When the cascade breached and spilled over the edge, Saan tumbled out of the well shaft, coughing and gasping, swallowing mouthfuls of water. Grigovar hauled him to the side, while the water flowed and bubbled around them, flowing across the hilltop.

Iyomelka crowed and danced. The *Al-Orizin*'s sailors applauded, laughing. Yal Dolicar cheered louder than the others.

Moments later, everyone saw the sprawled corpse ejected by the flowing water. Ystya recoiled in horror, while her mother ran to the body, dragged it to the side of the pool, and held it in an embrace. "My husband!" Iyomelka gazed down at the smooth, dead face that wore a wise expression unaffected by all the time he had been preserved in the water. "You have returned to me, my love." She kissed the forehead with her wrinkled lips. "As you can see, I am not the same woman you knew. But I will be again."

Without removing her garments, the crone plunged into the newly bubbling spring, stroking back and forth, drinking deeply.

Saan had swallowed plenty of the water on his way up the well shaft, and it drenched his hair, his clothes, his skin. Still, he felt no different. Grigovar shook his head, splashing water everywhere, and he too seemed unchanged.

Iyomelka, however, exhibited an immediate transformation. As the droplets flowed through the wrinkles on her cheeks, the imperfections miraculously smoothed. Her rheumy eyes brightened, her wet hair thickened and darkened to a steel gray, her body filled out.

Yal Dolicar pointed with the hook at the end of his stump. "She was telling the truth!" Without being invited, he ran to the spring, dropped to his knees in the fresh mud, and used his good hand to scoop water into his mouth, expecting miracles. He removed the hook attachment from his stump and looked down at the abrupt pinkish scar, waiting for his hand to grow back. But he was disappointed. "I guess the rejuvenation doesn't always work."

"Or maybe it just doesn't work on men," said Sen Sherufa.

Sikara Fyiri stood watching in anger and confusion. The others ignored her.

Iyomelka reveled in the bubbling spring, then climbed out to stand dripping in the island sunshine. No longer a crone, she was now a statuesque but stern-looking woman who appeared to be about fifty years of age. She gave Dolicar a withering look. "The magic was not meant for you. It does not work on mere humans."

Her words surprised them all. Saan said, "Mere humans? What are you?"

"Much more than that." With a flick of her hand, she drew a rectangular shape in the air, pulling both sorcery and substance from nowhere to create a long crystal-walled box. "Come, Ystya, help me place your father here, where he will be safe."

Worried, the young woman looked at Saan, then back at the corpse. "It's been so long, I barely remember him." Together, the two laid the old man inside the transparent container. With another gesture, Iyomelka called on the spring water to fill the coffin, like an aquarium Saan had once seen in a wealthy merchant's home in Olabar.

"Yes, the power is at last restored. The power of life, the power of youth, the power of creation." The island witch sounded pleased. She turned a triumphant smile to Saan. "Very well, you've done everything I asked, Captain, and I am true to my word. My gratitude is great. Choose whichever treasure you like, take what you will—so long as you depart this island. Everything has changed now, and there is much for us to do."

The lure of the reward salved Yal Dolicar's disappointment at not regaining his lost appendage. He glanced back toward the jungle, where the fabulous wealth of flotsam treasures lay in piles.

Saan raised his chin, utterly confident. "I have made my choice, Lady Iyomelka." Beaming, he took the girl by the arm. "Your daughter is the greatest treasure on this island. I choose *Ystya* as my reward. I'll take her with me when we leave."

109 *Calay*

After the storm winds finally chased the black clouds inland, heartened workers around the castle opened shutters and pried off the plank coverings that protected the delicate glass windows. Brisk salty wind blew in, as refreshing as laughter.

Anjine stared up at a patchy blue sky with the only glimmer of joy she had felt in some time. "Guard-Marshall Vorannen, escort me while I inspect my city. Let's see what this storm has done to us." Once he had returned safely from his patrols during the height of the storm, Vorannen had given her full briefings of what he had seen, and Enifir insisted that he stay inside the shelter of the castle; Anjine had reaffirmed that with her own order.

And now they were ready to depart again, into the aftermath.

Old Prester-Marshall Rudio hurried down the hall. His wisps of gray hair were mussed and his clothes rumpled since he had not brought a change of garments for the four days he'd remained in the castle. "I would accompany you, my Queen, but first I must attend to the presters in my kirk."

"We will be some time, Prester-Marshall. Meet us down at the harbor later this afternoon."

Sen Leo na-Hadra followed her and Vorannen through the Royal District, across the bridge to the Military District where soldiers were already working to repair roofs and walls on barracks that had suffered great damage. Some buildings had collapsed, and grim people dug through the wreckage, pulling out bodies. Presters walked slowly through the streets, calling out verses from the Book of Aiden, offering comfort and sharing prayers. Animals wandered loose; many pens had been smashed. A barking dog raced by, chasing a pair of ducks. Neighbors compared damage to each other's houses.

At the Sonnen forges, Ammur and Vicka rallied their apprentices and journeymen to rebuild fences and shovel debris from the work areas. A young man stood precariously balanced on the roof of the main house, whose chimney had collapsed; covered in soot, he moved bricks out of the way, looking forlorn at the prospect of reassembling the chimney.

Queen Anjine paused, realizing that this was Mateo's home, now that he had married Vicka Sonnen. She had stayed at the smithy, managing business matters, while Mateo carried out his military duties . . . including the terrible duty Anjine had given him.

The big blacksmith saw her and bowed, looking flustered. Vicka gave a quick curtsey, without a second thought to her muddy dress or unkempt hair. "Majesty, do you have any word when Mateo will be back? We could certainly use his help around here after the storm."

Anjine froze, realizing that Vicka didn't know about Mateo's orders. Mateo wouldn't have told her . . . no, he was too upset. This woman didn't know what her husband had done.

"I . . . expect the storm might have delayed his return. He has many responsibilities for the army." Anjine looked at the woman and recognized the beauty and self-confidence Mateo saw in her. He would not have wanted a wilting flower who pined for him every hour he was away.

"I do miss him, but I know where his heart lies, Majesty."

"You're his wife—his heart belongs to you."

Vicka flushed, wiped a hand on her skirt, and pushed dark hair out of her eyes. "Yes, but he also loves his land and his queen. I get only part of his heart."

And I get part of it as well. Instead of voicing her thought, Anjine said, "Tierra is lucky to have a man like Mateo to protect us against the vile Urecari."

"True enough, Majesty. Even so, I could use his help rebuilding that chimney." Anjine nodded to two of her soldiers, asked them to help with the work at the blacksmith shop; it was the least she could do, after sending Mateo—Vicka's husband—away. She let the woman get back to her tasks as she continued her procession to view the damage around the city.

In the Saedran District, families picked up debris, patched shattered windows, swept away muck that had spilled from flower boxes and vegetable gardens. Biento and Yura na-Curic stood before their small house, picking up shards of broken pottery. Their grandchildren ran about, chasing stray chickens. Sen Leo paused at the doorway to the Saedran temple. "By your leave, my Queen, I will see to my people, my wife, and my daughters now."

"Your people are in good hands with you, Sen Leo."

In the Butchers' District, the relentless rain had washed away the smell of offal and crowded livestock, but many of the pens had flooded; bloated animals lay covered in mud or sprawled in murky puddles. With a shudder, Anjine recalled the terrible mission she had given Mateo. She had known he would never refuse. He would have done anything for her—ah, but what she had asked him to do. . . .

The procession wound around the bays and points of the large harbor. Anjine listened to the conversations, complaints, grieving, and expressions of relief. By now, the magnitude of the damage overwhelmed her, and she longed to go back to the castle, but she had obligations here. She needed to show the people their queen's concern for her city. She knew Calay could rebuild.

When she and her entourage reached the merchants' docks, the damage was the worst she had seen. Many piers were smashed, cargo barges and tall ships battered about like toys, some of them driven up onto the wharves. Crates and barrels floated loose in the water along with tangled nets, waterlogged sails, and a few scarecrowish bodies.

People in small boats rowed toward the headlands and the mouth of Calay harbor, where the water was gray-brown, filled with silt, seaweed, and debris. "I suppose the beachcombers will find great bounty," Vorannen remarked.

Anjine nodded. "Who knows what the hurricane has stirred up from the bottom of the sea?"

Merchants picked their way across the precarious piers, using boathooks to snag drifting possessions, trying to recover scraps of their losses.

Out in the water, a man in a small dinghy let out a loud cry and flailed his oars. One of the oars was snatched out of his grip, and the boat rocked wildly back and forth, finally capsizing as the triangular head of a black-scaled sea serpent lifted itself high. The creature gave a shrill blast through its blowhole. The man clung to his capsized dinghy, cringing in terror as the black serpent swam past. Ripples of golden scales highlighted its ebony hide.

People began yelling up and down the docks. Ferrymen who had rowed merchants out to gather flotsam now struggled frantically back toward shore.

Farther out in the harbor, Anjine saw the head and neck of a second black-and-gold serpent rise in a cascade of water to hoot at its companion.

Aboard one of the intact tall ships, seamen who had been hanging fresh sails now dropped the wet canvas sheets and swung down from the yardarms to gather harpoons. Yelling, they threw the spears at the nearest monster. One iron-tipped harpoon struck the serpentine neck and pierced the scales, though not deeply. The monster roared and shook its head, knocking the harpoon free, then charged forward to smash the hull of the offending vessel.

Marshall Vorannen was already shouting orders. "Alert the city guard! Open the armories. We must defend Calay!"

Anjine watched in dismay as another pair of sea-serpent heads rose out of the water, and the four giant creatures moved deeper into the crowded harbor.

110 *Corag Mountains*

After riding into the mountains, Mateo and Jenirod met up with Destrar Broeck's mammoth army outside of Stoneholm. Though familiar with the big beasts from his training year up in Iboria Reach, Mateo had never seen so many of them all together in the same place. Jenirod could not believe the spectacle. "The Book of Aiden tells of great monsters, but I never dreamed of creatures such as this!" On the ride into Corag, he had been so proud of his horses, but even the best chargers from Erietta Reach seemed puny and ineffective when measured against woolly mammoths.

More than a hundred beasts shuffled around the open stony areas near the cliff city, bellowing and snorting as they searched for food. Soldier-trainees set up camps on the cold ground, and herders tried to keep the mammoths from wandering. Skilled Corag metalsmiths had fashioned embossed plates of body armor and fastened them to the shaggy beasts with leather straps and lengths of bright metal chain. The mammoths trumpeted as if proud to show off their new armor.

From the great hump behind the head of a bull mammoth, Destrar Broeck waved at them. "It's Subcomdar Bornan himself! Look sharp, Iaros, or he'll report you to the queen!"

Though the destrar's nephew tried to make an impressive show, his mammoth mount lumbered away, despite Iaros's tugging at its neck harness and yanking its soft ear.

Mateo laughed. "I hope your beasts won't be so unruly

in battle, Destrar. Will they follow commands when we strike Gremurr?"

"Almost certainly not. A beast this size does exactly as it likes. Fortunately, once we get them on the road and over the pass, they should charge all on their own—the Curlies won't know what hit them. We'll wreak havoc enough, don't you worry." He glanced down at Jenirod and their warhorses. "Just make sure your little mounts don't get stepped on. Isn't that Destrar Unsul's boy?"

Jenirod sat high in his saddle. "Yes, sir. Would you mind two more men in your assault? Mateo and I would like to join the march on Gremurr."

The Iborian leader shifted on his shaggy mammoth. "I thought you might be coming to take command, Subcomdar."

"No, I'm here in an . . . unofficial capacity, but we've got our reasons. You are in charge of this operation."

"You're welcome to lend your arms and your blades. You were always good at following orders, as I recall."

"And you were good at giving sensible ones, Destrar."

One of the mammoths in the herd let out a shrill roar, and the rest followed suit in a chorus powerful enough to knock rocks loose from the surrounding cliffs. Broeck heaved a long, grumbling sigh. "We've been here two days already, and these beasts are anxious to move. If we stay much longer, they'll get hungry and restless." His face darkened. "But that's not the only reason for us to march. I've waited long enough to avenge Tomas."

His comment burned like a hot stone in Mateo's heart. "The queen already exacted revenge for Tomas. A thousand Urecari paid the price. I did it myself, for her."

"I heard . . . but that was *her* revenge." Broeck glared at him. "This is mine. He was my grandson."

While the mammoth army prepared to move out, Jenirod paced, betraying a mixture of queasiness and excitement. "This *will* be different from my attack on Fashia's Fountain, won't it?" Haunted uncertainty had hovered behind his eyes ever since he'd caught up with Mateo in the rainy meadow. "This is a real battle? Against real enemies?"

"Yes, Jenirod. You'll face Urecari fighters who can actually defend themselves. They'll die like men instead of helpless victims." Mateo wondered if he would ever stop thinking of the thousand heads. Or Tomas's. "But I mean to see them all killed, nevertheless."

Broeck and Iaros led the huge beasts along the mountain road into the cold and windy wilderness. Along the way, the mammoths stripped the grassy meadows of all vegetation. As they climbed higher, Destrar Siescu's new road dwindled to a stony path across cliff faces, chipped out by countless prisoners.

Siescu himself waited for them at the last work camp on the pass overlooking the descent. Corag soldier-guards still watched the bleak-eyed Urecari prisoners who toiled at the rockpiles, shuddering in terror at the passage of the lumbering monsters.

Wrapped in thick furs, Siescu greeted Destrar Broeck and Mateo. "We've opened the gateway to Gremurr. You can march these beasts to the mines and chase the Curlies all the way into the Middlesea."

Mateo ran his eyes over the sullen laborers. "Keep your workers fed, Destrar. Once we capture the mines, we'll still need people to provide labor for the Tierran army."

Broeck adjusted the head harness of his mammoth, impatient. "Don't worry, we'll capture more prisoners at Gremurr, too. I don't intend to kill them all, though they deserve it."

Raga Var came up the path from the mountain pass ahead. "I just ran the route, and the way is clear. Your monsters will make the passage safely." He nodded toward the Eriettan horses, pursed his lips in appreciation. "Those are better creatures for a narrow mountain path. Mammoths are too huge."

The Iborian destrar laughed out loud. "Horses won't strike a tenth of the measure of terror these monsters will! Mammoths won't be too huge when we face the Urecari." Broeck slapped the bull mammoth, and the big beast plodded forward, taking one heavy step after another. The huddled Urecari slaves watched from their open camp.

111 *Gremurr Mines*

After stowing away aboard the ore barge, Villiki endured filthy and stifling conditions for six days as she remained hidden. When the captain tied up to the docks on the northern shore of the Middlesea, she was anxious to get off of the miserable ship.

Each night during the voyage, she had crept out of hiding, finding her way around the deck obstacles by starlight. She stole food and water, then slipped back into the shadows belowdecks, tucking herself into a cramped area behind crates of supplies destined for workers at the Gremurr mines.

The coarse barge captain and his boisterous crew maintained a lax watch, since no one could imagine a stowaway who *wanted* to go to Gremurr. From muffled conversations she heard through the boards and hatches, Villiki learned that the crew had made this voyage from Olabar to the mines dozens of times without any trouble.

Finally, once the men made preparations to unload the cargo, Villiki tore off the dirty outer rags she had used during her escape from the church. Now that she had arrived, she no longer needed to pose as a nondescript beggar. Beneath, she still wore the fine clothes that the sikaras had given her.

From being cramped belowdecks, she was grimy, her face and hands smudged, her hair badly in need of washing and perfuming. Nevertheless, Villiki did her best to make herself presentable. This was not how she had wanted her son to see her after so many years, but it would have to do. She used a corner of the discarded robe to clean her face, raked her fingers through her hair. Villiki's presence, her attitude, her hauteur would be her finest garment. Tukar would welcome her, regardless. She was his mother, and he had to love her.

She heard men clomping on the decks above, opening the cargo hatch and winching out heavy crates to carry them to shore. Villiki waited until the space was clear before walking into the shaft of sunlight that poured down from the open hatch. She climbed up the wooden ladder and emerged on deck to the utter astonishment of the work crew unloading the ship.

The workmaster of the mines—a barrel-chested, bald-headed man—stopped shouting orders in midsentence to gape at her. She strode imperiously up to him. "You there! I am Villiki, the mother of your lord Tukar. I command you to take me to him."

The bald workmaster closed his mouth so abruptly that his teeth clicked together, but he recovered from his astonishment and sketched a small bow. "Lady Villiki ... your presence here is most unexpected." His voice was laden with so much speculation and doubt that she had no doubt he recalled the circumstances of her banishment. "I am Zadar, in charge of the mines."

"Good, then you have the authority to bring me directly to my son." She glared at the dumbstruck barge crew, not even knowing which one was the captain. "I have had a long, hard journey, and the hospitality of this ship leaves much to be desired." The men let out astonished protests, but Villiki nudged Zadar to escort her along the dock.

Nearby, seven impressive warships were docked, and workers had begun to cover the hulls with armor plates like scales on a sea serpent. Omra, in his arrogance, had used poor Tukar as his slave to complete this massive project for his war. But the enemy in faraway Tierra held little relevance to Villiki, whose enemies were much closer.

Stepping off the dock, she surveyed the rugged cliffs, smoking factories, smelters, and open mine entrances with a skeptical eye. The clank and clamor of work echoed through the oppressive air. This was a stark place, far inferior to either the palace in Olabar or the main Urecari church ... but better than a garbage-strewn alley. Or a grave.

As he led her along, Zadar wisely held his tongue. He asked no questions about why or how she had come here, but his pinched expression made his disapproval plain. She followed him up a gravel path to a house decorated with cut stones and meticulously planted flowers. Flowers? Tukar would not have bothered with such prettiness, she knew, but she had heard that her son was married after all. The wife was probably a spy, with orders to assassinate Tukar should he ever plot against the soldan-shah—why else would she marry a man who had been shamed and exiled? Villiki decided she might have to take care of her, just in case.

She hardly recognized the man who emerged from the villa, it had been so many years. He looked like a common laborer with roughspun clothes and no jewelry at all. After many hard years, and in her current disheveled condition, Villiki knew she didn't look her best either.

Tukar barely gave Villiki a second glance as he grinned at the workmaster. "You're here early for our *xaries* game, Zadar? And who is this?"

She smiled and spread her arms. "Tukar, my long-lost son! I have returned to you at last." The last time he'd seen her was on that night his own father had stripped her naked and ordered his guards to beat and chase her out of the palace.

He blanched and began to stammer. "Mother! W-what are you doing here?"

She ignored the idiotic question. "Call your servants. I need a bath, fresh garments, and jewelry so that I may make a proper appearance."

A woman and a wide-eyed boy appeared behind

Tukar—the wife and son, Villiki supposed. A puppy came out to bark at her, and the boy did nothing to control it.

Tukar turned quickly. "Shetia, please tell Firun to begin heating water for a bath. Look through your own clothes and see if you have anything appropriate for my mother." He shot his wife a glance filled with confusion and silent apologies, then looked back at Villiki. "We have only one servant."

"Then you have indeed fallen far in your years of exile." Now that she was here, things would change. It was about time her son received the respect and wealth he deserved.

Tukar stiffened. "I have everything I need, and I do important work for Uraba." A quiet old servant appeared, a man obviously too weak to work in the mines any longer. "Show my mother to the extra bedroom, Firun. She would like some time to rest and refresh herself."

Villiki followed the servant. With a glance over her shoulder, she saw that Tukar and his wife looked very worried.

Villiki took a place beside her son as they ate a meager but adequate meal. Now that she was cleansed, perfumed, and wearing a few scant rings and chains—perhaps the finest things that mousy Shetia owned—Villiki felt strong again. Her situation would improve soon.

If Tukar had only listened to her when he was younger, if he had followed her training and advice, he would have been a powerful man today. He could have been the soldan-shah. Now, after so many years in the squalor of Gremurr, he must surely realize the error of his ways.

The wife spoke little. Shetia showed genuine affection for Tukar, and did not seem intelligent enough to serve as a useful spy, although it might be just an act. Villiki remembered her own fatal error in assuming that the Tierran slave Adrea's silence implied stupidity. She wouldn't make that mistake again. No, this wife was not to be trusted, and must be dealt with quickly.

Tukar joked with the young boy, who seemed to adore his father. Rather than learning how to be a great leader, though, Ulan seemed more interested in his dog. The creature had to be tied outside the villa, because Villiki wouldn't tolerate it during the meal, and now it continued to yowl mournfully. The boy looked forlorn as he picked at his food, avoiding his grandmother's gaze, silently blaming her.

If she hadn't known better, Villiki would have thought that Tukar *accepted* his lot here, and she wasn't going to stand for it.

Right now, Olabar would be in an uproar because of her escape—she couldn't begin to guess what must be happening in the church. Even so, it would take time before word could reach the soldan-shah in Ishalem. Villiki had a slim chance to alter events now, but only if Tukar did as he was told. Maybe with those armored warships at the docks . . .

As they ate their dinner, she took charge of the conversation. "You've had many years to reflect upon the terrible things that happened, my son. By now you can have no doubt that your wicked half-brother despises you and has ruined your chances for freedom and happiness. Look at you! Omra has earned his own downfall by taking that Aidenist slave woman to wife. As First Wife! He will bring about the end of Uraba. He will destroy the church of Urec. But you and I can make it right. We have an unprecedented opportunity here to change the course of history."

Tukar frowned and shook his head. "Mother, you don't know what you're saying."

"I know what I've seen!" She jerked a finger in the direction of the harbor. "You have seven warships there, nearly completed! When they are ready to sail, I will help you take them, with all the soldiers here at Gremurr, to overthrow the corrupt soldan-shah in Olabar. You, Tukar, can take your rightful place after all these years in exile."

He wore a look of astonished horror on his face. With a sweep of his hand, he knocked her goblet of wine off the table. "No, Mother. I refuse."

Villiki was astounded. She lashed out to slap him, but with an unexpected ferocity, he caught her wrist and forced her back into her seat. "I said I *refuse*. I am a loyal subject of the soldan-shah, and I will not hear such treason—even from my own mother. I am already pardoned, and I will take my family back to Olabar as soon as those warships are completed." His face reddened. "Now I see why you came here, and you are not welcome. I'm sending you back on the next barge, so that my brother can do with you as he wishes."

Outside the villa, the damned dog kept barking, louder now than before.

Unable to believe what she was hearing, Villiki was blinded by rage. "You've always been a fool, Tukar—weak and unambitious, and *I* have suffered for it."

"You have suffered because of your own character flaws, Mother, not mine."

Villiki lurched to her feet, but Tukar only looked at her

coolly and perhaps with ... pity? With sudden horror, she realized that if he cast her out of here, she had nowhere to go.

A loud banging from outside broke the tension. The slaves in the mines were shouting. The dog continued to howl. Guards pounded on the metal work bells used to summon crews to and from their shifts.

Ignoring his mother, Tukar rushed out of the villa to see what had happened. Villiki ran after him. Outside, the dog pulled against its rope, barking and barking. A guard stumbled up the gravel path, his cheeks flushed, his mouth agape. "My Lord Tukar, there are monsters in the mountains heading down toward us. An army of great shaggy beasts! We are under attack!"

112 *The* Dyscovera

On the morning after the ship encountered the undersea city and descendants of the original Saedrans, Hannes delivered his most blistering sermon yet. It was clear to Criston that the prester hadn't slept at all, but rather had wrestled with his words all night.

Over the course of the voyage, some sailors had grown tired of Hannes's fervent harping, while others became even more bonded to him, though they had no outlet for their anger. Remembering how he had nursed the haunted man back from the brink of death, Criston still respected the prester's faith and deferred to him in spiritual matters. However, after hearing Hannes deliver his pointed tale explaining that Ondun had created the *land* for His chosen people—clearly a jab at King Sonhir and the sea dwellers—Criston called the prester into his cabin, along with the Saedran chartsman, who was preparing for his first day of discussions with the mer-people.

The captain took his seat at a small table and moved aside the charts he had marked. "Please close the cabin door, Sen Aldo, so that we can have a private conversation."

Hannes spoke up before Criston could even begin. "I don't like this, Captain. I do not trust these people—not at all."

Aldo's nostrils flared. "And what have they done to earn your distrust?"

"They are cast out from Terravitae. They destroyed their own land, which was a gift from Ondun!"

An uncharacteristic flash of anger crossed the young chartsman's face. "These are survivors of *my* people, who left Terravitae voluntarily. They have been lost throughout our history, and now we can be reunited." He turned to Criston. "Captain Vora, Saedrans have dreamed of finding our lost brethren for countless generations. This is a great blessing, and not just for Saedrans. These underwater dwellers may have maps, knowledge of Terravitae—who knows what they might have discovered during all that time?"

"They do not follow Aiden. We must not rely on any information they offer." The prester scratched habitually at the waxy patch that scarred his face. "Can you not see it with your own eyes? They are God's *mistakes*."

A glint of dark humor shone in Aldo's eyes. "Prester Hannes, are you actually suggesting that God made a mistake?"

Criston pounded the table, halting any further argument. "May I remind you both of our true mission. Think of what King Korastine asked us to do. Think of the war, of all those who have died."

Hannes was perplexed. "Captain, I don't see what that has to do with—"

Criston folded his hands together, forcing himself to sound reasonable. "Sonhir and his people move freely in the waters, Prester. With their great underwater cities and large numbers, they could be valuable allies! If they fight beside us, they could sink the entire Uraban navy! We must form a bond with them so that they want to help Tierra."

Hannes narrowed his dark eyes, calculating. "If we were to convert them, show them the truth—"

"They are *Saedrans*," Aldo insisted. "You use Saedran chartsmen without trying to convert them." The prester did not find the argument convincing.

Criston continued, "You're both missing the point. As allies in our war, Sonhir's people could swim right up to the Uraban coastline. They could approach Urecari ships from underneath and smash holes in their hulls."

Hannes glowered. "I cannot argue with your logic, Captain, but this is a holy war. How can we trust any ally who denies Aiden? Perhaps if we convinced King Sonhir to accept the Fishhook?"

"They would not do it, Captain! It would only offend them."

Hannes raised his hand as if to strike Aldo. "The words of Aiden are not offensive!"

Criston reached out and caught him by the wrist, held it firmly. "I have to agree with my chartsman, Prester. This is a delicate matter." He leaned forward, leaving no room for argument. "I want your promise of cooperation, my friend."

Hannes pulled his arm free and knotted his hands into fists. When he spoke, each syllable seemed forced from his throat. "In the name of Aiden, and because you ask it, Captain, I shall . . . withhold judgment, for the time being."

"Good." Criston turned to Aldo. "It is your job to go out and learn more from these people, become their friend. Invite their king to come speak with me here, so that we can know each other better."

Aldo sat alone in the ship's dinghy, rocking on the open sea halfway between the *Dyscovera* and the mostly submerged tower that rose above the water's surface.

Deep below, he could see the most ancient buildings covered with a fur of green seaweed. He could make out windows, doors, and long-unused outer staircases. The newer buildings—constructed of coral, mother-of-pearl, and stone blocks excavated from the seabed—were more freeform, with sweeping arches and thin spires supported by the embrace of the sea.

Four of King Sonhir's daughters swam around Aldo, laughing and teasing. They splashed the Saedran in the boat, and he sputtered, trying to remain dignified, which only made the girls splash him more. Their pale skin had a beautiful shimmer, and their long, lush hair flowed behind them in the current. The young women seemed innocent, unafraid, and very curious. They peppered Aldo with questions about his home, about life on land, about the cities that men built from trees and stones.

In the Tales of the Traveler and other ancient legends, Aldo had heard of beautiful sea women called sylphs, and now he knew the origin of those stories. "Can you really change shape?" He watched the girls swimming around his boat. "We've seen dolphins, and then these forms. Are you . . . one and the same?"

They laughed, ducked under the water, and emerged on the opposite side of the dinghy. "It's all Saedran magic. You should know that."

"We take whatever shape we need—it is still *us* inside."

One young woman leaned close, resting her arms on the gunwale. "We can awaken the spell within you too, Aldo. You don't know how wonderful it is, to change shape and swim wherever you like. The sea is where you belong."

"Our father would welcome you home. Join us. We can make you happy here. Have you not seen how beautiful our cities are?"

"Are your towns on dry land as lovely as this?"

Aldo tried to sound confident. "Our cities are lovely, but different." Watching the young women play, however, he felt longing and curiosity. The submerged metropolis seemed to call out to him. "I can't live underwater like you."

"We can change you. We know how. You could stay with us."

Another said, "We'll make you one of our people, Aldo. This is where true Saedrans belong."

"You could be with us," the third said. "I promise *I'd* make you happy."

"*I* would make him happy!"

"We all would!" They laughed and swam in circles around the boat.

Aldo flushed. "I'm sorry, but I'm not tempted. I already have a wife and children back home." Lanni . . . and his little son and daughter.

The sylphs giggled, as if he had told a wonderful joke. "A wife and children back home!"

"But they're on land—that doesn't count. Swim with us."

Aldo blushed, then cleared his throat, embarrassed. "It counts for me." Even with beautiful, half-naked women splashing around him, enticing him, he recalled the clear images of his beautiful, devoted wife and children. His love had not faded over the course of the long journey; as a chartsman, he had a perfect memory of them, forgetting not so much as an eyelash or a strand of hair. "I love them, and I miss them very much. They need me." He paused, thinking about their mission. "All of Tierra needs me."

"Tell us about Tierra!"

He grasped at the safer conversation, and they listened while he described how Saedrans lived back in his homeland, as well as what he had seen in Uraba. When he told stories of the Great Desert and the arid sand dunes, they shuddered; when he talked about the war between Aidenists and Urecari, they seemed perplexed. Having lived in isolation for so long, they couldn't imagine such a great rift between fundamental beliefs.

Captain Vora expected Aldo to convince the mer-people to join the Aidenist side of the fight. Though he loved Tierra, Aldo was a Saedran, and did not necessarily espouse Aidenist goals. He had seen terrible acts committed on *both* sides, though neither the Aidenists nor the Urecari seemed to see what they themselves had done wrong.

Aldo could say one thing in all honesty, however.

"Captain Vora is a good man, an honest man. My captain wants to invite your king aboard so they can talk and understand each other."

"We'll tell him," said the girls.

"Our father will agree."

"Sonhir wants to see your strange ship."

One of the girls giggled. "And ... we know where Terravitae is."

He bit back a gasp, but the young women continued to taunt and tempt him. "But we'll tell you only if you promise to come back and spend more time with us."

Aldo nodded. "I'll take the boat out again tomorrow to see you, I promise."

The sylphs streaked off, racing one another toward the tower balcony, to find King Sonhir.

113 *Iyomelka's Island*

When Saan claimed her as his treasure, Ystya brightened with surprised delight and ran toward him. Excitement at the prospect of sailing away on the *Al-Orizin* glowed from her.

Despite her own promise, Iyomelka did not react well to Saan's request. The woman drew herself tall, and her skin and hair throbbed with all the power she had absorbed from the newly awakened spring. No one who saw it could doubt the magic the water contained. "How dare you!" Her eyes flashed, and a thunderstorm seemed to be building inside her. "I forbid you to take my daughter."

As if he didn't notice the impending sorcerous explosion, Yal Dolicar burst out laughing. "Oh, I didn't expect that one, Captain! Remind me never to play *xaries* with you."

"I learned by watching you, Yal Dolicar." Saan faced the island witch with a roguish grin on his face. "We fixed your fountain, and you gave your word. You said I could choose any treasure I wanted. I choose Ystya."

The older woman found no humor in the situation, and her voice was as sharp as the fin of a shark cutting through water. "You tricked me." Her anger drew buzzing energy from the island itself. The water that bubbled from the fountain now frothed and gurgled.

Dark, unnatural thunderclouds began to brew overhead, knotting like black smoke, and a rumble penetrated the air. Lightning struck twice not far away, searing lances of white energy that threatened to move closer. The gathered crewmen looked terrified.

Equally furious and unafraid, Sikara Fyiri clutched her golden fern emblem. "What is this dark magic? I warned you about this woman, Captain! We must pray to Ondun immediately!"

Grigovar couldn't suppress a rude laugh at her comment. "I doubt that would help right now, Sikara. Haven't you been paying attention? Ondun's right there in the crystal box."

"I refuse to believe it!"

Ystya clung to Saan's arm, her hopes dashed. "Be careful! She will destroy you and your ship, drown all your men. This can never be."

With amazing speed, the water around the island grew

gray and choppy, frothed with whitecaps. In the distance, anchored outside the reefs, the *Al-Orizin* rocked as the storms increased.

Saan wondered if there were any limits to the enchantment Iyomelka had summoned. He didn't doubt the seriousness of the threat, and he maintained his cool demeanor only with great difficulty. "There is no cause to threaten us, my Lady. We had an agreement, and the terms were perfectly clear. Why are you reacting this way?"

Nearby a lightning bolt struck a tall palm tree, shattering it into smoking splinters. The Uraban sailors gasped.

"You may not have my daughter. I will never release Ystya. Do not force me to summon havoc and sink your ship—like all the others."

Despite the danger to the *Al-Orizin* and the crew, Saan faced the older woman with indignant anger. He was not used to being cheated. "So you will not abide by your own terms? You are breaking your word?"

Iyomelka forcibly pulled the girl away from Saan. "Choose something else, and I will not need to break my word."

"You should be more careful when you make an agreement." He didn't dare risk anymore. He believed in Iyomelka's powers. With false deference, he added, "All right, then—we choose *all* of the treasure instead. We will fill our longboats with it." Saan stood firm, daring the island witch to deny him.

To his surprise, she agreed. "Take whatever you can carry aboard your boats, so long as you depart from here."

Yal Dolicar applauded, as if he suspected this had been his captain's plan all along.

Saan tried to match the older woman's anger. "Very well, we will sail away with the first light of dawn, as the tide changes. I give you *my* word—and *I* don't give it lightly. All of us will be gone, and you need never see us again." Lowering his head, Saan looked apologetically at the lovely Ystya. "I didn't think your mother would allow it, but I had to try. There is so much I could show you of the wide world." The girl began to cry.

Turning away from the crestfallen look on Ystya's face, Saan called out to his crewmen, "You heard Lady Iyomelka—go load the longboats with treasure. There's plenty for every man. We have earned it . . . and there will be more when we find Terravitae!"

The sailors cheered, and Yal Dolicar and Grigovar led the group to the jungles and the waiting mounds of treasure.

Standing by the silvery pool and the crystalline coffin that held the old man's—Ondun's?—body, Iyomelka looked grudgingly satisfied. But her daughter broke away and ran back to Saan, who automatically folded her into his embrace.

A shadow fell over the clearing from dark clouds that thickened in the sky overhead. Pebbles on the ground vibrated, bouncing from tremors at the heart of the island. Iyomelka said, "Daughter, you will stay here, *as I command.*"

Saan clung to Ystya just a moment longer, before extricating himself. He kissed the girl on the forehead and rested his head briefly against hers to whisper in her ear, then stepped away. He held her at arm's length and said with great reluctance, "Go back to your mother."

While Saan and his companions walked back to the beach, dragging armloads of treasure and then returning for more, the two women remained on the top of the hill, watching them. Ignoring them, Yal Dolicar and his fellow sailors loaded the longboats with treasure. The two craft rode very low in the water on the way back to the ship. From the rear of the second boat, Fyiri muttered a prayer and a curse, looking back at Iyomelka in the distance.

All the way to the *Al-Orizin*, Saan watched the coastline. Iyomelka and her daughter came to the shore to observe them, probably to make certain they stayed away, as promised. Saan waved, and Ystya waved back, but the island witch simply stood there, willing them to leave. Overhead, the storm clouds and the rumble of thunder circled the island like guardians.

Four hours before sunrise, in the dead of night Saan roused his crew and told them to prepare for departure. Aware of their captain's plan, the men moved quietly, setting the sails and making the ship ready. Grigovar lowered one of the empty longboats into the water again.

Yal Dolicar was delighted. "You continue to surprise me, Captain."

Sen Sherufa, looking concerned, wished Saan well as he climbed down into the boat. With powerful strokes of the oars, he and Grigovar rowed toward the island, making barely a ripple or splash. By now, the big diver could find his way through the hazardous reefs even in darkness.

Saan had told Iyomelka that the *Al-Orizin* would sail at dawn, but he too could break promises. The island witch had changed the rules. He didn't feel any qualms about cheating her in return. Sitting eagerly up front, his eyes adjusted to the darkness, he peered at the white strand of beach where he had hurriedly asked Ystya to meet him.

His heart leaped when he spotted a lithe figure there. The young woman rose at the longboat's approach and waved silently but excitedly.

Grigovar seemed amused. "She's waiting for you, Captain, just as you said."

"Who could pass up a chance to go with me? Ystya will fit in the front seat right there." He joked to distract himself from the nervous flutter in his stomach. "Remember, Iyomelka said we could take whatever we could carry in a longboat."

Grigovar chuckled. "She does need to be more careful with her words."

The young woman waded out into the water, eager to meet them. Saan leaned over and took her hands. Though she was smiling and breathless, he said, "Are you sure you want to do this? You can't ever go back." His heart ached to see her exotic loveliness, her doelike innocence. How could even the Key to Creation be more beautiful? "Your mother will be terribly angry."

"That is why I need to go, while I have the chance." Ystya climbed into the boat, with Saan's help. "She killed my father. I'm not safe."

Saan couldn't believe what he had heard. "What do you mean?"

In the moonlight, the girl told her story. "After my father found us on the island, we all lived together for countless centuries. I do not know why, but toward the end, my mother and father grew to loathe each other. One day my mother drowned him and dumped his body into the well. She had no regrets—until the magic faded and the spring dried up."

Ystya lowered her head. "How long before my mother grows bored or impatient with me? I am no longer a child. Now that she has her power back, she could lash out and kill me, too."

Saan put his arm around her. "I'll keep you safe."

A troubled Grigovar stroked quietly and swiftly away from the island, past the underwater wrecks of other ships that had fallen victim to Iyomelka's storms and traps.

Back at the *Al-Orizin*, Sen Sherufa placed a blanket over the girl's shoulders and led her to a cabin, talking to her with soft reassurance. Saan issued hushed orders. "Weigh anchor, and let us be off."

Catching the nighttime breeze, the *Al-Orizin* put a great distance between them and the island. By the time Iyomelka awakened and discovered what they had taken from her, the ship would be long gone.

114 *Calay Harbor*

Gliding together across the murky waters of the harbor, two black-and-gold sea serpents charged a battered merchant ship that was tied up to the docks. One of the monsters bit down on the ship's rail, which exploded in a spray of splinters. The second serpent rammed the hull, cracking the lapped boards of Iborian pine. The hissing sound from their blowholes was terrifying, echoed by other creatures that appeared in the harbor.

Six of the monsters now circled the waters, prowling.

Anjine shouted orders at the top of her lungs. "Evacuate the docks! Get off the ships, all of you. Head inland. Away from the water!" Bells rang, people shouted, picking up her words and passing them along.

She stared toward the narrow mouth of the harbor, a bottleneck to the Oceansea beyond. The storm must have dredged the serpents from the cold secret depths and driven them out of their territory. Lost in the shallow harbor, the beasts were confused and infuriated, attacking anything in sight. She couldn't think of any way to herd the monsters back to deep waters.

Out on the bay, one desperate man abandoned his dinghy and tried to swim away as a sea serpent rose up before him. Blinking its reptilian eyes, the monster regarded the panicked man with curiosity before it scooped him out of the water, almost gently, and gulped him down.

Carrying a torch, Vorannen ran to the end of a pier, waving the bright flame from side to side and shouting. One of the serpents glided toward the guard-marshall, hissing and hooting, more curious than frightened. Vorannen hurled the flaming brand like a spear, and the sea serpent caught it in midair, as if it were a morsel of food. As the flames singed the tender flesh in its mouth, the serpent roared and spat. It hammered its head down on the pier to smash Vorannen, but he was already racing back toward dry land.

City guardsmen ran in, drew their bows, and launched a flight of arrows. Several pierced and annoyed the creature, and in retaliation it destroyed the rest of the dock, uprooting pilings and shattering boards. The other five creatures in the bay hooted to each other as they swam to and fro.

A sea serpent hauled its sinuous body entirely over the deck of a small cargo ship that was already swamped. Coiling and squeezing, the monster smashed the rails, cracked the deck-boards, and finally broke the keel itself. The boat gurgled, sank, and the creature glided back into the harbor.

Prester-Marshall Rudio hurried down to the dock, followed by several young presters and acolytes. Panting, Rudio stopped before Anjine. "These are not simply monsters from the sea, Majesty. They are evil, and we need a kind of strength that surpasses mere weapons. *I* can call on that special strength." He held up his Book of Aiden and turned to his fellow presters and acolytes. "Pray for me. I need your faith and the vigor of your hearts."

He opened the tome and began to walk down the sloping street to the nearest pier. Though Anjine believed in the teachings of the kirk as much as anyone else, she felt a hollow dread to see the old man stride onto the dock, entirely vulnerable. She knew what he was going to do.

Rudio shouted verses at the top of his voice. "For dawn shall burn away the night, good shall crush evil, and the greatness of faith shall crush the cowardice of questions." He lifted his other hand and called, lips drawn back, "In the name of Ondun, Aiden, and Sapier, I command thee to leave this place! Ondun Himself gave us this land, and Aiden found it. Every speck of soil in Tierra is our kirk! You are not welcome here."

Two of the black-and-gold serpents lifted their triangular

heads, and slitted eyes blinked in fascination at the prester—marshall, a single small figure at the end of the dock. Rudio raised his hand again, clenched it into a fist. "Begone, I say!" He shook the Book. "Do not awaken the anger of our God! Heed my command."

A third sea serpent appeared and stared down at the old man ... then a fourth and a fifth. All of the great beasts seemed mesmerized. Rudio continued to read verse after verse. With his voice cracking from the strain, he yelled out Sapier's Prayer.

Anjine watched, transfixed. Vorannen and his men had ceased their attack. The gathered people waited in absolute silence. The prester-marshall finally finished and made the sign of the Fishhook in the air.

One of the black serpents opened its mouth and darted down to snatch up old Rudio in a single bite, leaving only the ragged ends of the prester-marshall's boots on the dock, with his feet still in them.

115   *The* Dyscovera

Before the *Dyscovera* set sail from Calay, King Korastine had presented the captain with a set of formal courtly clothes. "Wear these when you finally meet Holy Joron." Criston had left the clothes in the cedar trunk until that afternoon, and now they smelled fresh and aromatic. It felt strange to don such finery, and he hoped that King Sonhir would be impressed. He wanted to make these mer-Saedrans amenable to helping the Tierran cause.

With scissors, Criston snipped his thick brown hair, then brushed it back to make himself presentable for his meeting with the leader of the undersea people. He combed, then decided to shave off the thick beard he had grown during the voyage.

The captain stepped out onto the deck late in the afternoon, both pleased and embarrassed to hear the whistles of admiration from his crew. Kjelnar strode up to him and let out a good—natured laugh. "Ho, Captain, you look like you're about to attend a royal dance!"

"It's a dance of a different sort. Neither the mer-king nor I know much about the other."

Aldo na-Curic looked both eager and uneasy. "I'm guessing you'll want me there, sir? I can help interpret, make the conversation go more easily." Over the past two days, the chartsman had spent a lot of time with the mer-Saedrans, particularly the king's daughters, who found him fascinating . . . whether as a wondrous enigma, a pet, or a potential mate. Sen Aldo seemed embarrassed about it all, but he had learned much.

Prester Hannes joined Criston, a placid expression on his rough, scarred face. "I must be there as well, Captain. I can teach the leader of these poor people about the Fishhook. Just think if he accepts the teachings set out in the Book of Aiden!" Half a dozen of his most devoted followers had expressed uneasiness about these people who either did not know or had willingly turned their backs on the Tierran church.

"That would not be a good idea, Captain," Aldo interrupted. "Since these are descendants of Saedrans, we know their beliefs. You would only offend—"

Annoyed, Hannes focused on Criston, ignoring the chartsman. "We must ensure that their hearts and minds are not corrupt, and the best way to do that is for them to accept Aiden."

Criston raised a hand to calm the growing anger in the prester's voice. "I know your passion, Hannes, but I must think of our mission. If King Sonhir can give us guidance—"

"Our more important mission is to spread the word of Aiden, Captain. If we can save these souls, we will have accomplished much, whether or not we find Terravitae."

Rather than reacting with anger, Aldo shook his head in frustration. "We Saedrans have lived among Tierrans for many centuries, and we've shown we can work together for a common goal. Why do you refuse to respect our own beliefs and philosophy?"

Now Hannes looked at him. "The Urabans have Saedrans, too—who serve the soldan-shah. That gives me little confidence in your trustworthiness."

Criston felt himself caught between the storm and the rocks. "Enough of this. Sonhir and I will be able to communicate well enough. This will be a private meeting between the two of us in my cabin—without a prester or a chartsman."

Hannes was shocked. "But who will bless your meal before you dine, Captain? We should invoke the presence of Aiden, whether or not this mer-king believes the Truth. It would give him a chance to accept the church willingly. Don't we owe him that opportunity?"

Criston forced a benign smile. "I know you want to help, my friend, but Sonhir and I will each do it our own way, just as common folk do at their nightly tables."

Javian called from the bow. "Here they come!"

Several dolphins swam from the submerged tower to the ship, and the majestic king of the aquatic people climbed the dangling rope ladder with power and grace. When Sonhir stood on the deck, dripping wet, he looked around with great interest. "I am greatly pleased to be here, Captain Criston Vora. I have learned much about thee from Sen Aldo na-Curic. It is good that two great leaders become friends."

The undersea king nodded formally at Hannes, who responded with a cold expression. The prester touched his fishhook pendant and said, "May the Compass guide you."

Sonhir didn't understand the significance of the blessing. "A compass serves little purpose underwater. My people find their own way."

Seeing the prester's flare of indignation, Criston quickly gestured toward the stern. "I offer the hospitality of my private cabin, Sonhir. I trust you'll find our foods enjoyable, and I still have a bottle of excellent Windcatch kelpwine. You've never tasted anything like it."

Though his long hair and beard hung wet, and he was naked except for a scaly wrap around his waist, Sonhir walked as if he wore regal finery. Although they had seen some mer-Saedrans carrying weaponry for hunting fish or defending against sea serpents, the king had come aboard the *Dyscovera* without guards or weapons of his own; to Criston, that spoke a great deal about their undersea culture.

Behind the closed wooden door of the captain's cabin, Sonhir looked at the confining walls, perplexed but not afraid. He had the curiosity of a child. "I have beheld places like this in our old ruins, but no one alive holds memories of living in such"—he spread his arms wide and was almost able to touch wall to wall— "small places."

Sonhir took a seat in the offered chair, studying the furniture with delight. Two bright whale-oil lamps illuminated a small repast set out on the captain's table. Criston offered a plate filled with dried meat, ship's biscuit, a loaf of hard bread, and a small bowl of stewed peas. The Saedran king picked curiously at the food, then tasted a morsel of each. "Thou hast given me new experiences, Captain Vora."

"We have embarked on a voyage of discovery. The world is full of new experiences." Criston poured them each a small glass of the kelpwine from the heavy bottle at the table. "Sen Aldo has already explained much about our land of Tierra, but let me tell you about the terrible war we face. Then you'll know why I hope we can become strong friends—and allies."

Darkness set in after a very colorful sunset, and Aldo sat once more in the ship's boat next to the *Dyscovera*'s hull, continuing his conversation with the mer-king's daughters. Their endless fascination exceeded even his own. Precluded from attending the captain's dinner with Sonhir, he had decided to continue his own discussions. He knew that Captain Vora was an even-keeled and sincere man, and his dinner with the other leader would go well.

Balanced in the rocking boat, he leaned over to watch the swimming sylphs, who teased him about his limited movements. The girls were lithe and sleek, beautiful and innocent. "It's time you went swimming with us, Aldo!"

"Just for a little while? We'll keep you safe. We'll guard you from sharks and sea serpents."

"There are no sea serpents around here," scoffed a third.

"You never know!"

"The guards are out patrolling. They'll drive any serpents away."

The young women swam back and forth, endlessly splashing Aldo until he was soaked. "Swim with us, swim with us!"

One rested her elbows on the gunwale to lift herself half out of the water. She said in a husky voice, "If you come with us, we can show you our towers, our libraries. We even have a map of the oceans and the boundaries of land."

"And we know where Terravitae is. Would that interest you, Aldo?"

His heart leaped. "Yes, it would! You promised to show me." How could he have forgotten?

"But you have to come with us."

Finally, he relented. Their presence was mesmerizing. "Well, it is a warm night. A gentle swim wouldn't hurt." He removed his boots, but kept his shirt and breeches on. And they would show him the maps.

"If you do, you'll want to stay with us! Won't he?"

"He'll never want a home on dry land again."

Aldo hesitated, suddenly uneasy. "No, I've already told you. I have a wife and children—"

The girl made a rude sound by sputtering water from her lips. "You land people are so rigid. Wait until you see our city!"

As he leaned tentatively over the side of the boat, the

girls grabbed his arms and yanked him into the water before he was ready. He yelped, catching a mouthful of the salty liquid, which made him cough ferociously—much to the amusement of the sylphs. When he bobbed to the surface and caught his breath again, Aldo tried to regain his dignity by swimming beside them, but his clumsiness elicited great gales of laughter from the sylphs.

Chattering dolphins appeared in the deepening dusk—at first Aldo thought the sleek, dark shapes were sharks, but the young women grabbed the dorsal fins, telling Aldo to do the same. He held on, curious, and with a lurch the gray swimmers streaked through the water, pulling them along. Aldo laughed with surprise and exhilaration, then sputtered from the spray. Out in open water, they all released the dolphins and trod water; Aldo looked down to see phosphorescent lights that outlined the sunken city deep below with majesty and mystery.

When the sylphs saw that his heavy Saedran shirt was waterlogged and hindering his swimming, they scolded him and pulled at the fabric, jerking, ripping. He struggled. "Wait! That's one of my only shirts—"

But they tore it off him. "There, now you can swim better. Why do you insist on being so clumsy?"

As the tatters of cloth drifted away, he realized how far he had come from the *Dyscovera*, which was silhouetted in the darkness and spangled with the lights of lanterns on deck and through open portholes. His uneasiness increased, and the water around him suddenly felt cold. "I'd better get back to the ship. The captain might need me."

But King Sonhir's daughters clung to him, thwarting his efforts to swim as though it was a great joke. "But we haven't shown you our maps yet. Wouldn't you like to see them?"

"Come down and have a look."

He found that he couldn't remain angry at the sylphs. They had no malice in them, but were oblivious to his concerns, his obligations. They grabbed at his limbs. "Join us underwater. We'll show you our city—it's not far."

"I can't go all the way down there. I'm not like you." He tried to stroke back toward the *Dyscovera*, knowing it would be a long and exhausting trip. "I won't be able to breathe."

But the girls tugged him down. He struggled in growing alarm—they wanted to drown him! He continued to fight, but could not resist the four girls. They dunked him, let him surface again, spluttering and gasping for breath, then pulled him under, holding his ankles and taking him deeper and deeper.

His lungs were about to burst. They had lured him with promises of Terravitae, but instead wanted to drag him into oblivion. He let out a mouthful of bubbles in a scream—they were trying to kill him! The sylphs dragged him deeper until his ears ached. He was dying from lack of air.

Then, through his dimming vision, one of the daughters swam close and pressed her face to his in a passionate kiss. Forcing his lips apart, she breathed into his mouth a gust of refreshing air that sparkled in his lungs. He felt suddenly revitalized, and to his amazement, he was no longer starving for air. The effect lingered much longer than any normal breath. When he stopped fighting, the girls gestured downward, and he saw that they were now close to the glowing lights of the submerged city.

A second daughter swam up and gave him another long,

life-giving kiss as she breathed oxygen into his lungs. The sylphs laughed in a symphony of sweet underwater vibrations . . . and he realized that maybe they meant to keep him alive after all.

The girls pulled him along with as much ease as the dolphins had at the surface. When a third daughter kissed him and breathed into his mouth, Aldo finally relaxed. Despite his fears and suspicions, the sylphs merely wanted to show him their world. As they had said.

The girls drew him toward the coral-studded towers and remarkable arches. Forests of seaweed grew up from the softly undulating ocean bed, waving in the currents like tall pines in a breeze. Beds of shells were arranged into beautiful gardens decorated with sea anemones and antlers of coral. Fish swam past, darting in games of their own.

In the rippling, dim light Aldo spotted a group of male mer-Saedrans swimming around the buildings on some sort of patrol, carrying spears and daggers with blades made from sharpened shells.

Some of the freeform buildings shone with pallid blue light; encased globes of a phosphorescent glow made ghostly silhouettes of the windows and chambers. Faintly shining jellyfish floated around, like a living constellation. Even so, the submerged city was dark and sleepy as night penetrated the deep water.

Aldo swam on, and the daughters guided him to a cluster of five squat towers, their arched windows and doors offering numerous access points at various heights. The girls pointed, excited, as they swam up to one of the arched openings; Aldo sensed that they were going to show him something important.

Before letting him look, the sylphs offered him another life-giving kiss—one from each of them—and they propelled him into the tower chamber. Lagging behind, one of the girls waved her hands, stirring the water so that one of the luminescent jellyfish drifted inside with them. It shed a glow into the gloom, lighting up the tower's interior.

In the uncertain illumination, Aldo saw that the walls were covered with drawings, sketches of undersea topography, watery mountains, chasms, outlines of islands and unknown shores. It reminded him of something he had seen many times in the Saedran temple in Calay. Another Mappa Mundi, but from an entirely different perspective!

He drank in as many details as he could make out, though he caught only glimpses. The night shadows were too deep, but he knew that this could be the key, the direction that the *Dyscovera* needed. One of the large landforms was marked TERRAVITAE.

He would have to come back in daylight, when he could see more and study all the details. This was exactly the information Captain Vora had asked him to find! Sen Leo and the Saedran elders in Calay—and Sen Sherufa—longed for such a huge breakthrough in their quest to complete the Map of All Things.

Though he tried to squint into the gloom, memorizing as much of the map as he could discern, the sylphs drew him back out of the tower chamber. Eager and distracted, they had much more to show him of the lost, submerged Saedran continent, the origin of his people.

It felt like a dream. He swam along, drinking in the remarkable sights.

At the end of their meal, Criston was pleased with how their conversation had gone. The mer-king had been a receptive listener, learning about the clash between the Aidenists and the bloodthirsty Urecari, about the burning of Ishalem and the piratical raids that had destroyed Windcatch, taken Adrea, killed his mother.

Sonhir found such news astonishing and sad. "I comprehend why thy comrades are hurting, but I am not eager to join mine own people to this war."

Criston lowered his head. "I realize it would be a terrible strain on you, but if your Saedrans were to ally with the Tierran navy, we could save thousands of innocent lives. Surely, that is what Ondun would want? We do have common ground in our beliefs."

As the mer-king considered this, nodding slowly, Criston felt his hope increase.

Just then the cabin door burst open, and Prester Hannes stood there in his full vestments, fishhook pendant clutched in one hand, the Book of Aiden in the other. Startled, Sonhir turned to look at the prester.

Criston rose to his feet. "Not now, Prester. I asked not to be disturbed." He kept his voice calm and civil, but something about the other man's mood had changed. The veneer of friendship and respect was gone.

As if he were under some kind of compulsion, Hannes pushed his way into the cabin, holding the Book of Aiden like a shield. "You may be the captain of this ship, but I am accountable to a higher authority. I make no apology for what I must do. I have prayed long and hard about it."

Seven men stood behind him crowded at the cabin door,

ready for violence. Even Javian hovered at the back of the group, wide-eyed and uncertain.

Criston stood behind the table, trembling with anger. "Prester Hannes, I am asking you, *as your friend*—think carefully before you speak another word. I am the captain of this ship."

"I answer to the captain of us all." Hannes shook his head. "Were I a lesser man, I would let these orphans stay with their misguided beliefs. Were I a lesser man, I would simply shrug and let them be damned. But I can't do that. The light of Aidenism is too bright inside my heart." He stepped closer, his eyes locked on Criston's. "*This* is our true mission, Captain, to spread the word and save as many souls as possible, not just to find allies in a war—even a Holy War. I will compel this man who styles himself king to see the Truth. Once he accepts Aiden and instructs all of his people to follow our ways, then Ondun will smile on us. As a devout prester, I can do nothing less."

Sonhir stood now, looking outraged. "Thou hast betrayed me, Captain Vora."

"I have done no such thing. This man is acting against my orders. And *you* men!" Criston shouted to those crowded behind Hannes. "This is mutiny."

"We're saving our own souls, Captain," called one of the sailors, "and the souls of those undersea people as well. If we're wrong, we'll let Ondun judge us."

"You *are* wrong, and I promise I'll do the judging long before Ondun can."

"It's too late, Captain." Prester Hannes stepped aside to let the burly sailors push their way into the cabin.

*

Filled with wonder after all he had seen underwater, and knowing now that the mer-Saedrans did have a key portion of the map he so desperately needed, Aldo allowed the sylphs to guide him back toward the ship. Though he had been frightened and uncertain at first, now he found he was reluctant to let this adventure end. The things he had seen, sights no other landbound Saedran had ever witnessed!

With a last effervescent kiss, the daughters of Sonhir released him and let him swim upward. The *Dyscovera*'s wooden hull floated far above, like a craft in the skies overhead. He emerged with a splash, flinging water from his eyes, next to his small boat.

"Come back and swim with us tomorrow," one of the girls said, surfacing beside him.

"We'll show you more."

"I'd like that very much," Aldo said. "I want to study your map in daylight. Thank you!" Filled with joy, he wiped dripping hair from his face and drew great breaths of heavy, flat air. He could see the lanterns overhead, but the night was dark. He called up, "You there on deck! I'm back with a great tale to tell." A group of men came to the rail and chattered excitedly.

The sylphs swam up to him again, touching him in farewell. Then, with a whisper like fluttering wings, a large net fell upon them from above, weighted with lead sinkers. The four sylphs and Aldo became entangled as they struggled to escape.

Aldo clawed at the strands of the net and yelled, "What are you doing? Why—" He choked on seawater. The net pulled tighter as the men on deck snagged it with a long boathook.

The four frantic sylphs ducked underwater again and combined their voices in a loud, unnatural scream, a cry that blasted like thunder beneath the waves. The eerie sound made Aldo's hair stand on end, but the men above paid it no heed as they yanked their exotic catch out of the water.

"You're making a terrible mistake!" Aldo yelled.

With an added chill, he heard the creak of the capstan and the rattle of the thick anchor chain. In the starlight, he realized that the *Dyscovera*'s sails had been set, and the ship began to sail away from the underwater city.

116 *Gremurr Mines*

Astride their warhorses, Mateo and Jenirod followed the mammoths down the mountain path toward the Gremurr mine complex. As they toiled down the canyon, sending up dust and clamor, Mateo viewed the structures ahead: smelter furnaces belching smoke, row upon row of prisoner tents and soldier barracks. This was not just a camp, but an entire city. The Urabans had sullied the Tierran continent, building this place in defiance of the holy Edict.

Jenirod was scandalized. "For years, they've been stealing from us. Mining metals from our mountains!"

Mateo was more somber. "To create weapons that shed Aidenist blood."

At the front of the charge, Destrar Broeck raised his voice above the sound of the beasts. "The scimitar that beheaded poor Prince Tomas must have come from here. Prepare for battle! You have your orders."

The soldiers cheered, and the mammoths set up a resonating bellow. The Iborian destrar reached to the saddle holder beside him and grabbed one of his iron-tipped spears, much like the ones with which he had slain the ice dragon. Holding the jagged weapon high, Broeck drove his bull mammoth forward, leading the beasts in the initial charge. The mammoths lifted their trunks and trumpeted louder than any army's war horns.

Caught unawares, the Urabans looked up to see the oncoming army's shields and fishhook banners. Several ran to bang on metal bells and gongs, sounding the alarm. They were utterly unprepared for such an attack.

When the steep canyon opened onto the even terrain of the camp, Jenirod kicked his horse into a gallop and swung past the lead mammoths. Face flushed, the Eriettan waved his sword and howled, "Kill the followers of Urec! Kill them!"

Mateo rode next to him, eager for a battle that carried no guilt. "Don't harm the Tierran slaves there, though—and we'd better keep some Curlies alive so they can be *our* slaves and work the mines."

Broeck heard him and bellowed a response, "We'll try—but in the end, we may just have to let Ondun sort them out."

Jenirod spurred his horse into the milling Urabans and slashed with his blade, running down any enemy guards who scrambled for weapons. Keeping up with the charge, Mateo rode ahead with his sword high.

The mammoths stopped for no obstruction, knocking

down tents and pavilions, smashing storehouses. There were no strategic military maneuvers; the beasts were forces of nature unleashed.

Tukar ran back inside his house, frightened for his wife and son. Shetia waited for his instructions, confident that her husband would protect them. Ulan jabbered countless questions, but Tukar shushed him. "You both must flee. I have to get you to safety. We're under attack by *Aidenists*!" The word struck terror into them. The puppy kept barking.

Villiki looked affronted when her son ignored her, but Tukar focused only on his wife and son. "Shetia, you know where the old mine shafts are. Run now, climb up the canyons, find a place to hide. The Aidenists are using monsters to destroy everything—they'll kill anyone in their path."

The boy clung to his arm. "Father, you come too! You have to watch out for us."

"I have to watch out for all of my people here." Tukar bent down to look at his son. "That is my responsibility. I need you to take care of your mother."

The boy looked solemn. "I will bring my dog. We'll be safe."

Villiki barked a harsh laugh, her voice filled with sarcasm. "Forget about them, Tukar—it is time to *lead*! Put up a fight—or are you a coward? You have soldiers here, and you have slaves to defend the camp."

Tukar spun with such anger that he astounded her. "Why in the name of Ondun would the prisoners defend us, Mother? This is no game of *xaries* that you can win by cheating! I make my own decisions—in this house and in this camp. You and your schemes are not welcome here. You've always been good at taking care of yourself—so get out."

Villiki left in a huff through the front of the villa and strode off toward the fray, wondering whether she herself could command the people of Gremurr since her son was not willing to do so. Tukar didn't waste a second glance on her, as he helped Shetia and Ulan gather a few vital supplies and belongings. He gave each of them a blade and sent them out the back. "Run and hide in the canyons until this is all over. Then we will all go home to Olabar. I will pray for you."

Shetia kissed him, crying. "And I'll pray for you, Tukar." He gave the boy a hard squeeze and kiss and sent them away. Ulan untied the barking dog, which bounded after them, away from the mines. After his wife and son had disappeared into the underbrush, working their way up the wild slopes, Tukar left the villa as well, heading the other direction.

In the main camp, the bloodthirsty Tierrans and their demons continued to wreak havoc. He squared his shoulders, put on a brave face, and tried to imagine how Soldan-Shah Omra would want him to stand against this threat.

Riding high and feeling invincible, Destrar Broeck goaded his mammoth into the Urecari settlement. He had already lost one spear when he was unable to yank it free from an enemy breastplate before the momentum of the charge tore the shaft out of his hand. He grabbed a second iron spear and jabbed it at any Urecari who stood in the way.

The industrial smoke and noise maddened the beasts, and they went on a rampage. Broeck didn't care if they smashed everything. Thinking of his murdered grandson, he could have leveled the Gremurr mines into rubble and still not felt satisfied. He raised his spear and roared, "For Prince Tomas!"

He heard an echoing cry from the soldiers who rode around them. "For Tomas—and for Aiden!"

Nearby, Iaros let out an accompanying howl. "And for all the victims of this war!"

The mammoths thrashed their ivory tusks from side to side, goring anyone who got in their way—Uraban soldier-guards, aides, camp accountants, supply staff, metalworkers, maybe even a few Aidenist slaves. As the big beasts knocked down the canvas-walled guard barracks, they smashed stoves and braziers. Fire quickly caught hold. Flames raged through the clustered shelters and spread to the prisoners' tents. Many captive Tierrans broke free and scrambled through the camp, though they had nowhere to run. Some of them joined the fight, attacking their oppressors with bare hands.

Broeck guided his mammoth toward the large stone-walled buildings that belched smoke. The Gremurr smelters must be captured, their output turned to the service of the Tierran army. Twenty Urecari soldiers stood in a line, shoulder to shoulder, brandishing spears and shouting as they made a stand to guard the facilities. They wouldn't be enough.

The destrar urged his beast forward, leading a dozen

mammoths in a charge. Several Urecari defenders broke from the lines and ran, but the others remained in position to the last. The leader of the small squad threw a wooden spear, which clanked off the armor plate covering the beast's furry shoulders. The mammoths trampled the men, not even slowing as they ran toward the smelters.

Eyes stinging from smoke and cheeks flushed from the heat, Workmaster Zadar called out to the armed guards who had taken refuge inside the stone building. Crates filled with newly manufactured swords were stacked all around them, ready for shipment back to Olabar. An orange bath of molten iron filled a huge thick-walled crucible, ready to be poured into flat molds—armor sheets for the seven ironclad warships in the harbor.

As the tumult of battle increased in the camp, the sweating and grimy slaves paused in their work. Zadar regarded them. Having seen the size of the Tierran army, he knew that his handful of guards could never defend them. However, these workers had labored in the mines for years, and Zadar had treated them harshly but fairly. He had given them food and shelter; he had never been cruel. As prisoners, they must know that their treatment could have been far worse. They must feel some pride in their work, perhaps even regarding these mines as their true home. How could they not, after all Zadar had done for them? Faced with certain death from the invaders, he saw only one chance.

Outside, the shaggy beasts bellowed and charged toward the smelters, trampling the line of guards. Making up his mind, Zadar used the pommel of his sword to smash open the nearest crate of new weapons. He turned to the slaves who worked the smelters. "Will you defend your home against these invaders? You can hear what's happening out there. They will kill you all, you know it."

The guards were astonished, and the slaves hesitated, but Zadar roared out in his voice of command, "Arm yourselves! This is our only chance! You must stand against them."

The slaves looked at each other, at the guards, at Zadar—and at the weapons. The workers were gaunt, weary, and frightened, but they could hear the mammoths outside, the cries of pain, the clash of swords. It was obvious to all that these wild, chaotic attackers would simply kill everyone, regardless of their race or religion.

One of the slaves plucked a sword from the crate, hefted it in his hand, and glanced at its sharp point. Zadar faced the door and raised his own scimitar, waiting for the attack to come. Behind him, all work had stopped.

Without a word, the slave thrust the sword deep into Zadar's side, ramming the blade in all the way to the hilt.

Zadar gasped in astonishment before the pain thundered upon him. The slave's face held no particular hatred or disgust, just a matter-of-fact expression, as though this were an everyday occurrence. The workmaster looked into the blue Aidenist eyes. The slave yanked out the blade and gave Zadar a fierce shove into the roiling orange pool of molten iron in the crucible.

Then all of the slaves were smashing open crates, grabbing swords, and running toward the greatly outnumbered Urecari guards.

*

Villiki watched in disgust as Tierran warhorses rode down Gremurr guards, who fled before them in terror. "Pull together and defend yourselves!" But the mayhem drowned out her voice. *Poor leadership*, she thought. Even if her plans had come together and she had succeeded in setting her son upon the throne years ago, Tukar would still have failed miserably. "Why don't you fight?" she screamed at the panicked soldiers, but they ignored her.

She wore a bright red garment, one of Shetia's gowns, which had made her feel like a true sikara again. Had she not given up her church vows to marry bumbling Soldan-Shah Imir, she could have been ur-sikara by now. She could have ruled in finery. Now all was lost.

The mammoths continued their rampage and much of the camp was in flames. The freed Aidenist captives gleefully took up weapons to join the attack, killing their guards and slave masters. Two old men used rocks to bash the skull of a guard; even after he lay limp on the ground, they continued to hammer at him with a sound of breaking bones that crackled like a fire.

Villiki realized she had made a grave error in coming here. She glanced toward the salvation of the harbor, thinking that she could slip aboard one of the ironclad ships. Surely some of the wiser soldiers would set sail across the Middlesea and escape this onslaught. However, there was a death sentence upon her if she ever set foot in Olabar again.

Death here, or death there ... it was all the same.

Before she could decide what to do, Villiki heard a clamor and whirled to see four woolly mammoths smash down a nearby pavilion. Then they charged toward her, drawn to her bright red dress. Riding atop the lead mammoth was a young Aidenist soldier whose face glowed with excitement.

She tried to run, but the waving scarlet fabric enraged the beasts further. The lead mammoth shot forward, its footsteps falling like hammers on war drums. Why wouldn't one of the Urecari guards protect her?

Villiki's foot caught on the hem of the long gown, and she tripped. She screamed in fury, thrashing, and then the terror set in. Trying to scramble to her feet, Villiki rolled over just in time to see an enormous foot, as wide as a tree trunk, rise up and crush down upon her.

117 *Oceansea, Near Ishalem*

Standing at the bow of his Soeland patrol ship, Destrar Tavishel felt the strength of Ondun Himself. His ten refitted vessels closed in on Ishalem like hungry wolves about to pounce on a tender young rabbit. His decks and cargo holds were filled with small kegs of whale oil, each one ready to be rigged with a cloth fuse.

Master Carpenter Burnet had anchored, reinforced, and tested all the catapults back in Farport, pronouncing them fit for war. His crews had spent more than a week practicing, sailing around the islands and hurling kegs at artificial targets. Their aim remained sloppy, but once the ships entered the harbor, they could spatter the city walls with flaming kegs. The spilled oil, fire, and wind would do the rest.

A crewman came running up, his long red hair blowing in the warm wind. "Destrar, we have sighted Ishalem."

Tavishel squinted through the gauze of lingering mist and could see white walls of fresh-cut stone and construction scaffolding. What had once been an Aidenist harbor was now crowded with foreign ships emblazoned with the glaring Eye of Urec. Tavishel closed his eyes and invoked the assistance of Aiden's spirit against such obvious desecration. "The Curlies will keep soiling our sacred land unless we stop them."

Facing the brisk wind, he regarded his determined sailors. "Crank down the throwing arms and prepare the mangonels. Ready a line of men from the holds to the hatches to the deck so we can reload with oil kegs as quickly as we can shoot. We should be in range within the hour. Victory is ours."

The men pulled on the ropes and turned the cranks, bending back the small catapult's wooden throwing arm until it groaned with strain. The ratcheting wheel clicked one tooth at a time, quivering with pent-up energy like a cliff panther about to spring.

In the distance, they heard tinny sounds of banging alarms, and bright signal fires shone from the tall stone lighthouse outside of Ishalem. *Aiden's* Lighthouse! Oh, how those people deserved to burn!

Inside Ishalem, the people—perhaps the soldan-shah himself— would know that the Aidenists had come truly to conquer this time. No mere skirmish, but a full-scale bombardment.

"Ships approaching from the south, Destrar!" called the lookout. "Twenty—fifty, or more!"

"What ships?" Tavishel shaded his brow and peered toward Aiden's Lighthouse, where he saw many large, bulky sailing vessels approaching the harbor. He was confounded. "What sort of design is *that*?" They were squarish vessels with incomprehensible rigging and gray pleated sails.

"They may outnumber us, but we have the mangonels. Turn to an attack posture. We'll bombard them with our first round and frighten them off."

The word was shouted across to the other nine Soeland ships, and individual captains prepared their catapults. Sailing toward the much larger enemy fleet, Destrar Tavishel smiled; he was about to surprise the enemy.

Aboard Ruad's ship at the lead of the large Nunghal fleet, Asaddan shook his head. The sibilants hissed through the gap in his teeth. "Soldan-Shah Omra was correct to warn us that the Aidenists could attack at any time."

The shipkhan was neither impressed nor fearful. "Ten ships, cousin? If that is the most powerful navy they can muster against Ishalem, the Urabans have little to worry about." He glanced curiously at Asaddan. "What is your experience with these Tierrans? Are they as evil as Omra suggests?"

"Who could be that evil? My friend Saan is a Tierran, by blood, and his mother came from a Tierran village. They certainly aren't evil. Still, you saw all the severed heads dumped at the wall. A thousand innocent victims! What sort of people could do that? Their hearts must be blackened by their own hateful thoughts."

The line of Nunghal vessels drew closer, blocking the

Tierran ships from the Ishalem harbor. Crowded on deck, the Aidenist sailors scurried about, toying with some kind of device.

"What sort of gadget is that?" Ruad asked. "Have you ever seen such a machine?"

With a sharp jerk and spring, the catapults' throwing arms knocked forward, hurling small barrels into the air toward the Nunghal line. Two Tierran warships launched their projectiles first; then, as if startled into action, the other eight marauder vessels followed suit.

The barrels tumbled through the air, smoking and flaming. They caught fire and struck the water well short of the Nunghal vessels. When the kegs smashed into the water, flaming pools of oil spread outward.

Asaddan peered curiously as the Tierrans struggled to winch back their catapults again, drawing down the thick throwing arms to launch a second round. He scratched his head. "How quaint."

Ruad narrowed his eyes, much more cautious. "Yes, but what if Aidenist ships managed to enter the harbor and throw those flaming barrels into the city? We don't know the true range of those weapons."

The Aidenists launched a second volley, this time much more coordinated. The barrels flew farther, and Asaddan yelped in surprise as a whistling, tumbling keg spun overhead and overshot Ruad's ship. Two of the Aidenist shots were lucky enough to strike their targets. One keg smashed into the broad gray sails of a Nunghal ship and spilled fiery oil across the rigging. With astonishing speed, the great vessel caught fire. The other Aidenist projectile shattered against the hull of another vessel, also spreading fire. The

Nunghal sailors hauled up buckets of seawater, working frantically to douse the flames.

The shipkhan of the first vessel soon saw that his ship was doomed; he had the presence of mind to steer away from the other crowded Nunghal-Su ships even as his crew abandoned ship. The seafaring clans were familiar with the dangers of spreading fire in close-packed vessels.

Appalled, Ruad whistled for his men to load the cannons that were normally used to protect against sea serpents. "Fortunately, we have a much greater range." Ruad whistled for his crew. "Send word down the line." The shipkhans of the other vessels armed their cast bronze cylinders with fire-powder.

Asaddan did not take his eyes from the ten enemy ships, stunned by what he had seen. "This seals the decision. Soldan-Shah Omra is our friend, and it's clear that these Aidenists intend to cause havoc."

"We'll earn our alliance with Uraba by taking care of the problem," Ruad said with a dark grin. "A single broadside should be sufficient."

After the second volley of flaming barrels struck, Tavishel wasted no time. "You men, load the mangonels with a third round! They will be terrified by what we can rain down upon them." As the ten Soeland vessels continued to close the gap, the third round from the catapults would sow great devastation amongst the opposing fleet.

Aboard the foreign ships, the shaggy crewmen extended strange cylinders through openings in their hulls. Tavishel frowned as he watched.

Fire spat from the opposing vessels, accompanied by a

ricocheting sound of continuous thunder, boom after boom after boom. Tavishel looked up wildly to hear a whizzing sound, the screaming of impossibly fast projectiles hurtling through the air.

Explosions bombarded all ten of his ships. Hot stones or iron balls slammed into masts, cut into sails, shattered hulls. On Tavishel's ship, men screamed and dove away from their half-cocked mangonel, releasing the throwing arm just as the side brace snapped in half. The arm of the collapsing catapult snapped downward like a striking viper, ripping its anchor bolts and smashing into the deck.

An eruption threw Tavishel to the opposite side of the ship. Sharp wooden stakes flurried around him like snowflakes in a blizzard; he was cut and stabbed, but felt no pain. The screams, crashes, and roars deafened him. As his warship lurched and writhed from the bombardment, he struggled into a sitting position and saw mangled crewmen all around him. Looking through hazy black smoke, he realized that all ten of his vessels had been smashed into flotsam.

Fires caught on the numerous kegs of whale oil filling the holds. Nearby, one of the Soeland vessels exploded, as all of the flammable kegs caught. A clotting geyser of orange flames burst from the hatches. Men screamed as they burned like torches, covered in spilled oil.

Tavishel grasped a broken rail to pull himself up. Water rushed in through the breached hull, racing the spreading fire to see which could devastate the vessel first. With an inexorable groan, the mainmast toppled over, taking the rigging ropes along with it. The sails turned to sheets of flame.

The bulkhead collapsed in front of him, and the destrar

plunged into the sea amid the spreading debris. Fire raced and skipped across the floating pools of oil. Tavishel tried to swim, but could get nowhere, for some reason. He looked down, and saw with shock that the lower half of his left arm was gone. Everywhere, he heard screams and continuing explosions. The Soeland vessels collapsed into their own infernos.

The enemy ships did not even bother to fire a second round.

Floating, dazed, and dying now, Tavishel stared dumbly toward the distant shore. There, in the brightening sunlight, he thought he could see Ishalem.

118 *Iyomelka's Island*

When she did not find Ystya upon awakening, Iyomelka assumed the girl had gone somewhere to avoid her mother and sulk. A glance from the hill showed that the ship was gone with the sunrise, as Saan had promised. Her daughter had longed to go with the foreign sailors.

Oh, that young captain had a voice like honey, and he made lovely promises that the innocent girl would not recognize as false. Ystya had such great potential—didn't even know her own powers—but she was naïve and foolhardy, and needed to be protected. This island was the place to protect her, especially now that the vivifying spring had been restored.

Iyomelka bathed to gather the power that was her due, but when she emerged from the sparkling pool, feeling stronger than she had in decades, she still saw no sign of the foolish girl. She began to feel a dark dread within her.

The island witch had also been gone from the outside world for centuries and had forgotten just how devious and treacherous men could be. She searched for Ystya, going to all the places where the girl could hide, but without success. She could not find her daughter. It was several hours past dawn before Iyomelka knew with a sick certainty what had truly happened.

The *Al-Orizin* had sailed away, and Saan had lured her daughter with them. He did not know what he had done!

Iyomelka ran down to the beach, saw the girl's footprints in the sand, vanishing into the water where she must have met a small boat. The older woman stared out at the submerged reefs that had wrecked so many other vessels, but the Uraban sailing ship was long gone. She held out her arms and let her anger and despair build. She wailed louder than a thousand gulls, "Ystya!"

Summoned by her emotions, tropical winds whipped up around the island, stirring the jungles. Fan ferns brushed their leaves together with a dry, mocking sound. The palms swayed and bent until one of the tall trunks snapped with a loud crack, sending down a cascade of broomlike fronds.

The ocean currents responded to Iyomelka's call, as they always did when she grew angry. Whitecaps thrashed and foamed beyond the lagoon and spread like echoes toward the reefs. Black clouds gathered above the island at the center of a widening weather pattern that would become a vortex tugging at any sailing ships from far and wide. If she could snag the *Al-Orizin*, she could suck the ship back here and smash it up against the reefs.

But Captain Saan was a clever one; he would have sailed away at his vessel's top speed. Iyomelka knew he had tried to trick her all along. "Bring back my daughter!" The wind snatched her words away, and she doubted even magic could carry that threat far enough across the seas for Saan and Ystya to hear it. Still her anger continued to build. Forgotten now was the rejuvenating power of the reawakened spring.

Needing more strength, Iyomelka raced back up the hill to the bubbling well. The deep pool shone fresh and silver in the stormy morning. Her husband's preserved body lay next to it within his crystalline coffin, entombed in the pure water. His face looked maddeningly beatific, as if he truly didn't care that she had killed him. Maybe he was happy she had ended the misery of enduring her company! Ondun had always been a fool. Even the greatest love was not meant to last for thousands of years. . . .

Iyomelka drank deeply of the powerful water, stripped off her clothes, and plunged into the cold pool, bathing her skin, washing her hair, allowing the magical waters to infuse her pores, her flesh, her bones. It was not a process to be hurried. Unconcerned with the spring losing its potency now, she decided to take all of the magic and fortify herself . . . so much that she felt the energy building inside her, ready to explode. If Iyomelka didn't release some of the energy she contained, it would begin to eat away at her.

From the fountain, she could look out toward the ocean, knowing what lay beneath the surface of the reefs. The island witch extended her hands, spread her fingers, and sent forth a command. She called the tides, shifted the water, and drew together strands of seaweed, lumps of coral. Then she *pulled*.

The largest of the sunken sailing ships rose from beneath the waves, still dripping, its wood rotten with sea worms, its sails nothing more than green shreds. The webwork of rigging was nearly gone, leaving only a few dangling strands that had been gnawed at by fish and time.

As the wrecked ship heaved itself to the surface, made buoyant by her summoning, Iyomelka called swarms of starfish from the reefs. They detached themselves from their hiding places, rose up, and clustered in sufficient numbers to patch the holes in the hull. Seaweed twined up to weave into and secure the ropes. Anemones clung to the sides of the deck and hull, and a flourish of sharp coral antlers protruded from the bow.

Iyomelka would use this vessel as her own.

Before leaving, almost as an afterthought, she used more of her magic to raise the crystalline coffin, and the water-filled container followed her down to the beach. The old man's preserved body looked peaceful in its tank.

Standing on the shore, Iyomelka sent the waters away from the lagoon so she could walk across the mucky sea bottom to meet the vessel that balanced on the rough reef. Water continued to drip off the slime on the masts, spars, and deck.

She climbed aboard the resurrected ship, pulling herself up the peeling hull with a rubbery strand of brown-green kelp. Behind her, the transparent coffin rose to the deck and settled onto the warped boards, still exuding magic. Iyomelka did not give her husband a second thought, but she would need him later.

She climbed to the bow of her vessel, where the long spears of twisted coral pointed toward the open sea. Without looking back at her island, Iyomelka allowed the waters to return in a rush, calling the tides to float the ship, which lurched off of its jagged perch.

Ready to depart, Iyomelka whistled for her own winds and moved the waters to create a current beneath the starfish-patched hull. She drove her ship away from the island, away from the reefs. Her anger remained unabated as she set out after Saan and the *Al-Orizin*.

119 *The* Dyscovera

Hearing the commotion on deck, Kjelnar burst out of his small cabin to see what the shouting was about. Full night had fallen, and lanterns were lit around the ship; he had been resting for a few hours before he was due to take the late watch. Now he felt the *Dyscovera* lurch.

Two sailors at the capstan had already raised the anchor. He saw men up on the spars, tugging the rigging ropes, setting sail. They spoke to each other in furtive voices, not the usual cheerful bellows, repeating orders from the captain. Before Kjelnar could even catch his breath, the night breeze stretched the canvas and the ship began to move. He couldn't believe what he was seeing. Captain Vora had given no orders. "By the Fishhook, what is going on!"

The men paused, glanced at him, then went back to tightening the ropes, as if Kjelnar no longer mattered.

Mia emerged from where she had been hiding by the

crates near the chartsman's pigeon coop and ran across the deck to him, her thin face pale in the darkness, her voice hushed. He wondered if she had been assaulted again. "First Mate, they've taken over the ship, and they're sailing away."

"Who's taken the ship? What does the captain have to say about this?"

"Prester Hannes and a group of men locked him in his cabin along with King Sonhir."

"You're saying it's mutiny?" Kjelnar clenched his fist and looked for the nearest thing to strike. Of course, the others wouldn't have let the woman sailor in on their plans. "How many remain loyal?"

She shook her head. "I don't know. The other crewmen don't talk much with me, and I can't find Javian."

The big Iborian strode forward. "Come with me. We'll see about this."

Off the starboard side, a group of men had hauled up a net filled with struggling forms. He recognized Sonhir's daughters and Aldo na-Curic, all tied together, dripping wet. Kjelnar stormed over to them. "You there, stop what you're doing! What is this madness?"

One of the crewmen looked over at him, flushed with excitement, not even afraid. "We've snatched some of the fallen sea people so the prester can teach them to be good Aidenists. They'll thank us for it." He seemed to think even the first mate would agree with the scheme.

Kjelnar swung his fist squarely into the man's face, knocking him out cold with one blow. As the sailor crumpled, the big Iborian tore the other two crewmen away from the net. "I'll see you all cast overboard!"

The confused men tumbled to one side, stunned as their heads struck the wooden deck. How far did this mutiny go? Kjelnar handed Mia his dagger. "Cut them free. I'm going to see to the captain."

The big Iborian charged off toward the captain's state-room, where several men crowded the door. Not intimidated, Kjelnar grabbed two men by the collar and threw them behind him, then two more, as if he were plucking ticks off a hound. "Captain Vora, are you all right?"

He saw young Javian among the men, looking uncertain, most likely pressured into taking part. Kjelnar spun the cabin boy around and pressed his face terrifyingly close. "Get away from here. Go help Mia!" The boy skidded, stumbled, and ran to where the young woman still worked at cutting the struggling figures free of the net.

Inside the large cabin, a handful of mutineers held Captain Vora and the mer-king captive while a smug-look-ing Prester Hannes intoned from the Book of Aiden as if he were performing an exorcism. "I know what is best. You may command this vessel on her voyage, Captain, but in spiritual matters I am your master."

Criston struggled to break free. "I am the captain in *all* things concerning this ship." But the prester wasn't listen-ing.

Hannes's angry view of church teachings had annoyed Kjelnar plenty of times during the voyage, and he had had enough. "Prester, release the captain and King Sonhir now—or you'll answer to me."

But the scarred man looked beatific, utterly convinced of what he was doing. "I answer only to Aiden."

Shouts and screams rang out from the darkened fore-deck, far from the captain's stateroom. "*Dyscovera* is under attack!" Behind him, Kjelnar saw a handful of sailors face off against shadowy forms that scrambled up the hull and swarmed over the rails.

Sonhir squared his shoulders, even though the mutineers still held him in a tight grip. The mer-king's hair and skin had dried by now, and he looked like an angry god himself. "Stand aside. My people have come for me. They will destroy thee for such betrayal."

Kjelnar was still trying to understand all that had happened here, what Hannes and his ruffians really wanted—but most importantly, he knew that outsiders were attacking his ship. He shoved the mutineers out onto the deck, not caring about Hannes. "I'll deal with you men later—fight, damn you! You'd better help to defend this vessel."

Under the faint moonlight he could see ominous shapes rushing aboard, and dark sea creatures swimming in the water all around the moving ship. Then a large thump shuddered through the deckboards as something massive rammed the *Dyscovera*'s hull from below.

Mia sawed on the wet strands of the net with Kjelnar's dagger blade, cutting the struggling forms free. Aldo spluttered, thrust his head out, then tore his way free of the net ropes. He recognized her immediately. "Mia! What's happening? Why are they doing this?"

She helped him to his feet. "I don't know, but I'm not with them."

Javian came running up. "Kjelnar told me to help you."

As one of the stunned mutineers stirred on the deck, Javian expertly knocked him on the back of the head with a small wooden cudgel he carried, sending him sprawling again.

The terrified sylphs huddled against each other, still caught in the net. Aldo bent over and untangled strands while trying to calm the girls. "Hush. We're getting you out of this. I won't let anyone hurt you." Rising, the mer-king's daughters shivered in the open air, and Aldo continued, "I'm sorry, I'm sorry. I don't know why any of this is happening."

"Prester Hannes said it was necessary," Javian answered. "He told us that King Sonhir needed to accept the Fishhook at all costs. He said Aiden would protect us, no matter what we did. I think . . . I think he is evil."

Responding to the sylphs' underwater scream, mer-people climbed the sides of the *Dyscovera*, muscular warriors that seemed caught between their human and aquatic shapes. Frantic human sailors grabbed harpoons and spears, stabbing the mer-Saedrans, which only inflamed them to greater ferocity. The Tierran crewmen stood shoulder to shoulder, yelping for assistance as they tried to defend their ship.

Kjelnar charged out of the captain's stateroom, swinging both fists. Seeing nothing but a threat to the *Dyscovera*, he grabbed the wet-skinned aquatic warriors and unceremoniously tossed them over the side. "Get off my ship!" He picked up a wooden truncheon and struck hard, cracking the skull of a mer-Saedran whose hair hung in long ropy locks. The undersea warrior fell limp.

More and more mer-Saedrans climbed aboard, scaling the hull from all sides. Mutineers and faithful alike fought side by side in a panic, clumped in numerous small battles. Javian ran to join the fray, but even though Mia called after him, the young man vanished into the tumult.

Kjelnar threw himself upon several of undersea warriors, hoping to save fellow crewmen, but the big Iborian overestimated his own strength. As he grabbed two of the wet-skinned men, four more closed around him. They tore the truncheon out of his hand and tossed it skittering across the deck. Though Kjelnar bellowed and strained, they dragged him toward the deck rail.

Aldo saw what was going to happen and shouted at the top of his lungs. "No, please!" He turned to Sonhir's daughters, who had climbed to their feet, shaking. "I beg you, stop them!"

The sylphs wailed in terror, their voices shrill and vibrating, but the mer-Saedrans pulled Kjelnar overboard and down into the water with a huge splash. He was gone.

Inside the captain's stateroom, Prester Hannes slammed shut his Book of Aiden and grabbed a gutting knife from one of the shelves. "Those demons will vanish without their king." Looking plaintively at Criston, Hannes strode toward Sonhir, raised the knife. "Captain, this is the only way. We must save our ship!"

But Criston took the bottle of kelpwine and swung hard, shattering it on Hannes's head. With a look of astonishment, the prester crumpled, sprawling onto the table.

Criston turned to the mer-king. "Sonhir, I did not mean for this to happen. This is not what my people believe. This man did not act on my orders."

"Yet he did act." Sonhir shoved the prester away in

disgust. "He is the man who speaks for thy god. He has shown the poison in thy beliefs."

"No, not my beliefs! Those words were wrong. I didn't mean—" He shook his head. "Oh, it doesn't matter. You must go. Leave this ship, and please tell your people to retreat. We don't want to fight with you."

King Sonhir searched the captain's face for a long moment as a squall of anger rose and passed. "I shall tell my warriors to withdraw, and they will cause thee no further harm ... but too much damage has already been done. My people can never be allies with the followers of Aiden."

He strode out onto the main deck.

Terrified by the mayhem, some of the *Dyscovera* crew came toward the frightened sylphs, seeing easy targets, but Aldo and Mia stood protecting them. The young woman brandished Kjelnar's dagger in one hand and her own knife in the other, jabbing at anyone who ventured too close. "Chartsman, get them out of here!"

Frantic, Aldo urged Sonhir's four daughters to the deck rail. "Escape! Go back into the water. I don't want you hurt!"

Two of the girls dove over the side at once, arcing perfectly into the water and submerging with barely a ripple. Another stood shaking as the battle faltered; the last, boldest daughter leaned close to Aldo, gave him a quick kiss on the lips again, then backed away with a smile.

With tears streaming down his face, Aldo said, "I did not mean any harm, I promise." She dove quickly over the side, accompanied by her sister. He knew now that he would never see their charts of undersea lands and Terravitae, their own Mappa Mundi.

The mer-king appeared on deck and shouted a command in their archaic language, which made the aquatic people pause in their fighting. Looking disheveled, Captain Vora also stepped out into the night. "Lay down your weapons! You men, all of you—stop fighting!"

Grumbling, deeply shaken by the loss of Kjelnar overboard, the *Dyscovera* sailors backed off, keeping their weapons raised. Across from them, covered with blood and seawater, the aquatic people glared at the humans. Never letting down their guard, they gathered their wounded and dead and slipped over the side.

Two crewmen dragged Hannes's unconscious form out of the captain's stateroom. Criston looked around, studying the men, not sure whom he could trust. Young Javian came trotting back to the captain now, stunned and confused.

After the last of his people had retreated overboard, and he saw that all of his daughters had returned to the water, King Sonhir glowered at the unconscious prester. "I will take that man with me into the waters. The sea will dispense its justice."

Criston shook his head, even though he knew the mer-king's solution would be much easier. "I cannot allow that. He is one of my crew, and he is the prester of my church."

Sonhir's face was dark, and the two men stared at each other for a long moment. "So be it. You are the captain of your ship, and you must endure the consequences of your decisions—*all* of them." The mer-king turned his broad back on them, bounded across the deck, leaped into the air, and went over the side without touching the deck rail.

Prester Hannes groaned heavily as he returned to consciousness; he blinked his eyes and looked around. Ferociously, Criston shoved him toward Mia and Javian. "Tie him to the mainmast, and if he starts spouting his poison again, *gag* him! No one is to talk to or release him."

When he came awake again, the prester wore a broad grin on his scarred face. The *Dyscovera* sailed on, unguided, pushed by the night breezes.

120 *Calay Harbor*

After devouring Prester-Marshall Rudio, the sea serpents continued their attack on Calay harbor. Vorannen tried to rally his city guard troops, but the soldiers now wrestled with a new kind of terror. "Even Aiden has forsaken us. We must go to the kirk, to beg for salvation!"

Queen Anjine had seen how easily—how frivolously—the monsters had dismissed the prester-marshall's faith. Her wave of anger built to a crest. "This is my city, and these are my people!" Anjine was the queen of all Tierra, but she felt entirely powerless now. She didn't know how to begin a fight against these serpents. She clenched and unclenched her fists ... and in the back of her mind, she wished Mateo could be there.

Vorannen stood by her side, coiled with frustrated energy. "The soldiers are ready to fight, Majesty, but arrows, swords, and spears will do little against those beasts. Come with me, we need to get you to safety and hope that the serpents leave our harbor."

She flashed him a quick, hard look of assurance. "I will not abandon my people."

Archers launched another volley of arrows at the thrashing sea serpents, but most bounced off of the dark scales. "Majesty, I am your protector. After what those monsters did to the prester-marshall, I won't allow you to risk—"

"And I am your *queen*. I will do what I deem necessary."

Though the sea serpents had glided away from the docks, the scraps of Rudio's bloody boots remained there as forlorn reminders. She shook her head. "If Aiden did not listen to the prayers of a *prester-marshall*, what can I do? What other weapon do we have?" Suddenly, Anjine drew a quick breath. *The kirk!* "Wait—Prester-Marshall Rudio had the right idea, but the wrong method. Marshall Vorannen, come with me. There isn't much time!"

After only a flicker of hesitation, Vorannen nodded. "As you command, Majesty." Following her orders, he seized one of the city guard's skittish horses by the reins for himself and another for Anjine, holding the mount still so the queen could climb into the saddle.

Together, they galloped along the cobblestoned streets toward the stone structure that dominated Calay. Not knowing where else to turn, people had flocked to the protection of the kirk, where they begged the gathered presters to pray for them. Two old women clung to the cast bronze fishhook that stood at the entrance, refusing to be pried loose even though other terrified people wanted to take their places.

Queen Anjine knew that the fishhook could not protect Calay, though. Aiden had given them another weapon to use against such monsters, if only Prester-Marshall Rudio had thought to use it.

Outside the main entrance of the kirk, she and Vorannen slid off their horses and tossed the reins to bystanders. "Hold our mounts ready!" The guard-marshall threw the wooden doors wide.

In the nave, townspeople pressed together, swaying and trying to hear the words of three presters who stood at the main altar, reading from the Book of Aiden with a loud desperation that made their voices crack. Many of the faithful had come here seeking shelter during and after the hurricane, and now many more gathered because of the monsters attacking the harbor.

"Make way for the queen!" Vorannen pushed through the press of the crowd, forcing a passage for Anjine. "Make way!" She followed close behind him down the wide aisle to the main altar. The presters looked at the queen with surprise and relief, as if she had come to save them.

She was not here for the presters, though. The moment she spotted the long, curved object sitting in its cradle, she *knew* she was right. In addition to being etched with hundreds of spiraling key verses, quotes from the Book of Aiden, the milky ivory drew its magic from another source—if the tales were true. She flashed a hard smile at Vorannen. "There comes a time when we must choose to believe the legends. The power of Raathgir's horn must be more than a story."

The guard-marshall's expression brightened. "My wife has told me stories of Raathgir from her beloved Iboria. If there is strength left in this horn, my Queen, we will use it."

Together they ran up to the altar, scattering the astounded presters. Mounting the dais, Anjine and her guard-marshall rushed to the weighty ice-dragon horn.

When she touched the relic, Anjine thought she felt a spark pass through the palm of her hand and travel into her body to warm her heart. "As your queen, I take this relic to defend our land." She and Vorannen lifted it, and everyone muttered with awe. "With Ondun's blessing, it will be restored to you."

Vorannen bore most of the horn's weight at the larger base while Anjine held the narrow end steady. The crowd parted, clearing the aisle, as the two carried the long horn swiftly the length of the nave and out of the kirk to where their mounts waited. Vorannen slung the curved relic over his horse's withers and lashed it in place with a loose leather thong from the saddle, as the queen swung onto her horse without waiting for assistance. As people streamed out of the kirk behind them, the two horses raced downhill toward the harbor, hooves clattering over the wet cobblestone streets. Ahead, at the docks, they could still hear the roars of frustrated sea serpents.

When they could see the full harbor, Anjine pointed to one of the largest ships still tied up to the end of a long pier. With both of its masts shattered, the vessel would not sail anytime soon, but the deck looked firm. And because of the long pier, the ship was close enough to the prowling serpents.

"Out there to the bow of the ship. We will extend Raathgir's horn—and pray. If this relic doesn't have the power we need, then Calay is lost."

The ice dragon's horn wasn't a weapon like a catapult or a battering ram, and Anjine had never seen it in use. She'd only heard stories . . . and there were many stories in the world. Destrar Broeck had believed in the horn's power.

Anjine had to hope that he was right, but she didn't *know*. If the magic was just a myth, the monsters would devour her as easily as they had killed Prester-Marshall Rudio.

Leaving the horses loose, the two ran the length of the pier, carrying the horn together, until they reached the merchant ship. There, Vorannen tried to take the heavy talisman from her. "You do not need to risk your own life, my Queen. I can do this myself."

But she gripped the horn, refusing to let go. "This is *my* city. I must protect it." She knew that King Korastine would have done exactly the same thing.

The black-and-gold serpents hooted to each other and swam closer. The ice dragon's horn begin to shimmer with cold internal fire as Anjine and the guard-marshall carried it to the bow of the damaged merchant ship. Reassured as to the relic's true power, Anjine extended the horn's tip as far as possible, resting it on the wooden prow.

"Monsters, by the power of Aiden contained in this horn, I command you to return to the sea!" The eerie blue glow from the sleek horn bathed Anjine's face, hair, and body.

The serpents recoiled from the bow of the ship, as if they had encountered a great wall of heat. A loud hissing sound curled from their blowholes, and Anjine drew upon her determination, her heart, her need to protect her people. Power surged through her hands into the horn, which flared with a blinding blue-white light.

The six sea creatures, at first curious and fascinated, now backed away in fear.

"The horn will drive them away ... but the serpents don't know where to go." Holding the slick horn, she turned to Vorannen. "We need to herd them back out to the sea, chase them from Calay harbor."

"How do we do that, Majesty?"

"By taking a boat and driving them before us—force them to leave!"

"In a boat?" Vorannen looked around, saw small rowboats and fishing craft drawn up to shore or tied to damaged docks. They all looked incredibly fragile. "I can't let you be so vulnerable, Majesty. Let me get other guards. With enough men in patrol boats next to you, they can use spears and torches to fight off any attack."

But she had already seen the power cast by Raathgir's horn, and she did not know how long it might last. "The ice dragon will protect me in a way that your guards cannot." She took a deep breath. "I am the queen. I wear the crown—it must be me. My order stands."

Vorannen remained stony, then gave a curt bow. "As you command, Majesty." As the sea serpents retreated to the center of the harbor, circling uneasily after being thwarted by the magical horn, Anjine and the guard-marshall left the damaged cargo ship, Vorannen shouted to his guards. "Prepare a rowboat for the queen! We will drive the serpents from the harbor. *Move*, men!"

Three city guardsmen scrambled to right one of the overturned craft that had been tied up in front of a boathouse. With confident balance, Anjine climbed into the front and rested Raathgir's horn at the bow. As she stroked its scripture-etched surface, she summoned more phosphorescence and power, though she didn't know how. While the stoic guard-marshall took the oars and pulled them out to deeper water where the serpents waited, one of the anxious soldiers called from the shore, "May the Compass guide you, Majesty."

She continued to stare forward, holding the horn. "Aiden—and Destrar Broeck—have given me the only weapon I need."

As Vorannen rowed tirelessly, as fast as he could out into the storm-churned waters, Anjine sat rocking in the small boat. She remembered a day from her childhood when she and Mateo had stolen a rowboat to go all around Calay harbor on a romp. But this was no lighthearted adventure. Anjine leaned forward, grasping the horn with her sweat-slick palms. She was the queen of all Tierra, and she had an object of great power. She was not afraid.

As the fragile boat came closer, the black-and-gold serpents backed away, uneasy. Reptilian eyes glared at her like cracked gems washed up from the seabed. Their mouths opened, showing long fangs; one held a few tatters of cloth from the prester-marshall's robe. They retreated as Raathgir's horn continued to emit its silvery-blue shimmer.

Anjine dredged deep inside herself, calling up her beliefs and mental strength, as if by sheer force of will she could add fuel to the ice dragon's innate power. Vorannen kept rowing.

Pushed back, the angry serpents let out a chorus of roars, but the talisman and the queen continued to herd them toward the mouth of the harbor. "Begone! Back to the sea!"

Though the serpents tried to resist this unknown force, Anjine knew that they did not want to be enclosed within the harbor. They needed to be guided—or pushed—out.

As the strange procession reached the headlands, one of

the serpents noticed the opening, sensed the currents to the Oceansea. It turned to face the empty water and hooted.

Anjine yelled, "Back to the sea, where you belong!"

The monster needed no other encouragement. With an undulating ripple its sawblade dorsal fins scythed the surface one last time before it sank out of view. Following it, the five other serpents turned, similarly anxious to be away from the repulsion of the ice-dragon horn. With a splash, they curled their sinuous bodies underwater and streaked toward the open sea.

Vorannen heaved a sigh of amazement. Anjine let the ice dragon's horn slide back into the boat, and she felt dizzy. As the serpents retreated, the pale blue glow faded from the talisman, and the miraculous power rushed out of her, leaving her empty. She collapsed in utter exhaustion.

121 *Gremurr Mines*

The Gremurr mines had fallen, the battle won by the grace of Aiden. The mammoths continued their wholesale rampage through the camp's remaining structures, but the enemy had already been defeated.

Without sympathy, Broeck bellowed for his soldiers to round up the Uraban survivors who had surrendered before the shaggy beasts. "Put them all in chains. Who better to work in these dirty mines?"

"This time, they'll be making swords and armor for the *Tierran* army, in order to shed Uraban blood." Jenirod was exultant now. "Aiden has smiled upon us this day. Queen

Anjine will be proud of what we have done, Mateo. Truly proud, this time."

"She'll also be glad that we rescued so many kidnapped Tierrans, these poor prisoners of war." Tomas would never come home, but Mateo hoped that bringing these freed people back to their families would ease her bone-deep pain and grief.

Even though the Urabans had all surrendered, the Iborian destrar was not yet satisfied. Broeck rode his bull mammoth back and forth, looking for something else to trample, but finally slid down from the beast's back. He stepped in front of Mateo and glanced at the rocky cliffs and stony beach of Gremurr's natural harbor. "Very little food here for the mammoths. Iaros will have to lead them back up over the mountain passes. He knows how to handle the beasts by now."

"You're staying here, then?" Mateo asked.

"Did you see those armored warships in the harbor?" Broeck turned to regard the open waters of the Middlesea. "The fight's not over yet. The Curlies will try to take this place back once they know we've captured it. We should interrogate the guard captains, then put them to the sword."

"We'll need men to work the mines. Haven't we slain enough?"

"Those who fell today died honorably in battle, but others should face execution for their crimes. Remember what they did to Tomas!"

Yes, Mateo remembered . . . but how many more executions would it take to fill that empty well of vengeance? "You are in command, Destrar . . . but I urge you to execute only the worst ones."

The big Iborian let out a humorless laugh. "That's like asking me to choose the darkest shade of black. We'll learn what we can from them, and I'll decide which ones need to die."

The freed Aidenist slaves had extinguished the fires and worked to salvage supplies from the damaged tents. There would be a great feast, where the rescued Tierrans could eat as much as they wanted; the Uraban captives, on the other hand, could go without food.

Mateo established a main command tent using canvas from some of the intact barracks. Tearing down any sign of the unfurling fern, soldiers proudly mounted fishhook banners on either side of the opening flap.

For hours, Mateo sat with Destrar Broeck and Jenirod at a field table inside the command tent, discussing how to consolidate the mines. Interrupting them, guards ushered in a Uraban prisoner. He was a stocky middle-aged man with soft skin and a proud bearing that almost managed to mask his apprehension.

"We felt you should speak to this person, sirs. His name is Tukar, the administrator of Gremurr. Apparently, he is also the brother of Soldan-Shah Omra." The guard was accompanied by a scarecrow-thin former prisoner, who would act as interpreter. Among the freed slaves, they had found many grateful men who could speak fluent Uraban after all their years here.

Broeck rocked back in his field chair, bushy eyebrows lifted with great interest. "Well . . . a fine hostage."

Mateo rested his forearms on the table. "Tukar . . . sir." He didn't know how to address the Uraban, who was obviously a man of some importance—a defeated man.

"Gremurr is an illegal settlement, above the Edict Line. You know you're operating in Tierran territory?"

A translator repeated the words. Tukar nodded, then replied. "I deny nothing. I am proud to have served the soldan-shah and the will of Urec."

"He'll be a good bargaining chip," Mateo said, leaning toward Broeck. "As a hostage, he could help protect the mines against a retaliatory attack."

Waving Mateo aside, the Iborian destrar rose to his feet, his face red with building anger. His decision was already made. He fixed his gaze on Tukar's face but spoke to the translator. "Tell him this and say the words carefully: You Urabans made my grandson, Prince Tomas, pay the price for what others did. As the brother of the soldan-shah, you will understand that *you* must be held accountable for crimes committed by the followers of Urec." He paused, and his voice came out trembling, raspy. "Soldan-Shah Omra needs to feel the pain that his people inflicted upon all of us— upon me."

When the translator finished, Tukar's face turned gray, and he swallowed hard.

Down in the harbor, the Tierran army had seized the seven nearly completed ironclad warships. Studying them, Mateo could only imagine how much destruction those vessels could bring to unprotected Tierran coastal towns. By capturing the Gremurr mines, the Aidenist army had also confiscated the most powerful navy in the Middlesea. Since no Aidenist warship had ever sailed these waters, he doubted that the Uraban cities had any defenses from the sea. Mateo and his men could attack whenever and wherever they pleased.

"It still makes no sense," Jenirod mused. "Why would they build warships *here*? How does the soldan-shah intend to get them to the Oceansea? Or is there some other enemy he's worried about?"

"We're the only ones the Curlies need to fear," Broeck said, a deep growl in his throat.

"Maybe he meant to have Tierran slaves carry them on their backs across the isthmus and toss them into the Oceansea." Mateo's sour comment drew a laugh from both men.

Later, they learned from the Tierran captives, and confirmed the information through harsh interrogation of Urecari prisoners, about Soldan-Shah Omra's astounding scheme to dig a canal across the strip of land below Ishalem. A route for ships to sail from the Middlesea to the Oceansea. The idea seemed both ridiculous and impossible.

Mateo didn't doubt it for an instant.

Several ore barges had also tied up to the docks, and Mateo guessed that other ships would soon arrive at Gremurr. The Urabans would learn about the loss of the mines soon enough, and Destrar Broeck intended to deliver the news in his own particular manner—a personal message aimed directly at the soldan-shah. Layer upon layer of revenge, however, had not satisfied the Iborian leader.

A terrified Uraban sea captain had been found hiding in the hold of a dirty ore barge, and Mateo decided to use the man as his messenger. The fearful captain spoke no Tierran, but he groveled and apologized, insisting, through a translator, that he was just a sailor with no involvement in politics and no interest in other religions. The barge captain and a skeleton crew shuffled aboard, looking haunted and beaten; the rest of the sailors would remain in the slave camp and be put to work in the mines.

Broeck faced the captain and spoke in a rush so that the translator could barely keep up. "You, man. Sail to Olabar and tell the soldan-shah that the Gremurr mines belong to *us*. Say that Queen Anjine will no longer tolerate this intrusion on Tierran soil."

Broeck called his own soldiers forward, and one of them carried the sack with its grisly burden. Standing on the dock, Mateo squinted into the bright sunshine that glared off the water and steeled himself. "I'll do it."

"No." There was no flexibility in Broeck's tone. "Tomas was my grandson." He took the object from the soldier and marched to the prow of the ore barge, where he thrust Tukar's head onto a spike they had mounted there.

The poor man had not struggled, had not wailed; he had died bravely. Now Tukar's lifeless eyes stared across the water, and before long they would gaze upon Olabar again.

The captain and his barge crew couldn't sail away from Gremurr swiftly enough. Mateo watched the dirty ship sail south across the Middlesea.

"We need to make war plans," Jenirod said. "After we finish armoring those seven ships, we can raid the coast of the Middlesea. If we capture Sioara and establish our own outpost there, the Tierran army will have an easier way to cross into Uraba."

"I'd prefer that we strike Olabar directly," Broeck said.

"We have plenty of options," Mateo said. "When we strike, we won't do it merely to inflict pain or exact vengeance, but to win this war. Victory is ours."

The men walked back to the command tent. After all the destruction, death, and conquest here at Gremurr, Mateo didn't feel very triumphant, but he was coldly satisfied.

122 *Off the Coast of Ishalem*

It was nearly dusk by the time the fleet of Nunghal ships returned to Ishalem's western harbor. A victory light shone from the spire of what had once been Aiden's Lighthouse. Their cannon bombardment had utterly destroyed the Tierran attackers. By now, sea breezes had cleared most of the smoke on the water, but flames still burned from some of the wreckage and floating oil.

Two muscular Uraban men rowed Soldan-Shah Omra out to meet Shipkhan Ruad, where he asked to be taken aboard the large ship. "I would like to see what remains of those foolhardy warships. The 'Hooks came to Ishalem with hatred in their hearts, and received destruction in return." He drew a deep breath, smelling the lingering acrid firepowder from the Nunghal cannons. "Ondun is stern, but He is just."

Now that the reality had set in, Asaddan and Ruad were shaken by what they had seen and done. They had never witnessed, much less taken part in, such violence and bloodshed. When the sun was swallowed by the sea, the water turned orange, enhancing the angry fires that still fed on the shattered Tierran fleet. As dusk deepened to purple, Ruad guided his ship, taking the soldan-shah out to where the enemy vessels had sunk.

Omra stood at the bow, his face dark and grim. The catapults rigged to the foreign decks and the barrels of flammable oil made the Aidenist scheme all too plain. From the shore, the moment he'd seen them loose their first volleys of flaming oil-filled kegs, Omra had understood that the evil Aidenist captain meant to burn Ishalem again! And this after they had committed the barbaric atrocity of beheading a thousand innocent Urecari prisoners of war!

The rage felt like firepowder ready to explode within him; he no longer held any resentment toward Kel Unwar for what he had done to young Prince Tomas. These Aidenists were like mad dogs that needed to be struck down, and Omra could find no mercy in his heart. "Take me there. Let me gaze upon what remains of their ships and crews." His sense of justice demanded that he witness it with his own eyes.

Ruad's vessel approached the flickering flames that lingered on pools of spilled whale oil. All of the Aidenist attack ships had sunk, leaving only a widening archipelago of smoldering flotsam and jetsam that dispersed into the waves and currents.

Asaddan shook his shaggy head. "Listen, you can hear some of them screaming. Men are still alive and clinging to the wreckage."

Omra stared ahead, lost in his hatred. "I hear nothing. My ears were made deaf by the screams of the Uraban prisoners they murdered."

Asaddan looked unsettled, nauseated, but not from any seasickness. He stepped away from the soldan-shah, as if afraid of him.

As Ruad's ship picked its way forward, Nunghal

crewmen saw floating spars, tattered and charred sails, large splintered hull boards, and mangled bodies. Pale-skinned Aidenists drifted facedown, while several survivors clung to broken barrels or crates, or draped themselves over splintered yardarms. A few of the pathetic men waved and begged for rescue, but Omra glowered at them, unmoved.

Shipkhan Ruad closed his eyes and shook his head. "What destruction we have wrought. Nunghal cannons are to defend our ships from sea serpents. They have never been used for such things before."

"What you have wrought is God's vengeance," Omra said. "You saw what they intended to do to Ishalem. They received what they deserved. You have never seen actual war before, or its cost."

In the water, a man with a shaved head and squarish beard clung to a broken spar. Omra could see that one of his arms had been blown off, but the man still lived. He lifted his bloody stump and stared with glazed eyes up at the gray-sailed vessel. His tattered coat held the marks of a sea captain. Omra wondered if this had been the leader of the entire ruthless attack.

If so, he felt a steely thrill of pleasure to know that the enemy commander had lived long enough to see his utter defeat. Before he died out here, alone, the man would *understand* how Ondun Himself had turned against the Aidenists and their evil ways.

The Tierran captain lifted his head and stared blearily. From high up on the passing Nunghal ship, Omra gazed down upon him with no empathy.

"Soldan-Shah, shall we pick up the survivors?" Ruad asked in an anxious voice. "There are many men floating here. We should take them back, tend to their injuries—even if you keep them as prisoners."

By the light of the scattered fires in the deepening night, Omra saw triangular dorsal fins slicing through the water, circling the wreckage. The sharks had scented the blood of the dead and injured, and once full darkness fell they would have a generous and brutal feast.

Omra hardened his heart. "No. Turn the ship and sail back. I have seen enough."

Asaddan was aghast. "You mean just to abandon them? They're still human beings."

The comment earned him a glare from Omra. "I dispute your claim that they are human. If your ships had not stopped them, all of Ishalem would be ablaze right now. We will leave these men to the fates they chose for themselves."

Shipkhan Ruad gave the order, and the Nunghal ship sailed away from the fading fires. Behind them, they heard the sudden splashing of sharks, and the screams of hopeless men.

"That is the price they must pay."

123   *Olabar, Main Urecari Church*

Since the sikaras already hated her, Lady Istar could not issue the arrest order herself—there would be far too much of an uproar already—but the former soldan-shah had no such qualms. Imir took several of the highest-ranking priest-esses into custody, where they could be interrogated about Villiki's schemes.

In the palace, Kel Rovic guarded Naori and the soldan-shah's two heirs, watching over them night and day. Because he was worried that sikara agents would try some additional violence, every morsel of food was checked for poison; the "volunteer" tasters were drawn from the most belligerent sikaras in the prisons.

The suicide of Ur-Sikara Erima had sent the priestesses into a panic. Those who had attained the highest positions of power were now suspects, which left the church with no effective leadership. Any sikara who spoke out against Imir's reactionary decrees found herself immediately seized.

With all three of her daughters safely at her side, Istar made her way through the main church's secret corridors and chambers in search of clues that Villiki might have left behind. Riders were dispatched to Ishalem with urgent messages informing Soldan-Shah Omra about what had happened. But before her husband returned home, Istar wanted to understand the depths of Villiki's plans.

Cithara led her mother to the hidden chamber where the woman had lived. Without hesitation, Istar broke into Villiki's private trunk, ransacked her wardrobe and drawers, searched her possessions. Following them, young Istala gazed about herself with superstitious fear. All of her dreams and her faith in the church had crumbled around her—Fashia's Fountain desecrated, the ur-sikara dead, the church caught harboring a murderous traitor.

Lady Istar felt sorry for what her youngest daughter had lost.

From beneath Villiki's writing table, Cithara reverently withdrew a bound book whose interior pages had all been torn in half. "Mother Istar, I saw Villiki write in this very special book. It is connected somehow with the *Al-Orizin*."

Recognizing the sympathetic journal from which the ur-sikara occasionally read during church services, Istar sat down by the light of perfumed candles. Here, at last, were the true messages Saan's ship had sent back. She pored over the handwritten entries, scheming notes that Villiki had exchanged with Sikara Fyiri. These words were nothing at all like what she had heard Erima read aloud to the congregation. Some paragraphs described daily activities aboard the *Al-Orizin*; others were ruthless discussions of what Villiki planned to do here in Olabar. Istar read each line with great fascination. Even these distorted descriptions gave her a view into what Saan was doing on his long voyage.

Most thrilling of all, though, was the final entry, written in a different hand from Fyiri's. "This is Sen Sherufa na-Oa, chartsman of the *Al-Orizin*. Captain Saan has now acquired possession of this logbook, and henceforth all messages transmitted to Olabar will be accurate—unlike those of Sikara Fyiri." The Saedran woman went on to describe at great length their encounter with the island, the witch Iyomelka, and her claims of being the wife of Ondun and the mother of a mysterious young girl.

Istar smiled, suddenly understanding the reason why Ur-Sikara Erima had stopped reporting messages from the ship. Apparently, Villiki had never bothered to write back once she knew the logbook had been taken from her pawn Fyiri.

Istar smiled at her daughters. "Saan needs to know what has happened here, and we can trust Sen Sherufa to report precisely what we write. We can be in contact with your brother again—real contact." She tapped the torn pages of the journal, pondering possibilities. "Because the two journals are linked, if *I* write a message here, will the words appear for Sherufa to see—and Saan? Or must a sikara do the writing?"

"I'm not certain, Mother, but you could try," Istala said. "What happens to this volume, happens to its counterpart."

Though she was perfectly capable of writing for herself, she slid the book over to her youngest daughter. "Show us what you learned from the priestesses, my dear one. We'll write your brother a letter and explain all that has occurred. He'll know that we are now in secure contact with each other."

In spite of her ordeal, Istar drew a deep breath and felt a joy inside her. Just by touching these pages, she could touch Saan. She now knew her son was still alive, still healthy, still exploring. "And don't forget to tell him that we love him."

124 *The* Al-Orizin

With cool spray blowing in their faces and hair whipping behind them, Saan slipped his arm around Ystya's waist and held her close. Neither he nor the young woman regretted what they had done. The *Al-Orizin* cut through the water, her sails full, continuing into the wide unknown.

Away from the strange island that had been her prison for most of her life, Ystya continued to marvel at everything she saw: the spray dancing from the bow of the ship, the far gray horizon, the fish that leaped from the waves. He found her innocent joy refreshing and hypnotic. "So much ocean! What lies beyond there?" She pointed off toward the eastern horizon. "And there?"

"Unexplored lands. You and I will see them together, for the first time."

Since escaping from the isolated island, the young woman had remained fearful of Iyomelka, but Saan comforted her. "Your mother is far away, and we're safe from her." To pass the time as they gained more and more distance, he told her stories of brave Uraban voyages—some of them true and some completely fictitious.

Sen Sherufa also took the young woman under her wing, teaching her things she needed to know. Ystya was eager to learn about Uraba, about history, about the places on Sherufa's Saedran charts. Sikara Fyiri insisted on teaching Ystya about Urec's Log, but the girl just laughed, which the priestess found maddening.

Staying on deck for most of the day, Ystya continued to glance behind them from time to time, but she saw only a line of scattered clouds far on the horizon. "My mother will be very angry, you know." She looked at Saan. "She will try to capture us."

He gave a loud and confident laugh. "Oh, Iyomelka can rant all she wants, but what can she do? She has no ship, and we have been sailing for many days. Besides, now she has the island all to herself—maybe that's what she wanted."

"No, that is not what my mother wants."

Each night, Sen Sherufa attempted to read the star patterns overhead, but though the chartsman diligently recorded all the new information, she could not reconcile the constellations in the sky with the star patterns she had been taught.

Far behind the *Al-Orizin*, day after day, the line of storms continued to dog the ship, slowly gaining ground. Grigovar muttered that it might be something the old witch had called up after all, but Saan refused to consider the possibility.

For his own part, Yal Dolicar didn't seem concerned. "It was well worth stopping at the island, Captain. We got a hold full of treasure, and you got yours!"

Sherufa bustled out onto the deck in the afternoon, as clouds thickened overhead. She held the sympathetic journal in her hand. "There's a new inscription from Olabar!"

Saan grimaced, already soured by the idea. "And what poison does Villiki spread now? I'm surprised she bothered to write back. Did she take our warning to heart?"

The Saedran woman opened the book and pointed to the last half page on which words were written. "Villiki is gone! Read this." The script was different, carefully formed, the letters almost childlike.

Saan did not bother to hide his surprise. "It's from my mother—and Istala wrote it." He drank in the report of Villiki's treachery, the death of the ur-sikara, and the overthrow of the corrupt elements in the church. Saan called out, "Grigovar—go fetch Sikara Fyiri. This is news she needs to hear."

When the priestess emerged from her cabin, looking annoyed, Saan let her read the entry for herself; when she was finished, Fyiri pushed the book away. "I don't believe any of this. It must be a trick, some kind of lie. Anyone can write falsehoods."

Saan goaded her. "Ah, as you did? I trust my mother's report more than anything Villiki wrote."

Fyiri remained unrepentant. "If this is true, then a great crime has been committed against the church of Urec. The former soldan-shah and the corrupt First Wife will pay for this."

Saan chuckled at the empty threat and pulled Ystya close to him again. "This is a very good day."

The man in the lookout nest whistled and extended his hand toward the horizon. "Captain, something dead ahead—like a long black line, or a wall!" Saan shaded his eyes and gazed toward the horizon.

"Is it the edge of the world?" Ystya asked. "Are we about to sail off?"

Saan responded with a laugh that he hoped sounded reassuring. "That's just a silly story used to frighten children and superstitious sailors. It's probably the coast of Terravitae." The dark barrier extended as far as he could see. He took out his spyglass and peered through the lens. The strange black obstruction looked like a low *barrier* across the horizon, lying dead ahead of them.

And it was moving.

"It seems to have . . . *scales*," Saan said. "Giant scales."

Ystya took the spyglass from him and stared through it, using her keen eyesight. She had been fascinated by the spyglass and its magnifying lenses. Now she stiffened, and her skin went pale. Her hands trembled as she handed him back the glass. "It's Bouras—the Father of all Sea Serpents."

Fyiri insistently held out her hand, and after Saan let her use the instrument, her voice held genuine fear. "I think the girl is right—it's the snake that encircles the world from horizon to horizon." For the first time, the sikara appeared to be terrified.

Saan held up the spyglass once more, and saw that the image *did* appear to be the body of an inconceivably huge serpent. Its great scales blurred as it moved along, endlessly circling. This was a far larger creature than any other ocean beast he had ever encountered.

The lookout called again, "Captain! The storms are closing in behind us—and I don't think that wall of clouds is natural."

Saan turned the spyglass in the opposite direction to look at the localized knot of storms that defied the prevailing winds, cut across the currents, and headed straight toward the *Al-Orizin*. He adjusted the lens, scanned slowly across the froth of churned water, the sheets of rain. He saw a corona of lightning. Rapidly striking bolts danced across the water in a spectral illumination.

At the center of the storm rode a tattered dark ship that glided through the furious whitecaps like a sharp knife. The sails of the wreck were torn, her hull rotted, masts and yardarms splintered.

And at the prow stood a woman who seemed to be driving the fury of the ocean, riding the storms, creating the power with her anger. *Iyomelka*.

Feeling his chest grow cold, Saan held Ystya more tightly. He made up his mind.

If they had indeed found the enormous serpent girdling the world, he could not imagine how the *Al-Orizin* would ever get past it, but he would not go back to the wrath of Iyomelka.

"Hold your course," he shouted. "Continue straight ahead."

125 *The* Dyscovera

The Tierran sailors hauled up buckets of seawater to pour onto the deck so they could scrub away the bloodstains. His face stormy with anger, Criston Vora oversaw the efforts of the crew. Those men duped into following Prester Hannes did the worst jobs, guarded by the sailors who had remained loyal. The mutinous men appeared cowed, but several of them remained defiant and certain that Aiden's instructions to convert the mer-people had been clear.

They were all guilty, and they knew it. But if he executed every one of the mutineers by throwing them into the open sea, the *Dyscovera* would be little more than a ghost ship.

A shaken Sen Aldo had withdrawn to his cabin for a day, miserable over what had happened. He had been thrilled to rediscover his original people, but now he felt only failure. He had actually seen that the mer-Saedrans had a map to Terravitae . . . and now he had lost it.

Finally the distraught chartsman emerged to stand next to the captain. "I've tried to be tolerant, sir, even when Prester Hannes issued his inflammatory sermons. But those Saedrans were my lost brothers and sisters. His unreasoning hatred made me lose the greatest hope of my people! He had no right! How will they ever forgive us now?"

Criston shook his head. "Hannes may have triggered another war here. And Kjelnar . . . " He gave his head an angry shake. "We lost a good man, a brave sailor, and a friend. I considered him indispensible, but the *Dyscovera* will have to continue without him." Anger and grief warred in his voice. "I don't know how Aiden can pardon us for the foolish offense we committed in his name."

In all, they had lost six crewmen, only two of whom had been among the mutineers; ten more men were being held for defying the captain's authority. He had thought the cruel justice he had shown Enoch Dey would stifle any questioning of his authority. Prester Hannes had been the loudest voice calling for the would-be rapist's execution.

Yet Hannes had instigated this latest crime. Criston could not forgive himself for not recognizing the lengths to which the man's zeal would drive him. He had thought their shared tragedies, and recovery, would bind them together. Criston had believed he *understood* the man, but Hannes had turned on him.

Confined in his cabin and given only limited rations of ship's biscuit and water, the prester seemed ironically offended that Captain Criston Vora had turned against *him* and Aiden.

Criston knew that if he executed the man who represented their faith—not to mention their holy mission to discover the land of Terravitae—the whole crew would mutiny. And if the *Dyscovera* ever did reach their destination, how could he explain to Holy Joron that he had cast out the one man who spoke on behalf of Aiden?

Sen Aldo followed him as he walked toward the mounted compasses at the captain's wheel. During the fray with the mer-Saedrans, one of their three instruments had been irreparably smashed—the Captain's Compass, which pointed the way home to its twinned compass needle in Calay. The compass had been maliciously pummeled and destroyed, though no one had witnessed anything during the fight with the mer-Saedrans.

Criston could not shake the suspicion that someone had done it intentionally. But why? To prevent the ship from ever getting back home? It made no sense.

Nervous, the chartsman cleared his throat and held up small strips of paper on which he had printed dense coded characters. "Sir, we should send one of the *rea* pigeons to inform Sen Leo of what we found ... and what we lost. I have to be honest with him, though he will be devastated."

Criston felt the weight pressing on his shoulders. "Go ahead, Sen Aldo. They need to know. How many pigeons do we have left now, seven?"

"Yes, seven more chances to send a letter home. We are fortunate none of the birds were harmed in the recent fighting."

"Seven will be enough." Criston nodded absently, and Aldo went off in troubled silence.

A few moments later, having tied the letter securely to its leg, the chartsman brought his pigeon forward. They watched Aldo whisper something to the bird, then fling it into the air. With a steady beat of its wings, the pigeon circled upward and began winging its way into the distance.

Javian and Mia joined Criston at the compass station. "How far do you think we have to go to find Terravitae, Captain?" the young man asked.

Criston looked at the cabin boy, who stared at the

smashed compass, knowing they could not now find their way home. Javian had been partly caught up in Prester Hannes's uprising, but Criston wanted to believe that the boy had seen the truth and changed his mind. Or was he just weak-willed?

"We go as far as we need to go. The *Dyscovera* will not turn back until we have looked into the eyes of Holy Joron."

With a gasp, Mia pointed at the ancient relic of Aiden's Compass. "Look, Captain! I saw it move."

Beneath the polished crystal plate, the golden needle twitched. The needle hovered to and fro ... then reoriented, straightened, and pointed along a strong, true course. Toward Terravitae.

Glossary

ABILAN one of the soldanates of Uraba.

ADREA wife of Criston Vora, captured by Urecari raiders; now named Istar.

ADREALA first daughter of Adrea by Omra.

AIDEN one of the two brothers who sailed from Terravitae to discover the world. The descendants of his crew populated Tierra.

AIDEN'S COMPASS ancient relic whose needle will point back toward Terravitae.

AIDEN'S LIGHTHOUSE a tall lighthouse on the western side of Ishalem.

AIDENIST follower of the Book of Aiden.

AINI First Wife of Soldan Xivir from Missinia.

AL-ORIZIN Uraban exploration ship.

ALAMONT one of the five reaches of Tierra, rich agricultural land led by Destrar Shenro.

ALDO NA-CURIC, SEN Saedran chartsman aboard the *Dyscovera*.

ALISI sister of Unwar, kidnapped by Tierran traders.

AMMUR SONNEN blacksmith who runs the largest smithy in Calay, father of Vicka.

ANCHOR constellation in the Tierran sky.

ANDOUK soldan of Yuarej, father of Cliaparia.

ANJINE daughter of King Korastine.

ARDAN subcomdar of the Tierran navy.

ARIKARA capital city of Missinia.

ARKSHIP ancient vessel wrecked in Ishalem, believed to be the original vessel belonging either to Aiden or Urec.

ASADDAN Nunghal refugee who crossed the Great Desert to Missinia.

ASHA second wife of Soldan-Shah Imir, murdered by Prester Hannes.

ATTAR soldan of Outer Wahilir, brother of Soldan Huttan, poisoned by Prester Hannes.

BAINE former prester-marshall of the Aidenist church, martyred with his followers in the ruins of Ishalem.

BELOS, SEN revered Saedran elder.

BIENTO NA-CURIC Saedran painter, Aldo's father.

BOOK OF AIDEN Aidenist holy book.

BORA'S BASTION capital city of Alamont Reach.

BOURAS legendary father of all sea serpents, supposedly girdles the world.

BROECK destrar of Iboria Reach, father of Ilrida, grand-father of Tomas.

BURIAN NA-COWAY Saedran model-maker.

BURILO son of Soldan Xivir from Missinia, Omra's cousin.

BURNET master carpenter in Soeland Reach.

CALAVIK capital city of Iboria Reach.

CALAY capital city of Tierra.

CAPTAIN'S COMPASS a compass that always points home.

CHARTSMAN a Saedran navigator possessing perfect memory.

CHERR, SEN revered Saedran elder.

CIARLO brother of Adrea, lame in one leg, prester of the town of Windcatch.

CINDON Criston Vora's small boat, named after his father, sold before his voyage on the *Luminara*.

CINDON VORA father of Criston, a fisherman lost at sea.

CITHARA daughter of Cliaparia and Omra, now raised by Istar.

CLIAPARIA Omra's second wife, killed by Istar.

COMDAR leader of Tierran army and navy.

CORAG one of the five reaches of Tierra, a mountainous region led by Destrar Siescu.

CRISTON (2) infant son of Omra and Istar, murdered by Cliaparia.

CRISTON VORA captain of the *Dyscovera*, survivor of the *Luminara* expedition. Criston is married to Adrea (Istar), who was lost in a Urecari raid.

CUAR Uraban unit of currency.

DAVIC apprentice and helper to Prester Ciarlo.

DAWSON ORIN young recruit in Tierran army.

DELNAS, COMDAR leader of the Tierran military, both land and sea forces.

DESERT HARBOR new settlement on the edge of the Great Desert, from which sand coracles launch.

DESTRAR the leader of one of the five Tierran reaches.

DILORA, PRESTER young prester in Calay.

DOLICAR, YAL confidence man who moves back and forth from Uraba to Tierra.

DYSCOVERA Tierran ship built to explore the seas and find Terravitae, captained by Criston Vora.

EDICT LINE the boundary agreed to by the leaders of Tierra and Uraba, dividing the world in half.

ENIFIR Anjine's handmaiden, wife of Guard-Marshall Vorannen.

ENOCH DEY crewman aboard the *Dyscovera*.

EREO BORNAN father of Mateo, a captain in the royal guard who died saving the king.

ERIETTA one of the five reaches of Tierra, mainly rangeland, led by Destrar Unsul.

ERIMA ur-sikara from Lahjar, successor to Lukai.

EYE OF UREC symbol painted on the sails of Uraban ships.

FAAN protocol minister of Uraba.

FARPORT capital city of Soeland Reach.

FASHIA the wife of Urec.

FASHIA'S FOUNTAIN important shrine to Urecari faith.

FENNAN prester in the village of Windcatch, killed in Urecari raid.

FILLOK brother of the soldan of Outer Wahilir, killed in an ill-advised raid against a Tierran trading ship.

FIRUN old Aidenist slave at Gremurr mines, household servant to Tukar.

FURIC, SEN revered Saedran elder.

FYIRI prominent sikara in the church of Urec.

GAHARI Uraban merchant family.

GART young son of Destrar Unsul.

GOLDEN FERN fern with mythic properties, supposedly planted by Urec before he became the Traveler. Anyone who finds the fern is destined for greatness.

GOLDEN FERN First Uraban ironclad warship, armored at Gremurr mines.

GREAT DESERT arid wasteland in the south of Uraba.

GREMURR secret Uraban mines on the northern coast of the Middlesea, in Tierran territory.

GRIGOVAR member of the *Al-Orizin*'s crew, former reef diver from Lahjar.

HAKRI First Wife of Soldan Vishkar from Outer Wahilir.

HANNES prester who caused great damage to Uraba, was a slave at Gremurr mines, and escaped over the mountains to Tierra.

HIST subcomdar of the Tierran army.

HUREF soldan of Abilan.

HUTTAN soldan of Inner Wahilir, husband of Kuari.

IAROS nephew of Destrar Broeck, heir apparent of Iboria.

IBORIA one of the five reaches of Tierra, the region to the far north, led by Destrar Broeck.

ILNA NA-CURIC younger sister of Aldo.

ILRIDA daughter of Destrar Broeck, second wife of King Korastine, and mother of Prince Tomas; she died of tetanus.

IMIR former soldan-shah of the Urabans, father of Omra and Tukar, now retired.

INNER WAHILIR one of the soldanates of Uraba.

IREC Soldan-Shah Omra's second son, by his second wife Naori.

ISHALEM holy city considered the center of both the Aidenist and Urecari religions, burned in a great fire and now reclaimed by Uraba.

ISTALA second daughter of Adrea by Omra.

ISTAR (1) young wife of Zarif Omra, died in childbirth.

ISTAR (2) First Wife of Soldan-Shah Omra, mother of Saan, Adreala, and Istala; formerly Adrea, wife of Criston Vora.

IYOMELKA mysterious old crone living on an isolated island, mother of Ystya.

JAVIAN cabin boy aboard the *Dyscovera*.

JENIROD eldest son of Destrar Unsul of Erietta.

JERARD old prester aboard the *Luminara*, killed by a sea serpent.

JIKARIS khan of the Nunghal-Ari.

JILLAC military captain from Alamont, in charge of the prison camps.

JORON third son of Ondun, who remained behind in Terravitae when Aiden and Urec sailed away.

KEL rank of captain in the soldan-shah's palace guards.

KHALIG Uraban merchant, chosen by Kel Unwar as a messenger to Calay.

KHENARA port city on Oceansea coast of Uraba.

KILLIN NA-FAS Saedran apothecary.

KIRACLE Korastine's father, previous king of Tierra, killed by a lightning strike while out riding.

KIRK Aidenist church.

KJELNAR Iborian shipwright, builder of *Dyscovera* and her first mate.

KORASTINE the king of Tierra, father of Anjine and Tomas.

KUARI First Wife of Soldan Huttan from Inner Wahilir.

KURDA Soeland general in Tierran army.

LAHJAR port city on Oceansea coast of Uraba, the farthest settlement south.

LANDING DAY Aidenist festival commemorating the landing of Aiden's Arkship.

LANNI wife of Sen Aldo na-Curic, daughter of Sen Leo.

LEO NA-HADRA, SEN old Saedran scholar, adviser of King Korastine, teacher of Aldo na-Curic.

LEVIATHAN terrible sea monster that destroyed the *Luminara*.

LITHIO First Wife of Soldan-Shah Imir, mother of Omra, now estranged.

LUAREN sikara at Fashia's Fountain.

LUKAI former ur-sikara of the Urecari church, died after her involvement was exposed in a plot to poison Omra.

LUMINARA magnificent exploration vessel dispatched from Tierra to discover the world, destroyed by the Leviathan.

MATEO BORNAN childhood friend of Anjine, former ward of King Korastine raised in the castle after his father Ereo was killed in the line of duty. Now subcomdar in the Tierran army, liaison to the throne.

MIA sailor aboard the *Dyscovera*.

MIDDLESEA vast sea to the east of Ishalem.

MIOR sailor aboard the *Dyscovera*.

MISSINIA one of the soldanates of Uraba.

NAORI third wife of Soldan-Shah Omra.

NORGO new leader of desert bandits harassing Desert Harbor.

NUNGHALS race inhabiting the Uraban continent to the south of the Great Desert. They are composed of two branches, the nomadic Nunghal-Ari and the seafaring Nunghal-Su.

NUNGHAL-ARI nomadic branch of the Nunghals.

NUNGHAL-SU seafaring branch of the Nunghals.

OBERTAS marshall of the royal guard in Calay.

OCEANSEA vast sea to the west of Ishalem.

OENAR former soldan-shah of Uraba, great-grandfather of Imir, the subject of a large bronze statue that was melted down to make weapons.

OLABAR capital city of Uraba.

OLBA turbanlike head covering, usually white, worn by Urecari men.

OMIRR Soldan-Shah Omra's eldest son, by his second wife Naori; the zarif of Uraba.

ONDUN the creator of the world, father of three sons— Aiden, Urec, and Joron.

ONDUN'S LIGHTNING ship on which Aldo served as chartsman.

OUROUSSA port city on Oceansea coast of Uraba.

OUTER WAHILIR one of the soldanates of Uraba.

PELITON capital city of Erietta Reach.

PILGRIM'S PATH processional path up the hill to the Arkship in Ishalem.

PILGRIMS' ROAD main north–south road through Tierra to Ishalem.

POL young son of Destrar Unsul.

PRESTER an Aidenist priest.

PRESTER-MARSHALL leader of the Aidenist church.

QUANAS captain of the *Sacred Scroll*.

RAATHGIR Iborian ice dragon, whose horn is said to be a talisman to ward off sea serpents.

RAGA VAR mountain scout in Corag.

RAVEN small patrol ship on which Mateo served as first mate.

RA'VIR Tierran child raised by Urecari to become a spy and a saboteur, named after an opportunistic bird that lays its eggs in other birds' nests.

REEFSPUR Tierran coastal fishing village.

RENNY young son of Destrar Unsul.

RICKAR FENN young recruit in Tierran army.

RIEF, COMDAR TORIN—leader of Tierran army and navy.

ROVIK kel of the soldan-shah's palace guards.

RUAD Nunghal-Su shipkhan, once an outcast, now captain of his own ship again.

RUDIO old, conservative prester-marshall, successor to Baine.

SAAN son of Criston and Adrea, raised by Soldan-Shah Omra.

SACRED SCROLL Tierran trading ship where Alisi was held captive.

SAEDRANS "Ondun's Stepchildren," independent people not descended from either Aiden or Urec. Saedrans serve as chartsmen, engineers, doctors, apothecaries, and in other scientific professions.

SAMFAIR finance minister of Uraba.

SAND DERVISHES desert demons who lure travelers into the sand.

SAPIER grandson of Aiden, founder of Aidenist church. In a legend, he caught a sea serpent with a fishhook and rode it to safe waters.

SAZAR leader of a clan of rivermen; he calls himself the "river destrar."

SEN term of respect and accomplishment for Saedrans.

SENA first wife of King Korastine, mother of Anjine; died from pneumonia.

SHARIQUE wife of Yuarej soldan Andouk, mother of Cliaparia.

SHAY, CAPTAIN ANDON captain of the *Luminara*.

SHENRO destrar of Alamont Reach.

SHERUFA NA-OA, SEN Saedran scholar in Olabar.

SHIELTAR former soldan-shah, grandfather of Omra, who was njured by an arrow when he led an abortive raid into Tierra.

SHIPKHAN captain's title among the Nunghals.

SIESCU destrar of Corag Reach.

SIKARA priestess in the Urecari church.

SILAM HENNER crewman aboard the *Dyscovera*.

SIOARA a port on the Middlesea, capital of Inner Wahilir.

SOELAND one of the five reaches of Tierra, a group of islands led by Destrar Tavishel.

SOLDAN leader of one of the regions of Uraba.

SOLDAN-SHAH the soldan of soldans, leader of all Uraba.

SONHIR leader of the undersea people of the sunken Saedran continent.

STONEHOLM capital city of Corag Reach.

TAVISHEL destrar of Soeland Reach.

TEACHER mysterious hooded figure in charge of Omra's *ra'vir* program.

TELHA VORA mother of Criston, killed in Urecari raid on Windcatch.

TENÉR port city on Oceansea coast of Uraba.

TERRAVITAE the original land where Ondun created his people, from which Aiden and Urec departed on their voyage.

TESHA First Wife of Soldan Huref from Abilan.

TIERRA the northern continent, composed of five reaches; its population follows the Aidenist religion.

TIRA young woman in Calay, trained as a *ra'vir*.

TOLLI name used by Anjine as her alternate childhood identity.

TRAVELER wandering old man who leaves tales of his travels, rumored to be either Aiden or Urec.

TYCHO kitten given to Anjine by Mateo; also name used by Mateo as his alternate childhood identity.

UALFOR emissary from Soldan Huttan of Inner Wahilir.

UISHEL young woman from Soeland, Mateo's first love.

UNSUL destrar of Erietta Reach.

UNTRA former soldan-shah, grandfather of Imir.

UNWAR kel in the Uraban military, provisional governor of Ishalem, builder of the great wall.

URABA the southern continent, composed of five soldanates; its population follows the Urecari religion.

UREC one of the two brothers who sailed from Terravitae to discover the world. The descendants of his crew populated Uraba.

UREC'S LIGHTHOUSE a tall lighthouse on the eastern side of Ishalem.

UREC'S LOG Urecari holy book.

URECARI follower of Urec's Log.

UR-SIKARA lead sikara of the Urecari church.

USTHRA trade minister of Uraba.

VANOV, GENERAL military leader from Alamont.

VICKA SONNEN daughter of Calay blacksmith Ammur Sonnen.

VILLIKI third wife of Soldan-Shah Imir, mother of Tukar, disgraced and exiled for her part in the plot to poison Omra.

VORANNEN marshall of the Calay city guard, married to Enifir.

WEN NA-CURIC younger brother of Aldo.

WINDCATCH small Tierran fishing village on the Oceansea coast.

XARIES a Uraban board game similar to chess.

XIVIR soldan of Missinia, father of Burilo.

YSTYA beautiful young woman living on an isolated island, daughter of Iyomelka.

YUAREJ one of the soldanates of Uraba.

YURA NA-CURIC Aldo's mother.

ZADAR workmaster in the Gremurr mines.

ZARIF Uraban title of prince.

Author's Note

With the first Terra Incognita novel, *The Edge of the World*, we added an innovative dimension by developing a companion rock CD, with story and lyrics written by me and my wife, Rebecca Moesta. *Terra Incognita: Beyond the Horizon* was performed by the supergroup Roswell Six and released by ProgRock Records. The tracks featured music written by keyboardist/producer Erik Norlander (Rocket Scientists, Asia featuring John Payne) and performances by some of the legends of rock music: Michael Sadler (ex-Saga), James LaBrie (Dream Theater), John Payne (ex-Asia), Lana Lane, Gary Wehrkamp (Shadow Gallery, Amaran's Plight), David Ragsdale (Kansas), Chris Brown (Ghost Circus), Chris Quirarte (Prymary), Martin Orford (IQ, Jadis), Kurt Barabas (Amaran's Plight, Under the Sun), and Mike Alvarez. I wrote the connective story between the songs, and multiple award–winning artist Bob Eggleton supplied the paintings for the CD booklet.

Beyond the Horizon tells the story of young Criston Vora sailing off to sea and leaving his young wife Adrea behind; he places letters in bottles for her and throws them overboard, longing to come home—but Adrea is captured by Soldan-Shah Omra and taken off to a distant land forever.

Because the first CD was such a satisfying experience, listed among the Best Progressive Rock Albums on numerous sites, we decided to create a second CD for the next novel in the series, *The Map of All Things*. Again working with Shawn Gordon at ProgRock Records, Rebecca and I wrote the lyrics for the new CD, *Terra Incognita: A Line in the Sand*. This time, the companion album tells the story of Queen Anjine and Mateo and the ever-darkening, never-ceasing war against Soldan-Shah Omra.

> *Red was the flush of a young maiden's lips*
> *Now it's the color of blood.*
> *White was a blanket of pure mountain snow,*
> *Now it makes shrouds for our dead.*

A darker and grittier CD required a harder sound and a different mood from the songwriting and performances. To differentiate the two albums, we turned to Henning Pauly (Frameshift, Chain), whose music I have enjoyed for years. Henning— already a friend and a fan of my work—took on the project with great enthusiasm. He developed music that conveys the distinctive cultures and personalities of the two lands at war and the three main characters in the story. Rebecca and I crafted a set of lyrics focused on the war, targeting religious intolerance and the perpetual spiral of hatred.

> *You killed our fathers, so we kill your sons.*
> *How can you say you're the innocent ones?*

Because our guest performers have extremely busy careers of their own, and because *A Line in the Sand* tells a different part of the story with different characters, the second CD has some returning musicians and some new names. Grammy Award–winning rock, folk, and country star Janis Ian—whose song "At Seventeen" struck straight to my heart when I was in high school—cowrote the lyrics on two of the songs.

Among the new participants in *A Line in the Sand*, we are proud to have Steve Walsh from the group Kansas (whose powerful voice on songs such as "Carry On Wayward Son" and "Dust in the Wind" influenced a whole generation, including me)— as Soldan-Shah Omra. Sass Jordan (Album Rock's Female Vocalist of the Year) belts out the vocals for Queen Anjine.

Lee Gibbons created another fabulous iconic cover painting for both the book and the CD, and Bob Eggleton again provided interior art.

Smoke, like their souls, rises faint to the sky.

If you listen to the two CDs you'll see and hear a whole new dimension to the Terra Incognita universe. For samples and more information, go to www.wordfire.com.

A last note, the story of the map in *The Map of All Things*: Richard Ware is an aspiring writer who attended one of my writing workshops in Los Angeles. He is also a skilled tattoo artist by trade. He contacted me via Facebook after reading *The Edge of the World* and offered to draw the expanded map for the second novel, which is included here. Rich also graciously provided some excellent interior paintings for the *A Line in the Sand* CD booklet.

Thanks for joining me on these voyages to uncharted lands. I hope you enjoy the conclusion of the trilogy in *The Key to Creation.*

Acknowledgments

Words, artwork, and music—for the Terra Incognita series, I had to draw upon the talent, expertise, and excitement of many different people to fill in the gaps in *The Map of All Things*. Richard Ware volunteered to create a wonderful, expanded map of the Terra Incognita world. Lee Gibbons produced another magnificent cover that immediately conveys the feel of the novel.

The musical visionaries involved in the two *Terra Incognita* rock-opera CDs provided a constant flow of inspiration as they interpreted the story and lyrics: Henning Pauly, Shawn Gordon, Steve Walsh, Janis Ian, Sass Jordan, Michael Sadler, James LaBrie, John Payne, Kurt Barabas, C. S. Brown, Gary Wehrkamp, Chris Quirarte, Mike Alvarez, and Erik Norlander.

My typist Mary Thomson kept up with me, transcribing all 125 chapters as quickly as I sent her the audio files, and she also offered her expertise in many areas. My hardworking test readers went over drafts of this novel with sharp eyes and sharp pencils, adding their input, insights, and ideas to make this a stronger story—Deb Ray, Diane Jones, Louis Moesta, and of course my wife, Rebecca Moesta.

My editor Darren Nash and publisher Tim Holman have stood solidly behind this series, ably assisted by Jennifer Flax, Jack Womack, and Alex Lencicki. My agent John Silbersack at Trident Media Group continues to help ensure that the Terra Incognita series reaches the widest possible audience.

extras

www.orbitbooks.net

about the author

Kevin J. Anderson has written forty-six national and international bestsellers and has over twenty million books in print worldwide in thirty languages. He has been nominated for the Nebula Award, the Bram Stoker Award, and the SFX Readers' Choice Award. Find out more about Kevin Anderson at www.wordfire.com

Find out more about Kevin Anderson and other Orbit authors by registering for the free monthly newsletter at www.orbitbooks.net

if you enjoyed
THE MAP OF ALL THINGS

look out for

THE SUM OF ALL MEN

by

David Farland

1

IT BEGINS IN DARKNESS

Effigies of the Earth King festooned the city around Castle Sylvarresta. Everywhere the effigies could be seen – hanging beneath shopwindows, standing upright against the walls of the city gates, or nailed beside doorways – stationed any place where the Earth King might find ingress into a home.

Many of the figures were crude things crafted by children – a few reeds twisted into the form of a man, often with a crown of oak leaves in its hair. But outside the doors of shops and taverns were more ornate figures of wood, the full size of a man, often elaborately painted and coiffed in fine green wool traveling robes.

In those days, it was said that on Hostenfest Eve the spirit of the earth would fill the effigies and the Earth King would waken. At his wakening, he would protect the family for another season and help bear the harvest home.

It was a festive season, a season of joy. On Hostenfest Eve the father in a home would play the role of Earth King by setting gifts before the hearth. Thus, at dawn on the first day of Hostenfest, adults received flasks of new wine or kegs of stout ale. For the young girls the Earth King brought toy dolls woven of straw and wildflowers, while boys might get swords or oxcarts carved from ash.

All these bounties delivered by the Earth King represented but a token of the Earth King's wealth – the vast hoards of the 'fruits of the forest and of the field' which legend said he bestowed on those who loved the land.

So the homes and shops around the castle were well adorned that night, on the nineteenth day of the Month of Harvest, four days before Hostenfest. All the shops were clean and well stocked for the autumn fair that would shortly come.

The streets lay barren, for dawn was approaching. Aside from the city guards and a few nursing mothers, the only ones who had reason to be up so late of the night were the King's bakers, who at that very moment were drawing the foam off the King's ale and mixing it with their dough so that the loaves would rise by dawn. True, the eels were running on their annual migration in the River Wye, so one might imagine a few fishermen to be out by night, but the fishermen had emptied their wicker eel traps an hour past midnight and had delivered kegs of live eels to the butcher for skinning and salting well before the second watch.

Outside the city walls, the greens south of Castle Sylvarresta were dotted with dark pavilions, for caravans from Indhopal had come north to sell the harvest of summer spices. The camps outside the castle were quiet but for the occasional braying of a donkey.

The walls of the city were shut, and all foreigners had been escorted from the merchants' quarter hours ago. No men moved on the streets at that time of night – only a few ferrin.

Thus there was no one to see what transpired in a dark alley. Even the King's far-seer, who had endowments of sight from seven people and stood guard on the old graak's aerie above the Dedicates' Keep, could not have spotted movement down in the narrow streets of the merchants' quarter.

But in Cat's Alley, just off the Butterwalk, two men struggled in the shadows for control of a knife.

Could you have seen them, you might have been reminded of tarantulas in battle: arms and legs twisting in frenzy as the knife flashed upward, scuffling as feet groped for purchase on the worn cobblestones, both men grunting and straining with deadly intent.

Both men were dressed in black. Sergeant Dreys of the King's Guard wore black livery embroidered with the silver boar of House Sylvarresta. Dreys' assailant wore a baggy black cotton burnoose in a style favored by assassins out of Muyyatin.

Though Sergeant Dreys outweighed the assassin by fifty pounds, and though Dreys had endowments of brawn from three men and could easily lift six hundred pounds over his head, he feared he could not win this battle.

Only starlight lit the street, and precious little of that made its way here into Cat's Alley. The alley was barely seven feet wide, and homes here stood three stories tall, leaning on sagging foundations till the awnings of their roofs nearly met a few yards above Dreys' head.

Dreys could hardly see a damned thing back here. All he could make out of his assailant was the gleam of the man's eyes and teeth, a pearl ring in his left nostril, the flash of the knife. The smell of woodlands clung to his cotton tunic as fiercely as the scents of anise and curry held to his breath.

No, Dreys was not prepared to fight here in Cat's Alley. He had no weapons and wore only the linen surcoat that normally fit over his ring mail, along with pants and boots. One does not go armed and armored to meet his lover.

He'd only stepped into the alley a moment ago, to make certain the road ahead was clear of city guards, when he heard a small scuffling behind a stack of yellow gourds by one of the market stalls. Dreys had thought he'd disturbed a ferrin as it hunted for mice or for some bit of cloth to wear. He'd turned, expecting to see a pudgy rat-shaped creature run for cover, when the assassin sprang from the shadows.

Now the assassin moved swiftly, grasping the knife tight, shifting his weight, twisting the blade. It flashed dangerously close to Dreys' ear, but the sergeant fought it off – till the man's arm snaked around, stabbing at Dreys' throat. Dreys managed to hold the smaller man's wrist back for a moment. 'Murder. Bloody murder!' Dreys shouted.

A spy! he thought. I've caught a spy! He could only imagine that he'd disturbed the fellow in mapping out the castle grounds.

He thrust a knee into the assassin's groin, lifting the man in the air. Pulled the man's knife arm full length and tried to twist it.

The assassin let go of the knife with one hand and rabbit-punched Dreys in the chest.

Dreys' ribs snapped. Obviously the little man had also been branded with runes of power. Dreys guessed that the assassin had the brawn of five men, maybe more. Though both men were incredibly strong, endowments of brawn increased strength only to the muscles and tendons. They did not invest one's bones with any superior hardness. So this match was quickly degenerating into what Dreys would call 'a bone-bash.'

He struggled to hold the assassin's wrists. For a long moment they wrestled.

Dreys heard deep-voiced shouts: 'That way, I think! Over there!' They came from the left. A street over was Cheap Street – where the bunched houses did not press so close, and where Sir Guilliam had built his new four-story manor. The voices had to be from the City Guard – the same guards Dreys had been avoiding – whom Sir Guilliam bribed to rest beneath the lantern post at the manor gate.

'Cat's Alley!' Dreys screamed. He only had to hold the assassin a moment more – make sure the fellow didn't stab him, or escape.

The Southerner broke free in desperation, punched him again, high in the chest. More ribs snapped. Dreys felt little pain. One tends to ignore such distractions when struggling to stay alive.

In desperation the assassin ripped the knife free. Dreys felt a tremendous rush of fear and kicked the assassin's right ankle. He felt more than heard a leg shatter.

The assassin lunged, knife flashing. Dreys twisted away, shoved the fellow. The blade struck wide of its mark, slashed Dreys' ribs, a grazing blow.

Now Dreys grabbed the fellow's elbow, had the man half-turned around. The assassin stumbled, unable to support himself on his broken leg. Dreys kicked the leg again for good measure, and pushed the fellow back.

Dreys glanced frantically into the shadows for sign of some cobblestone that might have come loose from its mortar. He wanted a weapon. Behind Dreys was an inn called the Churn. Beside the flowering vines and the effigy of the Earth King at its front window sat a small butter churn. Dreys tried to rush to the churn, thinking to grab its iron plunger and use it to bludgeon the assassin.

He pushed the assassin, thinking the smaller man would go flying. Instead the fellow spun, one hand clutching Dreys' surcoat. Dreys saw the knife blade plunge.

He raised an arm to block.

The blade veered low and struck deep, slid up through his belly, past shattered ribs. Tremendous pain blossomed in Dreys' gut, shot through his shoulders and arms, a pain so wide Dreys thought the whole world would feel it with him.

For an eternity, Dreys stood, looking down. Sweat dribbled into his wide eyes. The damned assassin had slit him open like a fish. Yet the assassin still held him – had thrust his knife arm up to the wrist into Dreys' chest, working the blade toward Dreys' heart, while his left hand reached for Dreys' pocket, groping for something.

His hand clutched at the book in Dreys' pocket, feeling it through the material of the surcoat. The assassin smiled.

Dreys wondered, Is that what you want? A book?

Last night, as the City Guard had been escorting foreigners from the merchants' quarter, Dreys had been approached by a man from Tuulistan, a trader whose tent was pitched near the woods. The fellow spoke little Rofehavanish, had seemed apprehensive. He had only said, 'A gift – for king. You give? Give to king?'

With much ceremonial nodding, Dreys had agreed, had looked at the book absently. *The Chronicles of Owatt, Emir of Tuulistan.* A thin volume bound in lambskin. Dreys had pocketed it, thinking to pass it along at dawn.

Dreys hurt so terribly now that he could not shout, could not move. The world spun; he pulled free of the assassin, tried to turn and run. His legs felt as weak as a kitten's. He stumbled. The assassin grabbed Dreys' hair from behind, yanking his chin up to expose his throat.

Damn you, Dreys thought, haven't you killed me enough? In one final desperate act, he yanked the book from his pocket, hurled it across the Butterwalk.

There on the far side of the street a rosebush struggled up an arbor near a pile of barrels. Dreys knew this place well, could barely see the yellow roses on dark vines. The book skidded toward them.

The assassin cursed in his own tongue, tossing Dreys aside, and limped after the book.

Dreys could hear nothing but a dull buzz as he struggled to his knees. He glimpsed movement at the edge of the street – the assassin groping among the roses. Three larger shadows came rushing down the road from the left. The flash of drawn swords, starlight glinting off iron caps. The City Guard.

Dreys pitched forward onto the cobblestones.

In the predawn, a flock of geese honked as it made its way south through the silvery starlight, the voices sounding to him for all the world like the barking of a distant pack of dogs.

2

THOSE WHO LOVE THE LAND

That morning a few hours after the attack on Dreys and a hundred or so miles south of Castle Sylvarresta, Prince Gaborn Val Orden faced troubles that were not so harrowing. Yet none of his lessons in the House of Understanding could have prepared the eighteen-year-old prince for his encounter with a mysterious young woman in the grand marketplace at Bannisferre.

He'd been lost in thought at a vendor's stall in the south market, studying wine chillers of polished silver. The vendor had many fine iron brewing pots, but his prize was the three wine chillers – large bowls for ice with complementing smaller pitchers that fit inside. The bowls were of such high quality that they looked to be of ancient duskin workmanship. But no duskin had walked the earth in a thousand years, and these bowls could not have been that old. Each bowl had the clawed feet of a reaver and featured scenes of hounds running in a leafy wood; the pitchers were adorned with images of a young lord on a horse, his lance at the ready, bearing down on a reaver mage. Once the pitchers were set into their silver bowls, the images complemented one another – the young lord battling the reaver mage while the hunting dogs surrounded them.

The ornaments on the wine chiller were all cast using some method that Gaborn could not fathom. The silver-smith's detailed workmanship was breathtaking.

Such were the wonders of Bannisferre's goods that Gaborn hadn't even noticed the young woman sidle up to him until he smelled the scent of rose petals. (The woman who stands next to me wears a dress that is kept in a drawer filled with rose petals, he'd realized, on some subconscious level.) Even then, he'd been so absorbed in studying the wine chillers that he imagined she was only a stranger, awed by the same marvelous bowls and pitchers. He didn't glance her way until she took his hand, seizing his attention.

She grasped his left hand in her right, lightly clasping his fingers, then squeezed.

Her soft touch electrified him. He did not pull away.

Perhaps, he thought, she mistakes me for another. He glanced sidelong at her. She was tall and beautiful, perhaps nineteen, her dark-brown hair adorned with mother-of-pearl combs. Her eyes were black, and even the whites of her eyes were so dark as to be a pale blue. She wore a simple, cloud-colored silk gown with flowing sleeves – an elegant style lately making its way among the wealthy ladies of Lysle. She wore a belt of ermine, clasped with a silver flower, high above the navel, just beneath her firm breasts. The neckline was high, modest. Over her shoulders hung a silk scarf of deepest crimson, so long that its fringes swept the ground.

She was not merely beautiful, he decided. She was astonishing.

She smiled at him secretively, shyly, and Gaborn smiled back, tight-lipped – hopeful and troubled all at once. Her actions reminded him of the endless tests that one of his hearthmasters might have devised for him in the House of Understanding – yet this was no test.

Gaborn did not know the young woman. He knew no one in

all the vast city of Bannisferre – which seemed odd, that he should not have one acquaintance from a city this large, with its towering gray stone songhouses with their exotic arches, the white pigeons wheeling through the blue sunlit sky above the chestnut trees. Yet Gaborn knew no one here, not even a minor merchant. He was that far from home.

He stood near the edge of a market, not far from the docks on the broad banks of the south fork of River Dwindell – a stone's throw from Smiths' Row, where the open-air hearths gave rise to the rhythmic ring of hammers, the creaking of bellows, and plumes of smoke.

He felt troubled that he'd been so lulled by the peacefulness of Bannisferre. He'd not even bothered to glance at this woman when she had stood next to him for a moment. Twice in his life, he'd been the target of assassins. They'd taken his mother, his grandmother, his brother, and two sisters. Yet Gaborn stood here now as carefree as a peasant with a stomach full of ale.

No, Gaborn decided quickly, *I've never seen her; she knows I'm a stranger, yet holds my hand. Most bewildering.*

In the House of Understanding, in the Room of Faces, Gaborn had studied the subtleties of bodily communication – the way secrets revealed themselves in an enemy's eyes, how to differentiate traces of worry from consternation or fatigue in the lines around a lover's mouth.

Gaborn's hearthmaster, Jorlis, had been a wise teacher, and over the past few long winters Gaborn had distinguished himself in his studies.

He'd learned that princes, highwaymen, merchants, and beggars all wore their expressions and stances as if part of some agreed-upon costume, and so Gaborn had mastered the art of putting on any costume at will. He could take command of a roomful of young men simply by standing with head high, cause a merchant to lower his prices with a balking smile. Concealed by nothing more than a fine traveling cloak, Gaborn learned to lower his eyes in a busy market-place and play the pauper, slinking through the crowd so that those who saw him did not recognize a prince, but wondered, Ah, where did that beggar boy steal such a nice cloak?

So Gaborn could read the human body, and yet he remained a perpetual mystery to others. With two endowments of wit, he could memorize a large tome in an hour. He'd learned more in his eight years in the House of Understanding than most commoners could learn in a life of concerted study.

As a Runelord, he had three endowments of brawn and two of stamina, and in battle practice he could easily cross weapons with men twice his size. If ever a highwayman dared attack him, Gaborn would prove just how deadly a Runelord could be.

Yet in the eyes of the world, because of his few endowments of glamour, he seemed to be little more than a startlingly handsome young man. And in a city like Bannisferre, with its singers and actors from across the realm, even beauty such as his was common.

He studied the woman who held him, considered her stance. Chin high, confident – yet slightly tilted. A question. She poses a question of me.

The touch of her hand – weak enough to indicate hesitancy, strong enough to suggest . . . ownership. She was claiming him?

Is this an attempt at seduction? he wondered. But no – the body stance felt wrong. If she had wanted to seduce, she'd have touched the small of his back, a shoulder, even his buttock or chest. Yet as she held him she stood slightly away, hesitating to claim his body space.

Then he understood: a marriage proposal. Very uncustomary, even in Heredon. For a woman of her quality, the family should have easily arranged a marriage.

Gaborn surmised, Ah, she is orphaned. She hopes to arrange her own match!

Yet even that answer did not satisfy him. Why did not a wealthy lord arrange a match for her?

Gaborn considered how she must see him now. A merchant's son. He'd been playing the merchant; and though he was eighteen, his growth had not come in fully. Gaborn had dark hair and blue eyes, traits common in North Crowthen. So he'd dressed like a fop from that kingdom, one with more wealth than taste, out wandering the town while his father conducted more important business. He wore green hose and pants that gathered above the knee, along with a fine white cotton shirt with ballooning sleeves and silver buttons. Over the shirt, he wore a jerkin of dark-green cotton trimmed in finely tooled leather, decorated with freshwater pearls. Completing the disguise was a broad-brimmed hat, on which an amber clasp held a single ostrich plume.

Gaborn had dressed this way because he did not want to travel openly on his mission to spy out Heredon's defenses, to gauge the true extent of the wealth of its lands, the hardiness of its people.

Gaborn glanced back toward his bodyguard Borenson. The streets here were crowded, made narrow by the vendors' stalls. A beefy, bronze-skinned young man with no shirt and red pants was herding a dozen goats through the throng, whipping them with a willow switch. Across the road, beneath a stone arch beside the door to the inn, Borenson stood grinning broadly at Gaborn's predicament. He was tall and broad-shouldered, with a balding head of red hair, a thick beard, and laughing blue eyes.

Beside Borenson stood a skeletal fellow with blond hair cropped short. To match his chestnut eyes he wore a historian's austere brownish robes and a disapproving scowl. The man, simply called by his vocation, Days, was a chronicler of sorts – a devotee of the Time Lords – who had been following Gaborn now since Gaborn was an infant, recording his every word and deed. He took his name from the order of 'the Days.' Like every man of his sect, Days had given up his own name, his own identity, when he'd twinned his mind with that of another of his order. Days watched Gaborn now, keenly. Alert, eyes flickering about. Memorizing everything.

The woman who held Gaborn's hand followed his glance, noting the bodyguard and Days. A young merchant lord with a guard was common. One shadowed by a Days was rare. It marked Gaborn as someone of wealth and import, perhaps the son of a guildmaster, yet this woman could not possibly have known Gaborn's true identity.

She pulled his hand, invited him to stroll. He hesitated.

'Do you see anything in market that interests you?' she asked, smiling. Her sweet voice was as inviting as the cardamom-flavored pastries sold here in the market, yet slightly mocking. Clearly, she wanted to know if she interested him. Yet those around her would mistakenly believe she spoke of the wine chillers.

'The silver shows some decent handiwork,' Gaborn said. Using the powers of his Voice, he put a slight emphasis on *hand*. Without ever recognizing why, she would believe that in Understanding's House, he had studied in the Room of Hands, as rich merchants did. Let her believe me to be a merchant.

The vendor of the stall, who had patiently ignored Gaborn until now, lurched from under the shade of his rectangular umbrella, calling, 'The sir would like a fine chiller for the madam?'

Until a moment ago Gaborn had seemed only a merchant boy, one who might have reported to his father any interesting wares. Now perhaps the merchant thought him a newlywed, with a wife far more handsome than himself. Merchant lords often married their children off young, seeking monetary alliances.

So the vendor thinks I must buy the silver to humor my wife. Of course such a lovely woman would rule her household. Since the merchant did not know her, Gaborn imagined that she would also have to be a stranger to Bannisferre. A traveler from the north?

The young woman smiled kindly at the vendor. 'I think not today,' she teased. 'You have some fine chillers, but we have better at home.' She turned her back, playing her role as wife exquisitely. *This is how it would be if we married*, her actions seemed to say. *I'd make no costly demands*.

The vendor's face fell in dismay. It was unlikely that more than one or two merchants in all the Kingdoms of Rofehavan had such a fine wine cooler.

She pulled Gaborn along. Suddenly, Gaborn felt uneasy. In the far south, ladies of Indhopal sometimes wore rings or brooches with poisoned needles in them. They would try to lure wealthy travelers to an inn, then murder and rob them. It could be that this beauty had nefarious designs.

Yet he doubted it. A quick glance showed that Borenson was certainly more amused than concerned. He laughed and blushed, as if to ask, *And where do you think you're going?*

Borenson, too, was a student of body language – particularly that of women. He never took risks with his lord's safety.

The woman squeezed Gaborn's hand, readjusting her grip, holding him more firmly. Was she seeking a greater claim to his attentions?

'Pardon me if I seem overfamiliar, good sir,' she said. 'Have you ever noticed someone from a distance, and felt a tug in your heart?'

Her touch thrilled him, and Gaborn wanted to believe that, indeed, she'd seen him from afar and fallen in love.

'No, not like this,' he said. Yet he felt it a lie. He'd once fallen in love from afar.

The sun shone on them; the skies were brilliant. The air blowing off the river smelled warm and sweet, carrying the scent of hay fields from across the shore. On such a fine day, how could anyone feel anything but invigorated, alive?

The cobbles on the street here were smooth with age. Half a dozen flower girls strolled barefoot through the crowd, calling for patrons in clear voices. They blew past, a breeze rippling a wheat field. They all wore faded dresses and white aprons. They held the centers of their aprons up with one hand, making their aprons into a kind of sack, sacks filled with riotous colors – brilliant burgundy cornflowers and white daisies, long-stemmed roses in deepest reds and peach. Poppies and bundles of sweet-scented lavender.

Gaborn watched the girls drift by, feeling that their beauty was as stunning as that of larks in flight, knowing he would never forget their smiles. Six girls, all with blond or light brown hair.

His father was camped with his retinue not more than a few hours' ride off. Seldom did his father let Gaborn wander without heavy guard, but this time his father had implored him to take a little side excursion, saying, 'You must study Heredon. A land is more than its castles and soldiers. In Bannisferre you will fall in love with this land, and its people, as I have.'

The young woman squeezed his hand tighter.

Pain showed in her brow as she watched the flower girls. Gaborn suddenly realized what she was, how desperately this young woman needed him. Gaborn nearly laughed, for he saw how easily she could have bewitched him.

He squeezed her hand, warmly, as a friend. He felt certain that he could have nothing to do with her, yet he wished her well.

'My name is Myrrima . . .' she said, leaving a silence for him in which to offer his own name.

'A beautiful name, for a beautiful girl.'

'And you are?'

'Thrilled by intrigue,' he said. 'Aren't you?'

'Not always.' She smiled, a demand for his name.

Twenty paces behind, Borenson tapped the scabbard of his saber against a passing goat cart, a sign that he'd left his post at the hostel's doorway and was now following. The Days would be at his side.

Myrrima glanced back. 'He's a fine-looking guardsman.'

'A fine man,' Gaborn agreed.

'You are traveling on business? You like Bannisferre?'

'Yes, and yes.'

She abruptly pulled her hand away. 'You don't make commitments easily,' she said, turning to face him, her smile faltering just a bit. Perhaps she sensed now that the chase was up, that he would not marry her.

'No. Never. Perhaps it is a weakness in my character,' Gaborn said.

'Why not?' Myrrima asked, still playful. She stopped by a fountain where a statue of Edmon Tillerman stood holding a pot with three spigots that poured water down over the faces of three bears.

'Because lives are at stake,' Gaborn answered. He sat at the edge of the fountain, glanced into the pool. Startled by his presence, huge polliwogs wriggled down into the green water. 'When I commit to someone, I accept responsibility for them. I offer my life, or at least a portion of it. When I accept someone's commitment, I expect nothing less than total commitment – their lives – in return. This reciprocal relationship is . . . it must define me.'

Myrrima frowned, made uneasy by his serious tone. 'You are not a merchant. You . . . talk like a lord!'

He could see her considering. She would know he was not of Sylvarresta's line, not a lord from Heredon. So he would have to be a foreign dignitary, merely traveling – in Heredon, an out-of-the-way country, one of the farthest north in all the Kingdoms of Rofehavan.

'I should have known – you are so handsome,' she said. 'So you're a Runelord, come to study our land. Tell me, do you like it enough to seek betrothal to Princess Iome Sylvarresta?'

Gaborn admired the way that she drew the proper conclusion. 'I'm surprised at how green your land is, and how strong your people are,' Gaborn said. 'It is richer than I'd imagined.'

'Will Princess Sylvarresta accept you?' Still, she was searching for answers. She wondered which poor castle he hailed from. She sat beside him on the edge of the fountain.

Gaborn shrugged, feigning less concern than he felt. 'I know her only by reputation,' he admitted. 'Perhaps you know her better than I. How do you think she will look on me?'

'You are handsome enough,' Myrrima said, frankly studying his broad shoulders, the long dark-brown hair that fell from under his plumed cap. By now she must have realized he was not dark enough of hair to be from Muyyatin, or any of the Indhopalese nations.

Then she gasped, eyes going wide.

She stood up quickly and stepped back, unsure whether to remain standing, curtsy, or fall down and prostrate herself at his feet. 'Forgive me, Prince Orden – I, uh – did not see your resemblance to your father!'

Myrrima lurched back three paces, as if wishing she could run blindly away, for she now knew that he was not the son of some poor baron who called a pile of rocks his fortress, but that he came from Mystarria itself.

'You know my father?' Gaborn asked, rising and stepping forward. He took her hand once again, trying to reassure her that no offense had been taken.

'I – once he rode through town, on his way to the hunt,' Myrrima said. 'I was but a girl. I can't forget his face.'

'He has always liked Heredon,' Gaborn said.

'Yes ... yes, he comes often enough,' Myrrima said, clearly discomfited. 'I – pardon me if I troubled you, my lord. I did not mean to be presumptuous. Oh ...'

Myrrima turned and began to run.

'Stop,' Gaborn said, letting just a little of the power of his Voice take her.

She stopped as if she'd been struck by a fist, turned to face him. As did several other people nearby.

Unprepared for the command, they obeyed as if it had come from their own minds. When they saw that they were not the object of his attention, some stared at him curiously while a few started away, unnerved by the appearance of a Runelord in their midst.

Suddenly, Borenson hovered at Gaborn's back, with the Days.

'Thank you for stopping, Myrrima,' Gaborn said.

'You – may someday be my king,' she answered, as if she'd reasoned out her response.

'Do you think so?' Gaborn said. 'Do you think Iome will have me?' The question startled her. Gaborn continued. 'Please, tell me. You are a perceptive woman, and beautiful. You would do well at court. I value your opinion.'

Gaborn held his breath, waiting for her frank assessment. She couldn't know how important her answer was to him. Gaborn *needed* this alliance. He needed Heredon's strong people, its impregnable fortresses, its wide-open lands, ready to till. True, his own Mystarria was a rich land – ripe, its markets sprawling and crowded – but after years of struggle the Wolf Lord Raj Ahten had finally conquered the Indhopalese Kingdoms, and Gaborn knew that Raj Ahten would not stop there. By spring, he would either invade the barbarian realms of Inkarra or he would turn north to the kingdoms in Rofehavan.

In reality, it didn't matter where the Wolf Lord attacked next. In the wars to come, Gaborn knew he'd never be able to adequately defend his people in Mystarria. He needed this land.

Even though Heredon had not seen a major war in four hundred years, the realm's great battlements remained intact. Even the fortress at lowly Tor Ingel, set among the cliffs, could be defended better than most of Gaborn's estates in Mystarria. Gaborn needed Heredon. He needed Iome's hand in marriage.

More important, though he dared not admit it to anyone, something deep inside told him that he needed Iome herself. An odd compulsion drew him here, against all common sense. As if invisible fiery threads were connected to his heart and mind. Sometimes at night he'd lie awake, feeling the tug, an odd glowing sensation that spread outward from the center of his chest, as if a warm stone lay there. Those threads seemed to pull him toward Iome. He'd fought the urge to seek her hand for a year now, until he could fight no more.

Myrrima studied Gaborn once again with her marvelous frankness. Then laughed easily. 'No,' she said. 'Iome will not have you.'

There had been no hesitancy in her answer. She had said it simply, as if she'd seen the truth of it. Then she smiled at him seductively. *But I want you*, her smile said.

'You sound certain.' Gaborn tried to seem casual. 'Is it merely my clothes? I did bring more suitable attire.'

'You may be from the most powerful kingdom in Rofehavan, but ... how shall I put this? Your politics are suspect.'

It was a kind way to accuse him of being immoral. Gaborn had feared such an accusation.

'Because my father is a pragmatist?' Gaborn asked.

'Some think him pragmatic, some think him ... too acquisitive.'

Gaborn grinned. 'King Sylvarresta thinks him pragmatic ... but his daughter thinks my father is greedy? She said this?'

Myrrima smiled and nodded secretively. 'I've heard rumors that she said as much at the midwinter feast.'

Gaborn was often amazed at how much the commoners knew or surmised about the comings and goings and doings of lords. Things that he'd often thought were court secrets would be openly discussed at some inn a hundred leagues distant. Myrrima seemed sure of her sources.

'So she will reject my petition, because of my father.'

'It has been said in Heredon that Prince Orden is "much like his father."'

'Too much like his father?' Gaborn asked. A quote from Princess Sylvarresta? Probably spoken to quell any rumors of a possible match. It was true that Gaborn had his father's look about him. But Gaborn was not his father. Nor was his father, Gaborn believed, as 'acquisitive' as Iome accused him of being.

Myrrima had the good taste to say no more. She pulled her hand free of his.

'She *will* marry me,' Gaborn said. He felt confident he could sway the princess.

Myrrima raised a brow. 'How could you imagine so? Because it would be pragmatic to ally herself with the wealthiest kingdom in Rofehavan?' She laughed musically, amused. Under normal circumstances, if a peasant had laughed him to scorn, Gaborn would have bristled. He found himself laughing with her.

Myrrima flashed a fetching smile. 'Perhaps, milord, when you leave Heredon, you will not leave empty-handed.'

One last invitation. *Princess Sylvarresta will not have you, but I would.*

'It would be foolhardy to give up the chase before the hunt has begun, don't you think?' Gaborn said. 'In Understanding's House, in the Room of the Heart, Hearthmaster Ibirmarle used to say "Fools define themselves by what they are. Wise men define themselves by what they shall be."'

Myrrima rejoined, 'Then I fear, my pragmatic prince, that you shall die old and lonely, deluded into believing you will someday marry Iome Sylvarresta. Good day.'

She turned to leave, but Gaborn could not quite let her go. In the Room of the Heart, he'd also learned that sometimes it is best to act on impulse, that the part of the mind which dreams will often speak to us, commanding us to act in ways that we do not understand. When Gaborn had told her that he thought she would do well in court, he had meant it. He wanted her in his court – not as his wife, not even as a mistress. But intuitively he felt her to be an ally. Had she not called him 'milord'? She could as easily have called him 'Your Lordship'. No, she felt a bond to him, too.

'Wait, milady,' Gaborn said. Once again Myrrima turned. She had caught his tone. With the word 'milady,' he sought to make his claim on her. She knew what he expected: total devotion. Her life. As a Runelord, Gaborn had been raised to demand as much from his own vassals, yet he felt hesitant to ask as much from this foreign woman.

'Yes, *milord*?'

'At home,' Prince Orden said, 'you have two ugly sisters to care for? And a witless brother?'

'You are perceptive, milord,' Myrrima said. 'But the witless one is my mother, not a brother.' Lines of pain showed in her face. It was a terrible burden she held. A terrible price for magic. It was hard enough to take an endowment of brawn or wit or glamour from another, to assume the financial responsibilities for that person. But it became more painful still when that person was a beloved friend or relative. Myrrima's family must have lived in horrible poverty, hopeless poverty, in order for them to have felt compelled to try such a thing – to gift one woman with the beauty of three, the cleverness of two, and then seek to marry her to some rich man who could save them all from despair.

'However did you get the money for the forcibles?' Gaborn asked. The magical irons that could drain the attributes of one person and endow them on another were tremendously expensive.

'My mother had a small inheritance – and we labored, the four of us,' Myrrima said. He heard tightness in her voice.

Perhaps once, a week or two ago, when she'd newly become beautiful, she'd have sobbed when speaking of this.

'You sold flowers as a child?' Gaborn asked.

Myrrima smiled. 'The meadow behind our house provided little else to sustain us.'

Gaborn reached to his money pouch, pulled out a gold coin. One side showed the head of King Sylvarresta; the other showed the Seven Standing Stones of the Dunnwood, which legend said held up the earth. He was unfamiliar with the local currency, but knew the coin was large enough to take care of her small family for a few months. He took her hand, slipping it into her palm.

'I . . . have done nothing for this,' she said, searching his eyes. Perhaps she feared an indecent proposal. Some lords took mistresses. Gaborn would never do so.

'Certainly you have,' Gaborn said. 'You smiled, and thus lightened my heart. Accept this gift, please. You will find your merchant prince someday,' Gaborn said, 'and of all the prizes he may ever discover here in the markets of Bannisferre, I suspect that you will be the most treasured.'

She held the coin in awe. People never expected one as young as Gaborn to speak with such grace, yet it came easily after years of training in Voice. She looked into his eyes with new respect, as if really seeing him for the first time. 'Thank you, Prince Orden. Perhaps . . . I tell you now that if Iome does accept you, I will praise her decision.'

She turned and sauntered off through the thickening crowd, circled the fountain. Gaborn watched the graceful lines of her neck, the clouds of her dress, the burning flames of her scarf.

Borenson came up and clapped Gaborn on the shoulder, chuckling. 'Ah, milord, there is a tempting sweet.'

'Yes, she's altogether lovely,' Gaborn whispered.

'It was fun to watch. She just stood back, eyeing you like a cutlet on the butcher's block. She waited for five minutes' – Borenson held up his hand, fingers splayed – 'waiting for you to notice her! But you – you day-blind ferrin! You were too busy adoring some vendor's handsome chamber pots! How could you not see her? How could you ignore her? Ah!' Borenson shrugged in exaggeration.

'I meant no offense,' Gaborn said, looking up into Borenson's face. Though Borenson was his bodyguard and should thus always be on the watch for assassins, the truth was that the big fellow was a lusty man. He could not walk through a street without making little crooning noises at every shapely woman he passed. And if he didn't go wenching at least once a week, he'd croon even at the woman who had no more shape than a bag of parsnips. His fellow guards sometimes joked that no assassin hiding in between a woman's cleavage would ever escape his notice.

'Oh, I'm not offended,' Borenson said. 'Mystified, maybe. Perplexed. How could you not see her? You must have at least smelled her?'

'Yes, she smells very nice. She keeps her gown in a drawer layered in rose petals.'

Borenson rolled his eyes back dramatically and groaned. His face was flushed, and there was a peculiar excitement, an intensity in his eyes. Though he pretended to be jesting, Gaborn could see that Borenson had indeed been smitten by this northern beauty more than he cared to admit. If Borenson could have had his way, he'd have been off chasing the girl. 'At least you could have let her cure you of that vexing case of virginity you suffer from, milord!'

'It is a common enough malady for young men,' Gaborn said,

feeling offended. Borenson sometimes spoke to Gaborn as if he were a drinking partner.

Borenson reddened even more. 'As well it should be, milord!'

'Besides,' Gaborn said, considering the toll a bastard child sometimes took on a kingdom, 'the cure is often more costly than the malady.'

'I suspect that *that* cure is worth any price,' Borenson said longingly, with a nod in the direction Myrrima had gone.

Suddenly, a plan blossomed in Gaborn's mind. A great geometer had once told him that when he discovered the answer to a difficult calculation, he knew that his answer was right because he felt it all the way down to his toes. At this moment, as Gaborn considered taking this young woman home to Mystarria, that same feeling of *rightness* struck him. Indeed, he felt that same burning compulsion that had drawn him to this land in the first place. He yearned once again to take Myrrima back to Mystarria, and suddenly saw the way.

He glanced at Borenson, to verify his hunch. The guardsman stood at his side, more than a head taller than Gaborn, and his cheeks were red, as if his own thoughts embarrassed him. The soldier's laughing blue eyes seemed to shine with their own light. His legs shook, though Gaborn had never seen him tremble in battle.

Down the lane, Myrrima turned a corner on a narrow market street, breaking into a run. Borenson shook his head ruefully, as if to ask, *How could you let her go?*

'Borenson,' Gaborn whispered, 'hurry after her. Introduce yourself graciously, then bring her back to me, but take a few minutes to talk as you walk. Stroll back. Do not hurry. Tell her I request an audience for only a moment.'

'As you wish, milord,' Borenson said. He began running in the swift way that only those who had taken an endowment of metabolism could; many in the crowd parted before the big warrior, who wound his way gracefully between those who were too slow or clumsy to move for him.

Gaborn did not know how long it might take Borenson to fetch the woman, so he wandered back to the shadows thrown by the inn. His Days followed. Together they stood, annoyed by a cloud of honeybees. The front of the inn here had an 'aromatic garden' in the northern style. Blue morning-glory seeds were sewn in the thatch of the roof, and a riot of window boxes and flowerpots held creeping flowers of all kinds: palest honeysuckle dripped golden tears along the walls; mallow, like delicate bits of pearl, fluttered in the gentle breeze above the snow-in-summer; giant mandevilla, pink as the sunrise, was nearly strangled by the jasmine. And interspersed with all of these were rose vines, climbing every wall, splotches of peach. Along the ground were planted spearmint, chamomile, lemon verbena, and other spices.

Most northern inns were decorated with such flowers. It helped mask the obnoxious scents of the market, while herbs grown in these gardens could be used for teas and spices.

Gaborn stepped back into the sunlight, away from the heavy perfume of the flowers. His nose was too keen to let him stay.

Borenson returned in a few moments with his big right hand resting gently on Myrrima's elbow, as if to catch her should she trip on a cobblestone. It was an endearing sight.

When the two stood before him, Myrrima bowed slightly. 'Milord wished to speak to me?'

'Yes,' Gaborn said. 'Actually, I was more interested in having you meet Borenson, my body.' He left off the word *guard*, as was the custom in Mystarria. 'He has been my body for six years now, and is captain of my personal guard. He is a good man. In my estimation, one of the finest in Mystarria. Certainly the finest soldier.'

Borenson's cheeks reddened, and Myrrima glanced up at the big guard, smiling discreetly, gauging him. She could not have failed to notice by now that Borenson had an endowment of metabolism to his credit. The hastiness of his speeded reactions, the apparent inability to rest, were sure signs of it.

'Recently, Borenson was promoted to the rank of Baron of the Realm, and given title to a land and manor in . . . the Drewverry March.' Immediately Gaborn recognized his mistake. To give such a large holding was impetuous. Yet now that the words had been spoken . . .

'Milord, I've never heard—' Borenson began to say, but Gaborn waved him to silence.

'As I say, it was a recent promotion.' The Drewverry estate was a major holding, more land than Gaborn would normally give to a distinguished soldier for a life of service, if he'd had time to consider. But now, Gaborn reasoned, this sudden act of generosity would only make Borenson that much more loyal – as if Borenson's loyalty would ever waver. 'In any event, Myrrima, as you can see, Borenson spends a great deal of time in my service. He needs a wife to help him manage his holdings.'

The look of surprise on Borenson's face was a joy to behold. The big man was obviously taken by this northern beauty, and Gaborn had all but ordered them to marry.

Myrrima studied the guard's face without reserve, as if noticing for the first time the strength of his jaw, the imposing bulge of muscle beneath his jerkin. She did not love him, not yet. Perhaps she never would. This was an arranged marriage, and marrying a man who lived his life twice as fast as you, one who would grow old and die while you floundered toward middle age, could not be an overwhelmingly attractive proposition. Thoughtfully, she considered the virtues of the match.

Borenson stood dumbfounded, like a boy caught stealing apples. His face told that he'd considered the match, hoped for it.

'I told you I thought you'd do well in court,' Gaborn said to Myrrima. 'I'd like you to be in my court.'

Certainly the woman would take his meaning. No Runelord could marry her. The best she could hope for would be some merchant prince, burdened by adolescent lust.

Gaborn offered her a position of power – more than she could normally hope for – with an honorable and decent man whose life doomed him to a strange and lonely existence. It was no promise of love, but then Myrrima was a pragmatic woman who had taken the beauty of her sisters, the wisdom of her mother. Having taken these endowments, she would now have to assume responsibility for her impoverished kin. She knew the burden of power. She'd be a perfect woman to hold a place in Mystarria.

She looked up into Borenson's eyes for a long moment, face and mouth suddenly hard, as she considered the offer. Gaborn could see that now that the proposal was made, she realized what a momentous decision this was.

Almost imperceptibly, she nodded, sealing the bargain.

Borenson offered none of the hesitancy that Myrrima had found with Gaborn. He reached out and took her slender hand in both fists.

He said, 'You must understand, fair lady, that no matter how sturdy my love for you grows, my first loyalty will always be to my lord.'

'As it should be,' Myrrima said softly, with a slight nod.

Gaborn's heart leapt. I have won her love as surely as Borenson shall, he thought.

At this moment, he felt strange – as if gripped by some great power. It seemed he could feel that power, like a buffeting wind, encircling – invisible, potent, overawing.

Gaborn's pulse raced. He glanced around, certain the source of this emotion must have a cause – a shifting in the earth in preparation for a quake, an approaching thunderstorm. But he saw nothing out of the normal. Those around him did not seem troubled.

Yet he could feel . . . the earth preparing to move beneath his feet – the rocks to twist or breathe or shout.

It was a distinctly odd sensation.

As suddenly as the rush of power had come, it dissipated. Like a gust of wind passing over a meadow, unseen, but subtly disturbing all in its wake.

Gaborn wiped perspiration from his brow, worried. I've come a thousand miles to heed a distant, unheard call. And now I feel this?

It seemed madness. He asked the others, 'Do you – do you feel anything?'